The Meaning of Grace

Deborah Forster

16
EasyRead Large

Copyright Page from the Original Book

A Vintage book
Published by Random House Australia Pty Ltd
Level 3, 100 Pacific Highway, North Sydney NSW 2060
www.randomhouse.com.au

First published by Vintage in 2012

Addresses for companies within the Random House Group can be found at
www.randomhouse.com.au/offices

National Library of Australia
Cataloguing-in-Publication Entry

Forster, Deborah
The meaning of grace / Deborah Forster

ISBN 978 1 74275 534 2 (pbk)

A823.4

Cover image by Kirsten Mckee/Getty Images
Cover design by Natalie Winter
Internal design and typesetting by Midland Typesetters, Australia
Printed in Australia by Griffin Press, an accredited ISO AS/NZS 14001:2004 Environmental
Management System printer

Random House Australia uses papers that are natural, renewable and recyclable products
and made from wood grown in sustainable forests. The logging and manufacturing
processes are expected to conform to the environmental regulations of the country of
origin.

Deborah Forster grew up in Footscray, Melbourne. She worked as a staff and freelance journalist for many years and was a 'This Life' columnist on *The Age* and *The Sunday Age.*

Deborah is married to Alan Kohler and they have three children. Her first novel, *The Book of Emmett,* was shortlisted for the Miles Franklin Literary Award in 2010.

Praise for The Book of Emmett

'Deborah Forster's debut novel, *The Book of Emmett,* is wonderful ... Immediately engaging, it tells with grace and humour, panache and simplicity, the story of a broken family ... This is a story not of how people are crushed, but the many ways in which they survived. With humour and pain in equal intensity, Forster rips through one family's search for love and acceptance.' Jennifer Levasseur, *The Sydney Morning Herald*

'Brilliant. A story of such gently savage emotional intensity it stays with you long after you've turned the last page.' Susan Duncan

'Deborah Forster is a writer in a class of her own. When a book makes you breathless with fear and love for the characters, and says a Kombi van 'handles like a dog on lino', you know it's wonderful. Deborah Forster has used an angel's phrasebook to make a story that's as beautiful as hope, as real as truth and as Australian as 50–50 cordial and Tic Toc bickies.' Kaz Cooke

'A powerful story. In this mature and strangely uplifting book, Forster neither sensationalises nor trivialises the enormity of the pain for those whose childhoods are denied them.' Mary Philip, *The Courier Mail*

'The central story is not new: a family growing up under the overwhelming shadow of domestic violence and the generational legacy that entails. But the inventiveness of the telling, the dark seductiveness of the language and the prickly complexity of the characters make this most familiar of stories original and surprising.' Jo Case, *The Age*

'In an impressive debut novel that vividly evokes Australia in the 1950s and 1960s, the dark, disturbing experiences are illuminated by innocent and happy ones. The children are wonderful and it's their indomitable spirits that make this book fly.' *Australian Women's Weekly*

'A first novel of subtle achievement, *The Book of Emmett* stands out from a flood of tales on domestic abuse. Written with no-nonsense poise and leavened by wry humour, it never shies from the stunting consequences on the lives of those affected of the trauma of emotional and physical violence. Despite this, it is a poignant story of survival with memorable characters – a salute to tenacity and a touching marker of lost potential.' Judges, 2010 Miles Franklin Literary Award

'Beginning with a fractious funeral ceremony on a hellishly hot day in Melbourne's west, *The Book of*

Emmett ... patiently and painfully traces the lives to this point of an ordinary family. The father, Emmett Brown, is by turns cruel, capricious and charming. Forster analyses the physical and psychological damage that this combination of qualities causes Emmett's wife and children, as well as the bonds that they are compelled to form with each other. The novel's prose is elegiac. Its scenes of domestic life are jaggedly vivid. Forster has created an insightful anatomy of suburban Australia.' Judges, 2010 Prime Minister's Literary Awards

'This is a powerful and emotional debut novel. Forster beautifully portrays the fear and shame experienced by this family, but also the love and courage that sustains them.' Professor Robert Dixon, Chair of Australian Literature, University of Sydney

For Alan

PART I

Chapter 1

Cellophane

Crumbs of fog lay on the sea that day, and the stillness was unbroken. On the poplars, yellow leaves shiver on their stems. Next door the maple, red as a new wound, towers over the little house. On the way to the car for the drive to chemotherapy, Edie puts her arm around her mother's shoulders. Grace mentions the leaves, but all Edie is aware of is her incredible lightness. The word 'cancer' hurtles through her and blocks out everything all over again, but she thinks maybe she says 'yeah' about the leaves.

Grace had been slow to open her eyes that morning and it seemed even the blue of them was being claimed by the grey future. And yet the map of her life in the lines of her face is kindly, is her, is Grace. 'How you going, darlin' mum?' Edie had asked, kneeling beside the bed, and Grace had touched her hand to her daughter's cheek and said, 'Better now for seeing your face, my girl.' She tucked a strand of Edie's hair behind her ear. Edie smiled but wanted to weep. Maybe she always loved me, she thought, and we find out at the end.

Setting out, Edie sees yesterday's sheets and Grace's blue nightie on the line, and that the thin May stillness holds them silent and unruffled. Should have brought them in yesterday before the day went, she thinks, backing out on the disintegrating gravel drive. Hope I'm back in time to get the clothes in before the birds shit on them. The radio in the car is on Grace's favourite talkback station and the morning host is Stuart Apple. 'Stewie's fired up,' Edie remarks. The station has taken a bit of finding in Edie's car radio, but there he is, going on about dumb government, train timetables and what makes an Australian? A refugee? Jangling ads fertilise the mix. Driving through islands of low cloud, Edie worries that Stewie, who she thinks of as Spewie, will get to her, but Grace treats him as an audible newspaper, just another diversion in a sea of them. 'Bit of company, love. Bit of a diversion, that's all,' she says, 'on a long drive.'

Warmth is late coming to the sky; the sun seems too far away today. The car seats cup them and they drive the twenty or so kilometres to the hospital. They swerve to avoid a dead fox smeared on the road like a broken jar of jam. In the distance, on the green paddock, black-and-white dairy cows stretch and munch. Grace clears her throat so Edie mutes Stewie on the radio. 'You have to watch foxes around calves. They're cruel too. Take a calf's eyes out for the fun of it.'

'Isn't that crows and lambs?"

'Well, they will too. Nature can be cruel, you know, Edo. I spent some time on a farm when I was a girl.'

Edie hasn't heard Grace speak about that time for so long, it's half-remembered. She thinks she might raise it but maybe mentioning the days when Grace was away from her own mother ... well, right now that might not be good. So she leaves it. Leaving it is the wisest course, she has discovered. In all things.

In the warm car, crocheted rug on her knees, Grace appears to doze and Edie is careful with the driving. She stays back from other cars and gets tooted twice for her trouble – Mrs Slowpoke at the lights. As they're turning into the hospital Grace says, 'Don't worry about those bastards. You're a good driver, darlin' ... Long as you know your way, of course.' Edie glances over and sees closed eyes and nothing short of benevolence but still, out of habit, she holds the comment for further perusal.

And then somehow it all takes so long finding a spot in the car park lined with dusty cars and utes that Edie isn't surprised when her mother whispers, 'You know, I don't think I'll be able to walk today, love.' But Edie is unprepared for it; each decline is like another leg of the marathon. And some kind of alarm switches on and makes her want to run to get help, or maybe even just run away. The idea of fleeing swoops on her like a bat in the night, surprising and efficient, but common sense stops that rubbish. 'Right, Mum, stay here. Rest. I'll get a wheelchair.'

Edie tears off with no idea where the wheelchairs might be, and of course there are none to be had. She sprints to three different booths in the foyer: information, volunteers and lost property, all empty. She should've known better – no wheelchair booth. Bastards, she curses. This dashing about gets her so hot that sweat rolls freely and into her eyes. For a minute she doesn't know whether she's crying or not. Tears don't sting, she thinks – maybe sweat is tears with muscle. Oh God, could you be more pathetic? Blood thumps. That'll be the high blood pressure. Unfit, pale, on the wrong side of forty-five and you can't even find a wheelchair for your poor old Mum. Useless.

She's dressed wrong too, for though it was cool earlier on at Yarrabeen, this place is a bloody hot-house disguised as a hospital. Edie's parka and dangling red scarf draw unhappy attention to her, and could it be that her second-best jeans really are trying to drown her as she wades through the foyer? It must be so.

At the moment when it seems she'll have to carry Grace, she spots a nurse pushing a big woman folded into a plaid dressing gown. Edie takes off after the wheelchair, already apologising from a distance. 'Excuse me, nurse, would you mind if I took the wheelchair after...' The patient snores and a tremor jolts her left hand. The thought flies through Edie that getting old is always going to be a major disappointment. The nurse in blue scrubs, ponytail swinging, stops, turns and surprisingly, agrees to give Edie the wheelchair. 'Okay,' she says, cross and kind at once, 'but only if you bring it back to the ward. Promise on your life! These chairs are rare as bloody hen's teeth round here.' Edie wipes the sweat off her brow, subtle enough, she believes, to escape detection and blots it on her jeans. 'Yes, I definitely will. I'll bring it back for sure,' she lies, wide-eyed and convincingly with no intention of bringing the thing back. She wrangles it through the sliding doors, out to the car, to find Grace's head resting against the window. God, how did it happen so fast? She lifts her into the wheelchair, groaning with effort, but Grace seems to rally.

Once inside the hospital they pass the op-shop where they'd bought things for each other: a slimming black shirt for Edie, a set of knitted bed socks in gelato colours for Grace, a doily, a small pewter vase, all souvenirs of the days of better health. She could list them, maybe she could chant them. And they pass the coffee shop where Grace loved to watch Edie devour her roasted-vegie focaccia while she dallied with her pie. Today, they hurry on to the oncology ward and then get redirected to the emergency department because there's no point having chemo now. They hurry so as not to be late for the hours that stretch ahead of them like a traffic jam. Against a wall of windows they take their place in the grey, arching room overlooking a car park. Outside, smokers lean on pillars and look at the sky. 'Makes you think of that cyclone up north, where all the bananas got wiped out,' Grace whispers after a while in the waiting room.

'And the people and the houses as well as the bananas, Mum,' Edie admonishes, before setting off on a helpful list of disasters, including earthquakes, tsunamis, bushfires, cyclones and floods, and soon their neighbours join in with other remembered Acts of God. One old woman with a sprained ankle the colour of a storm wonders why there still aren't many men's names for cyclones, and someone says they alternate these days between male and female. Someone else says, 'Wasn't there an Oscar?' and all of them fill in time as if they were filling in holes with shovels. Grace can wait though. 'Don't worry. You get patient when you get old.' Edie hears her mother as a breath. Scattered clouds come and go outside the high windows, and Edie presents at the admissions and says, 'Please take a look at my mother.' She can't bring herself to demand pity when she looks around and sees the others in the same boat. That she doesn't set her mother above the others doesn't come back to her till later. Now, the answer is the same: they're doing their best. It won't be long.

She gets a cup of coffee from the vending machine and manages to drop it on the floor and then skid in it. Grace doesn't comment on her clumsiness but it brings a faint smile. While Edie's cleaning up with a few tissues donated by others, somehow time elapses and Grace is being taken into the inner sanctum and given a trolley bed. Then a new set of waiting begins. A blood-pressure cuff is placed on her skinny arm and her shirt is opened so that red and blue stickers can be placed on her chest to measure her heart rate. Her breath is slowing. Edie thinks Grace says, 'Ian', her husband's name, which Edie hasn't heard for years, and then it seems that Grace is just sleeping.

The nurses and doctors decide to admit Grace and agree that, while today is a very bad day, it won't be the day she dies.

Not today, she tells herself in a rush of gratitude, thank God it's not today. Still, she can't stop the wave from breaking within her when she realises she must ring Juliet, her sister, about the question of hospices, but she'd rather not think about that just yet. It seems that though everything is flimsy and shredded, the kids are nothing to their mother now, which is only right because Grace can't listen anymore. She need not be troubled by Jules and Edie. This love for her mother quietens her. She will be calm. She releases Grace's hand with a regret that feels elemental. It seems all warmth leaves with her, and her mother's quiet fingers rest like a pianist's waiting for new music. Edie leans forward and kisses the hand. Tears fall, heavy and clear. She pulls down her sleeve to mop them up, and as she's doing this in the softness of the moment her mother places the other hand on her daughter's head and out of sleep whispers, 'Matey, my little mate.' And Edie must leave to escape this falling sadness.

Outside the booth, in a corridor of pushing people, she pulls the curtains across to screen her mother and leans against a fragment of wall, shaking with the loss that is coming at her now out of the dark like a comet. She wipes a hand past her eyes but still feels like a child. And then a teenage boy is wheeled past with a head wound, his hair matted with blood.

10

Her eyes harvest his hot fear. It seems to Edie that in here they're all swimming in the deep end now.

She steps into the cool air in the car park, next to an ambulance, and takes a deep breath. She calls Juliet and gets the lilting message: *Hi, you've called Juliet Fisher. Feel free to leave a message.* 'Juliet, it's Edie, Mum has taken a turn for the worse, the cancer is back and they think she's going to need more care. Though she won't die today apparently, so don't worry about that, but she's failing. You better come to St John's Public Hospital.'

***

Standing beside the bed again in a room on a ward now, she watches Grace sleep. The disease has reclaimed her, split apart and travelled like an alien across her brain and spine and taken her away. She remembers a younger Grace filing her nails at night, pale fingernail dust floating in beams of light while they watched telly and devoured chocolate. Edie imagined inhaling her mother with the chocolate. On those nights, Grace would laugh with an ease the kids understood was hard won and all the damned better for it. The peace of those nights still hangs within Edith like a pearl moon. Once, out of nowhere, after Ted was put to bed and before the telly went on, she announced, 'Girls, never let anyone take your freedom.' And then she handed out scorched almonds as if they were tablets of wisdom. The girls took them solemnly and they were more than their taste. They thought about it but still secretly only hoped their respect might get them another chocolate. It didn't. Grace was always pretty tight with chocolate.

Afterwards the girls pondered the mystery of chocolate rather than the mystery of freedom. Why were they were called scorched when they sure didn't taste burned? In the photo album in Edie's mind, Grace that night is happy as a box full of birds, a general in charge of a cellophane bag of scorched almonds.

And now here she is and everything is falling apart, like some kind of ending. How can this all be happening on a day in May, right here and now, when it's coming up to the right time for Grace to die, for the force of Grace to be released? And on a day when it's been decided Edie's old enough to be able to cope with the death of her mother? No. Well, she won't ever be that old, not for that kind of desolation. She smooths the cotton blanket with the red stripe. That won't be possible.

Like an everyday angel, Karen the social worker arrives in the shining corridor. Karen says Grace should stay with them now, move across to the nice new hospice down the street behind the whispering grasses. The words 'we can control her pain and help her die with dignity' register in Edie, but still she blurts, 'We have Rodney the district nurse.' The social worker looks at her with modulated pity. 'I see,'

Karen says with a small smile that, despite the comfort, makes Edie feel nervous.

Abruptly, Karen roughs up her short, tufty hair with one hand. Her eyes have seen it all and she knows Edith would like someone to tell her what to do. She's willing to be the one. She rests a hand on the bed and places her unruly papers beside Grace's feet like a sleeping cat. Edie feels that finally the understanding has come and soon caves in to agreement, which because it's so easy doesn't stand a chance. Karen offers to ring Juliet and run it all past her, and Edie accepts with unglued fatalism. Her heart thuds. 'She might not be too happy. She wants Mum to die at home.' Guilt seeps from her. She remembers the raging row they had after the first diagnosis. Edie never cared for the whole dying at home argument and Juliet, who had travelled for most of her life, cared passionately for it. They took the fight to the backyard so Grace wouldn't hear, but nothing mattered in the end because Edie had no stomach for the fight.

If Karen can pull this off there must be a God, Edie thinks. And here she is trying to duck under the rope without asking Juliet or Ted. How many times before she learns? It's one of those decisions you get to relive, and she starts the reliving even before Karen leaves. Then the taste of regret fills her mouth like sour milk. The thing she understands is that they have some time now and they need to get organised.

When Juliet does arrive, she's upset and terse. 'Could I speak to you, Edith? In private. We won't be needing you, Miss Berger. This is a family matter.' Juliet has dyed her hair red again. They are shepherded to a room at the back, a lunch room with tartan couches.

'We've had this talk, Edith. Mum wants to die at home. She told me this. Many times.' Juliet's eyes are wide, her face now about the same colour as her hair. 'She won't be going into any hospice. Ted is in full agreement with me.'

Edie knows Juliet will get her way and that the work of it will fall on her own shoulders again. Still, she will have her say. 'Listen, Julie, Mum told me she didn't want to be a bother. She couldn't stand the idea of that. She didn't want me wiping her bum, said she couldn't stand it. That she didn't bloody well care where she died, as long as she had a bit of dignity.'

Edie's eyes start to water. Juliet is not impressed – they are fighting over long-held territory, the country that is their mother – and she has always been more determined. There will be no give and take.

'Get organised, Edie. This is how it's gonna be, mate.' Juliet leaves and Edie sinks onto the highlander couches looking at the kitchen with its jar of broken 'Nice' biscuits. Is it pronounced *nice* or *neece?* she wonders. It's not too long before she takes herself off, past the hospital bed where Juliet is holding Grace's hand, down the ship-like hospital stairs and out into the cool night. In the privacy of the car, still holding Grace's bag and the bright rug she had over her knees this morning, she weeps.

Chapter 2

A Trinity of Kids

Ian worked down at the new grey power station kneeling by the river like an elephant. But he had become a sore disappointment to Grace and he was not the man she had married at all. Then again, maybe she'd just been deceived. How he kept his job these days was a miracle because he seemed vague and lost. At work, camouflaged in his overalls, he was said to be a genius at installing the intercoms in the vast new building. No one, it was said, could install them like Ian Fisher. Well, he reasoned cautiously, completely unused to any kind of certainty connected to himself, I suppose I *am* a trained electrician. But Grace never heard any praise of Ian and had none to give. She thought he was a dropkick and that there was something wrong with him, as if the intercom in his head was all static.

Joseph Fisher, the first Australian Fisher in Ian's family, had come from Ireland via Northampton as a convict. He got seven years for stealing something. In New South Wales, his assignment went badly and he threatened the farmer/master with an axe, which was unwise. Actually, he just gestured toward it leaning against the shed when the Mister wanted more wood chopped. Joe Fisher was dispatched to Port Macquarie. Defeat followed defeat now and always, though he did have three children with the energetic Isabella Dawson, a runaway servant. After consideration, Isabella decided the new mines opening down south could be the answer to their problems, but in the end Joseph was just another clumsy, hopeful miner until he managed to blow his head off with a stick of explosive. His five-year-old son Norman was standing outside the tent when it happened.

Ian Fisher was steeped in these stories of the past. He held them close, counted them and wove them into his belt. In addition to poor old Joe, the ill-fated miner, there was his dad, Paul the sailor, his great-great Nan Isabella, who made a fortune selling grog on the goldfields – and, of course, lost it all again when she trusted a shyster. Little Normie, the boy by the tent, became a boilermaker in a brewery and was always good for cheap beer. All of these stepped forward to make a circle around Ian.

Ian's quick brain got him an apprenticeship as an electrician, which was a definite step up from the ranks of the unskilled. When he married Grace Bell, people thought he had it made. She was beautiful and smart, a secretary for a big mining company HQ in the city. While there were those who thought she was spoiled by her kindly parents, most people loved Grace for the light of her, for her calm blue eyes and the way she saw things so simply and happily.

Edie and Juliet were born in quick succession and they had decided not to have any more, but then Ian got drunk one night a few years later and along came Ted. Ian reckoned sex was overrated anyway, but then, according to him so were drinking and eating. On the list of his pleasures, looking at Grace was number one and being alone was number two. He loved his kids – they were the people who mattered – but though he knew it, he didn't always feel it. His feelings had become a weight to him.

In those first years, Ian kept his anxiety and depression quiet, taking himself off on long walks in the nights when he couldn't sleep. He found their dog Hodge, a dull, scruffy thing living in a stormwater drain, on one of those walks and she followed him home. She was named after Samuel Johnson's dog because he loved the doctor. When he sat with the family, he'd rest his hand on Hodge's head, as if she were a portal to another place. As if he needed to be somewhere else.

But the truth of it was that as anxiety overcame him, his concentration waned and the possibility of making a big mistake down at the power station by the river was all he thought about. It sang to him like a siren's call. He became clenched and permanently tired. There was no sleep to be had, except in the car sometimes, and often when he was driving, his eyes would lower like lead weights. Having no one to talk to became a habit. After months of this, planning how he would kill himself became a refuge.

***

One Saturday morning in what would be the first of her three olive-green kitchens, the distance between Ian and Grace is as fixed and cold as the moon's orbit but he looks at Grace anyway, something he hasn't done much lately. And strangely, there seems to be some kind of hope in him this morning. 'Look. Gracie. I've wanted to talk. I'm all finished with working at the power station. I'm going to set up a radio repair shop. Be a self-made man. There'll be plenty of moolah, you'll see. Plenty.' He rubs his thumb and forefinger together in the air for a bit too long, trying to make her smile. But his eyes falter. She isn't so hard, seeing hope in him reminds her that she'd loved him once. She never expected him to be like this. There were no signs. She stirs her tea and waits for him to tell her he's already chucked the job in but it takes a while.

He chucked it in without saying anything more to Grace. I'll get it right now, he decided, and I will be better than I am now. A bit of severance pay was used to set himself up as a radio repairman. He got hold of a long tan dustcoat and had 'Fisher's Radios' embroidered on the pocket. The embroidery alone cost nearly a pound. Grace discovered the dustcoat on the back seat of the car and couldn't believe his compounding stupidity – everyone knew that radios were finished because television was taking over. Then she got mad. What she made at the plumbing factory would never cover anything. It was years since she'd worked as a secretary in the city. She'd wanted to be closer to home for the sake of the kids. Things would need to change.

In the kitchen she waits but she doesn't expect him to understand anything. His limp impracticality has them all by the throat. He just doesn't get anything really. He's never seen the importance of money and Grace doesn't even know the half of it, though she'd believe anything of him. Last night on his walk he gave a fiver to an old bloke sitting at the footbridge. Could have been some kind of insurance with God, but probably it wasn't. Ian reckoned God couldn't care less what anyone did, specially him. If there was a God, he was busy.

Through the kitchen window Grace sees the kids on the grass under the endless sky so blue that it becomes violet, sees them messing around on the spongy bit of grass in the middle that Ian does manage to mow. He leaves the edges to grow wild because he can't be bothered with edges. Seeing the kids with their ceaseless tumbling and chasing, it becomes clear: they are her responsibility, not Ian's. The other clarity is that there *is* something wrong with him, and while she knows she might feel sorry for him, if she had the time and the money, right now there's nothing beyond it and she can't fix it. He disgusts her. Everything: his mouth, his hands, his clothes, his empty eyes. His filthy hair. Repellent. Ugly, dirty and sad. How can a grown man be so pathetic? she wonders. He hides, won't talk and quits a perfectly good job. She decides to wait and see. But to Grace, quitting a job is surely a sign of madness, and so he must be mad.

Ian sets up in a corner of a TV repair shop just down from their house. The kids are impressed that he has an electric kettle *and* a white mug on the bench in the corner. They stay with him on Saturday mornings while Grace goes to the shops. She lets them out at the front door of the TV shop and they troop down the aisle past all the legs of all the TVs, Edie carrying Ted and trailing his blankets, dropping his dummy and stuffed toy rabbit. All the faces are on the same TV channel at the same time as they pass by. They camp under Ian's desk and watch each of the dozens of TVs, trying to spot differences.

One rainy day they watch *Curly Top,* the old Shirley Temple movie. Ted, with his half-drag, half-crawl, is pursuing the inlets and plains of the shop, but before they are halfway into the movie they become aware of their mother's shiny legs and her high-heeled shoes and her reliable animosity towards their father. Edie and Juliet absorb Shirley ardently, dazzled by the beautiful child and bitterly disappointed that Grace has come early to pick them up. They hear her with sinking hearts.

'What do you honestly think you're doing here, Ian?' she asks, a tight line of pegs in her voice. 'Do you really think you're going to support us like this?' She opens her arms. 'You are just a joke of a father and a pathetic, hopeless husband.' She reaches down to drag the first child's arm she can grab out of the desk cave, and all the Shirley Temples scatter into curls and smiles. As they walk home without their father, holding on to the metal sides of Ted's pram, the rain is fine and cold and it sinks into them.

Trouble is, transistors are sturdy little machines and these days TV has everyone in its thrall. The transistor repair business lurches towards failure, so to stave it off, Ian tapes a few signs to light poles and in shop windows advertising himself as others advertise for lost cats. 'Your Transistor Reliably Repaired by Ian Fisher, Rear of Advance Televisions, 22 Field Street, Smithton.'

***

The factory girls on the droning assembly lines at Pab's Plumbing Parts call Anna-Maria di Benedetti, Betty. It's easier and she doesn't seem to mind, none of this carry-on about how to pronounce her name either. She's just a damn good worker, quick and accurate, and anyway, Betty Benedetti has a ring to it. She smiles the brown-eyed smile in a way that makes you trust her, and pretty soon Grace befriends her.

One Easter, when Juliet gets sick with chicken pox, Betty brings in a little egg with a chicken on it for her. 'Oh, Betty,' Grace says, holding the little yellow thing. 'No one's ever given me anything for the kids before.' Tears push at her eyes and the other women in the glary lunch room have stalled the volume to witness the scene. Some prickle – gifts set precedents – some feel shamed they didn't think to make such a gesture, and some wonder about wasting money.

Betty thinks Grace needs a holiday. 'Come with me this Christmas, we go down to Yarrabeen with my parents. There is caravan park by the sea. Is beautiful. You could stay here. I will fix it.' She laughs. 'And don't worry, not much, not much money. Yarrabeen is so cheap it's practically free!' She laughs and claps her hands and says, 'So it's done!'

Being Italian, Betty's father had been corralled into a detention camp for migrants near Yarrabeen during the war. But Gino surprised himself by loving it. The sea and the cliffs and the penguins and the tea-trees and the big sky and the locals who didn't seem to mind them, apart from calling them wogs with no idea of the effect it had on them.

After the war her mum and dad bought a little plot near the back beach and built a hut, and this was where Betty's life began, her father working as an odd-jobs man and fishing most days in the bay in his boat, her mother sewing piecework at home, mainly uniforms for girls' schools.

As Betty fills Grace in about Yarrabeen, they're handling taps, putting the wheel on the handle. When the kids came there didn't seem to be any work for secretaries around where they lived and she wanted to be close to the kids, so she got a job down at the big tap factory and she likes it more than she expected to. It's easy work and the other girls are a laugh and assembling the taps has a kind of rhythm to it. Truth is, she'd just die if there wasn't somewhere to go every day. She loves her kids but she loves being away from them too. Before she got the job at Pabs she remembers the lonely house with the little kids looking at her all day, waiting for her to do something that was fun, or else howling. And while money is money, the best thing about work for Grace is other people. Friendships grow while hands are busy. While Betty chats about the beach and about her family, Grace remembers something about Yarrabeen. She recalls Kevin Culp from down that way and that he was tall, gentle and gawky. Those were the days when you met others at dances, she thinks, not pubs. She remembers Kevin at a dance in New-town, and she liked him even though he was ridicu-lously tall.

Then there was Ian at another dance, and suddenly Ian was everything. His moods, his smile, his plans, his poems, his clothes. Now look at him. What happened? Pathetic. What else do you call a man like that?

Grace has the green buttons and Betty the red, and you have to be damn quick to keep up with the line. She wonders what it would be like not to have Ian around for a week and it doesn't take much imagination. Since she's never in her life had a holiday, this, she decides, will be the year. The money she's hidden from Ian might even be enough.

＊

After his job goes, their father loses everything but his habits. He sits in the corner and reads poems from faraway countries over and over, he makes milky cups of tea he doesn't drink, and he stays away from home a lot. He tries to cook when he's there, odd food they always hate: curries, dark red stinky stews and something he calls tripe. He says it's cheap and nutritious. He doesn't clean up like their mother does, just puts things down and wanders away. He sleeps most of the day and never at night, but even so, to them he seems no more hopeless than ever. His hair is longer than the other men's and he doesn't wash or shave much. He wears the same clothes day after day and they develop a smell that never leaves the kids, the smell of sadness. They get that their mother doesn't like him anymore, she never even looks at him, but then this isn't so new either.

These days it seems his only job is making the toast in the morning because the toaster has a delicate constitution that he understands. Buttering and listening to commands about 'not too much vegie' and which jam and how the toast should be cut – Ian's on top of all that. One morning, early that December, he's buttering toast and the sun is sifting through the curtains onto his hands, covering them. He's like a strand of spaghetti with his long, light-brown hair and skin so pale. He's quiet but it's a listening quietness. When he does talk, it's startling.

'Girls,' he says, turning, up on the balls of his feet like a fighter. He's ready to say something, still holding the butterknife. They look up from their plates, sleepy, wild hair, and the steam seems to go out of him. 'I have something to tell you and you're not going to like hearing it. I'm sorry, but the truth is there will be no Father Christmas this year. I've spoken to him and he just can't come to our house – he's got too many other kids who need him. Especially those poor little African kids you see on the telly. And you kids will be fine without him. Won't you now? You are very special kids, better than most, so you'll be fine. And since he asked me, I told him you would be.' He watches as the tears creep up on them, the heavy tears turning the toast in their mouth to sludge.

He turns back and butters energetically. Finally, Edith responds, 'I said I want jam, not vegie. I said, Dad.' She stares at his hands while beside her Juliet's eyes well again at the thought of the absence of Christmas. Ted is dragging himself up on anything – chairs, table legs, people's legs. Not long before, he fell and banged his head on the floor and Juliet gave him her ragdoll, Junie, but only for a while. Now she thinks Ted won't even get a present for his first Christmas, and when his crying stops he sucks on the doll's nose until it's wet through. He still can't have Junie for keeps though.

It doesn't surprise Edie about Father Christmas. She's known for a while he's really her parents anyway. She thinks it's her Dad's fault that they haven't got any money since she believes he got the sack, and their mum's money pays for everything. Still, she thinks, Ted should at least get something because he's a baby. It's not fair otherwise.

***

On Christmas morning, as early as they can get away with getting up, the two girls are creeping towards the lounge room. They move through the house in the khaki light of morning, when outside magpies call on the grass and the day holds the promise of real heat. They pass Ted, already awake in his cot in the passageway, sitting up dribbling and cooing and playing with the corner of his blanket in a halo of light stealing past the end window. 'Come on, you little rat, might as well check out Chrissie for yourself,' and with some effort Edith on tiptoes hoicks him to her. He grabs a hunk of her hair and holds on.

In the small lounge room the listless Christmas tree is peppered with a couple of baubles and a thin snake of silver tinsel. The tree's been there a good three weeks, standing in a red bucket with a few scummy inches of water giving off a rank sourness. On the windows the paper blinds against the brilliant light are like a pair of paintings on the bare wall. They seem to have been gnawed at the corners.

Like a little stalking party of hunters, the three approach the room and there, in the middle of the floor, before the purple vinyl couch with the wonky leg, is something completely unexpected. It's a child's inflatable paddling pool blown up to its full size. There's a pond in the lounge room with dolphins and fish cavorting along its puffy sides, and if these sea creatures had sprung to life and swum towards them singing Christmas carols, they could not have been more amazed.

No sound comes from their parents' room and the trinity of kids in their raggedy night clothes huddle before the pool. Then they move towards it as one and catch the glint of its riches together. And the closer they get, the more it shines. Before them is a carpet of shining lollies all over the bottom of the paddling pool. More lollies than they have ever seen – red and green and blue and yellow, some wrapped, some loose, redskins and cobbers and chocolate bullets and smarties and crunchy cellophane-wrapped lollies. They stand beside that little pool, considering their options in silence. Should they get in? But even given the beauty of the vision, the question weighs on them: is this for *us?*

As they well know, Father Christmas is not coming this year, a fact made crystal clear by their dad, though curiously Grace had given Edie a pair of yellow thongs two days ago when she stood on a bindi in the backyard. 'Might as well give these to you now rather than waiting for Christmas, sweet, can't have you walking on all our good bindi-eyes.' Grace had smiled, winked and gone back to hanging out the washing in the bright gale where bees were dispersed through the cyclone fence. Apart from reckoning that they had the windiest yard in the whole world, Edie hadn't missed the reference to Christmas.

There weren't many other houses where they lived then. It was a new estate way out west and the plain, like a prairie, swept into blue distance. The fence seemed to pull the wind onto them. Grace had to anchor the line by hanging onto a towel, and when she let go the washing line spun like a top in a carnival. When her mother had said it was 'a good drying day', it felt like the loveliest thing a person could say. She had handed her mother the pegs and glanced down at her new cushiony thongs and decided there was probably something else going on about Christmas, despite what her dad had said, because everyone knew he was not the boss.

But with the wading pool in the lounge room, well, it could go either way. What if Father Christmas *had* snuck in and done all this, well then he'd want them to jump in and have a go. But what if Grace had done it and she didn't want them to touch it yet until she was up, and what if Uncle Bill and Auntie Shirl from next door had done it? Or their gran? Maybe they should wake their mum. Edith puts Ted down on the floor for a minute and he solves everything. He drags himself and his heavy night-wet nappy right into the pool and starts grabbing lollies, cellophane and all, and shoving everything into his little mouth as if it were a magic cave. Edie grabs him so he doesn't choke himself, pulls the lollies out of his mouth and makes his knotty little hands let go of all these glorious things. Then Juliet starts laughing and jumps in and chucks lollies around, scoffing as many as she can. 'Woo hoo,' she whispers, loud as she dares. 'He came. I told you, Min, Father Christmas came and I knew he would. He always comes, specially when I ask him.'

Grace and Ian are at the door together smiling, sleepy and rumpled. Grace is knotting her blue rose dressing gown and Ian is making his hair stay down. Edie, holding fat Ted back from the shiny treasures of the pool, wonders which of them has done this, which one has made the magic. She never works it out.

Later, they tip the lollies out and put the pool on the grass and daisy weed, filling it with lapping, sunlit water. The kids skid and slide and squirt each other until their parents trail away, tired of smiling, tired of this long day of best behaviour. Grace has things to do for the holiday and Ian is always occupied with the business of not being with them.

'I'm just off to see a man about a dog,' he tells them, ruffling Juliet's hair and winking. Edie wonders why his eyes are always sad. Still in his pyjama top with shorts and thongs, he walks away from them through the simmering Christmas streets, past children trying out new bikes, past people in dressing gowns gathering to chat, all saying, 'Good morning and happy Christmas.' He imagines he smiles. The sun pushes through him but he's always paler than everyone, as if he's a faded photo. To be alone and not be anyone's father or husband, just for half an hour. He gets to the park, which is empty of people and full of sunlight, sits on the bench and, until he hears someone coming, weeps without restraint.

The kids and Grace set the table for Christmas dinner in the little lean-to kitchen that Grace has painted olive because it is her belief that everything looks better that colour. She's made some curtains with a pattern that looks like the raffia wine bottle she's so proud of, the one scrounged from the tip. She fitted it out with the dribbly candle and it sits on the laminex table, never lit, a dream of Italy in a bottle.

Opaque glass louvres run along the short wall and, now open, a hot wind aims right at their hearts as they eat. Each mouthful seems hotter than the last. Ian arrives back in time for the meal but stands looking at the Christmas tree. Juliet calls him over to have some of the chicken. 'Look, Dad, the parson's nose, I saved it for you.' Edith thinks that's pretty sucky but Grace pats Juliet's head and says she's a kind little girl, and Juliet looks at her sister with a superior air and a little shark smirk. Ian seems deaf but after a while says he's not hungry. The day seems so long, Edie wonders if it will ever be over. Then they have a bit of tinned plum pudding boiled in the saucepan (Big Sister brand, Edith notes with a kind of pride) and custard from the shop, which Grace says is better because it's always perfect. The shop makes sure of that, darling, she says, so we don't need to worry.

The kitchen throbs with heat and then it seems as though Grace has forgotten the threepenny bits, which spoils things, really, even though the girls say it doesn't matter. And then Grace leaves the room – maybe she's in tears – and the kids stare at their hot pudding in the hot room and the hot custard in the little jug begins to form a skin. Juliet says she's going to be sick but it's something she always says and, as usual, she isn't. Their mother doesn't come back and after a while they ebb away from the table on a tide of relief.

Ian seems to get sadder and sadder, and after Christmas pudding the little girls go and stand by their father but don't speak. Edith leans into him as if there was a wind pushing her. She's never noticed that he has eyelashes before or that there's prickly stuff covering his face like a rash. He's crying again. He stinks. She touches his shoulder as Juliet shrinks from him; she says later it was because he was dribbling. Edith saw that too but the wave of pity that arose made her kiss his face anyway. The lines in it are long and deep, and the tears fall heavily. And then Grace is there, brisk as ever. 'That's enough of that. Come away now, girls, just leave him be. Christmas always makes Dad sad.' What occurred to Edie, though, was not to do with the isolation of her father, it was to do with herself. It seemed that while Grace approved of Juliet being kind, this was not okay for Edith. All this would take some working out.

Grace says men always feel sorry for themselves, so there's no point anyone else feeling sorry for them. 'Because if you do,' she'd say all exasperated, 'then they really go for it and have a good old wallow. Believe me, Edie, I know all about your father.' She'd say this with her usual dose of sad experience at the conspiracy that dragged her into their father's path.

Chapter 3

Something Unnameable

On Boxing Day, the plan begins. She intends to go to Yarrabeen just for the holiday, but Grace will never come back. Betty and her kids pick them up for the trip to Yarrabeen in their old blue station wagon. Each kid holds a gaunt, faded towel. School bags stuffed with clothes, bats and hats are crammed into every crevice of the car. Grace sits in the front seat with red-faced and wretched Ted on her knee, who's fussing and dragging at his sunhat till it nearly strangles him. Despite Ted, Grace in sunglasses and shorts looks so happy that Edith is mildly scandalised. It doesn't seem right when Dad is so sad. When Dad is not even invited.

Betty's husband died in a work accident, falling through a roof two years ago, so she's well used to being her own boss. The absence of men is unusual and liberating, and the women laugh and then lower their voices for serious talk. And when she can tear her attention away from Betty's son Davey next to her, Edith listens ardently to the women.

Betty's daughter, Lily, and Juliet (or, as Betty infuriatingly calls her, Guillietta) take it in turns to kneel in the middle of the front bench seat, their heads just skimming the car roof. They hold their mother's shoulders and look like loyal servants.

34

Edith shares the back with Davey, Betty's other son Leo, plus the spare girl from the front seat, then the bags. The food, much of it Grace's tins of baked beans and tomato soup, weighs heavily in the boot and the back of the car is low to the road.

Edie's hair is sucked through the window in the fast, dry heat, and everyone sweats with abandon. Edith does her best not to let her leg touch Davey's whose golden thigh, she has noticed, has golden hair to match. Wow! she thinks. All this takes a bit of concentration, and when Davey speaks to her, she loses it immediately. 'Why does everyone always call you by your full name?' In those days she was known almost always as Edith. His blue irises are circled by dark blue and his hair is shining and loose. He seems like a boy from another planet. 'I don't know,' she says, though she's always thought it's because no one likes her. People who are liked get nicknames. 'Well, my full name is Davido Michelangelo Benedetti. I'll call you Edie.' Davey laughs. For the first time, Edie feels elated by her name and not even slightly carsick.

And it's not long before Yarrabeen folds itself into her. All her life she will see the tidal pools of shining water by the sea. The sweep of sand. The tinfoil ocean. The baby brother and his toy yacht in the tidal pools, his milky skin and eyes bluer than the sea. And she will recall holding Davey's hand in the sand dunes.

Chapter 4

The Gimlet

If you squint, the gimlet at Blanket Bay looks a bit like a crooked telescope. The bay, the shell of water that merges lightly with the Southern Ocean, is so cold and vast that whales call it home. The sea gnaws away at the cliff, laying bare the dark seams in the rock. In the evenings, shearwaters, their wings wide and slow, circle home to their burrows on the ridge, wailing like ghosts. Through the gimlet the sea is revealed and framed, and sometimes you see whales breaching, calling and sighing. Kids nag fathers to lift them to look through the gimlet because it's said to be lucky, and they oblige because who really knows about luck?

Before the highway, Yarrabeen was just a holiday town clinging to the lip of the sandy bay. Now people commute to the city. The YB fish shop was there then, always supported by peeling paint and doleful awnings. It sells battered fish as big as cricket bats, fat scallop pouches and hamburgers chocked up with beetroot.

The little supermarket sells grog, carrots and cabbages, smokes and newspapers – and not much else. It's still there, just. In the early eighties, the bakery came third runner-up in a competition for vanilla slices. The prize involved a bronze medallion window sticker, which hangs there still. The bakery is the heart of Yarrabeen and its pies swathed in soft beige pastry define comfort. Grace Fisher started work there when she arrived in Yarrabeen, and for twenty years she spent most days in a mantle of flour.

People recalled happy days in Yarrabeen, scrambling over the rocks, hair whipped behind them, the clean wind shearing their chests and faces, and then later, after climbing the ninety-eight stairs to the lighthouse, they'd come down for some ambling on the sand, shoes in hands, swinging like weights. Yarrabeen brought them back to a time when things were good, even if it was just for that day. The little town wasn't too far from the city. Hour and a half max. And these days the highway cut it down to an hour. It was a place of caravans and mutton-birds gliding in at dusk on big wings and fairy penguins hurrying before the night sea. And the hum of the mutton-bird wings is stored within Edith – heard, remembered and locked away. And the sound recalls her mother. Grace often sent the kids to bed before dark and, waiting for sleep, the wings seemed to bring the night with them, to release Edith from the waiting and guide her towards sleep. There's something in the wings, in the waiting, that brings Grace. That's what she thinks. Waiting was what Edie did best.

***

Kevin Culp, with his question mark shoulders and cupped chest, was once the tallest man in Yarrabeen and Mango Lakes combined but lately, privately, he feels a change and reckons he's begun to shrink a wee bit. That'd be due to the cartilage between the spine, he fancies, apparently it disintegrates as you get on. Typical of bloody life, save the worst till you can handle no more. Likes that word, though: 'disintegrate', got a bit of class. He heard it on a science show on the radio. Amazing what you can find out on the ABC, which he reckons is a good thing since it's all coming out of the public purse. Anyway, he thinks, I do digress and he smiles his bent smile at the sink where he's doing the washing up for Grace.

***

When he was a young man, Kevin Culp met Grace Bell at the dance in Newtown and thought she was the loveliest girl he ever saw. Thought she liked him, which was a huge bonus because it wasn't easy to get girls interested in a tall, skinny baker from Yarrabeen. But Grace's parents hadn't long died and she still wasn't sure of anything but her job as a junior secretary. It occupied most of her brain, and this was a good thing. Kev and Grace courted for a while. He'd take the train down to the big city on Friday nights and stay at the YMCA. They walked through the botanical gardens, ate ice-creams, visited her Auntie Millie at their rented house in South, and then suddenly, Grace up and settled on that damn Ian Fisher who to his mind was a complete dropkick. Something unstable there, he thought. You wouldn't read about it. He'd told her all about Yarrabeen, though, every detail. Well, he'd come back to Yarra and married Sandra Polites, but that was all a long time ago now. Truth is, though, he'd often thought of Grace, so when she turned up at the caravan park and asked for help, he was delighted. He fixed her and the kiddies up in Seacrest, the place in Cedar Street, nice enough but hard to rent down here, what with things being so tight these days. 'Ah, it's an ill wind that blows nobody good,' he says to Nell, his dog curled on the mat. 'Ain't that right, Nellie girl?'

Being a tall baker means a lot of stooping at ovens, which is murder on the back. He bends now to clean the cold ovens, bringing out a bit of blackened bread. Ah, he was bloody wasted on baking, should have been a basketballer, though he's not sure they even had that in his day. Footy or nothing, he reckons. The first thing people always remarked on was his height. 'How tall are you?' they'd ask, looking up. 'Never measured,' he'd say, though he knew it to the quarter inch. His height still underlies everything about him and is arresting even to himself. Why he should be tall is a mystery because most Culps weren't. He used to think he must have had that Abraham Lincoln thing – gigantism or giantism, something like that anyway. It used to bother him until one day height seemed the least of his problems.

Life pushes problems at you, he thinks, and you gotta just push bloody back.

The rain is trying to shake itself from the sky, and he thinks of wringing out the sheets like his mum used to do on wash days. He'd hold onto one end while she twisted the other, and often he'd drop it in the dirt and mess up the whole process. Today the sky is wresting the rain out of itself like those sheets, with about the same rate of success. A few flurries cast upon the dust, the scatterings of intent. The greyness, though, is some comfort this summer, where even the sky feels seared. But then Kevin has always liked dull weather, and if he'd had his druthers he'd have gone off and lived in a cave in some damp place, maybe even Trout's cave down by the beach – that would have done, somewhere he could get cosy. Or maybe somewhere English, where the trees have lime-green leaves soft as feathers. He saw this amazing photography on a nature show once. Saw the leaves replacing themselves each year, rising up on branches like the beaks of baby green birds. Yeah, somewhere soft like that might suit his skin.

Kevin is patchy with skin grafts from skin cancer scraps, some of them layers deep with repairs serious enough to leave dents. Still, he wears his khaki overalls with a sense of purpose. The remains of his hair are a frizz of electrocuted ginger. Yarrabeen needs people like him, he reckons, people prepared to go the distance to build a new future. He votes for the National Country Party and he's not ashamed of it either. Reckons he'd be a member if he had a farm to go with it. But ah, this may come one day, he thinks. None of this commie stuff from the lefties in town gets past him. He lets them know the error of their ways. Currently, he's working on his proposal for a Big Gimlet on Main Street, where the solitary soldier now stands. He draws the project up at night on the kitchen table on a lined pad he bought at the newsagents for twenty cents, just because it lost its cover – what a find! Being a baker, he's never had a lot of time for watching TV at night, and now bed calls to him earlier and earlier. Before he heads off, he gets his son's old coloured pencils out of their tin and draws the Big Gimlet. It isn't all that challenging but he does take his time with it. Alexander wanders in holding a plate of toast with vegemite for dessert. He's dark like his mother was but not as tall as Kev. His eyes are just as blue as his, which is definitely a plus, thinks Kev.

The boy is terse, though. And miffed. 'What you doing with those pencils?'

'Using them, as you can see, my good young man. Making something. You should try it sometime.'

Alex hovers next to his father. He's sixteen, vigorous unwashed hair springing from his head and pimples scattering across his cheeks like tailings. Crumbs stick to his fingers and he licks at them unpleasantly.

'You want to use blue for the headings. Blue looks better.'

'Thank you for your input, Mr Van Gogh, but I'll be using the red.'

Alexander picks up the plate and the toast slides across it, landing on his father's hand and then on the drawing.

'Well then.' Kev steps back, looks at his son and detects a small smile. Alex leaves the toast on the plate next to the drawing. 'Sorry, Dad,' Kev hears when Alex is down the hall.

***

Kev's pushing the construction of the Big Gimlet for the tourists who are, to his way of thinking, the lifeblood of the place, so moving the gimlet up to the main street would save them the trouble of walking all the way down to the beach. 'Ya gotta make it easy for people, see? It's like the Big Prawn and the Big Banana. Put us on the map! The tourists come here for a bit of a break, a little holiday. They don't want to have to drag themselves all that way down there where there are no coffee shops. Do they? No, 'course not. These rich folk, they love their coffee. I'm telling you, build the Big Gimlet out of fibreglass, be absolutely bloody beautiful and what a pull for the town. I can guarantee a real goer,' he tells anyone who'll listen. He's thought about developing the main street himself but, like many a would-be developer, luck has never been on his side. Though with Grace showing up, maybe this changes things.

***

The ute rolls to a stop at the one set of traffic lights. He's folded into it like an origami crane, all angles, and he seizes the chance to eject a bit of air. He rises up slightly on the seat and expels a long, slow and – even to himself – surprisingly loud fart. It doesn't smell much, not that he really minds the smell at all, but he opens the window anyway and waves to poor old Beryl Marks hobbling across the road, hanging onto her shopping jeep as if it were a plough. She sees Culp in his ute and nods back cautiously, as if she'd caught a whiff of something. His radical ideas for a new Yarrabeen have caused a few issues with some of the oldies, and Beryl Marks is one of them. 'She's absolutely ropeable about your plans,' one of his neighbours told him. Old bat, he thinks, and takes off just a bit too fast and nearly clips the jeep. She glares at him from the footpath.

His days are full, though, because apart from the bakery work he delivers wood in the winter afternoons and then, since the ice trade disappeared years ago, mostly he just bludges in summer, which means fishing when the tides are right. Just working at the bakery making good, sound, crusty loaves would be enough for anyone, but being busy makes life pass in a controllable way. The one-foot policy he calls it: one foot in front of the other. World's your bloody oyster, and if only the kids realised it, we'd all be better off. His own son, Alexander, has been a worry for years, well, since he lost his mother he supposes, and after that it wasn't long before he was dropping out of every bloody school round the place. Next thing, he thinks, he'll take up bloody drugs and that'll be all I need.

44

Chapter 5

Min

When Grace first takes Edie and Juliet to Yarrabeen, they're pale girls of eight and six who, if they'd had a bit more conviction, might have had their mother's dark curls. But alas, as they have heard a thousand times, they went the other way and took after their father and went pasty. Grace, however, believes there's still time for redemption. They have that dishwater hair that's now just waiting to turn brown, and she remarks more than once that even Marilyn Monroe wasn't born a blonde, you know.

It's true, there's something of the squaw in the child that is Edie Fisher, though maybe she's a bit more speckled than most Indians. She has the small, round face and the secret brown eyes, but, whatever it really is, the long plait says 'squaw' to Jules, who has her radar squarely tuned in to what will truly shit Edie.

She taunts her with 'Min-min, Minnie Mouse' and sometimes, when Jules feels just that little bit more wacky than usual, she'll call her 'Mini-minor'. Edie reckons people only like Juliet because she got the good name; if Edie had scored Juliet, things would've been different. But *she* had to get Edith Eileen Fisher. When she was little, Grace called her Bobby Bear and lately, after Davey, she's become Edie, which is some improvement. She can appear sullen in the eye-averting way of the shy. Scabs seem to gather at her joints like pink petals, but it's just eczema. Already, she likes to retreat from the gaze of others and clothes are a sore trial. Grace makes their outfits and dresses the girls alike brightly. Today they're in check pants and shirts with orange groves sprouting all over. Edie pulls her brown cardigan into her as if it were a shell. The things that are important to her are all beyond her reach, up on the highest shelf. What happened to her Dad? Is Uncle Kev coming to live? Does that mean Alexander comes too? Does her mother love her? Then why'd she give her such a rotten name? And why is she always so busy? And Juliet, why is she mean to me? What did I do?

When Juliet starts calling names, she gets Edie's full attention. As she ages, Edie is amazed that so many taunts can be derived from the innocent Min-nehaha in 'Hiawatha's Childhood'. But even then, Juliet was thrilled that it upset her sister so much to be called names. But clarity is often elusive and late in arriving and the only truth is that time, with its own reasons, sees to it that the nickname 'Min' lasts longer than Edie's plait.

Ian would read the poem to them on good nights at the old house. The rhyming of the verses and his guiding voice in the single yellow light of the kitchen come back to Edie in shafts. On those nights, it always seems to have been winter – the orange stripe of the bar radiator bolted to the wall above them, a fan of heat splaying across the dusty wall. The lean bamboo blinds restraining the black night. At the table, their mother is knitting moss-stitch jumpers. She only likes moss stitch. Her fingers ricochet, elastic as echoes, the clacking needles like dentures speaking another language, speaking the language of mothers.

'By the shores of Gitche Gumee,' Juliet whispers when the meanness rises, and her sister's eyes glisten instantly, reliably. Being reminded of their father hurts both of them, but for Jules it's always better to give than to receive.

She closes her eyes and chants:

'By the shores of Gitche Gumee
By the shining Big-Sea-Water,
Stood the wigwam of Nokomis,
Daughter of the Moon, Nokomis.
Dark behind it rose the forest,
Rose the black and gloomy pine-trees,
Rose the firs with cones upon them;
Bright before it beat the water.
Beat the clear and sunny water,
Beat the shining Big-Sea-Water.
There the wrinkled old Nokomis
Nursed the little Hiawatha.'

Juliet glances at Edie, who seems to be both open and closed. And then, like a switch flipped, she flies at her. Missing her dad has become something alive in Edie. Once she's on top, Jules is a goner. For Juliet, who loves the poem and remembers way more of it, getting Edie to start a fight is perfect. It makes her feel better somehow and getting Edie into trouble feels like Christmas. And she hadn't even got to Minnehaha...

Chapter 6

Swim and Fish

That day down by the beach, the seagulls huddle on the limited grass in the park, sleeping against the weather like stones. The car advances and parks. The birds rise.

Maybe it's the winter sky and the white sea before them, or it's the food or the undivided company of their mother, but that day was special.

The kids call a truce on their usual flicking, pinching, name-calling and sly kicks. Peace seeps in and, dazed by the moment, they begin to feel a bit like a family. It won't last. And without their father, it's not real anyway. But Edie thinks they took the moment and shaped it to fit, and it seems that they could live like this forever.

Then again, Jules is being very nice today, which makes Edie suspicious.

She's sneaky, she thinks, and she'll be twice as mean to make up for it. Mild dread is a way of life. Juliet, with her fine light hair, sits in the front seat with Grace, whose hair is darker, but still they're a matching pair like lace curtains, dusted with pale freckles. Edie believes their freckles are better than hers, less spotted and more subtle and isn't that typical?

In the back seat of the dented white Datsun is the baby Ted with the resolutely runny nose. His first word was 'more'. He's standing on the seat, accepting chips like a seagull from Edie, consuming sauce and grime. He's getting over some cold or other again and coughing and laughing. He pokes too many chips into his mouth and jigs on the seat, nappy big under his corduroy overalls, palm out for more. His hands make starfishes on the window against the shadow of the big trees.

Picking through the chips in the greasy paper nest, Edie reckons the feed today is better than scrounging in the cupboard for a tin of baked beans. On the downside, Juliet has beaten her to the front seat again. Very annoying.

Plus, Juliet seems to think she's the equal of their mother – plainly ridiculous. She thinks she's the Queen of Sheba. And here I am, she thinks, sadness in her mulish heart, babysitting Ted again. When she pulls him away from the window and gives him the chip paper, families of ghost starfish nest on the glass.

As they absorb the salt, oil and vinegar like sponges, the day wraps them in itself and they are happy. And then out of nowhere talk gets serious and Grace makes a pronouncement about dying. And about the disposal of remains. The kids are stopped. The chips begin to taste cold. They swallow the gathering lumps. The thought of their mother dying rushes at them and in the silence they feel their hearts going about the lonely business of staying alive.

She starts off brightly enough but that's sadness in her voice, thinks Edie, not fooled for one moment. 'Now I don't want to make a big deal of it, but you all know that I'll die one day. Happens to everyone. Every living thing must die.' Though Edie's listening with a kind of desperation, she drops out and her eye follows a man passing by in the street who looks a bit like Dad – same sloping shoulders, same washed-out look. She truly did hear most of her mother's ramble, even the part 'and God, I hope none of you ever do die and I'm here to bury you, but that's another story and I suppose I won't be the one telling it'.

Grace catches Edie looking away in the rear-vision mirror, gazing down the street, and a pulse of annoyance grabs her. Honestly, sometimes she could just thump that girl. She'd try the patience of a saint. She turns. 'Now,' she smiles sadly at Juliet. 'I know you miss your father.' She wants to be kind but it doesn't come out right. She snaps raggedly at Edie, '*I* miss him too you know, Edith, but the fact is he wasn't much chop, not much chop at all, and he left us high and dry, a fact that will become plainer as you get older. *Edie.* You listening, Edie?'

She's not listening. The girl's swelling mind trails the man in the street with a muted longing that becomes an ache that turns her mother down like a radio. Grace turns around to glare at Edie and she wonders how her mother always knows the moment she's lost her. Some kind of mother magic? Or maybe it's not that mysterious. While she's being examined she notices that even now, after eating chips, though possibly no more than one or two, her mother's lipstick is still straight and not even slightly smudged. Well, thinks Edith, *I* won't wear lipstick when *I'm* old. It's yucky and *I'd* be sure to mess it up, and that's worse than wearing none at all apparently.

'Edith darling, just pay attention for a few seconds, will you? Honestly. I try.' Grace consoles herself with the thought of her effort and breathes in. 'Well anyway, I don't want to grandstand. We'll leave that to the blokes, eh?' She laughs, embarrassed, and chokes up but the kids don't get it. 'Anyway, girls, the thing is I want you to bring my ashes down here when I die. Bring them down here and put them into the sea. Just chuck them in. That shallow patch over there shouldn't be too hard to get to. Okay?'

The kids, with the patience of children who've seen a lot of things, are silent.

Is she going to die? Edie wonders with a kind of clamping in her guts. What about Dad? She starts to feel queer, too many chips working on her. She's always been a delicate girl, stricken with bouts of dizziness, motion sickness and even hives. And maybe this is Grace's way of telling them something. She thinks of all the times Grace has said stuff about death lately. 'Knock me down with a feather' and

'Blow me down' and 'You wouldn't be dead for quids'. Something's going on. Must be.

Probably cancer like Pamela Lavender's mother. It took ages before she died. Everyone cried a lot. Kids were nice to Pamela, though. People brought them casseroles and lasagne.

If she dies this would mean Edie would be in charge of the others, because there is no one else. No one else. But she doesn't say anything, groaning and holding her stomach and watching the man who looked like Dad disappear. She thinks her father might have once carried her on such shoulders.

And in the little car now swathed in steam, Jules cracks the window and the swimming cold air enters to examine them like a doctor. She opens the window further and hurls a handful of chips into the air. The birds with their kaleidoscope eyes rise up, hanging before them like white flags.

Grace seems to be wiping her eyes but the kids cheer for the seagulls anyway. She believes she's done the right thing, coming up here to live. Instead of saying this, she reaches for her bag and takes a moment for a smoke. Around the car window, scalds on the upholstery from burning ash are woven like braid. Smoking is her one weakness, she often says. And she lights up, relishing the steps in the ritual: the selection of the cigarette, the trip to her mouth, the match striking the box. Next comes the hungry breath and then the smoke holding the children like small fish in a net. The girls crack their windows at the same time. They don't say anything about the smoke. That would be rude.

***

Edie knew her sister was her enemy before thinking began. It didn't matter what told her, she came to believe all was lost on that first day. The day Juliet was born. Edie still wonders how you make your mother love you. They love you when you're naughty and funny. Like that day Jules told her she wasn't washing the baking tin and put it around the back for the dog. When Grace found it, she chased a skinny, smiling Jules round the yard and out the front, the blackened tin still clanking in her hand. The day was hot, the sun yellow as frying butter. The wind rustled in the lemon gums and in the grasses. In the end, after a few yards of panting, Grace gave up, laughing so much she couldn't catch her breath. Looking out at Jules, the bare-legged laughing girl, ready to take off any second, Edie was awed by her sister. Jules is just so damn good at all of that stuff. If you can get your mum to think you're funny, well, then you're really made.

Edie decides two can play at that game. And she plans a joke after tea in the kitchen one night when the gingham curtains breathe against the open window. She'll tell it right, she promises herself. She readies herself. She needs to get her head settled for the laughs. 'Mum,' she begins. 'Mum, I've got a joke for you. You'll really like it.'

Grace is ironing their school dresses with speed and precision, pounding the ironing board as if she were hammering something, but her listening seems opaque. The cigarette smoulders in the ashtray. She pauses for a drag now and then. 'Hmm,' she says.

Edie's delivery speeds up. 'Jimmy told me this one at school the other day. It's a good one. You'll love it. So, you ready? Here goes: what do frogs eat with their hamburgers?'

Grace breathes out more smoke in the halting way she sometimes does when she's thinking and smiles, 'I don't know, darl, what do frogs eat?'

Edie can barely contain herself because she knows she will remember the joke. 'French flies,' she burbles. 'Get it? Get it, Mum?' Pause.

'What a beauty, Edie. Absolute beauty.' Grace smiles, though she doesn't laugh. Her mood is always in her voice and now you'd call it well disposed. She reaches out her hand and rests it on the nearby Juliet's head instead of Edie's, mixing the girls up again, this time with the long white cigarette burning between her fingers. Edie flinches. That's it for jokes, she thinks, they are not reliable, and she flops onto a chair. But like the guardian of something important, the thought rises in her: get that cigarette away from my sister.

***

Smoking is horrible. She hates it so much. Always has. What a weirdo, a true weirdo. Everyone smokes. She's got a reason for hating it, though, she tells herself – and it's not just because her mother smokes. It happened when Ted was a little baby and Grace was holding him when she lit a match. It was hot that day. The burning match head flew off and stuck to his chest, burning itself out on him. The small lump of a scar remains.

'Well, your mum was lighting up, see,' her father explained when Edie asked about the mark, 'holding Teddy on one arm and the smoke in the other. See? She was stuck. She couldn't put either down so she blew at the match head. Only made it worse, you see. It melted. You screamed your head off for poor little Ted. Yes, you did, and it made things worse.' He was watering his favourite plant at the time, a young daphne he was hoping would flower this winter. 'Reminds me of my poor old granny, whose name was also Daphne as you already know, young Edith, and her daughter, Grandma Nerry. Now, *there* was a mother.' He smiles at her and plays the hose across her bare toes and she squeals, 'Dad!'

He straightens up and starts putting the hose away, wrapping it around his forearm like a whip. 'Though you've got nothing to complain about in that department either, young lady. Nothing at all. I want you to remember that.'

***

56

And suddenly Edie has had enough of everyone today, especially Juliet, and something boils over and her voice breaks, tight and old. 'Don't give everything to the birds, Juliet, and save that potato cake for later. Jeez. Anyway, you're not supposed to feed the birds. It only encourages them, doesn't it, Mum?'

Grace wraps up her newspaper parcel and pauses. 'Edie girl, I've got to tell you something. And you should listen with all your ears, my darling. Sometimes you've got to make up your own mind on things. And sometimes you've got to leave people alone. Two simple facts.'

By now Ted's complaints are impossible to ignore. He's jumping on the seat and plastering snot everywhere. Grace reluctantly dashes out the smoke in the ashtray, breaking its slender neck. She wipes her fingers on the paper for any traces of grease, straightens her grey skirt, turns the key in the ignition and, after a few stutters, the car comes to life. Backing out, they see the darkening change in the sky and the giant trees moaning against the heavy wind like chained beasts. Everything has become the colour of slate. Juliet is still heaving chips to the retreating seagulls and Edie is nursing a salvaged, solitary, cold potato cake on her lap for later.

***

This must have been the week their father, Ian Fisher, electrocuted himself in a panelbeaters in

Broadmeadows. It's a machinist's shop now, corrugated iron sides, rusting into oblivion. Apparently, they still do sheet metal work these days when they can get it, even though the premises are pretty dilapidated. Ian was fitting it out. He'd got himself a job on a freelance basis. When he died there, it was run by a panelbeater named Neil Nim. The sign out the front read: 'Bingles Fixed: Best For Less'.

When Nim found him, Ian's bent head was thrown back onto a stack of old tyres that Nim thought might be viable retreads one day. In death, Ian's eyes were wide and white as silver fish in the sea and his mouth was closed and brimming with blood after he'd bitten through his tongue. His light hair was floppy as ever, and yet that day it was soft and clean.

Apparently, he'd made a mistake with the live feed. A strange thing for an electrician to do. Beside him on the concrete floor was his metal toolbox, the keys were in his pocket.

That night after work, Grace got a phone call from Mr Nim. Neil Nim, a name Grace would never forget. Ian had her down as next of kin when he signed on for the work. There would be an inquiry into Ian's death, though, the panelbeater said. Nim was catarrhal and coughed in hard, clearing barks before apologising for his sad news. The pause between their words seemed eternal. The police wanted to clear things up about the manner of death, all a workplace formality, really. Nim said he was sorry again and then, no longer hacking and hawking, he just went away. As the numbness entered Grace, she went to the children's room and sat on the end of Edie's bed. Hours passed until she realised she must sleep or she would be useless at work the next day, but all night she thought, *What happened to you? Where did you go?*

Ian kept his toolbox neat to the point of perfection. Pliers, longnosed and blunt-nosed, screws and fuses and fine wires and tiny screw drivers that he tells Edie are for fixing the fairies' houses and little pliers that he once used to take out the kids' baby teeth. It was heavy and he used to say it was the most valuable thing in the house. 'Not that there's much here, eh? A man's tools are his worth,' he'd say. 'Worth more than bloody anything, more even than most of the cars around here, and there's nothing much else.' On the nights when he put the grey slab of the metal box on the table for a bit of a clean out, the kids were allowed to hold the tools, but only if they put them back in the right spot.

***

Four months after Ian died, the toolbox came down to them on the train, the keys posted separately. Ian had known where they were in Yarra-been because Grace had sent him a letter explaining that she needed a break, but that he could write to them at 5 Cedar Street, Yarrabeen. She never heard from him. The police held the toolbox until the coronial inquest was over and a verdict of suicide was made.

She picks the toolbox up from the train station in the next town and her arm feels the weight of it. The kids are at school on this rainy morning when she's nicked off for half an hour from the bakery. She puts the heavy box in the boot and can barely look at it because it seems that Ian inhabits it. She sits outside the station in the Datsun and has a smoke. How do you tell children such a thing about their father? Maybe you never have to, she decides, just remember to keep with the accident. As she smokes, the interstate express passes through, sleek as a jet, pulling people to different places. She feels the sudden need to go with them, to leave all this. The speed of the train shakes a coat of leaves free from the trees. They drop like gold eyes onto the shining wet path. She thinks of Ian, but it's best not to think.

Early one morning, a week later, in her blue rose dressing gown and old thongs, Grace drags the toolbox out of its hiding spot under her bed in a frenzy of wanting to know everything there is to know. Suddenly she finds herself wondering if the damn tools really do have any value. Probably not, knowing Ian's ways with money, she thinks briskly. She removes the keys from the envelope that arrived last week along with a letter saying the coroner had opened the toolbox but placed things back the way they were found. Grace unlocks the thing on the kitchen table. And Ian surprises her again. On top of the tools is an envelope addressed to Edith, Juliet and Edward. She opens it with a horrible sense of foreboding. Seeing his handwriting, neat and sure and so completely him, is like holding his heart. Here is the same Ian who wrote her love letters. The earthquake of old love shakes her and her tears slip away and she must sit down to read this:

My Dears,

I want to tell you so much, but you can't tell everything you feel. You just never can. Let me tell you this, though: being your father was the best thing that ever happened to me. I love each of you. Edie, my sweet little Minnie, it will all be all right, and Juliet, you will be a beauty. Wear your glasses and do what your mum says. Ted, my baby boy, such a lovely child will grow to be a special man. I know it and I will be with you every day of your lives. I love your mother. It's not her fault what happened. You kids make sure you have a good life in Yarrabeen. Swim and fish. Swim and fish, and I will be with you while you do.

I am not myself anymore, and it's not fair on anyone to have me around. I just can't get better. I've forgotten how to get things right. I'm just a burden. This is the best thing for everyone. I am tired. I want it to stop. You're all better off without me.

Love,
Dad
XXX, a kiss for each one of you on the top of your heads.

Grace holds the letter to her. She's riven by this and yet, she's still mad at him. Bloody idiot, she thinks, bloody, bloody idiot – you didn't have to tell them. They don't need this. *What on earth happened to you, Ian?* She knows she should pack things away – knows it – but the shock is in her and some part of her just wants the comfort of her kids. Of their kids. Of Ian. Ian who is so lost. And yet still so present. The weeping lasts until she hears kids coming out of their rooms and Grace, knowing they will see the toolbox, stands up to be in front of it. She tries to make her face normal, dashing away tears and straightening up her hair, but then suddenly Edie is there asking what's Dad's toolbox doing on the table, and what's she reading? Grace stands up straighter and surprises herself utterly by giving Edie the letter.

Reading her father's handwriting is like seeing him again, like looking at his face. He taught her to write. Her face is white, eyes round. She looks up, horrified. 'What does it mean, "better off without me", Mum, what does that mean? Where did this come from? Who gave it to you? What really happened to Dad? I thought it was an accident at work.' She's buttoned her yellow pyjamas up all wrong and part of her white stomach winks out. Her feet are bare and she looks older than a child.

'It doesn't mean much, Ed. Some people get a feeling before they die and he must have had that. That's all.'

Edie doesn't buy this and never will, and she wants to know why he thought they didn't want him around. 'I love Dad. Didn't he know that? Why didn't he know?'

Juliet is still holding the crackly lined paper up as if she might see through it. Slowest reader in the grade, Edie thinks snidely, even now finding advantage. And yet a feeling like pity seeps into her – he was her dad too. 'I can't read this writing. I don't know what it says. Read it, Edie.'

She grabs it and, with surgical delicacy, fillets the text to do less harm. 'Dad says your eye will be better and he wants us to swim and fish. He calls me his "sweet little Minnie".' And she starts to cry and her legs fold her down onto the little stool.

'Oh Edith, that's not all it says and you know it. Come on now.' Grace wants this to end now, wants Ian to leave them. They were all right. They will be all right again. Won't they? Wants the day back on track with school and work and babysitters and not thinking about painful things. No more painful things. This has dragged on too long. She stands near Juliet, wondering whether she should just read the thing out to them.

Juliet persists with the letter, holding it like a raggedy hanky, shaking it and demanding as if she were an angry lawyer in a courtroom of her peers, 'But why didn't he come and live with us if he knew where we were? If he wrote us a letter then he musta known. I was waiting for him. He didn't hafta work at that rotten, awful factory where he made the mistake. Did he? Did he? What happened to him? Why didn't he come and live with us here?'

Grace kneels before her, crying against her will, pulling Ted between them. 'Darling, Dad was sick. He was not well, and sometimes when you're not well it doesn't matter what anyone does, you are just gonna die.'

Juliet's hair is wild with sleep and shock, her plaits on the verge of flying out of themselves. Even her fringe is standing up. The toolbox rests like a tomb on the table. She's mad as she's never been mad before, standing in her pyjamas with little blue boats, and her voice becomes shrill. 'Well, Mum, if he was sick why didn't someone make him better? Why didn't you take him to the doctor? You take us to the doctor when we get sick. No. Mum. No. I just want my dad and so does Edith. I want him to come back and he can live in Yarrabeen with us.'

Chapter 7

Skeins of Birds

Now, all these years later at Yarrabeen, watching the sky from the kitchen window at Seacrest, Edie sees a string of seabirds passing and thinks of that day in the white Datsun. She's sipping boiling hot mint tea in a pea-green mug, possibly with too much honey, and thinking, Mum must have known about Dad then and thought it better not to say. That would have brought on the talk of death and dying. But she didn't seem very emotional, that's for sure.

Edie believes she remembers but concedes it may well have been her own mood she's remembering from the days when empathy was a long way over the border. And now the old voice she reserved for her mother has crumbled away like the rocky face of a cliff. When Grace first got breast cancer five years ago, much seemed irrelevant and the hope of reprieve from it fluttered within her like a flag on a bright spring day, all green and blue. And then they got over the hurdle and things sagged again. The new clarity from this latest diagnosis is another clean wind.

When she became a mother, she got that her mother was just trying to get by all along. She never did have a great big plan. Ah, she thinks sadly, grabbing a stool and dragging it up to the window to watch the sea, I used to even blame poor old Mum for Dad's suicide. And for his depression, can you believe it? she asks herself. Now, depression reaps so many. Maybe it always did. Then, people treated it like a secret weakness.

Poor old Dad. He got no help from anyone. And when we did find out, it was all to do with the rotten toolbox.

Edie still thinks it was better they knew. Grace told her later that she thought about not telling them, but on the morning of the toolbox it all came out, just spilled over them like some low, black cloud. And anyway, Edie thinks, what is the correct procedure for dealing with suicide?

And now the cancer is back and it's Grace's turn. And so it goes for everyone.

Grace had been tired for a while and it seemed she couldn't shake the flu. 'Just keeps hanging onto me, Edie,' she'd say, 'and I'm completely stuffed.' Turned out the flu was really cancer again, this time back for good. Apparently, it will take four or five months for the disease to do its work and then one of them – Edie or one of the others – will do what Grace asked all those years ago: take her ashes to the beach and deliver her into everything. Liberate her from us needing her so much, Edie thinks guiltily, knowing the loss will never leave. And yet Grace had gone on after her own mother died. How? she wondered. And the hollow stretches; you live with your mother and you live without her.

Through the window, the birds are still passing and she watches absently until it seems that the way birds fly, making small adjustments to stay in formation, reminds her of Grace. Grace at the head of a skein of birds travelling intently across the graded sky, leading them through it all: weather, drama, sorrow and happiness. All of them – Edie, Juliet, Ted and all their families – follow Grace solidly, wing beats paired. Each correction lifting them to stay with the flight. And each one in each family is together and alone.

Chapter 8

Seacrest

A skin of age and salt stains the 'Seacrest' brass plate near the front door, and by it the hide-a-key is parked under a succulent as grey and soft as an aged pensioner. At first it seems the house swarms with ghosts. The verandah creaks and wind rushes at them through chinks round the windows. Creepy big cracks flow like dark rivers across the walls and seep dusty old insects. The girls shadow their mother. Lucky, Ted is too young to be worried. In the end, the girls start a collection of dead insects and getting all competitive about it helps.

Snubbing the sea is what the forebears did, maybe so you could open the door without getting blown away. Or because humans believed they were more important than the elements. Whatever the reason, the early settlers turned their backs on the immensity. The back of the house faces the water and the front looks onto the street. At night, the house strains against the wind and on still nights, as it settles, the slowing pulse of the cooling timbers counts them to sleep and they hear small dumpings of the waves below. Other nights, rain beats across the tin roof. And as the nights pass they begin to notice the house accepting them.

The landlord, Kevin Culp, is in and out, bringing bits and pieces – a bucket, an old bench seat, some parsley seeds. He introduces them to Ivy and Roy Jackett, the neighbours. Tells them which is the good butcher. The kids like him and he loves a chat. And he tells Edie a couple of times about knowing her mum before. 'Your mother was such a beauty, little mate,' his splintered voice gears up like an old truck to the run of his thoughts. 'We called her the Teenager. She'd have been one of the first of them ever bloody well invented! Loved all the latest style and that kind of thing...' And he'd stop, put his heavy hand on Edith's head and slip her a consolation prize of two bob, quietly though, so no one would notice, then wink in a way that made them both smile. He'd move off, tinkering here and there, stalling for the chance of a cup of tea with Grace.

The doors at Seacrest are unreliable closers. They swing loose and easy on their hinges, and the bottom of each door has been well planed. Draughts glide through like voices from other places. Apart from the sinkage and the big trees around the house, the weather dictates if the doors will close. No one locks anything in Yarrabeen anyway, so it doesn't matter much, except to Edie to whom the idea of locks seems like perfection. She likes the completion that locking brings.

Long, printed curtains trail with faded flowers. The two big front rooms with their high ceilings and fireplaces are compensations for all the cracks, for

69

the kitchen with rusted taps and stained sink. There's an early Kooka stove with gas jets like geysers that have taken a few eyebrows over the years. The house has two bedrooms. The three kids have the big bed which, once Ted settles down from being a baby, is not even so bad. There's something about being together that feels good. Though the endless needs of babies are a trial for everyone, Edie thinks, maybe even the babies. Grace gets the small bed and is glad because sleeping on her own is pure delight. She wakes hearing the morning birds arrive, jawing with the light. Sometimes there's the blessing of kids sleeping in, which gives her a few moments to herself. She goes out the back with her thongs on, a cup of tea and her morning puff, and looks out at the shining sea. Inside, the toast is in and the working day ahead beckons. Grace Fisher would not call a king her damn uncle.

Seacrest was the first house built on Cedar Street, but there are a few other old ones – Roy and Ivy Jackett next door, and over the road are the Joneses, the Theodakises, the McKennas. The gardens are worth a look and people in car coats and cardigans pull up out the front some Sunday afternoons, looking for a break in the winter. They're pleased to see the magnolia trimmed with blooms like ruby birds. The McKennas across the road are proud of their garden, and Mr McKenna's mown nature strips are famous for being both short and cushiony. Week after week he mows the others down to his level and Sunday mornings come laced with the stuttering, sawing sound of the mower scalding the grass and flicking out sticks and stones. He is still always the best.

**

At first Grace and the kids make do with what's in the house – the beds, a table and one vast lounge chair. The kids sprawl at her feet on the floor at night and draw everything they've seen that day. Seagulls crop up a lot. Grace reckons their talent comes from her side of the genetic set-up. Her proof is in the picture her mother, Molly, painted of a Tasmanian farmhouse from a book. It's the only picture in the house. She thought to bring it with her for some reason and she thinks it was her famous intuition leading her, some kind of early knowing that she would never go back to Ian.

Her own mother had dreams, though Molly's dreams were mostly about houses. Sometimes when she's passing that picture it's as if Molly is showing her something, but she never works out what that might be. Molly and Henry have both been dead for so long.

When Grace was sixteen and working as a junior secretary, her mother and father were killed in a train crash near Geringup. They'd been visiting friends and were on the Sunday night train. The train derailed and nine others were killed. Grace went to work on the Tuesday after speaking to the police on the Monday. She organised the funerals, and her mum's old friend Millie moved in with her. She sold the house and put the money in the bank. She never told anyone about it. It's still in the bank. Having that money there gave her the freedom to leave Ian. Even though she didn't touch it, it allowed her to get away. She missed Molly and Henry so much that she couldn't speak of it. Such losses are not forgettable and only sometimes are they manageable. She plans to give it to her kids when the time comes, and this gives her comfort.

***

After a while, Culp the baker in overalls starts coming around every Saturday for lunch with Grace. They'd bring the leftovers from the shop and have a bit of a feast. After a couple of months around the kitchen table with cups of tea and plenty of pastry, Grace says they can call him 'Uncle Kevin' if they want to. The girls steal a covert glance at each other and seem to keep eating.

Later, Edie and Jules are under the house in the dry, sandy dirt engaged with a couple of leftover sausage rolls the width of their forearms. Kev's dog Nell appears on the warm drift of the scent of pastry. She dribbles politely beside them.

Edie is bothered. 'Why would she want us to call him "Uncle Kevin"?'

'He likes us, I s'pose.' Juliet picks at the pastry with her little white fingers.

'That's not the reason, you dill. There's more to it than that. Now that Dad's died' – she crosses herself because she saw Betty Benedetti doing it and she loves Betty Benedetti because of Davey – 'there's something going on, I tell you. I know I'm right.'

Half of Juliet's sausage roll flops off and lands in the dirt.

'What *is* going on then? What d'you mean? I don't get it.' Juliet gives the rest of the pastry to the happy dog, who downs it in a gulp and settles into the dirt to stay with them forever.

'We are going to end up with a new father and,' she pauses for drama, 'a new brother. A horrible new brother. I'm telling you. That's what's going on.' She tosses her food to Nellie and makes handprints in the dirt. *Dad, Dad, Dad,* she writes with a twig in each handprint.

Chapter 9

Some Kind of Waiting

Something about the mouse's eyes reminded Edith of her Grandma Nerry, their dad's mum, but it's hard to work out what it really is. Fear or love or some kind of waiting that looks like love. She doesn't know, not for sure. The mouse died when someone sat back on the couch in the old house where they lived with their dad, without even knowing she was hiding there. A couple of days later the stiff little body rolls out of the cushions during a casual pillow fight, and when Edie puts her hand on the stony body, the sickness of irresponsibility invades her. Oh no. It's my fault.

If she's honest, she'd admit that Tammy was doomed all along just because she was hers. And here was proof. Most of her other pets had ended badly – Dazza the budgie got out when she left the cage door open; her dog Blue, run over (gate open); Bun, her piebald rabbit, eaten by next door's greyhound Sarge, who remains a very nice dog, and it was explained that he could not have been expected to resist a rabbit wandering into his own yard. And yet against the odds Edie remained an enthusiastic, if doomed, pet owner.

Right from the start, that first day in the pet shop, she saw in those tiny mouse eyes a kind of hovering fear, just like her Nan's. She felt sad for it and thought she should leave it alone and not drag it into her crazy family, but she picked up the shivering creature anyway because her mum was willing to buy her a mouse and now was not the time to waver. One qualm and there would be no mouse. 'I'll call her Tammy,' she said bravely, looking up, but her mum was already at the counter paying for the innocent little creature.

Of course, not looking for Tammy in the first days she went missing was the biggest sin. There were no posters about poor old Tammy. Nothing. Edith just brushed her out of her mind like crumbs off her jumper, telling herself she'd run away with all the other mice or that she'd show up when she was hungry.

Juliet reckons this is all boring Edith-rubbish, as usual.

'She's a mouse,' Edith says when Tammy is first lost, 'if she can't survive, who can?' Juliet says she 'hates these meeces to pieces' and falls about laughing at her own jokes which to Edith is such bad manners.

Ha, ha, thinks Edie darkly. Very funny. But now, on viewing the corpse, Juliet changes her tune to extravagant pity. 'Poor little darling thing, searching for crumbs at the bottom of the couch.' She does a little mouse-searching-for-crumbs act, brushing little paws across her round cheeks, and snickers with a *hee, hee, hee* that is actually heartbreakingly mouse-like.

Jules laughs luxuriously. When she can bring herself to breathe and speak at the same time she says, 'Honestly, Edo, it's just a mouse. You weren't even worried about it till you found it dead. You're such a hypocrite.'

'You don't even know what that means, Juliet. You're so dumb, so shut your rotten trap.'

'I do so. Mum said Dad was one – and his whole family too – because they don't help us.' Juliet is getting mad now, tearing off hangnails with her teeth and spitting missiles of skin just short of Edie.

'She did NOT say that!' She's screaming now, and not far away from crying, and then the thought rushes in that Jules has overheard this. 'Well, come on. Who did she say it to then?'

But Juliet won't say and steers her back to the mouse accident, which has less to do with her or her sources. Her logic is faultless: everyone knows Edith is the big bum in the family, so she's got to be the one who squashed the mouse.

'Drama Queen of New Orleans. Hypocrite Head, your mouse is dead,' Juliet chants to her sister's plopping tears. 'Starved her mouse to death. And then sat on her. You ought to be reported to the RSPCA.'

When Edie tells Grace about the demise of Tammy, she's cleaning the stove and her hands are slick with grease because she doesn't believe in gloves. Complete waste of money! When Edie shows up, her nose is suddenly madly itchy. She swipes it with the back of her hand, and somehow she sees the funny side. The poor dead mouse tickles her.

'Honestly, Edie, you should have kept it in the cage like I said,' she chides, trying to be sympathetic and contain herself. No success on either score. Edie trails away, leaving her mother smiling at the stove, hoping she might just fall in. Always busy, she thinks scandalised, always doing some damn thing, doesn't even care about poor Tammy. What sort of mother, she asks herself, doesn't care about her daughter's mouse?

Later, to punish Grace, Edie steals her lily-of-the-valley box from the old soap boxes. At least Tammy's coffin will be nice, she comforts herself. I'll teach her to laugh at the death of a poor mouse. Death is serious and so, she realises on reflection, is having your father leave you forever because though she knows he died, she prefers to think he's just not around. Maybe it's even the same thing. Her mum wouldn't let them go to their dad's funeral – she didn't believe in kids at funerals. 'You don't need to see all that yet,' she'd said to Edie as she pulled on her best brown skirt and her trench coat, but Edie remembers wanting to see all that, whatever that was. Wanting to say goodbye to Dad. Wanting people to know he had a daughter who loved him. But her mum didn't listen, and she remembers the buckles tapping on the heels of Grace's shoes as she left for the funeral down in the city. Remembers the hammering of them.

Well, she thinks, sniffing, Tammy will have a real good funeral, because I will make sure.

Lining the box with fresh green leaves from the immense maple tree, she buries Tammy in the compost heap which, it turns out, is another big mistake. A week later when Grace is turning the compost there's an impromptu exhumation and she discovers the small rotting corpse all tucked up in her nice box and secured with a rubber band.

After a moment's reflection, Grace puts Tammy's earthly remains back in the box and gives the mouse a second burial in the rich soil beside the compost. Before she goes in, she wonders when Edie will stop trying so bloody hard. She breaks off a daisy from a frothy bush, sticks it in the mound and shakes her head and it comes to her that the big battle is with ourselves, that we must all fight our natures and that poor old Edie's in for a long fight.

***

The last time the girls see their grandmother they're ten and twelve, sitting at the end of a restaurant table in Yarrabeen, drinking fruit juice with little umbrellas at jaunty angles. Ted wants one too but Grace is having none of that – they're too dear to waste on a four-year-old. He's stuck with water and he grizzles and kicks the girls to compensate. Tino's is Hawaiian themed. Dusty orange and yellow plastic leis are draped around the room and Tino

Gamberi wears the same Hawaiian shirt covered in palm trees, day in, day out. He sells the idea of summer accompanied by tinned pineapple along with smoothies, lime spiders, pizzas, pastas and toasted sandwiches.

The autumn weather is falling apart outside, the side flap of the restaurant is open and the Fishers watch the rain falling heavily, their shiny hair the brightest thing about the day. They pick at their pineapple-strewn pizzas, ripping the cheese off in flaps and eating the waxy strings, showing off like mad for Nan Fish or Grandma Nerry, depending on what they feel like calling her.

They never saw much of Ian's mother when they lived in the city. There was always an exasperated, elastic tension between her and their mother that threatened to snap. It was the differences that got both women. Grace smoked and Nerida hated smoking. Nerida cooked with an extravagant love of food. Grace ate if something was put in front of her, but otherwise abstaining was good for the figure. The differences are deep but the common territory was Ian, and since he died, now the kids are at the heart of that old ground.

Nerida thought Ian was the good guy in the marriage, but she knows she's biased – how could she see it any other way? Ian loved Grace too much, and it bothered Nerida that there might have been a streak of coldness there in young Grace. Ian was the giver, bringing in wages and talking to the kids in a way his own father had never managed. She knew he was a little down but it's not uncommon, and there was a streak of the blues in both sides of the family. Still, men are so different. They have their urges, you know, and most of the urges are to run away, though her own husband never thought of that. Which leads to the old sadness, the cage she's lived in since her boy died. She blames herself, of course, for all of it.

Maybe if she'd done what Grace did and nicked off with the kids, got them away from their father, she would have ended the tyranny. Ah, who knows? There's plenty of tyranny around. He would just have found them anyway.

When she met Paul Fisher as a young woman, he was a sailor on a merchant vessel. He seemed decent and she was getting on, already twenty-six, and the family she thought she'd never have was suddenly on offer. She said yes and the gates opened on her. She didn't know what to expect and he turned out to be a carping, defensive, sex-mad drongo. Her life with him was one of muted sadness with fear thrown in for variety. Now, each morning they read their part of the paper in silence, he finance and sport, and she gets the rest, their dog moving from one pair of legs to the other, looking for love or scraps of toast. But then Ian died.

She wants to give Grace some money she's saved from her knitting. And she's made the girls a couple of jumpers, Fair Isle, very pretty if she does say so herself. And a lovely little Aran for Teddy, though the cream colour will be a problem, she can see that. He is a grub of a boy. She only hopes it's big enough. He's so like Ian, she feels her heartache ease up when she looks at him and words come out slow as stones. What can you say? What can you say when you lose your son and then, there he is before you again, a little child you barely know.

Thinking about those kids gives her a pain between the eyes. She'd say it was her brain but it's much worse. The loss of your grandchildren is a double blow because you're so ready to love them, so able to. Finally you know how to love without limit.

Today, while Paul worked at the marine hardware shop, doing his cryptic crossword in the breaks between customers, she'd driven all the way down here in the old teal Valiant, attending to the wet road as if it were alive, the jumpers in the back and a hundred dollars in an envelope in her bag. She doesn't have long. She prays he won't notice the extra mileage.

That they're meeting in a restaurant she reads as a bad sign, but she's in no position to bargain with anyone about anything. She's timid and grey with faded green eyes. The girls watch with Ian's eyes, like a pair of owls, and Ted is as always transfixed by the pineapple. She wishes Grace didn't hate her and she doesn't remember what caused the strain between them, probably something as simple as not bringing a dessert to a family do, but time has unravelled and there's nothing much she can do about that anymore.

In the restaurant Grandma Nerry watches them all mousey and un-asking, and keeps her car keys and scrunched-up hanky on her floral knee ready for a quick getaway. Grace has suggested she not mention Ian. 'They're so young, Nerida, and Edith for one, will never get over it.'

So Nerida, while pained at this request, goes along with it and asks them about school. Grace, whose face is a mask of orangey make-up, reveals that the girls read a lot for children these days. Juliet basks in the flicker of attention when her mother names her as 'the little one', as if her grandmother had forgotten her. 'The little one has read her latest Agatha Christie book five times, even though she has the eye problem.' Juliet is wearing her glasses today, one side blocked out to correct the slight turn in her eye. Edie seethes at the smugness radiating from her sister.

Juliet takes off: 'My teacher Miss Panno says Agatha Christie is a genius and she has so many great characters. But–'

Edie snorts and loads up with a floppy triangle of pizza. Chewing fast, mouth still full, she expostulates and bits of pizza are sprayed around: 'Ha! I don't even read Agatha Christie anymore.' She swoops on a stray ejected scrap and casually eats it again.

'What are you reading at the moment, then, darling?'

'*My Family and Other Animals* by Gerald Durrell.'

'And who's your favourite character?'

'Well, I don't have just one favourite. The best books have lots, don'tcha reckon? I like Roger the dog and Achilles the tortoise and Quasimodo the pigeon – oh yeah, and Spiro the taxi driver. I've read it far more than five times. In fact, I've lost count.' She shoots a withering look at her sister. 'It's the only book I read now. There's a lot of wisdom in it, I reckon, and I want to go to Corfu one day. It seems to be mostly blue.' She sucks determinedly at her almost-finished drink. The slurping is too loud to ignore, still her grandmother agrees it's wonderful to read.

'But,' Juliet continues as if her conversation never veered off, 'I really like Hercule Poirot, but not as much as Miss Marple – she's my best favourite because she reminds me of you, Grandma Nerry.' Juliet glances at Edie and smiles.

Nerida laughs and clamps Juliet to her in a confined hug and turns her eyes to Edie, who sees in a stab of clarity that her grandmother is sad even though she's laughing. And that she looks like her father.

Leaving the cafe into the wet curtain of rain, Edie furtively gets close to her grandmother and manages to hold her hand briefly though it's full of keys, plastic bags, hankies and the umbrella. She feels a bit in the way, so she hangs back. She doesn't ask about their dad because she'd heard before that their mother doesn't want any of that stuff brought up. 'What's done is done,' Grace always says.

Ted and Juliet are kissed goodbye first, then Edie, and the girls are told to go and stand under the shelter on the verandah and wait. There's a puddle shaped like a bottle of milk and they take turns splashing each other from the top of it, which is harder than you'd think.

Edith looks over and Grace, holding Ted's hand, is hugging Nan for a long time, maybe crying because Nan is patting her back but it's hard to tell with all the rain. Mum's got the plastic bags with the jumpers and an envelope and her make-up is all streaky. She's waving as the Valiant finds its way onto the road like a green barge on a long black river.

Chapter 10

The God of Bees

Juliet and Edith pass through serene periods of friendship and other times they seem to hate each other's guts with a wild extravagance that mystifies their mother, an only child. Often their worst fights happen after Ted is put to bed and Grace retires in front of the telly or, if she's got a basket of ironing that she'll get paid for, then she sets up in there and concentrates. They're meant to be keeping it down and doing their homework. Juliet is skinny and moon-pale, and the slight turn in her left eye makes her seem shy and intriguing.

At the kitchen table, a little ball of light hangs over them, throwing the cupboards into shadow. Their drowsy cat sprawls on the kitchen table and offers his soft presence as a balm. Edith suggests that Juliet should be wearing her glasses with one eye blocked out more because she's so dumb she needs all the help she can get – at last she's found a way to get under her sister's skin. Life is good.

'What rubbish, shit-for-brains.' Juliet flares from placid to outraged in an instant. Edith looks up, her opinion confirmed that stirring Jules was far easier than even she would have believed. You just need the right tools. 'Why should I wear them? *Why?* You wear them, Edith, you ugly horrible thing ... You're so smart, you wear them.'

Edie tries to hide the sly smile.

Jules hurls the glasses and they catch Edie's nose in passing. Jules marches over and grabs them off the floor, carrying the specs as if they were a live crab. She takes them to the rubbish bin and holds them above it, looking at Edith through red, teary eyes.

Edie's calm voice barely gives her anything. 'Mum will kill you if you break them, moron, and you know it.' She briefly glances up from colouring in a map of the counties of England in pastels and puts a hand out to settle the stirring cat. Now, where *is* Sussex? she wonders. I always lose Sussex. She might do Scotland in a tartan pattern, maybe just black and red. Ireland, surely that has to be green. Whoa, are Scotland and Ireland counties or countries? And what's the diff? Suddenly it seems calmer in the kitchen. Has Juliet put a hold on the tantrum? Edith could barely give a shit, feeling brave enough to think in swear words now. She glances up from her colouring again and sees that Juliet has let the foot pedal drop on the bin and put the specs back on. She's wiped the tear tracks away with the back of her dry little hands and like a politician embarks on a policy statement.

'For your information, Edith, Mum will not kill me no matter what I do. You're such a fool, Edie

Fisher, you don't even know how much she loves me. And she loves me way, way more than she loves you.' The kitchen door slams hard behind her and Edie looks briefly at the door before consuming herself with the colours of Scotland, a small smirk playing across her mouth.

***

The next week it's suddenly turbulent spring, all random heat or blue wind rushing at them off the Southern Ocean like a fisherman's knife. Juliet likes it, the feeling of change, in the weather, in anything picking you right up off the street like a scrap of paper, and in a flare of daring she decides just to ditch the hated specs and bugger the consequences.

All day she harbours the happy decision. She tells Edie that she needs to count the pylons at the end of the pier. She's doing a project on piers, she says. Edie squints and something in her understands where this is going. Still, she holds Juliet's bag, watching her race down the pier like she's late for something. At the end of the rough boards she takes the glasses off and drops them without a qualm. They're received into the deep and she feels instantly released. Strolling back, she waves wildly to Mr Wilson, who's bringing his green boat across the slanting green sea. She's so happy now, it's like everything is beautiful.

As Edie waits, she picks up shells as if by chance, half-believing she's distracting people from what her sister might be doing out there. All is confirmed when she sees her. No specs and a smile like a slice of watermelon. Later, when they walk back through the town, Edie remarks with casual relish, 'Well, moron, you've really done it now. You're a goner this time. Ha!' And she laughs, half-hoping to make Jules cry because this enormity surely requires tears at the very least. Jules is already onto the tears part of the equation, working out how to make herself blub. It's harder than she thought, though. She doesn't cry much. There is stuff to cry about but Edie's better at it. She misses her dad, she thinks, but she likes it here and she didn't like the way he was: always sad, always asleep, always out at night.

At school it's been some consolation to be regarded as rich city kids even though they are hollowed by Ian's death. Edie thinks about her father most of the time but can't find ways to speak of him. Juliet burbles on that she doesn't ever think of him but should she say his name – and strangely she often does – he lives in that moment and that is comforting.

Today they walk down a back lane, past flapping gates, weeds, trees and bins. Jules is thinking hard about their dad and it's not too long before he has provided tears. She even manages a hiccup or two, but fake tears don't impress Edie, who suspected all along she'd use the idea of their dad for a few cheap tears. Now here's Juliet blubbering, as if she's the only one who ever loved him. The utter gall.

Unexpectedly, when Juliet sees her mother, genuine guilt and shame well in her and she starts up like a fountain. Edie thinks, you'll never get away with it but, watching the scene unfold, she realises she will. 'Sorry, Mum, some boys from the Point took my glasses and broke them. And my bag, but they gave that back, so that was good, wasn't it?' she stutters through her sobs, glassy tears rolling free. Grace wipes them away with the tea towel that's always in her hand, the one that smells of toast. She takes the child into the back of the bakery and gives her a pink donut as big as her face, and even unwilling Edie is moved by the performance and bothered by the way her mother is so willing to be taken in. She can't speak. It was consummate.

On the way home they're quiet, only the happy sounds of donut consumption accompany them. Each has something to think about – Jules about what a devastating beauty she'll now be and Edie about her favourite subject, the nature of unfairness.

Jules waves the donut at Edie. 'You want some?' Edie ignores her. 'Don't be such a snob, Edie, come on, you know you want some.'

Disapproval comes easily to Edith and she keeps to her withering silence. Jules laughs are runs ahead. 'Bugger you then, I'm having a picnic.'

She heads over to the little park where the see-saws creak in the wind. Three hibernating barbecue cubes near the toilet block still wear their coats of summer grease. Behind them, the pewter sea goes all the way down to Tassie. Edie heads for home.

And then she hears a scream from Jules who, it seems, has managed to sit on a bee. Serves her bloody right, Edie thinks, and a smile overcomes her stiffness. Something makes her help anyway. Juliet's yelling draws passers-by and other kids. The pink cottontails are pushed down to reveal a throbbing red lump, and Edie surgically extracts the bee's stinger between her fingernails. 'You should be more careful where you sit, idiot features. Poor bee, dead twice over. First you sit on it, then,' she laughs with true enjoyment, 'they die, you know, when they sting you. It's not something they want to do. And when I think of how you carried on about my mouse, I ought to stick the stinger back,' she says. 'You did deserve it, you little liar. It was probably God did this. I reckon it was the God of Bees.'

'Oh God, you go on, Min. Just shut up, will you? You think you know everything and I've got news for you. You just don't.'

The late summer sun is harvesting their whiteness like cream off the top of milk. After the bum surgery and examining the offending sting, Juliet flings herself back onto the thready grass dotted with tiny pink flowers and yellow daisies, wiping her damp face with sticky hands. She won't get stung again, she's sure of that. She thinks wildly that she wouldn't mind if Edie tells their mum about the bee because that would get a bit of sympathy, but she probably can't have one confession without the other so it's best to clamp down. 'Thanks, Edo. You're the best,' she says, laughing, and then gets serious. 'Don't tell Mum about this or the glasses or I'll kill you.'

Edie looks into her face, so like her own but only better. Stupid girl, who ever heard of getting killed over glasses and a bee sting? But she feels sorry somehow for something between them. For something they will never really fix.

Juliet adds toughly, 'And I know about bumping people off from all those Agatha Christies.' In the lovely yellow light, with dandelion threads wafting past, they get the giggles and Edie laughs so much that she starts coughing but manages to get out, 'What'd you have in mind? Poison, stabbing ... worth it to see you in jail.'

'Shut up, Edith,' Juliet says, spitting on her hand to anoint the sting gingerly before picking up her school bag and the remains of the battered donut and taking a bite. 'Let's go. Wanna finish this?' She hands the donut remnant over and Edie downs it in one claggy, shocking pink clump.

***

'I can sing,' she yells at Edith to complete silence and adds, as if it matters, 'way better than you.' And then she starts up, exactly like a lawnmower, Edith thinks, shaky then way too loud. They're on the beach in the elbow of the evening, waiting for their mother to come home from the bakery maybe with leftovers for tea. Ted is at Auntie Ivy's. They could go there but Ivy makes them wash their hands. They could go home but there's nothing to eat there. They've checked the cupboards and the mice have even eaten the crumbs. There are a couple weevilly Weet-Bix hanging around and some butter, but no milk, bread or biscuits. The beds aren't made and there are dishes to do, and if they're home they'd be expected to do all those chores. It's better to stay out. There's a nip in the sea air tonight and both are hoping for a hot pie. One each would be good – you can always hope.

The sky is layered with high peach cloud drifting like smoke. Edith digs a cave hole in the sand. It keeps her busy and warm. She mumbles that Juliet can't sing to save herself and says sourly, 'Shut your face, shit head, shit head, shit head,' which, because she's said something – anything – encourages Juliet to start on 'A Hard Day's Night'.

Edith looks up from her digging and sees her weird little sister playing a pretend guitar like one of The Beatles. She chucks sand at her and laughs reluctantly. 'Honestly, what an idiot. Such a bloody little idiot.' She sighs the world-weary sigh to the delight of Juliet who, spurred on, only cackles like a little red chook and bounces around, singing loud and flat.

Truth is, Edith's a hard nut to crack. Their mother calls her Hard-hearted Hannah – she who never laughs and since she got older cries much less. So on the strength of this little victory over her sister, Juliet saunters along to help with the hole. After a while they climb in and try not to get sand in every part of themselves, which Edith had already discovered is futile. Sand is a magnetised, she reckons, and humans are full of iron. Her mum said so. She wipes her eye and it crusts over. When the hole is deep enough, they pop their heads out like submarine commanders. Finally, they see their mother coming down the street carrying Ted, who's grizzling with his molars coming in. Grace is laden with bags of bread and they scramble out, surging towards her like commandos, and lighten her load. The fragrant warmth within the bags is a living thing. Edith holds Teddy, who laughs when he sees them, and each girl takes one of their mother's hands, soft and white from flour.

***

They invent Test of Courage to pass the hours after school when they can't face going home. All tests involve pain and fear, though they try not to leave any marks. Who can climb highest in the Lebanese cedar in the park by the beach? Who can hold her breath under water the longest? Who can stand the Chinese burn on her wrist the longest? Have their arm twisted up their back? Run across the big road the most times? These tests are timed and there are no concessions for age.

Handstands is a hard test but one most favoured by Juliet. They dig a deep hole and then do handstands in it. Whoever lasts the longest upside down in the dank hole is the winner. Juliet usually wins because she's got balance. There's no reason why that won't happen again tonight. Probably why she's keen on it. They dig and dig, getting up a sweat in the last of the still day. This basement sand is familiar to both – damp, cool and mostly obedient. They dig with the old salt of competition and the possibility of triumph pushing them. Though Juliet often wins, Edith can always refuse to admit defeat. There's no prize but pride, the only prize that ever counts.

They laugh and speed through the sand, slinging it behind them. The hole ends up about half their height, deep and clammy. The wind picks up and the big cedar tree laments the way of things.

'Right,' says bossy Edith, 'I'm first – you went first last time. And remember, timing. Do it properly, Juliet. Don't get distracted and stop counting. You can't get sick of it. I'll be counting too, so no cheating. We have to measure properly or else it doesn't mean anything. Remember, it goes "one-cat-and-dog" for each second. Got that, dumbo?'

After three goes, Edie's up and only teetering a bit. She's counting and gets to eight when it happens. The sides of the hole cave in and she's buried head-first to her waist. Juliet doesn't know what to do. She grabs Edie's ankles, hauling away, but she can barely move her. She huddles beside the reduced hole, hugging her skinny knees, and tries to think. Then she's running around, yelling, 'Edie! Edie! I'm sorry,

Edie!' When Grace discovers the scene, she sprints over, dropping Ted and falling to her knees, shopping bags in a heap. She manages to pull Edith out, and the girl seems to be dead. She clears sand from her mouth. 'Get help,' she yells at Juliet. 'Go now!' The child runs to the Top-Shop across the road where old Jim Briggs is stacking the fridge with milk. Juliet bursts in, the doorbell pealing. 'Hi, Jim,' she yells. 'Mum says to get help. I think my sister died in the sand.' Juliet's eyes are wide and her freckles seem illuminated.

Gerry Farmer, the ambulance officer, glowing in his white shirt with epaulettes like small wings, is breathless from running. The ambulance couldn't get in that close. He kneels gravely beside the child, uses the stethoscope and announces that Grace's mouth-to-mouth skills have saved Edith's life. 'Sand can be a killer,' he says with feeling. 'If only more people understood this.' He knows Grace through the bakery, which is a help because he'll need to explain to her the possible complications of foreign bodies entering the lungs. Though the child is breathing now, she could suffer a multitude of problems. 'Well, your lungs are a tricky part of the body, there's silicosis, for one thing, and then there's the possibility of scarring on the lung. Pneumonia is another possibility, of course.' Gerry has never known as much as he thinks he knows, and scaring people at their worst moment with his medieval diagnoses is only one of his flaws. He's been warned about it before, but restraint doesn't come easy. He busies himself with a blanket.

Cautiously, Juliet edges back to find Edith sitting up, shivering violently while she's wrapped in a blue blanket, sipping water from Gerry's special ambulance bottle. Then an oxygen mask is placed over her mouth and nose, and she's propped up on the trolley and tucked in like a baby. Grace is talking to Gerry in the ambulance's glimmering red light.

Edie can't stand to look at Juliet and closes her eyes. Finally, she croaks though the mask, 'Did you push the sand in? And don't bother lying because I know you did. Liar.'

Hysteria's warm grip begins to close on Juliet. Her voice is too high and she seems so small in all this evening air. 'NO! I didn't. Honest, Edo! It just fell in. It wasn't my fault. And you were too big – I couldn't move you!' She weeps a little.

'Sure,' sighs Edie, adjusting the mask.

Gerry takes her to the hospital for the night, just to keep a check on her lungs, but she's so tired she doesn't even enjoy the sounds of the siren scaring everyone just for her. Still, for a few moments she's well enough to be peeved that her little sister and brother get to come along in the ambulance with her mum, just because there's no one at home to look after them. Shoulda got Ivy. It's never just me and mum, she thinks, drifting off into the land of extreme sleep.

Chapter 11

What Men Are For

Grace always told Juliet that men were nothing but a damned nuisance. 'Once you've got your kids, what do you need 'em for, I ask you?' They're on their knees planting potatoes in soil, that looks way too good to be from around here. Grace made compost from just about the first day in Cedar Street; it's a point of honour with her. They mound the soil over the spuds like small graves. So despite her advice about men, it wasn't long before Grace accepted Kev's offer to dig her a big vegie patch and fence it with chicken wire to keep the damn rabbits out. They already have cabbages and pumpkins growing, and the sight of the rabbits feasting got her blood up. But she draws the line at killing them because, she explained to Kev, they look a bit like cats and she likes cats. Kev shook his head and got on with his fencing. 'Women and their fancies,' he said to himself.

This morning they pulled out the last of the green tomatoes, the leaves curling and smelling like spices. Ted has a bucket full, and later they'll make pickles. Snails hiding under the cover of big leaves are fair game for Jules. She flicks them out with a stick and then smashes the sticky lumps with her gumboot. Helpful to the core. Got to be quick or Ted will eat them, though now that he's nearly four he's getting a bit more sensible.

Grace wipes a hand across her forehead and smiles. It amazes Juliet that Grace never really gets dirty. How do you manage that? Her mum's wearing bottle-green crimplene slacks and a shirt covered in daisies, both of which she made herself. Her shoes are small, light slip-ons – she likes to be quick on her feet. Grace darts rather than moves, always seeming to get anywhere fast. Effortlessly. She stops, smiles at the child and tells her something as if it's just occurred to her, the power of the message burning through her like an ember. 'You remember this, young Juliet. No woman ever needs a man. You may choose one, but that is very different. Truth is, they need us more than we need them, but it's not something they like to admit.' She plants another spud and the soil over it is like chocolate cake.

The girl hears her father in what Grace says, hears Uncle Kev too, but says nothing – questions would make her mother stop talking, always easy to do. So, blinking and smiling, her hair glowing in the sun, Juliet smiles at her mother and at her own secret. And behind the secret is an ache, and the ache is so strong some days, but naming it would be too hard because she doesn't have a name for it.

Grace plants so many potatoes that they're sure to have a huge crop in this year. 'Your own spuds are like life, little Julie, rich and sustaining, unlike men.'

98

She stands up and surveys the spud mounds. 'Bloody good job.'

As she gets older, Juliet thinks about that day planting. She imagines that she might have said something to disagree with her mother. She would have liked to have said that men might be handy for sex, but since she didn't know that stuff then, she couldn't. She imagined there was a mystery between men and women. Something her mother must have been leaving out. She saw it. Saw the thing between them, some kind of love, something nice. Something she knew she'd want for herself one day. Later, when it's obvious that she knew a whole lot about sex and Grace kept on saying men were useless, Juliet could only smile. Now she thinks of the day in the garden fondly. Sex always changes everything, she thinks.

They did most of their talking on Friday nights at the bakery. Juliet would shake Edie off, often leaving her fervently digging caves down at the beach or over at Ivy's watching telly, and slip into the back room after school to set up the possibility of homework on the pine table. The bakery stayed open till seven on Fridays and, though there weren't many customers, there were always sausage rolls, pies and sometimes a cake and cordial. Grace kept a cask of wine there and another at home – always red. To celebrate the end of the week, she'd have half a glass topped up with Coca-Cola, but only ever the one. 'I like a bit of sweetness,' she'd say mid pour, laughing 'bit sharp without a touch of Coke.' Then she'd be in and out, serving customers their family pies.

That's what Juliet remembers. All this while her sister was not there or with Auntie Ivy, the messiest woman in Yarrabeen, so disorganised she once lost Ted. Grace arrived to pick him up and he was nowhere to be found. It turned out he was asleep in the long grass down the back of Ivy's yard, a loaf of white sliced for a pillow.

But mostly there were no brothers and sisters at the shop, and Grace would join Juliet out the back in her white apron and dark pants with floured hand-prints, where she would have a fag and point out spelling mistakes. She knew all this from being a secretary. 'You got the wrong "there", love, it's the possessive: "t-h-e-i-r" apples.'

'Eat something, Mum,' Juliet says, 'and don't smoke so much – it'll make you sick.'

'Don't start on me now. This is my little recreation, my hobby. Keep that nagging up and you'll remind me of your sister. Oh, I suppose she means well enough, but nagging never works. Draw me something, Jules, draw me something beautiful.'

Juliet draws a daisy or a bird or a pair of shoes. The fridge in the workroom flutters with her pictures. Her mother squints and holds the newest one out at arm's length to clear her eyes of the smoke. 'My little maestro. My talented one. Put that on the fridge – and now down to this essay. Juliet, how do you spell "quality"? This is a word you need to know. This is a word just for you.'

Chapter 12

Earwigs

For Edie, medical shows take the place of anything else – the more intimate the surgery, the more she loves it. Pale bones revealed through layers of yellow fat, tendons lying flat on a surgeon's gloved hand like linguine and tumours the size of grapefruits, eggs, golf balls and tennis balls.

Kev sits with Grace in the shed as she irons for extra money. He loves the warm smells of the back shed. Truth is, that ironing smell reminds him of his mum. Who else irons these days? He does a few odd jobs too, mends a fence or whatever she asks of him. He's always there, despite having his own house. He'd like to get married but Grace won't have a bar of it – nothing personal, she says, just doesn't like the idea of it anymore. Still, things are discussed between them out in the shed. Grace and Kev reckon Edie's weird telly habits are probably due to her father. At least that's what Kev's taking in, perched there on a stool like a crane. He hints that Ian was weird too. 'Wasn't he?'

'Mmm,' Grace says, working a collar.

But young Edie changes his mind one night at the dinner table. She's been listening to him and her mum make the dinner. Tuesdays were always Kev nights and usually featured sausages he picked up at the butchers. Tonight, because Kev had a hand in it, they were going all out and having sausage casserole. Left to Grace, they'd eat the same thing. Food was chaff to Grace and as little as possible of whatever was easy was what she was looking for.

He's chopping parsley when he says dolefully, 'I tell you I think I might be dying, Gracie. It's grim. The pain is shocking and I sit over the toilet for at least half an hour and even then, I can barely shift a damn thing. It's starting to upset me.' He lifts the carrots into the casserole. Even Edie listening in the hallway finds this unsettling.

Grace, peeling potatoes, smiles at him. 'Maybe you should go and see the doctor. It's probably nothing, so don't get all het up about it, Kev.' Through the window over the sink, moonlight is on the sea.

'Don't like bloody doctors. Every time you go see them they reckon there's something wrong with you.'

'Honestly, Kevin. Isn't that why you go to them?'

Soon, Edie's called to set the table and scrambles from her earwigging place.

When dinner is served she waits to grab the seat furthest from Alexander, knocking Jules away in doing do. The steam lifts off the pyrex casserole dish when Kev removes the lid with a flourish. He gave it to Grace a while ago but he's the only one who uses it.

He serves up and Edie plunges in with her diagnosis. 'Ever thought of piles, Kev? Could be something that simple.'

He looks at her as if for the first time, and so impressed is he that he gives her an extra sausage.

The doctor agrees with Edie and sends him off to a specialist. Rubber bands see to it. He has to wait for the bands to drop off, though. And it's not a pleasant business.

***

As a child Edie is as solid as a rain tank with thin beige hair inclined to curl but, getting no encouragement, adopts a gravity-fed limpness instead. Her big eyes are as green as Ian's and her mouth is straight as a clothes line. Maybe a box of freckles spilled on her. It sure looks like that. Her teeth are miles too big for her mouth, but this will soon be cured by the extraction of six teeth at the State school dentist which, to her mother's delight, will be free.

Edith Fisher hates the way she looks and often seems to be in some checked fabric because her mother thinks checks give her some definition, which she's in sore need of. And she has that shit name given to her by a shit mother, she thinks, and these are words she only says to herself. But what really galls her is that she's still being treated as a damn child! And just because her mother wants to live here in Yarrabeen, then they all have to. Why couldn't she have taken us to live in Paris, eh? Like in the Madeleine books, where they wear uniforms and everyone's neat and kind. Her dad would have taken them to Paris for sure. If he had any money, he would.

When she lies in the dark in bed she plaits the tassels of her dressing gown cord to stop herself from scratching the rotten eczema on her arms and the tender part behind her knees. She's convinced she gets it because the words eczema and Edith go so damn well together, and the 'E' God decided on it. Every night calamine lotion coats her. The itchies will go, she tells herself again and again, it will definitely pass, but even when she's saying this a little snake of electricity crackles in her arms, sparking its way through her, driving her mad. Soon she puts the tassel down and the urge to stop the hungry itch makes her scratch without restraint, within the limits of relief. Afterwards, she holds her fiery arms and checks for hot, wet blood. Not much – a good thing because if she gets blood on her sheets she'll be in for it, what with the extra washing.

Today she ate half a chocolate cake in one go, which seems a lot even to her. She stole it from the bakery when her mother was serving a customer, put it into a plastic bag and then into her school bag. She couldn't leave it there. It was beautiful: a glossy chocolate sprinkled with hundreds and thousands. When Grace came back into the kitchen after the theft, Edie leapt as if she'd been stung.

'Oh hello, love, what're you doing here?' Grace asked.

'I just wanted to see you, Mum,' she said in a high little voice, surprised. 'It's me. It's me, Bob, who else?'

'Well, I'll go home, Mum. Homework.'

Grace was storing the morning's scones into a plastic container for the old people's home. 'Poor old wretches,' she said to herself about the oldies after Edie had gone, 'always so grateful for anything.'

Edie broke off a chunk of cake on the way home and it tasted like heaven. She brushed the crumbs from her school dress, happy that at least the ants would enjoy this feast. 'Eat up, ants, you won't taste anything like this again.' The icing coated her fingers like paint and she swung them in the cold air, hoping they would harden so she could flake off the icing, but they remained soft and buttery. Edie said hello to Ivy next door, not knowing that a stripe of chocolate icing stretched her smile almost to her ears. Ivy, the constant pruner, was worrying away at some bush in the front yard when Edie waved. She paused with her little fork by her blue hydrangea and smiled, thinking what a lovely smile young Edie had.

Eating the cake took a while, and then she was sick in the hallway on the way to the bathroom. She used her cardigan to clean it up and threw the lot into the rubbish bin, covering it all up with newspaper. She'd tell her mum she'd lost the brown cardie. Well, it worked for Jules, she thought, but then she was not Jules.

That night her mother sent her to bed even earlier because she couldn't eat her chop and mash, and because of the missing cardigan which was soon discovered in the bin. And lying there in the bedroom that still didn't really feel like home, she heard the little dumping sounds of the waves. The real questions were:

Why do I still have to go to bed at seven – summer or winter – just because Juliet has to? Why?

Does mum love her?

When will she be old enough to stop Alexander?

Why did Dad have to do that to himself?

When will I stop stealing?

How can it be so easy to steal? The one answer to these questions was about stealing. Maybe I'm just really good at it, came at her with all its shameful truth.

It's getting so that she can't stop thieving lately: the birthday card for Grandma Nerry with the flowers trailing out of the teacup; the writing paper for her mother who was so pleased with it; the chewing gum, half of which she gave to an unappreciative Juliet. All of it.

Okay, she says to herself, I will think about Alexander. That'll stop the itching. Alexander used to be all right, but now he's so strange that she'll never work him out. He's older, taller, stronger and smarter. He works at the bakery with her mum. Edith sees him in his floury baker's apron and thinks about how she'll kill him with the big testing skewer for the loaves –

skinny thing straight through his rotten heart. She tries to plait the tassel again but after the last scratch, her fingers are wet with blood. She didn't think there'd be so much. But that horrible Alexander. Who can I tell? No one would believe me anyway. She thinks that everyone probably has an Alexander around, someone who touches you in the wrong place, who laughs at you, calls you muffin thighs and says if you tell anyone he'll eat your eyes first. If she'd been smarter, it wouldn't have happened. If only Uncle Kev wasn't her mother's best friend in Yarrabeen. Maybe she could tell Grandma Nerry, but she already looks so sad, and she doesn't see her much.

Uncle Kev gave her mum Seacrest to live in and the job. Why'd he do that? Is it because Alexander gets to do stuff to me? Edith doesn't know, not really, but she understands something, that it's to do with kissing and that. Uncle Kev visits after work some nights and her mother talks to him in her sensible way at the kitchen table about bills and the old days and fixing the house and how clever the kids are turning out to be. The way she used to talk to Dad. They play cards and her mother laughs and with every laugh it feels like her father is more lost. Edie doesn't know what to say, but there's this meanness inside and it only happened since they got here. Juliet's got it too, whatever it is.

Occasionally they go to Uncle Kev's place on a Sunday for afternoon tea. He lives further down toward the bay in an old red house with a white verandah. The sky is open around it – no trees, just mowed weeds and a solitary white daisy bush standing like a bunch of flowers thrust from the hand of the earth next to an old dragging gate. Uncle Kev is against trees near houses. 'Bloody dangerous,' he rants, but after she's heard it a few times it washes over her like fly spray. Most things do, she finds. Uncle Kev's okay, Edie reckons, a bit like some kind of cocky boss, not like her dad who would tell stories and smile at her with his eyes. Kev just raves on: 'Bloody idiots with all their greenie notions. God made chainsaws for a reason, you know.'

When he laughs his poor old teeth reveal the dark work of his diet. He's an all-meat, no-veg man. He's just had another skin cancer whipped off his variegated face and today, blood seeps through the bandaid on his sausage-roll nose.

At afternoon tea, the ooze goes unmentioned but Edie enjoys watching it. She takes a scientific interest and another wedge of Boston bun and, in a reflexive act, her mother jerks the plate back. Juliet notices and says meekly, 'Oh, I couldn't,' and smiles.

Later, Juliet and Edith go outside. They say they have to go to the toilet but they don't, they just want to have a bit of a snoop. BUY AUSTRALIAN is banged onto the toilet door with bottle tops from VB beer and the kids wonder who would disagree with such a sentiment. Apparently, the previous owners drank all the beer. Inside, the toilet is a long-drop dunny with a heavy wooden lid that doesn't quite meet the seat.

Dankness comes out to meet them and then hangs in a low cloud with flies suspended in it. Both girls would rather burst apart than use that toilet, but still there's something mighty interesting about such conditions. They poke around the sheds, pat Nell the lovely kelpie, pull weeds beside the shed, blow the heads off dandelions and waste time in the privacy of the yard while the adults waste time inside. They climb the little mulberry tree, and if the purple fruit is ripe and dropping, the soft sourness is a revelation. They stay outside as long as they can.

Chapter 13

A Slip of Icy Air

At eighteen, Alexander's restless energy spills from him like something leaking. His hair is trapdoor black and the darkness rising from him is like a warning. His eyes ache for something, but not for long. He sits with one leg crossed over the other and jiggles the foot around, crazy as a mosquito, and then leaps up to sweep crumbs from the table into his hand, jittering over to the bin to drop them in. According to the locals, and despite knowing the truth, they reckon there's a hint of the Afghan in his genes. The truth is that Alex's grandparents were Greek bakers, the entrepreneurial Polites family, who came to Yarrabeen years ago to set up the bakery, and later the fish shop.

Because the Polites were known and loved, there was some disappointment when their beautiful daughter Alexandra, known always as Sandra, married that great streak of misery Kevin Culp, the baker's apprentice from Long Gully, but the marriage seemed happy and a child was born. Then, the sniper that is fate took aim and changed everything. Sandra and her parents were killed in a car accident down in the gully one wet afternoon when they slid along the road and slammed into a tree. They'd been at a funeral in Newtown for a Greek friend on that grey day. It was thought they were probably trying to miss something on the road and blame fell on Doreen Wilson's dog Slick, who was by the wreck, as if he'd seen the souls out of the bodies but now must wait for them to be claimed, like a kind of angel. Everyone agreed that the patience of dogs is a wonder and Slick was delivered home to Doreen, with warnings. A working bee was organised to fix the fence.

On that day, Alexander Culp was the six-year-old boy waiting in the red house in Yarrabeen. He and his father didn't sleep much after the accident and they didn't comfort each other either. They lapped each other in the lonely house, passing through the rooms liked faded copies of themselves. Kev could think of nothing to say to anyone, let alone to a child who'd lost his mother. He was so like his lovely mother that to look at the boy made him feel quite sick. Kevin took his loss out on the bakery, baking too much bread, watching the dough thrash through the mixer with a fixed expression, sweeping the drifts of flour until every speck was gone, cleaning everything over and over. He worked every hour he could, sleeping on flour sacks in the corner of the bakery and sometimes his weeping woke him.

Alexander was alone much of the time or with neighbours. His disappointed eyes fixed on something within. At night, he slept with his mother's blue jumper. Though he could, he didn't speak English for a while, but soon and inevitably the Greek flew away from him. The sympathy of the town became the coat he wore, and loneliness followed. He decided to act as if he was all right and the secret of that pretending consumed him. He never learned to make friends but he did learn stuff: to get by, to make his bed, to look after his room, carefully folding the crocheted rug his Nana had made him. That was years ago. The blue jumper is still under his pillow.

'Okay if I take the girls to my room to read comics? Give you guys a break.' Alex asks with a yawn and Grace, pouring more tea, readily agrees to a little break. She doesn't think this odd coming from a grown-up, as Alexander now clearly is. She just thinks he's a bit odd, probably because he lost his mother, but it's always nice of him to offer to look after them, considerate really. Anyway, lately she doubts her own powers as a mother. She's begun to think of the girls as the Bicker Twins. They grate on her nerves with their thready arguments, needling each other like wasps. Unlike Ted, who plays peacefully with some faded blocks scrounged from Alexander's childhood. In her heart, she believes boys are easier and most of her friends agree.

Alex sleeps in a little room off the verandah. It's long and thin with cloudy louvres along one wall. Little draughts eddy through. In summer, crickets often come along with the draughts. In winter, he stuffs socks into the cracks and sleeps in a slip of icy air. On the wall, a map of the world with a circle around Greece has been up a long time. He doesn't see it anymore.

These days he likes stamps. He collects them and has four leather-bound books of them sandwiched in acid-proof paper. His best album is bound in fake red leather. The girls are permitted to look but not touch the tiny, pretty stamps of flowers and of the Queen. He says one of them is worth nearly as much as a car, and certainly all of them are worth more than *their* car. When he laughs loudly, his mouth is huge as a tunnel. Edith thinks, what are those black things in his teeth?

Fillings, Juliet explains later. 'Sugar gives 'em to you. You'll end up like that, Miss Piggy. For sure,' she says, hoisting up her shorts and twiddling her plastic multicoloured bangles.

'Shut your face.'

'Honestly, why don't you just shut yours.'

***

Alexander Culp's bed hunkers against the other wall. He draws the frail, papery blinds down on the louvres, saying, 'It's too bright, don't you think?' and he gets the girls to lie down on the floor before the promised pile of new comics. Boy, are they in for a treat, he says, lying down between them. He says he's a bit cold so he grabs the crocheted rug off his bed and hurls it over the three of them. His leg is against Edith's hip and it feels strange, but that first time she's not scared.

She's never really been crazy about Alexander, not since they first got there, not since the time he was chopping wood in the backyard for her mother and he split a log so hard it flew at her like a stray bullet. As she turned away, it clipped the back of her head, neat as a stab. Just as she started yelling and crying with the shock of it all, a flock of white cockatoos screeched past. They sat enthralled in the big gum deciding that the wheat could wait. Edie put a hand up to her head and felt something wet. The cockies squawked.

'Oh no!' Edie yelled, her face white and round. Alex rushed at her, yelling, 'Don't tell!' Then, on one knee before her, he beseeched her, 'Aw Edie girl, you won't tell, will you, Edie? You can have all the comics. But only if you keep quiet, though. Gimme a look at it. See, it looks worse than it is. It's not that bad.'

She'd never been beseeched before, but when you get hurt, telling is the only good part of it, she reasoned. It means people are nice to you – people like your busy mum, and your busy teacher, and sometimes even Juliet.

Sensing she might not go along with him, Alex tried to shoosh her, dragged her to the tap and turned on a rush of freezing water. Her shoes got wet. He dunked her head under the tap and rinsed the cut. He covered it with her soggy hair, but the blood seeped forth, warm on her cold head. Still, she could tell by the feel of it that it wasn't a very big cut. The cockies screeched, lost interest and moved on, leaving silence with a rotting feeling of betrayal. At home, Edie got ticked off for her wet hair and shoes. She'd liked to have told on Alex but something warned her. It took a long time to discover that if someone wants you to keep a secret, that person is not your friend.

***

There's still something wrong with him, she thinks, stretched on the floor in his skinny little stampy bedroom that stinks of sweat, flour and dirty clothes. She can see cricket corpses under the bed, feet pointing straight up. The room is neat but sour. There's some kinda creepiness in him. Plus, his hands are always freezing, even in summer. He puts one arm over her middle and moves his hand down a bit. What's he doing? she thinks. Is this normal?

And then, unbelievably, he seems to be taking her pants down. And then, fairly quickly after the first shock, there's another – he moves his fingers into her private parts. It doesn't hurt but it's not nice and it feels so wrong. She might be sick. She's so puzzled by this that her brain goes funny: what is this? Such things don't happen, do they? She must be imagining it, or maybe it's okay, this is just what some grown-up people do to you.

Her breathing slows down until it seems she's breathing only from a flat dish of air.

All the time he's doing this to the child, he's talking to Juliet about the comics. She turns the pages for him so he can balance on one elbow. 'I love Richie Rich, don't you? He's my favourite. I want a servant. Yeah. How good would that be?'

So it must not be happening, thinks Edith, because it's invisible. After a while of his intrusive prodding, Grace calls and he takes his hand away and puts her underpants back. He says nothing about it, ever.

He's done this every time they've been to Kev's house for four years, telling Grace he's helping the girls with their maths, with their English, until Edie is twelve. She doesn't know if Alexander is doing the same thing to Juliet, though she reckons he probably does since she's regarded by everyone to be the pick of the sisters.

She doesn't speak of it though, and it stays with her. The clammy shame of it like a noose. She tells no one about it because even then she thinks no one would believe her. And anyway, it must have been her own fault. Somehow.

***

Getting out of going to Uncle Kev's becomes the major event of the week. She invents stomach aches, headaches and homework. She sulks and is mean to her sister – meaner than usual – so that she won't be allowed to come, but not much gets her out of anything.

Then, accidentally of course on the last visit, when she is twelve, she feels a grown-up and she puts a stop to it. Next year she'll be going to the high school, and something in her tells her she doesn't have to put up with Alexander Culp anymore. There's a new girl in her now and this one is brave. She likes this girl, this little Viking. When Alex suggests some help with long division, red-faced, she says rudely, 'No, thanks, I can manage just fine.' The adults turn and look at her, as if for the first time. They know she's hopeless at maths, and in not taking help she's messed up the order of things. It's summer and the boundless blue sky swings away over the universe and the small house. The back door is open to the soft day and out there the mulberry tree is a green lagoon. Nell is snoring on the mat. The gentle snores enter the kitchen. Bakery treats are piled on the table and there's cordial for the kids.

Grace almost pleads with her. 'Come on, Edie love, you want a little help, get you ahead a wee bit? Eh? Off you go with Alex now. He's helped you so much already.'

Edie, hunched on her stool picking a scab on her knuckle says, 'Nup.' Long pause. 'No way.' Her shorts have ridden up again and her top with the cherries on it totally appals her. Everything is too small. Today, Edie is a young seal shedding her first skin. She must find a way to get her own clothes. And she will not be prey to this creep another second. She balances her pink thong on the tip of her toe, slips it back on properly and prepares for change.

Grace is ruffled. She sits up straight and tries a commanding tone. 'Come along now, Edie girl, off you go. Give the grown-ups a little time.' The girl sits on the red stool at the table. The kids all have to sit on stools of various colours. At Uncle Kev's, only grown-ups get chairs and tea.

And then Grace misses one of the most important thing her daughter will ever say to her: 'Nothing would make me go into Alexander's room ever again.' Juliet smiles like a clown from her yellow stool. You beauty, she thinks, there goes Edie. Total nut job.

Alex, perched on a blue stool, looks stunned, embarrassed and his face colours. He's holding a yoyo out and Ted is tangling the thing.

'And,' Edie glares at him defiantly, 'I don't think anyone else should go into his room either.'

Grace stands up, affronted on Kev's behalf. Each parent frequently takes their partner's child's part over their own: bonding, the complications of bonding. Alexander is widely regarded in Yarrabeen as a dill, but he's excused for it – who wouldn't be a dill if that happened to you? Your mother so young?

'Apologise to Alex, Edith, immediately,' Grace says. Edie just glares at her. 'You complete brat of a girl.' Grace slaps her arm hard enough to leave a red handprint.

'No. I won't apologise.' Edie's eyes are dry, green slits and the air heaves with the sick heart of the damaged and the complete mystification of everyone except Alexander and Edith.

Uncle Kev suggests another cup of tea to settle things down a wee bit and sets about making the brew, getting down the old tea tin with the sad swaggie on it, swirling hot water round in the pot, drying the mugs. His hands seem to be shaky but he'll soon be himself again. You know teenagers, they can be a bit highly strung, he tells himself. Edith forces herself not to cry. She goes to the fridge and gets out milk and passes the sugar to him.

Edie feels like she's in a trap that will make her tell the whole lot, spill it all, but she can't do that because it happened to her and that makes it secret. She blames herself for everything. Alexander just makes her feel sick. She reckons she might just get out of it, if she's smart and holds on. She'll act her way out of it. Act normal, she tells herself, just be the same. But then they're in the kitchen, all the adults, her mum who never asked her anything about anything and weedy, cold Alex sitting there playing with Ted as if he were a normal person and getting away with everything. Well, he better not touch Ted, she thinks.

And then, in the gap between thinking and knowing, it just happens – she comes to the conclusion that she should chuck a mug of hot tea on Alexander Culp. The idea of it soothes her and she is there, watching Kev pour the tea from the pot with his usual long, flourishing pour. Carefully, she carries the green striped mug over to Alex in what seems an act of reconciliation and then, Edie seems to stagger, just a bit, and then bang, she drops it on him.

His face contorts with pain and she remembers not to smile. She studies him as if he was a blow-fly doused with Mortein, and it feels good enough to last her until she sees how upset everyone else is, how they still care about him. And really, even tipping the tea is not enough – no, she'd like to really hurt him, but that'll have to wait.

Though the tea appears to be a complete accident, she's punished for her bumbling anyway. Grace explodes that she's 'a stupid, clumsy oaf, and rude with it'. Her mother bristles while she's cleaning up with the dishcloth. 'Say sorry to your cousin,' she demands, holding tea towels out to Alexander, who's carrying on like a pork chop. 'Say sorry. I'm telling you, Edith.' Then she addresses Alex and Kev as if Edie isn't there: 'Honestly, she's just so sullen lately.' Kev has the mournful look of a waterbird a long way from home. Edie says nothing but she's stewing. Finally, it pours forth and makes her scream at her mother, 'He's NOT my cousin. And YOU say sorry TO ME.'

For that she cops a decent slap on her face and is sent to walk home on her own under the stippled early evening sky, fiercely stripping innocent leaves by the roadside, letting tears fall secretly and freely and thinking, boy, I just hope that tea hurt.

Chapter 14

The Wombat

Edie has grown taller in the past few months, though she's still dappled with freckles. Her teeth have straightened out but remain disappointingly small. Her hair is darker and longer. Her father inhabits her face. The memory of his sadness maybe. Womanhood inches closer with all its surprising changes. Her eyes are green as spring on a sugar gum.

Now that she's free of Alexander she owns herself almost entirely, and this is so good. Walking back and forth from high school is where she does her good thinking. The boiling tea, well, she brushes that off as an impromptu first act. No, she thinks, I need something more lasting.

So, day after day, she considers her problem as she walks past the pier with the waves agitating beneath it. Past the citizen's park with the muted swings moving lightly with ghost children. Past the rows and rows of little houses like faces under their tin roof hats. Through weather that is changing because everything is always changing, especially the sky round Yarrabeen.

She walks with her friend Peg Yardy, a stretched-out girl, pigeontoed as a fast bowler. She loves to talk about sex and what will happen when their time comes to partake. Edith never mentions that she knows something about the subject. This knowledge is the boulder she carries.

'D'you reckon Kenny Blake has a big one?'

They're walking home through a dank, overcast afternoon. Peg lives round the next corner.

'Helen Logan reckons it's huge. Put your eye out.'

'God, shut up, Peg. Who cares? Really, who cares about that dork and his horrible willy?'

'Don't you think it's interesting?'

'No. I think it's boring. *I am* interested in love though.'

'Come off it, Edie, blokes aren't interested in love.'

'Well, if they're not then I won't be interested in them.'

The silence hangs on the girls, strange and awkward, until Edith says, 'Want to come to my place, see if there's something to eat? Probably not though.'

Peg is able to resist.

She thinks about Alexander for weeks, undecided, mad and guilty that she let it go on for all those years. The thought turns in her. Then, one afternoon in late summer when the eucalypts are crackling with their veins of heat, she passes clumps of red-hot poker thrown down like spears beside the road. Well, that's the day she reckons she might have something. First thought is fire, but that's not on, she's no arsonist and besides, it's too dangerous for everyone else. The time from thought to execution is short but, really, there's so much comfort in decisions, she reckons. She takes a couple of things out of her pencil case before she stashes her schoolbag in the bushes near the pier.

The walk down there is spiced with her decision: the sun is warm, the sky is limitless, the birds call like church bells and she barely feels the hole in her shoe that catches gravel and needs taking off and shaking every so often. This mission feels right. The round, brown bus passes, chugging along like a wombat. She sees herself as a bit of a wombat in this matter and just hopes she doesn't come a gutser like a wombat in a trap.

She waves to Harry Greber from school in the front yard of his mum's flaky grey miner's cottage. Apparently, Harry's dad went mad and did something awful when he was little. Edith tries not to find out what exactly, but it must have been bad. His mum never looks into anyone's eyes, and after it Harry was not the same boy. Some people think there's something wrong with him. They reckon he's retarded or something, but she's not so sure. Can't boys just be nice? she wonders. Can't they like little kids and kind dogs? Can't they just be gentle?

'Hazza-man,' she says quietly, swinging back on the short wire fence, 'watcha doin?'

He's playing catchie with his dog Kanga, an exuberant, shaggy thing with amber eyes. The dog stops playing now and then for an emphatic scratch. Edie thinks of her own eczema and feels for the poor old dog. Harry puts his hand on Kanga's head, which stills her long enough for Edie to lean over and grab a drink from the tap in his front yard without getting flattened.

'Wanna go down the creek and get some taddies?' Harry holds a stick up from Kanga, who wants it single-mindedly. The air feels navy blue behind them. Bees feast on some wallflowers by the porch. 'There's plenty down there. Deadset. I saw 'em yesterday.' He avoids her eyes.

Edie stands up from the tap and wipes her mouth from the sliding water. 'Not today, Haz. Got something I hafta do, maybe tomorrow, eh? Wanna chewie?'

She squeezes out a battered Juicy Fruit into Harry's smudged palm.

'See ya then, Haz. Kanga.'

She starts chewing and the sugar hits her mouth, reassuring her that she is alive and well and ready for her task. Leaving Harry feels like leaving all safety, but she will do what she's about to do. She is resolute. Like when she steals. That's when she gets strong, as if iron has entered her soul, and she sidles up to something in the op-shop: a glass dome that has bubbles like stars trapped in it for her mum, a card she might like, a bunch of tattered pink carnations that dripped all over her leg when she shoved them under her raincoat at the fruit shop.

She's been thieving for years, and by now she's pretty good at it. Stationery is by far the easiest – pens, rubbers, little clips, food, chewies, lollies, chocolate bars. Truth is, nothing tastes as good as something nicked. Edie passes along the road with her thoughts following like seeds on the wind and her mouth working hard on the chewie.

Soon, as the road dips to the wonderful sea glinting like ice, Uncle Kev's muted red house is revealed. Edie looks younger in her school dress, and the hat makes her look like a button mushroom. She takes if off. Where's her bag? Fear shoots through her and then she remembers that she stashed it. She chucks out the chewing gum and feels her pocket for her supplies. Doesn't matter, the bag will be all right. She knows Alexander won't be home because he's helping at the bakery, either that or at uni. Kevin, as she's taken to thinking of him, will be away too because he's always at the bakery, probably still sorting out tomorrow's orders with her mum now.

She walks towards the house, smelling the dusty paddock. The smell of straw and oxygen her father said, is the millions of little creatures all eking out a living. She smiles to think of him and, as always, wonders how a person can get that sad. She's got a feeling she'll find out. Dust reminds her of rain, though she barely remembers it. The sea air smacking into the verandah is as fresh as toothpaste.

The door, like all others in Yarrabeen, is not locked and she lets herself in, identifying the smell of Uncle Kev, tobacco, fried sausages and tea. She's scared. The feeling of being in that little room with Alexander Culp comes back at her and suddenly she feels crook enough to chuck. It takes all her courage to stay, to calm herself. Behind her, the leadlight in the front door shines on her face. Red and yellow, green and blue lilies. Her face is wet with tears just doing their thing. It's odd to say she hates the house – she doesn't. She hates Alex, though, and the years of being mauled by his cold hands.

A stab of fear hits her and she wants to run. She wipes the tears away with her forearms. She might be sick, which would be a dead giveaway – what if she chucks in the hallway? – but she tells herself that now is the time to keep going and so she holds her breath. She tells herself her mum would be proud of her. She goes into Alex's room, just as she has done so many times before. In there, she wonders why she ever did go with him. When she was a little girl he'd take her hand and steer her; it never seemed real or right to make a fuss. And later she went because he was kind and interested in her and she thought it couldn't happen again. Not again. And sometimes because she wondered whether she'd understand it this time. She still doesn't understand it.

She takes out the round-tipped little school scissors she brought with her, goes to the crocheted rug and starts cutting, which is not easy because these scissors are as blunt as rocks, but she gets a run and starts pulling. It isn't long until the whole thing is an unravelled tangle of bright wool. She puts the scissors back in her pocket, and a gust of weeping seizes her.

'Not yet. You,' she tells herself sternly, 'you are not done.'

She goes to the desk, to the albums of stamps, and sitting down she takes out the carefully selected texta from her pocket and lifts the crackly paper. Carefully, she puts a black cross over every single stamp. It takes a while, there are a lot of stamps and the pen wafts its texta-smell all over everything. Then, on the wood of the oak desk, she writes, 'I HATE YOU' in her best handwriting. Disappointingly, she messes up the 'a' and has to go over it again. She thinks, it would be the 'a', the important letter.

As she lets herself out of the house, she's juddery and high as a falcon soaring over the dry paddock that fringes the house. She feels the tears again and her throat is sore from holding them back, so to take her mind off herself she goes down to the beach and dares the waves to wet her school shoes – she loses the bet. She walks all the way home with a squelch to her step, but Grace doesn't notice the wet shoes. The sea leaves a white tide mark on them, a reminder of treachery. For days later she looks at her feet and waits to hear the news that she'll be going to jail, if not be executed for her crimes. After a while she dares to believe that the news might not come. And while retribution doesn't come, the mark of the sea stays on the shoes, a mark of warning and of victory. Whenever Edie notices it, she's proud but stunned by what she has done. And the secrecy of the victory is a lesson: sometimes the best wins are the quiet ones.

Chapter 15

The Colony of Women

Winter rolls in fast in Yarrabeen. Mornings still and cold and breathing the chilly air is a sweet novelty that catches them unaware. And then damp afternoons with sea fog banking against the pickets, the white sky low and quilted. Edith looks out from the backyard and the bay is constantly changing. She's not constantly changing, though – she's stuck. Always reverting to thoughts of childhood as if they're scenes in a movie. She can recite them, but what does she remember and what is true? Juliet is always off somewhere, usually dragging Ted along. Still. There it was again, the bell of her laughter. Edith can hear her laughing, always having a go, saying, 'Edie, you lazy dog. You never finish the dishes properly, never even wipe the sink after you or hang up the bloody tea towel...' She sees herself swinging the tea towel and connecting with a satisfying *thwack* on Juliet's thigh. She sees Grace standing beside a teenaged Ted as he swigs a drink of water from the tap. 'Get a glass, would you, Ted?' and Ted looking up at her cheekily and laughing, mopping his wet mouth. She looks out the window into the summer day and sees the gold of an insect moving on its own stream of air. She sees it and yet she sees

Juliet too. Juliet has been gone long years now, and the space she left has become an old quarry.

Juliet's ashy eyes are bold and dangerous and her wavy hair catches light. It ripples around her face. Everything abides in that voice, which is honey till she gets mean. And she always gets mean. They were born a year apart, Edie cunningly named in hopes of inheritance from Auntie Edie on the farm in the Mallee, but then those farms up there rarely make money, plus, she had her own kids. The occasional birthday card reminded her that she had a bush auntie, and when she dies, nothing comes her way anymore, not even cards.

Juliet was named when Grace took one look at the baby and a feeling of pure joy ran through her. She had to find the loveliest name. She'd never seen *Romeo and Juliet,* but the name appealed like an idea of perfect love. Well, Jesus, thinks Edie each time she hears this story, I get Edith for a useless fat old bush auntie and she gets Juliet. Honestly, how do you work that out? Still, she allows, things hardly worked out well for Romeo and his Juliet.

Cherishing hurts becomes a habit for Edie, and it also becomes a habit to reproach her mother. She never hears her say that when Edie was born she was too confused to love anyone, except maybe the lactation consultant. Still, Edie's not surprised – if she had to choose a child to favour, she'd pick the others too. Edward Bell Fisher was born with a cow's lick and a set of lungs he knew how to use. There were plenty of arms for young Edward to find solace in because he was loved completely and secretly. Edith believed he'd been named for her, which didn't hurt one bit.

'None of you kids were planned, you know. You were all accidents.'

Grace is out in the garden battling with the weeds. She makes them help on Saturday afternoons for an hour after lunch – the sleepy hour, she calls it. If you don't work, you'll fall asleep.

'What do you mean "by accident", Mum?' Juliet is digging a hole for the new apple tree. It's hard work and she'd like to stop regularly.

Edie's interested to see how Grace gets out of this one. She's been saying this about accidents forever, and each time it occurs to Edie that there's something wrong with the equation. Being the first born a year after the marriage, shouldn't she at least have been expected?

'Never you mind, nosey young miss. It just means that God made you is all that means.'

Ho, thinks Edie, that's a beauty. Drag poor old God into it.

Juliet laughs. 'But Mum, what did God actually do?'

'Enough cheek, now, dig your damned hole.'

'Well, it's clear that Ted wasn't planned, otherwise someone would have revised his nose.'

After that kind of crack it was always on. He must have been about nine the first day Juliet mentioned his nose. It was a picnic day down the cliff at the beach. The heat pulsed, the salt crusted on them and the foamy surf rolled in. Yet Ted always has the energy for a stoush. Mentions of Ted's 'perfectly normal nose' always get his goat.

'Right, Romeo,' he says to Juliet, leaping up and kicking his towel into a tangle, 'you wanna go then, eh?' The sand scatters and his skinny boxing stance frames him, tight fists up near his face as he prances around on his toes, dead serious. Juliet in her daffodil-yellow bathers reaches over and puts her hand on his head. He swings good and hard at her guts, but misses and hot tears of frustration start. 'Hate you, Julie-shithead.' Then he grabs the thermos flask, unscrews the top and pours the sticky lemon cordial over Juliet's head, and they wrestle in a way that involves shoving jaws away from each other. Sand sticks to the cordial on them, and when a plate still laden with sandwiches slips from the card table and the food is ruined, that's it. Grace stands up, grabs her flowery beach bag and heads back up the cliff. Edie watches the idiots dissolve into helpless laughter. Soon enough they're rolling in the salad sandwiches and Ted has beetroot on his cheek.

'Dickhead,' she says.

'You are!' He pulls the beetroot off and hurls it at her. It slaps into the back of her leg and starts a slow purple slide.

Today, a few years later, he chucks his load of weeds into the hole she's digging and whispers, 'Bitch-woman.'

132

'Take those weeds out, Edward, or else you'll be digging the hole for the apple tree yourself, my boy.' Grace is taking time for a smoke. 'Hopeless, the lot of you. Why can't you just get on like normal people? The three of you can do this whole job. I'm telling you. Longer it takes, the longer you'll be at it. It's your choice.'

***

Asking a child to be a mother is asking for trouble. Because of everything – the move, Ian's death and Grace's busyness working through them – Edie got used to standing in for her mother. One night doing the dishes with Ted's help, it occurs to her that Ted *is* on the nose.

Truth is, she thinks, he's growing and needs to pay more attention to washing himself, especially after cricket training. She knew he wouldn't want to hear it in front of Juliet because she'd turn it into a barb. She could see it now: 'Ted, we have something to tell you. Listen, little dick, you smell like dog turd' followed by hoots of laughter, a few headlocks and maybe some broken china.

No, I'll do it without her, Edie decides, do it without any agony. Once again, they are stuck with the dishes. She passes Ted a wet plate covered in froth and imagines she begins conversationally. The boy's stringy dark hair hangs long and his face is well hidden. 'You're growing, mate. You know, getting older.

Body'll be changing, I suppose. That's the way of it, eh...'

She notices Ted daydreaming and says, 'Ted, are you listening? You look like a stunned mullet.' Lately he's not listening as much. He seems to have been transported to somewhere far from Yarrabeen.

'What?' Ted asks blankly, drying the disc of the plate over and over with the soggy tea towel. He isn't daydreaming, he's just part of somewhere that involves clear skies. Out the back door, down the cliff, the sea is a swirling mass that blends into the sky. This means he won't be able to get out his trusty little telescope tonight. No point, no stars tonight, he thinks bleakly. Now what do I do?

'Jesus,' Edith says, annoyed. The water's too hot. She perseveres and when she finally pulls her hands out they're poached. The cold tap goes on. Her annoyance is aimed squarely at Ted. It's bloody hard enough, little rodent, she thinks. For a start, he's got to stop wearing his school shirt to Saturday cricket, thinking he's Dennis Bloody Lillee or something.

'Look, I'm trying to say something, Ted. About you. It's just that you're, well, now that you're getting older – what are you now, twelve, soon be thirteen? Well, anyway – and it happens to everyone, remember – you're starting to stink up just a bit, after cricket ... you know, getting a bit pongy on it. And your hair too could use a bit more attention. Use my shampoo instead of the soap. Mate,' she smiles weakly, her own hair flopping subversively, 'it's nothing personal, it's just well, shampoo has really taken off lately. They even make it for men now.'

The boy is deeply stung by such a personal slap. A pause lingers between them and the wind shakes the house. The mention of his person by his own sister is just too much and a feeling of his lonely maleness in this horrible colony of women captures him. Tears drill at his eyes and then they narrow.

'Well, you know you can just shut your face, Edie. I don't nag you about your stinky farts. Or Juliet with that awful perfume of hers. And I never say anything about Mum and her disgusting smokes. I never say anything about anyone and all the rest of you do is talk, talk, talk, and you know what? I'm sick of the bloody lot of you.' Carefully, but with solemn dignity, he places the plate he's been drying for some time onto the bench. The rat's tail tea towel is piled. As he walks away, the kitchen door slams like a full stop.

***

One night she came home later than usual from a study group. She'd walked under the ivory stars to the back door, and smack into the sound of Van Morrison. In the front room her mother and brother are deep into *Astral Weeks.* Their eyes are closed. Grace is in the big chair and Ted lies on the floor with a pillow under his head. Ted has saved for six weeks to buy this record. He's put his dollar a week pocket money all on George Ivan Morrison.

Ted sees Edie and reaches over to the record player and turns it down. 'New record. Just got it. This is our third listen.'

'Hi, Mum, I've been at the study group, remember? At Jenny Jones's joint.'

'Oh yeah, how did it go? This is so lovely. "Cyprus Avenue" is just...'

She has her feet up on the cracked brown leather pouf ottoman (their dad liked them to call it by its whole name). Her slippers are sheepskin and her trackie daks are covered in bobbles. Grace is happy. There's a smoke going in the smoker's stand and a glass of red wine and coke beside it. She's sharing a bag of scorchies with Ted. Life at this moment, thanks to Van, is pure perfection. Uncle Kev took himself off after one listen, muttering 'early morning tomorrow'. Edith is miffed that her mother likes Van Morrison. *She* likes Van Morrison better than anyone. Even Ted.

Ted yawns a Luna Park yawn. 'I better go to bed, Mum. School and all that.'

'Righto, I'll just have a little bit more. Absolutely incredible, reminds me of my mum.' Edie listens with her and they fall asleep with the arm of the record jumping little jumps in the quiet ditch.

PART II

Chapter 16

The Small Book of Mistakes

Maureen Frances Morgan escaped a damp farm outside Tipperary in the province of Munster in the greenness of Ireland and came to Melbourne as a lady's maid. Leaving her mother, six brothers and four sisters behind on the dairy farm being treated as slaves and lackies was hard. But when you get a chance, you take it.

To Molly, home meant never enough to eat and living with mud, shit, cold and rain, but her ma knew a woman who worked for the Lady Erin MacLeish. She got the girl in with the big house as a junior maid, starting in the kitchen and working her way upstairs by dint of brains and charm. It wasn't until Molly was set to the job of tending Lady Erin's hats, feathery things in pale colours, that she glimpsed another future. It wasn't long before she was charged with the responsibility and honour of actually placing the hats on the ladyship's head. That was the day she knew she was safe from the farm. She left with Lady Erin and the MacLeishes for Australia and her mother, Mary, wept for a while. Soon enough all she really missed was the girl's pay packet but still she wished her girl a better life than her own. When they parted, Molly watched her mother walking up the green hill bearing two heavy buckets, and the sight of her – a victim of the church, of fertility, of her father – never left her. As far as Molly was concerned, all three could be done without.

So the Irish in Molly made her sound like bells and her curls were soft and her eyes were violets, but her nose was a scythe and her jaw was stronger than beauty allowed. Men tended to read some kind of warning in her and decide against her, and she was a bit too thin so time passed in packets of years. Molly was an acquired taste. Too skinny, too sharp, too quiet and she saw into them like a lighthouse sees into the dark – for a while and for only so far. She always turned away.

Over the years she had a few exchanges with other servants. Mr Williams was a nice man to walk down to the seaside with on a Sunday afternoon but, really, she was happy being a fully-fledged old maid, happy with a room, a ginger cat, a good recipe for boiled fruitcake and ghost-memories of a day by the sea at Connemara with her sisters and brothers and her mother when she was a girl. Her father had spent the day in a pub. Molly wrote to her mother every Christmas and sent money and a lace handkerchief, all of them much too good to use and kept in a soapbox that once held lily-of-the-valley soap.

Soon enough, though, Lady Erin with her new-found squatter husband, an Australian with a big voice and brown hands, planned to move to a property in the Western District. Molly already knew the country life was not for her. She liked the city, with real pavements under her feet and umbrellas in their stands by the door and shops that sold bread, white and fine as hotel sheets. When she left, Lady Erin presented her with one of her old hats, a pale-blue velvet one that had always reminded Molly of a tortoise.

Wearing the hat, Molly found a job at the biggest hotel in the southern city and took an attic room upstairs with pigeons for neighbours something that pleased her ginger cat.

***

In no time it seemed she'd been a maid at the city hotel for years. Making beds, cleaning lovely rooms, picking up after people – none of it ever bothered her. All of it was better than dealing with cows and brothers, who were little better than beasts themselves, she truly believed. Being happy seemed a matter of organisation and memory; she never forgot where she came from and so looking around made her smile.

She became head maid at the Hotel Imperial in the city and answered to Miss Gladys Prichard, the overstuffed housekeeper with fragile hair who lolled about in her office eating from a cache of complimentary chocolates taken from the guests' rooms. Consequently, she'd become very fat and found most of her job too hard to manage. In this weighty problem, Molly was her right arm. Glad's tasks whittled down to just counting sheets and pillowcases and gossiping with people in accounts over cups of tea. This left Molly to keep order with a crew of careless, smoking, laughing girls she doggedly turned into quality maids.

Behind her back, they called her Mad Molly Morgan because she'd done the unthinkable. As a single woman, Molly, with her fading curls, had given up the hunt for a husband, to them, proof of madness. Plus, she could be pretty sharp. They gossiped over harsh words delivered for toilet seats left up or a harmless forgotten feather duster resting on a mahogany chest. Such minuscule provocations.

The consequences of crooked pillowcases and towels could be ruinous because when she came upon them she marked the offences down in the small book of mistakes she carried dangling from her apron at her waist. At the end of each shift she went through them, never satisfied until the maids repented and yet a lavish repentance still didn't go far with Molly. Three marks in the book and you were out on your ear. With the pure daring of youth, though, the maids took it in turns to stir old Molly but she only ever sacked Enid Mills, who really was a renegade.

'Things have got to be done right,' she told the maids in white uniforms. 'People are paying for this hotel with their own good money.' The maids, with their caps on straight and their smiling moon faces turned to her, would have liked to have yawned. But that would be foolish.

Henry Bell had pale hair and eyes like a Nordic God, but he was just a poor Englishman. Henry was born in Leeds and came to Australia with his thieving mother and his brother, Horace, when he was five years old. Mrs Sarah Bell had light fingers and left her husband behind working in a bicycle factory. He came home on Tuesday to find the place cleaned out and a note saying, 'Goodbye, Norman. I took the savings in the tea tin.' Sarah was a step from jail. And Australia, as everybody knew, was a good twenty years behind England in all things. She really hoped they still liked thieves.

Henry and Horace didn't see much of their mother who was usually busy being a tea leaf, and they grew used to having nothing or everything. Without bothering to divorce their father, she married an Australian grocer from Carlton when Henry was sixteen. The boys weren't invited to the wedding or to live at the house behind the grocer's store. Horace wanted to find his father, so he took a job as a steward on an ocean liner and worked his way back to Leeds. Henry liked the sun, so he stayed and got an apprenticeship as a carpenter and in the end he became an expert at repairing old furniture, working for an antique dealer. He liked the stability of old furniture.

Henry might have been an aristocrat until he opened his mouth. He was fair with even features and an easy gentleness, but when he spoke he sounded like an Australian worker whose voice was a shade too high. He was mocked for this by those who love to mock, and it made him quiet. Mostly he wore overalls, but for pleasure he wore tweeds. When he rode his old black bike to work, his overalls tucked into his socks, he looked like a golden matador, his brown arms sheathed in a fuzz of golden hair. His was the soothing kind of beauty that wrapped itself around those he loved.

Henry came one day to the Imperial to fix a wardrobe door. It was finer work than the house carpenter could manage. The wardrobe was a hundred and fifty years old and had been kicked by a guest. It upset Henry just to witness the damage. Kneeling, he stroked the wardrobe's grain as if it were a child's forehead.

'What do you think, Mr Bell. Can it be repaired?'

'It can. But it will take some time.' And when he looked up at Molly, she found herself blushing like a school girl.

It was Molly's job to stand beside him while he worked to ensure he didn't steal anything. These were the house rules. Liking him was so unexpected. That they became good friends, and later lovers, was surprising. She had never encountered such tenderness in anyone. That he wanted to marry her was astonishing, nearly as surprising as being pregnant. They married two months before Grace was born in the summer of 1932. Molly squeezed herself into her good grey suit and the zip needed to be down, but she decided no one noticed. She wore a little black hat with a half net, and he wore a suit borrowed from another carpenter who had recently married. The witnesses came from among the maids. Afterwards, they had a drink in the ladies' lounge of the Imperial. Lemon squash and a pot of beer. Some snaps taken that day had Molly looking baffled and Henry smiling.

At forty years of age, Molly gave birth to Grace Mary on the first day of 1933. The labour took three days, and by the third she had to be restrained from trying to throw herself from the second-storey window. If it won't end, she thought, she must end it herself. Finally, the midwife wiped her hands and told Henry it was time to go for the doctor. He brought Dr Egan back on his bike, dinking him up the hill like a man whose legs could pedal to the moon. The doctor brought chloroform and he soon sent Molly to sleep, extracting Grace from her like a pip from a plum.

Molly woke to a swimming feeling of illness, loss and confusion. For a moment, everything was wrong – the baby must have died. Then she saw her young husband holding Grace, and she believed in God then and there and forever after.

Henry was twenty-two on that day and the eighteen-year gap between them underlined everything forever. He spent his youth looking to be older while Molly Morgan tried for youth with various creams and potions, like a fisherman casting for luck till her face took on a look of tight preservation, and then she just let it all go, aging with her quilted skin and her fine netted hair like a woman from an older time. They lived within the endless secret compression of time and somehow made it a place of safety for Grace but, regardless of their love, time was a tug of war with one at each end of that rope. And some days, it would seem, Molly might have been Henry's mother. As they aged, the gap grew.

From the moment she was born, everybody loved Gracie. Her hair curled and her mother's dark eyes peered out of her round face. Henry took her everywhere. Molly never restrained the love she felt for her. And then the war came and Henry enlisted. He went away when she was six years and three days old. He left her with a doll in a blue dress they named Winnie because he'd read her Winnie the Pooh every single night of her life.

When Henry went away, Molly went back to work at the Imperial, leaving Grace with Millicent, one of the upstairs maids whose shift alternated with hers. Though they missed Henry and worried for him, they did all right. And then the thing they were dreading happened to Molly instead of Henry. She fell down the back stairs and cut her shin to the bone.

The healing was slow, walking was impossible, and finally infection set in. The doctor told her she must go to hospital or lose her leg. There was no one to leave Grace with, until Millicent said she'd take the child home with her to the country. 'But I don't like the country. I don't want her there. It is too hard. It is not kind enough for my little Grace.'

Millie told her she was mad. 'You're talking about Ireland. This is not like that. We have good things for children. Ponies and laughing and kittens and swimming. She'll love it. You'll see.' It was that or the orphanage.

In the hospital, sitting up with her leg in a cradle, Molly was visited by Millie and Grace and there were many tears. Grace climbed under Molly's bed and sat there until two nurses dragged her out.

Millie and Grace boarded the train before the brownout and rode a long way west past mountains and yellow paddocks thick with wheat, always leaning with the wind it seemed, and every paddock with a lone gum tree, white as bone.

Bill Boyd, Millie's dad, bred sheep for money and horses for love and he and Grace became friends over apples. He'd peel them and give her a piece off his knife, and they'd take the cores out for the horses.

She followed Bill around on all his chores, lifting buckets far too big for her and brushing down the horses where she could reach. At night he ate her vegetables because she hated them. He was a kindly man. Grace stayed with Bill and Millie a year because Molly just could not be repaired, the leg ulcerated into a crater. Henry spent the last part of the war in Crete, starving, outnumbered and often unarmed. He wrote letters to 'darling Mollie and Gracie'. He never did work out how to spell Molly. After the year, Grace didn't want to go home, and

Molly felt it was a poor home she was providing anyway: no Henry, no horses and not much money. That was when Grace began to feel some kind of embarrassment about her mother, ashamed of this woman who loved her too much. At eight, it seemed to Grace that you can be too kind.

Chapter 17

There Are No Ordinary Cats

One windy afternoon, Edie's out scrounging for pressies for her mum. She'd decided to give up thieving because of the inevitability of getting nabbed, though she still needs things for her mum. The net was closing in the small town, and she could just about feel the heat. Anyway, the freedom to roam Yarrabeen was the best thing about the place, the only good thing in her opinion, and she could not afford to lose it. Freedom made her feel bigger, more in charge of her own self in a way she never was in town. And so did walking out the door and seeing the sea clouding the land with mist and walking through it, hidden. These things softened Yarrabeen and they even softened the idea of jail. And the rubbish tip *was* purely a treasure trove and a free one at that! On days when she was bored shitless (and now she said it out loud!), she took herself down there. She has already found her mum a beautiful blue biscuit jar, minus only the lid! Unbelievable. Musing in the wind of that clear, glassy day, she sees the smile her mother will give when she presents the latest find. Pleasing Mum makes life better, she thinks amiably, not noticing at first that weirdo from school Bernard Sedge looming in the distance. *Yuck* is the first thought, and then she really sees him. When she looks harder, she believes he's stabbing at something in his mad way and her fear deepens until she flies over the empty tins and sacks and then she's in a little rubbish cove, watching him stab at a mother cat huddled in a cardboard box. His spear is whittled from a white gum branch.

Words stop in her. 'Ah!' she screams before managing to yell, 'You! Bastard! Ah...' She kneels to find the body of the mother cat, still so small itself. She kicks the boy in the leg. This is the worst thing you could ever see. The kittens, little pockets of life, black and white, a tabby and a black, call out for their mother. Bernard takes off and she chases him with long strides over the rubbish. Suddenly he stops, panting and heaving, and makes out that he'll spear her too. 'Right in the fucking face, Edith Fisher!' he screams. She ducks, stumbles and he catches her by the foot, causing her to fall and cut her hand on a tin can. Seagulls witness it all, hovering like rescue choppers. 'Bitch!' he yells. 'Why don'tcha just mind your own bizzo, you bloody bitch.'

He holds the spear at her head and suddenly the sight of him – his crazy white hair standing up, his mean little scared eyes – causes outrage to replace fear. 'Ha!' she yells, 'as if!' In her head she hears Grace say: how dare the little twerp.

Edie gathers phlegm from the deep and spits it right at him. Though he dodges, a splodge of it lands right in the middle of his jumper and he wipes it off without looking. When he laughs, his teeth are curiously sharp. Edie crouches to catch her breath and, holding her own hand, she yells, 'You're a true moron. How could you hurt that poor cat? You're really sick.' She's breathless from running. 'I'm telling my mother on you, Bernard Sedge, that's for sure.'

His teeth are revealed again, he's enjoying the exertion and the attention. His hair is standing straight up. He's aroused by hating her. 'Not scared of you, Fisher Street, or your dumb mum neither. My mum says you're no better than you ought to be and neither is your mum. Town trash, anyway.'

She wonders what he means and thinks she notes a melting in his eyes, and she reckons that he's scared too. She rises from the rubbish. 'Get stuffed, Bernie, you cretin. You're a goner and I'm getting those kittens, so don't go near them. You want to rack off, Bernie, you dill, because I'm dobbin'. The police will be real interested in this and that you tried to stab me too.' He slowly backs off, and then he runs – runs so fast she soon loses him in the foothills of the tip.

By the time Edie and Grace return, the mother cat is a cold ball of sorrow with five kittens still pushing at her. They wrap the kittens in a towel, take them home and feed them with eye droppers until they're old enough to give away. One dies. Feeding those kittens is the closest Edie will ever feel to Grace. Feeling the small animals grow. The night feeds and changing of the towels. Their blind cries and murmurs of pleasure. Their growing personalities. It made Edie see that mothers are everything and without them we're lost.

One night, together by the kittens, Grace says her mother Molly always loved cats. 'She quoted someone wise who once said there are no ordinary cats and that it was true – their beauty is perfect. My mother was very, very kind.' She puts the kitten back into the box and looks at Edith. 'These kittens make you think about mothers, don't they?' They refill the hot water bottle for the kittens and go back to their own beds, passing through the cold house united in mothering, united as any football team.

***

Next morning she decides to tell her mother all about Bernard Sedge's slander but Grace isn't inclined to go into it. 'Leave things as they are,' she says. 'He's nothing much, just a little hoon, just the town fool.' Edie never asks what 'town trash' means, probably doesn't matter anyway. They give kittens away but keep the little black one they name Willy-Boy.

Bernard Sedge still bothers her. At school, he whispers obscenities and, once, he pisses on her bag. She sees him after she's left it at the lockers and she forgets something and goes back for it. He runs away, dribbling and laughing. He calls her Fisher Street because there's one in the next town up. Pathetic reason. He reminds her of a hyena. She'd seen them on

TV, slinky things always looking to take a lion cub. He still scares her though.

She tells Grace about him one evening. Tea was over with, dishes done, nice and early, just how Grace likes it. The kettle's on and Grace is painting a wooden stool cream. She aims to distress it later with the grater. Pretty it up. Maybe add a stencil or two, a heart and ribbon would be nice and perfect because she's already got it! The radio plays and the suave voice of the evening guy is tackling everyday issues with a sense of humour: neighbourhood disputes, telephone marketing and in-law problems. Fence disputes are Grace's favourites. Edie half hears someone ring up about a neighbour who keeps too many cats. This is the spur; it reminds her. Cats and mothers and the closeness they had. She sits down at the table and instantly puts her hand in a blob of cream paint under the stool. She swats at it and it smudges. Willy-Boy manages to avoid all paint, unlike Edie, who now has it on her school dress. The cat sashays around and settles down on the kitchen table like a sunbather at the beach.

'Mum, remember that Bernie Sedge? The boy at school from the tip? Well, he keeps following me and he peed on my bag.' She transfers most of the paint smudge onto the newspaper and her mother sighs.

'You'll be imagining that, Edie love.' She takes a drag at her cigarette and lets the smoke stream out.

'I'm not. I know he is. He weirds me out, Mum. I'm telling you, he touched me.'

She stops painting and holds the brush upright so it won't drip. 'Where? Where exactly did he touch you?' She peers at her daughter like a judge on the high bench.

'Here.' Edith touches her breast area shyly, the paint smear still visible.

'Well, you've got nothing there anyway, so that's all right then.' She begins to paint again with long strokes, caressing the wood with the brush. 'Boys can be a bit of a trial, love. Try not to take them too seriously or personally. If it wasn't you they were annoying, it would be some other poor lassie. That only encourages the poor wretches. You get on now. Help Juliet with her homework. She's hopeless at her maths.' Grace smiles, dragging some more newspaper under the stool. 'Not like you. You are my clever one.'

Chapter 18

Honey

In time it came to Edith's attention that there was a boy named Tom Southey in high school, two years above her, who was said to be a major spunk. On viewing, she agrees with this diagnosis and pursues him like a guided missile. He is hers, she decides, and he *will* love her. The craziness for him must have come from the loss of her father. She almost understood this then, but not quite and Southey, he was a pure innocent, outside of all these things.

They start out together when he's in his final year at the high school. He's noticed her shining hair and hasn't missed her smiling at him. There's the dance coming up and he reckons he'll see what comes of a bit of a chat. She's at the lockers, ferreting for a lost book, one leg holding her bag against the bottom locker, when suddenly she feels the presence of someone else. She pulls her head out and there's Southey, long dark hair kicking up at the ends, olive skin, green eyes and white, white teeth. She feels the heat of life pound through her and her heart speeds up as if she's been injected with something. He just seems a bit nervous.

'G'day,' he says, smiling, 'How's it going?'

'Good.' Silence has clamped her and towed her away.

'Oh good, righto then. Listen, you going to the dance?'

'Err, yeah, reckon I might be.'

'Well good, I'll see you there.'

And he's gone and her eyes follow him leaving, already missing him. She wants to hurl herself onto his back and plead, 'Take me with you, make me new, make me someone else because I can't do it on my own!' But she knows she's always been a bit sudden about these things. Instead she looks into her bag and extracts the lost book, some version of science for dills, and then with maximum force wedges the bag into the battered grey locker.

They have reached an understanding: Edith loves him and he thinks that's pretty damn terrific. That he seems more interested in his mates than in her isn't really a worry. She can conquer these quibbles. When Edie first kisses Tom Southey, nothing much happens, which is disappointing – shocking, actually, considering how high her hopes were. How could she have got him so wrong? Who'd have thought he was a bit of a wet rag. Just shows you can't tell and that looks don't even matter. He's just not passionate. There's nothing much to Southey. He's nothing more than a passing sparrow.

It's been a while since the botched kiss and still Edie hangs around with him anyway, though she's possibly considering ways to exit, not letting on how cast down she feels. And then one evening they're sitting on the front doorstep of Seacrest holding hands and eating lemonade icy poles.

It's late in the January school holidays and the cicadas are singing high in the trees at the back of the park. Soon Edie will be going into Year 11 and Southey will begin his apprenticeship. He's old for it, but his mother wanted him to finish school.

Across the road, Mrs Mac's aspen has begun to shed its leaves and the small gold pennies float down to them. Edie hears the cicadas but watches seagulls as they track through the fading heat of the sky, diligent wings always occupied with the question of food. She's looking at her feet and the leafy currency spotting them when Southey reaches over, puts his hand on her chin and kisses her mouth softly. He tastes of lemonade. 'That still wasn't right,' he says urgently, 'let's have another go.'

He turfs his icy pole into the bushes and grabs her with both sticky hands. They begin again with a slow sweetness, and then she feels it – the strange shift that signals the change. Ah, so this is it, she thinks, but then with a rush she worries that anyone can see them. In time they plan a weekend. Tell lies to cover their time together, say they're with friends camping in the Grampians. They bring food – apples, bread and hard cheese – and Passiona to drink. The lies have no consequences because love is like that when it wants to be.

They rent a little bubble caravan in the park between Newtown and Yarrabeen, ten dollars for the two nights, and at this time of the year the caravan park is deserted. School's back and the workers are stacked back into the city like bees into hives. Though here, the tea-trees seem to be filtering the heat from the inland and the sea breeze cools the evenings.

Timing is everything. On Friday night they both walk from their homes carrying school bags stuffed with clothes, shopping bags and Edie brings a small Dutchman's Puzzle quilt she made at thirteen. It's mostly red.

She knocks at the little green door, thinking she's first to arrive, but there he is filling the doorway with his smile and his eyes and the gravity of it all. This is so different from every day, she thinks, and even better; he is so different to me. She puts the bags down and touches his face, the beginnings of a beard are there. He seems so wildly incomparable, he can be excused anything. It is such a delight to be away from herself, to be in this net of Southey. He pulls her inside the caravan where things all seem to be red. The windows are portholes and the tea-trees whisper that it's all right, that it will always be all right because Southey loves her and love is alive within them both.

Though something does nag at her that this is not the love she'd imagined. Something more equal, less one-sided – not how it is here with her doing all the towing, all the thinking, all the planning, all the worrying – was what she wanted. But now that they are naked this seems much less of a problem and somehow it seems Southey has discovered initiative. He's beside her on the little bed that's been converted from a table. He's covering her with the red blanket and kissing her again, and she thinks his eyes are bees.

***

They begin to talk later in the caravan on that starry evening, in the grip of a new kind of honesty and she is amazed to find herself telling him the story of Alexander. It's as if she's been waiting to tell.

'The touching didn't progress much. He didn't do much else. It made me feel sick. His hands were cold and thin. Oh God, this is awful, I shouldn't tell you. I know I shouldn't. You will hate me now, but at the time I couldn't stop him. I didn't know how. It went on for four years.'

She tries a laugh to ease the distress in her voice but it misfires and, anyway, the summer drifts in through the sliding window. 'I'll always hate him. But sometimes I think I hate my mother more because she never thought to protect me from it.'

Southey listens in silence and then after a while says, 'I was molested too. The cliché scoutmaster at First Yarrabeen. I was just turned thirteen. He was married. But he got me, made me feel special and I trusted him. Took me years to get away from the bastard. My parents were the same, completely trusting and utterly useless. I did tell them after I got free of him, but the news seems to have had no impact. They looked embarrassed and puzzled. So I just gave up on them. The police finally got involved and I made a statement, along with many others, but he escaped and hasn't been heard of again. People said he killed himself and I bloody hope he did. He left his wife and his own kids too. I remember their little cream brick-veneer house, and the grass so long and green and neglected. I saw her once at the service station and I said hello, but she looked through me. I was just another kid her husband had meddled with. I suppose to her, we kids were like the other women.'

***

Tom Southey was the son of a plumber from the outskirts of Yarrabeen towards the western side of Blanket Bay. His father, Henk, was Dutch, a clumsy olive-skinned fellow with iron-grey, childishly upstanding hair. Skin furrows ran down his face like dry riverbeds. He grew up near Antwerp and felt the war coming with a dread born of experience. Each day the threat seemed to grow. He had lost his father in World War I, and the idea of coming through that kind of slaughter again seemed impossible. His mother died when he was seventeen. At twenty he decided to make a clean start. When an immigration fair came to town he stood looking in through the door of the echoing hall. The queue for America was long and knotted, but there was no queue for Australia. The Australians on duty, one of them a pretty woman, laughed behind a table decorated with plastic flowers like red brushes. He went up to the table, coughed and they smiled at him. When one called him 'mate', he thought, they'll do. When a passport official asked him where he was headed, he said, 'South,' but there was a mix-up at the Immigration office and he wrote down 'Southey'. Not a bad name, Henk thought later.

As he stood on the pier surveying the width of the new country, it really didn't seem that hot – and where were all the kangaroos? He made his way further south and then when the war spilled across the world, he suddenly wanted to do something to belong, something that mattered, so he joined the AIF and fought in the capturing mud of Papua New Guinea. And after that, any soldier was his brother.

Maggie Lonergan, Southey's mother, once had clear blue eyes and dark wavy hair, but now the trappings of youth have departed and she's pale as a pebble. Her eyes are doubtful and, to Edith, seem close to beige. At least there's certainty in the darkness still in her grey hair. Her round cheeks seem young, though her skin is old.

Maggie married Henk Southey when he came back from the war, a hard man ready to settle down with a house, a backyard and a lawnmower. Maggie, he believed, could be taught how he liked things. She loved his name and his hands, and then, so many of the young men had died in the war.

She called her baby Thomas Sebastian Southey and in time the feeling for everything flew to the goodness of the baby. Henk was left out of that feeling so completely until it came to the point where she could not even look at him.

He would come home from work and find her still playing peek-a-boo with the baby or just holding him in the rocking chair, letting the evening fall around them. Henk would start making noises in the kitchen. Once he hurled the coffee pot into the sink and it broke into slivers and cut him. She put Tom down and went in to see Henk, his thick hands covered in blood and his eyes looking at her as if she knew something. 'What happened?'

'Nothing much.'

'Are you–'

'I'm not hurt.' He looked around, his hand in the tea towel like a great big fist and his face filling with sorrow.

'This place is a tip, Maggie. When are you going to get organised?'

'The baby–'

'The baby doesn't need to be held all day.'

Henk's frugality, his absent sense of humour and imagination, his austere distance and his ineptness made him hard to love. And he was not like other men. He even hated sport, for God's sake, cursing their addiction to it as juvenile. So in the end he became a dour know-all who'd even tell her how to make scones (despite not knowing how himself) because her last batch wasn't light enough.

When she has a visitor, Maggie's tongue loses all caution. She doesn't know what causes it, maybe it's the loneliness that seizes her, but give her a visitor in her own kitchen and she becomes the soul of indiscretion. Neighbours are all wary. Who wants other people's secrets?

At Edith's first afternoon tea, Southey and Henk chat about tools and lawn edging, while the women eat pound cake compact as carpet and remark on the weather for the time of year. Then, as they both know she must, Maggie gets up to take plates into the kitchen. Edie follows with the cups.

In the patchy light of the blue-and-white kitchen she meets another Mrs Southey, no longer repressed but free and light, laughing and chatting about recipes, cats and hay fever. The sink is filled with frothing water. The girl grabs the tea towel in an effort to look helpful.

For a bit, Maggie tries to fight against the temptation to drift into this young girl's life. She's always felt she can move in and out of other people. Henk's always thought she wasn't all there, but what would he know? It's just what happened when she likes someone enough, she feels the drift come into her and she begins to understand. Her heart pounds and she even feels taller and wiser. She swims with the swallowing tide of another life. It's delicious. It's funny. Why resist? And, today, there's just the utter relief of having another woman around.

She looks upon this girl, so young and sweet, eyes wide as a deer's, and she grabs her by the shoulders and says, 'It's wonderful to have you in the family, Edie. God, bloody wonderful! I needed a girl and you needed a boy and the Lord brought you to me. Southey will make anyone a fine husband. He's a kind boy.' And then the mysterious bolt of indiscretion. 'You'll be glad to know he's nothing like his father.'

The bushfire of menopause sweeps across her poor red face. The heat from her sink hands stays clamped on the girl's shoulders like pegs on a clothesline. 'Thanks,' Edie manages, smiling idiotically, 'for the welcome.' She tries to duck out and laughs a bit.

The sticky silence swells and the dishes settle in the froth. Edie wants to bolt. Mrs Southey sure is weird, she thinks and she misses her own mother so much she can almost conjure her up in the old kitchen, quilting at the table, fabric strewn around her feet like bright leaves. She swallows. She must think of something to say.

'Blossom's out early this year...' she ventures a bit too brightly, trying to stop the intimacy. She's relieved to have said anything, seeing she nearly commented on how clean the floor was. Through the kitchen window, a battered old plum tree has managed a few feathery sticks of blossom. At the mention of the tree, Maggie pulls her hands out and flaps them free of soap bubbles. She shakes her head and, like a tic, 'no, no, no' rushes out.

She gets close to the girl and whispers, 'It's a wonder there's any tree left out there at all, the way he prunes things. Not to mention blossom. Before he noticed it, the thing was absolutely covered in glorious blossom. Loves to cut things down. He's got a heavy hand, does Henk.'

Maggie is now drying a flowery teacup with close attention, as if she might hurl it at the wall in a little fit of everyday kitchen savagery. In Maggie's tearing little sentences, Edie sees all the crabbed, constrained years that went into making Southey and she nearly weeps at the thought. Never let Southey and me be like this, she beseeches the universe, placing Maggie's cups in the cupboard over the kettle. Then, she changes tack again. 'These are such nice cups,' she says in a gentling way.

But Maggie's not really with her now. She's set into some future. Wiping her hands on her flowered apron she declares, 'One day they will be yours, but first my dear, a grandchild, because when you have a child, then you will understand love.'

Her red-faced laugh is high and her eyes are squinty with the pleasure of boldness. 'Well, gee,' she says into the awkwardness. From behind the door, Maggie grabs the broom, the straws curled into a tick. She's sweeping with vigour when Southey opens the door and leans in smiling and apparently, it seems, quite sane. 'Mum, I hope you haven't been scaring poor old Edie off now.'

She hoots. 'Take more than me to scare this one off.' Happily, she surveys the pair of them together like a couple of baby budgies.

Chapter 19

My Eyes Betray Me

An hour and a bit away from Yarrabeen, the flat city sprawls, scattered with grey birds pitching across the mirrored sky. Sparrows and pigeons run the place as far as Edie can tell and are far more intelligent than people think. For three years she lives in Shaw, in a drowsy, compressed, bricked-in corner where the birds hover around her in the afternoons while she feeds them bread and lets herself dream of the future. The broad highway that passes behind the house in Yarrabeen runs all the way to Shaw. It's lined with yellow sword grass giving way on the windy plain near the city to weathered sheds sheltering hibernating trucks.

The distance between Yarrabeen and Shaw is salt to her and all the flavour comes from distance. Shaw seems so completely hers – the desiccated brown river, the little crepe myrtles dotted along the street in summer like red flares. Knowing Shaw makes it home instead of just some big crazy city. And not being known here is delightful to Edie. The peace of Shaw seems eternal and kind and a long way from Yarrabeen. Here in the palm of the city, where occasional parachutes of wild pink bougainvillea spill from brick walls like lava, she walks the streets anonymously and she is free. She doesn't think of anything but now. She is also unaware that problems can be bigger than work, paying rent and bumping into ratbags at the shops, but youth is her shield and thinking doesn't go too deep.

Anyway, Yarrabeen's gone now. It belongs to anyone who's ever been there, spent a couple of days in a caravan or even just wandered on the beach and put a toe in the water. Everyone has stories to tell about the place. How they spent their holidays there when they were kids, the caravan selling hot jam donuts in brown paper bags. They crowd in with all their details, seeming to know the place she knows. But the truth is that Yarrabeen is not what it had been. Her dismissal of Yarrabeen is her way of leaving home. Her mother represents Yarrabeen. Her mother, who these days dresses in Indian caftans coloured like jewels and carries her tarot cards wrapped in their black silk scarf, holding the answers to all things. Holding séances with Kev and their cronies. Holding hands and drinking moselle. No, it was well time Edie moved on.

***

Edie lives with Southey in Drum Street, Shaw, a street laced up tight as a knitted scarf. Cars circle their house like prowlers and some people striding by the thin street speak Greek, and everyone seems to dress in black. She hears snatches of student conver- sations earnestly designed to make things better for the working classes. Sometimes in the night, on the way from the Nobby's Retreat Hotel up the road, the few students who still can afford to live in Shaw throw empty beer bottles into the gutter. The clash and shatter makes her skin jump, but then she's always been easily startled.

She loves the dark-haired Southey in her extreme way and thinks about him more than about any other single thing: what he wants, whether they will go out, who he wants to have dinner with, whether his clothes need washing or his pillowcase is clean enough. She guards the idea of him within herself and it occurs to her that he has become something more, that perhaps he's the absent man at the centre of her. Although she comes to this conclusion, she doesn't take the door that leads away from it that would ask her why anyone needs one of those. It all just seems the way things are, the way they should be.

She comes up with the idea of 'bleshing' – blending and meshing – and tells him all about it. 'We'll be one person, a better person. No one will ever love you like I love you. We are made the same, we love the same, dream the same.'

They're sitting on a little couch covered with a bedspread full of green and brown flowers the size of saucers. She tugs at the white-fringed edges to get it straight without even noticing that she does it, and Southey rises up a bit to let it move beneath him. Edie likes things shipshape. Southey smiles at the idea of bleshing. 'Love you too,' he agrees readily and ruffles her hair, holding onto a long strand between his fingers and looking through the window where some of the horizontal weatherboards of the house next door bend like an ache.

He feels a quiver pass through him when she talks about such things and a suspicion that this is not normal. Trouble is, he likes being him. It's the way he wants to go on being and he's not about to apologise for it either. He wonders how you tell someone you don't want to become them. Surely this will not go well.

A chimney flanks each side of their house and there are four rooms, each with a thin casement window. The tin roof has rusted to the colour of dried blood. In the front, the bull-nosed verandah could be a hand shading eyes. A little plot of leggy greenness sits between the house and the street. Water has so long been a scarcity, it seems a memory. Each day after her work as a secretary to the principal at Our Lady of Goodness, Edith sits on a little orange aluminium deckchair parked out next to the bins. Being there in the fold between day and evening, waiting for Southey, is like the promise of something.

She's feeding the birds when it occurs to her that she doesn't actually mind the new school either. Even the kids aren't too mental and every now and then a little girl smiles when she brings the attendance rolls in from the teacher. 'Miss Fisher,' she asks sweetly, 'could you check the roll?' Edie huffs at them as if they've annoyed her, but sometimes she watches them and finds herself smiling.

Considering his name is Angus Dolt, the principal of the Catholic school is happy enough. He's short and wide and his check shirts stretch over his hard belly like plaid skin. Each day he wears the same muddy maroon tie scattered with tiny dull suns. He believes in being positive. His wide, sandpapery nose is huge. His tiny eyes are hidden by brimming black brows, and she can see that some hairs in there are blunter than others due no doubt to the Gentleman's Helper trimmer she's seen in his top drawer. 'Morning, Miss Fish,' he bellows, singsong style, advancing into the little anteroom office like the Salvation Army. 'Another beautiful morning in Shaw – sky, sun, traffic and lovely kiddies – and here we are doing the work of the Lord.' Her silence rebuffs him. She adjusts her glasses, thinks briefly of Juliet's resolute battle with spectacles, feels a familiar tug at such old thoughts, and then she settles to her newspaper. She shouldn't dare to read the paper in front of her boss but she thinks, just let him say something. There's something about religious types that makes her eczema come alive and she can feel it stirring. Or it could just be she's jealous of A. Dolt (as she likes to think of him) because she'd love his kind of certainty. But then it seems unwise to be certain of anything, apart from Southey, she reflects with a smile in her heart. Under the desk she drops her new slingbacks from her feet

172

like stones into the river. She never could work with her feet in shoes.

***

Southey likes stews so she makes an Irish stew with lamb forequarter chops, carrots, potatoes, onions, parsley and peas. The stock is made. The moment she gets home from work, often with her coat still on, she races to ready herself, cleaning and ordering things. The knives are laid out. The potatoes are peeled and placed in water. The table is set. She's pinched some daisies from a bush on the way home. The daisies remind her powerfully of Grace, who with her characteristic eccentric sternness had declared daisies are the best flowers because they were cheap and grow like weeds. Nothing elitist about your daisy, nothing fancy. Ha, she'd laugh, hard and sharp, and take a drag on her cigarette, letting the smoke out slowly in a dreamy, considered way that said she was happy with that pronouncement. Edith thinks she might name her first daughter Daisy as a way of pleasing her mother but doubts that it would work.

Sitting here after the dinner preparations is Edie's reward for the work of the day. A Turkish family next door yells at each other near mealtimes, and she enjoys that too though she knows it's bad to take pleasure from the pain of others. The teenage boy with the skimpy dark moustache is by far the loudest and 'you bitch' aimed at his mother rolls round like a marble in a bowl. The Turkish words elude her but the feeling doesn't. Although she's weary from school, she wonders why you'd speak to your mother in such a revealing way. And yet as she cranes her head towards the ruckus, it's thrilling to hear such bold-faced cheek, whatever the language. She envies the boy his freedom, and the shame in enjoying someone else's troubles resonates.

Chapter 20

Her Eyes So Open

After three years of life with Southey in the city, listening for his hand on the door every night, lifted by the sight of him, she's seeping away. She can't name it, but it's running out. There's no child; he doesn't want one – does she? She thought she did but who knows? Maybe she's not the maternal type. Maybe later they'll think again when the business is on its feet.

She doesn't see Grace much these days, though sometimes they talk on the phone. The days that pass without each other are links in the chain, and each day makes Edie stronger, more her own woman. The gaps mean she can think about her mother without interruption, though the thinking leads to no understanding. She's still locked into yearning for love the way she wanted it, but the space allows light to fall on her and makes her feel free.

For Grace, without Edie, the days are long. She wonders what she did. She doesn't call because she doesn't want to be in the way. She puts a picture of Edie in grade five on the kitchen mantelpiece, right next to the tea tin. She remembers her smile, teeth just crooked enough to be lovely. Her eyes so open. So ready. So young. She takes the tea tin down often but she never knocks that picture over.

Chapter 21

Moths

Parties are not easy for Edie. But Southey really, really likes them. Often she says, 'You go – I'll read a book and we'll both be happy,' and off he goes. Something niggles in her though, and Nancy at work has said she's mad to let Southey out on his own all the time. 'Men just cannot be trusted,' Nancy says jiggling a teabag in her favourite tea-coloured mug. She teaches grade three where, in her opinion, children reach their peak. She's claimed that class for the past eleven years and plans never to let go. Edie, reading *Jane Eyre* at the big table, says, 'Men are men, it's a fact, but Southey is different.'

Nancy laughs and shows her yellow horsey teeth. 'Wise words spoken by the wife at the table ... Who used the last of the milk and put the carton back?'

'Jonesie for sure,' Edie says and closes the book. They laugh. He's the only male teacher.

The next party invitation that comes along causes minor dissent. 'I'll come too,' Edie says that night as they eat spaghetti alla vongole in the little backyard. They throw the hinged shells into the weeds where they lie, looking like small white wings. The starry leaves of next door's tulip tree are shuffling and green, and beyond them the light is leaving the tent of the sky. 'Yeah,' she says scooping up the last wine and shellfish flavours with her spoon. 'It's time I got out more.'

'No,' Southey says quickly, 'don't worry about it, Edo. I know you're not mad on parties. I won't be late. I'll just see if Charlie's there and have a quick chat and shoot straight back. It's just a little work do.'

And this is where the niggle gets her. 'That's okay, we'll have fun and I'll just take myself off if I get bored.'

***

The party spreads through the tiny house like water in a dry dam and soon the back room is all knots of people and thudding music. For a while Edie chats and holds her warm, smudged wineglass, making conversation with those of Southey's friends who are talking rather than drinking. When the first man she chats to hears that she works at a school, he assumes she's a teacher. He likes that in a woman. Interest wanes when she says she's the secretary. A man with a ponytail and Buddy Holly glasses gives her vinegary wine and she wonders about this business of swapping pleasantries with strangers. She decides that these people are looking for partners. She's wasting everyone's time and she wouldn't mind getting back to *Jane Eyre* and the slow revealing of the goodness of Rochester. The book's in her bag. Hmm, she thinks, I wonder if I dare.

She fades into the long, narrow hallway and opens a door to find two people entwined, writhing on a bed. 'Oh!' she squeaks, alarmed. The amorous pair takes longer than she might suppose to spring from each other and then *they* glare at *her.* Amazing! Embarrassed, she slams the door. In the hallway, to calm herself, she pretends to muse over modish pictures of tin sheds, or maybe they're jam tins or shearing sheds, until she reaches the next bedroom. This is right beside the front door, which is flung wide open, and she sees moths hounding the light and drawing spindles of luminance upwards from a camellia. The glassy green leaves have tips like darts. She ducks into the room. The foot of the bed is piled with handbags and, while she knows that technically it's a breach of manners to be alone with them, she decides her need is greater. Besides, her stealing days are well over and it is some comfort that her mother never even suspected. Ah, surely no one will begrudge a poor bookworm a sneaky read. The yellow glow from the porch light leaks through the window and she sits on the floor with her back to the wall and for a while she manages to read undisturbed.

She's at the part where it seems Rochester has left and Jane is bereft, and then Edie is dragged from Thornfield Hall because she hears her name. Two women are out on the porch seat, a rickety old cane thing. She lifts her head, listening like a labrador in a duck hunt. Through the sheer curtain she steals a look at their profiles. They're smoking a joint! The window is open and the sour smell writhes its way into the room. One woman has fair, wispy hair, the other is wearing a strange pull-on hat with a bell in the middle. She's not averse to attention then, thinks Edie.

'Have you seen Southey's wife, what's her name? Edith, is it?' The woman holds her breath and then exhales the smoke in a rush. Edie's senses are pure animal now, and the air brings her information – of their voices, their relationship, their perfumes and their drawled vowels that speak of privilege.

'God, what a name. *Who* would name a child Edith?'

'Yeah, well, I feel for her though, she clearly has *no idea.*'

'Well, she came at the wrong time, that's for sure. He's in the thick of it with Wendy; they're so hot for each other it must be hard for them to keep their hands off. God knows why she decided to come tonight. Still,' she pauses, holding her breath, 'it wouldn't have mattered when she came. He's always into it with someone.' She passes the joint over, cackling as if she might choke. Edie registers that this hilarity seems a little much, even for such revelations.

'I mean, who hasn't that boy fucked?' she laughs.

'Come off it, Sue. Did you sleep with him too?'

'Many times, right in that very bed in there.' Sue's breath is suspended on smoke but soon laughter is rushing her.

The coldness that runs through Edith is familiar. It was there when she learned her father had killed himself. It was there whenever Alexander touched her, and it was there whenever she saw Bernard Sedge. Now here it is again and she recognises the cold, reliable truth of it. She waits, her back curled against the wall. Her eyes are burning but she's not weeping. Her head is hurting; her hands shake; her heart feels like a red rubber ball cut loose inside her chest. She puts the book with all its deliberate uncertainties back into her bag, steadies a hand on the cover to draw strength and sits there quietly absorbing the end of her own certainty. At first she thinks, well, what did you expect? Nothing ever lasts. Who did you think you were to have someone like Southey? Always too good for you. He was never such a great partner anyway, truth is he always had his eye out for something else. You were just a stop on the way.

When Sue and her friend leave the porch, rage begins to make its move in Edith. She puts her head in her hands. The shock is white and the shaking slams her again and again. Maybe my heart will stop, she thinks hopefully. She has to do something. She thinks of Grace. Grace will know what to do. But first there is the measure of her anger and it will be released. She walks to the dressing table, picks up a bottle of moisturiser and spreads it like icing all over the pillows. The bed-cake will be iced! Then she turns back the bedclothes and picks up something else –

maybe it's shampoo – and empties it too, careful not to get any on the bags. She decides she must move the bags so that they don't get messy and carries them to the place under the window where she had huddled, reading and learning that she was not only a fool but widely regarded as such. Bags safe, she continues with the desecration of the bed. She lifts off the cover and spreads unctuous, fragrant liquids all over the place. It can't come out fast enough. She pulls back the bedspread and smears Sue's fancy lotions across every layer. She pulls the bedclothes back up as they were and replaces the bags at the foot of the bed.

At last she picks up her own bag from by the wall and takes herself off, shutting the door tight. For a moment she holds on to the doorknob and leans her forehead against it as if she were sick, which she may well be. She sees Southey in the kitchen near a guttering candle by the stove in deep conversation with a woman she doesn't know, who she reckons is probably Wendy, and she stands watching till he sees her. She waves and he waves back, and she feels like her heart has been sucked out of her and all hope with it. Who is he? is all she can think. Who is he really? She walks home that night, a long, long way to the tulip tree that hangs over her yard, shading the stars from her tired eyes.

Chapter 22

Silent Reading

The day after the party, when he had gone some-where else to think about things, Edie sits out the front in the deckchair in that gap between afternoon and evening and writes about Southey in the Southey book. She still expects that he will show up and tell her he's made a big mistake. But the day passes and he doesn't come back.

She immerses herself in the memory of him until she can take no more. No detail escapes her. How when they first got married they hiked all over the state and when she got tired he carried her pack without complaint. Some nights he'd bury foil-wrapped trout and potatoes and cook tinned corn in the billy. She remembered he could occasionally be funny and sometimes, if he was in the mood, he laughed at her jokes. It didn't seem much to be grieving over. And, she thought, money might become an issue because he was always able to waste his pay with incredible ease.

***

Some things can neither be worked out nor cleaned away. At the end of her time in Drum Street, the mean son next door is still yelling at his mum. And just as surely Edie thinks that no matter how much she cleans the window frames, door frame, doormat, concrete floor, path, fuse box and the sentry bins, all of them will be covered in dust again. The more it goes...

Other nights she watches the lights from the cars move across the ceiling through her beautiful curtains. She waits for the trucks to begin. She hears the boy going at his mother and suddenly one night, after all these years, she hates him. It's not funny anymore. She opens the window and yells at the top of her lungs, 'SHUT UP. JUST SHUT THE FUCK UP. Your mother is good to you, idiot! Don't you even know that?' Oh dear, she thinks, now you've done it. This kid clearly has a big temper and he's bound to take it out on me. Oh boy. She assumes there would be a knock at the door and he'd be there with a hammer. Secretly, she may even have welcomed that, but she never heard anything ever again from next door, which was a mildly disappointing outcome. The mother, she believes, may have smiled at her one day in the grey street, but if she did it was a moth smile, small and light, and they passed like the trucks in Drum Street.

Edith stops cooking but cleans more, as if there is some stain that needs to be scoured away. She purges everything in her path. The empty fridge in particular gleams and it seems a shame to put food in it. She gets thin and shaky.

***

'People always think betrayal is the end. Doesn't have to be,' says Edie confidently at school. 'We managed this.' Nancy looks very doubtful. They're at a square table in the staffroom, Nancy having left the kids to silent reading. A stray nub of chalk rolls across the table as she reaches out and puts her hand on Edie's forearm. 'No, it's all right,' says Edie, 'we're stronger now than we've ever been, possibly.' Nancy doesn't know about all this forgiving.

In the end, truth is Edie got sick of his tears and pleading and apologies and stories of how nothing he did with the others meant anything. She decided she liked him anyway. Sure, he'd slept with other women, but he wanted to *live* with her. He would never do it again. This was an oath and she believed him. She did. Grace said there was more to a relationship than sex, and maybe it's true. Nancy doesn't know about all that, but she does know that a cheat is a cheat. She also knows that she hates Tom Southey and would gladly stab his eyes out for the distress he's given to her dear friend. She thinks Edie's a poor weak fool who will never believe what she's got herself into until he leaves her, probably for another woman. She doesn't say that though. She just pats Edie on the shoulder and says, 'You know what you're doing, Edie-girl. It's just good to see you smile again.'

Chapter 23

Reconciliation

Juliet had up and gone, too, to Sydney. She was determined to be a cartoonist on the big paper up there. She wanted to be famous in a secret kind of way, which is the way of cartoonists. She liked the cultish idea of them. And she could draw, which was some advantage, but the real advantage was the way she looked at things, Juliet saw the joke. And she was even funny enough to make the crusty old blokes smile a bit. But after a couple of years Sydney has paled for Juliet. Women have to be so much better, she thinks. Bastards have got it all sewn up. She comes back home for a bit, to have a rethink, and it seems Southey has run into her at the Shaw library this blue-green Saturday afternoon when hay fever abounds and the pollens spin around them. He's been out all afternoon with some work mates, drinking and watching the football finals, he explains, breathless and smiling. He decided to drop into the library to find a book by that new detective writer he likes, whatshisname? The Swedish dude, or was it Scandinavian bloke? He'd had no luck because it's reserved to the hilt but, lo and behold, there was the extremely cool Juliet reading magazines in a corner of the library. Well, he called Edie and suggested he bring her home to eat with them.

Edie is making some kind of fish soup, thick and fragrant with chillies, tomato, rice, chorizo and prawns. She shopped early at Mr Polack's in the main street and he rewarded her with an extra piece of flathead for being his first customer of the day. Funny, she thinks, how much she likes being known by strangers. Jenny at the flower shop asked her about her mother. And over the months she'd shared some of Grace's philosophies and sayings. 'Dig me a hole and bury me, it just doesn't get any better than this' went down well. This morning, outside the door, the first daffodils stood up straight in their buckets like hooded sentries. On the phone, Grace had told Edie she was 'cold as a polar bear's behind' because spring was 'dragging its heels'. Jenny laughs and Edie feels slightly ashamed that's she's been unfair to Grace.

She's well into preparations by the time they arrive. Juliet kisses her cheek and calls her Minnie Ed the Big Head to ruffle her, and it sort-of does. Just a little ruffle, but then she has a coughing fit that leaves her spluttering and pink. 'Jules, want glass of cordial? Fruit cup, yeah...' she gasps all croaky and watery-eyed and fades. Juliet looks at her as if she's mad.

'Just that I thought you might be thirsty.'

'Goody-two-shoes, Minnie,' she taunts with just a bit more than an edge to it. Edith understands in that second that her sister doesn't really like her all that much and never really has. But the territory they fought over was far more neutral than either would have admitted. Most of their battles were wasted, but it was all so long ago.

Juliet taps out secret messages on her empty wineglass with her hard, shiny nails. 'Open that bottle, Southey-boy, before I come over and do it myself.' Glass topped up and sipping, she surveys the little room. 'Oh, doesn't the house look cosy? Love the Miro, I had one. Yes, and the Kandinsky too. Very nice. Is that's Mum's old table? And I recognise that vase? Did she make the curtains?'

Juliet scans the room, Edie thinks, like a shopper at a sale. Pokes around in the bedroom for a while too, and the wardrobe door is still open when Edie goes in later. In the bathroom she's more like a poacher, little jars and pots with lids off and moved about. Edith's favourite moisturiser is spilled on the bench and she scoops it up onto her face with a feeling of violation, dread and guilt. What happened? Why couldn't I change it? Edie forgets that in the last few years she has hardly thought of Juliet, that she left childhood with all the haste in the world. That life took her off, and she let it.

Back in the kitchen, Edie lifts the lid of the big blue pot to see how the soup is going and the aroma wafts out. And the evidence is all there. It's her fault her sister doesn't like her. Juliet is perfect. Look at her: pretty, funny and even interesting now that she's doing well in Sydney. Southey is clearly enthralled. And then the singing thought comes to Edie out of nowhere, the one that is always right: why was Jules in the Shaw library reading magazines when she lives miles away? Must have come for the daffodils, Edie thinks flippantly staving it off, but she knows truth when it's there and though she won't say anything to anyone, a quietness settles within.

'Hand me the basil, will you, Southey?' Edie asks and he eagerly (*when is Southey ever eager?*) scoops up the tender green leaves and arrives at her side, asking if there's anything else he can do. It's when she looks into his eyes and they seem clouded, as if they are veiled, that she really knows. Proof will be unearthed one lie at a time, but now she tastes betrayal again, heavy, bitter and entrenched. The force of knowledge waits in her like a virus. She touches the back of her hand to her forehead. Clammy. Cold. Hot. Eyes, my eyes betraying me. And across the room her sister is sitting there on a stool, sipping her cool wine, like the Queen Bee.

The utter calm, the slyness, she rails inwardly. She turns the soup off, drops the basil leaves in and for a few seconds they hold themselves on the surface like small green boats. She stirs. Her heart has fallen down and her hands shake with the motor of knowledge that whirrs within. Should she serve the Spanish fish soup into the big white bowls? Which is worse? Who's the biggest betrayer, your sister or your husband or yourself for acting as if nothing had happened?

Juliet is now over at the table chatting about what makes the soup Spanish, and Southey, cutting bread, answers, 'Anything with chorizo,' which is Edie's standard line, and she laughs. Edie sits down and picks up the spoon. The other two eat and don't notice that Edie doesn't. Nor do they notice the extra spoon of chilli she deposited into her sister's bowl.

Chapter 24

The Lioness

He'd set up in Shaw thinking he'd make a fortune out of the city where good plumbers are hard to come by. Real workers. Reliable ones like him and his partner, Charlie Buckley, who only ever calls him Tom. He calls Charlie by his surname just to get back at him. Charlie is tall with blue eyes but he's all nose and much less chin. His hair is light, fine and moving out fast. He and Southey went to primary school together and found each other again when they did their apprenticeships at the same firm. They decided they could make a go of it as businessmen as well as tradies, with Tom Southey offering the charm and Charlie Buckley the nous.

One afternoon just before knock-off, Charlie discovers Southey and Juliet are nicking off to the Northern Territory. They call in to the kitchen renovation job in Beale Street to tell him, just as he's setting in a double sink. He could have used a hand with the job but it seems that Tom is having some kind of breakdown or something, and now he's nicking off altogether. Charlie's surprised, to say the least, but he is cool.

Juliet wears jeans and a pink silky top that to his mind is skimpy and doesn't go with her long (now) auburn hair – and yet, even he can see she might be considered beautiful. Those red painted nails, though, make him feel quite uncomfortable. He's never liked that 'claw' look women go for, and he's feeling tense just being near her. No one mentions Edie, which makes him want to, but instead he just scratches his chin hard and locks his hands behind his head, calmly watching the pair of them. So this is love, he thinks, feeling banished, an idiot who will never experience it. Well, there you go. Seems like you've got to be bloody good-looking for a start. And bloody pleased with yourselves too. Precluded from love and cursed by being both plain and balding, he has this mad urge for a cup of tea – a big one with two sugars, hang the expense – but it'll have to wait.

The grey kitchen seems unable to hold the three of them. Juliet and Southey's excitement is sharp and tense; they're catching a plane that afternoon. And they're not coming back. Juliet seems lazily sexual, even to Charlie. He gets the feeling that she's coming on to him in front of Southey, but he suspects it's what she does to blokes. It's nothing personal. The idea is just a vibe though, he could never prove it. Poor old Southey, lamb to the bloody slaughter. She runs her hand along his arm, lovingly, suggestively. Southey watches her intimately. It gives Charlie the creeps to see anyone, even Southey, drugged by sex. He's always thought sex should be a comfortable, friendly thing, but then he knows he's unusual among men.

'Geez, Tom, it's pretty sudden. You sure of this whole thing?' he asks his mate when they go round the back for a piss. 'Well, be careful. People get hurt pretty easy,' he says, offering advice casually as they zip up, like you might offer a biscuit to go with a cup of tea. Southey laughs at him. His hair is long and he looks tired, but he also looks happy. He borrows five hundred dollars from the wad he knows Charlie always carries for unforseen events. Charlie reckons that's the last he'll see of that.

***

Each day Charlie works alone at their old sites, places where they'd been so happy even to land a job. Now look at Tom, totally off the rails. And here he is, stuck doing everything in the work department and wondering whether he should go and see Edith, offer something to the poor girl, do something. Money maybe. Looking back, he couldn't say if Tom had been unhappy, but he had that kind of toxic restlessness, where you get yourself totally pissed just so you can feel alive, where you screw some woman just 'cos she'll have you. Bad stuff, ah, but who isn't restless? Who isn't damaged? Doesn't give you the right to damage everyone else.

When he does go round to Drum Street he finds a reduced Edith, her dull hair is plaited and she seems so damn small. How could anyone hurt someone like this and just walk away? Both her sister and her partner as bad as each other. It seems Edie flinches when anyone speaks to her and yet her careful eyes watch Charlie with too much interest, as if she were reading him, just because he knows Tom Southey. 'He said they'd be heading up north, maybe to the Territory.' He feels abashed at being able to tell her about them. Edie wonders whether he could know that hearing him talk about Southey and Juliet is torture, a strange torture that she actually invites because every mention of him means it's not over. And if it's not over, then he might come back.

Charlie doesn't get all the subtext, but he's always really liked Edith. He's long had a thing for serious girls. There's something about them, their brooding, careful ways and their unwillingness to bullshit that inspires him, gives him hope that a smart girl might like him just for himself. He knows he's not much of a catch, given the hair is on the wane, but still. Maybe if he shaved it off and looked macho, he thinks, you know, all bald and shiny, knowing the whole time he won't – the sunburn issues alone rule it out. And there's something about sweat beading up on a bald head that turns even him off.

One hot night not long after the lovers' departure, he calls round again. He knocks for a while before he gets any answer. 'Edith,' he says brightly when she cracks open the door. She's in a grubby pink checked dressing gown. It's six o'clock on a luminous evening. Her hands hold the door and her face is creased; she looks like she's been sleeping. She says nothing. She's blank, like she's never seen him before.

'It's Charlie, Charlie Buckley. Tom's partner. I came last week.'

And then there's almost a car crash on Drum Street. Brakes squeal and a round bloke yells, 'Moron! Not really interested in life, are you, mate? Bloody maniac!'

Charlie smiles in a comradely way. 'Traffic, eh? Worse every day.'

'What d'you want?' Edie asks quietly.

'Well, I brought Tom's tools over for you.'

'Keep them. I don't want anything to do with any tools,' she says, turning away from the door.

'Look,' he says to her departing back, 'the least I can do is give you the fee from the last jobs we were working on together.'

'Do whatever you like but take the damn tools with you,' she yells and slams the door. He can hear the flimsy jiggling of the little snib. He backs off the verandah as if she might get him. Some lionesses might seem tame.

Inside, Edie takes herself, shaking, to the couch. The idea of the toolbox tears through her. She remembers the letter inside her father's toolbox. And she feels like she can take no more.

A few days later, though, Charlie brings over more money from Southey's jobs and she lets him stay and pretend to watch the droning crap on telly with her. Some game show where everyone wants to win something. She doesn't move her eyes much. He places the money on the kitchen bench as he leaves.

He drops by again one evening after tea, with a couple of Golden Gaytimes and finds the screen door already unlocked, and it seems things might be getting better. The first time, Edith eats the icecream out of surprise, but the next time she rushes to the sink and runs hot water over them, holding onto the tap and weeping in the coiling steam.

Charlie stands just behind her, caught between the impulse to flee and to comfort. 'S'pose I better push off then,' he says, hands sunk in the pockets of his shorts, his blond tradie's boots just like Southey's. He reaches over to turn the tap off and then she gets it. Charlie with his poor disappearing hair and his lack of a chin is so different from her beautiful Southey and, well, she just turns and seizes him, shaking with sobs. She wants Southey back, but Charlie at least knows him, so he'll do. She looks up at him, still weeping, and says, 'I want you to fuck me, Charlie. Come one, come on.' Her tears are free-falling. 'Just do it.' The dressing gown has a nasty egg yolk stain running the length of the lapel and she smells like old clothes.

Charlie puts his arms around her and pats her oily hair. 'Darling girl, you don't want that at all. You're just a bit stuck here at the moment. You want things to be better – and they will be better in the end – but it takes time after a shock like that. You have to be patient.' He strokes her hand but she keeps crying. He gets her to sit on the couch, his arms still around her. 'Edie, Edie, lovely Edie, it'll be all right, believe

me. Other days will come and they will be good days.'
He holds her and kisses the top of her head, wipes
her face with the corner of his shirt and stays into
the night as she sleeps against him.

Chapter 25

Careless

It took some time for the pregnancy to be understood by Edie, seeing she'd never been there before. Motherhood was like a stop on the bus she'd always missed. She'd wanted to go there for so long that, now with Southey gone, it couldn't be possible. When she understood what was going on, understood the legacy, the thought of the child made everything bearable. But then at twenty weeks, in the little house in Drum Street, Edie started to bleed and then the pain came. She rang Grace. 'Mum. I've got blood. Fresh and red. Is this the end?'

Her mother's heart sank. 'Now Ed, stay still and calm. Remember to be positive, love, remember. It's probably nothing. Probably just some old blood finding its way out. And if it isn't, then we must accept that there was something wrong. It happens, sweetheart. It does happen.'

'Did it ever happen to you?'

'No, it didn't. But it's happened to lots of women and it doesn't mean you won't be a mother one day. Edie, don't give way to despair. This is bad. It is bad now, darlin', but in the long run it may not be the worst thing.' Edie breathes in her mother's words and plans to be positive. She thinks of green, the shade that is deep and peaceful.

The baby was a boy.

***

Before she leaves Drum Street she digs for nearly an hour under the tulip tree and drops Southey's shoes, like coffins for lost babies, into the hole and covers them in the winter-dark soil. Walking away from the shoe grave, she swears that she will waste no more tears on anyone, ever. When she wipes her face, she feels the weight of dirt on her skin.

Edie moves back to Yarrabeen, into Khartoum Street, near Grace, and she's lost. There's no job, so money is draining from her bank account like sand. She still eats tea and toast and sits around watching daytime television. These gaudy colours and coarse emotions populate her life, though they seem muted. She's as resentful as a teenager and a trial to everyone. Everything is muffled.

Grace tries to break through. 'You know, Edie, you might have to move on from Tom Southey,' she says, standing behind her while she's on the old fawn couch. 'He made his choice and you must make yours.'

'You mean he chose Juliet over me?'

Grace sits with her through those weeks, brings her dinner over on foil-covered plates, draws the curtains, washes her clothes, runs her baths, endures her anger. She knew about the affair before Edie told her because Juliet rang, guilty and drunk one night. Grace listened like a priest with a creeping feeling of horror that one of her children could do this to another, and that she must have caused it somehow. That she'd been careless with them. Her scalp prickled at the thought.

When it now occurs to Edie that Grace knew, it seems the circle of betrayal is complete.

'How long did you know?' she demands when Grace is sweeping the yard and Edith's on the step. It's windy so there's little point. Flurries of sweepings rise and fall. Edie is so tense she's shaking.

'Oh, Edie darling, a while. I've known a while.'

'Why didn't you say anything?'

'What could I say? I didn't want to interfere, Edie love. It's not my business.'

'That's where you're wrong, Mum, it's all your business. You spoiled her rotten and I've paid for it.' She chucks her mug into the bushes and stumps inside. Grace walks over to the bush and picks up the mug, the one with the bird on it.

Grace is washing the mug. How did it come to this? I thought I tried to be fair to them both and to Ted. It seems that nothing is ever good enough now. My mother was such a mother to me, but I never understood brothers and sisters. I just thought they'd be the best thing.

She stands there with the tea towel, drying the mug for too long. I thought I was loving them, not spoiling anyone, but if I did I would have thought it was Ted. I thought it would all even out, she tells herself. She lets herself out the yellow back door and walks home past the soft green nature strips. Yielding to the thought that she caused this failure.

***

Out the front window, over a span of months, Edie watches the world pass. Leaves change colour and jitter in the wind against the encircling sky. Storms make her feel alive. Maybe they'll take the house away, she thinks darkly and smiles at her own taste for disaster. She thinks she hears her dad in her grimness, but there's no comfort there. The postie leaves bills that remind her she'll have to change her name back from Southey. Why did I ever change it in the first place? she demands of herself, mystified by the urge to ditch her own name, her very self. And for what? At least at school, where she'd kept her own name just because she couldn't be bothered with the hassle, the kids always managed to end up calling her Miss Fish, which in its own way was a small, sweet consolation.

Grace comes through the back door every day. Sometimes she brings little presents. A rose powder puff. A perfect avocado. Three lemons from her favourite tree. She tries to clean, though there's not much mess, so she swipes at the benches in arcs with the dishcloth. She folds the cloth, hangs it up to air and makes yet another cup of tea. And all that is unsaid hangs heavy and swaying. Yet she remains.

***

Somehow time passes. By the time Edie finishes a blue-and-cream quilt, the mourning is over. She's working at Yarrabeen Primary for Principal Karen Ducker. She knows her mother has saved her. One Saturday morning, Grace brings her tarot cards and places them, wrapped in their silk scarf, on the round wooden table. Edie puts down her sewing and comes over.

'I thought you might like a reading.'

'I would. Thanks, Mum.'

When she was a child, the cards were strictly held. Children were not to touch them because the magic within them was not to be taken lightly. Readings are still a rarity. That Grace has some kind of vision that reveals the future and the paths of others is long known. She had it as a girl when she knew a horse would crash through the group of children she walked to school with. She could see the out-of-control animal, heavy and pale, and took her neighbour, little Jim, to dawdle behind the others and pick weed flowers. The horse did come careering through, and young Norah Kennedy got hurt.

Grace knew no one would have believed her. They didn't believe girls then. Girls were not serious. She stayed with Norah while the other kids ran to get help and Jimmy asked her how she knew. 'Shoosh,' is all she said. Norah's twisted leg, the dirt road, the guilt, the fear still pounding through her – none of it ever meant happiness. Knowing stuff doesn't help, but sometimes she reckons you need to act like it might.

Now, in the still kitchen where the garlic in the chicken soup wafts around, she hands the cards to Edie and tells her to shuffle and cut three times.

'New Beginnings. The Star means new life. Woo-hoo!' says Grace, laying the cards down and laughing. Edie watches her celebrating a card and realises that the love she feels for Grace is the biggest thing in her life. And she remembers the Yeats poem Grace used to read to them, and the line, 'For peace comes dropping slow,' and she felt that peace within her.

Chapter 26

The Air Is the Same

The idea of telling her mother about Alex Culp occurs to her in the spirit of cleansing, fitfully at first and then it takes up roost like some wild bird. She doesn't know when she'll tell Grace, only that she will because keeping it to herself now feels like walking around with a live bomb in her pocket. She hates it that Grace gets to be calm in her ignorance. She decides she should know what was really going on, but forgets that to tell a mother such a thing will stay in her blood forever, whether she shows you or not.

Edie chooses a neutral territory, back at Tino's under the jaunty striped umbrella. He runs the place on the smell of an oily rag. His regulars are important. He nods and gets them two cups of tea. He knows Edie is not herself, so he balances little pineapple-shaped shortbread on their spoons. At first they seem not to be talking about serious things, and then they just are. They move from changing the colour of the kitchen at Seacrest to child molestation in a heartbeat, just like ripping a bandaid off a sore.

She clears her throat. A car passes. A drop of water plops from the umbrella. 'You know Alexander was fooling around with me for years, don't you, Mum?'

The pause surrounds them. Edith is holding her breath, and it feels like she's looking through time. She has given her mother this chance, slipped it in, hoping that she sees the real betrayal, her own betrayal as a mother, the failure to look after the child she was. Maybe it can be forgiven. The clock is stopped, but who's the umpire?

Grace puts her cup down abruptly, slapped with shock but only, it seems to Edie, sorry that she doesn't get to drink her tea in peace. She doesn't like histrionics. 'What?' she says, utterly incredulous. 'What did you say, Edith?' Her voice and her eyes are serious. She's grey at the temples and appears to be aging instantly. Edie wonders how she can get out of this now. God, she thinks, why did you raise this? How can you talk about it? Isn't there enough misery around?

It flashes through her that her mother needs to rest and then she swallows, knowing with the weight of ancient sadness exactly how the revelation will go.

People pass. Cars swim by. The air is the same. The shortbread is on the saucer. And yet the secret is breaking apart. Every detail must be perfect or she won't be believed. It feels like testifying in front of a hostile jury, so she rushes it.

'What I have to tell you is that from the time I was eight until the time I was twelve Alexander Culp was feeling me up in his room. He ended up going further. Behind the shed, he made me do oral sex on him. Couple of times. I was so afraid ... He never raped me, though, so there is that and I am grateful.'

Then Grace says the wrong thing. 'Juliet?' and Edie feels like she might have been shot. She struggles not to shout.

'God knows if he was doing it to Juliet too, I never thought to ask. I was too concerned with what he was doing to *me.* Maybe you could ask her. But no, on thinking about it, maybe he was having it off with her too. Maybe that explains her. I think it certainly explains me.'

She stops speaking, picks up her tea with a trembling hand, decides she doesn't want it and slams the cup down.

Grace is watching Edith as if she were a foreign film.

'Southey knows about this but I've never talked about it with anyone else. Remember when I tipped the tea in his lap? Well, that was no accident. I thought you knew I hated him. I thought you could at least see that. Remember that time when somebody vandalised their house?' She's locked onto her mother's eyes and they are like mirrors. Finally, she thinks, you get her attention and you don't want it. She blinks. 'Well, Mum, that was all me. A thirteen-year-old vandal and bloody proud of it too.'

She sits in silence, angry to feel ashamed, to feel penitent, her head bowed while Grace stirs her tea. Tears seem paltry compared to the rest of this shit, Edie thinks. A rebel storms her and she believes she might as well tell her she was a thief too, but ah, what's the point? Enough is as good as a feast, and telling people things doesn't change anything telling your mum, though, that feels serious.

Grace looks like all her years have just fallen on her. She's frozen and awkward and squashed. She looks up, circumspect. The air itself waits to hear her words. She rubs her eyes.

'I don't know what to say, Edie. That was so long ago. It's just so hard to believe.' And although it's what she suspected would happen, Edie is still stung, and still outraged. Her voice is tight with what she has suppressed. She holds back all of her rage against this woman who could have protected her but was just too busy.

'Well, Mum, I don't know what to say either. But the thing you might want to start with is belief, that you absolutely believe me, and the second thing I want you to hear is that I never want to see or hear about Alexander Culp again.'

The deep lines on Grace's face seem deeper. Her eyes hesitate but she says it anyway. 'Edie, how can I explain to you what being a parent is like? It's the disappointment that gets you. Your kids are always disappointed in you. No matter what you do. You try your best, we all do, and there's always something you get wrong. I didn't know Alexander would do any such thing to you. Honestly, I didn't even consider it. How could I? Who does these things? Nothing was planned. I wanted to be with Kev and it just kept unravelling, like a ball of string. I am sorry.'

She bows her head. 'I am so sorry, love.' She wipes her eyes with a balled-up tissue and reaches across to Edie's hand. And Edie feels guilt tearing away at her, but whose guilt?

Nothing changes. Grace smiles when they see each other, kisses her hello and goodbye, and they simply don't mention it again. Sooner or later Alexander ends up around at Grace's for tea, and at that point Edie always just goes home. Says she's not hungry. That she's confessed nothing before, she realises, weakens her case, and it *has* become a case she supposes. What did she want to happen, anyhow? Layers of shame are like earth over her coffin. It's hard to say how much you hate someone who took something from you as a child. And now she must put up with him bringing his kids around when he's collecting the ironing. When she's talking to her mother.

'G'day, Edie,' he says, putting his daughter Beth down. She's six now, a fair-haired child in her blue cotton dress printed with yellow chickens.

Alex's wife, Clare, works in Newtown as a receptionist for Dr Adams. She wears dark skirts and white shirts and drives a little red Ford. Alex is a building surveyor and works a lot in the city. They have a life, probably a better life than hers, she reckons. They are paying off their house while she is here, doubly betrayed by the same bloke and always waiting for something. Maybe she *did* imagine those years lying next to Alexander. Must have just made it up. He shows no signs of acknowledgement. Maybe he thinks she's forgotten.

He kisses her cheek. He sits near her at the table. He looks at her, asks her how she's going and, every time he does, she shrinks, hating herself for the silence that makes her complicit. She believes she wants to kill him but wouldn't have the guts, which is a relief, really. Instead, she seems detached, a cold woman with a frozen heart. Does she really have to remind him of it to stop it finally? Well, she can't look at him or address him. And Grace, ironing in the shed, musing to the radio, doesn't get it either, and the iron moves across the plains of fabric like a ship.

Chapter 27

Foggy Gardening

Even though Edith is not yet awake and still pulling on the threads of dreams, she fumbles for her slippers and moves towards the front door. She opens it to the dull softness of fog, stops and yawns. When she moves, her breath stays on the air. Each day she's idly compelled to get the paper first thing to look for news of Southey and Juliet, see if they've been crushed to death by a boulder or something. Sadly, so far nothing. She's been in Yarrabeen for nearly six months now. She feels kind of together but a bit like what her mother calls a 'shag on a rock', alone and surrounded by water. Well, at least she's earning a living, always Grace's first criterion of every bloody thing, she thinks with a smile. 'Another day, another dollar,' she says.

Still, she's becoming used to sleeping alone, and maybe the hate is seeping away. The plan is simply not to think about it, but there are challenges. Her mother, for example, keeps asking her how she is, though not as often as Edie thinks she does. Grace is relieved by the signs of stability in her, by work and shopping and gardening, and even by chitchat about last night's telly. Edie complies but it all feels like a lie. Sometimes though, she thinks, you've got to lie your way to good health.

'Yeah, good,' she'll answer Grace, barely suppressing the urge to blurt, *I bloody hate everything. I hate my sister, my husband, my life, but I still watched* Four Corners *last night, so I mustn't complain, mustn't grumble.* After all, she reckons if Grace hadn't spoiled Juliet rotten, she wouldn't be in this mess. Still, gardening is where she thinks least about anything and so it suits her best. Another good day is forecast, which seems mad looking out into this but then everything has gone mad, possibly including Edith, who believes she can see the day's ration of dust in the morning. The feel of it in her throat is magic, and magic in all its guises is what will save her – whatever magic maybe.

She picks up her tarot pack every night and places the cards carefully on the old round table. Usually she gets death, destruction and disaster cards, which she thinks is her own fault because her vibe is so flat. She also believes it's because she uses the pack too often. This drains the knowledge and taints things. Sparingly, you've got to use the cards sparingly, she tells herself. But she has to try to see this damn future somehow. Realistically, she thinks what she probably needs is the real thing, a fortune teller.

Instead, she makes do with vitamins, standing by the sink gulping water and pills the size of pencil stubs, thinking they must surely start to work soon. Either that or she'll choke to death.

The breath of fog rolling up the cliff holds onto them for longer each morning, before the sun burns it away. Its damp feeds Edith as she moves through it, subtle as a spy. Undercover work would have suited her she decides, stabbing at the ground with the shovel. Women spies are always so thin though, like Juliet, like good old Juliet, she repeats until her shovel snaps a strand of perfectly good root. Shit.

Foggy gardening. The fog hides you while others are still hunched into question marks under their blankets. Edith strips off the stiff gardening gloves, tosses them into the old bucket, breathes the damp sky as if it were wine and reluctantly goes in to get ready for work.

***

Even on Monday, early before school, she's on her knees planting hyacinth bulbs at the front of the cottage. She's actually excited to have something to look forward to over winter. It became embarrassing at the school fair on the weekend when, standing before the hyacinths, she started to cry. The old poem came back to her:

If of thy mortal goods thou art bereft,
And from thy slender store two loaves alone to
 thee are left,
Sell one,
And with the dole,
Buy hyacinths to feed thy soul.

Suddenly she's startled by footsteps. The gate swings open, and there is Charlie Buckley. Charlie is smiling, carrying something. Charlie is carrying a baby basket. And from it comes a cry.

Chapter 28

Making Something

Down by the Yarrabeen Primary School at the rusty chain-mesh gates, the fence hemmed with crummy melaleuca, a little knot of parents gather anxiously. The heat, as usual, has saved itself for this benchmark day, the first day of school. It must be at least forty. People cluster in the paltry shade of a stray gum. Faces have aged, worry etched a bit deeper. Some parents are old hands at this business and love to expose the new chums. Charlie Buckley chats to Sandy Oxford, whose third child has also started school today. She's full of her own heroics about parenthood. 'You get used it. 'Course the first one's hard, though if I'm honest it was a happy day when Marcie went off to school too. And this one, honestly, I couldn't wait to get the little rat out of my hair.' Charlie feels himself recoil. 'This'll be your first I'm guessing by the way you keep looking at that door.'

'Yep, Lorrie is my one and only.'

'Unusual these days.'

Charlie scans the schoolyard. 'You reckon?'

'Planning on more?' The rudeness of strangers, he thinks, should never be underestimated.

'Perfection requires no furthering. Now, I really must check my messages, sorry.'

It's so hot that the bitumen is tacky. Heels are impaled. But could you actually melt glass on it? he wonders. This is the real question. He's still tall and thin with mild blue eyes, knobbly knees, a few scattered freckles on his nose and a mobile phone like a big black tumour clipped to his belt. He's unusual at the school gate in Yarrabeen. For a start, he's the only male. A white paper bag is stuffed into his pants pocket – one metre of butterfly ribbon for Lorrie from the haberdashery. First days are special.

When he finally sees her through the flow of confused preppies, his heart lifts at the beetroot-faced little girl in a blue gingham uniform, collapsed pony tail, stray bits of hair sticking to her round face.

'Daddy,' she says, all relief and surprise.

'Little possum.' He surprises himself by feeling a bit teary. He sweeps her up and carries her on one arm to the white ute, which reads along both sides: *We Plumb Yarrabeen and Surrounds.* He clips her into her seat and ducks around into the car, out of the heat.

'Well, how did you go, sweetie? Was it all right? How was lunch? Got you a pressie, young miss, just 'cos you are so good.' The little paper bag has her full attention. 'Wow, butterfly ribbon. I love it.' She laughs, unfurling it. 'I'm gonna wear it tomorrow. It's ace, Dad. Ace-a-rooney.' She high-fives him and then gets serious.

'Yeah, I ate most of the lunch at playtime, Jimmy Kolchak pinched my muesli bar but the Tim Tam melted. It still tasted good though.'

They pull up out the front and, when she sees her house, says, 'Dad, I'm tired. I'm no good at this school thing. When is Mum coming?'

'Little while, darlin', not long. She has to stay at school longer than you. You got me now. Let's get out of this bloody hot day, my girl. Cool you down and have a talk, eh?'

Inside in the old weatherboard's tepid kitchen, he sets the fan whirring, darts into the bathroom and comes back with a tightly wrung-out blue face washer. 'Towel treatment?' asks Lorrie hopefully and she puts her head back as Charlie drapes the cool towel on her face. Then he gently pushes into her eye sockets and finishes with a grand, fanning sweep. He chucks it over to the sink and goes to the fridge, gets out the bottle of cold water and two glasses, fills them up and then quarters and cores a fridge-cold apple. 'It's okay at school,' Lorrie says, 'but I'd rather be here with you and Mum.' The fan blows her hair back. 'Is school like my job? You know how you and Mum go to work, well, this is what I have to do, isn't it?'Cept I don't get paid. Miss Bollocks is pretty nice.'

'It's Miss Bald-Oaks, possum. She's got two names. Try to say it right and you'll get on better with her. People like it when you say their name right. They just do. Who did you sit next to?'

'Tiffany Bigtoe. She's a cheat too. She copied my picture and then hers got picked to show everyone.'

Charlie smiles. 'I think her name is Bristow, darling, I looked at the class list today when I was thinking about you. Life can be cruel, sweetheart, especially when you're a true original, but sometimes we must rise above the slings. Look ... here's Mumma!'

Lorrie flings herself out of the kitchen, down the hallway and into her mother's arms. Edie kneels at the door and the heat falls in behind her like storm troopers. But it doesn't even matter. She's grabbing armfuls of Lorrie saying, 'Well, my little one, how was it?' Edie glanced in on Lorrie several times at school but kept away because it seemed more sensible. She doesn't know if she'll keep the policy going.

'It was fun and good, and I like "Pearly Plum" a lot but I do not like Tiffany Bigbum or Lewis Cold.'

'Bigbum, eh? I've met a few in my time and they can be tricky at first, sometimes they can be a bit on the defensive side but often they turn out to be great friends.' She laughs, so relieved to have the child back in her kitchen again. 'Give Tiff a chance, little cat.' Edie stands up and shuts the door. Holding hands, they walk down to Charlie, who holds out a glass of cold water and a wet face washer to Edie. 'Can you believe this very big girl has just had her first day at school?' she says.

'First day of uni doesn't seem that far off now,' he says, pouring some more water, 'and it won't be long before she's got her HECS debt to worry about.' They both groan.

Lorrie asks if they can go to the beach and they say in a little while, when the sting is out of the sun, which is what they always say. They don't like the sting in the sun, but Lorrie can't see what difference it makes because they make her wear hats and long-sleeved rashies and smother her in sticky suncream. They even put zinc on her nose because they say she's got fair skin, but it isn't as fair as her mum's or dad's. She knows they aren't her real mum and dad, that her mother's sister, Juliet, is her mother and someone named Tom Southey is her father. They died or ran away or something and she got found by Dad and Mum, and she's glad they are hers because they are the best. She's heard them talking about Juliet and Southey since she was little, but it never meant very much. They will tell her more but she doesn't care when, though it feels like the day is coming soon.

Her parents are tidying up and chopping things for later, gassing on in that grown-up way of talking that doesn't mean anything but they sure seem to like doing it. She catches her dad saying something about her mangling names and wonders what 'mangling' means – it seems to be funny. Sometimes she thinks they love each other more than they love her, but she doesn't mind that, that's kinda good because she doesn't have to worry about them so much. She likes that they like each other. Some kids' parents are mean to everyone, to the kid and *even* to each other. Hers laugh, hug and call her beautiful names, like 'Darling' and 'Sweetheart' and 'Precious Toes', her personal favourite.

As she fishes her new pink lunch box out of her schoolbag and empties most of it into the bin, she thinks about the stinging sun, the blue waves and her old purple bodyboard, and how she wants to be the world champion of surfing like the lady who came from Yarrabeen once and now has blonde hair and lives in the city. World champion surfers don't really have to go to school ever again or listen to what Miss Bollocks says, but she supposes she'll go because it makes her mum and dad happy.

At the beach, in the shelter of a dune sprouting grass, they set up their early evening picnic on the green tartan rug. Before they eat, they swim in the warm sea. Lorrie says hello to it privately, which she always does because the sea is the most beautiful thing there is and you should be polite to beautiful things. Also, she thinks it might be nicer to her if she says hello. In the still air, little insect puffs hover over the rock pools like atoms.

Charlie and Lorrie cut through the long stretch of glassy water out to the waves, and the girl loops through them on the board like a dolphin. Charlie catches her each time like a sack of wheat as she slides into him. He talks to her after each catch, telling her how to balance herself even better next time.

218

Meanwhile, Edie walks along the beach, picking up shells for Lorrie, and after a while they wrap the girl up in towels and eat. They have lemonade because it's a special day and warm barbecued chook, chopped salad and fresh bread, being careful not to let sand enter the food. The tomatoes are just past their peak, yet their freshness and sweetness is still in them, although Lorrie hates them with feeling and knows she won't be getting used to them, no matter what her mum and dad say.

After tea Lorrie digs in the sand with the sea now lapping before her, and the evening is laced with high clouds. Edie's head rests on Charlie's leg and he watches Lorrie, concentrating with her beautiful reverence.

'We really got lucky, you know, Edie, when Lorrie came into our lives. I for one was lost. I wouldn't have known what to do. I loved you but I didn't know how to tell you, and I thought you were still grieving for Southey. Well, you were.'

Edie smiles, drifting and yet listening. She holds the sand in one hand. Holds and releases. Her toes are dug into it and she can still feel the buried warmth of the sun. 'We walk a crooked mile.'

'You said it.' Charlie laughs. 'When I saw you that day in the garden I felt this certainty that, while it may be crazy, we were meant to raise this little baby together. That this was important.'

'You said she cried all the way from the airport ... How didn't you freak right out?'

'Well, I did. I was so scared. I could hardly keep my hands on the wheel, they were shaking so much. And I had no baby restraint or anything. Waiting for Tom at the airport after his crazy phone call, and then there he was with the baby in that little green cocoon thing. She was so incredibly small.'

'"Where's Juliet?" I asked, and he shook his head, saying she'd shot through to New York as soon as the baby was born. I looked at her there, a little dark-haired thing small as a baby seal.'

The story is well known to both of them, how when Charlie asked Tom 'What's her name?' he said, 'You can pick,' and then he got all choked up and said he couldn't look after a baby – he didn't even want Juliet to have it. That's when he thought of Edie. At the airport, on one of the beige seats welded together in a line, Southey gave the baby a bottle he'd made earlier and kept in a little carrier. There are some details that Charlie doesn't tell Edie. That Southey cried all through feeding the baby, wiping tears off as they landed on her. That he'd said, 'Don't tell my mother there's a baby, for God's sake, or Edo will never get rid of her.' That he'd wondered how Edie was, whether she'd got over the betrayal and Charlie had been unwilling to tell him. Didn't want him to know. Wanted him to just piss off and leave Edie alone.

'You've done more than enough damage there to last a lifetime, Southey, and what with it being with her *sister,* I mean for God's sake, it's unforgiveable.

It's unbelievable. And now you want her to bring up your child. I just don't understand you, man. This is such an enormous ask, and look at you, sitting here blubbering about yourself. Selfish, selfish bastard.' He looks disgusted and the furrows on his forehead are raised with his questions. The fluffy hair on the side of his head stands out like wings.

The baby squeezes every bit out of the bottle and Southey's clumsy attempts to burp her lead to Charlie just taking the baby away from him. As the eldest of six he knows plenty about babies. He places the nappy over his shoulder and supports her as he rubs her back gently. Southey seems relieved not to be holding her. And then, in a flight of fear, he gets panicked at the thought of Edie.

'Well, what do you reckon, Charlie, will she take the baby? Will she look after her? Does she hate me that much? Not that I blame her, bloody hate myself more than enough for anyone. Wish I'd never even seen Juliet.' Charlie is in work gear, navy shirt and shorts. Southey's in shorts and a T-shirt, but he still wears those big work boots. Sitting there side by side in the busy terminal with clumps of people around them, they stand out like sore thumbs, especially the handsome one weeping a lot. In the end, he grabs a blue bunny rug and holds it to his face and Charlie feels a stirring of something like pity for the poor bastard. 'Listen, mate, it's not the end of the world. Look at this wonderful child here right in front of you; she's gonna grow up and change the world. She's your own daughter. That's something, it really is.'

And though he doesn't know, to comfort him he says Edith will want to look after the baby. 'She's family in more ways than one, and her mum will help her. I think you're doing the right thing if you can't manage the child on your own.'

He pauses and looks at the baby, round and little with a lick of dark hair. 'Though this whole thing is pretty damn strange, I'll give you that.' Then he adds with a rush of feeling. 'And look, if Edie doesn't want to for some strange reason, like she has her own life or she hates you both, then I promise you this: I will look after this baby and I'll do it properly.' It feels like he's said a momentous thing and nothing's happened. His eyes start to water at his words and a sinking feeling gets him. *God, what have I said?*

'Edie,' Southey says as if he didn't even hear Charlie, 'will be good to her.'

'Bloody long way from the airport to Yarrabeen with a poor little howling baby, I can tell you. I thought the police would arrest me or something. I made Tom give me her birth certificate and write that little note saying he was giving her into my care for me to deliver to you, her aunt. I tell you, I thought he might have murdered Juliet; she's just the sort who'd bloody get herself tangled up with idiots. No offence, Edo. God knows it was all so incredibly strange.' Charlie and Edie look on as Lorrie walks along the hem of water washing at her feet.

Southey went away to PNG; he said he wanted to help out over there. Charlie got a postcard after a year with a scene of a tropical sunset at a beach and the words. 'This is where I am. I'm not coming back. Thanks, Charlie. I will send money when I get it.' He tore the card into shreds and threw it away. Juliet never got in touch.

Whenever Edie hears the story, she wants to cry, but for Southey – such a weak fool who didn't know what love was, went out hunting for sex instead and found nothing. She looks out at the reach of the sky and thinks there's everything in the world before us and none of us gets what we want. The trick is to make something out of what we get.

Chapter 29

The Betrayed

One Sunday morning when the future is still lying in wait like a sly thief, Edith unearths the old blue address book with the daisy on the cover from one of her mother's oddly ordered junk drawers. There's string, screwdrivers, hooks, tacks, little hammers, tape measures and old handles, all corralled like countries in the continents of long thin drawers under the kitchen bench. Edie has come to believe that she should be in touch with Juliet because she has her daughter, after all, and they should talk or something. She hasn't thought it through. She's just been nagged by it for some time.

Under Juliet's name many numbers are scrawled and crossed out, evidence of her journey – this is something else to Edie, who went from Drum Street back to Yarrabeen. All of the numbers are in her mother's looping hand that's hard to read. A bolt of cold, unsurprised anger passes through her. Of course Grace has kept in touch with Juliet. But, honestly, how could she? A wave of betrayal breaks over her and she thinks it was the same as with Alexander Culp. Always the same, they say they love you but they never let it inconvenience them.

***

She dials the latest New York number and a man answers, saying, 'Yellow,' and it starts again, immediately. *Wanker,* thinks Edith blackly, involuntarily, right when she's trying not to think such things. She's trying so hard to be a good person, but it just breaks through and the bile gets out. Turns out his name is Dorfman, which sounds like a surname to her but all that Edith really hears is that he isn't Southey. 'I'm looking for Juliet Fisher,' she says, knowing she sounds both prim and unreliable because she hasn't managed to rein in her rickety voice. She probably even sounds English to this bloke.

'Yeah, right you are,' he says 'and who might I be talking to?'

'Oh, sorry, this is her sister, Edith.'

'She never told me she had a sister,' says Dorfman, and Edith is instantly outraged. How *dare* she not tell people about her. But he sounds like he might be ready for a chat. 'She's not here now, don't know what she's doing today. Fancy her having a sister. As hot as Julie?' He laughs hugely with a honking resonance, and after a long pause asks, 'I mean, do you look anything like her?'

Confusion assails Edie. There's a meaning that she can't get a hold of. 'Not really. I thought you were talking about the weather and I'm afraid it's a bit chilly here at the moment. Unseasonable.'

'Oh,' says Dorfman, 'that's a damn shame.'

There's a long pause before Edith regains her momentum. 'Well, Dorfman, could you tell her that Edith called, her *sister* Edith, and here's the number.'

He dutifully writes them down and says, 'Oh, and by the way, Dorfman is my last name. My first name is Bob.'

Edith doesn't care what his name is. 'Oh goodo, sorry,' she says, 'could you just tell her to call home?'

'Excuse me, let me just get the front door. It could be her,' he says, deepening her fury because it's costing good money to make this call. While she's stewing and debating whether to hang up, there, in the breathing silence, a child picks up. 'Hello?' a girl asks. 'Hello, who is this?'

'Hello,' says Edith cautiously. A small panic works through her and dries out her voice. 'I'm Edith. And who is this?'

'Aggie,' says the small voice, boldly imparting big news, 'I'm Agnes Fisher Smith. Mum says my name is nearly a sentence and special because there are no other Aggies around. I got a long name.' She laughs a rippling little laugh, and then Bob comes back and takes the phone, saying, 'Bloody kids, friends of Liam's, always where you don't want them to be.'

'Your daughter is very bright,' Edith says, a rogue croak in her voice.

'No, no, she's not mine. She's a bit of a remnant really of an earlier bloke, but she might as well be mine, seeing as how I do all the paying around here.' He groans ruefully and Edith thinks with a stab of relief, not spitefully, *Oh, Southey. Oh, Charlie.*

Chapter 30

Winter Birds

Jules Fisher is quite a name in New York magazine circles, well, maybe a bit of a name, considering the strength of the competition. Nothing stops the cartoonist in her from always scratching around for ideas, though. Maybe last night's dream, she thinks, maybe I could use that. She dreamt she was a blue whale tethered in her study singing songs and no one could hear. Or maybe she could do one on pregnancy or infidelity, always a juicy combination. All grist to the mill. She'd definitely do something on dreams, if not the whale unless, she thinks subversively, holding her breath, she already had. Which was more than possible. The old memory was not what it should be. Early onset or something. That and motherhood, or maybe it was all those drugs, all those years ago. Ha. Whatever. Now that there are two children to provide for, things are very different. Not that she doesn't love Liam and Aggie. The love surprises her considering how easily she abandoned Lorrie. She tries not to think about her. Ever. Some shame runs deeper than the deepest fault lines. No, she snaps herself out of it, that whale dream won't do at all.

There are days when it seems the cartoon will never come but she has to pay the babysitter for those hours anyway. There are hours when she pounces on ideas as if they are prey, a little toying and then the kill. Ideas come and go like winter birds landing on the wire outside her window. Getting either to come to you is another thing.

She knows something will turn up, she's been drawing for magazines for ten years and never missed a week unless one of the 'Formers', as she thinks of the past men in her life, insisted on a holiday. Holidays were not much fun, certainly not after the children, seeing they couldn't quite afford to pay for the help to come along too. But until the idea comes to life, the discovery dance goes on, the waiting and the considering. She looks out the window and ice is forming. Inside her study, washing is draped over the radiator blocking the heat. She's wrapped in a blue mohair rug her mother sent last Christmas. Having it around her is like having Mum there and, just as an idea begins to take hold, the phone begins, and for two beats she watches it warily, hoping the bloody thing will stop.

Probably someone about a bill. Or that eternally whingeing Woolly – isn't it always? She urges the caller to give up and then shocks herself by swooping on it. It is indeed her neighbour and fellow Australian, Woolly Freeman. She grew up on a sheep farm and as a child it was said she liked to eat wool, or at least lick it. Her real name is Clare but that's long forgotten.

Woolly's husband is an investment banker with enough money for them to have a Mexican housekeeper named Elena, which is a very comforting thing. Still, money does not always bring happiness. Most days on getting back from dropping her kids at school, Woolly zaps her cold cup of coffee in the micro and, with her coat still on, grabs a biscuit for comfort and phones Juliet to touch base with another member of humanity, in particular one with the right vowel sounds.

'What's up, Wool?' Juliet barks, clasping her rug to her and settling back.

'Nothing much. Just that I can't face this place another second. Elena is late and Jake's sick again. D'you think he's allergic to something? I sent him to school anyway. They're better equipped to see what's wrong with him than I am. I can't handle him right now. He's so needy. Must be an allergy, gotta be.'

'I'll put you on speaker, Wool, I've got to get on,' and she begins to draw a cartoon about loneliness that, she thinks, just might win her a prize at next year's press awards. 'Do you ever miss home, Wool?' she says, working at her little figures with the kind of care mothers lavish on small babies.

'Absolutely not.' She laughs. 'All those wankers and macho men more interested in football and beer than women; and the women, well, what can you say? You get neglected enough, you start to feel unworthy. It's tragic. You must be joking. I love it here. It's civilised, apart from the weather and the guns and the wars and whatnot. Oh, and the food, well, it can be a bit gross, I suppose, but it is great fun.' She laughs at her own ambivalence. 'But it could be just me.'

Jules looks out the window. 'Well, I miss home. I miss the sky. I miss my mum.' She sips her cold tea and the idea begins.

***

When Juliet and Bob and the kids decide to come to Australia, they all live in Newtown, the next big town on from Yarrabeen, hunkering beneath a dance studio on the main road. The shops are herded together like lost animals in a shelter, shabby and unloved, with smeared glass and saggy signs.

Bob Dorfman is a nice man. Quiet, heavy, tidy, a good cook and kind enough. He's hairy everywhere except his head, but this is just a small issue. There's something of the potato about him. Juliet's had so many handsome jerks that Bob is truly a blessing. When she was last down with a cold, he even made chicken soup. 'My mother's recipe. Pure fat and garlic. If this doesn't fix you, nothing will,' he said and spilled a good deal of it on her, but the scalds soon faded. He calls the kids 'Buddy' and smiles a lot. Juliet thinks a smile is worth thousands of words and there can never be enough of Bob's smiles.

Next door, Mai at the Sew Quick can be quite a handful. She's the cheapest dressmaker for miles and so she has all of Newtown at her command. 'No,' she barks at Jules one bright morning, 'you not first. You wait!' She commands the obedient mass of customers who stand in line patiently, garments over their wrists, like sheep waiting for the shearer. No one ever fought back, ever said, 'If you don't mind, I think I was next.' It wasn't worth it to go against Mai. She might take a set against you. If they didn't get their repairs and alterations done with her, the next place was miles away, dearer and the quality nowhere near as good. Sometimes, though, like all good dictators, Mai could be beneficent. Customers flinch at her smiles warily.

Waiting in the line, Juliet tells herself she's had enough of all this nonsense. She's lost her ticket. She's sick to death of this woman's outrageous attitude. She's been a New Yorker, for God's sake. And besides, she should be able to sew – God knows her mother and sister tried hard enough to teach her. So she seethes in the moment, though it might have been more tremulous than seething. Through the filmy window, people out in the weather pass by, oblivious to the tension mounting within the walls of Sew Quick. So what if she has to pay an extra two dollars for jeans to be hemmed, it still isn't worth being bullied. Bob's outside, illegally double-parked. He's the one who lost the ticket and cravenly sent her in to face the music; she can't decide who she's really mad at. Still, the jeans *are* his favourites.

'Ticket,' says Mai without looking up.

Juliet is bold. 'I'm sorry but we lost it.' Mai turns her hard eyes on Juliet, red nails clicking busily with fabric and pins. 'No ticket, too hard. Look at all these clothes, which one yours? Busy woman. You look.' Juliet steps behind the counter and rifles through the racks. She's aware that everyone's watching her and that her jumper is too short. She tugs at it, squats down behind the racks and sees jeans galore – wide, skinny, blue-greenish and grey. Finally, Mai drills Juliet's upper arm and says, 'I tell you, too hard. No ticket, no jeans. What name?' In a moment of inspiration Jules parts the hangers and there they are, waiting.

Juliet grabs them and strides out without paying. Mai sprints round the counter shrieking, 'YOU PAY. YOU PAY. YOU PAY, MISS.' Juliet turns, pulls at the bottom of her jumper and says, 'You know what? You can just get stuffed. You want to learn some manners, love.' She sinks into the passenger's seat and bellows, 'Drive. Just bloody drive...' She's still shaking when they get home and she realises Mai's probably got her phone number. Ah well, she thinks, let her ring.

Bob and Juliet have been in Australia for a little over eight months, time enough for the souring to have begun. They married to avoid immigration issues. Bob didn't mind moving to the apartment beside the railway line – it's cheaper and his savings are extremely helpful while Juliet struggles to get work, but the market for cartoonists here is pitifully small. She's been told she might get something placed if she's prepared to do it for nothing! It's all a matter of people developing a taste for her, the editor says. She smirks at that idea, what an absolute joke. Bob has no such problem, easily finding work for a small goods company travelling around to supermarkets, checking on their stock supplies and convincing them to order his lines.

He's home every night and talking to them, laughing and cooking, helping the kids with their homework. He's starting to think he's got more in common with the kids than their mother, certainly the three of them sound like Americans, unlike Jules who has slipped back into the old accent with glorious ease.

Aggie seems a bit interested in him as a father – she helps him every night with the dishes and they chat about school – but the caution is always in them. They've seen a few dad replacements in their time and it's made them wary. 'Partner fatigue' he calls it and he wouldn't blame them one bit. But he's got news: he intends to stay.

There's something about Juliet, her eyes or her humour, so cruel sometimes but funny – and she's still a looker. He's hooked. Still, whether he manages to stay is another question. Juliet is something special: an artist, a cartoonist. Once she wanted to be a poet and then switched to playwriting, and apparently she even won a grant for a little off-Broadway production. Grants are the key. Saves on all that experimental stuff, weeds out the most intensely boring. She was in with that set in New York and both the kids have different playwrights for fathers.

In New York, every now and then, she'd get a babysitter and go to a bar, usually Apothecary a few doors up. That's how she met Bob, 'the nice man', which is how she thinks of him. He does slobber when he kisses, and there's a little twitch under his left eye that betrays him when he's stressed. At least he's never hit her, never cheated on her. He's a hefty bloke, but she enjoys being the recipient of kindness.

***

The magazine she'd been working on all those years closed down one day, just like that, though it had been struggling for a while. No one will pay for journalism anymore. Everything is online and free. And what will become of us? she wondered. Freelance was offered on one of their other publications but there was never a contract. Still, she made a good living there and had really liked New York. Big and anonymous. Fast and full of men who, for longer than she would have believed, seemed impressed by her.

She never thought about Southey because he was a mistake, even though she admits it was fun at the time. And he had such gorgeous hair, didn't he though? She did think about Edith though, and always mixed into it there was her mother and the clandestine relationship they had kept up, because Edie could not know that Grace still contacted Jules. Jules resented the constriction in the end. Edith's husband dumped her and Jules was supposed to lose her mother. She believed the woman who took Southey from Edie could have been anyone; it was always just a matter of time. No man was going to stay with a droob like Edie, not in the long term. Anyhow, she didn't have to think about the baby because her mother gave her updates. Lorrie is tall. Lorrie is dark with curls and her skin is not so fair as ours. Lorrie is good at maths, wonder of wonders. Grace seldom spoke about Edith and though sometimes Juliet longed to hear about her, when she did it wasn't the same. Hearing her name spoken by her mother raked through the old feelings, the love and the hate. It was always strange to hear her name however much she professed to hate her.

***

In Newtown one Sunday morning, she's in bed with Dorfman and he's eating toast, reading a newspaper and using the edges of the paper to soak up the butter on his fingers. His coffee in the yellow mug breathes its dark smell into the musty bedroom. The phone rings and it's Grace. 'How are you, love?'

'Good, Mum, all well here. Work's work, not too bad I suppose, kids are good. Bob's cooking is fattening me up.' They laugh in the way of mothers and daughters, the familiar love that forgives and blesses, that smiles with the years behind it. 'And you?'

'Well, darling, truth is I'm a bit under the weather at the moment. Work is getting a bit much, I think, might have to cut down on it a wee bit. Uncle Kev sends his love. He had a nasty accident the other day, damn near sawed his finger off with the circular saw, but we got him to the hospital. Edith came from work and took us. She was very good.'

The hairs on Juliet's skin stand on end at the mention of her sister and she waits to hear more like a fox waits to catch another glimpse of a rabbit.

'Loves a crisis, does old Edie.'

'Anyhow, good to hear you're all well. Jules, you let me know when you want me to visit again and see Liam and Aggie. Just give me a bit of notice, darl, and I'll be there.'

Juliet hangs up the phone and thinks, Uncle Kev, eh, what's he doing cutting himself? He was always big on taking care with tools. And where was Alexander in all this? You'd think he'd help. And Grace doesn't sound one hundred per cent. Edith, however, sounds exactly the same.

***

Juliet has been living in Newtown, not far from Grace, for a year now and the kids go to schools nearby. She's working at McVeigh's Real Estate part-time as a receptionist while she trains for her realtor's licence. She tried the newspaper offices but one has closed and the others are not hiring; there's really only one broadsheet now, and it seems no one in there is that interested in anyone over forty. These days cartoons need to be drawn in a retro style and be about binge drinking or worrying about your fertility or hating women, none of which concerns her.

She's always seen herself as something of a feminist, so she'd be useless at the hate stuff. Still, you never know what you're capable of if you need a feed. Jules thinks you need that tug in the heart to draw, need to feel it, whatever it is. She used to think it was like fishing. But, anyway, that's all over with now that she's in real estate.

There's been a bit of a downturn in the economy apparently, though she wonders what on earth this has to do with her, but things are slow out here in the land of the lost souls as she's beginning to think of this place. Until she gets her estate agent's licence she helps with preparations for sales, advising people on getting their houses ready for sale. The houses she looks at are in about the same state as her own, piles of clothes and toys, the odd shoe, a manky cat dish in the corner, the stove looking like someone had a party on it and then went to bed, dishes everywhere (in stacks though!), everything stale-smelling, a nasty dark greyness in the bottom of the toilet, thriving weeds in the parched gardens, screaming kids – she could go on, but isn't everything so much worse when it's not your own?

She does enjoy looking into the little houses, particularly when she visits them at dusk, not long after the women get home, glimpsing into people's lives through the uncurtained windows: a child doing homework, a woman doing a stir-fry, the glowing blue light of the television with kids sprawled before it, wasting time as if there were plenty of it. These scenes are still lives waiting to be painted. If only she had the time.

She enjoys instructing her clients on how to present their places to get a better price. Clean out the clutter. Whack a bit of neutral, possibly stone-coloured paint on a wall, fresh flowers, healthy palms (reasonable size), whizz the furniture round to let in more light. She's always been a bit of a genius at placing furniture, and she's not too fine to get her jacket off and help anyone move a sideboard or a couch. This makes her unusual. Bob's amazed that she managed to talk her way into the job but he'll give her that: she's got the gift of the gab. He gave up the soul-destroying job in the supermarkets and now he's working in the kitchen of the Gee Whizz café in the main street. At lunchtime, the lines of heavy men grow every day. His New York hamburgers are legend.

Chapter 31

Hard Flat Voices

Although the kids both have sticky American accents, even those seem to fade under the blowtorch of Australian English. 'You suck,' Liam tells his mother when she's trying to explain to him that she expects him home by nine on a Friday night. Down there, skinny little girls with long hair appear bored as boys risk their necks – they are not so good at ignoring the girls. Skateboarding at the skate park dotted with its grungy concrete hills and valleys is totally awesome! And everyone hangs out there!

'Come off it, Mum, you don't have to be such a wowser...' Liam whinges and his mother reckons he's got his inner Aussie spot on. Delivered in his hybrid voice, there's something endearing in it. Still, there are times when he does remind her of his father, a firebrand playwright always raving about his rights, especially his right not to be a father.

'Still, my dear,' Jules says, looking up from her *Harper's* magazine with a straight gaze into his brown eyes, 'be home by nine or I will be down there in the car picking you up in my dressing gown and uggies. Your choice, Liam.'

'You're such a pain, Mum.'

'Thank you, my dear. I try.'

Juliet smiles and settles back into a nice long article on American architecture.

***

Mostly Aggie likes Australia because of Woody Farr-Harber, a handsome, dark-haired little boy with half a dozen freckles on his nose that she counts when they are colouring. At school some kids call him Would-He-Fart-Harder, which gets Aggie all protective. The first time he brought his colouring pencils around the corner to their place was bad because the only colouring book around was Australian marsupials, and brown colouring isn't much fun.

When Grace and Uncle Kev first came to visit Liam and Aggie, Uncle Kev tried to teach them little important things like the principle of a fair go, as in 'fair sucka the sav' – or sauce bottle depending on where you're from – and 'carn the Aussies' in the cricket and all that stuff. The kids humour him, the poor old bloke in his overalls, mauve nose getting bigger everyday and usually with a chunk missing off a finger or two. He's a bit too energetic and it makes them wary because he might get them to do something useful, like put out the bins or pull up a few weeds for their mother. It has happened before. 'By jingo, those weeds are taking off over there by the fence. C'mon, kids, let's have a go at the buggers.'

Grace's calmness, on the other hand, is intoxicating and being their own actual blood stands her in good stead with them. They can't remember their fathers who left, before birth in Liam's case and a few weeks after in Aggie's, and they were never introduced to extended family. There's never been any other parent to arbitrate their cases, no shoulder to rest a head on, and now here they are in Australia and they have family. It looks like Bob Dorfman is sticking around too and, unlike their mother, he seems to like to listen. Maybe Australia is not that bad.

***

On clandestine weekend visits, mostly Grace sets up Juliet's ironing board in the kitchen and presses anything she can find in the clean washing pile. If there is one. She just finds she thinks better on her feet with a bit of heat in her hand. The steam rises in clouds from the board but needs topping up often and she does this while she's chatting. Before you know it, a decent pile of folded things emerges. 'Nice little iron you got there, Jules. I'd get the steam setting checked though, could be on the blink. I'll get Uncle Kev to have a little look.'

Before they leave, it's been dismantled and repaired on the outside table, the cord wound tightly round itself, good as bloody new. The dishes have been done and put away, benches worked over with bicarb and vinegar – all without missing a line of conversation on what Ted's up to now that it looks like the lovely Lisa really has cleared off, how politi-

242

cians are all the same regardless of the decade, how the weather is definitely getting hotter, how to cope with the earwig problem when growing vegetables and dahlias (in particular), how there's never anything on the telly anymore and Kev's latest development thoughts and possible projects, though they seem to be trailing off these days. They always bring a load of whatever vegies have reached picking point – straggly silverbeet, dense pale cabbages, lanky rhubarb, all nibbled and spilling trails of dark soil.

'Organic. You pay a fortune for it in the shops,' Kev says. 'Been washed, probably could do with another one though, love.' He snorts, pushes his chair back and reaches over for the old Brown Betty teapot he gave Juliet when she came home. He tops up his tea liberally and adds a good two spoons of sugar. 'She still makes a nice brew, does this old girl.'

When the ironing has aired long enough, it's ready to go away. 'No point tempting fate with dampness. Damp is something you do not mess around with,' Grace says, giving Aggie's shoulder a hug as they go upstairs. They're attempting to put away the sheets, but the linen press barely has any space. The light at the end of the hallway travels to them and unravels something in Grace. 'You know, darling, you look so much like one of my daughters when they were girls. I can't really remember which one, but there's no need to tell your mother that, darlin', she'll have me locked up for treason.'

Grace laughs her crackly, sweet laugh and she is a pure good thing. Before she leaves, she's re-folded everything in the linen press and shown Aggie how to fold a fitted sheet. 'It's all about the corners, darlin'. This will stand you in good stead, my love. You're never too young for the real knowledge. Skills are at the heart of a successful life. Remember your old Nan told you that and you'll be right. And try not to panic – that's important too.'

Aggie follows her downstairs. My grandmother knows everything, she thinks, feeling elevated by genetics. She's even smarter than Mum, and way nicer too.

'But Liam,' her Nan says coming down the stairs one at a time, creaky as an old boat, 'now Liam, well, he is the spit of my boy Ted, that's for sure.'

***

All his life Kevin Culp was up with the birds and since he had the new pup to worry about, these days he was up even earlier. Up, dressed, put the old Akubra on the old scone and away they went. Some mornings they went down to the beach and the pup pulsed along the sand, burning up her youth as if there were plenty more years where that came from. She made him laugh. But the beach had rules about dogs and such and he was over it today. Today he went to his second-favourite place, down the road to where the bush fringed Yarrabeen. Beyond the dry grass lay the river and a little swimming hole. It was known for its snakes this time of year, but experience taught him roughly where they'd be and with that in mind, he chucked a ball around for the little one in the cool of the morning. She was a sweetie all right and nearly a year old now. A little border collie cross, light and fine as the summer morning. Her name was Wavy on account of her rippled coat and she was shaping up to be, he thought, the love of his life. Not counting Grace, of course. Grace was something outside of everything. Most wonderful woman he ever met, even though he never managed to get her to marry him. Ah, he thought, you can't force people to do what they don't want to do. He sat down on a big old tree fallen and splayed on the ground and Wavy was still flitting around like some crazy spirit, happy as Larry, coming back every now and then for a bit of reassurance. After a while, Kev felt himself sitting there for a wee bit too long and then he felt that he was not able to move. Wavy came along and sat beside him and he put his hand on her head. He was feeling strange. 'Something going on here, Wave,' he said to the dog and then he seemed to slip down a bit onto the bleached grass. Then he thought he was speaking but maybe he wasn't. The dog stayed beside him, the ball at her feet coated in saliva, and it wasn't long before Kev knew he was dying. Having a heart attack, he reckoned judging by the pain of it, and he was probably a goner. Things flashed through him. Grace. Alexander, the distance between them that he never fixed. The loss of his first wife. Then for a moment it seemed Grace was standing over him, offering to help him up. He was found later that day by some kids out walking to the swimming hole in the river. He was next to Wavy, his hand on her back for support. His hat over his eyes.

Chapter 32

A Cage of Memory

Seacrest sits low against the dimming sky. Inside, the yellow lights will soon come on. Out on the porch Spud seems easy, but he's slyly alert, his tail moving slowly as a club. Mouth just open, his steamy breath smells of seaweed. When Ted, with a new soft brown beard, goes through the front door alone, the dog scratches round a bit, allows himself a little moan and circles into the mat.

Ted walks down the hall to the back, feeling the house absorb him pore by pore. Then there's the back of the house and all he sees is his mother at the kitchen table, looking out at that streaky sky.

Grace gets up slowly, hands on the back of the chair and smiles, saying, 'You look well, my boy.' For Ted, it's as if he has entered a world of certainty, and she puts her arms around him and holds him like she'll never let go. This is the thing about Ted, she thinks, he always comes when I need him. She calmly discounts what Edith does for her because that's what girls do. She discounts again what Juliet doesn't do, because that's just Juliet – the free spirit. Which brings her back to Ted, her boy, and boys are not required in the same way. They bring a kind of joy to a mother that's inexplicable and when he hugs you, you stay hugged.

At the other side of the room, Edith notes with a heavy heart that even while she's pleased at her brother's arrival – better late than never – she's caught in a sudden gust of envy at the sight of them holding each other. She holds the blue teapot as if she was about to pour, hand jittering. She puts the thing down and a trickle of tea stains the shining bench.

Should she push in? Should she leave them? She hovers at the fringes until Ted lifts an arm and the three of them make a wounded knot in the little kitchen. Ted's in his dense dark coat, still cold from the air outside, and they're all crying and patting each other on the back.

Grace needs to sit down, so Ted eases her onto the chair as if she were made of glass. He kneels beside her, picks up her bent old hand and, holding it, says in a lumpy voice, 'You are my sweetheart, Mum, always...' and the words stop with a shudder. He weeps as if his heart will break at the thought of a life without her. She strokes his hair.

'Ah, Edward, my darling boy, it's not good, mate. We know that, darling boy, it's not good but I'm not scared and you shouldn't be either. I'm not. I'm ready. I just don't want you kids to be upset. It's natural, darling, it's the way things are. Everybody has to die. All of us.'

The tears give way and she looks at them both; the furrow between her eyes is deep and her eyes waver. She puts her hand to her mouth as if to stop herself from saying anything that might cause pain. Edith is back fooling with the tea and feeling useless. She looks at the calendar on the wall near the clock and sees the day of the visit to the doctor marked there in wonky pen. Three weeks ago. Since then chemo has begun. The mark on the calendar says Dr Ganges, oncologist, in her mother's looping hand. Edith thought they were getting used to it and then bloody Ted shows up with his beard making him look like Jesus Bloody H Christ and upsets Mum. Now they're right back where they started from. Then pity stirs her and she sees he's just made it real again. Just when it settled a bit and it looked like the chemo might have some effect, might have slowed the thing.

These things, brothers and sisters and squabbles and love, will all go on when her mother is dead. She knows this just as she knows her mother and her brother have always had the magic of ease. She remembers the times she took him down to watch the penguins and he wanted one for a pet. She'd like to remind them of that time but not now. As she wipes the bench where she spilled the tea she knows she must raise the subject of Juliet, who must come home for Mum's sake. She takes the pot over to the table, pulls the striped tea cosy onto it and clears her throat, twice.

'Mum, maybe I should call Juliet again.' The silence that surrounds the sentence is long and circling. Ted has his arm on the table and Grace's hand is resting on his sleeve. In the window, they are a trio of ghosts lightly etched on the room. Edith grabs at the blue checked curtains Grace made not so long ago and can remember that day at Spotlight in Newtown, see the happiness in her mother's face at the bargain fabric and the sausage they ate later outside the hardware store in the showering sunlight, holding themselves back from the drip ping sauce. A cage of memory is always around families. She finishes with the curtains and gets out some eggs. An omelette, she thinks. Yes, an omelette.

'Well, I would like to see Juliet again,' Grace says. She folds her hands around the mug. 'I have missed her.' Ted nods. Edie will see to it. Before Ted was very old they left their father. Now Grace is dying. Darkness descends and stays like a dark bird holding its wings over you. You can nick off now, bird, Edie thinks gloomily, I've had enough of you to last me. She sets the table. The wind comes up the cliff at them. She lights a candle, hoping to tempt beauty back to their table.

***

Juliet likes filing her nails at her desk, right there for all to see in the window of McVeigh's when the boss is out. That little thrill of danger has always been her friend. When she's feeling truly daring, she paints them red and allows plenty of time for them to dry, giving them a bit of a blow now and then.

She's at the desk one October day, gazing out at the tree full of snowballs of white flowers across the road, thinking that Roy and Ivy had one like it, when the phone rings. She answers with her best bright, chatty voice, 'McVeigh's Real Estate, Juliet speaking.'

'It's Edith Fisher here.' Juliet's mouth dries out and her natural flippancy deserts her. They have spoken once about Lorrie, when Edie sought to finalise things. Juliet told her there was no need. The call stalled and they hung up, both stung by the surge of feeling.

Now she actually feels happy at hearing Edith's voice, which is intensely surprising. 'Geez, Edie, good to hear from you. How are you?' she says but fails to convey happiness as a precaution.

'Listen, Juliet, this isn't a social call. Mum is the reason I'm calling you. I assume you know something about her health. I know you're in touch with her because that's how I got your number – from her phone book.' And, perhaps innocently, Edie touches on the old spleen in Jules again.

'Yeah, so what? Why shouldn't I be in touch with my own mother?'

'If you don't know, I am not going to be the one to tell you.' Juliet is offended again. It's the same old shit.

Cold tension passes through Edie and she begins to shiver. 'And did your own mother tell you she's got cancer? Stage four cancer? Tell you she's dying? Mention that at all?'

'What are you talking about, Edith? I spoke to her the other day and she was fine. She was asking about the kids and Bob and saying she might come up for a visit.'

'Well, you know what, she'll be fine for about three months, if we're lucky. She's not fine and she needs to see you. Soon.'

Afterwards, when Edie speaks to Ted about Juliet, they agree on getting in touch again and that maybe Ted should do it.

'Yeah, I suppose it is hopeless,' Edie says, 'but she deserves to be here. I'd want to be, wouldn't you? Well, we are, I suppose.' She's folding washing while she speaks on the phone.

Ted mutters something and then clears his throat. 'Wouldn't it be better if you two pretended to get along, just for Mum's sake? Try to be grown-ups.'

After a long pause, she says, 'You're right. I know you are.'

He sees himself reflected in the black glass. The kids are also reflected, watching some show about renovating in the yellow glow of the TV.

'How come she's so different from us? You ever wonder what happened?'

'She threw everything away, Edie.'

***

Ted comes down to stay with Grace when she's first diagnosed, which was a while ago now. Back in his old room that has become Grace's sewing and painting room, he sleeps on his single colonial-style bed. Years ago he shrewdly carved initials underneath so that Grace wouldn't notice. The big discovery there was that what Grace didn't know about didn't matter. Deceit is nothing until it's revealed, until then it has no taste. After that he swore off hiding things. Load of useless garbage in the end.

And now he sleeps better back in the old place, but he knows it's the sleep that comes with knowledge: the storms are coming but they're not here yet. He rings the kids each night at Mabel's and it's so clear that they don't miss him that he thinks he might as well stay away. And wouldn't that be easier? After, 'Hi Dad, good, okay and see ya,' he speaks to Mabel.

'Thanks,' he says. 'I don't know what I'd do without you.'

'S'okay,' she says easily in her cloudy Latin voice. She is Argentinian but despite that everyone refers to her as the Mexican. She's very sensitive, he thinks, and then she hammers him with, 'You heard anything from Lisa?'

He exhales hard. 'Geez, no. Nothing, never, why? The kids askin' for her?'

'Nah, but they get a look sometimes, just a look, and I think it's that mother look, like they are lookin' for their mother and she is not here. I try to be something like a mother for them, but it's not somethin' you can try at – it's got to be real.'

There's a pause and the truth of Mabel soaks into him. She should not be exploited and his intention is that he won't. She asks chattily, 'How's your mother? You must give her my love and the prayer for well-being that I am sending, Ted, even though I do not know her. I know you and I know she has been a good mother.' A fight breaks out between the nine-year-olds and something breaks in another room. Mabel says she must go now to avoid the war between the children.

Each evening Ted basks in the quiet enveloping love of his mother after long days of talking, reminiscing and planning. She's planning her funeral because it seems that chemo may not save her, just give her some time. Grace has always liked to master the details. She mastered the details for Kev's funeral, and many remarked on it. Wavy was tied up outside the funeral parlour, and Kev's hat sat on the coffin. It was sad, but she was controlled. At home, she felt she had lost her best friend and that the gate was closing behind her. For her own funeral she wants daisies, a few bunches, not too many – 'we won't go mad'– and plenty of Van Morrison. 'The Mystery' will be played in between people's talks, either that or 'Astral Weeks', she'll leave it up to Ted.

She'd like a cardboard coffin 'for the environment', but if they can't get that then 'anything cheap will do'. She's serious about this.

'Do not spend money on nonsense. These funeral blokes are total rip-off merchants,' she warns. Ted agrees. He finds the old vinyl record of *Poetic Champions* in his bedroom and plays it on the record player in the corner. Grace closes her eyes to listen. He thinks 'Queen of the Slipstream' as the coffin is carried out, and tears overwhelm him.

Before the diagnosis, Grace had almost finished a painting of an old house with blue wisteria around the verandah. She paints only houses, in honour of her mother. Her mother had a thing about houses, picking out her favourite in every street she ever passed. Picking out the one she'd have. 'What is the world without somewhere to live?' she says about her pictures. 'What are we without a comfortable place?' It sits in Ted's room on the easel. The colour comforts him and reminds him of Grace. As he drifts to sleep he imagines living in that house, looking out from under the wisteria onto the grass. The dream of the perfect home.

Over the years she had made their home beautiful. Jugs of flowers, paintings and polished wood, and her curtains sewn on the little machine that behaved itself only for Grace. She sewed new covers for the couch three times, and each of the chairs had changed too. Over the next few days they continue to talk and cry. They walk on the beach. They get fish and chips when hunger rushes at them and find themselves staring at golden piles. Once they get Chinese from Ming's, and not having the appetite to eat it is like turning away a friend. It's a reasonable idea to eat but too hard to actually do it.

PART III

Chapter 33

Her Mother's Voice Moves Like the Tide

At first when she retired from the bakery, Grace moved into her own ironing business. Most of her money came from men's business shirts, which she tackled in the lean-to wooden garage to the side of Seacrest. The new people in Yarrabeen were all of a sudden building houses with decks the size of warships and windows like department stores. And a lot of them had to drive back to the city on a Monday morning, so they'd bring their shirts to Grace and she'd convert them into order. She charged two dollars a shirt, which she admits was pricey. Through the back window she'd glimpse the sea, and through the splintery doors out the front the road spills out.

These days, though, her shoulder is giving her gyp, and she's tired for a woman with so much energy. As she irons, the radio runs on with old dance songs framed with tales of outrage and woe, with crime and calamity. A thin Persian-ish cotton rug spreads over the dimpled dirt floor like a red puddle. For stability, the ironing board rests on two bits of kindling. The hollows and bumps under her feet are all well known. The heat of the iron is tested by wetting her index finger and dashing it against the searing surface, the spitting hiss never failing to jolt her. A ladder of white scars from old burns climbs her forearm. Her war wounds, she laughs. She steers the iron across the shirt like a pilot in a blue sky. On the shelf, her workmate, the little radio piping out talk radio, is a hot plastic city gathering bolts of ropey fear and wrapping her in them. 'They ought to string him up,' she mutters occasionally, jamming the iron into a tight sleeve corner. 'Like a chook. Or a sheep.' Today it seems another football player has gone astray and tampered with some poor girl, and it's enough to make you spit, which she does, straight onto the iron.

The pain in her shoulder turned out to be breast cancer, coming at her backwards. Incredible. Still, the doctor told them it was early enough to be stopped and so they set about doing that. Chemo at the hospital. Hair falling out, a slow recovery and all of it done with Kev. She'd speak to him when she was sitting in chemo pretending to read the paper. Tell him what was going on in the world. Laugh at the silly buggers winning Tatts and then losing it. He was her mate.

It wasn't long before she put the very idea of cancer behind her. Her hair grew back in no time. The only thing it left her with was a sense of being tired. Sometimes when she thought about cancer she could not separate it from the loss of Kev.

On rainy days, the window holds the breath of steam and, when it's warmer and drier, it melts. At all times, the chorus of radio voices surrounds her like the lost. As she irons, the memory of her mother and Auntie Millie rises from the hot fabric and comforts her. As a child she saw their backs at the table, the blankets and the sheets ironed smooth with the scorched layer uniting them. She saw the women ironing before they saw her, and she loved them in a crush of feeling and slid round the table with a bright child's hello. And now, Grace thinks, they are all gone and I am ironing and then I'll be gone and my memories will be too. She doesn't think about it more than that, because if she does the sense of loss will take her, she just knows it. The best it gets is when there is nothing to think about. When the work of it just takes place in the vacuum of time. She must haul herself out of these wretched memories, so she smartly recognises that some days there are forty men's shirts to be getting on with: sleeves first, then front panels, then shoulders and collar. Seven minutes a shirt. Linen and pure cotton extra, though these aren't common in Yarrabeen.

'The truth is, Edie,' she'd say in the hot shed with the long queue of ironed shirts for company, 'the only thing everyone worries about is money. I'm telling you. And sure, we had the class issue here too, rich and poor really. Well, the middle classes care more about themselves than anyone else, which means they don't matter tuppence. And, well, I never met any upper-class types, so I can't comment.'

Grace laughs with a silent shaking of her shoulders, as if there's a spring in her, and then Edie sees that her false teeth are too straight and a bit too white, so they look a bit like the chompers of a laughing clown. Her eyes are cornflowers and her skin is like something woven. Hessian springs to mind, but that seems hard. Every reminder of her age slaps her. Grace wears a nautical stripe, navy and white, a long navy bobbly cardigan and beige pants with an elastic waist. Gives you a crisp edge, she says. Flat vinyl shoes of taupe with a sheepskin inner sole. Variations on taupe and navy. Grace can sometimes press a shirt in less than five minutes and, while she does, she continues on with the theme of the good old days. The white shirts, Edie notes, are almost all stained yellow in the armpits, as if someone peed on them. Her mother's voice moves like a tide. 'Pity people don't learn to wash a shirt properly. Pity people don't spend more time sweeping the path than wasting all their time on Facebook or whatever the hell it is, or flying about here, there and everywhere. Now what was I talking about?

'Well, yes, there were a few swarthy Europeans around in my day, some of them handsome lads too, but you'd never marry them. Imagine the cooking! They expect a lot you know.

'I remember some of their wives when I worked at the plumbing factory. Poor, sad things they were. No time for themselves. Not a skerrick. Always lonely and so far from home. My poor old mum left Ireland but she never minded, she always said she came to a better place, but you wonder. There's only one home for each of us, eh?' Then she'd pick up her smoke, draw on it, and her thoughts would be held in with the smoke.

Through the steamy little window in the shed, the constant sea rolls on and the sun is absorbed by it. Light falls onto the daisies in the yard and they glow like white stars. The blue hydrangeas nod in the shade. Sleeping flowers. 'I do like a blue hydie,' Grace always says, 'and it's worth a bit of effort to get some blueing tonic into them, Edie. They always make a good show.' Edith, sitting on the stool in the shed, says nothing and reflects on being a daughter. She's heard every single thing her mother has ever said to her – and disapproves of much of it – but still she waits, listening for more, for the key to her mother, to herself. The part that will make it all fall into place. Surely her mother has this key. She has been there from the beginning, though Edie thinks not from any sense of duty or love, more because it was an accident of birth that tied them together. Maybe the key to herself might fall by accident and be lost.

Grace thinks Edie should have something better to do than listen to an old woman's ramblings. You'd think so. Edie can listen or not as she pleases, as she worries out loud about her new pink lady apple tree that's failing to thrive. Maybe she should ring the helpline on the radio, that nice, capable young woman – what's her name again, Edie? Is it Kate or Caroline? It's a nice old name, whatever it is.

Grace's views of the past and of the way this country once was and now is are not something she shares with anyone except maybe Edith if she's feeling loose, and even then Edie always goes her for it. She's just so disapproving lately, Grace thinks wistfully. I suspect it reflects some deep inner problems, I mean, she's hardly a girl anymore; her looks have faded. It's not Grace's place to tell her, but no one else will.

'You look like you've been dragged through a hedge backwards,' she'll say, acting shocked but keeping it light to get a laugh from Edith. Or she'll say, 'Look what the cat dragged in,' another oldie that drives the point home gently, no need for anything heavy-handed here. Edith would reply, 'I didn't think I needed to get dressed up to see my own mother,' which has the desired effect of making Grace feel guilty, so she drops it and makes a cup of tea.

Grace still lives in the past, in a place where women dressed up to go into town or even just pulled a comb through their hair to go to the shops. She always managed to put on a bit of lippy. No one wants to look at your drab face, she'd think, looking at someone who hadn't bothered. Make an effort is her motto.

Trouble is, these days you just can't say what you like, on any topic. If you can't say what you think when you're old, when can you? This is the beauty of the radio – anonymous folk can say any old thing. They can single out various groups and blame them for violence or drinking or for picking on the young girls. What, she wonders, is the world coming to? The violence is terrifying. Grace catches these threads of lives agreeing or not, as each call takes her.

She awaits the courage to ring up the radio and believes it will arrive shining and hard as a pair of angel's wings. It never does. Trouble is, the person she's bravest with is Edith, but bravery just doesn't count there. Ah, at this age it's probably best to let others do your talking for you. She listens like a hawk for the caller who'll speak her mind for her, who'll put it just right on her favourite subjects: the disappearance of standards of appearance and manners.

Lorrie often sits with her as she irons. After school over the years, she did her homework on the little wicker table, and as she grows older she just drops in for a chat. After she's eighteen, Grace lets her sneak a smoke, and in that they are united conspirators against Edith.

'Give the radio station a ring, Nan, you've got plenty to say.' Lorrie smiles, holding her cigarette awkwardly. She doesn't really like smoking and she wonders why she does it.

'Why don't *you* ring them, about you and your mates?' Grace replies, adding, 'and we can talk about your partying down the dunes. I can see the bonfires from here, my girl, don't think I can't.'

'Nothing much going on down there, Nan. Truth is there's nowhere else to go around here. People having a bit of a drink, bit of a cuddle, usually ends in a bit of a chuck in the sand.' She laughs.

'Well, be careful. You know all about contraception, don't you? Your mother would have told you about that.'

Now Lorrie is getting bothered. She reties her ponytail. This conversation is veering off road fast. She suddenly feels bad. She dashes out the cigarette.

'Yeah. I know, Nan.' As she leaves, Grace thinks about the dual currents running through Lorrie with her mothers. Lorrie is as beautiful as a memory of her daughters in their youth: long silky hair, tall and slender as a willow reed. And she even looks like her own mother, Grace thinks, only better. And she's quiet and kind. Lorrie kisses Grace on the cheek and says, 'Nan, that's the last one. I've just given up on the fags. Maybe you should too.'

'If only I could, darlin', but I'm glad to hear you have. Good on you, little L, and goodnight, my darlin'. Sleep well.'

Lately Grace has been feeling a bit average. Maybe taking a bit of time off from waiting in the talkback phone queue will make a nice change. In the end she can't even hold herself back from ringing up, and that's a disappointment too because she doesn't trust herself to be true to herself anymore; it feels like she's always agreeing with someone. What is it that blocks us from saying things as we want to say them? she ponders, but there's no answer. Never is.

It's her teeth that get her to the call. She's had false teeth since she was fifteen, when the dentist took the lot out, which seemed sensible since he was so positive they were only going to rot anyway. Well, things do rot, don't they? Over the years she's had a few different sets of dentures and they've been pretty good, but this last lot, well, that's a whole different story. A Russian novel, in fact. She was ripped right off and had to go back to this charlatan of a dental technician in Newtown, named Ricky Santamaria, no fewer than nine times. She notes each trip in her diary.

After Ricky finally gets the dentures to stop bucking around on her gums like wild horses, the top plate just breaks in half. So she goes back to her old bloke down the road, who in two fittings gives her a very nice set of dentures in just the right shade of white. She has nothing against Ricky Santamaria personally, he's a nice young man, but in truth he's an inexperienced dill, probably without proper qualifications, let loose to wreak havoc.

So she rings up her talkback bloke, Stuart Apple, a drunk with a head like a crumpled paper bag, who she thinks of as Stewing Apple. She calls one quiet morning in a public, spirited kind of way to warn people against cheap dental technicians. Esteban, the producer, sternly reminds her to name no names. She agrees but finds her voice is not behaving. 'You must speak up, Janet,' Esteban says, and she has already forgotten that she gave herself the name 'Janet of Yarrabeen' to protect her privacy.

She waits on the line for what seems like hours, swallowing her heart and twining the telephone cord around her fingers. She notices that the phone looks pretty grubby when you get up close and gives it a little clean with a bit of spit on her finger. Suddenly, with no warning, there's Stewing Apple, urging in his booming, puppet voice, 'Go ahead, Janet of Yarrabeen, you're talking to the big city.'

Funny there should be someone else from Yarrabeen ringing up, she thinks. Wonder if I know her? The silence lies heavy on the radio waves. He asks twice – 'Janet, hello Janet, you there?' – and finally it gels and she utters, shocked and tremulous, 'It's me, oh dear, Mr Apple, I remember now. Here I am, it's me, Janet!' Then she goes on to talk about the perils of the denture industry, and the only thing to do when your falsies don't fit is to keep going back. 'Though all the going back in the world didn't work really, ended up I had to go to someone else.'

Stewing Apple chats about Yarrabeen. 'How's the weather down there today, and the fish shop?' which snaps Grace out of her softness. She takes weather seriously. 'Well, since you mention the weather, Mr Apple, there's gale-force winds for all waters west of the lighthouse, and my palm tree is nearly bent in two. I've been waiting on the line so long for you that I think now I'd better be off and checking things.' All at once she's sick of being on the radio, with every

Tom, Dick and Harry hearing her, and sick of Apple and his bullshit, palavery voice. 'Better be off then. There's things to tie down.'

People have always tired Grace promptly and irrevocably. Television programs do it, probably Ian Fisher did it, and now the talkback bloke does too. Stewing Apple bids her farewell. She counts this as a victory because usually he rudely chops people off or else gives them Larry-doo. Must've wanted to look like a good bloke, she concludes, and suddenly the idea that this is all nonsense comes upon her. She decides that what she most wants in all the world is just to put her head down and sleep.

Chapter 34

Raining Mansions

The road beside the burnished paddocks is dusty, flat and easy to drive. Ted Fisher is driving from work to Grace's into the flaring sun and the windscreen is smeared with dirt. Seeing is an optional extra. Though he doesn't see her often, he thinks about Grace a lot, and every time he gets into her car it folds around him like her arms. The old white Datsun with the brown stripes that remind him of men's pyjamas is a long way from the gorgeous Monaro at Roy and Ivy's but still, if Grace were a car, this would be her. The scorches remain tattooed around the door and now the seals are just about gone too, and yet when a slice of crusty air sneaks in, it brings the smell of her. If he's honest it's the smell of her smokes, but still. He's heard about the day in the garden when the head flew off a match. How it fizzed into his skin and he screamed. 'Stay still, Teddy,' but soon enough the moisture of him had stopped it. 'You're all right now,' she said, 'it was just a little fire.' Edie took him off to play with Juliet on the trampoline in the sea of grass. And after a bit of hiccoughing, he was okay again.

He takes his hand off the wheel and touches the lumpy scar in the hollow beneath his neck. That's the thing about Mum, she's always everywhere, he thinks, not knowing whether that makes things better or worse. As usual there's no clear answer. Possibly both. On the seat beside him sits the bread and milk he's bought. Nothing fancy in the bread department, nothing artisan, just white. He does get a loaf with a bit extra in the fibre department; the kids won't even know he's sneaking pure health into them. He smiles and wonders what they will hold against him as adults. Plenty, he decides, more than bread that's for sure and his lack of energy will be cause for serious discussion. Something else to look forward to.

The crook car seals are just another bloody problem, that and the carbie. And how much will it all cost? Molto bucks. Still, he soothes himself, the seals can be left, it's so bloody dry these days, probably won't have to worry about rain ever again. Then again, with the contrary nature of every single thing, you never know. Juliet used to say that if it was raining mansions he'd get hit by a shithouse. Spot-on there, Jules. He can't think about her, though, or about anyone he loves. The kids are different – nothing complicated there. He's got a job to do and he's trying to do it.

He snaps the radio on and a wash of talk pours forth and spills into a song by a band he can neither name nor stand and he snaps it over to talk. Out the side window, he can see by the dust that the dry goes on, spreading itself through the bristling grasses running alongside the road. He passes clumps of Scotch thistles tall as men and his eye hooks onto their alien, purple crowns that remind him of the ribbons on his grandfather's medals. And then, in a pulse, he thinks again of his sister Juliet, who was said to have got Pa's good looks. She boils up in his brain sometimes. Ted might have loved Jules once. He certainly loves Edie, and always will, but he hates Jules because she crushes people without even noticing. It's a simple equation, and some transgressions are never forgiven. To take Edie's husband away ... well what can be said about that? To see the pain it caused. He honestly thought Edie would not recover. And his mum too, caught between her daughters like that. And now the dust is coming in; it gets too much and his damn eyes are tearing up. He jabs at the radio and silence falls like a curtain. And Jules, he thinks again touching on the sore spot, despite it all, he misses her. She was funny and smart. She was beautiful and exciting. And while he won't be doing anything to see her again, he suspects she will be at Seacrest sometime soon. It's all done.

***

To distract himself on the drive Ted thinks. He likes to think about home, and what he likes best about home is the paddock. At least there are some chooks. He always thought he'd do something with the block, definitely grow vegies, maybe even keep a sheep or, ambitiously, a pair of pigs. He'd put in a row or two of fruit trees, but since it stopped raining, the dry red dirt lapping up against the house made it all look so dustbowl, he just gave up. Even the sky takes on a rose tinge at night and seems to glow behind the A-line pine house that reminds everyone of a Swiss chalet.

Lisa Montello, the woman he chose above all other women, had Swiss–Italian heritage she wanted to celebrate, so she prevailed on the look of the house. Now she's gone and the forlorn chalet remains. Ted sometimes thinks he might be stuck in a sci-fi movie. The flatness, the round pitted rocks, the thistles, the city in the distance all spread out. The few remnant chooks clucking in the chook house (also A-line with red trim) spoke of old plans, but plans are what you have when you have choices. They were but a stage on the road to completion, and when Lisa left everything changed. He had to admit there were times when he wished she had taken the kids with her because it would be true to say he wasn't coping. If it wasn't for his neighbour Mabel he'd be well up shit creek.

***

Last night, he felt happy with his chooks as he locked them up. He loved each little clutch of roundness, balls of feathers scratching and pecking away, and he didn't even mind the dust. And now they're sleeping the sleep of the innocent on the perches he made, 'Wacko' seeming to twitch. Do chooks dream?

He sure wished he didn't. Going to bed last night, he realised he had forgotten to lock the door. So rob me, he thought, addressing the cartoon robbers in balaclavas slinking around inside, probably deserve it seeing how I turned out pathetic, just like the old man. Poor bastard couldn't cope with anything.

Ted talks to the pretend robbers. Take the bloody lot, whatever you can find! You're welcome to the lot. In the kitchen last night he grabbed the whisky bottle, slopped a few slugs into a dirty glass, downed it, shambled along the hallway past Tara and Honey's bedroom where they slept like free-range creatures with the blankets shrugged off. He covered them, relieved they were finally asleep. His jeans sagging and his blue jumper carrying little pockets of old food, he slumped across his bed and soon began his snoring. The holes in his black socks set his big toes free. In the hall beside the door, Spud the black lab curled and settled, a protective circle warily watching over everyone until sleep overtook him too.

Ted's been trying not to think about anything and driving home is not a good place to start. He knows it's the best policy and he knows that too much thinking leads to problems, but thoughts rush in like they're trying to strangle him.

He's a draughtsman and all day he draws up plans to architects' specifications. Plans for people with the money to build houses with two lounge rooms. Home theatres! It never fails to amaze him. What's wrong with going to the pictures? he wonders. He knows what he'd be building if he had the dough, sees it in his mind. He used to talk about it with Lisa, who smelled like honey. He wanted one of those straw-bale houses with walls a foot deep that would keep things both cool and warm, with a low roof made of grass and a view out onto a bend in the river. All rambling and unplanned, nothing to do with drawings or regulations. He'd seen it as a hobbit hole, but when he told Lisa, the look on her face should have given him a clue that things weren't great. She'd never heard of hobbits and when he told her a bit about them it seemed she wasn't crazy about either their housing designs or his building plans.

Still, he's been keeping on in his own deliberate, solid way. He indicates to change lanes and grabs the wrong side for the indicator. How long's he been driving this car? He's stressed and knows it, headache arriving at the edges. *Mum has cancer again, Mum has cancer,* hammers into his head until he believes he knows it. Stage four, that's got to be really bad. It's the last number they have on that scale and the cancer has spread to her liver – it's a miracle she's still here. Miracle. It's been two weeks since Edith called him at work to say he'd better come over.

'Find a babysitter, Teddy-boy,' she'd said, her voice heavy with restraint and sadness that she knew she was stirring up. 'I've got to tell you something bad and I want you to get ready for it. It's a sad thing ... Mum's got the cancer again, mate, doesn't look good.' She'd intended not to be blunt but it just tumbled out and she hated hurting him with this news. But Edie never worked out how not to tell the truth, because for her the truth was something she could see earlier and plainer than most people. Then she started her silent, aching, breathless crying as he looked at the kids sprawled on the floor in front of some gaudy video.

He asked Edith whether she could hear him or not, that he'd ring back later. 'Nah, I can't talk now,' he said and hung up. He felt strangely sick, light-headed. Then he left the kids and walked through the paddock next to door to see Mabel Diaz. She'd been watering with the grey water from the washing machine, siphoning and then lugging vats of scummy water out to the Beurre Bosc pear trees she'd planted near the fence. She longed for their fruit. To hold the perfect brown fruit in her hand was worth the wait. This watering routine occupied her completely as she spilled the water carefully into the trenches around the two-year-old trees. Come on bees, she thought. Her children, Constance and Theodore, cantered within her reach and she silenced them easily when they got too loud. Their laughter fell lightly in the early evening.

When Ted stumbled towards her house she knew something was wrong. She felt a lurch within and thought of his girls, hoping the problem didn't concern them.

'Mum is dying,' he said and they stood looking down the wire fence with the sky spread out around them, and he thought, why am I blubbing here now and I didn't with my own sister? Through the weight of it all, he was aware of the heat of the tears – the fading heat of them – and that he could not take much more. Yes, Mabel would take care of the kids, take them to school and feed them and the chooks too with any luck. 'This is not a problem, Eduardo. I will always help,' she said.

Chapter 35

All the Tired Horses

It's about half past four and the afternoon wave of sorrow pushes through him but still he likes it up here in Yarrabeen. He misses his kids, misses his life, but he wants to help. It's just knowing how that is the problem.

Last night's phone call was about Pizza Day or some such something to do with Italian classes. Tara doesn't understand anything at all to do with maths and Honey is so smart it's alarming. It sounded like they missed Spud more than they missed him though. He didn't tell them about their grandmother yet. Just said Nan was not feeling too well. She'd soon be better though. How do you tell kids that stuff? He must ask Mabel how to go about it. And his job at Ben King Developments, knocking up plans for huge houses, well, that had turned out to be a disappointment too, and yet they were pretty good about time off. They gave him a few plans to work on and he sees them now and then, still unrolled.

Ted's at the back door taking his boots off and putting them upside down on the bench. When it rains, only the soles will get wet. Organisation is the key to life, he reckons. Spud is poised, ready to enter the warm house like a dolphin ready to enter a pool at an aquarium. He fails to see what difference a bit of sand will make. They're all friends here, are they not? Apart from that appalling cat. Through the glass panel in the back door he sees Edith in the kitchen by the phone.

The sky is darkening. It might just rain and the wind has a fine edge to it. It's getting on in the year and cold is a constant companion. It moves into the pockets of your coat and lies on your hair, a shadow always with you. Ted and Spud walked the four miles down the beach and back again, scooping up the surprisingly soft pats of horseshit for his mother's garden. They could only take the solid ones not washed away by the foaming surf. As he always did, he used the camping shovel and tin bucket he'd made in the workshop in form two. Only five pats today though they've got a surprising bit of weight to them.

It had been his job as a child to pick up horseshit for Grace's garden. She liked to call it 'horse manure', which annoyed him no end for being fancy, and then she'd get him to dry it out before it went on the roses. He remembered her back then, a woman strong in the shoulders with a wide mouth mostly outlined in red. Glossy hair that held its shine long after it should have departed, done up in a low bun with plenty of wispy bits escaping. And her blue eyes, he thought, the only eyes that always looked pleased to see you. Still the only ones he thought, remembering his ex-wife, Lisa, looking away as he walked in the back door. She'd offer a cheek to him as if it should have been quarantined afterwards. And that was on the good days.

The tired horses pass Ted and Spudley, as he's taken to calling his dog lately. They heard them in the distance and followed the plaited crescents of their hooves down the beach. And suddenly, they were upon them: their soft whiskery noses, the shuddering steam of their breath. Something about the trail rides tickled Ted. The better riders were always up the front, then down the end of the line came the poor whackers hanging on, grimly being jolted along. Poor bastards, Ted thought, can't even let go of the reins to wave, which is clearly the best part of the whole thing. What's the point of riding along the beach if you can't have a wave to the landlubbers below? And this was supposed to be fun after all. Didn't look like it. Looked like they'd been caught in a washing machine. The riding school had been using their beach for years, and in all those years it never made him want to go on a little jaunt. To have impact, he believed, recreation must involve something lasting. He liked things that involved a project. Building a shed, a chook house, a cubby or maybe, he thought, a water feature. Renovating a classic car would definitely work.

Now that he's here, he remembers Grace as a whip-crack mother. Sees her standing at the door yelling. 'Ted, what you doing in there? Get your bum out here and help me! I'm feeling pretty snakey about your lack of effort around here lately. Time to pull the finger out, my boy.' She'd get him holding the bottom of the cream check curtains she was making for Mrs Plym up the road. 'Hold 'em up off the floor, Teddy,' she'd say, and you could tell that she was a bit happier now. 'Don't want any complaints from old Mrs P. Want the full whack of her dollars riding in my purse.'

Spud beetles in as soon as he opens the door and scoots under the table before anyone notices anything and there he lies, breathing fast and shallow. He might be grinning.

'Edith,' Ted says, trying a bit of friendliness to alleviate his mood, 'how 'bout a nice cup of tea?' He goes to the sink with the kettle. He knows Grace is sleeping, so he keeps his voice down.

He supposes she might like to talk about the topic that has them in its thrall but he will not oblige. 'Any footy on?' he asks, trying to cheer himself up.

'No, well, I haven't looked,' she says tartly, folding a tea towel that's too dirty to be of any use.

'Got five pats,' he says at the telly, looking for a hint of the praise his mother might have shelled out and gets none. 'Northerly blowing up, getting quite nasty.'

He's not surprised to find that Edith pays no attention. She never really did anyway. Always disappearing up her own arse. When she looks up and says, 'I'm trying to get hold of Juliet again,' he tries not to show that he's surprised, winded even by the mention of their sister's name. He acts casual though swallowing hard.

'Yeah? How'd you go then?' He's bending over to light the gas with the latest of his mother's gas guns. She has a jug full of them next to the stove, saving them all because she never believes in emptiness. The mystery that is gas can always be coaxed, if you just hold the gun at the right angle. When his face is level with the bottom of the kettle, he clicks away and the gas flashes blue and catches the spark. He moves back swiftly, hoping his hair hasn't caught fire. He pats it furtively.

He stands up and looks at Edith, with the greying hair, and her face and hands start to soften as she tries to address the pain of speaking Juliet's name. 'Good of you to try to find her again.' He turns to get the blue mug that is Grace's favourite and 'The World's Best Nana' mug for himself because he likes its size and shape – he couldn't give a root about what's written on it. The small, blue-and-white striped one is for Edie because it's always been hers.

Chapter 36

Another Family

On Sundays, Ivy and Roy were there with roast lamb and vegies, and on Mother's Day they arrived with little presents for the kids to give Grace. On hot days they passed icy glasses of lemon cordial over the fence, brought in the washing when Grace was at work and mowed the backyard when Kev forgot. Most of Ted's early years were spent in their care. Roy took Ted down to the Yarrabeen Football Club to play footy every Saturday morning for the Comets. He coached all his teams over the years. When Ted realised he wasn't as fast as he thought he was, he lost interest at around fourteen. Roy still enjoyed seeing the boy out there but he gave up graciously too, saying he was tired of coaching, now that he thought of it.

When Ted comes home he usually calls in for a quick g'day to Roy and Ivy. Their aging is inevitable. It's been coming for so long because they were always so much older than him. He calls them his family as Roy once called him his son. Now Roy's smile is blank as a wall and seeing him lose himself is like watching slowness itself. The trickle of loss takes him away by pieces and shuts him out of himself.

Before dementia fully set sail, Roy developed an extended curiosity for detail. He'd pick up some stray leaf or packet of tissues or used tea bag and look at each intricately, ready for the mystery of the thing, find some kind of answer to it all. Sometimes if Edie stood beside him while he was examining something he'd pass it over to her and say 'Hey?' and wink, and that would make her smile. And so, even though she never noticed him much when she was a child, Edith began to love Roy now that he was baffled.

It's a Saturday and Charlie and Lorrie are having a late breakfast at the Penguin Café by the roaring fire. After Tino closed up and moved to the city, a young couple renovated, ditched the Hawaiian theme and opened up the old fireplace and brought in lots of old enamelware jugs to place everywhere. Edie likes Charlie and Lorrie to have some time to themselves every now and then and she doesn't want to worry them about Grace too much. She shakes out the tea towel on her shoulder and bits of parsley flick away. She's been making a casserole for her mother's tea for later and keeping an eye on her. Now she's sitting by the back door on the bench she made when she was at woodwork classes at Yarrabeen High, believing that forcing her way among adolescent boys was a blow for equality. The blow-for-freedom bench. Just another one of life's quirky little mistakes, like the idea that you can make people love you.

Still, the famous yellow bench remains upright and its age reveals itself in its creaks as she sits there in this pocket of the day. When she made it she was fourteen and unable to get out a full sentence, something that can still be a problem. Life gets better, she thinks and scratches at the pale stripe of an old oven burn flaking on her wrist. She sees Blanket Bay in a burst of sunlight with its blue folds, and then when the sun leaves and it seems so cold.

Ivy appears in her good camel coat, the dilapidated shopping trolley is propped by the gate. 'G'day, love,' she says. 'You well?'

'Well enough, Ive.' They don't kiss or hug in greeting. They are way better friends than that.

She's off to the supermarket and recites a list of things she doesn't have – milk, sugar, teabags, tissues – as if Edie cared. Honestly, she thinks, I might be in need of some more stimulating company.

Ted is down again for a few days to check what's going on with Grace. He's fallen back into adolescence easily and is still asleep in his old bed, so Ivy's thinking she wouldn't mind if Ted dropped in for a chat with Roy later on. Do them both a bit of good.

'Roy's all right today, love, seems calm enough. Basil the budgie has got his full attention at the moment, so we'll be right. Just watch him with the car, though. I've hidden the keys and he'll never find them, but he has had a bit of a fascination with them. Anyway, darl, I'll be off, enough of this chitchat, the shops await.'

Ivy stopped driving when she was forty or so, hounded into it by Roy who believed she was potentially a danger to herself and others. This pronouncement delivered him the car, which made him feel a whole lot better, not that he said he minded Ivy driving it. As the dementia engulfed him there hadn't been time to get rid of it. Maybe Ivy didn't really want to. Something within her whispered that she might one day drive again but maybe not the Monaro. She had a muted little dream of getting something small and yellow with excellent brakes. She'd renewed her licence over the years so this was always possible. Today she's off down the street, towing her old jeep behind her, ungainly as a three-legged chair. Edith watches Ivy's fawn back and carroty hair disappear with a kind of tough sorrow. It is beginning to occur to her that good people don't live forever.

The Buddhists say the way to manage this is to live in the present, so she tries. While she's doing the breakfast dishes she looks over at Grace by the fire with the warmth reaching her and it makes Edie feel good to see her at peace. She gets on with her mother's washing.

Outside in the Jacketts' driveway is the classic Monaro that Roy once took such pleasure in tending to, washing and drying it with the chamois apparently made from special sheep that live only on the eastern side of Mt Blanc. Ted was charged with drying the chamois on the verandah afterwards, watching it stiffen like parchment, damping it and rolling it up for Roy, ready for the next wash. Without a father, Ted received fathering with a sense of wonder and Roy dispensed it easily, much of it channelled through the car for which nothing was too good. The Monaro is pea green, alarming and almost mystic. Possibly it's

Ted's favourite material thing in the whole world and it's not even his. He learned to drive in it. Sometimes, just looking at it brings tears to his eyes.

It's cold now under the cloud. The wind, always stronger in Yarrabeen, is up. Winter in Yarrabeen is cave deep, Edie thinks, and after she's tended to the fire for Grace she looks through the front window and notices that there's someone in the green car. And on the right-hand side of it, too.

'Oh my God,' Edie says quietly to no one in particular. 'It's Roy. It's bloody Roy. Ted! Ted! It's Roy, he's gonna drive the car!'

'What, darling? What did you say?' asks Grace.

Edie drops the pile of wet sheets by the front door. 'Nothing, Mum. I'll just be out the front for a minute. I gotta check on Roy. You right in here?'

'Yeah, I'm fine. Nice and warm in here.'

Soon enough Ted staggers out, plucked from a rumpled field of warm dreams. 'What's up?' he says, claggy and blinking, hair suspended. She points at the car and Ted groans. He grabs a coat from the hook by the door and runs out in bare feet and red boxer shorts.

As Ted approaches the car, Roy looks up and smiles a beautiful, toothless smile of pure joy. Blue eyes shining, wind flipping around him, a brown leaf lifted here and there, his collar up, hair falling in his eyes – but he's sealed in the capsule of his car. His hands are on the skinny old steering wheel and he's raring to go.

'What you doin', Roy-boy?' Ted bellows. He doesn't mean to shout. The panic is in him like an illness and he knows that was too loud and people passing by are glancing over suspiciously. Roy is just like Mr Magoo. Smiling away. Ted reaches for the car door and it's locked. Each door is locked. Roy, always the stickler.

'Roy, mate, open the door, come on now. Just pull up the little black knob, the little button, Roy.' Ted keeps smiling, and then he sees the keys swinging in the ignition.

'Oh dear bloody God,' he beseeches.

There will be a disaster, he knows it. Truth is, he always feels a bit like that, a man in which reason is a swamp and help is a popular concept but it's not all that real. Edie is there, talking way too loud, too high and with her contagious fear. Some passing boys stop for a bit of a gander and obliquely edge closer, just like a pack of dingoes.

Edith and Ted keep smiling at Roy and he keeps smiling back. Apart from the approach of the boys, time could be standing still. Edie's shivering in her thin jumper and Ted has lost feeling in his feet.

The boys are wearing hoodies – grey and black – and their eyes are covered by their hair in varying shades of greasiness. When one says, 'Want some help?' Edith wants to hug him. Ted says, 'Be good, yep.' And doesn't move.

Edith says, 'Good on ya, boys. Yes, we do want help. Poor old bugger's got himself locked in and he can't get out. He's got Alzheimer's – you know, "old timer's", you heard of it? – and we're just looking after him and he does this.' Her voice rises and the questions start: 'God, what if he drives off? What are we going to tell Auntie Ive?'

She stops to smile at Roy, who waves at her and puts his hands back on the wheel, and also on the key. 'Ted, he will drive off. He's the memory of it, look at him with that gear stick.'

Ted reckons if he had the memory to put the keys in the ignition, he could easily drive the thing away. Maybe they should just call the police. Instead, Ted decides the time has come for action and throws himself across the windscreen. His thinking is that if Roy can't see past him, he won't go anywhere. He hopes he hasn't wrecked the windscreen wipers, though, or taken one of them through the liver. His feet, sticking out over the edge of the green car, are white as sheets.

The boy, whose name it turns out is Tallie or Tell but probably not Terry, volunteers the information: 'Well, we're pretty good at getting into cars.' He smirks. The others laugh.

'Yeah, but,' one adds with a note of caution, 'never tried one this old.'

Undeterred, they start fiddling with small tools taken from big pockets. It takes a while and nothing happens. Edith and Ted keep smiling at Roy, and the effort is telling on them. Soon Ivy comes bumping down the street pushing the wobbly jeep like a pram.

A house-length from the car, she drops the jeep and rushes at them. 'Ted, Roy...' she says, tears clouding her eyes. 'Oh. Oh. Well, I don't know. Well, I don't know. Will he drive off?'

The boys keep fiddling and Ivy takes over smiling at Roy. Ted, retrieving his dignity, gets down and says, 'Don't worry, Auntie Ive. Be right back,' and runs into the house to call the RACV. Then he finds his ugg boots and brings Edie's blue parka out for her, and everything feels much better for it. The problem is more or less resolved now that Ivy's here, so he sits on the Monaro's bonnet now, looking at the sky and feeling the wind. The maple will probably take the house in the end, he decides.

But Roy seems to be thinking of getting himself out with no idea how to do it. He's stopped smiling and rises against the window. They can't settle him. Fright, of all things, has got him now and he bangs on the windows. Ted and Ivy talk to him, about football this time. It doesn't work.

'Sometimes I sing to him when he gets scared.'

'Well go on, Ive, do it, get going nice and loud.'

The sky is crouched over them and it seriously looks like rain. Tallie finally pops the lock just as Wayne Pidgin, the RACV guy, pulls into the street, yellow light flashing in the grey day. Ivy is singing 'Danny Boy' in a quavering old voice that calls up distant lands and sorrow, and it gives everyone pause while it settles Roy, who watches her with rapt attention. Ted opens the door with Roy none the worse for wear and gets him inside. Ivy gives the car keys to Edie to hide. As she walks in she sees the little silvery boat on his key chain.

Tallie and the boys are thanked profusely and head off into the coldest day of the year, a trio of sudden kindness. 'Shithouse getting old,' one says. 'Sure is,' says another.

Grace has suspended her knitting; these days she still knits moss-stitch scarves but only in neutrals and this one is the colour of wheat. It lies piled in her lap like a rope. 'Bit of a commotion out there. I saw the yellow light of Pidgin's ute. Did you get Roy out?'

Edie flops into the chair beside her, still in her parka. 'Yeah, it's all right now. Ted is settling him and Ivy down. A cup of tea and a lie down. We thought Roy would just take off in that bloody old car of his.'

'Why did you think that?'

'Because he had the keys in the ignition.'

'There's something about getting old. Suddenly everyone is worried about you and you can't understand it because if you don't look in the mirror much you wouldn't notice the difference. You are still the same girl you always were.

'And Roy, well, he's moved to another place in his head but wherever he is, he's still young – we all are. He was probably just waiting to drive Ivy to the shops.'

She picks up her knitting and moves it along the needles like she's pushing up sleeves. 'Not a lot of fun, this getting old business. Still, we're the lucky ones, I suppose, we get a choice.'

Edie is settling down after the cold and the fear of Roy's excursion, but she thinks she might have heard an opening about her father. She'll risk it. She pulls her socks up really high, puts wood on the fire and asks, 'When did you know Dad had died?' The silence snags them. Fugitive breaths escape her. Grace sits straighter in her chair.

'Well, I knew he'd died pretty early, when we were down here and that he was electrocuted, but I thought it was an accident for a while. The police told me. The truth took a while. There was an inquest because it was at his work place and it was found to have been suicide because of the note they found in the toolbox. You've seen the note.'

Her knitting slows but is just as sure. Her fingers are thicker and bent with age. She believes knitting is good for her hands but soon it will be too hard.

'Ian was not well. I knew it and I ran away from it. I had you three; there was nothing I could do for him. I didn't even know what was wrong with him. He was not the man I married, that's all I knew. He slept all the time. Then he would cook and fly into rages if we didn't eat it. And he never slept at night. How do you explain that? You forget that people did not help each other with hospitals and medicine like they do now. Oh sure, maybe if you had money,' she lets out a sound something like a laugh, 'but we never had any of that.'

She stops knitting. 'Poor Ian. I think of him more these days.' She looks at Edith. 'I think about him when I look at you kids. He's in each of your faces, so he's always here.' Tears are falling onto her knitting. Edie goes over and kneels beside her. She puts her hand on the knitting and says, 'Gee, Mum.' When Ted comes in from Roy and Ivy's, he sees her kneeling beside Grace as if she's praying and he recoils. He's had enough for one day. Honestly, so much drama cannot be good for you.

He tries to be quiet so that he doesn't disturb them but they spring apart anyway and Edie laughs at his bare, knobbly knees. Grace says, 'You'd better put something warm on, my boy. Catch your death dressed like that in this weather.'

Chapter 37

Resilience

Ted takes Spud to the new Petbarn near his house for his long overdue bath. It's midwinter and the girls have started to complain about the rich smell of Spuddie which, combined with his silent-but-deadly farts as he soaks up the warmth of the fire, means that something really has to be done. In the end, it comes down to him. He'd seen this new place advertising $2.50 do-it-yourself baths and thought that sounded fair, about all you should pay for a dog bath which by rights should be done with a hose and a bar of Velvet soap. He leaves the girls with Mabel again and, like a man on a mission, aims himself at Petbarn, where he takes advantage of the free year's sign-up and feels a kind of pride swelling in him, as if he's a man who can live his own life, even get the dog washed at some fancy joint for not very much.

In the big basin Spud complies with a soulful expression in his brown eyes and a coat that resists soap but absorbs water. He shakes himself and a whip of cold, stinging water lashes Ted's eyes. He rubs more shampoo into the dog's thick neck, and as he does he feels something give. By the time he notices it, his wedding ring is off his hand and slipping down the plughole like a memory. The first moment of panic doesn't hold for long and is mainly that the ring is gold, but then a sense of relief sweeps through his heart. Ah, bugger the bloody useless thing, he thinks. He's been meaning to get rid of it and now, at least, some poor bastard might find it and get some use out of it. He can't get over how simple it was to lose and he feels somehow transcendent, as if some divine hand had slid the ring down the plughole.

He rinses the dog for some time until he realises he's on a timer. He begins the drying but it turns out each ten minutes is worth a dollar and you could go through a hell of lot of dollars like that. He gives up and the dog follows him through Petbarn, only pausing for a quick piss on a shiny bag of imported dog food. Why didn't you piss in the sink? Ted wonders.

In the street Ted pauses and attaches Spud to the lead. He puts his hand on the dog's wet head and says, 'Where to now?' and the wind cuts through them. The streets are bare of green and the air is the colour of smoke. Nothing moves much, it seems, but cars passing everything forever. Inside a café he looks out onto the grey street slowed by Antarctic winds and he's glad to be inside the steamy warmth. He doesn't think about Spud tied up to a No Standing sign with the old purple lead. A dog's a dog, is his philosophy and he orders a cappuccino because he loves the froth of the thing, and then his phone begins its clamouring.

'Yep, you got Ted.'

'It's Edie. What you doing?'

'Just sitting here waiting for the dog to dry.' It strikes him how foolish it sounds and he begins to snicker. He tells her about the dog wash and the price of hot air and both laugh, which sets the tone for the conversation.

'God, you're an idiot, Ted. I hate to tell you this but the dog's not going to do much drying today. It's freezing cold, in case you didn't notice.'

'You reckon? What's the temp then? Anyway, dog'll dry, won't it? Dogs always dry in the end.'

He casts a defensive glance out at the huddled dog and the familiar guilty feeling that she's right begins to creep up on him, so he changes the subject but keeps watching the poor wet dog.

'What's cooking with you anyway, how's Charlie and Lorrie?'

'Good enough. I dunno, it's me I suppose, I haven't seen them much lately. I know you've got a lot on with the girls and all, but I reckon I'm a bit down. Must be looking after Mum, she's going downhill. She reckons she'll go into remission but that's not even a possibility. I could use a bit of a hand, Teddy. This is going to take some time, and with Mum in denial mode it's harder than I thought.'

He places the cup back in its saucer and the froth rocks around.

'You reckon you might be a bit depressed then, Edie?'

She's quiet because there's a lump in her throat at the peripheral kindness offered by her brother. She hopes he might be about to offer to help but it seems unlikely, given his own problems. Because of the silence, Ted keeps going. 'I don't seem to get depressed. Must be lucky, I suppose. No, I know what I am! I'm resilient, that's what I am.'

Edie can't resist. 'And how do you know that, Ted?'

He takes a sip of cappuccino, wipes his mouth with one hand and knows this will sound silly but smiles anyway. 'I took a test, one of those free ones on the computer. Said I was resilient. Maybe you should take one of those tests. You never know, you might be pleasantly surprised.' Silence greets his wisdom. 'Now I better get hold of that dog before he freezes, and you will be pleased to hear that I do wish I'd brought a towel for the car. See you, short sister.'

'Ted,' is all she gets out but she knows he'll do what he can. He just hates being asked.

Chapter 38

The Hide

Ted never picks up the phone till he hears who it is; he lets the answering machine figure it out. 'Hello, Ted, pick up the phone will you? There's no time for your screening business now.' It's Edie again. He hears the tone and recoils like someone has stepped on his innards with a cold boot. He doesn't mean to but there's something about his sister that speaks to him of work. She never calls unless there's a reason and the reason will involve effort.

Ted puts the iron down and it tips over, spilling hissing water. He can't quite reach while he's straining for the phone. 'Hey, Edo.' He uses his deflecting name for Edith. The girls are in bed and he's ironing his work shirts and watching TV – crime shows are his weakness, anything forensic will get his attention. All those test tubes full of secrets. He mutes the TV, stands the iron back up and cradles the phone against his ear, still watching some lab scene involving beakers and blood-soaked fabric trying hard to delay orders from Edith.

'Listen. You need to help me deal with this.' And though he doesn't want to, he hears the portent in Edith's choking silence.

'Deal with what?' he says in a small voice.

'I thought since she was doing chemo that she'd be all right like last time. I thought there was time.'

Just when she thinks that Ted acts like a child, then he goes and proves her right. 'Anyway, what about Charlie and Lorrie? Aren't they helping?'

It's the day after that phone call when the idea comes to him, when he decides on the construction that will be a monument to his mother. He'll build a penguin hide, a little refuge where they could watch the penguins without being seen. What a brilliant idea! Took him a while to come to it. Reckons he probably needed to think. Always been a bit chicken-shit, really. Plus when he was first up there with Grace he could think of nothing but loss.

Taking in information like this about your own mother, he believes, is nearly impossible. Your brains just fall away and your heart becomes a little red balloon filled only with the promise of loss. And the loss of your mother, Ted thinks, staring into a frying pan full of strips of searing chicken fillet, is just so big. The chicken is duly trimmed of any yucky bits because of Honey's intense squeamishness with stray tendons of meat, not to mention fat or her personal hate: the mysterious 'boogery bits'.

Mum is the reference point. If you ever get con-fused about anything, there she is, waiting with all her knowledge of you. She is the library of me, he thinks. The idea that he will have to be in charge of himself, even responsible for himself is too much, morally, emotionally, every which way there damn well is.

When it's time – you can tell this by the bubbling and the smell – he drops some soy sauce onto the chicken and throws in the strips of wilted red capsicum and snow peas. The rice in the next pot is all but done and the fragrance humming out of it seems, well, *motherly.* 'Tara-girl, Honeybee, your dinner is ready.' Then he finds he's crying, just streaming tears without effort, like some kind of actor. He drains the rice and is comforted again briefly by the nutty smell of its heat. He wipes his hands across his face and then onto his pants, sits down at the table with the cooling pint-sized meals and starts eating chicken aimlessly to direct the sadness away from his heart.

Tara arrives out of nowhere and slaps his hand away from the food. 'That can be Honey's because it's got Dad's boy germs,' she decides imperiously. And then she sees the watery eyes and says, 'Daddy, what's wrong?'

He smiles at her dark hair and tortoiseshell eyes and says, 'I'm getting a cold, baby girl, now eat your tea.' He drags himself out of the seat as if he were an old heavy machine, kisses her forehead and then calls Honey again.

Honey is a small replica of Tara with the wild brown hair and a fringe over dark eyes. She has a mole on her cheek that could be a leaf and her hands are smudged with crayons and dirt. No one tells her to wash tonight. She brings her drawing to the table and says it's not finished – Daddy can look at it but not Tara. Calm as a queen she announces, 'If Tara touches it, I'll empty her dolls' clothes into the bin.' Tara eats her capsicum first because she hates it most and aims a big swinging kick at her sister under the table but misses and her chair thuds forward. Ted pours water for them and it registers that they must not be getting on today. 'I'll just be on the porch, girls. Be good and eat up your tea and I'll read you some stories afterwards. *Hairy Maclary,* maybe, if you're good.'

Out on the porch, on the striped deckchair and beside the cacti, another shaft of weeping spears him but he makes sure to keep the noise down because of the girls. He wipes his face on his corduroy coat sleeves, the one he hasn't taken off all day so it sags around him a friendly way. He's no more than the smallest speck in the span of the coral sky. And the sorrow sets in. When the severity of the weeping passes, he leans back in the deckchair and reaches a hand down to Spud's smooth head. He recalls Grace saying that we all have to work out how to comfort ourselves, because that's part of the job of growing up. Mum, he tells her in his mind, this dog of mine is such a comfort.

Somehow, he feels refreshed by the sadness though he doesn't see how this can be. So much has weighed in him since Lisa went and because he really thought she'd be back, he just left it there. He can see that life without Lisa is bearable; at least the fights have stopped. But life without Grace will be impossible, and he feels a solid pain when he tries to think of it. He remembers how she'd take him down to watch the little penguins moving Indian file along the cliff behind their house in Yarrabeen when he was a kid. It was the one time they had together that was just theirs and it only happened when he asked, and not even always then. Often she was tired, or sorting through piles of bills on the table with the grey calculator clicking away beside her or folding piles of washing that seemed to have bones of sunlight holding them up or she'd be making tomorrow night's dinner which usually involved mince or yapping on the phone to Uncle Kev. She was often listening intently to the bitter people on the radio whingeing that the world wasn't what it should be, that things were still not going well enough, that some kind of end was on its way, maybe even some kind of perfection. He believes he's heard this stuff all his life and who was he to argue?

And so it was a solace to watch the penguins shuffling along, to marvel at their steady certainty. Just doing what they had to do. How do you get that? he wonders. When Lisa took off (how many months ago now?) leaving him with the girls, he thought he'd die, just pass on somehow. He could not be the only parent. This was too hard. Much as he loves them now, and he's sure he does, he never really wanted to have them anyway, Lisa pushed it and he went along just to keep her happy, and now he's Mr Single

Parent. The bitterness of the trick played on him was so large he could touch it. Either that or his own failure. So he slumped and sulked and hated Lisa for dumping the girls on him and maybe hated them as well. And sometimes watching their eternal bickering, it even seemed he'd been transported into a weird parallel universe with his sisters again. God, he pleaded, spare me from the endless scoring of women and girls. Leave away, Lisa, he thought, just don't leave me in charge of the kids.

Work seemed the best answer and for brief moments in the office he managed to forget about the burden, then he remembered, and each time it was that he had to be a father. But his own father died when he was only a baby. Mothers, well, he could only base his parenting on Grace and, if he's honest, he wanted more from her. He puts his feet up on the other deckchair and looks out onto the dirt and sees a couple of backlit sparrows tussling in the golden dust and idly wonders which one has the upper hand. The sun is nearly finished with them for the day.

It's hard to analyse the love he has for Grace. Kids can never remember properly, he thinks, and I always put myself at a disadvantage in my memory. Poor me, yeah, poor old me. Maybe it was normal, though he knows normal is an extremely dodgy concept; the teasing sisters were a bit much. Though none of it matters anymore, he realises. He can see the hide in the backyard near the cliff, not far from the goat track down the cliff to the water. He only hopes the

302

penguins still pass there. He sees no reason why they would have changed their route. Penguins are creatures of habit and he could spot the differences between them when he was a kid. Blinky and Mrs Jones, for his teacher, and Igor, for the one with a tiny flipper. All gone now but there'll be others just as special.

The backyard in Yarrabeen is full of Grace's trees but he reckons there's nothing that special there. The apricot Edith Curnow rose, the one they all loved so much, he'd be careful of it or his life wouldn't be worth living. Maybe he could get it to climb over the penguin hide, even though there's not much time and it's in the wrong place. It's also not all that thorny, so it's not the greatest climber. Still, he thinks, a bit of trellis and a bit of fertiliser will perform miracles. The lemon tree looks very seedy, underfed he suspects – more likely never fed since Kev died – but the grass and shrubbery near the cyclone fence can't matter much. The grass is long and largely weed.

He'll have to dig down quite a way so that he and Grace will be level with the birds, but that's all right, he'll just build a little tin shed over a trench with one long window and a door and insulate it all so Mum will be snug and warm. There might be a bit of soil left over from the dig, but he'll organise a skip and barrow it into the thing. It'll be fine and she'll love it, which is the main thing. A labour of love. He could see himself and Grace in there at night, watching the little bowling ball penguins stumping by, industrious on their way to the sea for a night's fishing. The hide will make Grace feel better. No doubt about it. Have to get hold of some second-hand timber and a bit of corrugated for the roof. Mum will have some money for that, unlike me, he thinks ruefully. Anyway, it won't cost much and think of the improvement to the property. He considers ways to camouflage the hide and wonders whether you could get camo paint ready-made, or if you have to make it yourself. Maybe the army would have some or, he thinks, struck with one of those lightning flashes of genius, he could get camo nets from Aussie Disposals and put leaves and other natural paraphernalia in it! Perfect! Outside, as he looks out from the porch, more sparrows have flown in and they bathe in the dust like children in a happy family and he feels a bit better, feels them feeding his light heart.

Inside, he can hear from the surge in the bickering that the girls are way past being able to deal with each other alone. Food is scattered around their plates and baleful looks spill out at their dad staring into the yard again. In the end, he gets to his feet and flings the screen door open, feeling better now that he's got a plan. 'Come on then, you two, bath time, eh? And I think it's time we tackled your hair. No, none of that, this applies to both of you. After that we'll ring your Nan and have a little chat. Come on, little Miss Bee, no messing around now or Tara-girl is gunna beat you to the bathroom if you don't look out.'

Chapter 39

Tact

A gumtree is coming down in the swaying wind a few houses away in the street. Chainsaws tethered to men's belts reduce its limbs, each machine singing in a different key. The tree folds into itself, always getting smaller. Inside, the green suede account books that her mother turned into diaries are stacked at Edie's feet.

She reads: 'I'm just so happy. I need to tell someone. Ian sang 'Walking My Baby Back Home' to me the other night (the night I broke my heel!) and it was so wonderful, the clear night, the stars, and his arms around me. Honestly, I couldn't think of anything better. His name is Ian Patrick Fisher. He is twenty-four and an electrician. Qualified already! He took me to the Bijou and we danced every dance. He says he likes me but he's still hooked up with some other girl in the country. I suppose I am too, but I haven't heard from Kevin Culp for some time so I don't think it counts anymore. I think it's good that Ian told me. I wanted to be told. I went around to his work and waited for him till closing time on Friday night, and he got a phone call from the other girl and had to come out into the front office while I was there. He tried not to let me hear but I think there were tears. He told her he'd be back soon to fix the heater (apparently he's the only one who can do it). I nearly left, but something made me stay. I want to marry Ian and the only thing that bothers me about him is that sometimes he might be too kind. Can you be? I know he's very sad about the girl from the country.'

When Edie hears young Grace in the diary, all breathless and loving, and then looks over at the bed and sees her mother occupied with sleep, the past slides opens like a bolt on an old door. Time and its consequences. Oh, my darling mum, she thinks, once you were a girl.

***

Grace reckons this chemo thing sure makes you tired, and it's a good thing she's having the treatment again next week because it will make all the difference. A little top-up does wonders though she's doing it purely for the kids, who all seem to be a bit of a mess about the whole thing. She's sitting in the backyard in a bit of warmth. She kicks her thongs off and looks down at her bare feet on the concrete path and registers their intimate defiance, their bareness and familiar beauty, and smiles because they're so white, and she thinks of ghosts. Not much sun this year. The idea of herself as a ghost is not something she will share. The strange thing is that though they move like an old lady's feet, they look young, which supports her theory on aging. People seem to think she's old but really, she knows better. People don't look hard enough. Her feet remind her of being young and this makes a tear well. But that will not do, you can't sit here feeling sorry for yourself.

***

Grace and Edie addressed the cancer when it first broke out. The unspoken fear came too. All day they'd been in the big hospitals where giant machines scanned little Grace, photographing her as if she were a butterfly pinned to a wall. Edie waits in the soviet-style room in the old grey battleship hospital in Newtown. The hard chairs against the chipped cream walls with the equator of the room a pale green stripe. The high window reveals the heat in the day and seagulls pass languid as witnesses. A stack of magazines without covers are frayed and missing their recipes. This cannot be good, Edie thinks, diverting herself with thoughts of dinner and lovely distractions in possible new quilts in many yellows. Then Grace is walking towards her, so small and fragile it would break your heart, but soon they're laughing and joking with the relief of being set free from that bleak old place. Yet her eyes are sad. They both know that news will come that will change everything forever, but they don't speak of it.

Though it's not yet summer, the car, sitting in the sun during one of Yarrabeen's on-again/off-again heat waves, is so hot you could fry an egg on it. Edie plunges into the oven, trying not to touch any surface with her bare skin, but Grace is glad of it. 'Lovely warm car,' she says, 'lovely,' and closes her eyes against the radiant day and Edie drives home without the aircon on and the windows up, as if she's carrying a basket of eggs, and sweat rolls down her face like tears.

Chapter 40

The Energy of Decisions

Then the results come in. The kindly, helpful Dr Satsum delivers the news. His hands are beautiful and his amber eyes are washed with tears when he looks at Grace, which is really disconcerting. Doctors don't cry. He scratches at something on his blotter and on a shelf behind him are three little knights with English flags. Grace waits as she has always waited: polite, quiet and ready. When he tells them, she reaches her hand out to Edie and it is cool and steady. The doctor confirms that it is terminal cancer with major diffuse secondaries noted. The news is absorbed like a dose of poison.

Grace pats Edie's hand and takes her own back. 'Doesn't sound good, Doctor.'

'Let me say this to you, my dear. Whatever you do, don't go and have chemo. It will not be worth it.' Dr Satsum's gilded English vowels seem out of place in Yarrabeen. If only they'd listened to him.

***

The oncologists' rooms have something of a sea-side villa about them. Rope frames around pictures of little boats, oars propped in corners. A jaunty toilet door banded in blue and white. A skylight lets in the sun. They approach the rooms with measured hope while Dr Satsum's warning retreats like the tail of a storm. He's the ghost of Christmas past, now is the time for the ghost of Christmas present, Edie thinks. Dr Ganges is young, and through his office window his sports car awaits. It's a deep taupe colour and Grace whispers treacherously with a little laugh, 'His skin matches his car *and* his suit.'

Edie groans, 'Oh God, Mum.' And gropes in her bag for the health-care card.

On the phone they'd been promised the possibility that there will be no sickness from chemotherapy, even though the two drugs Dr Ganges proposes are as toxic as any on the planet. Pain, he says, will be controlled every step of the way. He advances this possibility as a firm guarantee.

'There is nothing to fear,' he says, his kindly eyes pleased to deliver such a benediction. 'We will review your progress regularly and we can change what we are doing at any moment.'

'Will I still die, Doctor?'

'Mrs Fisher, this will happen to us all but I assure you we can put this off for quite a while yet.'

And then Grace, who had entered the cheerful nautical rooms determined to stick to her policy of not buying promises, changes her mind completely.

'Yes, I will take you up on your offer,' she says. 'Doctor Ganges, you have put it all so well, there is little more I can say. I owe it to my kids.'

She turns to Edith sitting beside her, nursing both their bags like children on her knee – Grace's big tan leather sack and her black one. Grace is bright with the energy that comes with decisions, a new cocky Grace. 'So what d'you think of that, eh, Edie?'

In the yellow room where the doctor has three gel pens lined up like bullets before him on the blotting paper, Edith is staggered. The doctor will later say it's not uncommon for people in these rooms to decide to extend their lives. 'Who wouldn't want more time?'

Through the window, the wind whips a forlorn banksia on the street and the power lines rise and fall before the row of shabby houses. One of them has a little hedge, Edith notices. What is she hearing here? She smiles at Grace's almost drunken enthusiasm but as she begins to speak a feeling of dread takes hold. She thinks she hides it. 'Well, I don't know what to say, Mum. Are you sure? If it's what you want then, yeah, I'll be with you all the way.' She reaches over and covers her mother's hand with her own. 'I love you, Mum,' she mumbles, teary now. She feels as if her blood has been called away from her brain to pump her slowing heart, as if she's seen an accident that she'll be called on to report later.

Behind the shield of his desk, Dr Ganges seems pleased and is writing out scripts for steroids and sleeping pills and orders for chemotherapy in a self-contained, charitable way, and her mother is smiling as if there's been some kind of victory.

Chapter 41

The Old Indignation

'Edith, it's me, you've got to get over here now. It's Ted. I tell you, he's ruining my garden.' Though there's a breathless quality to Grace's voice, this kind of tirade has become routine lately and Edie is not too roused by it. A crack of light falls through the window and onto Edith. While she's soaking up her mother's anger, she briefly admires her own lovely curtains as she rummages under the bed for her missing slipper. 'Hiya, darling mother. I'll be there as soon as I get dressed.'

'This is a catastrophe, Edith. I'm not joking.'

'I'll be there in a sec, Mum. I'm just down the road, remember?'

It's six-thirty on a limpid morning, transparent with summer, and small white waves slide into the beach like paper planes. From the chair she gets dressed in yesterday's clothes. Charlie had to leave early that morning for a job in Benjeroop but he made his side of the bed, which always moves her.

In Lorrie's room, Edith opens the curtains just enough to see Lorrie's sleepy face with its traces of the people she has loved. 'What?' the girl says, drifting. 'Nan again?'

'Stay there, Lorrie. You've got another hour before you have to get up,' Edith whispers. 'I'm going down to Nan's. I'll see you before you go.' The early sun is already basking like a cat on the windowsill and Edith hopes with a certain futility that it won't be as hot as yesterday. She grabs a couple of towels off the floor and folds them, knowing she's wasting time and wishing she could think of other ways to waste it.

There's a note on the chest of drawers near the back door. She grabs it and reads. 'Love you, Edie. See you tonight, yours C.B.' Her sandals are by the back door, waiting for her like good soldiers. She will wear them to work, regardless of what anyone thinks. The weather insists.

Outside, along the porch, the only Tibetan prayer flags in Yarrabeen fly in the threshing wind. Do they bring any blessings? Are blessings even possible? Mild blessings today would be welcome. Edith, watching the flags, considers being lifted away on the wind and spared the next few weeks. That would truly be a blessing. Can you arrange them? she wonders. But soon her hand is on Grace's gate and she's bracing herself and deciding that all blessings should go to her mum. She deserves them all.

Pacing the garden and smoking fiercely, Grace is a pulsing clone of herself this morning. Her new wig is raised slightly, which makes her look comical, but she's a long way past caring. She smokes with an intensity that in a cancer patient is upsetting. 'I won't have it,' she seethes at Edith as if she's been there all along, 'he's ruined my bloody beautiful garden. All my work. Left it like a complete tip and he hasn't been here for days – days! To leave it like this is unbelievable. What's wrong with him? Wouldn't work in an iron lung.' A blast of smoke. Grace's eyes are hooded and her hands shake violently. In the distance towards the cliff, Ted's inspired penguin hide reclines in rakish disarray, proving that time means nothing to the unfinished project. A shovel has fallen and a hammer rusts on some weathered crusts of timber. Mounds of soil nestle up to it with shoots of grass emerging like green fingertips. They gaze upon the pitiful building site, Edie with forbearance and Grace with rage. In this, the last of Grace, the old indignation has welled.

'It's okay, Mum, don't worry about that today,' Edie says, reaching out a hand to her mother's arm.

'Well, Edo,' she says, savagely dashing out her smoke on the sole of her shoe and tossing it into the depths of the garden, 'I haven't got many other days to worry about it, have I?' Suddenly she rips her wig off as if it were a beanie and chucks it on the table. 'And this bloody thing can go to the shithouse. It's as itchy as buggery.' The wan bundle of fake hair lands on the table, felled like an old chook.

Edie almost smiles but Grace remains stiff, her shoulders locked and her face a ruin of itself. This is not the mother she recognises. She wishes Ted were with her, just to be calm, just to be her brother, and then the thought comes to her that the steroids might be responsible for this seizing of her mother. The chemist said to watch it.

'Mum, how many of the white tablets did you take?' Edie asks, keeping it light. 'The small white ones in the box, you know the little box, with the little compartments.'

'I don't know, Edith. Honestly, what's that got to do with that mess down there?' Grace says, shortly gesturing with her shaking hand, one cigarette following another. And the smoke passing through them reminding them of all the times they tried to get her to stop smoking and how in the end every-thing passes for nothing. Her hard eyes are not really Grace's at all, though the anonymity is something she recognises from childhood. But she sees it's just a reference to the mother who scared them, who wanted them not to bother her, at least not all the time, and whose fury was well worth avoiding. That mother is lost and so is her kindness. Growing old has revealed all the mothers she once was.

In the last month Grace has gone away to a place where she has begun to hate those who will go on living. Everyone cops the fury. Grace tells Ted he's a bastard because he was not respectful of her darling Edith. This made him a low-life, pompous prick.

Edie begins to cry, and Grace thinks she's upset because of her brother, but hearing Ted spoken about like this is worse than hearing it of yourself. Edie stuffs bedclothes into the washing machine, feeling like she's stuffing her heart in there too. She can't look at Grace, agitated as boiling water, and when her mother drifts away Edith folds herself over the machine and weeps for this drawn-out thing. But she has mistaken this moment for an important one: in Grace, hating everything is just a stage.

Ted was always beloved to Grace. His blue eyes, his olive skin, his artistic nature. The penguin he carved for her when he was ten is in her bedroom – a one-footed penguin with startled eyes. No, to hear her disparage Ted is to hear the end of things, like watching a boat crash, first the splintering and then the sinking into the cold. Edith weeps for her absent mother and for herself. She wouldn't have believed Grace could think such things. Has Grace been holding these thoughts for so long that they are bursting out of her now like hand grenades? How, she thinks, could I have not known my own mother? To see a whole other side of someone a month before she dies is baffling, like one of those impenetrable maths equations. She wonders who will cop it today.

She tells Edie that Juliet is a whore – a cheap one too – we all know that. Later, each child will reveal that they, too, had heard their mother say such things. Edie, according to Grace, is completely mad, a depressed bully and a bad driver to boot. Ted cops that one.

You look into the face of the beloved every day, Edie thinks, and then one day you notice a stranger with a crook memory looking back at you and you wonder where it all went, those lucidly endless days I had with you. The days I didn't count because they were just my life. And in those best days, each of them perfect even in their faults, Grace was in every one.

That love is still there, she thinks, but it has left Grace already and I am only a half of it. If your mother forgets you, Edith decides, you must remember everything for her, especially yourself. That's your job. You must continue because you are carrying her within.

Clenched like a fist, Grace sits on the stool outside the back door waving the cordless telephone at Edith. 'I want to ring Ted and tell him, this is not working. Fair crack of the whip! I don't want this stupid thing he's building. He can shove it!' Edith would like to groan. Instead she hovers, hand out to take the phone.

'Give him a bit longer, Mum, Ted's got to get the kids off. Do you want me to ring him later?'

'No. I don't. Anyway, what can you do about it? I'm his mother, for God's sake, not you.' She's quaking with rage and her eyes are shiny with unspent tears. Later, Edith realises it would be a mistake to believe all the rage over those weeks was caused simply by too many steroids or by the hide. When you find out you're dying, some rage is always there lying around in everyone, like a bit of uranium.

In time, Edie comes to see that dying won't be silenced and nor should it be. You can't pretend it away. Disguise it with all the medication, delay it with the chemotherapy, ameliorate it with all the kindness you can find, but the mind knows the score and it doesn't want to go.

'Come in now, Mum, come on,' she says and speaks of Lorrie, who is their language. 'Lorrie's got to get going soon and you know how she keeps sleeping through the alarm ... You know how the alarm plays music? I'm convinced her brain thinks she's just drifted off rather than being told to wake up. She ended up sitting on our bed again last night, so evidently she's sleepwalking again. It used to frighten the life out of me, but now I don't get such a fright – to be honest, it's nice to wake up to the little L. Though she's practically a woman now...' While she's speaking she remembers that her mother never let any of them sleep in her bed, so when they were frightened they would take their blankets and lie outside her door, feeling soothed by her breathing presence through the walls.

Grace clears her throat. 'Juliet,' she says. 'Juliet used to sleepwalk, remember when she went out in the street in the middle of the night and was about to take off? You found her, didn't you?'

Edith doesn't remember any of that and reasons that Juliet was probably nicking off to meet some boy and concocted the whole sleepwalking story, but there's no point going into it. Edie sits down beside Grace; she'll have to go to work soon. Juliet and Ivy will check on Grace and then Charlie and Lorrie. Maybe this is not enough. Lord knows Juliet is useless.

318

Though Grace insists on her independence, since Kev died she's never really let anyone else help.

That Grace answered normally is a good omen and Edie seizes it. 'Hey, Mum, what d'you say we open up the house like you used to when we were kids – all the doors and windows – for an hour or two before a hot one, remember?' She sits her mother at the table and goes around picking up mugs and plates and wiping down benches like a waitress. She cracks the window open and a cool sliver of air trails in like a ghost, and it feels like the house is breathing in the morning.

When the door opens with the sigh of hot timber, Wayne Newton, her cat slides in on plump paws with a single *mew* and leans on Grace's foot. She reaches down to pat him and feed him a corner of the Vegemite toast Edie has placed before her. She eats nothing herself and after two sips her tea goes cold. Next week another cycle of chemo begins and the black tiredness will swamp her. Even the false energy of the steroids can't mask this. Edith stands behind her mother and suddenly wraps her arms around her. Wayne, sensing a chance, transfers his affections and comes scrounging to Edie for another corner of vegie toast to eat.

Chapter 42

The Random Will Be Just as Good

Late at night, still at her mother's house in the cove in Yarrabeen between the bay and the big highway, everything becomes sticky and green with disappearing memory. Edith is stilled with fear at the imminent loss of her mother. She sees the caterpillar trail of the departed – her father, their grandparents, Uncle Kev. Without Grace, the family will be left with just the clucking of the tongues with no heart.

Edie puts the syringe down. She's administered the two drops of morphine into her mother's mouth and now Grace stirs. Her eyes flicker and the moons in them show. 'Can I sleep now? I'm so tired, love,' she whispers, feather soft.

'You go off, Mum, I'm here.' She puts a hand on her mother's small, bald head. A couple of days ago she asked Edie to cut what was left of it. 'Sick of it all over the pillow like some kind of damn pox.'

When Edie asked if she'd like to get hold of a hairdresser, Grace was indignant as a queen: 'What, and waste good money? No way, my girl. You can cut it.' So she placed one of Grace's faded old ruby towels around her shoulders. Grace handed her the good dressmaking scissors with the chipped black handles.

The steely weight of them in her hand was really the authority of her mother.

'Go on. Doesn't matter anymore, love.' What's left of that translucent hair was quickly cut and fell slowly, soft as dandelion down, and Grace was impatient for it to be done. Before Edie finished she ran her hands over her head and seemed almost happy. 'Better. Definitely. Better than a poke in the eye with a burnt stick, eh?' She smiled her sunburst smile. Edie gathered up the towel and what was left of the hair, strands of it sticking to her tears. She took the towel outside and put the whole thing in the rubbish bin by the back door because she wouldn't ever be able to see the towel again without seeing Grace at that moment. She knew her mother wouldn't see she'd thrown away a perfectly good towel and this made her feel bad about being lazy, sneaky and wasteful. Old habits die hard.

The morphine has moved into Grace quickly and settled the restless pain like a warm cloak. Edie holds her mother's white hand. She strokes it. In the cleft of the room, the house surrounded by sea noises and the growing wind, she puts her mother's hand back under the last quilt they made together. The one with the pale blues of summer and a touch of peach, just the hint of that gold light of evening. As every quilt they'd ever made together did, this one became the only one. The joy was in making it. In mixing colours and talking while they sewed.

The accidental beauty of the quilts is always in them, like finding flowers in the garden.

She remembers kneeling on the floor arranging the blocks and Grace in the doorway, enthusiastic at first, saying, 'Move that centre blue floral three up next to the grey check' and then laughing at clumsy old Edie. The next time Edie glanced up, she saw Grace was leaning in the doorway; an ash from the smoke had fallen onto the quilt and Edie thought it's time for Grace to give such things as quilts and good food and dreaming and watching telly on rainy nights up and yet she can't let it happen, even in the face of it.

And Grace said, 'I need to go and rest, Edie love. You keep going anyway. The random will be just as good. It always is.'

Outside, the wind moves in the tea-tree, down through the goat track to the beach. On nights like this, above the sea itself the wind seems a nesting noise, a circling of safety. Maybe it's just the penguins, she thinks. Weather is irrelevant now, breathing is irrelevant, but she still has time for the wackiness of 'it's a good thing the knowledge of the penguins are still there looking after us', but even her smile feels tired.

Edie loves and hates the peace. The business of the day with its chemotherapy and nurses and concerned visitors holding little bunches of flowers, the phone calls reporting back to Ted and Juliet, the trying to take it all in, the justifying of medical decisions, the medications – everything is taken over by these long, quiet islands of night. Work is taking a backseat and many days she drowses through the afternoons. She's working three days a week for a while and Ivy helps out on the other days.

In Grace's living room, her eyes fall on the dusty studio picture behind the plastic frame on the mantelpiece, where her mother is shining forth from the brightness of the past with the old calm, the steady gaze and the hidden heart. She picks up the old photo, dusts it with her sleeve and looks into that face, and it gives a hint but not the full story. This is the mother she didn't know. The young woman with life before her all laid out like some beautiful table. Who told her daughter about meeting Ian Fisher, the man who would be her father, about dancing all night at the Bijou and how when she broke her heel on the dance floor he swept her up and carried her home.

'How could you not fall in love with a boy like that,' she used to say, laughing, her eyes so happy. 'Though I was pretty light, he was straining badly by the time we got home.' Her laugh so sweet and very pleased at the instant effect she'd had on him.

She puts the collapsing layers of the frame carefully back on the mantelpiece and sinks into the old flowery couch. Grace is sleeping in the bed in the far corner.

Like a message from a better time, Wayne Newton is forwarded from around the corner. Before settling, he perches on her knees, pricking her with what Lorrie used to say were the pins in his toes. Her jeans save her but then she idly fears she may be getting too old for jeans anyway. The gloom descends. She's the eldest and aware of her age, which sets her apart from her sister and brother who don't seem to be. It's her claim. Honestly, how can you think of such shit at such a time? she asks herself dully.

Stroking Wayne means stray cat hairs settle on her leg like broken beams of light. He dribbles with the pleasure of affection. The comfort of him has eased them both. He moves between her house on the corner and Grace's house, following the trail of Edie's scent past the grass and the tea-tree, making each place his home.

Outside, the dull sky passes itself off as calm enough, though somewhere in it there's a fresh wind urging it on. Edie puts the cat at the foot of Grace's bed. 'Storm rising, Wayne, good thing we're in, wouldn't like to be out in it tonight.' The detached Wayne settles roundly into the aerial layers of cat sleep, and as he rises, his purr fades.

The other old pictures of her mother on the mantelpiece tell their stories, and though they're black and white she knows the colours and the stories behind them. Grace's blunt fringe had been cut way too short the day before and she'd made the check jacket herself from wool purchased at Higginbotham's for quite a lot per yard.

And those wide lips are coated in Revlon's Flame-Red. 'It was my colour from the moment I wore it,'

Grace had said over the years, forgetting each time that she'd said it before. How many times had Edie heard that, she wonders – more than ten, fewer than three? And what makes you recall such words? There was a core of glamour in Grace that was magnetic to the girl. With your mum, she thinks, you're always the girl and she's the woman.

And now Grace May Bell the teenager is an old woman who has about a month to live, but even given the diagnosis Grace half expects a cure. She's that kind of woman. She was heard telling Ivy only a few days ago that there was a cure for her. 'Yeah, I'm in remission. I am.'

Ivy, clearing away glasses of melted ice, stopped for a moment and said, 'Well, me old darlin', you deserve to be in that place, wherever it is, more than anyone.'

Grace remains true to the cult of optimism. But Edith's pessimism is just as entrenched. When Grace began to sleep away the afternoon hours like someone who'd forgotten life, it seemed to Edie that death had taken her in and was giving her dying lessons. Edie must keep her opinions to herself though because talking about death is not allowed except when Grace says such things as, 'I'm not afraid to die,' and, 'Everybody must die, Edith,' all of which Edie thinks is the purest crap.

This is not *everybody,* this is *you,* and why can't you ever admit to *anything?* But like a good daughter she agrees and says in a cheerful voice, 'That's the right approach, Mum.' But all of this is spelling out the terrible, unfathomable intimacy of mothers and daughters. And the insect clocks are busy eating time.

Chapter 43

The Papery Light

In the holiday season, Ivy and Roy rent their house out for six weeks. Always have done. Brings in enough for the pensioners to live on for months. Ivy worries with a strangling fear that damage will be done and never repaired, but Roy's always been the boss. Despite his health problems the budget still calls for it, so Ivy goes ahead. As she always does to prepare for the onslaught, she packs each little vase and cup away into the big locked cupboard. Then they go and live in a caravan on the other side of the bay for six weeks.

Each year, like an incremental graph, it appears the tenants get wilder. They know this from the neighbours, though Grace never complains – she knows they need the money and this will be the last year for all of them anyway. And tonight next door at the Jacketts' people down beer as if it could cure them of everything. They fight and laugh and booze on.

'You dick,' Edith and Grace hear one man drawl from the backyard. 'Can't even apologise properly. Mean as cat shit and twice as ugly.'

'Yeah, and what would you know, you stupid prick? Your own bloody mother gave you away.'

This last remark is greeted with silence from the women. 'Take no notice of the idiots, love. He's just full.' More proof if anyone needed it about holidays, thinks Edie.

Around midnight, Edith walks her mum outside to the toilet. Grace looks up at the spine-thin strip of sky between the houses and is refreshed with the love of every single thing.

With one arm over her mother's shoulder, Edith places her other arm around her back, and they pass the slumping fence dividing them from next door like a zip. On this side of the fence, before the wide-open toilet door, Edie waits, gently leaning on it. Inside the dark dunny, a small trumpeting fart echoes in the bowl and then the stream empties. Grace is past embarrassment these days and while seated, some-times talks, still bright from her long day of sleeping. 'Nice night eh, Bob ... What? Come closer, darlin', so I can hear you. Oh, I tell you, it's so good to be up and out of that bed...' And the pleasure of her mother's familiar, airy energy lifts her as if she were a child on a swing. 'Nice night, it is, it is.'

'Yep, it's a beauty, Mum,' she says too loud and too fast and runs her hands though her hair, realising she hasn't washed it for a while. Its greasiness reminds her of her own self, of a time before nursing Grace. Her eyes are tired rivers flowing into everything. Her clothes are not clean. Truth is, everything is falling apart.

Even while enjoying herself with a revelry of normal things laid out in the wide night, the retreat of energy in Grace begins, stealthy and demanding. 'Okay, Edie girl, I'm ready now,' she says, quietly placing her hands on each wall and bracing herself against it. As she stands, Edith ducks in with the toilet paper she's been holding and wipes her mother's bottom, hoping she does this tactfully, which involves not talking and not being rough with the delicate flesh. She drops the paper into the pan, lets the nightie down and stands up, guiding Grace out into the papery light of the bony moon.

Tonight her mother's gaze rests on her but her mind is flowing inward. Edith has missed her chance to say anything about love or this time together, and the time just gets shorter. A moment escapes like a breath.

'Bobby,' Grace sighs, 'let's get in, darl. I've had enough of nature for one night.' They hear the clink of next door's glasses above the constant sea. Grace leans into Edie, thinking of genes and circumstance. Old faults sewn long ago into their seams. Behind them on the highway cars slip by in bursts of certainty. And then Lorrie is standing at the screen door, outlined like an angel. She slips a shining arm around her grandmother and moths, crazy for light, hurl themselves at the door in a tangle of blurs. 'I'll take over for a while, Mum, go and have a rest.' Edith relinquishes the weight of Grace and stays out in the warm night on a yard chair, harvesting night sounds near the penguin hide.

Chapter 44

The Dream of Whales

Next morning there's a rattle at the door and it seems someone is trying to get in with their hands full. 'Oi, Edith. You there?' she hears and slowly, without curiosity, gets up to tend to the door, annoyed that the seal between her and her mother is broken again. Without thinking she carries the last diary with her to the door to let in Rodney Cooley, the palliative care nurse – not her favourite among them.

'You took so long I thought someone had died,' he says softly, smiling with his little pursed lips. He glances into Edith's eyes to see whether he's gone too far and briefly sees her anger. Then, just as quickly, she does not feel angry because there is no time for anger anymore.

'Come in, Rodney,' she says and the door swings open to allow the wide slice of clean day. Blinking at the nakedness of it, she places the diary on the old bookshelf so that she can grab the grey commode chair Rodney thrusts at her.

'Buck up, missy, none of your long faces on my shift. And how is our darling Gracie this fine morning?' He bustles in carrying a bed brace, unwieldy as a set of antlers, along with a stack of catheter bags and a pile of blue-and-white disposable bed underlays.

('These are the only ones to bother with, I'm telling you, and I speak from years of experience.') He also totes an ungainly clanking IV drip stand.

He's always annoyed her and here it is again to-day. Why doesn't he have more sensitivity? She asks Rodney if he'd like a cup of tea and he agrees heartily, stage-whispering, 'Yes please, my love, three sugars and the merest hint of a dash of milk.' He puts his bits and pieces down gently so as not to disturb Grace, who seems even more tired than usual today.

Edie heads off to put the kettle on, even though he never lets her actually make the tea, and when she comes back he's holding her mum's hand and stroking her face, saying, 'It's all right, my dear. All will be well.' It seems there has been an accident. 'Come on, darling, don't you worry about a thing, we'll have you cleaned in a jiff, before you can even remember what happened.'

Rodney gets up to grab his nurse's bag and stumbles over one of the extension cords that feeds out from Grace's hospital bed. Even so, he doesn't let go of Grace's hand. 'My mum always said clumsy was my middle name,' he says. Grace doesn't notice. On the other side of the bed, Edie wipes her hands with the sanitiser gel and flaps them through the air to dry them which, as usual, takes longer than it should. Rodney shows Edie how to drape towels over her mother to keep down the amount of skin exposed and to clean in sections. Grace doesn't mind; they have her on her side facing the window and even balanced like this she seems to be sleeping in the winter half-light as if their ministrations are not real.

Once cleaned, she sleeps again while Rodney perches with Edie beside the diaries on the green velvet couch. The sleek cat circle that is Wayne doesn't move. Rodney picks up both her hands and, being close to him, Edith thinks of apples and smells their freshness lifting from him. Though he's tall, his face is round and brown. He's bald but for a low ring of hair. His eyes are kind little triangles and his buckle mouth is, as usual, pursed and ready to speak. 'Now,' he says, 'my darling, it's time for the next talk and this one is about you. You must not take it too hard because I'm not criticising, please understand this is *not* a criticism.'

Oh dear, thinks Edie, preparing to be criticised. She watches Rodney with flinching eyes, believing she can take it.

'There is only one truth in this dying game and it's this: it's too much for one person. The dying. It's always too much for one person. I have seen it again and again. It's no reflection on you, personally as such, but the dying need more than you think and also, strangely, they need less. It's a very mysterious business and I could talk for hours about the insights as well as the things I've missed – and believe me, darling Edie, I've missed a few in my time. But the important person here is not you or me. We must remember that. It's Grace who matters. And it's our job to help her pass in the best way possible. This is the thing: it isn't about us. I brook no intervention in this, dear Edie. We all have to get our arses into gear, and now is the time.'

Her hands have dozed off in Rodney's mollusc grip and his vision swims around her like the dream of whales in winter seas, true and compelling, even thrilling, but he isn't taking her somewhere – he's waiting for an answer.

'There's my brother, Ted,' she speculates, tentatively looking to Rodney for guidance. 'I could ask him.'

He stands up in his dark nurse's uniform with his name tag skewwhiff on his navy short-sleeved shirt and the wings of an angel are spread out beneath and his name. He looks down at Edie. He seems disappointed with her. 'Pardon me, my dear, but there is no option. Now, unfortunately, I must resort to bluntness and you must brace yourself. Grace told me you have a sister named Juliet. It would mean the world to Grace if you could make up with her and get her here. The healing would be truly beneficial. I mean no offence, Edie, I'm just the messenger.' She would like to defend herself. She believes she has asked them both and not got far.

Rodney collects his stethoscope and blood-pressure monitor and places them into his black bag. 'Look, Edie, I hope you can forgive me for what I'm about to say. Every one of my patients is unique, but they all have something in common.' He straightens and looks at her with his hand on his bag. 'The truth is they really are never coming back. When they love someone they don't see, the departure cannot be peaceful. See what you can do about getting Juliet to visit your mum a bit more before the time comes because, my dear, that time is winging its way toward you.' He stops over by the door, seeming to remember something. 'At the very least, get your brother to come and stay now or your husband or your daughter involved in this before you fold. You've done ninety-five per cent. You need help now.'

Chapter 45

A Buttery Morning

When Juliet arrived the night before to take part in the nursing of their mother, it was dark and Grace was already in the arms of morphia. Edie, sleeping beside her on a camp bed, heard her sister but decided to pretend she was asleep. She saw Juliet lean towards Grace and kiss her and even she was touched. Better late than never crossed her mind but the truth is, Edie did not know the half of the story between Grace and Juliet. Each night Grace was in hospital after the emergency admission Juliet would call her and they would talk for as long as they could. And then on the days when Juliet would come in, Edie would leave hearing them laugh and chat as she walked away. Juliet was up to date in the life of Grace.

When Juliet does come to the house to nurse Grace, it seems to Edie she comes in her own sweet time. Rodney Cooley's words echo. After all those fights about the type of care Grace needed, now the time was here for something to happen. For some order. If it was going to be at home as Juliet had insisted, then let it begin, let the final Test of Courage begin.

***

Juliet's dressing gown is, to Edith's mind, utterly slatternly. It's some kind of slippery pink stuff, a colour she's always thought a big mistake for anyone over five years of age. And besides, it barely even covers her sister's fat, freckled breasts. Juliet is a solid woman now and the taut, short Tweetie-Pie-festooned nightie induces incredulity. Her hair, long and wild, is now dyed buttercup blonde. She's wear-ing purple thongs, her painted nails are black and chipped, and it's true that even Edith wouldn't have hoped for such a florid deterioration. This is way too much. She herself, she reflects soberly while appraising her sister, has merely faded like some poor old stained tea towel. But then with Jules, looks were premium.

'What'd I miss?' Juliet wonders and, child-like, stands rubbing her eyes before the toaster, waiting, as Grace used to say, for the toast to put itself in. 'Toast anyone?' she yawns. 'Edie, put the kettle on, would you?'

After putting a bit more water in the kettle, Edith slams it down harder than she intends. Her wrist is not what it should be since she sprained it last year and suddenly she feels it. Juliet looks softly at her but Edith won't meet her eyes. 'It's good to see you,' Jules says.

'Yes, I suppose it's good to see you too,' Edith snaps and silence laces them down. It's as if someone broke the dial on all her actions and everything is cranked up. She regrets the accidental snapping, if only because it wasn't that much fun. When you snap you should at least mean it. And she starts a little debate within on the Etiquette of Snapping when she is standing in front of the sister she hasn't seen since the last fight at the hospital. The one who ran off with her husband and had his child and then sent her home for Edie to raise, which turned out to be the kindest thing anyone has ever done for her. Still, she hates this woman and, so it seems, she always will.

She gets out the mugs, even though she doesn't want tea and her mother's earlier cup is again cold, which gets her considering the place of tea in the life of Fishers. The Australian tea ceremony. Could we even speak to each other without it? she wonders. One of the mugs is chipped so she puts it aside. Make a good place for toothbrushes, she thinks carefully, grasping at a little blip of the everyday. Juliet makes a small, irritating cough, what Edith always said was her 'play-cough'. Turns out, though Edie still doesn't know it, to have been asthma.

'I'm looking forward to seeing Lorrie.'

Coldness spreads through Edith, right to her fingertips, along with fear. What if Lorrie loves her more than me? Followed by, of course, she'll love her more, are you kidding? This has been the story of your life and you will have to be the strong one not to let it show. Lorrie doesn't need you carrying on about yourself now. Now is massive: she meets her mother and her grandmother is dying. All we need now is for Southey to show up and ... Please, God, no.

'Well,' Edie manages to get out, 'I suppose you would be looking forward to that. It's been a long time.' Restrained, she thinks, and better, but still not perfect. She wants to stop the inner dialogue, but then she thinks, maybe Juliet seems less tawdry now or is it the buttery light of morning?

Grace is on the couch by the stove. Early in the morning she sometimes likes to sit out of bed and follow the sea through the kitchen window. But now she seems to be fading. Her head sinks back and her eyes close as she feels the anger between her daughters.

'Look,' Juliet begins, impatiently pulling her hair back into a fast, smooth bun, jabbing it down with hair clips drawn from her mouth like little black twigs. 'I didn't mean to get into all this – now is certainly not the time, that's for sure. Maybe we should just get Mum back to bed. We can have a talk later.'

Edith sees she's right.

The daughters each take a side of their mother and slowly walk her from the couch back to the bed, bringing the oxygen tank and the IV drip stand with them, looking straight ahead. With their mother between them, they don't see each other.

Once Grace is in bed, Edith says, 'Back later, Mum,' to no response.

When, a little later, Juliet asks Grace what's on for today, she replies, 'Nothing much, darlin',' in a tight, exhausted voice from deep within the hard old pillow she's had for years. 'Apart from killing your brother for leaving that hole in the garden.' A small, light gust of laughter is sucked out the door and follows Edith home on wings.

Chapter 46

Walking My Baby Back Home

Juliet is adamant about the cleaning of Grace's false teeth. There's a right way and a wrong way and Juliet knows both very well. It seems to Edith that her sister still knows everything there is to know. She'd like to swallow her irritation but it keeps getting stuck. She has a basin, a toothbrush, Steradent and Listerine.

This is a good morning and Grace is sitting up with Wayne curled at her knee. 'You can only really rest with a cat nearby,' she says, musing to herself more than to anyone, reaching a hand towards Wayne. They hear the words and see the words but are shocked because it seems her pleated mouth has shrunk without its teeth. Mum was always so private about her false teeth and now they are everyone's business. Lately their mother is divided into a series of jobs, and each job requires full concentration. Stand back to look and you'll get lost in the maze. Dance music from the fifties, all blithe beat and subterranean sexuality, emerges softly from the tape player and Grace has her still hands in her lap and her blue cardigan around her shoulders. She loves having the kids around her. It's her essential role, being their mother. Sun pushes in from the window and seems to glance over the carpet, looking for something lost. Dust, like small, winged angels, moves about within the streams of light. Juliet scrubs Grace's false teeth with a toothbrush and the intensity of a wrestler. Edith hasn't seen anything like it since their brutal fights as girls. 'These little falsies will be clean,' says Juliet, 'clean as they possibly can be clean.' Her light dyed hair flops forward, far too long for a woman of her age, Edith thinks tartly.

The grinning dentures fizz in a bowl of white Steradent and Juliet bumps the bed with the passion of her scrubbing.

'Take it easy, Juliet,' Edith says evenly, lightly, and is ignored.

Grace has a fungal infection of the mouth but at least the herpes in her left eye is healing. The chemo has left her immune system a holed and leaking vessel. There have been eye drops every two hours, which it seems that Ted is best at administering. He takes a firmer hold on the red lower lid and yet still manages to be gentle. Grace's sore eyes are more closed than open now.

It's a week before she will die and the price of the few extra months has been high.

The chemotherapy treatments have taken place at the local hospital, with Edith sitting beside her for every one of them. The hospital was the same one where Edith spent a week with a mysterious fever when she was thirteen. She recalls the place with its strangely nautical theme full of rounded stair rails like an ocean liner. She recalls waking to see her mother knitting beside the bed and singing that old song, soft and sweet: 'Walking my Baby Back Home'. Edie thought, staying as quiet as she could, that if she could remain there forever listening to her mother sing that old song she'd always be happy. The light fell around her and Edith couldn't bear to wake up fully because the vision would be gone. She wondered whether she dreamt her mother.

When Juliet thought about her mother, it was always with a kind of certainty. She knew she was loved and knew she was the favourite child – no doubt about it. There was something between them, something in the eyes, something damn near perfect. Juliet even felt a bit sorry for the others, especially poor old Edo, who really could not compete. Edith had worked it out too, which just made it worse. She believed Juliet was loved first and foremost by her mother for her beauty. For that reason, at first, she discounted it. If it's that damn dumb, who wants it? Still, it was always a nice fallback. Better than nothing. And poor old Edie, scrabbling around, always giving mum things – how pathetic. And Ted, well, Ted was just a lost boy and then his damn wife up and leaves him floundering around until the time when some other woman takes him under her wing. What happened there? she wonders.

That time with the glasses, she thinks. Mum knew I'd lost them, didn't know the half of it but she knew something was up. Still, she let me have my way. Let me feel believed. Edie was disgusted – well, tough luck, Edo. You never understood that you needed to be audacious around Mum. She wanted us to have guts. She was enthralled by courage because she had it. Took guts to leave Dad. She never disapproved of me, even when I ran off with Southey. Never said a thing. Just got in touch when she could. When I sent the baby home with Tom Southey, Mum thought I was brave because I knew I couldn't do it. She was always with me. Always. That's why I had to see that she got what she wanted in the end. If she wanted to die in Seacrest, then that's what had to happen. Uncle Kev would have done the same thing. Bloody Edie, so weak, caving at the first hurdle, always wanting the easy way out.

Jules is outside raking up leaves on the footpath in Yarrabeen, not because she enjoys it but because after her years in the US she figures she'll get sued if some poor bugger goes head over turkey on their wet leaves. Be just our luck. As she rakes, a fine film of sweat creeps up on her and her face shines. And then, maybe it's the work – to her mother, work was life – but she begins to feel Grace and to believe she's standing with her, even telling her how to rake, though she knows Grace would be helping her rake rather than telling. 'You teach by showing, darlin',' she used to say, and then there is it – the memory of Grace has settled in her eyes and the tears fall hard and it hurts, and she stops raking and holds onto the damn rake, and there is such a void within her. She holds the rake tightly, just so she'll stay standing, and the leaves in the pile are as loose as memories. When the wind comes in on them they rise and scatter, and Juliet is still weeping with the rake.

Edie, coming back from the shops, sees her sister standing there crying. She gets out of the car and she's thinking 'She's missing Mum,' and before she knows it she's over there hugging Juliet. Holding her, cradling her head, telling her it will be all right. Then Edie says something she's been thinking about for a long, long time but doesn't mean to say. 'Thank you for Lorrie. I never said. I was so mad at you. I just couldn't think straight. But thank you. I will never be able to thank you enough.'

'Oh God, you were the best person I could think of. She is so lucky to have you and I am so sorry. I was horrible. I've hated myself all these years for what I did to you.'

The raked leaves rise and fall in flurries. Edie wipes her eyes. 'Let's call it quits, mate. We've got Mum to worry about now.'

Ted, over by the house, is watching and reckons he's seen a miracle. There's someone who should know about this. He leaves his boots at the door. 'Mum, you would not believe what I just saw. Juliet and Edith having a hug. They're both blubbering. They're holding onto a rake and there's leaves flying around all over the ship.'

Grace, lying in her clean bed, smiles at Ted. Her hand reaches out for Wayne. 'Go on. Isn't that something. Those two girls have their daughter in common. I wondered when they'd get that.'

Ted sits a while with Grace. He's reading *Middlemarch* to her and enjoying the expanse of the story. When finally the sisters come in they are a bit wiped out with all the emotion but they bring with them a sense of peace and everyone feels it.

Chapter 47

Five Baths

Before it gets too bad Edith runs a bath each morning for Grace. She brings in lavender lotions, soaks and a bath pillow. And a candle apparently scented with gardenias. The bathroom has stripped wooden floors, stained with water marks near the foot of the pink bath. A dense glass–mesh gold screen hides the shower. The pink basin is deep with two solid taps – one buttoned green, the other red. The joke is that Grace might have sorted these at Pabs all those years ago. Who knows?

The care of Grace has been divided into Edie in the mornings, Juliet in the afternoons, Ted in the evenings and all of them rotate the nights. The one good thing about cancer, Grace says, is that she gets to say goodbye to them, to tell them she loves them. This time is gold.

In the bathroom there's a cupboard above equipped with Steradent and Quick-Eze and a lonely pumice stone. The window is high and meshed with wire. Opened out you can see a scrap of sky and the leggy lilac tree dahlias that bob around in the wind like dancers.

She runs the bath before she takes her mother in and changes her bed. Grace waits in a side chair. When the bath's ready, Grace sits on the side, waiting before she's strong enough to get out of her nightclothes. She takes her first bath by herself and Edie, hovering, calls through the door, 'You right, Mum?'

'Yeah, right as rain, my darlin'. Come in and talk.'

Edie takes a pew on the toilet seat and, while Grace sinks into the healing warmth, her eyes are closed. Edie finds silent tears slipping while she chats about the idea of new curtains in here. 'Something sprigged,' she says and Grace says, 'Mmm,' and Edie wipes the tears away with her mother's nightie. She holds it on her knee, aware of its waning warmth.

For the next bath, Edith helps. That night's bed-clothes always huddle in a pile under the basin. Edith helps her mother into the bath carefully, fearfully. The idea of an accident looms at her like an oncom-ing train. In the bath, the thought comes to Edie that her mother is once again a baby floating in amniotic fluid, this time scented with lavender. She says, 'You're a better daughter than I was, young Edie.' Edie picks up the bedclothes and the nightie. 'Edie, stay a while.'

She sits back down.

'I meant what I said. I've never told you. I never told my own mother. I was a busy woman, I know, didn't mean I didn't love you. Didn't mean I didn't notice all you did. I wish I'd been a better mother.'

Edie hands her a flowery face washer, warm from the tap she's just run it under.

'Put it on your face now, Mum. You were the best mother I could have had. Mothers don't come better, and I reckon your mum would have said you were the best daughter there ever was too. So let's think about what nightie you'd like to wear today.'

'No, Edie. I want to talk to you.' She takes the face washer and drapes it over her chest to give herself a bit of dignity. 'I want you to listen now. I have something to say to you and you will be surprised, I think.

'You know Mum and Dad died when I was young and, you don't know this, but they left me everything they had. It wasn't so very much, but it was a lot more than most young girls have.' She begins to cough and it takes a while for her to settle. Edie cleans out the toothbrush glass and gives Grace a drink of water in it.

'Thanks, Ed. I'm better now. Well, I never told your father or anyone about it. I reckoned it was really my mum and dad's money; I was just looking after it. I put it in the bank and it earned interest. I worked and never thought about using it.' She smiles. 'But, you know, that money gave me so much courage. It was always there behind me, telling me I could do things. I know that. It's how I felt strong enough to leave your father and set up in Yarrabeen. In those days women, well, we didn't get any help from anyone, but I knew I could make it because Mum and Dad were still helping me. I always felt they were with me, and I still do. I've got the money, and I want you to know where the bankbook is. When I die, I want you to share it with the others. I know you will.'

She is tired now, faltering, and her words slide away. 'Will you make sure everyone gets some? Just share it out evenly. Mum and Dad would have liked that.' She closes her eyes. 'And I would like that too. Like to hand it on from them to you kids. Like the idea of you having a little nest egg. A nest egg, darling, that's all it is.'

Edie tops up the warm water in the bath, and steam rises and curls up to the window. Soon she helps Grace out of the bath, gets her clean and dry, and they head back to the bed by the window.

Later, Edie finds the bankbook and the money is all there, and there's enough for everyone to feel safe. Edie sees all her mother's frugal ways over the years – all the saving and the kindness – and it hits her that there are so many ways to love and that, when you look at a life, you must see them all before you know any of it.

***

During the third bath Grace rests in the warmth of the water like a pale waterlily, her head on the pearly fleur-de-lis bath pillow. She looks up at her daughter and says, 'Yes, this is so good,' but she seems to be drifting off to sleep so Edith sits and watches, trying not to look at her mother's body but failing, noting all their shared similarities: the breasts, the paleness, the shape of the limbs, the lack of hair. Finally, she thinks, are there any differences?

The fourth bath is not a success. Grace is so tired they turn around halfway to the bathroom.

On the fifth day the struggle is harder, the struggle for every single part of the pleasure the bath gives. Edith sits beside her, watching and thinking, and after they get her dressed and back into bed her mother opens her eyes as if she's never seen her before and says, 'My darling, Edie, you have the most beautiful nose. Did I ever tell you that you have my father's nose?' And this is how the time of baths ends.

Chapter 48

A Parcel of Feathers

Now that it's autumn, in his own good time Ted disperses the dry horse manure around his mother's garden. Each shovelful is from him, and in this way he's telling her that he loves her. It's everything to him that she knows this. He works most of the morning it seems and for a while he keeps avoiding the penguin hide, which looks pretty well abandoned down there at the bottom of the garden. The manure is ripe with hay and soil. Each time he lifts it, he remembers that we're all made of the earth. We're nothing too fancy, none of us, despite what we think.

Waiting for this death has been like being in a trance, slow and muffled. When Juliet decided the hospice was out, Grace said she wanted to be with Juliet at her house in Newtown. And this threw everybody. Ted watched the battle between his sisters, then he took them out into the hospital corridor. 'We'll take Mum to Seacrest and draw up a roster. Make it work.'

What he's moving through now is something else. This is his mother. This is his Grace. It was one thing when Lisa left. She just up and said he wasn't for her, packed the old black wheelie suitcase and took off with the wheels laying tracks in the red dirt yard, hair whipping around, eyes hard as diamonds. She decided she could do without the kids, just like Juliet did with Lorrie. Took off with some bloke from her work – well, that's when you lose respect. She did me a favour, he thinks, though he's not sure whether she did the kids a favour. Poor little buggers. That will all be dealt with later. He doesn't know what he'd have been like if Grace had left him. He will have to be the one who makes his kids the best they can be. Be the best person in their lives, just like his mother was for him.

It's cold for this time of the year and he's spread all the manure around by nine. Feels like he's been working for several hours though. Time is definitely slowing. He checked Grace before he went out in the garden. He'd been on since four when Edie took over, stumping down the street in her uggs and trackie daks the colour of sludge. He'd done everything: given Grace the morphine, checked her eyes, put the drops in, checked on the bag of mahogany-coloured piss and found it needed emptying then swapped it for another. Put a teaspoon full of ice smashed fine as rice into Grace's mouth, held her hand, kissed her forehead. Read a bit.

The garden and the morning are as fresh as a slice of apple. He knows now he has to complete the hide and, you know, he just does it. No more mucking around. Doesn't even take much effort. He finds a can of grey acrylic paint in the shed and paints it inside and out. Then he stands there looking at it for quite a long time, as if he's speaking to it or listening, waiting for it to tell him what to do next. He gets the trellis in under the rose and carefully arranges it over the hide, and it looks like it's been there a while. He transplants some agapanthus and acanthus around it. He scrounges the plants up from other parts of the yard. Then he mows the grass, a spray of it flying up and sticking to the damp hide. He thinks he's a dill for not waiting till it was completely dry, but then he smiles and thinks, well, it'll just hide it better, eh?

You always feel better when you've got a plan, he tells himself. He understands that Grace had said that to him so many times and now it's the river voice of his own consciousness. That quiet voice that loves him. Jesus, how are you supposed to get through this stuff? he wonders. He takes his boots off at the back door and goes past Grace. Edie's chatting about Lorrie's new boyfriend and how nice he is, that he's still studying too, and goes into the spare bedroom without washing, curls up on the bed and falls asleep.

That night he's on again at midnight. Outside there's a steel moon in a light sky, no wind and the big tree is holding its leaves in pairs like wings. Grace is awake when he comes in and performs all the checks again. She's bright for that moment and tells him to sit beside her and have a rest, so he does and tells her the plan. She thinks the plan is right, but she wants her teeth back in. He cleans them and inserts them delicately. She smiles. 'How did I get such a son as you?' she asks and he holds her fine hand but he's past being able to use his voice properly. 'Mum,' is all he can say.

He wraps Grace in her blankets and carries her out to the yard, to the hide, where he's put pillows and his bedspread and an old coat of Kev's. She's so light she could be a parcel of feathers.

The sea is luminous and still. Grace says, 'So lovely, my boy.' They reckon they may have seen a penguin or two passing by, using the goat track, but it might have been anything. The owl in the big tree keeps lookout. Now and then she hoots a warning. In the hide, Ted has his arm around Grace and it isn't long before the morphine takes over and she slips away. Ted stays out there for some time in the silver light, holding her, just being with her as the warmth of her ebbs away.

He's lost the ability to recognise what is real. Seconds take hours sometimes, but when it seems right he carries her inside, tenderly, and puts her back into the bed. He holds her still hand until Juliet comes in for the next shift. When he tells her that Grace is gone, he doesn't go into detail.

Acknowledgements

The Meaning of Grace is a work of fiction. I'd like to thank my publisher, Meredith Curnow, an inspiring professional and a lovely, lovely person. Thanks also to my editor, Brandon VanOver. He's a pleasure to work with because he's wise, calm and funny. You could not find better people or publishers.

Thank you to Carmel O'Toole, whose kindness is legend. And to my husband, Alan, and our children Phoebe, Alice and Chris, the family I live for.

Back Cover Material

'The emergence of a significant literary voice. An author with a promising future' AUSTRALIAN BOOK REVIEW

'Deborah Forster is a writer in a class of her own' KAZ COOKE

One day Grace Fisher, mother of three, changes every single thing in her life. She takes off to the coast with her three kids and never comes back. She leaves her sad, hopeless husband behind and soon enough he falls apart. And as Grace sets up in Yarrabeen, holding down a job at the bakery and ironing for extra cash, the kids struggle with the mystery of how Dad got so swept away. Fending for themselves becomes the way of things.

Edie, the eldest, locks herself into a dream of romantic love that can't help but fail. Juliet struts through life, filling it only with what she can seduce, steal and manipulate. Love comes easily for Ted, the youngest, but when his wife walks out and he must raise his two daughters alone, he starts to wonder about sisters, his own abilities and how to be a father.

Grace is kind, selfish and full of imperfect love. With her serious lipstick, slapdash cooking and inspired gardening, she is entirely herself. When she's diagnosed with terminal cancer, her children must confront each other again as adults, and try to understand their mother so they can understand themselves.

Written with her hallmark warmth, humour and deftness of observation, Deborah Forster's follow-up novel to the Miles Franklin-shortlisted *The Book of Emmett* is a moving story of the loves and rivalries that live at the heart of every family and the meaning that comes from loving Grace.

Books For ALL Kinds of Readers

At ReadHowYouWant we understand that one size does not fit all types of readers. Our innovative, patent pending technology allows us to design new formats to make reading easier and more enjoyable for you. This helps improve your speed of reading and your comprehension. Our EasyRead printed books have been optimized to improve word recognition, ease eye tracking by adjusting word and line spacing as well as minimizing hyphenation. Our EasyRead SuperLarge editions have been developed to make reading easier and more accessible for vision-impaired readers. We offer Braille and DAISY formats of our books and all popular E-Book formats.

We are continually introducing new formats based upon research and reader preferences. Visit our web-site to see all of our formats and learn how you can Personalize our books for yourself or as gifts. Sign up to Become A (RHYW) Registered Reader.

www.readhowyouwant.com

Printed in Great Britain
by Amazon.co.uk, Ltd.,
Marston Gate.

MVS COBOL II
Power Programmer's
Desk Reference

Books and Training Products From QED

Database

Migrating to DB2
DB2: The Complete Guide to Implementation
and Use
DB2 Design Review Guidelines
DB2: Maximizing Performance of Online
Production Systems
Embedded SQL for DB2: Application Design
and Programming
SQL for DB2 and SQL/DS Application
Developers
Using DB2 to Build Decision Support Systems
The Data Dictionary: Concepts and Uses
Logical Data Base Design
Entity-Relationship Approach to Logical Data
Base Design
Database Management Systems: Understanding
and Applying Database Technology
Database Machines and Decision Support
Systems: Third Wave Processing
IMS Design and Implementation Techniques
Repository Manager/MVS: Concepts, Facilities
and Capabilities
How to Use ORACLE SQL*PLUS
ORACLE: Building High Performance
Online Systems
ORACLE Design Review Guidelines
Using ORACLE to Build Decision Support
Systems

Systems Engineering

Effective Methods of EDP Quality Assurance
Handbook of Screen Format Design
Managing Software Projects: Selecting and
Using PC-Based Project Management Systems
The Complete Guide to Software Testing
A User's Guide for Defining Software
Requirements
A Structured Approach to Systems Testing
Storyboard Prototyping: A New Approach to
User Requirements Analysis
The Software Factory: Managing Software
Development and Maintenance
Data Architecture: The Information Paradigm
Advanced Topics in Information Engineering
Software Engineering with Formal Software
Metrics

Management

Introduction to Data Security and Control
CASE: The Potential and the Pitfalls

Management (cont'd)

Strategic and Operational Planning for
Information Services
Information Systems Planning for Competitive
Advantage
How to Automate Your Computer Center:
Achieving Unattended Operations
Ethical Conflicts in Information and Computer
Science, Technology, and Business
Mind Your Business: Managing the Impact of
End-User Computing
Controlling the Future: Managing Technology-
Driven Change

Data Communications

Data Communications: Concepts and Solutions
Designing and Implementing Ethernet Networks
Network Concepts and Architectures
Open Systems: The Guide to OSI and its
Implementation

IBM Mainframe Series

QMF: How to Use Query Management Facility
with DB2 and SQL/DS
DOS/VSE: Introduction to the Operating System
DOS/VSE: CICS Systems Programming
DOS/VSE/SP Guide for Systems Programming:
Concepts, Programs, Macros, Subroutines
Advanced VSE System Programming
Techniques
Systems Programmer's Problem Solver
VSAM: Guide to Optimization and Design
MVS/JCL: Mastering Job Control Language
MVS/TSO: Mastering CLISTS
MVS/TSO: Mastering Native Mode and ISPF
REXX in the TSO Environment

Video

DB2: Building Online Production Systems for
Maximum Performance
Data Architecture: An Information Systems
Strategy (Video)
Building Online Production Systems with
ORACLE 6.0
Practical Data Modeling

Programming

C Language for Programmers
VAX/VMS: Mastering DCL Commands and
Utilities

This is Only a Partial Listing. For Additional Information or a Free Catalog contact

QED Information Sciences, Inc. • P. O. Box 82-181 • Wellesley, MA 02181
Telephone: 800-343-4848 or 617-237-5656 or fax 617-235-0826

MVS COBOL II
Power Programmer's
Desk Reference

David Shelby Kirk

QED Technical Publishing Group
Boston • Toronto • London

Library of Congress Catalog Number: 91-14091
International Standard Book Number: 0-89435-305-5

Printed in the United States of America
91 92 93 10 9 8 7 6 5 4 3 2 1

Library of Congress Cataloging-In-Publication Data
Kirk, David Shelby.
   MVS COBOL II power programmer's desk reference / David Shelby
Kirk.
      p. cm.
   Includes bibliographical references and index.
   ISBN 0-89435-305-5 :
   1. COBOL II (Computer program language) 2. MVS (Computer system)
I. Title.
QA76.73.C252K57 1991
005.13'3—dc20   91-14091
                                                            CIP

DEDICATION

This book is dedicated to the many mainframe professional programmers who want to do their very best, yet often have neither the time nor the resources to improve their skills. The opportunity to have worked with so many of them through the years has been a blessing to me, as they continually impress me with their ability to "get the job done" and with their commitment to our profession.

I also dedicate this book to my wife, Linda. Without her encouragement and support, the manuscript for this book would never have been put to paper. Her faith and inspiration have brought me through many valleys to many mountaintops. This book is one of those mountaintops.

Contents

List of Figures

Preface

What This Book Is

Writing quality, high-performance code is what this book is about. This book was written for the professional COBOL programmer who wants to always write the best, most efficient, and cleanest code possible and who needs a ready reference for day-to-day use of COBOL II in an MVS environment. With that focus, the book is not organized in the way in which COBOL books for the novice are. This book, knowing the demands for maintenance and compatibility that the professional programmer faces, devotes a majority of its pages to explaining differences and demonstrating techniques. While COBOL II is the foundation of the book, other techniques are also given. The book will also be useful to managers and others planning to convert to COBOL II who want to understand more about its features. Many topics appear in several places because I felt you might look for the topic in several places.

While the majority of the book focuses on COBOL II, it attempts also to assist you in other challenges you face in the programming process, such as interfacing with programs written in OS/VS COBOL and using the Linkage Editor and DFSORT. There are reference aids on other topics, too, ranging from hexadecimal tables to the EBCDIC collating sequence and even to a summary of JCL. These references are not complete, but they include the information most likely to be needed by a COBOL programmer working with MVS.

In addition to providing reference material, this book includes suggested design and coding guidelines for programs. While your shop may already have guidelines, those in this book focus on simplicity, compatibility with prior versions of COBOL, and on avoiding terms that may be unfamiliar. Emphasis is on clarity, structure, and style, using the minimum syntax required.

What This Book Is Not

This is a desk reference, not an encyclopedia. This book does not contain every facet of information available about COBOL II or MVS, nor does it attempt to tutor you in programming fundamentals or elementary COBOL syntax (e.g., you won't find the definition of a COBOL paragraph or the purpose of a SELECT statement in this book). This book also does not attempt to explain the ANSI standards and their many levels, because those topics typically do not interest the professional programmer who has little or no say in such issues, anyway. There are references to specific environments, such as CICS and IMS but, again, there is no tutorial information on basics of programming for their environments.

How This Book Is Organized:

Chapter 1: Introduction. Read this chapter thoroughly for an overview of COBOL II features. If your shop hasn't yet converted to COBOL II, this chapter will highlight some of its benefits.

Chapter 2: Coding Differences. This chapter is designed to help you get over the hurdle of learning a new version of COBOL by answering the question, "What's different?" This is the chapter of instruction. You will want to read this chapter more than once.

Chapter 3: Programming with COBOL II. This chapter is designed not to be read sequentially but to be used to address specific COBOL design and coding issues. The chapter is organized by topic, not by feature, so some COBOL features may appear more than once or be cross-referenced. Included in the chapter are information on JCL, the Linkage Editor, and DFSORT. If it is a topic related to coding, compiling, linking, or executing COBOL II programs, you will find it here. Where Chapter 2 explained the new features of COBOL II, this chapter demonstrates how to use the new features (and some old features) effectively.

Chapter 4: Debugging Techniques. No, this chapter does not teach dump reading, although it does have a brief tutorial on debugging concepts for the less experienced reader. Instead, this chapter gives some tips and information on debugging facilities that are new with COBOL II and that are most likely to be used. This includes several tips and techniques for your "testing toolkit."

Chapter 5: Design Guidelines. This chapter is designed to assist those professionals who do not have well-defined standards for program design at their shop or who have difficulty developing GO TO-less programs. Techniques to design SORT applications are also included.

Chapter 6: Coding Guidelines. Several topics in this chapter are also in Chapter 3. The difference is that, where Chapter 3 focuses on using COBOL II effectively, this chapter focuses on the mechanics of coding, with a suggested coding format for each COBOL division. Even if your shop already has a set of COBOL coding standards, you may find that this chapter provides different ideas to consider.

Chapter 7: Summaries, Tables, and References. If it isn't here, either I overlooked it or you don't need it. This summary includes charts and information on much besides COBOL. Information on JCL, acronyms, comparisons to OS/VS COBOL, and common ABEND codes are among the topics available here for instant reference.

Chapter 8: Sample Programs. These sample programs demonstrate some COBOL II features, plus examples of OS/VS COBOL compatibility. All examples demonstrate the design and coding guidelines from Chapters 5 and 6.

Chapter 9: Related Publications. Earlier in this preface, I mentioned that this book doesn't contain everything there is to know about COBOL II or about MVS. No book could. This chapter serves to help you quickly locate related texts from QED and IBM. As a professional programmer, I know one of your personal goals is to build and maintain a library of useful reference materials. This chapter can help you make those choices.

Who This Book Is For

If you have difficulty with some topics in this book, the reasons may be that the topics add depth to subjects you thought you already knew or they uncover areas of MVS of which you were unaware. As the saying goes, "Just do it." As you explore the various topics, you may find yourself learning about more than the topic at issue.

Programmers who see their jobs as just a way of earning a paycheck will benefit little, if at all, from this book. They know all the COBOL they need to make a program function. The readers who will benefit from this book are those who continually seek a better way. Making a program function correctly is part of the job; making the program work better and more efficiently is a higher goal. They know, as I do, that being a professional programmer is one of the most interesting and challenging of the technology professions. By having this book in your hands, I assume you are one of us. Welcome. I hope you find the book useful.

To any grammarians among you, I confess that I knowingly used "programmerese" when discussing many topics. I used this approach because that is how most programmers discuss programming. For example, you will find that the word ABEND has been used as a noun, as an intransitive verb, as a transitive verb, and as an adjective. While that may not be proper use of the language, I doubt that any programmer misunderstands such expressions as "the program ABENDed," or "locate the ABENDing instruction."

To paraphrase a sentence in the first paragraph of this preface, this book was written for you, the professional programmer. If I've omitted some useful topic, made a technical error, or included information you haven't found to be useful, please let me know. I would enjoy hearing from you.

David Shelby Kirk
Cicero, New York

Acknowledgments

No book that attempts to move COBOL to a higher level can do so without acknowledging that much has been done by others through the years to bring COBOL to its current level. It was not only improvements in COBOL, but improvements in many other technologies that have made it possible to write this book. I have attempted to list here specific acknowledgment of those efforts.

Extract from Government Printing Office Form Number 1965-0795689:

Any organization interested in reproducing the COBOL report and specifications in whole or in part, using ideas taken from this report as the basis for an instruction manual or for any other purpose is free to do so. However, all such organizations are requested to reproduce this section as part of the introduction to the document. Those using a short passage, as in a book review, are requested to mention COBOL in acknowledgment of the source, but need not quote this entire section.

COBOL is an industry language and is not the property of any company or group of companies, or of any organization or group of organizations.

No warranty, expressed or implied, is made by any contributor or by the COBOL Committee as to the accuracy and functioning of the programming system and language. Moreover, no responsibility is assumed by any contributor, or by the committee, in connection therewith.

Procedures have been established for the maintenance of COBOL. Inquiries concerning the procedures for proposing changes should be directed to the Executive Committee of the Conference on Data Systems Languages.

The authors and copyright holders of copyrighted material:

FLOW-MATIC (Trademark of Sperry Rand Corporation),

Programming for the UNIVAC (R), I and II, Data Automation Systems copyrighted 1958, 1959, by Sperry Rand Corporation; IBM Commercial Translator, Form No. F28-8013, copyrighted 1959 by IBM; FACT, DSI 27A5260-2760, copyrighted 1960 by Minneapolis-Honeywell,

have specifically authorized the use of this material in whole or in part, in the COBOL specifications. Such authorization extends to the reproduction and use of COBOL specifications in programming manuals or similar publications.

References in this book to the ANSI Standard or to ANSI 85, are to the American National Standard Programming Language COBOL, X.3.23-1985.

Use of the following terms in this book are references to these specific IBM products:

Term used	IBM product and program number
MVS	MVS/SP, MVS/XA, and MVS/ESA, unless noted
COBOL II	VS COBOL II Compiler & Library & Debug (5668-958)
OS/VS COBOL	OS/VS COBOL Compiler & Library (5740-CB1)
DFSORT	DFSORT (5740-SM1)
Assembler H	Assembler H Version 2 (5668-962)

The following terms used in this book are trademarks of International Business Machines Corporation:

MVS/SP, MVS/XA, MVS/ESA, CICS/MVS, DB2, IBM, SAA, DATABASE 2, Systems Application Architecture, System/360, System/370

Introduction to COBOL II

This first chapter of the book is different from those that follow. Instead of dealing with the day-to-day issues you face as a programmer, it addresses concepts and features of COBOL II that are appropriate for a wider audience than programmers (maybe your boss would enjoy reading it on a cold winter's night). Oh, reading the other chapters will also help your boss, but those other chapters are designed explicitly for you. They are intended for desktop reference, to be used for specific questions, or for design and coding issues.

   This chapter addresses the programmer who is new to COBOL II and wants to know the differences between COBOL II and earlier versions and who also wants to know what some of the benefits of using COBOL II are. As a professional programmer, you take pride in your skills, and the need to learn a new version of COBOL may seem threatening. It won't be. While there are many differences, you will find that much of what you've always done in COBOL programs will still work. In many ways, COBOL II frees you to do tasks more simply, more efficiently, and with better structure.

1.1.   WHAT IS COBOL II?

As a reader of this book, you already know the fundamentals of COBOL, so you may be wondering, "Why is COBOL II considered a different animal?" Let's hold that question for a moment and cover some COBOL history. COBOL II (the proper name is VS COBOL II) is only the latest in a long line of COBOL compilers developed by IBM.

   Until the early 1970s, COBOL was bundled with the equipment (i.e., if you bought/rented IBM's hardware, COBOL was available at no extra charge). For reasons beyond this book, IBM began pricing hardware and software separately, and while customers considered it a disadvantage at the time, it proved to benefit everyone. With a fee being charged for software, IBM and other vendors began to develop a software industry, providing superior software designed to run on IBM or compatible hardware.

IBM's first proprietary version of COBOL was COBOL Version 3, which provided some enhancements such as debugging assistance. This was followed a couple of years later by COBOL Version 4, which also included an optimization facility. Then, around 1976, IBM released OS/VS COBOL, embodying all features of earlier compilers, plus many more. Until the announcement of COBOL II, OS/VS COBOL was the major version used. If you've been programming in an MVS environment, you've been using OS/VS COBOL. Throughout this book, key differences between the two will be identified.

Compiler	Approximate year	Standard level
COBOL F	1968	DOD (Department of Defense)
ANS COBOL Ver 2	1970	ANSI 1968
ANS COBOL Ver 3	1972	ANS 1968
ANS COBOL Ver 4	1974	ANS 1968 and extensions
OS/VS COBOL	1976	ANS 1968 and ANS 1974

Figure 1.1. COBOL releases for OS/MVS prior to COBOL II.

Now, back to your question, "Why is COBOL II considered a different animal?" There are two primary reasons, and I'll try to give you some information as well as background on each.

One, COBOL II supports the American National Standards Institute (ANSI) 1985 standards, which are the first major upgrade to the COBOL language since its inception, embodying structured programming components and removing obsolete features. Since IBM introduced COBOL II prior to approval of the 1985 standards, the earlier versions of COBOL II (versions 1 and 2) did *not* meet ANSI 1985 standards and are not covered in this book. My assumption is, since version 3 has been available since 1988, your shop is using version 3.0 or a later version.

Two, IBM developed COBOL II to be a part of the operational environment. What does that mean? It means that COBOL II is not just a compiler, but it is an active part of the resident software environment on your mainframe and the compiler-generated code expects to run within some degree of control by the COBOL II run-time facilities. It also means that COBOL II can take advantage of new operating software, such as MVS/XA and MVS/ESA. It means that COBOL II is an environment in itself, not just a compiler, and recognizes other environments such as CICS and IMS.

The importance of those two reasons isn't obvious until you assess the history of COBOL. When COBOL first became available in the early 1960s, many people felt it would eliminate the need for programmers, allowing business analysts to write application logic in English. COBOL's terminology supported that belief, using terms such as verb, sentence, statement, and paragraph. While the dream of eliminating programmers proved untrue, COBOL remained a language that had no proper structure, as did other procedural languages. COBOL was shackled by its attempt to appear as English prose.

PL/1, for example, has DO and END structural components to contain procedural substructures, allowing procedural control of any grouping of statements. For COBOL, the only structural components available in earlier versions of COBOL were paragraphs, sections, statements, and sentences. For structured programs, sections are too big to control effectively (and open to misuse of GO TOs), sentences are uncontrollable, and statements are controllable only within the confines of a sentence. That left only the paragraph as an element that could be controlled, normally with the PERFORM statement. The restrictions imposed by the other structures, combined with the limited conditional logic of IF, ELSE, and NEXT SENTENCE, left the professional programmer with few structural tools. With ANSI 85, COBOL now qualifies as a professional's language. With COBOL II, true structured code is now possible. The opportunities for structured code will be addressed in other parts of the book, including Chapter 3 (Programming with COBOL II), Chapter 5 (Program Design Guidelines) and Chapter 6 (COBOL Coding Guidelines).

Also true in earlier versions of COBOL was a total dependence on a shop's technical staff and trial and error to determine what compile and link-edit options should be used with COBOL. COBOL object code was insensitive or unaware of the presence of CICS or IMS and reference manuals for the earlier versions of COBOL rarely, if ever, acknowledged the existence or programming considerations necessary for MVS, CICS, or IMS. Today's IBM manuals are a far cry from those earlier versions, with extensive information and guidance on using COBOL II with other environments.

COBOL II, then, is no longer just a language. As such, it is more complex, more flexible, and more sensitive to an environment. Therefore, the need exists for this book. As you read through it, the importance of these issues will become apparent.

1.2. IMPORTANCE OF UPGRADING TO COBOL II

Converting your applications to COBOL II has many benefits, some for the application (user) and some for you, the professional programmer. Since conversion is a one-time process, it isn't a special topic within this book. If your shop has COBOL II, your technical support area may have installed some conversion assistance software, either from IBM or other vendors. If such conversion software is available, your efforts to change your programs from OS/VS COBOL to COBOL II will be less: not eliminated, but less. For more information that may assist you in such a conversion from OS/VS COBOL to COBOL II, see Chapter 2 (Coding Differences) and Chapter 3, section 2 (Module Structures).

1.2.1. Newer IBM Features Supported

One of IBM's major points when COBOL II was announced was that this language would be kept current with IBM's plans. IBM has kept its word on this, as COBOL II has had major upgrades and enhancements since its announcement. As new announcements continue, OS/VS COBOL will be left further and further behind. Keeping your applications (and you) current on technology is important. You will stay aware of new technology and continue to grow in your profession and your application takes advantage of new operating opportunities. What follows is an overview of some of the enhanced capabilities of COBOL II. Where a technique requires a conscious effort on your part, it will be covered in detail in later chapters.

31-Bit addressability.

With COBOL II, your application can use features, either consciously or automatically, of your shop's operating environment. For example, if your shop is running MVS/XA or MVS/ESA, there is memory available beyond 16 megabytes, yet OS/VS COBOL programs are unable to be loaded there. COBOL II can generate object code with 31-bit address capability, allowing COBOL II programs to be loaded into any memory space. The address space above the 16 megabyte level can be compared to the sunshine above the clouds during a storm. Down below, most programs and systems software are thrashing and competing

<table>
<tr><td>

There's not much up here . . .

16-megabyte line
</td></tr>
<tr><td>Large components of systems software (e.g., MVS, VTAM)</td></tr>
<tr><td>On-line applications (e.g., CICS, IMS)</td></tr>
<tr><td>Batch applications</td></tr>
</table>

Figure 1.2. Symbolic representation of 31-bit opportunity.

for the same memory space. Up above, the memory is virtually (pardon the pun) empty. This is a significant part of COBOL II's ability to improve application performance.

You may be wondering why current programs can't run in that upper address space. The reason is that application programs written for the IBM System/360, System/370, 4300, and 30xx series, prior to the availability of MVS/XA, used a 24-bit addressing scheme, allowing a maximum address of 16 million. Not too many years ago, that sounded like an infinite number. No longer.

Reentrant code.

Your applications can also be reentrant, making the applications available to multiple users without being reloaded into memory. This applies especially to a CICS environment, where an application may be used concurrently by many terminal users. Before COBOL II, reentrant code was available only from skilled assembler programmers. The RENT option will be covered more thoroughly in Chapter 3.

Faster sorting.

Although there are restrictions, most SORTs will run more efficiently in COBOL II. In addition to this enhancement, you will find much about using SORT within COBOL programs throughout this book.

VSAM enhancements.

If you use VSAM files, COBOL II now provides the opportunity for your application to get detailed feedback from any VSAM I/O request. This is not a replacement to the FILE-STATUS clause, but an enhancement to it.

Higher compiler limits

If you're like I am, you never think about compiler limits. The size of an 01-level, the number of data items possible, and other such limits seldom interfere with designing an application. By increasing the limits significantly (due largely to availability of MVS/XA and successors), COBOL II provides the opportunity to rethink how WORKING STORAGE should be used in a program. Imagine what you could do if you could define an 01-level to be 16 million bytes. That is larger than many databases. What if you loaded that data file into a table in memory to improve response time for that critical application of yours? Hmm . . .

1.2.2. ANSI 85 Support

Being at the latest ANSI level may not seem important to you, but this issue has a wide ripple effect in the industry. New features implemented from the latest ANSI level represent the evolving sophistication of COBOL. As COBOL continues to evolve, the language gets more power and becomes more consistent across multiple platforms. When COBOL was new (early 1960s), people envisioned that a COBOL program would be able to operate properly on any computer with no need for a conversion. In hindsight, those early dreams had little chance of success. Every vendor implemented COBOL a little differently, and there was little consistency even within the products of one vendor. The industry now has an opportunity to achieve a level of standardization not possible back then. With your application compatible with the ANSI 1985 standard, you will stand a better chance than ever that much of it will be compatible in a future environment.

Although books could, and have been, written about the many modules and levels of ANSI, you won't find that information in this book. Programmers rarely want to know what modules and subsets of ANSI are available. Instead, they want to know what works and what doesn't. This isn't to criticize those other books. Some people need to know that information (I did, to write this book), but the scope of this book is what you probably need on a regular basis. *The major benefit you will see with ANSI 85 features is the ability to do true structured programming.*

1.2.3. Standards Control Opportunities

You'll need to check with your shop to find if this feature is implemented. COBOL II can restrict what statements are used (yes, some programmers still use the ALTER statement), provide customized messages for designated statements, and even restrict what compile options are allowed. For an individual programmer, this isn't a benefit, but for a large MIS shop, knowing what options are specified and what statements are or aren't used is important for departmental planning. Good standards can also protect you, the programmer, from inheriting maintenance responsibility for programs that only work correctly with a nonstandard use of compile options or with unfamiliar statements.

Actually, COBOL II provides the opportunity to do much more, such as providing shorthand for certain statements or even support for languages other than English. Since that pertains to customizing COBOL II for an entire installation, it isn't part of this book. For more information on how to do this, see Chapter 9 (Related Publications).

1.2.4. SAA Opportunity

IBM's strategic plan to integrate a variety of operating platforms is called Systems Application Architecture (SAA). This is a major step for the industry and provides impetus for companies to start standardizing how they use computers. One of the SAA building blocks is COBOL II. If your company has decided to move toward an SAA environment, COBOL II provides a monitoring facility to warn you if incompatible features are used.

SAA is an exciting concept, especially if your company wants to share applications across mainframes, midframes, and PCs. With COBOL II, programs you develop for a mainframe environment can be more easily transported to other environments, freeing you from the requirement to program for different platforms. For more information on how COBOL II fits in with SAA, see Chapter 9 (Related Publications).

1.2.5. Improved Tuning and Cost Control

Although much of this is done by your systems programmers, COBOL II can be configured for specific environments. There are new compile options that cause different code to be generated, depending on how data are defined and used within your application. These options are explained in Chapter 3 (Programming with COBOL II).

Optimization.

Have you ever placed an "*" in column 7 to comment out procedural code that was not to be executed? Most of us have, at one time or another. Now, COBOL II locates code that is out of the logic flow and flags it and doesn't generate code for it. So, if you have code that is not to be deleted but is not to be executed, just move it out of the logic path and you're done. Providing that service is part of the enhanced OPTIMIZE facility, but it does much more. COBOL II will restructure the object code if that is more efficient, and, in some situations, it will even eliminate redundant computations within the application.

Batched compiles.

Another cost control feature is the ability to batch several programs together and invoke the compiler once to generate several object programs. This concept was available in OS/VS COBOL, but required special control statements to activate. COBOL II further builds on this facility by providing the option to generate appropriate Linkage Editor statements to cause separate load modules to be generated in one invocation of the Linkage Editor.

Preloads.

COBOL II now provides specific opportunities for your systems programmers to preload IMS/DC applications and improve their performance. Systems programmers may also package specific COBOL runtime modules to improve performance of specific environments, such as CICS. Since those tasks are specialized and do not affect the development and coding of COBOL programs, no additional information on preloading is provided in this book.

1.3. BENEFITS OF COBOL II TO AN APPLICATION

Applications benefit from many of the above features, primarily because they reduce resource usage and allow programs to be created that are less costly to maintain. Some of the features, however, provide the opportunity for applications to expand and to incorporate new services. Until MVS/XA broke the 16-megabyte barrier, many shops had been facing a continual problem: finding virtual storage constraint relief (VSCR) for their mission-critical applications. This means that there wasn't enough memory for the application to run efficiently. This occurred for two reasons. One, the application probably continued to grow in size as new functions were added. Two, IBM and other vendors kept adding new functions to the operating software to meet customer needs. A shop running CICS, TSO, IMS, VTAM, MVS, JES, and other software, in addition to your application, eventually finds that memory is full.

IBM's introduction of 31-bit addressability provided the opportunity for programs to operate above the old environment of 16 megabytes, thereby freeing the programs from the constraints of competing for memory with other applications in a finite space. This ability to free a program from memory constraints is one of the major benefits an application can realize with COBOL II.

Another benefit the application realizes is the opportunity to develop programs that are cleaner and easier (cheaper) to maintain. By consciously applying the new structured components of COBOL II, you create applications that are easier to read, easier to debug, and less costly to maintain.

1.4. BENEFITS OF COBOL II TO A PROGRAMMER

Much of what COBOL II means to you has already been mentioned, and after you finish this book, you will probably feel this list is too short. COBOL II provides such a large menu of features that it is difficult to sample them all. These are what I believe are the features most impressive to programmers.

Structured programming.

Yes, for the first time, COBOL has the ability to implement a true DO-UNTIL or CASE statement and can contain nested conditional statements within a paragraph. With prior levels of COBOL, a programmer could always justify a situation where the GO TO statement was necessary. Not so with COBOL II. This gives you the opportunity to create cleaner code than you could with OS/VS COBOL.

Documentation.

Okay, so documentation isn't the programmer's favorite word. All the more reason to use COBOL II. With COBOL II, you can control what error messages you get and where they appear. The cross-reference facility even tells you where data fields are modified, not just referenced. There are summaries of statements used, programs CALLed, and you can even control what portions of the source program are listed. The operative word is CONTROL. These features weren't in OS/VS COBOL. You will find more information on these techniques in Chapter 3 (Programming with COBOL II) and in Chapter 4 (Debugging Techniques with COBOL II).

Another documentation improvement is more subtle. Finally, you can mix upper- and lower-case text, making the program more readable. No longer must you code

```
IF DS1-INCOME IS NUMERIC
   MOVE WS1DTAXDID TO PR1-TAX-ID.
```

Instead, you may now code

```
If Ds1-income is numeric
   Move Ws1-tax-id to Pr1Dtax-id.
```

Many people feel that mixed upper- and lower-case text is easier to read than all upper case. Whether you prefer that isn't the issue, however. The point here is that you are in *control*. An extension of this concept is that you may now specify whether you want the COBOL II messages and other information on the source listing to appear in upper case or in both upper and lower case. Again, your choice. In this book, for purposes of contrast against the text, all COBOL statements will be upper case.

Debugging.

What I haven't mentioned yet is that COBOL II includes improved debugging facilities that have their own chapter (see Chapter 4, Debugging Techniques). There, you will find that COBOL II provides even more debugging aids than were available in OS/VS COBOL, including a new COBTEST debug tool that has three modes: full-screen mode, line mode, and batch mode. The on-line facility receives little mention in this book because, being on-line with instant help available, using it is largely a matter of practice, probably much the same as learning ISPF.

There are two other debugging aids you will find useful and easier to use than COBTEST. One is the new subscript range intercept feature (SSRANGE), which intercepts subscripts that go beyond the range of a table. If you've ever had the 2:00 A.M. phone call for an 0C4 ABEND of a critical productional program, you will appreciate the benefits of this new feature.

The other debugging aid is the new formatted dump (FDUMP). Whereas OS/VS COBOL's equivalent facility required additional JCL and was somewhat clumsy (few programmers I've met ever used it), the new compile option for formatted dumps imbeds the debug code directly within the object code, eliminating the need for additional compile-time JCL. This new dump presents your DATA DIVISION areas in readable format and can save valuable time when you need to determine the content of a number of data fields.

CICS enhancements.

Do you use CICS? If so, the coding becomes simpler with some coding requirements removed. For example, no longer do you need to maintain base locator pointers (BLLs) for your LINKAGE SECTION. More details for CICS are in Chapter 3 (Programming with COBOL II). Yes, you will need to convert CICS COBOL programs that make heavy use of LINKAGE SECTION, but there are software aids for that. See your technical support staff for availability of any in-house conversion aids.

1.5. DEVELOPING AN APPROACH TO LEARNING COBOL II

When you first learned COBOL, you probably studied many parts of the language before you were able to code a simple application. My recommendation to learning this new version of COBOL is quite different. Rather than read this entire book before attempting any of the new facilities, just jump in and swim. Here is my recommended approach to get you up and running in COBOL II quickly:

1. **Compile a known OS/VS COBOL program.** Assuming that you know the name of the COBOL II JCL PROC to use for your shop (I'll cover JCL in Chapter 3), compile a program with which you're familiar using the COBOL II compiler. This will give you some immediate feedback on some of the errors that might occur. If you've been using the LANGLVL(2) and MIGR options in your OS/VS COBOL compiler, you might find no errors at all. If so, you are positioned to move quickly toward mastering COBOL II. If there were errors, don't worry. Most are not difficult to correct. Don't attempt to correct the errors yet, as I'll get to that shortly.

2. **Read Chapter 2.** In Chapter 2 (Coding Differences), you will discover the more visible differences between the two compilers. Although CO-BOL II can't be so easily dissected, I have attempted to organize the chapter by three categories: what was dropped, what was changed, and what is new. In your first reading, focus on what was dropped and what has changed, not on what is new. Your immediate goal is to learn which, if any, of your current programming techniques must be changed. Since changing old techniques is much harder than learning new ones, address this first. Also, Chapter 2 does not cover every nuance of COBOL II. Instead, it covers the most likely features you'll encounter or use.

3. **Compare compile options.** There is a summary of compile options in Chapter 7 (Summaries, Tables, and References). Don't worry about new ones, just concentrate on the differences (e.g., the equivalent of PMAP in OS/VS COBOL is LIST in COBOL II). With this information, you can use COBOL II as you used OS/VS COBOL.

4. **Remove syntax errors from a known program.** Now, go back to that listing you compiled and start removing syntax errors. If you've used some coding techniques that aren't in this book, you may need additional assistance. With new compiler releases, there are usually

several little known or undocumented features that are changed. Your goal is reaching the level of proficiency where you can use COBOL II to compile programs without using new features. (Note: If you are going to be working in an environment where you must continue to maintain applications in OS/VS COBOL and also write applications in COBOL II, you will find specific help in Chapter 3, section 2 (Module Structures) and Chapter 8 (Sample Programs).

5. **Try EVALUATE and remove all occurrences of FILLER.** By now, you're familiar with COBOL II and have successfully compiled a program with the COBOL II compiler. Now is the time to experiment with some new features, preferably those that are visible and that will let you feel comfortable with new features. I recommend some experimental use of the EVALUATE statement, since it can replace a variety of nested IF statements, or even replace some table searches. If you are using an online text editor, such as ISPF, also try replacing all FILLER by spaces. Although a small item, this makes a DATA DIVISION noticeably more readable.

6. **Reread Chapter 2 and remove unnecessary items.** On the second reading of Chapter 2, focus on removing all paragraphs and clauses that aren't needed. You might remove some that are still in your shop standards, but your standards may need to be reviewed and updated if they still reflect OS/VS COBOL (Chapter 6 in this book might be a good place to start). For example, the LABEL RECORDS ARE STANDARD clause and the DATA RECORDS clause are required in FDs at many shops, yet both are obsolete statements in ANSI 85, and COBOL II treats them as comments—so why bother coding them? You will also discover that the ENVIRONMENT DIVISION isn't needed at all in several circumstances (e.g., an on-line IMS/DC application with no FD statements).

   By removing every item that doesn't cause the compile to fail, you will start to discover changes you may want to make in how you develop applications. Clinging to old techniques and continuing to code obsolete statements prevents you from improving your coding productivity—and may cause you to spend extra time at some future date removing those statements because a future release of the compiler might no longer recognize them.

7. **Set a goal to use three new features in your next program.** This is the hard part. Now that you feel confident with COBOL II, there is a normal tendency to get on with it and to stop learning new features. As an example, over the years I've encountered many OS/VS COBOL programmers who did not know how to get a Symbolic Dump (SYMDMP) or to use a binary search (SEARCH ALL). It happens. Learning all the primary features of a compiler takes work. Otherwise, the pressure of the project causes all of us to keep doing things the same old way.

SUMMARY

This chapter has touched on the differences you will experience in using COBOL II. The following chapters will provide information that clearly demonstrates that COBOL II is, indeed, a different animal. In teaching COBOL II, I am continually enthused by the excitement of programmers who suddenly see COBOL as a true programming language. I'm sure you will too.

Coding Differences between COBOL II and OS/VS COBOL

To learn COBOL II, your first priority is to understand what you must unlearn. This is normal, as new versions of COBOL have traditionally dropped some features and modified others. This chapter is intended to serve as a periodic reference on these features for you, and to serve as a first-time tutorial on the differences between COBOL II and its predecessor, OS/VS COBOL.

For purposes of readability, the terms *components* or *elements* are used throughout this book when referring to a collection of terms that form the syntax of COBOL programs. This includes, but is not limited to, paragraphs, clauses, statements, sections, divisions, and data description entries. The term, *feature*, will normally be used to describe a capability of COBOL, which would also include any components that implement that feature. For example, Report Writer is a feature, but GENERATE is a component of Report Writer.

To assist you, this chapter is organized in decreasing order of importance from a maintenance or conversion perspective, covering first the elements that are no longer available, followed by the elements that have been modified, followed by elements that are new to the language. Determining whether a feature was dropped, modified, or new wasn't always obvious and was subject to my interpretation. You may feel, after reading the chapter, that some features I listed as modified were, indeed, sufficiently changed to be classified as new.

Overall, most changes reflected here are because COBOL is evolving into a cleaner, simpler language. The trend is to

- Remove elements that belong elsewhere within the software inventory (such as the Communications feature).
- Remove features that were hardware or vendor dependent (such as ISAM or CLOSE WITH DISP).

- Eliminate overlapping elements (e.g., EXAMINE and TRANSFORM).
- Remove requirements that have outlived their intent (such as SEG-MENT-LIMIT and LABEL RECORDS ARE STANDARD).
- Remove requirements for elements where a general default is sufficient (such as SOURCE-COMPUTER).
- Provide a debugging language that is separate from the source language (e.g., READY TRACE is removed).
- Provide new facilities to improve program-to-program communications and to use memory more effectively.
- Provide new facilities to give the programmer more control of processes and more opportunities to use structured techniques.

With practice, you will soon find that your programs use fewer lines of code and are easier to read.

How to read the syntax charts.

Throughout this book, and in IBM books as well, you will encounter a new format to represent COBOL syntax. The format is simpler than earlier versions, but let me explain briefly. Below is the syntax for minimum items for the IDENTIFICA-TION DIVISION. The basic rules are

- Entries appearing on a top line are mandatory.
- Items appearing beneath a line are optional for the above line.
- Entries appearing beneath another entry are alternatives.
- New elements will be shown in **BOLD**.
- The symbol to continue to the next line is shown by "—>".
- The end of a statement is shown by "—><".

In the example on the first line the format is indicating that IDENTIFICA-TION DIVISION is mandatory, but since there is an element beneath it, that element may be used instead.

On the second line, PROGRAM-ID and paragraph-name are mandatory and may be followed, optionally, by either COMMON or INITIAL or both.

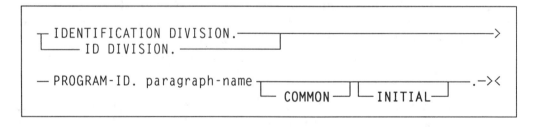

Figure 2.1. Example of COBOL syntax chart.

If you compare the charts in this book with those in IBM reference manuals, you will find that IBM's are more complete and identify all options. The ones used in this book are subsets intended to highlight new features. Options rarely used and those that haven't changed may not appear. These charts are usually all you will need if you are already comfortable with the basics of COBOL syntax.

2.1. OS/VS COBOL FEATURES THAT WERE DROPPED IN COBOL II

This section lists the most visible (most commonly used) elements of OS/VS COBOL that are not in COBOL II. The dropped elements were either ANSI 1968 components or were early IBM extensions of COBOL. If your shop used ANSI 74 COBOL, you should have few problems in a move to COBOL II. If you are unfamiliar with any particular element, so much the better, because that means you won't need to unlearn that element. Most, if not all, of the elements in this section may be converted to their COBOL II equivalent (if one exists) by using conversion software on the market. Your technical support staff can assist you.

2.1.1. Report Writer

Many shops didn't discover Report Writer until the 1980s, although it has been in use at some shops since the 1960s. Report Writer is still a module in the full ANSI 1985 standard (although an optional module), and IBM chose not to incorporate it into COBOL II.

When COBOL II was introduced, there was no choice: you had to abandon use of Report Writer. Since then, IBM has developed a Report Writer preprocessor that converts Report Writer code into equivalent COBOL II code, allowing a shop to use the preprocessor either 1) on a one-time basis to convert existing applications, or 2) on a routine basis, converting programs with Report Writer prior to each compile. The choice here is not easy or simple. Consider:

1. If a shop does a one-time conversion, the shop is free from the Report Writer issue, but loses the productivity feature that caused the shop to use it initially.
2. If a shop continues using Report Writer, the preprocessor increases the cost of each compile, the generated COBOL code does not match what the programmer wrote and may be more difficult to debug, and when report output is incorrect, the problem may be in one of three places: the compiler, the preprocessor, or the program logic.

Whether Report Writer should be used at your shop, then, is something I can't tell you. It is not part of COBOL II, but you can continue to code Report Writer if your shop uses the preprocessor. Neither choice is perfect.

Report Writer

Communications

ISAM & BDAM

Segmentation

Macro-level CICS

EXAMINE & TRANSFORM

READY/RESET TRACE, EXHIBIT, USE FOR DEBUGGING

CURRENT-DATE & TIME-OF-DAY

NOTE & REMARKS

ON (the statement, not the clause within statements)

WRITE AFTER POSITIONING

STATE & FLOW Compile options

OPEN & CLOSE obsolete options

Figure 2.2. Major OS/VS COBOL components absent in COBOL II.

2.1.2. ISAM and BDAM

If you use ISAM or BDAM, you need to convert such files to an equivalent VSAM format before using COBOL II. While conversion software may address all, or most, of the COBOL changes, the files must be separately converted.

2.1.3. Communications Feature

This feature, which required a CD entry and used SEND, RECEIVE, ENABLE, and DISABLE statements, has been removed, and no equivalent feature exists. This was a feature that allowed COBOL programs to interact with a user-written TCAM program. Most likely, your shop uses other software for sending and receiving messages, such as CICS or IMS/DC, anyway.

2.1.4 Segmentation Feature

While this is no longer supported, any such references are treated as comments. With virtual storage, the need for segmenting COBOL programs is considered obsolete.

2.1.5. Macro-level CICS

If you have CICS programs at the macro level, they need to be converted to CICS command level before using COBOL II. There are some conversion programs on the market that address this conversion issue.

2.1.6. EXAMINE and TRANSFORM

EXAMINE and TRANSFORM have been eliminated in favor of INSPECT. OS/VS COBOL supported all three verbs.

2.1.7. READY/RESET TRACE, EXHIBIT and USE FOR DEBUGGING

COBOL II is evolving to a point where no debugging facilities will exist in the code proper. At this writing, READY TRACE and RESET TRACE are obsolete. USE FOR DEBUGGING is still supported, but it will be removed from the next revision of the ANSI standard, so I don't encourage its use. For debugging assistance, IBM provides the COBOL debugging facility (see Chapter 4, Debugging Techniques). If READY TRACE or RESET TRACE appear within a COBOL II program, they are ignored. The EXHIBIT statement will cause a compile error.

2.1.8. CURRENT-DATE and TIME-OF-DAY

Removing CURRENT-DATE and TIME-OF-DAY is part of COBOL's evolution toward using procedural elements to accomplish objectives, rather than relying on special registers. OS/VS COBOL supported both ANSI 68 and ANSI 74 facilities to access date and time. These ANSI 68 statements are not allowed:

```
MOVE CURRENT-DATE TO data-name
MOVE TIME-OF-DAY TO data-name
```

Whereas these ANSI 74 statements work in OS/VS COBOL and in COBOL II:

```
ACCEPT data-name FROM DATE     (implicit PIC is 9(6))
ACCEPT data-name FROM TIME     (implicit PIC is 9(8))
```

The PIC definitions are *changed* from ANSI 68. In ANSI 68, CURRENT-DATE was X(8), for MM/DD/YY (slashes were included) and TIME-OF-DAY was X(6), for HHMMSS. In COBOL II, DATE is 9(6) for YYMMDD (different order and no slashes), and TIME is 9(8) for HHMMSShh (for hours, minutes, seconds, and hundredths of seconds).

For more information on additional options of ACCEPT, see the next section of this chapter.

2.1.9. NOTE and REMARKS

Neither of these is listed in the IBM OS/VS COBOL Reference Manual, but both were acceptable. Use the * in column 7, instead.

2.1.10. ON Statement

This is part of the debugging extensions IBM provided with OS/VS COBOL. You possibly have never used it. This is *not* a reference to ON clauses, such as ON SIZE ERROR, which continue to be valid.

2.1.11. WRITE AFTER POSITIONING Statement

This statement was a carryover from pre-OS/VS COBOL compilers. It is replaced by WRITE AFTER ADVANCING.

2.1.12. STATE and FLOW Compile Options

While not COBOL elements, these two debug options were popular in some shops and unknown in others. Their functions are available in the new COBTEST debug facility.

2.1.13. OPEN and CLOSE Obsolete Options

Those optional clauses that were hardware dependent, the LEAVE, REREAD, and DISP options for the OPEN statement, and CLOSE WITH DISP and CLOSE WITH POSITIONING are no longer valid. In both cases, other options have been available for several years, so I don't anticipate these changes will cause application problems. Also, these OPEN and CLOSE options, as were many of the changes listed in this section, were *not* specified as being part of OS/VS COBOL proper, but they were documented in the appendix as IBM extensions.

As I mentioned earlier, the best way to evaluate the implication of the dropped features is to compile one or more of your programs. Also, specifying the LANGLVL(2) and MIGR options when compiling with OS/VS COBOL will help sensitize you to incompatible elements.

2.2. MODIFIED COBOL COMPONENTS

This section requires a careful reading because the fundamental syntax of these components existed in OS/VS COBOL. Features identified in the prior section (e.g., Report Writer) will not be repeated here.

Only those options and syntax that are sufficiently different to warrant your interest will be presented. The examples shown in this section may be incomplete, not displaying all options of a particular clause. The purpose for this approach is to focus on what has changed without requiring you to cope with the full syntax of COBOL. (Note: A listing of COBOL II statements and their syntax is in Chapter 7, Summaries, Tables, and References). I have classified entries in this section as "modified COBOL components," rather than as "new COBOL components" because the features are made available using clauses or statements with which you are probably already familiar.

2.2.1. IDENTIFICATION DIVISION

The major change in the IDENTIFICATION DIVISION is that it now allows you to specify how the program will participate within a run unit. This is accomplished by the PROGRAM-ID clause. No other entries are required, nor should they be used.

Required entries (those that must always be present): IDENTIFICATION DIVISION or ID DIVISION, PROGRAM-ID.

Obsolete, treated as comments: All other entries, including AUTHOR, INSTALLATION, DATE-WRITTEN, DATE-COMPILED, and SECURITY.

Obsolete and not allowed: REMARKS.

Enhanced elements (descriptions follow this list): PROGRAM-ID.

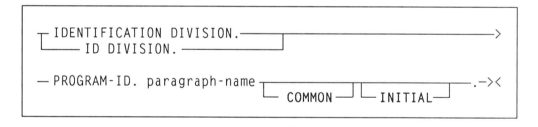

Figure 2.3. IDENTIFICATION DIVISION requirements.

PROGRAM-ID modifications.

The new features of PROGRAM-ID are intended to provide additional features for multi-module structures, where one program is CALLed by another. The optional clause, COMMON, specifies that the program may be accessed from any other programs sharing a nested run unit (see Chapter 3, Programming with COBOL II, for more information on module structures). Unless your shop starts using nested programs, you won't have use for this feature.

The clause, INITIAL, specifies that the program is to be in its initial state every time it is CALLed. Even without INITIAL coded, a program is in its initial state the first time it is CALLed and on the first CALL following a CANCEL statement. Use of INITIAL should be reserved for those structures where a subprogram does not reinitialize variables, does not maintain any information from one CALL to the next, and the program logic always assumes that it will be CALLED only once. Your use of INITIAL will be dependent on how your shop writes and mixes subprograms.

Recommendation for using IDENTIFICATION DIVISION features.

Instead of using the obsolete elements, use the COBOL comment facility (an * in column 7) to provide any needed documentation. The date the program was compiled appears on source listings and is imbedded within the object program. Be careful not to misinterpret COBOL II syntax messages (this applies to all divisions, not just the IDENTIFICATION DIVISION entries). For example, consider this error from a compile listing (notice how COBOL II embeds the error message in the source listing—a nice improvement):

```
        PROGRAM-ID.
            DKA101BN.
        AUTHOR.
==> IGYDS1128-W "AUTHOR" PARAGRAPH COMMENTARY WAS FOUND IN AREA "A".
            PROCESSED AS IF FOUND IN AREA "B".
            DAVID S. KIRK.
        REMARKS.
            THIS SUBPROGRAM CALCULATES VACATION DAYS.
```

It appears that AUTHOR is incorrect, yet no error appears for using REMARKS. This appears to contradict my previous statements. In fact, because COBOL II ignores obsolete elements, the compiler saw REMARKS in column 8 and assumed it was part of the AUTHOR paragraph. Errors such as this can be confusing.

2.2.2. ENVIRONMENT DIVISION

The major change of the ENVIRONMENT DIVISION is that you may now get full VSAM status code feedback for your VSAM files. This is provided by the FILE STATUS clause. Other notable changes are a continuing reduction of required and optional clauses. In fact, there are now many situations where this division serves no purpose and need not be coded.

Required entries (those that must always be present): None. (This would be true if all defaults were acceptable and there were no files to SELECT.)

Obsolete, treated as comments: MEMORY SIZE, SEGMENT LIMIT, and MULTIPLE FILE TAPE.

Obsolete and not allowed: ACTUAL KEY, NOMINAL KEY, TRACK-AREA, TRACK-LIMIT, PROCESSING MODE.

Optional entries (ignored): ORGANIZATION IS in SELECT statement.

Enhanced elements (descriptions follow this list): FILE STATUS.

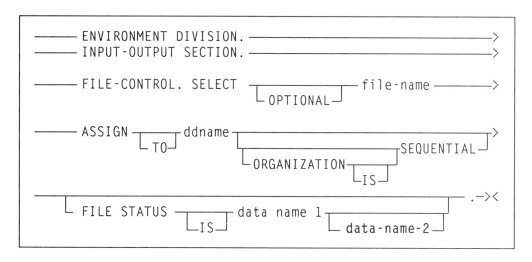

Figure 2.4. Example of FILE STATUS for sequential file (all SELECT options not shown).

Use of expanded FILE STATUS codes for VSAM.

From the example in figure 2.4, the "data-name-1" entry is the normal FILE STATUS field from OS/VS COBOL. The new entry is "data-name-2," which must be defined in the WORKING-STORAGE SECTION (or the LINKAGE SEC-TION, if appropriate) as a six-byte group item. The group item must contain three subordinate entries, each a half-word binary entry. An example:

```
01 VSAM-STATUS-CODE.
    05  VSAM-RETURN-CODE      PIC S99  BINARY.
    05  VSAM-FUNCTION-CODE    PIC S99  BINARY.
    05  VSAM-FEEDBACK-CODE    PIC S99  BINARY.
```

This new feature allows a COBOL program to access the status for a variety of VSAM processes. The returned codes are from Access Method Services. For more information on the content and use of these fields, see the appropriate VSAM Macro Instruction Reference manual (chapter 9, Related Publications). (Note: Notice the use of the word *BINARY* in the example. COBOL II allows programs to use BINARY in place of COMP, and PACKED-DECIMAL in place of COMP-3 if desired. COMP and COMP-3 still work fine.)

Recommendation for using ENVIRONMENT DIVISION features.

The ENVIRONMENT DIVISION contains many optional entries that are rarely used. If you use VSAM files, you already know what options are necessary and where the new VSAM status codes will help your applications. From programs I've seen or worked on, the example in figure 2.4 exhibits the complete syntax that is adequate for more than 90% of programs. If your application uses the default collating sequence (most do) and has no special names to define (few do), then you need to define the ENVIRONMENT DIVISION *only* when there are files to process.

2.2.3. DATA DIVISION.

Most of the big changes in the DATA DIVISION were identified earlier in Section 2.1 (COBOL Features Dropped). Other changes reflect an on-going process of cleaning up the COBOL language, removing the requirement for clauses that are either irrelevant or self-evident. For example, labels for a file are handled via MVS and JCL, so the LABEL RECORDS clause is irrelevant. The 01-level that follows an FD is always identified with the FD, so the DATA RECORD clause is also irrelevant. Since FILLER always means a data description with no name, the word FILLER only documented what would be self-evident if FILLER were omitted. Now it can be.

These changes don't require that you modify existing programs, but they do allow you to code less and achieve the same results.

Required entries (those that must always be present): None. (Having no entries would be rare.)

Obsolete, treated as comments: LABEL RECORDS clause in FD (illegal in SD), DATA RECORD clause, and VALUE OF clause (in FD).

Obsolete and not allowed (see Section 2.1): Report Writer statements, Communications statements, ISAM & BDAM statements.

Optional entries (Described below): FILLER.

The FILLER entry.

This is an easy and optional change that improves readability of a program. The word *FILLER*, used to define data descriptions with no name, may be replaced by spaces. For years, it was a meaningless entry in COBOL. Now, it is no longer needed. Consider the example in figure 2.5. The second entry for the record is easier to read.

```
With FILLER:


01 WS1-RECORD-AREA.
   05  WS1-NAME            PIC X(20).
   05  FILLER              PIC X.
   05  WS1-ADDRESS         PIC X(25).
   05  FILLER              PIC XX.
   05  WS1-JOB-CODE        PIC X.
   05  FILLER              PIC X(30).

Without FILLER:


01 WS1-RECORD-AREA.
   05  WS1-NAME            PIC X(20).
   05                      PIC X.
   05  WS1-ADDRESS         PIC X(25).
   05                      PIC XX.
   05  WS1-JOB-CODE        PIC X.
   05                      PIC X(30).
```

Figure 2.5. Example with and without FILLER.

Enhanced elements (descriptions follow this list): USAGE clause, VALUE clause, OCCURS DEPENDING ON, and COPY statement.

Modifications to the USAGE clause.

One of the changes to USAGE was mentioned earlier: the ability to use BINARY instead of COMP, and PACKED-DECIMAL instead of COMP-3. This is nice, but old habits die hard. In developing example programs for this book, I continued to use COMP and COMP-3, and I plan to continue using them since they require fewer keystrokes.

The addition of POINTER, however, opens up new doors that will be explored more in the next chapter. POINTER provides to COBOL programs the facility to treat addresses of data as data, a technique that was previously available only to assembler programmers.

Modifications to the VALUE clause.

The extension to VALUE that will be most appreciated is that it may now be used in OCCURS statements. In OS/VS COBOL, a table could not be defined and initialized in the DATA DIVISION, requiring either a REDEFINES entry or a PERFORM VARYING statement in the PROCEDURE DIVISION. Consider

In OS/VS COBOL

```
01   JOB-CODE-TABLE.
     05   JOB-CODE-ENTRIES OCCURS 8 TIMES INDEXED BY JOB-CODE.
          10   JOB-TITLE      PIC X(8).
          10   JOB-MAX-SAL    PIC S9(5)V99.
          10  JOB-MIN-SAL     PIC S9(5)V99.
                .
                .

     PERFORM 0100-INIT-TABLE VARYING JOB-CODE FROM 1 BY 1 UNTIL
         JOB-CODE > 8.
                .
                .

0100-INIT-TABLE.
     MOVE SPACES TO JOB-TITLE (JOB-CODE)
     MOVE ZEROS TO JOB-MAX-SAL (JOB-CODE)
                   JOB-MIN-SAL (JOB-CODE).
```

In COBOL II

```
01   JOB-CODE-TABLE.
     05   JOB-CODE-ENTRIES OCCURS 8 TIMES INDEXED BY JOB-CODE.
          10  JOB-TITLE      PIC X(8) VALUE SPACES.
          10  JOB-MAX-SAL    PIC S9(5)V99 VALUE ZERO.
          10  JOB-MIN-SAL    PIC S9(5)V99 VALUE ZERO.
                .
                .
```

Techniques such as this can save procedural complexity and reduce programming efforts. Later on, you will see a new statement, INITIALIZE, that can replace the above PERFORM logic when needed in a program.

Another option in the VALUE clause is that you may now code in hexadecimal, just as assembler programmers do (Note: The hexadecimal literal may now be used where other alphanumeric literals are valid, not just in the VALUE clause). The literal must be preceded by *X* and the data must follow hexadecimal conventions (a multiple of 2 bytes, with values of 0 through 9 and A through F). Nice trick, but should you use this feature? One of the strengths of COBOL is its avoidance of machine dependencies. There are several situations, primarily between COBOL and non-COBOL modules, where hex literals may be effective, but I encourage you to be c-a-r-e-f-u-l. Here is an example of possible use:

```
05  WS5-PROCESS-SWITCH  PIC  X  VALUE X'01'.
    88  BIT-0-SET            VALUE X'80'.
    88  BIT-0-1-SET          VALUE X'C0'.
    88  BIT-0-2-SET          VALUE X'A0'.
    88  BIT-0-3-SET          VALUE X'90'.
    88  BIT-0-4-SET          VALUE X'88'.
    88  BIT-0-5-SET          VALUE X'84'.
         .
         .
```

This initializes the field to a binary value of 1 and provides 88-level entries to allow setting or testing of various bit combinations. This technique might be helpful if your system interacts with assembler programs that use one byte for multiple switches. This does *not* mean you can change individual bits. The down side of hex values is that it is easy to make mistakes with them and difficult to figure them out. For more information on bits and hexadecimal, see Chapter 7.

The new NULL option can't be explained without first laying some groundwork. NULL is related to POINTER. I'll show NULL and POINTER to you later.

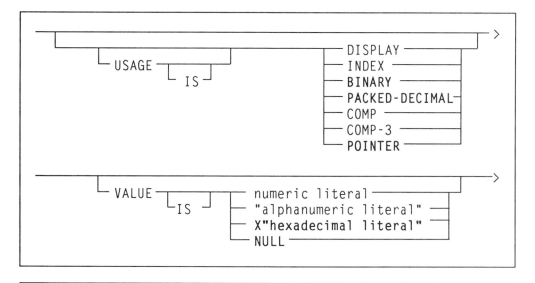

Figure 2.6. Example of USAGE and VALUE clauses (all options not shown).

The modifications to OCCURS DEPENDING ON.

With COBOL II, you may now have variable length data subordinate to variable length data, as demonstrated in figure 2.7. Notice that the control fields (named here VALUE-A and VALUE-B) are in the fixed portion of the record and are not allowed to be in the variable portion. While this facility is now available, do you want to define files this way? The strong move towards data normalization has significantly reduced the number of variable length records and I applaud the change.

```
01   RECORD-NAME.
     05   1ST-GROUP-NAME.
          10   VALUE-A          PIC S9     COMP.
          10   VALUE-B          PIC S9     COMP.
     05   2ND-GROUP-NAME OCCURS 1 TO 10 TIMES
          DEPENDING ON VALUE-A.
          10   FIELD-C          PIC XX.
          10   FIELD-D  OCCURS 1 TO 30 TIMES
               DEPENDING ON VALUE-B.
               15 FIELD-E       PIC S9(5) COMP-3.
               15 FIELD-F       PIC XXX.
```

Figure 2.7. Example of nested OCCURS DEPENDING ON.

The COPY statement.

OS/VS COBOL supported both the ANSI 1974 standard and the IBM extension to the ANSI 1968 standard. COBOL II supports the ANSI 1974 and the ANSI 1985 standard. The format of the COPY statement that met the ANSI 1968 standard is no longer allowed. That format was

```
01 data-name COPY membername.
```

whereby data-name replaced the associated data-name from the copy member. See the example in figure 2.8. COPY statements in OS/VS COBOL that follow the ANSI 1974 standard should work satisfactorily.

An additional change in COBOL II is that you may have COPY statements imbedded within other COPY statements. This nesting was not allowed in OS/VS COBOL. In writing this, my first feeling was "Why would anyone want to do this? Programming is hard enough without adding this complexity." I encourage you to not use it unless you have a very specific need for it.

Recommendation for using DATA DIVISION features.

Assuming you aren't using Report Writer or other no-no's, these changes in the DATA DIVISION do not require that you change the way you code COBOL programs (Exception: The COPY statement example I mentioned). Also, making any of these changes prevents your program from compiling with OS/VS COBOL again.

```
COPYbook member EMPREC:

01  EMP-REC.
    05    EMP-NAME       PIC X(30).
    05    EMP-JOB-CODE  PIC X.
```

COPY statement extension in OS/VS COBOL:

```
01  WORK-REC  COPY  EMPREC.
```

Generated source code with OS/VS COBOL:

```
01  WORK-REC.
    05    EMP-NAME       PIC X(30).
    05    EMP-JOB-CODE  PIC X.
```

Generated source code with COBOL II (causes syntax error):

```
01  WORK-REC
01  EMP-REC.
    05  EMP-NAME         PIC X(30).
    05  EMP-JOB-CODE   PIC X.
```

Example of allowable format:

```
COPY EMPREC.
```

Figure 2.8. COPY format that is no longer allowed.

I recommend you take advantage of the opportunity to omit FILLER and the opportunity to leave obsolete statements out of your FDs and SDs. Anytime you can stop coding obsolete statements, the program becomes cleaner. Also, if you continue coding LABEL RECORDS ARE STANDARD and DATA RECORD IS, all COBOL II will do with the statements is check if you spelled them correctly. If you did, it ignores them. If you didn't, you will get a syntax error. Is that any way to play the odds? So stop it, already.

2.2.4. PROCEDURE DIVISION.

Changes to existing statements in the PROCEDURE DIVISION add several new options to your tool kit. Many of the changes qualify as all new. They are included here because they are extensions to existing statements. The issues that will require you to change any entries in this division were highlighted earlier in Section 2.1 of this chapter (OS/VS Features That Were Dropped).

Required entries (those that must always be present): None. (This would be true for a program within a run unit that consisted of no procedural code. I'll show you an example in Chapter 3.)

Obsolete, treated as comments: Not applicable in PROCEDURE DIVISION.

Obsolete and not allowed (see section A, above): References to CURRENT-DATE and TIME-OF-DAY, EXAMINE, EXHIBIT, READY/RESET TRACE, TRANSFORM, Report Writer statements, Communications statements, ISAM and BDAM statements, NOTE (use * in column 7, instead), ON statement (was used primarily for debugging), and OPEN and CLOSE obsolete options.

Enhanced elements: Scope Terminators, CALL, PERFORM, READ and RETURN, SET, SORT, and NOT ON SIZE ERROR and NOT INVALID KEY.

Scope terminators.

Scope terminators are the easiest of COBOL II's new PROCEDURE DIVISION enhancements to start using. Until now, the scope of a conditional statement extended for the duration of a sentence (i.e., the scope was terminated by a period). That sometimes caused clumsy coding practices. Consider the following from OS/VS COBOL:

```
2100-PRODUCE-REPORT.
    PERFORM 2300-READ-RECORD
    IF NOT END-OF-FILE
        IF VALID-CONTROL-BREAK
            PERFORM 2400-WRITE-SUBTOTALS.
    IF NOT END-OF-FILE
        PERFORM 2500-ASSEMBLE-DETAIL-LINE
        PERFORM 2600-WRITE-DETAIL.
```

While you may have done that code differently, this technique is not unusual and is an example where a period was necessary to end the scope of the nested IF statement. Because there were additional processes dependent on the first IF statement, that statement had to be repeated. A *scope terminator* is a new COBOL II element that allows you to define the end of a conditional statement's scope without the need for a period. The syntax is straightforward: the letters *END-*, followed by the name of the affected verb. For example:

END-IF is the scope terminator for the IF statement
END-COMPUTE is the scope terminator for the COMPUTE statement

(remember, with an ON SIZE ERROR clause, any arithmetic statement can be conditional)
END-READ is the scope terminator for a READ statement.

Any statement that has conditional elements may use a scope terminator where a period is not needed (and my philosophy is *never* to code anything that is not needed—more on this in the chapter on program design, Chapter 5). There is an exception to the first sentence in this paragraph, as a new format for PERFORM has a mandatory scope terminator, yet it is NOT conditional. More on that a bit further on when new PERFORM features are addressed. For now, let's redo that prior example:

```
2100-PRODUCE-REPORT.
    PERFORM 2300-READ-RECORD
    IF NOT END-OF-FILE
        IF VALID-CONTROL-BREAK
            PERFORM 2400-WRITE-SUBTOTALS
        END-IF
        PERFORM 2500-ASSEMBLE-DETAIL-LINE
        PERFORM 2600-WRITE-DETAIL.
```

Notice how the logic is clearer. I finished the example with a period as it is the end of the paragraph, although an END-IF could have been coded if the logic flow were to continue. My preference is to code scope terminators every time I code a conditional statement and to avoid using periods except at the end of paragraphs. Scope terminators make the structure clear and, as I never use unnecessary periods, I never have to worry about an improperly placed one.

Changes to the CALL statement.

The opportunities that come with the new features in the CALL statement are not immediately apparent. The new features are extensions of, and do not conflict with, CALL statements from OS/VS COBOL (Exception: In OS/VS COBOL, you were allowed to have a paragraph-name as an identifier following USING. COBOL II does *not* allow that). There are several changes, each of which needs clarification. Let's look at each option, keeping in mind that they can be combined within the same CALL statement.

Use of BY REFERENCE or BY CONTENT in CALL statement. This new option lets you control whether your program will let a subprogram have access to the data in your program or only the value of the data in your program. Confusing? Remember, in OS/VS COBOL, a subprogram that accessed a passed parameter list (CALL USING . . .) was accessing the data directly within the CALLing program. That meant the subprogram could modify the data, even if you didn't want it modified. Now, by specifying BY CONTENT when you CALL

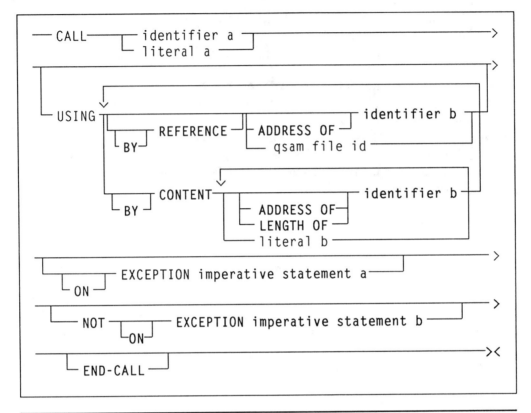

Figure 2.9. CALL Syntax in COBOL II.

a subprogram, the subprogram receives what appears to be your data area, but it is actually a separate area. If the subprogram changes it, your program's data area is not affected. If you code neither of these options, BY REFERENCE is assumed, as that is compatible with OS/VS COBOL coding conventions.

Use of LENGTH OF clause in CALL statement. Did you ever want to pass data to a subprogram, but the length of the passed data varied? Now you can also pass the length of the data, so the subprogram can respond according to your intent. This is useful whenever variable data must be exchanged between programs. Errors can still occur, of course, if the program logic is incorrect, but now the information is available so such a program can be cleanly constructed. The LENGTH OF clause is not restricted to the CALL statement, as it is a new special register provided by COBOL II. The receiving program must have an identifier defined in the LINKAGE SECTION with PIC S9(9) COMP. Here is an example of that technique:

```
CALL 'SUB1'    USING WS3-WORK-REC
               BY CONTENT LENGTH OF WS3-WORK-REC
```

The subprogram, SUB1, would need the following:

```
LINKAGE SECTION.
01  LS1-WORK-REC.
   .
   .

01  LS2-LENGTH     PIC S9(9)  COMP.
PROCEDURE DIVISION USING LS1-WORK-REC LS2-LENGTH.
```

Use of ADDRESS OF clause in CALL statement. This will be covered later, along with POINTER data elements. The ADDRESS OF clause is not restricted to the CALL statement, as it is a new special register provided by COBOL II.

Use of ON EXCEPTION and NOT ON EXCEPTION in CALL statement. These are conditional expressions that receive control depending on whether the subprogram was accessed by your CALL statement. They apply only to dynamic CALLs. For example, your program periodically CALLs a large subprogram dynamically, but the REGION may be of insufficient size. You might code

```
CALL LARGE-PROG USING data-name
    ON EXCEPTION
        DISPLAY 'Program not loaded, increase REGION'
        MOVE 16 TO RETURN-CODE
        STOP RUN
END-CALL
```

(OS/VS COBOL had an option, ON OVERFLOW, that was equivalent to ON EXCEPTION. COBOL II supports that syntax, also.)

Changes to the PERFORM statement.

The PERFORM statement has always been one of my favorites and now it has even more flexibility, although the new features are a mixed blessing. First, I want to tell you about the new features, and then I'll get back to that point about a mixed blessing.

PERFORM now has two major new syntax structures that can be useful if you do structured programming. The first is full implementation of the DO-UNTIL format. (Refresher: a DO-UNTIL statement executes the code before testing the condition; a DO-WHILE tests the condition prior to executing the code.) Until now, the PERFORM UNTIL (a DO-WHILE statement) had to serve both needs. Now you can specify the PERFORM UNTIL statement adding WITH TEST AFTER to it and it becomes a DO-UNTIL format. (Note: If not coded on a PERFORM UNTIL statement, WITH TEST BEFORE is assumed for compatibility with existing code.)

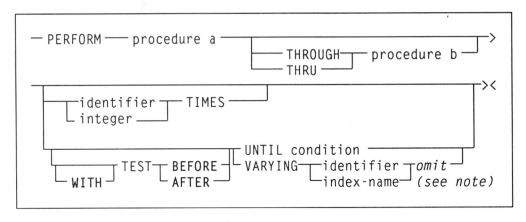

Figure 2.10. Basic PERFORM syntax. (Note: For clarity of new features, the syntax following VARYING is omitted from the diagram where omit appears, including FROM, BY, UNTIL, and AFTER.)

For me, the big question was "When would I ever need the WITH TEST AFTER clause?" I never found a satisfactory answer, but I can offer an example. WITH TEST AFTER has a potential advantage when you are using the VARYING clause to load a table and want the index-data-item to reflect the number of entries in the table, not one greater than the number in the table. Consider these two options:

```
PERFORM 3300-LOAD-PREMIUM-TABLE VARYING PREM-INDEX FROM 1 BY
   1 UNTIL END-OF-FILE

PERFORM 3300-LOAD-PREMIUM-TABLE WITH TEST AFTER VARYING
   PREM-INDEX FROM 1 BY 1 UNTIL END-OF-FILE
```

Assuming there were 1,000 premium entries to be loaded to the table, the contents of PREM-INDEX after the first statement would refer to a 1,001st entry, whereas the contents of PREM-INDEX in the second example would reflect that the table had 1,000 entries, not 1,001. Assuming the END-OF-FILE condition-name is not already set at the time either statement is executed, the choice becomes one of style.

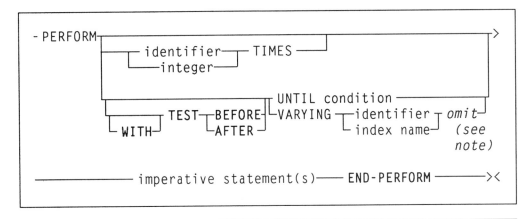

Figure 2.11. Inline PERFORM syntax. (Note: For clarity of new
features, the syntax following VARYING is omitted from
the diagram, including FROM, BY, UNTIL, and AFTER.
This is where omit appears.)

The second option is the inline PERFORM, with all PERFORMed code
following the PERFORM statement. From the syntax in figure 2.11, a sample
inline PERFORM might be

```
PERFORM VARYING STATE-INDEX FROM 1 BY ONE UNTIL END-OF-FILE
    PERFORM 2100-READ-RECORD
    IF NOT END-OF-FILE
        MOVE STATE-DATA TO STATE-TABLE (STATE-INDEX)
    END-IF
END-PERFORM
```

Earlier, I mentioned that the PERFORM verb was an exception to my
statement about using scope terminators on conditional statements. The END-
PERFORM statement is the *only* scope terminator that applies to a
nonconditional statement. Also, it must be coded at the end of all inline
PERFORMs.

In my first paragraph on these PERFORM enhancements, I mentioned a
mixed blessing. Although I admit it is a matter of style, I prefer not to use either
statement. Why? While teaching programmers I learned that most programmers
do best when they have a few simple tools. The PERFORM WITH TEST AFTER
is so subtle in its difference that many novice programmers may not recognize
what you are doing with the code. The inline PERFORM is nice in concept, but it
can increase the density of paragraphs and reduce readability, especially when
the code is to be maintained later by less experienced programmers.

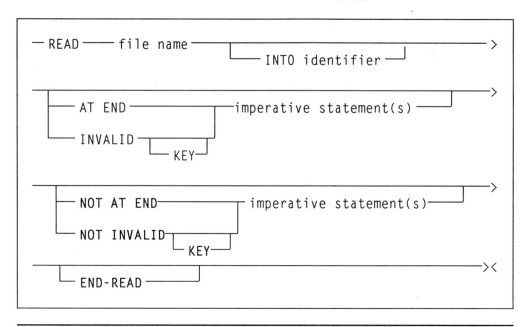

Figure 2.12. Basic READ syntax. For clarity, I omitted little used options, such as NEXT RECORD. (Note: AT END/NOT AT END *cannot* be intermixed with INVALID KEY/NOT INVALID KEY.)

Changes to READ and RETURN statements.

The changes to these two statements are so obvious and easy that one might wonder why these enhancements weren't done years ago. Anyway, they provide some interesting program structure opportunities. (Example 8.2, in Chapter 8, Sample Programs, is one.) By adding a NOT AT END clause, much of the clumsiness of READs and RETURNs is eliminated.

In OS/VS COBOL, I typically had a paragraph similar to this:

```
2300-READ-PAYROLL.
    READ FD3-PAYROLL-FILE
      AT END
        MOVE 'Y' TO FD3-EOF-SWITCH.
    IF FD3-EOF-SWITCH = 'N'
        ADD 1 TO FD3-RECORD-COUNT.
```

Now I can use the following replacement:

```
2300-READ-PAYROLL.
    READ FD3-PAYROLL-FILE
      AT END
        MOVE 'Y' TO FD3-EOF-SWITCH
      NOT AT END
        ADD 1 TO FD3-RECORD-COUNT
    END-READ.
```

I think you will agree that the COBOL II approach is much cleaner. (Being the end of the paragraph, the END-READ wasn't required. I use it for clarity.) This feature also provides the opportunity to change a typical programming style that is common in structured programming.

Typical PERFORMed READ, followed by test for end of file:

```
PERFORM 2300-READ-PAYROLL
IF FD3-EOF-SWITCH = 'N'
    imperative statements to process data
    .
    .
```

Opportunity for a different approach with COBOL II:

```
READ FD3-PAYROLL-FILE
  AT END
    MOVE 'Y' TO FD3-EOF-SWITCH
  NOT AT END
    imperative statements to process data
    .
    .
```

It works, but I suggest you use the approach carefully. I prefer decomposition of a program to keep I/O statements in separate paragraphs. While the READ statement fits well in the above example, it will tempt a maintenance programmer to add another READ statement in the future. Your shop may have standards on that, too.

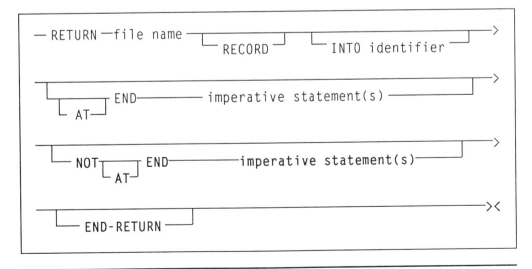

Figure 2.13. RETURN syntax.

SET enhancements.

Many programmers have never used this statement. Lack of use is indicative of a lack of experience with managing indexes in programs (more on that in Chapter 3, Programming with COBOL II). For now, let's look at a new capability. The SET statement may now reference 88-level condition names. Demonstrating is easier than explaining.

```
01   WS3-EMPL-DATA.
     05   EMPL-NAME            PIC X(30).
     05   EMPL-JOB-CODE        PIC X.
          88   PROGRAMMER      VALUE '1'.
          88   ANALYST         VALUE '2'.
          88   MANAGER         VALUE '3'.

01   FD2-PRINT-REC.
     05   FD2-EMPL-NAME        PIC X(30).
     05   JOB-TITLE            PIC X(10).
          88   PROGRAMMER-TITLE    VALUE 'PROGRAMMER'.
          88   ANALYST-TITLE       VALUE 'ANALYST'.
          88   MANAGER-TITLE       VALUE 'MANAGER'.
          88   UNKNOWN-TITLE       VALUE '**********'.
```

Where the application is to interrogate EMPL-JOB-CODE and move the appropriate value to JOB-TITLE, in OS/VS COBOL, you might code:

```
IF PROGRAMMER
    MOVE 'PROGRAMMER' TO JOB-TITLE
ELSE
    IF ANALYST
        MOVE 'ANALYST' TO JOB-TITLE
    ELSE
        IF MANAGER
            MOVE 'MANAGER' TO JOB-TITLE
        ELSE
            MOVE '**********' TO JOB-TITLE
```

In COBOL II, you can code this:

```
IF PROGRAMMER
    SET PROGRAMMER-TITLE TO TRUE
ELSE
    IF ANALYST
        SET ANALYST-TITLE TO TRUE
    ELSE
        IF MANAGER
            SET MANAGER-TITLE TO TRUE
        ELSE
            SET UNKNOWN-TITLE TO TRUE
```

As you can see, this use of SET removes literals from the PROCEDURE DIVISION and moves them where they belong, to the DATA DIVISION. Readability is improved too, as all options appear beneath the data name. When you get to the EVALUATE statement in the next section, you will discover an even cleaner way to write the above logic by using both the EVALUATE statement and the SET statement.

I haven't yet covered all the new features of the SET statement. I have more on SET in the next section, where I include it with a definition of POINTER data elements.

SORT enhancements.

People have debated with me on whether what I'm about to describe is an enhancement or not. To me, anything that makes a program cleaner is an enhancement. SORT hasn't changed, so what's the big deal? Well, SORT no longer requires that procedural logic be organized by SECTION names. That's it. Why is that important? Anytime an unnecessary coding element is removed, you have the opportunity for a cleaner structure. This is what I call a style issue. If you consider that most programmers never use SECTIONs except when they do SORT programs, there is a tendency to use both paragraphs *and* SECTIONS. This practice creates programs that are unstructured and rife with GO TOs. It is not unusual to find SORT programs where an INPUT PROCEDURE is something like this:

```
1000-INPUT SECTION.
1010-INITIALIZE.
    initialization logic
    .

    .
1030-PROCESS-DATA.
    PERFORM 1040-READ-RECORD
    IF EOF-SWITCH = 'Y'
       GO TO 1050-EXIT.
    process record...
    .

    .
    GO TO 1030-PROCESS-DATA
1040-READ-RECORD.
    input statements
    .

1050-EXIT.
    EXIT.
```

Have you seen programs such as this? Often, they occur because the requirement for a SECTION caused the programmer to think that all paragraphs had to be within the SECTION, mandating a GO TO statement. It wasn't true, but it happened a lot and I've even seen corporate standards manuals that *dictated* this technique. Removing the requirement for SECTIONs lets programmers write simpler SORTS. (See Chapter 8, Sample Programs, for an example.) (Note: later versions of OS/VS COBOL did not require SECTION names, but many programmers used older manuals and the compiler continued to issue warning messages.)

NOT ON SIZE ERROR and NOT INVALID KEY clauses.

These are straightforward. Wherever you may currently place an ON SIZE ERROR clause (e.g., ADD, SUBTRACT), you may now also, or instead of, place the NOT ON SIZE ERROR clause. Likewise, wherever you could place an INVALID KEY clause (e.g., READ, WRITE), you may now also, or instead of, place the NOT INVALID KEY clause.

Recommendation for using PROCEDURE DIVISION features.

My first recommendation is that you rethink how you do nested IF statements and start restructuring with END-IF and other scope terminators. This quickly improves your program structure. Next, I suggest using EVALUATE and the expanded features of READ and RETURN, as they also improve structure and readability. Familiarity with the new option of SET comes quickly if you already use 88-levels. To help you change your approach to SORT programs, I included an example in Chapter 8 (Sample Programs).

The extensions to CALL and PERFORM should be approached more cautiously. The CALL enhancements offer some opportunities for new systems you are developing, but make sure you're comfortable with the features before committing to a large project. As I indicated earlier, the PERFORM enhancements are powerful, but you may want to postpone using them until you have more experience with scope terminators.

2.3.   NEW COBOL COMPONENTS.

By now, you may feel that you've already read about the new features of COBOL II. New, yes, but the components described in the prior section were enhancements to existing COBOL elements. This section introduces some new features that have their own syntax. Making the decision to separate COBOL features this way was not easy. As I mentioned at the beginning of this chapter, my guiding light was to address the learning requirements of the maintenance or conversion programmer. By first learning what was dropped, followed by learning what is different, and ending by learning new features, you will be more productive more quickly than if I had glossed over differences and jumped here immediately.

While these elements are new, many benefit from using them in combination with each other or with the expanded capabilities described for current components.

2.3.1. Nested Programs/END PROGRAM Statement

I've picked nested programs first because it is an interesting concept that may take time to absorb and your shop may decide never to use this approach to application development. From previous material in this book, you have probably surmised that program structure is more flexible with COBOL II (e.g., INITIAL in PROGRAM-ID and extensions to CALL and PERFORM statements). If so, you're right on target. This feature, and those that follow, support and expand on flexibility in program structure.

First, let's get our terms straight. A *nested program* is one that is contained WITHIN another program, a concept that did not previously exist in COBOL, although PL/1 and FORTRAN have always had such capabilities. Placing a program within another program requires that a means be defined to identify the end of a program. That new COBOL element is the END PROGRAM statement. See figure 2.14 for an example.

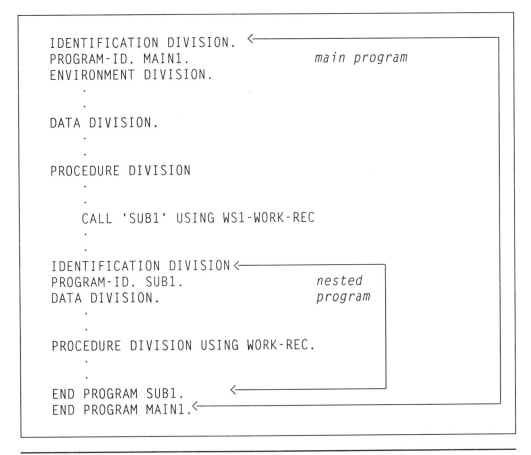

```
IDENTIFICATION DIVISION. ←
PROGRAM-ID. MAIN1.                    main program
ENVIRONMENT DIVISION.
        .
        .
DATA DIVISION.
        .
        .
PROCEDURE DIVISION
        .
        .
    CALL 'SUB1' USING WS1-WORK-REC
        .
        .
IDENTIFICATION DIVISION ←
PROGRAM-ID. SUB1.                     nested
DATA DIVISION.                        program
        .
        .
PROCEDURE DIVISION USING WORK-REC.
        .
        .
END PROGRAM SUB1.      ←
END PROGRAM MAIN1. ←
```

Figure 2.14. Sample of nested program. SUB1 is CALLed by MAIN1, yet exists within MAIN1.

In the example, MAIN1 calls SUB1. Notice how the END PROGRAM statements make clear to the compiler that SUB1 is within MAIN1. The program name in END PROGRAM must match that in the PROGRAM-ID statement or a syntax error occurs. Because SUB1 exists only within MAIN1, it has no identifier within the object module from a compile and is invisible to the Linkage Editor (i.e., SUB1 cannot be CALLed from separately compiled programs).

When used, END PROGRAM must be the last statement for a program. The statement may be used, if desired, for any program, even one that is not nested, as a means to let the compiler validate the last statement. Other terms that have meaning to nested programs are COMMON (in PROGRAM-ID) and GLOBAL (in FD and data descriptions).

You are probably wondering "Why would I ever use such a structure?" When I first learned about nested programs, that was my question too. At first, it appears to be an unwieldy structure with nothing positive about it. Actually, it is more a change in the way you build structure than in the way you write code. This is an exciting feature, one that will receive special treatment in Chapter 3 in a section titled Module Structures. For now, it is sufficient that you are aware of the concept and how the basic structure is formed. There is an example of a nested program in Chapter 8.

2.3.2. EVALUATE.

The EVALUATE statement is an extension of the IF statement and provides the CASE concept for structured programming. Many programmers attempted to implement a form of CASE in earlier versions of COBOL by using the GO TO DEPENDING ON statement. That worked with limited success, but it required many GO TO statements to support it and had other restrictions in its structure.

The EVALUATE can take one or more data elements or conditions and specify the action to take. The entries following the word EVALUATE specify *what* will be evaluated and *how many* evaluations will be made. For example:

```
EVALUATE WS1-SEX-CODE ALSO WS3-MARITAL-STATUS
```

The above statement specifies that there will be two evaluations, each against a data-name. Entries following WHEN could then specify values that might be in those fields. The number of comparisons following WHEN must match the number of entries following EVALUATE. For example:

```
EVALUATE WS1-SEX-CODE  ALSO  WS3-MARITAL-STATUS
WHEN        'F'        ALSO        'S'
```

would be a possible entry. The imperative statement(s) following that entry would be executed if BOTH conditions were true. For example:

```
EVALUATE WS1-SEX-CODE   ALSO   WS3-MARITAL-STATUS
WHEN        'F'          ALSO      'S'
                         PERFORM 3100-SINGLE-FEMALE-EMP
```

The appearance of the next WHEN entry or END-EVALUATE terminates the scope of the WHEN clause. It is easier to understand the statement by looking at one, so I refer you to the following examples. Keep your use of EVALUATE simple at first as you build on experience. You will find EVALUATE can make what would have been long IF statements much more readable and much easier to maintain.

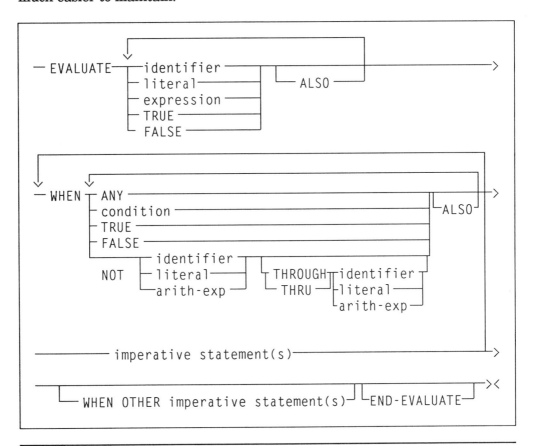

Figure 2.15. EVALUATE syntax.

Generally, the TRUE options provide more flexibility because a condition may be any valid COBOL condition (e.g., 88-levels, data-name followed by relational operator followed by literal or data-name, conditions separated by AND or OR). Although the syntax in figure 2.15 may imply that you can mix and match, you cannot. The combination of possible entries must provide three components:

1. A value (e.g., data-name, expression, or literal)
2. A value to compare to the first value
3. A condition (e.g., true or false)

For example, an 88-level-name defines a data-name and a value and could be used with TRUE or FALSE, but it could not be combined with literal or identifier as those are already defined by the 88-level-name. Likewise, condition entries and 88-levels may *not* be used where a data-name follows the EVALU-ATE verb because that provides more than the three required components. The following examples do not include all options of the EVALUATE statement and are intended to show examples of concept, features, and format. There is an IF statement following each one for comparison purposes.

Testing value of a single field:

```
EVALUATE WS1-SEX-CODE
    WHEN 'M' PERFORM 2100-MALE-APP
    WHEN 'F' PERFORM 2200-FEMALE-APP
    WHEN OTHER PERFORM 2300-ERROR-RTN
END-EVALUATE
```

IF equivalent:

```
IF WS1-SEX-CODE = 'M'
    PERFORM 2100-MALE-APP
ELSE
    IF WS1-SEX-CODE = 'F'
        PERFORM 2200-FEMALE-APP
    ELSE
        PERFORM 2300-ERROR-RTN
    END-IF
END-IF
```

Testing truth of a single 88-level or condition:

```
EVALUATE TRUE
    WHEN 88-level-name   PERFORM 2100-RTNA
                         PERFORM 2300-RTNB
                         MOVE 'Y' TO WS1-SWITCH
    WHEN 88-level-name2 OR condition-a
                         PERFORM 2500-RTNC
    WHEN OTHER           MOVE 'N' TO WS1-SWITCH
END-EVALUATE
```

IF equivalent:

```
IF 88-level-name
    PERFORM 2100-RTNA
    PERFORM 2300-RTNB
    MOVE 'Y' TO WS1-SWITCH
ELSE
    IF 88-level-name OR condition-a
        PERFORM 2500-RTNC
    ELSE
        MOVE 'N' TO WS1-SWITCH
    END-IF
END-IF
```

Testing more than one 88-level or condition:

```
EVALUATE
            TRUE        ALSO        TRUE
    WHEN 88-level-a  ALSO condition-b
                        PERFORM 2100-RTNA
    WHEN condition-c  ALSO 88-level-d
                        PERFORM 2200-RTNB
    WHEN 88-level-e  ALSO ANY
                        PERFORM 2300-RTNC
    WHEN OTHER          MOVE 'N' TO WS2-SWITCH
END-EVALUATE
```

IF equivalent:

```
IF 88-level-a AND condition-b
    PERFORM 2100-RTNA
ELSE
    IF condition-c AND 88-level-d
        PERFORM 2200-RTNB
    ELSE
        IF 88-level-e
            PERFORM 2300-RTNC
        ELSE
            MOVE 'N' TO WS2-SWITCH
        END-IF
    END-IF
END-IF
```

Testing more than one data field:

```
EVALUATE
    WS1-SEX-CODE  ALSO WS2-MAR-STATUS
    WHEN 'M'      ALSO     'S'  PERFORM 3100-SGL-MALE
    WHEN 'M'      ALSO     'M'  PERFORM 3200-MAR-MALE
    WHEN 'F'      ALSO     'S'  PERFORM 3300-SGL-FEM
    WHEN 'F'      ALSO     'M'  PERFORM 3400-MAR-FEM
    WHEN OTHER                  PERFORM 3500-ERROR
END-EVALUATE
```

IF equivalent:

```
IF WS1-SEX-CODE = 'M' AND WS2-MAR-STATUS = 'S'
    PERFORM 3100-SGL-MALE
ELSE
    IF WS1-SEX-CODE = 'M' AND WS2-MAR-STATUS = 'M'
        PERFORM 3200-MAR-MALE
    ELSE
        IF WS1-SEX-CODE = 'F' AND WS2-MAR-STATUS = 'S'
            PERFORM 3300-SGL-FEM
        ELSE
            IF WS1-SEX-CODE = 'F' AND WS2-MAR-STATUS = 'M'
                PERFORM 3400-MAR-FEM
            ELSE
                PERFORM 3500-ERROR
            END-IF
        END-IF
    END-IF
END-IF
```

Testing expressions and literals:

This short example demonstrates that you may use EVALUATE for situations other than comparing data names to values. All other above combinations may also be used here.

```
EVALUATE LOAN-BAL + NEW-LOAN-AMT
    WHEN 0 THRU LOAN-LIMIT  PERFORM 3100-ISSUE-NEW-LOAN
    WHEN LOAN-LIMIT + 1 THRU LOAN-LIMIT * 1.10
                            PERFORM 3200-WRITE-CHECK-DATA
    WHEN OTHER              PERFORM 3300-REJECT-LOAN
END-EVALUATE
```

The easiest way to learn the EVALUATE statement is to start using it. I have found novice programmers pick this statement up quickly because it is easier (and quicker) to code than nested IF statements and the logic is easier to see in the code.

2.3.3. CONTINUE

CONTINUE is a new statement that does *nothing* except meet the requirement of having a procedural statement where required. You might be thinking, "Wasn't that what NEXT SENTENCE did?" No. NEXT SENTENCE is really a GO TO statement that transfers control to an unnamed sentence following the current sentence. By now, you can probably guess that I don't like the NEXT SENTENCE clause for that reason. A GO TO is a GO TO, even when it is a NEXT SENTENCE clause. In COBOL II, there is never a need for NEXT SENTENCE if you use the new features of COBOL II and use periods sparingly.

In the previous paragraph, I stated that the CONTINUE statement did nothing. Well, that's not exactly true. What it does is allow the procedural logic to continue to the next procedural statement within the program. Unlike NEXT SENTENCE, it does not determine what that statement is. Let's look at some examples where CONTINUE fills a gap.

Example 1

```
EVALUATE  FD3-SEX-CODE
WHEN  'M'  PERFORM 3200-PROCESS-MALE-APP
WHEN  'F'  CONTINUE
WHEN OTHER MOVE 'Y' TO FD3-INVALID-TRANS-CODE
END-EVALUATE
```

Here is a situation where CONTINUE allows the EVALUATE syntax to contain a WHEN condition for code "F" when no processing is to be done on that condition, preventing the WHEN OTHER from being executed for what is a valid code.

Example 2

```
IF APPL-AGE > 17 OR APPL-PARENT-CONSENT = 'Y'
    CONTINUE
ELSE
    PERFORM 3100-ISSUE-REJECTION-NOTICE
```

This is a less obvious example. Often it is much clearer to code positive logic than to code negative logic, even when the processing is for the negative condition. If example 2 had been coded for the negative condition, it would have read:

```
IF APPL-AGE NOT > 17 AND APPL-PARENT-CONSENT NOT = 'Y'
    PERFORM 3100-ISSUE-REJECTION-NOTICE
```

The need for the two NOT conditions and the use of AND are sometimes lost on novice (and a few senior) programmers. Turning the statement around is cleaner and the CONTINUE fills the requirement that a procedural statement be present.

Here is a more typical case, where a nested IF has a condition that is not to be processed. Coding CONTINUE makes the logic clearer, as it denotes (in this example) that if SEX-CODE is 'M" and MARITAL-STATUS is other than "M', nothing is to process.

Example 3

```
IF SEX-CODE = 'M'
    IF MARITAL-STATUS = 'M'
        PERFORM 3100-MALE-MARRIED-APP
    ELSE
        CONTINUE
ELSE
    PERFORM 3200-TEST-FEMALE-APPS
END-IF
```

Without CONTINUE, the following is also valid (just in case you were wondering if END-IF could work also.)

```
IF SEX-CODE = 'M'
    IF MARITAL-STATUS = 'M'
        PERFORM 3100-MALE-MARRIED-APP
    END-IF
ELSE
    PERFORM 3200-TEST-FEMALE-APPS
END-IF
```

2.3.4. INITIALIZE.

Have you ever had some initialization (or reinitialization) code in a program where you had to reset a myriad of program switches or storage areas? It is usually tedious to code and you always wonder if you remembered all of them. That's where INITIALIZE can help.

First, you need to organize your data areas so one statement can reset all of them. I recommend placing all accumulators or switches that affect a particular logic path into a single 01-level entry. This is important because the INITIALIZE statement acts on data fields based on their data type, not their data name.

The function performed by INITIALIZE is to reset numeric fields to zero and alphanumeric fields to spaces, although there is an optional clause that does a REPLACING BY. The most common use of INITIALIZE is:

```
INITIALIZE data-name.
```

Here are some examples. If you have the following data areas,

```
01  WS2-COMMON-ITEMS.
    05  WS2-TRANS-SWITCH    PIC  X.
    05  WS2-HEADER-SWITCH   PIC  X.
    05  WS2-LINE-COUNT      PIC  S999    COMP-3.
    05  WS2-TOTAL-DEP       PIC  S9.
    05  WS2-JOB-CODE        PIC  X.


01  WS3-PREMIUM-TABLE.
    05  WS3-PREM-ENTRY      PIC   S9(5)V99   COMP-3 OCCURS 100
                                TIMES   INDEXED BY PREM-INDEX.
```

you can set all of them to appropriate spaces or zeros by:

```
INITIALIZE WS2-COMMON-ITEMS WS3-PREMIUM-TABLE
```

Compare the simplicity of this with the extra coding you would need if using OS/VS COBOL. Your programs may never need to do this type of processing, but if your programs do need the logic, this is the way to go.

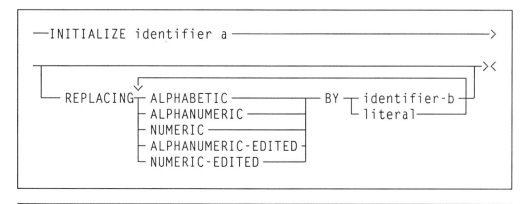

Figure 2.16. INITIALIZE syntax.

I have been criticized by a few technicians for recommending INITIALIZE, since it generates a few more machine instructions than the proper number of MOVE statements. I mention it here because these technicians may also work at your shop. If machine cycles become more expensive than your time, I'll change my views, but I think the industry passed that mark two decades ago.

2.3.5. TITLE.

I like the ability to place comments in a document where they will be seen more than once. TITLE generates no code and is active only during the compile process. It serves to place a custom title line on your source listing on every page until another TITLE statement is encountered. Here is an example:

```
TITLE  'PREMIUM CALCULATION PROGRAM'
IDENTIFICATION DIVISION.
    .
    .
    .
PROCEDURE DIVISION.
TITLE  ' TERM POLICY CALCULATIONS'
    .
    .
    .
TITLE  ' WHOLE LIFE POLICY CALCULATIONS'
    .
    .
    .
```

In addition to printing a title on your source listing, TITLE also causes a page eject to occur. If you're thinking, "Doesn't the "/" in column 7 do that, too?", you're right. The difference is that the "/" causes the comment to appear only one time, not on all following pages. This simple line of text improves a program's documentation. As a matter of style, I like to use it just prior to the IDENTIFI-CATION DIVISION statement.

2.3.6. Data Manipulation Enhancements/Changes

I've saved these enhancements until the end because they add subtle opportunities for rethinking program structure and data manipulation techniques. Because they are different, your shop may not allow their use, so you may want to get the corporate scoop before using these particular features. Topics here relate to the many new ways data may be defined both for system management and for data manipulation. Most of the entries here are new features, although some changes may require that you change how you write some pre-COBOL II statements.

LENGTH OF and ADDRESS OF special registers.

You saw these two elements previously as part of the CALL statement. They are new special registers (some other special registers you may be familiar with are TALLY, RETURN-CODE, and several relating to SORT, such as SORT-CORE-SIZE). Special registers are facilities provided by the compiler and are not defined within the source program.

The LENGTH OF special register is a value kept by the generated code for each 01-level item. You may never have need for it in your programs, but it makes a significant improvement to CICS programs by eliminating the need to manipulate or specify LENGTH in EXEC CICS statements (covered in Chapter 3).

The ADDRESS OF special register is a value kept by the generated code for the address of each 01-level item in the LINKAGE SECTION. (Use of ADDRESS OF with POINTER is explained further in this chapter.) In addition to being used in the CALL statement, it also simplifies CICS programs by eliminating the need for CICS programmers to use BLL cells (covered in Chapter 3).

GLOBAL and EXTERNAL data elements.

This is a major enhancement, providing extensive new options for program design. In OS/VS COBOL, data elements were part of the source program in which they were defined. Access to the data elements from other programs could only be done via a CALL USING statement. No more. COBOL II can define data areas separately from the program in which they are used or where their definitions appear (more on this in Chapter 3). Let's examine each term separately.

Global. When appended to a data or file definition (01-level or FD), that data element or FD may be referenced by any nested program within the run unit. I reviewed the concept of nested programs earlier, but I didn't explain why it might have advantages. Here is one possibility: being able to define an FD or 01-level that is directly accessible from within other programs. See figure 2.17 for an example. The module, SUB1, has no DATA DIVISION, yet can reference all defined GLOBAL entries in the program in which it is nested.

That prior sentence is important. A GLOBAL item is global ONLY to those programs that are contained *within* it. Programs that do not share the same parentage do not have access to the data. Examine figure 2.18. While most COBOL code is missing from the example, the structure is based on the module relationships that follow: Outermost module: MAIN1. MAIN1 may access data or FDs only from within itself. (MAIN1 isn't contained within any other module.)

Directly contained modules: SUB1 and SUB2. SUB1 and SUB2 may access any data area or FD within their own programs or that are GLOBAL in their parent, MAIN1 (i.e., SUB1 may NOT access any data area or FD defined in SUB2).

Indirectly contained module: SUB2A. SUB2A is directly contained within SUB2 and indirectly contained within MAIN1. It has no relationship to SUB1.

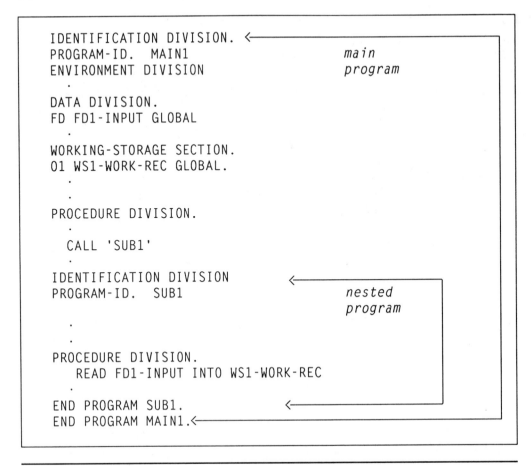

```
IDENTIFICATION DIVISION. ←─────────────────┐
PROGRAM-ID.  MAIN1                 main     │
ENVIRONMENT DIVISION               program  │
     .                                      │
DATA DIVISION.                              │
FD FD1-INPUT GLOBAL                         │
     .                                      │
WORKING-STORAGE SECTION.                    │
01 WS1-WORK-REC GLOBAL.                     │
     .                                      │
     .                                      │
PROCEDURE DIVISION.                         │
     .                                      │
   CALL 'SUB1'                              │
     .                                      │
IDENTIFICATION DIVISION    ←────┐           │
PROGRAM-ID.  SUB1               nested      │
                                program     │
     .                                      │
     .                                      │
PROCEDURE DIVISION.                         │
   READ FD1-INPUT INTO WS1-WORK-REC         │
     .                                      │
END PROGRAM SUB1.          ←────┘           │
END PROGRAM MAIN1. ←────────────────────────┘
```

Figure 2.17. Sample of GLOBAL file and record definition.

Therefore, SUB2A may access data areas within itself, that are GLOBAL within its parent, SUB1, or within SUB1's parent, MAIN1.

Use of GLOBAL is an excellent technique to maintain control of data accessibility and eliminate the need to code definitions of the FDs or data areas within each module.

External. The external clause may be used on FDs and 01-level entries also. Where GLOBAL applied to nested programs, EXTERNAL applies to traditional, external structures where each program in the run unit is separate, often being separately compiled (and link-edited, if DYNAM is used). This can be advantageous if it is desirable for several programs to share the same files or data areas. Whereas GLOBAL elements were accessible only from programs that were

```
IDENTIFICATION DIVISION. ←
PROGRAM-ID.   MAIN1                     main
DATA DIVISION.
FD FD1-INPUT GLOBAL
WORKING-STORAGE SECTION.
01  WS1-WORK-REC  GLOBAL.
PROCEDURE DIVISION.
   CALL 'SUB1'
   CALL 'SUB2'
IDENTIFICATION DIVISION? ←
PROGRAM-ID.   SUB1                    nested
   This program has access to FD1-INPUT
     .                      and WS1-WORK-REC
   This program does NOT have access to WS5-DATA
END PROGRAM SUB1.          ←
IDENTIFICATION DIVISION? ←
PROGRAM-ID.   SUB2                    nested
This program has access to FD1-INPUT
     .                      and WS1-WORK-REC
01 WS5-DATA GLOBAL.
   CALL 'SUB2A'
ID DIVISION.               ←
PROGRAM-ID. SUB2A                    nested
This program has access to FD1-INPUT,
       WS1-WORK-REC and WS5-DATA
END PROGRAM SUB2A. ←
END PROGRAM SUB2.          ←
END PROGRAM MAIN1. ←
```

Figure 2.18.   Sample of GLOBAL access by subprogram.

contained within a program, EXTERNAL elements may be accessed from ANY program in the run unit that has the same definitions.

From a coding perspective, the difference between GLOBAL and EXTERNAL is that the EXTERNAL items must be coded in all programs *exactly* the same. If the element is spelled differently, for example, it compiles with no errors, and executes, but the defined EXTERNAL element is unique and processing errors (or ABENDs) will depend on the process attempted. Elements that will be EXTERNAL should be defined as COPYbooks to eliminate this possible error. Also, EXTERNAL 01-level items may NOT have a VALUE clause.

For an example of EXTERNAL, assume the following COPYbooks:

PAYSEL

```
SELECT FD1-PAYROLL-FILE
    ASSIGN TO PAYMAST  FILE STATUS IS FD1-STAT.
```

PAYFD

```
FD FD1-PAYROLL-FILE EXTERNAL
    RECORD CONTAINS 100 CHARACTERS
    RECORDING MODE IS F.
01 FD1-PAYROLL-REC.
    05  FD1-EMP-NUMBER PIC X(5).
        .
        .
```

PAYWORK

```
01  WS1-PAYROLL-WORK EXTERNAL.
    05 FD1-STAT     PIC XX.
        .
        .
```

Using these three COPYbooks, you could develop the program structure in figure 2.19. It helps to visualize the structure by considering that all EXTERNAL elements are separate from all programs. The true in-memory structure for the example in figure 2.19 is:

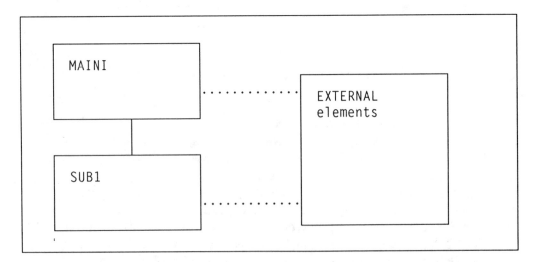

Note: EXTERNAL elements are treated as 24-bit addressable items that will be placed BELOW the 16-megabyte line.

```
ID DIVISION.
PROGRAM-ID.  MAIN1.
ENVIRONMENT DIVISION.
INPUT-OUTPUT SECTION.                          Unlike GLOBAL,
FILE-CONTROL.                                  there is
    COPY PAYSEL.                               nothing unique
DATA DIVISION.                                 about the
FILE SECTION.                                  main program
    COPY PAYFD.                                regarding use
WORKING-STORAGE SECTION.                       of EXTERNAL.
    COPY PAYWORK.
PROCEDURE DIVISION.
1.   OPEN INPUT FD1-PAYROLL-FILE
     CALL 'SUB1'
        .

END PROGRAM MAIN1.
ID DIVISION.                                   This subprogram
PROGRAM-ID.  SUB1.                             could be
ENVIRONMENT DIVISION.                          CALLed either
INPUT-OUTPUT SECTION.                          statically or
FILE-CONTROL.                                  dynamically.
    COPY PAYSEL.
DATA DIVISION.                                 The linkage
FILE SECTION.                                  is established
    COPY PAYFD.                                at run-time,
WORKING-STORAGE SECTION.                       not during
    COPY PAYWORK.                              compile or
PROCEDURE DIVISION.                            link-edit.
1.   READ FD1-PAYROLL-FILE
        .

END PROGRAM SUB1.
```

Figure 2.19. Example of EXTERNAL use.

As you saw, EXTERNAL and GLOBAL bring new structure opportunities to COBOL programs. Both offer their own advantages that may change the way you design programs. Also, you can use EXTERNAL and GLOBAL definitions together. Suggestions on when to use these features in program design are in Chapter 3 (Programming with COBOL II).

NULL value, POINTER data items, SET, and ADDRESS OF.

Earlier in the book, while describing changes to the USAGE and VALUE clause, I mentioned that NULL and POINTER were new terms and would be explained later. I also postponed an addition to the SET statement and use of ADDRESS OF with the CALL statement. This is as good a place as any to discuss those features. The features here are needed to replace BLL manipulation in CICS programs and allow use of dynamic SQL (SQLDA) in DB2 programs (see Chapter 3). Some programmers will probably never need to code any of these entries, but they create interesting opportunities for new structures (also in Chapter 3).

All of these elements relate, since they support manipulating addresses within an application. I don't foresee these options being used much (other than for CICS and DB2), but they do offer unique opportunities. While they don't have to be used together, it will be simpler to grasp them that way. Let's start with ADDRESS OF. The term, ADDRESS OF, represents an internal register for each 01-level item in the LINKAGE SECTION. One of the new CALL formats uses it this way:

```
CALL 'SUB1' USING ADDRESS OF  WS3-DATA-AREA
```

This CALL statement passes the address of the data element *as data*. The CALLed subprogram must move it to where it can use the address to access the data the address points to. Here is an example of a CALLed subprogram, demonstrating the concept.

```
LINKAGE SECTION.
01  LS1-ADDRESS               POINTER.

01  LS2-DATA-AREA.
    .
    .
    .
PROCEDURE DIVISION USING LS1-ADDRESS.
1.  SET ADDRESS OF LS2-DATA-AREA TO LS1-ADDRESS
    .
    .
    .
```

Before the program can work with the data elements in LS2-DATA-AREA, it first establishes addressability to it. That is accomplished by the SET statement. The SET statement takes the passed address in LS1-ADDRESS and establishes it for addressability to LS2-DATA-AREA. LS1-ADDRESS is defined as a POINTER item. This is because it contains an address of data, not data. Notice there is no PIC clause.

If this were the typical way of using POINTER items, it would be easier to code in the traditional way, since COBOL has always provided addressability to data areas in CALLing programs. For example:

Calling program

```
CALL 'SUB1' USING WS3-DATA-AREA
```

Called program

```
LINKAGE SECTION.
01  LS2-DATA-AREA.
        .
        .
        .
PROCEDURE DIVISION USING LS2-DATA-AREA.
```

This typical structure passes the address of the data-name, but it does so as an address for the internal code to manage, not as data for the application logic to manage. Obviously, POINTERs are not intended for use in traditional CO-BOL-to-COBOL structures.

While this technique isn't needed in typical COBOL applications, there is a use for it if your application must interact with assembler programs that pass addresses of addresses between programs instead of addresses of data. With CICS, for example, the list of BLL cells is an address of addresses that requires attention prior to using the data areas.

The example showed one form of the SET. Here are the two basic forms it takes when ADDRESS OF is used.

```
SET pointer-item TO ADDRESS OF data-name <— This stores the
                                             address of the
                                             data-name in the
                                             pointer-item.



SET ADDRESS OF data-item TO pointer-item <— This establishes
                                            addressability of
                                            the data-item
                                            within the COBOL
                                            program.
```

To summarize the elements described here:

- NULL may appear in a VALUE clause for a POINTER item or within a SET (SET pointer-item TO NULL).
- POINTER items are valid only for use as one of the operands in the form of the SET statement using ADDRESS OF.
- ADDRESS OF exists only for elements in the LINKAGE SECTION.

Examples of these techniques are explored in Chapter 3 under the sections, Module structures, and CICS/IMS/DB2 issues.

Class tests—alphabetic and numeric.

This is a good news/bad news situation. The good news is that you may now test for ALPHABETIC-UPPER and ALPHABETIC-LOWER when you are validating an alphanumeric field for all upper-case or all lower-case text. The bad news is that ALPHABETIC now allows both upper- and lower-case text. In OS/VS COBOL, the statement

```
IF data-name ALPHABETIC
```

would only be true if the field contained characters *A* through *Z* and the space. Now, it will be true if the field contains *A* through *Z*, *a* through *z* and the space. If you will be converting programs from OS/VS COBOL to COBOL II, I suggest you change all occurrences of ALPHABETIC to ALPHABETIC-UPPER.

The NUMERIC situation is not as clear. The NUMERIC class test operates differently, depending on a compile-time option, NUMPROC. Your shop has set a default value for this option and your technical staff can probably answer your questions about this. The NUMPROC option is explained in chapter 3, along with all other compile options. The good news about the NUMPROC option is that it provides some performance improvements if your numeric data elements are always properly signed.

Reference modification.

Reference modification is another addressing technique that has been lifted from other languages. This is a technique whereby you may access part of a data area without using the REDEFINES clause in the DATA DIVISION. For example, assume you have a data area defined that contains a phone number, including parentheses, [e.g., (555) 555-1212]. Counting parentheses, spaces, and the hyphen, that comes to 14 positions. With the data area defined as

```
05 FD3-EMPL-PHONE-NUMBER    PIC X(14).
```

you could access the area code (you know it is the second, third, and fourth characters in the field) by coding

```
MOVE FD3-EMPL-PHONE-NUMBER (2:3)  WS1-AREA-CODE
```

In case you didn't figure out the example, the first digit specifies the starting byte within the field. In this case 2 for the 2nd byte. The digit following the colon represents the length of the field (in bytes) for this statement. In this case 3 because the area code is 3 bytes long.

Since reference modification applies to bytes, this technique should be used for alphanumeric fields. (It could be used for other data types, but it would become a maintenance nightmare.) The complete syntax is

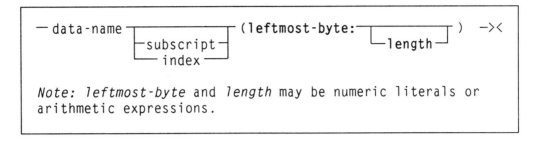

```
— data-name ——————————————————— (leftmost-byte: —————————— )   —><
              ├─subscript─┤                         └─length─┘
              └── index ──┘

Note: leftmost-byte and length may be numeric literals or
arithmetic expressions.
```

Figure 2.20.   Reference modification syntax.

From figure 2.20, you see that if subscripts or indexes are used, they are placed first, following the data name. The length operand is optional. When length is omitted, the compiler assumes a length that represents the remaining bytes in the field. Therefore, to use the previous example of a phone number, the code to move the seven-digit phone number and the hyphen would be

```
MOVE FD3-EMPL-PHONE-NUMBER (7:8)  TO WS3-LOCAL-PHONE
```

or

```
MOVE FD3-EMPL-PHONE-NUMBER (7:)  TO WS3-LOCAL-PHONE
```

As you can see, this can be non productive. Counting the bytes in the field to code this statement takes time and can be difficult to read. When not needed, I don't encourage this approach because it adds one more element to possibly debug. Finally, if you use an arithmetic expression to compute the starting position and length at run-time, results may be unpredictable if your computations do not fall within the defined data field length (e.g., a starting position of -5 or a length of 0). A new compile option, SSRANGE, can assist in debugging. (SSRANGE also supports debugging OCCURS clauses and is covered in Chapter 3 and in Chapter 4, Debugging.)

De-editing numeric data.

The term *de-edit* means to be able to MOVE from a data element that is edited (i.e., has PIC characters such as $, Z, and decimal points, as in PIC $,$$$.99) to a numeric data element that is not edited [i.e., has PIC characters that depict a numeric value for computation, such as PIC S9(5)V99]. This was never possible before. This can be handy if you are pulling numeric entries from a data entry screen (e.g., CICS) and want the screen to be edited for the terminal operator but also want it in numeric format for processing. This ability requires no special coding on your part. It is just a capability for the MOVE statement that was not allowed in earlier releases of COBOL.

DAY-OF-WEEK.

Earlier, I explained that CURRENT-DATE and TIME-OF-DAY were replaced by a form of the ACCEPT statement. That capability existed in OS/VS COBOL, since the ACCEPT statement is an ANSI 74 statement. Here is an additional extension to the ACCEPT statement you can use with COBOL II:

```
ACCEPT data-name FROM DAY-OF-WEEK
```

where the implicit PIC for DAY-OF-WEEK is PIC 9(1). The values range from 1 for Monday through 7 for Sunday. For example, the value 5 represents Friday.

Extended compiler limits.

Normally, you probably never think about how large a data item can be. In fact, you probably never knew the limit when working with OS/VS COBOL programs. I didn't. Since data elements were used to store copies of data records in memory, the limit didn't usually matter because the limiting factor was usually the data record size. That has changed with COBOL II. Consider the following comparison:

	Maximum data size	
	OS/VS COBOL	**COBOL II**
Working-Storage	1 megabyte	128 megabytes
01-level size	1 megabyte	16 megabytes
Linkage Section	1 megabyte	128 megabytes

Note: A megabyte is not one million bytes. It is 1,048,576 bytes. That means that 128 megabytes is really 134,217,727 bytes and 16 megabytes is really 16,777,215 bytes.

This extension offers possibilities of using an 01-level for an in-memory database, something you couldn't consider in OS/VS COBOL. While there are always other considerations when designing a high-performance application, one option might be to load a database into a table in memory and then access it by using an index. MVS/XA offers programmers the opportunity to reevaluate their use of memory, once considered more precious than other resources.

SUMMARY

This has been a hefty chapter of the book. I encourage you to read it more than once, highlighting and underlining those elements that affect your programming techniques. COBOL II is a major step forward for COBOL. You don't need to read the next chapter (and probably shouldn't) until you have experimented with several of these different features and developed a feeling of comfort with and enthusiasm for COBOL II. The language structure should feel natural before you start looking for new techniques.

Programming with COBOL II

This chapter is designed to provide some tips and techniques for day-to-day programming assignments and for maximizing a program's design and performance. I assume you have read the previous chapter and also that you have experimented some with COBOL II. This chapter does not, however, focus solely on COBOL II components. Instead, it focuses on whatever technique is appropriate to the topic. This will often include a new feature of COBOL II, but not always.

This chapter is not written to be read from beginning to end as was the previous chapter. Instead, use this chapter as a ready reference for COBOL techniques. You will find many topics are duplicated to some degree elsewhere in the book and you may be wondering why some topics appear twice. I did this because, as a desk reference, you should find topics where you look for them, not where I think they should go. So, this means many topics appear in several places. I hope they appear in a sufficient number of locations to ease your use of the chapter.

3.1. USING STRUCTURED PROGRAMMING COMPONENTS

First, if you're not familiar with structured programming, see Chapter 5 (Program Design Guidelines). For the rest of you, you know whether or not you use structured programming practices. Structured programming means

- no GO TOs (that's right, *none*)
- no EXIT statements

- no PERFORM THRU statements
- one entry and one exit for all statements/paragraphs/modules

If you coded those statements only in OS/VS COBOL SORT or CICS programs, that's ok, as there was often little choice. EXIT and PERFORM THRU don't explicitly violate structured programming concepts, but they do violate top-down design techniques since they do not decompose logic. This section is a brief review of COBOL statements that provide structured programming components (SEQUENCE, SELECTION, DO-WHILE, DO-UNTIL, and CASE).

3.1.1. SEQUENCE Component

SEQUENCE means that a statement's scope places it in sequence with the preceding statement. A set of sequence statements are, therefore, all sharing in the same scope. When you execute the first statement in a sequence, the structure takes you through all of them. So, what does that mean? It means that you must *not* contain the scope by inserting any periods that aren't required.

```
MOVE A TO B
MOVE C TO D
```

are two statements that meet the definition of SEQUENCE. The first is executed and then the second. If we were to precede those two statements by an IF statement,

```
IF condition
    MOVE A TO B
    MOVE C TO D
```

we know that both MOVE statements would be executed. However, some programmers are in the habit of placing periods after *every* statement. Preceding such statements with an IF statement would give us this:

```
IF condition
    MOVE A TO B.
    MOVE C TO D.
```

Obviously, that would be an error. It has been this practice over the years that has sensitized many people to "always check for missing periods." In truth, the reverse is the proper approach. Instead of checking for missing periods, you should avoid placing unnecessary periods and spot check for them. They are only appropriate at the end of a paragraph. Throughout this book, the approach is "if you don't need it, don't code it."

3.1.2. SELECTION Component

If you're thinking that this is accomplished by the IF and ELSE statement, you're correct—but there are many more selection statements. For example, other statements that provide selection options are

```
Statement    Selection clause

ADD          ON SIZE ERROR, NOT ON SIZE ERROR
CALL         ON EXCEPTION, NOT ON EXCEPTION
COMPUTE      ON SIZE ERROR, NOT ON SIZE ERROR
DELETE       INVALID KEY, NOT INVALID KEY
DIVIDE       ON SIZE ERROR, NOT ON SIZE ERROR
EVALUATE     WHEN
MULTIPLY     ON SIZE ERROR, NOT ON SIZE ERROR
READ         AT END, NOT AT END, INVALID KEY, NOT INVALID KEY
RETURN       AT END, NOT AT END
REWRITE      INVALID KEY, NOT INVALID KEY
SEARCH       WHEN
START        INVALID KEY, NOT INVALID KEY
STRING       ON OVERFLOW, NOT ON OVERFLOW
SUBTRACT     ON SIZE ERROR, NOT ON SIZE ERROR
UNSTRING     ON OVERFLOW, NOT ON OVERFLOW
WRITE        INVALID KEY, NOT INVALID KEY
```

Because all of these provide the SELECTION component, all of them also have scope terminators associated with them to avoid prematurely terminating the scope of the statement (for example, END-MULTIPLY, END-WRITE). It is the extensive use of scope terminators for SELECTION statements that maintains the integrity of your structured program, since scope terminators ensure the SELECTION components are also eligible to be SEQUENCE components as well.

3.1.3. The DO-WHILE Component

Nothing new here. The PERFORM UNTIL statement accomplishes this. You have a choice of using the traditional approach, where the executed code is in a separate paragraph, or using the new inline format where the executed code immediately follows the PERFORM statement. Remember; a DO-WHILE component tests a condition BEFORE executing the code, whereas a DO-UNTIL component tests the condition AFTER executing the code.

Traditional

```
PERFORM 2300-PROCESS-RECORDS UNTIL EOF-SWITCH = 'Y'
```

Inline

```
PERFORM VARYING TAB-INDEX FROM 1 BY 1 UNTIL END-OF-FILE
    PERFORM 2400-READ
    IF NOT END-OF-FILE
        MOVE FD1-REC TO WS3-TABLE (TAB-INDEX)
    END-IF
END-PERFORM
```

Remember, the inline PERFORM requires the scope terminator END-PERFORM.

3.1.4. The DO-UNTIL Component

This was never before available in COBOL and many analysts who develop programming specifications for COBOL applications avoid using DO-UNTIL. Anyway, you now have it with the WITH TEST AFTER clause appended to a PERFORM statement. You have a choice similar to that offered above for the DO-WHILE component, either using the traditional PERFORM where the executed code is in a separate paragraph, or using the new inline format where the executed code immediately follows the PERFORM statement.

Traditional

```
PERFORM 2300-PROCESS-RECORDS UNTIL EOF-SWITCH = 'Y' WITH
    TEST AFTER
```

Inline

```
PERFORM WITH TEST AFTER VARYING TAB-INDEX FROM 1 BY 1 UNTIL
    END-OF-FILE
    PERFORM 2400-READ
    IF NOT END-OF-FILE
        MOVE FD1-REC TO WS3-TABLE (TAB-INDEX)
    END-IF
END-PERFORM
```

This example appears identical to the earlier example for DO-WHILE. The difference is in the status AFTER execution. Remember, the inline PERFORM requires the scope terminator END-PERFORM.

3.1.5. The CASE Component

This component is provided by the new EVALUATE statement, of which there were many examples in the previous chapter. Do NOT use the GO TO DEPENDING ON statement to attempt this.

3.1.6. How to Avoid the GO TO Statement

There is additional material in Chapter 5 (Program Design Guidelines) that addresses this topic. I include the topic here because it is a common concern of programmers who have trouble with the concept. My approach is to concentrate on decomposing the program design and not to concentrate on GO TOs. The need for GO TO statements disappears in an application where each paragraph decomposes downward and outward to accomplish the scope of the paragraph.

When dealing with structure, I create analogies with an office environment where the main module/paragraph is the "manager" and the other modules/paragraphs are "subordinates" or "junior managers." For example, a manager wanting to review records for employees eligible for a pay raise in the current month would not say to a subordinate, "Please get me all the employee records." Instead, the manager would say, "Please get me the records of the employees eligible for a pay raise this month."

Sound simple? Compare that simple logic to a program that needs to read a file but wants to process only certain records. Often, we see something like this:

```
2100-PROCESS.
    PERFORM 2300-READ-RECORD
    IF NOT END-OF-FILE
        IF ELIGIBLE-FOR-PAY-RAISE
            process, etc
                .
                .
        ELSE
            GO TO 2100-PROCESS.

2300-GET-READ-RECORD.
    READ FD1-PAYROLL-FILE
      AT END
        SET END-OF-FILE TO TRUE
    END-READ.
```

This is poor code, primarily because the process of getting input has not been decomposed. Why not try the office analogy approach and do this:

```
2100-PROCESS.
    PERFORM 2300-GET-VALID-RECORD
    IF NOT END-OF-FILE
        process, etc
        .
        .

2300-GET-VALID-RECORD.
    PERFORM UNTIL END-OF-FILE OR ELIGIBLE-FOR-PAY-RAISE
        READ FD1-PAYROLL-FILE
          AT END
              SET END-OF-FILE TO TRUE
        END-READ
    END-PERFORM.
```

This "delegates" the process of simple validation to a subordinate module, freeing the "manager" module to make processing decisions instead of doing simple edits as well. You will probably find your programs have more paragraphs, and smaller ones at that. You will probably also find that junior programmers can maintain them too. The use of the GO TO statement will continue to be used by a portion of programmers, but it will always be indicative of either an inadequate or incomplete program design.

3.2. MODULE STRUCTURES

This section contains suggestions and tips if you are building a new application, adding a subprogram to an existing structure, or contemplating different ways to link your logic subsets together. If you're unfamiliar with combining programs, read the first two topics for an overview.

3.2.1. Main Modules and Submodules

This section introduces the term *run unit*, which appears throughout the book. A run unit is the logical collection of programs executed under control of a main program. This may be one or more programs in one or more languages formed into one or more load modules. For example, in a batch environment a run unit begins at the JCL EXEC statement.

A main program/module is one that is invoked from MVS (for example, PGM= on JCL EXEC statement). A main program is to a great degree coded the same way as a subprogram. Differences lie in the way they are terminated (see next topic) and how they share data with other programs in the run unit (see topics on Sharing Data and on Sharing Files). For example, a main program using the PROCEDURE DIVISION USING statement is receiving data from MVS (via the JCL PARM parameter) in a format different from the same statement being used in a subprogram. Where a LINKAGE SECTION is used in a main program, it is typically to store the above-mentioned PARM data from a JCL statement. The main program is the highest element in a run unit. As in other components of a run unit, a main program should have one entry point and one exit. (Note: If the first COBOL program is CALLed from an assembler program, there are some differences. See that topic later in this section.)

Subprograms/submodules are invoked from another program (CALLed from another application or from a software environment, for example, IMS or CICS). Subprograms use PROCEDURE DIVISION USING to accept data from a calling program in a format determined by the CALLing program. Subprograms can in turn also CALL other subprograms. As in other components of a run unit, a subprogram should have one entry point and one exit.

Example of a batch main program and subprogram

```
//    EXEC PGM=MAINPROG
```

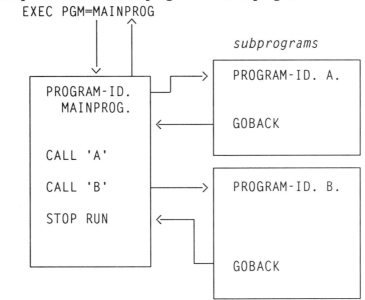

From the JCL, MVS gives control to MAINPROG. MAINPROG in turn transfers control first to program *A* and then to program *B*. The subprograms use GOBACK to return control and the main program uses STOP RUN to return control to MVS.

3.2.2. Terminating a Program/Module

COBOL provides five ways to terminate an application.

1. **STOP RUN.** The STOP RUN statement, used by main programs, returns control back to the system environment. The system environment is normally established by MVS at the time the first program (the main

program) is initiated. Therefore, a subprogram should NOT use STOP RUN. Another function of the STOP RUN statement closes any files in the run unit that are still open. One STOP RUN, at most, should be within a run unit. While COBOL II has removed many of the restrictions on using STOP RUN for CICS and IMS applications, I recommend you not use it. (Note: For other considerations on the environment, see the topic on assembler language.)

2. **GOBACK.** The GOBACK statement returns control to the CALLing program and should be used by subprograms. GOBACK is the preferred statement for CICS and IMS applications. (Note: GOBACK may also be used by main programs, but the resource cleanup that would have been done by STOP RUN is dependent on various installation defaults, primarily the RTEREUS run-time option. Check with your technical staff before standardizing on this approach.)

3. **EXIT PROGRAM.** The third option is the EXIT PROGRAM statement, which performs differently depending on whether it is executed from within a main program or from within a subprogram. If executed in a CALLed subprogram, it functions as GOBACK. If executed in a main program, it is ignored. Note: An EXIT PROGRAM statement is implicitly defined at the end of every COBOL program, (that is, if the last statement in a program falls through to the next available statement, an EXIT PROGRAM statement will be executed). This is avoided by PERFORMing paragraphs and not allowing fall-through logic (for example, PERFORM THRU or GO TO). Most shops do not use EXIT PROGRAM; they use GOBACK instead. Because CICS and IMS applications treat this statement differently depending on whether EXIT PROGRAM is in the highest level module or not, I recommend that you do not use it. Anytime a statement acts differently in different settings, it is only a matter of time before you forget which setting you are in. This is a statement to avoid.

4. **EXEC CICS RETURN.** The fourth option applies to CICS programs. CICS provides a specific statement, EXEC CICS RETURN, to terminate run units in the CICS environment. CICS programs should use EXEC CICS RETURN when the run unit is finished and control is to be returned to CICS. Note: Under COBOL II, STOP RUN no longer crashes the CICS environment as it did in OS/VS COBOL, but it lacks environmental cleanup functions of EXEC CICS RETURN.

5. **ABEND.** The final option is to force an ABEND. While this isn't a clean technique, there may be times when you do not want the application to appear to have terminated with no errors. Any ABEND code you use should not be in the range of 1000 to 1999, as those are used by the COBOL II run-time routines. Your shop may have some home-grown subprograms that do this, or for CICS you can probably use the EXEC

CICS ABEND command. If so, use them. Otherwise, here are some techniques to consider:

Use IBM's ABEND routine, ILBOABN0. This subroutine is supplied by IBM with other COBOL run-time modules and requires a parameter passed to it that is PIC S9(4) COMP, containing a value between 0 & 4095 (this will be the ABEND code). Here is an example:

```
05  WS1-ABEND-CODE    PIC  S9(4)  COMP  VALUE +5.
        .
        .

    CALL 'ILBOABNO'  USING WS1-ABEND-CODE
```

This example produces a printed dump if there is a SYSUDUMP or SYSABEND DD statement in the step. In this example, the User ABEND code is 0005.

Use your own ABEND routine. You can control whether the dump is printed. This can be advantageous when you need the ABEND termination code but do not want the added expense and waste of printing a dump. While I don't guarantee this assembler program for all environments, it does work and it is simple. (Note: As with all other assembler examples in this book, this module is not reentrant, although it does execute in 31-bit or 24-bit mode.) It uses the same parameter list as IBM's, but there is no dump produced.

Sample assembler program to ABEND with no dump

```
ABEND    CSECT
ABEND    AMODE 31
ABEND    RMODE ANY
R1       EQU   1
R2       EQU   2
R12      EQU   12
R13      EQU   13
R14      EQU   14
R15      EQU   15
         USING ABEND,R12
         SAVE  (14,12),,*
         LR    R12,R15
         LA    R14,SAVEAREA
         ST    R14,8(,R13)
         ST    R13,4(,R14)
         LR    R13,R14
         L     R1,0(,R1)
```

```
          LH    R2,0(,R1)
          ABEND (2)
SAVEAREA  DC    18F'0'
          END   ABEND
```

Using the above example, this would be executed as

```
CALL 'ABEND' USING WS1-ABEND-CODE
```

One benefit (drawback?) of this module is that, if it ABENDs, it does not activate any debugging function, such as the FDUMP option. Be sure to assemble it with IBM's Assembler H product. (Note: Changing ABEND (2) in the above listing to ABEND (2),DUMP causes it to force a system dump, if that is preferred.)

STOP RUN versus GOBACK.

Some people are confused by differences between STOP RUN and GOBACK. If a subprogram uses STOP RUN, it exits back *past* the program that CALLed it, defeating the concept of structured programming (Note: also affected by RTEREUS run-time option). Consider this example:

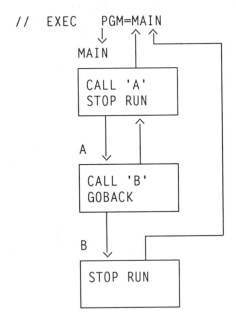

Module MAIN does a STOP RUN back to the system. That's proper. Module A executes a GOBACK to return control to the CALLing program. That's proper too. Module B executes a STOP RUN, bypassing all prior modules, creating a GO TO environment. That can cause structural problems in an application.

Some programmers writing in IMS or CICS code STOP RUN (in error) because they visualize their program as receiving control from MVS. Actually, the program that receives control from MVS is the IMS or CICS control program, which in turn invokes the application program. An IMS or CICS application then is *always* a subprogram. IMS applications should use GOBACK to terminate processing. If you're ever in doubt, GOBACK is safer than STOP RUN since GOBACK works with both main programs and with subprograms. CICS programs have a specific CICS statement, called EXEC RETURN, which should be used for the highest level module. (Note: COBOL II now allows CICS and IMS programs to use STOP RUN, primarily (my opinion) because so many programmers kept using it. My suggestion is to follow the above guidelines, using GOBACK and EXEC RETURN, because they are compatible across all supported environments for IMS and CICS.)

3.2.3.   COBOL II to COBOL II

This is the simplest approach to a multimodule application. When all COBOL programs in a run unit are COBOL II, you may use all functions available from the COBOL II environment. This includes the ability to use reentrant code, to reside above the 16-megabyte line, or to share data and files as documented later in this section. There are no special techniques to use here, but I mention it to encourage you to develop (or convert) all modules that constitute a run unit to COBOL II to minimize any incompatibilities and to ensure you full access to COBOL II facilities. (Note: "Mixing and matching" is not allowed in CICS. All COBOL programs must be either COBOL II for a run unit or OS/VS COBOL. See your technical support staff for more information.)

3.2.4.   Nested Programs in COBOL II

Nested programs, with examples, were introduced in the previous chapter. The primary advantage to this approach is the extra features that are available to you when sharing data or files with other programs (explained later in this section). A secondary benefit is that the compiler sees the programs as one program, not several. This means the documentation from the compile process (for example, cross-reference listings, program assembler code, or offset listings) is more thorough and you never encounter a situation in which one of the modules has several different object copies and the Linkage Editor used the wrong copy. You also receive a listing from the compiler showing the hierarchy of your structure, which can be helpful to a maintenance programmer unfamiliar with the application.

From a structured programming point of view, the benefit of nested programs is that you can insert new subprograms quickly. One technique I encourage is putting subprograms in COPYbooks, making it simpler to share them across an application.

The debugging advantage is that there is only one true program. The added complexity of doing hex arithmetic to determine in which module the ABEND occurred is history.

From this material, you probably feel I think it is a good approach. I do. Having all the code together, getting one cross-reference listing, not having to pass data back and forth to subprograms, not having to remember to insert COPY statements for all the common items are big benefits to a maintenance staff. Let's look at an example: If we have a new application that has been designed to use several subprograms and share a common file and table data, the traditional approach would be to develop several COPYbooks, develop the various applications using the COPY statements, compile and link them and then test to see if they communicate together. Whew! Here is a nested way: Develop all common data and files and place them in one master COPYbook, something like this:

COPYbook   Name: PAYMAST

```
    IDENTIFICATION DIVISION.
    PROGRAM-ID.  PAYMAST.
    ENVIRONMENT DIVISION.
    INPUT-OUTPUT SECTION.
    FILE-CONTROL.
        SELECT FD1-PAY-FILE ASSIGN TO PAYDD
            FILE STATUS IS PAY-STAT.
    DATA DIVISION.
    FILE SECTION.
    FD FD1-PAY-FILE GLOBAL
             .

             .


    WORKING-STORAGE SECTION.
    01 WS1-PAY-WORK GLOBAL.
             .

             .

    PROCEDURE DIVISION.
    1.  CALL 'PAYRUN01'
        STOP RUN.
```

Now, all you need to do to use this program is to code

```
    COPY PAYMAST
    ID DIVISION.
    PROGRAM-ID.  PAYRUN01.
    PROCEDURE DIVISION.
             .

             .

    END PROGRAM PAYRUN01.
```

This is much simpler than coding all the normal entries for a program and remembering which COPY statements to code.

The down side of nested programs is that you must recompile all of them even when you changed only one of them. Whether that issue is more important than the benefits is something for your shop to decide. (Note to CICS users: A nested program, including all nested CALLed modules, must be processed as one unit by the CICS translator.)

3.2.5. Assembler Language to COBOL II

Assembler language has special considerations because it is outside the COBOL environment. By COBOL environment, I am referring to the run-time modules that are invoked to provide integrity from one COBOL module to another. There are specific differences depending on whether the assembler program is the CALLing or the CALLed module.

Assembler programs as subprograms

There is no problem for COBOL programs to CALL assembler programs provided that the assembler programs follow standard IBM linkage conventions (see the following sample programs for an example) and are able to function in the appropriate addressing mode (31-bit or 24-bit). If you are migrating an OS/VS COBOL application to COBOL II and the application CALLs some assembler modules, those modules may need to be reassembled using IBM's Assembler H product (and may need some coding changes) to operate properly in 31-bit mode. Your shop probably has a technical staff already familiar with the coding adjustments, and actual coding of assembler is beyond the scope of this book.

Assembler programs as main programs

First, let's identify the concerns. The first issue to fix is the possibility that the assembler main program has only 24-bit addressability. If so, you have two approaches:

1. Reassemble the main program with IBM's Assembler H product (and possibly change some code) to get the program to have 31-bit addressability. If full reentrant access is desired, the effort increases considerably.
2. Compile the COBOL subprograms with compile options NORENT. This option prevents the run unit from taking advantage of MVS/XA and MVS/ESA performance enhancements in virtual memory, so while it is the easier of the two approaches, you will be better off to reassemble the assembler mainprogram.

The second concern is that COBOL II programs operate in a COBOL environment that is normally established when the COBOL main program is initiated. This environment stays active throughout the run unit without needing to be reinitialized for entry/exit of each COBOL module. If an assembler program is the *main program*, the possibility exists that, while the programs will function properly, the run-time environment will be reinitialized frequently and affect performance. Using assembler language, therefore, can create a performance issue if it is the highest level module in the run unit. (Note: In a CICS environment, assembler programs may not CALL a COBOL program.)

There are four ways of initializing the environment to prevent the performance degradation:

1. Use the RTEREUS run-time COBOL option (documented later in this chapter). This is probably your shop's default setting for non-CICS applications (RTEREUS is ignored by CICS). The section on compiler options shows a way to determine what this setting is. This is the easiest approach because it requires nothing on your part. If RTEREUS is not your shop's default and does not conflict with your shop's standards, your systems programmers can establish the option for your particular program (more information on this facility, IGZEOPT, is in the section on compile options). Doing so requires a modification to your link-edit control statements (documented later in this chapter).

2. Use a COBOL program as the main program. Where RTEREUS is not the default and there are reasons not to establish it, this is the next simplest approach for you. By creating a small stub driver program, you cause the environment to be initialized for the run unit. For example:

```
ID DIVISION.
PROGRAM-ID. DRIVER.
PROCEDURE DIVISION.
1.   CALL 'assembler-program-name'
     STOP RUN.
```

The following chart depicts the possible structure:

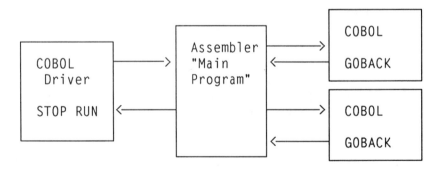

3. Modify the assembler program to initialize the run-time environment prior to the first CALL. IBM provides a module called IGZERRE that does this. (Note: This technique is not recommended for CICS or IMS/DC applications.) The main assembler program would need to include these statements:

Prior to first CALL

```
LA    1,1
CALL  IGZERRE
```

After last CALL

```
LA    1,2
CALL  IGZERRE
```

Simple assembler program to CALL a COBOL module

This is a simple program (it works) that initializes the COBOL environment and CALLs a program called MAINPROG.

```
          TITLE   'CALL COBOL subprogram and Initialize '
CALLCOB   CSECT
CALLCOB   AMODE 31
CALLCOB   RMODE ANY
          SAVE    (14,12),,*
          USING   CALLCOB,12
          LR      11,13
          LR      12,15
          LA      13,SAVEAREA
          ST      13,8(0,11)
          ST      11,4(0,13)
          LR      4,1
          LA      1,1                 A '1' in register 1 will
          CALL    IGZERRE             initialize environment
          LTR     15,15
          BZ      OKAY
          WTO     'IGZERRE Error',ROUTCDE=(11)
OKAY      LR      1,4
          CALL    COBPROG             Call PROGRAM-ID of 'COBPROG'
          LA      1,2                 A '2' in register 1 will
          CALL    IGZERRE             terminate environment
          LTR     15,15
```

```
          BZ      QUIT
          WTO     'IGZERRE Error',ROUTCDE=(11)
QUIT      L       13,SAVEAREA+4
          LM      14,12,12(13)
          XR      15,15
          BR      14                    RETURN TO MVS
SAVEAREA  DC      18F'0'
          END     CALLCOB
```

For more information on parameter lists for IGZERRE, see the IBM COBOL II Application Programming Guide (Chapter 9, Related Publications).

4. Use the OS/VS COBOL assembler interface, ILBOSTP0, instead of IGZERRE. I include it here because you may encounter CALLs to that module in your current assembler programs. If so, that module is still supported by IBM, so there is no need to change it, other than possibly relinking it for 31-bit addressability. That should be done by your systems programmers using the RMODE and AMODE options of the Linkage Editor.

STOP RUN considerations when CALLed by an assembler program.

As stated elsewhere, subprograms should use GOBACK to return control to the CALLing program. That applies here, too, even if the CALLing program is written in assembler. However, there may be a reason you want to use STOP RUN at the highest level COBOL program and still treat it as a subprogram. The problem you face is that the STOP RUN statement normally returns control to either the program that CALLed the program that initiated the environment or to MVS, if MVS initiated the environment. To get around this, you need an *additional* assembler program between the high-level assembler program and your program. This will make it appear that the CALLing assembler and the CALLed COBOL program are communicating directly. (You also face *severe performance problems* if the COBOL program is CALLed frequently, because it must be reinitialized each time STOP RUN does resource cleanup.)

Anyway, assuming you're determined, here is a sample program that can be tucked between the assembler main program and your COBOL "main program." This example assumes the RTEREUS option is invoked. If not, use the previous example that included CALLs to IGZERRE. This works, but I don't recommend it. Here is the flow, showing both STOP RUN processing and GOBACK processing:

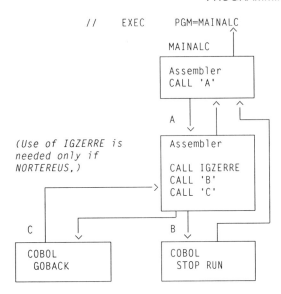

Sample program to CALL COBOL program without initialization

```
          TITLE 'CALL COBOL Main Program '
CALLMAIN  CSECT
CALLMAIN  AMODE 31
CALLMAIN  RMODE ANY
          SAVE  (14,12),,*
          USING CALLMAIN,12
          LR    11,13
          LR    12,15
          LA    13,SAVEAREA
          ST    13,8(0,11)
          ST    11,4(0,13)
          CALL  MAINPROG            Call PROGRAM-ID of MAINPROG
          L     13,SAVEAREA+4
          LM    14,12,12(13)
          XR    15,15
          BR    14
SAVEAREA  DC    18F'0'
                END   CALLMAIN
```

The COBOL program in the diagram, module B, returns control at STOP RUN, not to module A that CALLed it but to MAINALC, the program that CALLed the program that CALLed B. The complexity of this solution may cause you to rethink why you prefer STOP RUN. As I mentioned earlier, GOBACK eliminates the need for the intermediate program.

All the considerations for assembler language are not addressed here, the goal of such a technical topic being to make you aware of issues to address if you are developing or maintaining such an application. If you are developing COBOL applications with no non-COBOL modules, your shop's run-time environment considerations have already been addressed by your technical staff.

This treatment of the topic is elementary, at best. If your shop is heavily into assembler interfaces, the complexities could fill several books. Check with your technical support staff for more assistance and direction and prior to using these sample programs. The issue of using non-COBOL languages with COBOL, especially if IMS or CICS are involved, often requires involvement and tuning considerations that are beyond this book.

3.2.6. COBOL II to OS/VS COBOL

If you are maintaining an application where some of the modules in a run unit have been migrated to COBOL II while others remain in OS/VS COBOL, you have some special considerations. You should view a mixed environment as a temporary approach, because there is performance degradation when both CO-BOL versions are used. First, if it is a CICS transaction, either keep all modules OS/VS COBOL or convert them all to COBOL II. A mixed approach is not supported in CICS (other than by EXEC CICS LINK, which introduces its own performance degradation). There are also some headaches for IMS (see CICS/IMS/DB2 Issues for more information).

Since OS/VS COBOL modules must reside below the 16-megabyte line, you must use appropriate COBOL II compile options for downward compatibility to the OS/VS COBOL module. The options are NORENT for a static CALL and DATA(24) for a dynamic CALL. (See Static and Dynamic CALLs for more information.) See figure 3.1 for a depiction of the structures available.

In all examples in figure 3.1, the data areas will be below the 16-megabyte line. The COBOL II module above the 16-megabyte line does this because one of the compile options is DATA(24). The other structures accomplish this by specifying NORENT, which causes data areas to be allocated within the object module. No changes are needed for an OS/VS COBOL module if it was compiled with RES and the appropriate (static or dynamic) CALL statement. Of the three structures, only the one with RENT (above the line) offers any COBOL II performance advantages, although all of the examples are less efficient than an all-COBOL II run unit.

If the OS/VS COBOL program were compiled with NORES, you would have one or more additional steps, since my assumption is that you will want to use RES for all COBOL II programs. (COBOL II requires that all modules in a run unit share the same RES option.) Your choices are

1. Convert the OS/VS COBOL program to COBOL II for a complete solution (all modules in run unit are COBOL II).

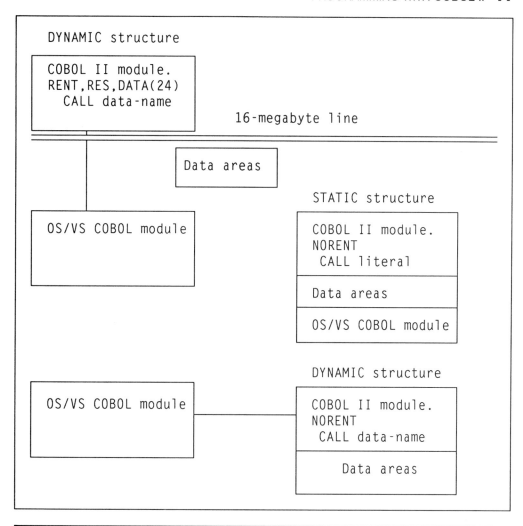

Figure 3.1. COBOL II & OS/VS COBOL structures.

2. Recompile and link the OS/VS COBOL program with the OS/VS COBOL compiler, specifying RES, for a temporary solution.

3. Compile the COBOL II program with NORES for a temporary solution (You give up the performance opportunities provided by MVS/XA and MVS/ESA, as NORES requires NORENT.)

4. If the OS/VS COBOL program is not to be converted or recompiled with RES, ensure that, during the link-edit process, all OS/VS COBOL versions of the ILBOxxxx modules are replaced by their equivalent modules from the COBOL II subroutine library. (See Creating a Load Module for

more information on REPLACE.) This step can be combined with step 3 for a NORES environment, or with step 5 for a mixed environment.

5. If your choices from the above options cause you to have a mixed environment, use the COBOL II run-time option MIXRES until the OS/ VS COBOL modules have been converted.

If your choices included option 5 (MIXRES) you must ensure that MIXRES is specified as a run-time option. The section on compile options explains how to determine your shop default options. My guess is that it is not set to MIXRES. If it is not, you must ask your systems programming staff to assemble a special run-time module for you (IGZEOPT). You must explicitly include the IGZEOPT module in the link-edit process for any load modules in the run unit that contain the NORES option. (See the section in this chapter, Specifying COBOL II Options, for more information.)

After reading this information, I hope you agree that converting the OS/VS COBOL applications to COBOL II is the preferred approach. The effort to create a coexisting environment of COBOL II and OS/VS COBOL modules will almost always be more costly than migrating the older programs to COBOL II and getting it finished.

3.2.7. Using RETURN-CODE

Every time a program returns control to a CALLing module, a return code is passed back to the CALLing module. At the highest level, this return code is made available to MVS. With the COND JCL parameter, this value can be tested. This technique may also be used within applications (even those with a mix of assembler and COBOL II, or COBOL II and OS/VS COBOL). This is because in every COBOL program there is a special register called RETURN-CODE. It is initialized to zero at program initiation and the value is updated following each CALL statement. RETURN-CODE is implicitly defined as PIC S9(4) COMP VALUE ZERO. (Note: Prior to COBOL II, this was not allowed for CICS applications. Since EXEC CICS commands affect the RETURN-CODE, you need to test or change its value with that in mind.)

Using this special register requires no special coding on your part. What it does require is a disciplined set of values to be used within your application. The most widely known set of disciplined values are those developed by IBM for use by its language processors and utility programs. For example, we all know that

- A return code of 0 means no errors.
- A return code of 4 means minor warnings.
- A return code of 16 means serious error.

This is not magic. It just proves that when everyone on a project agrees to use certain values, communication improves. To send a value in RETURN-CODE to a CALLing module, all you need do is code:

In subprogram

```
MOVE numeric-literal  to RETURN-CODE
GOBACK
```

In CALLing program

```
CALL 'subprogram' ...
IF RETURN-CODE = numeric-literal...
     .
        ·      insert appropriate processing here
     .
```

In the above example, the CALLing module must also include logic to set the value of RETURN-CODE prior to returning control via GOBACK or STOP RUN. Otherwise, it will contain the last value returned.

3.2.8. Sharing Files Among Modules

Sometimes, it is desirable to have several modules in an application have access to a file. I don't recommend it, preferring to keep tighter control on the read/write process. However, I recognize the need for it, as there are probably situations when good functional decomposition dictates it. There are different considerations for file sharing: one for assembler programs and two others for COBOL II programs.

Sharing files with assembler programs.
You have very little control here, and there is the (mostly theoretical) possibility that IBM will redo the format of the Data Control Block (the phrase "when pigs fly" comes to mind, but then I've been wrong before). Anyway, if the file is QSAM, you can share it with an assembler program by specifying the file name in the CALL statement. (*Don't* try this with COBOL subprograms.) The format is

```
CALL 'program-name" USING fd-name
```

This passes the address of the DCB to the assembler program. This can work if there is clear agreement on which program OPENs, CLOSEs, READs, and WRITEs to the file.

Sharing files with COBOL II programs.

There are two ways to share files with other COBOL II programs. One technique works with nested program structures and one with traditional, separately compiled structures. Since a program can have both nested modules and separately compiled modules, the two techniques can appear in a single run unit. (If any terms in this topic are unfamiliar to you, reread the sections on nested programs and on GLOBAL and EXTERNAL data elements in Chapter 2.) In both applicable cases, the logical processing of the file must not be violated. The options presented still require, for example, that the shared file be OPENed prior to issuing a READ to it, and so on.

For nested programs

In a nested program, use the GLOBAL clause on the FD, e.g.,

```
FD  FD2-PAYROLL-MASTER  GLOBAL
    RECORD CONTAINS 100 CHARACTERS.
01  FD2-PAYROLL-REC PIC X(100).
```

If this is specified in an outer program, all contained programs (both directly and indirectly) can access the file just as if the FD appeared in each contained program. Any program within the subset may issue any valid I/O statement for the file and has access to the 01-level entry for it, as well.

For separate programs

For separate programs, each participating program must have a common DATA DIVISION entry for the shared files and shared I/O areas. The FD entry must be similar to this:

```
FD  FD2-PAYROLL-MASTER  EXTERNAL
    RECORD CONTAINS 100 CHARACTERS.
01  FD2-PAYROLL-REC    PIC X(100).
```

The file description entries must be an *exact match*, even to the spelling. This is best done by COPYbook entries. There are examples of this in GLOBAL and EXTERNAL Data Elements in Chapter 2.

Note: External files are accessed below the 16-megabyte line. This should normally not be a major consideration, but you still need to be aware of it. EXTERNAL files may also be GLOBAL files.

3.2.9. Sharing Data Among COBOL II Modules

Sharing data other than files has many options, all of which can be combined with the file-sharing techniques if desired. Let's start with the simplest and proceed to the more complex:

Pass selected data via CALL BY REFERENCE statement.

This is the most common approach to sharing data, as a CALL statement uses, by default, the BY REFERENCE format. Until COBOL II, this was the only way to pass data to another program, so I encourage you to also consider the other options. In this approach, the original data exists within the CALLing module and it makes the data available to the CALLed module with something like:

```
CALL 'proga' USING data-name
```

Actually, this passes not the data, but addressability to the data, to the CALLed program. The CALLed program can not only reference the data, but it can change the data as well. This approach is well-documented, as the CALLed program must establish a LINKAGE SECTION to describe all data being passed from the CALLing program. The problem with this approach occurs when the two programs have different definitions of the data. Consider this:

CALLing module

```
01    WS1-REC        PIC X(24).
01    WS2-REC        PIC X(80).



      CALL 'suba' USING WS1-REC
```

CALLed module

```
LINKAGE SECTION.
01    WORK-REC      PIC X(50).

PROCEDURE DIVISION USING WORK-REC.
100-PROCESS.
    MOVE ZEROS TO WORK-REC
    GOBACK.
```

Examine what happens in this simple example. The CALLing program passes addressability of WS1-REC to suba. The CALLed subprogram uses this addressability to address not the intended 24-byte record, but the 24-byte record PLUS 26 bytes of WS2-REC in the CALLing program. This happens because the PIC clauses have different values. By moving zeros to WORK-REC, both WS1-REC and much of WS2-REC are set to zeros.

This is not untypical where the CALL statement is used, and it is a major cause for problems created by CALL statements. My recommendation is to use COPYbooks for passed data items and to have walkthroughs of all CALL statements and associated ENTRY or PROCEDURE DIVISION USING statements. (Although I included reference to the ENTRY statement, I don't recommend it. It gives more than one entry point to a COBOL program, a violation of structured programming rules. If you're thinking it is required, such as for IMS programs, it is not.)

Passing selected data via CALL BY CONTENT statement.

Similar to the above example, this approach is desirable if your program must pass selected data to another program, but the other program has no need to update the data. This also ensures some added control. The downside is that there is additional overhead: the system makes a copy of the data for the CALLed program. The format is

```
CALL 'suba' USING BY CONTENT data-name
```

With this format, the subprogram can change the data, but doing so does not change the data in the CALLing program and the potential problem in the previous example is avoided. This format, BY CONTENT, may be mixed with the previous approach, BY REFERENCE (that is, passing some fields by reference and others by content).

Passing variable selected data by CALL statement.

This technique can be combined with either of the two previous examples. It is useful if the data being passed may have a varying length. The format requires the clause, BY CONTENT LENGTH OF data-name. A sample CALL might be

```
CALL 'suba' USING WS1-WORK
            BY CONTENT LENGTH OF WS1-WORK.
```

The subprogram must be prepared to receive two data items:

```
LINKAGE SECTION.
01  LS-WORK.
      .
      .
01  LS-LENGTH      PIC S9(9)  COMP.

PROCEDURE DIVISION USING LS-WORK  LS-LENGTH.
```

The procedural code of the subprogram must include logic to interrogate LS-LENGTH and act appropriately according to application specifications.

Sharing data within a nested program.

This technique uses the GLOBAL clause discussed earlier for files in Chapter 2. If you use my recommendation earlier to use GLOBAL file structures, this complements the approach, making a complete set of data accessible from one program or COPYbook. The format applies to 01-level entries in WORKING-STORAGE. The format is

```
01 data-name GLOBAL.
   05...
    .
    .
```

GLOBAL may be combined with EXTERNAL if desired.

Sharing data externally.

This technique uses the EXTERNAL clause we discussed earlier. There are examples of this in Chapter 2. The advantage is that there is no need to pass data with the CALL statement, which can be a plus if specifications change for an application. As with EXTERNAL files, the data is maintained as DATA(24), below the 16-megabyte address. The clause may only be used at the 01-level in WORKING-STORAGE. The format is

```
01 data-name EXTERNAL.
   05...
    .
    .
```

A note of caution: With EXTERNAL, the generated run-time code allocates a new data area if the EXTERNAL element cannot be located. (Remember, even the spelling must match. That is why I recommend use of COPYbooks for all such elements.) If, for example, a data item were spelled differently in a subprogram, the CALLed subprogram would access a new, uninitialized data area (VALUE clause isn't allowed for EXTERNAL) instead of the intended EXTERNAL data area. This causes no warning message to occur, as COBOL II cannot detect what the spelling should have been. This may, or may not, cause an ABEND, depending on how the program accesses the data. Finally, any indexes specified in an INDEXED BY clause are treated as local, not as EXTERNAL.

Accessing data within a CALLed program.

I include this technique, not because I anticipate frequent use of it, but to demonstrate that it is possible. This technique is appropriate if (1) there are data areas in a CALLed subprogram that the CALLing program wishes to access, and (2) you have decided that the data should not be EXTERNAL. Prior to COBOL II, this was impossible.

The technique is to establish a POINTER element in the CALLing program and have the CALLed program return the proper address for it. We accomplish this by using a combination of the POINTER data element and the SET state-ment with the ADDRESS OF clause. In the following example, note that the two SET statements are slightly different.

In this example, there are three programs:

1. MAINPROG, which desires direct addressability to the table in SUBPROG called PREM-TABLE. It CALLs SUBPROG, passing it the POINTER item in which the address of the PREM-TABLE is to be stored.
2. SUBPROG, which is CALLed by MAINPROG and contains a premium table that needs to be shared. It CALLs SETADDR, passing it PREM-TABLE and a data element in which to receive the address.
3. SETADDR, a necessary subprogram to establish the address of PREM-TABLE in SUBPROG. This process must be done in a separate program because the ADDRESS OF value exists only for entries in the LINKAGE SECTION. Since PREM-TABLE is in WORKING-STORAGE for SUBPROG, a third subprogram is needed. This program, upon receiving control from SUBPROG, uses the SET statement to store the address of PREM-TABLE.

Here is the structure:

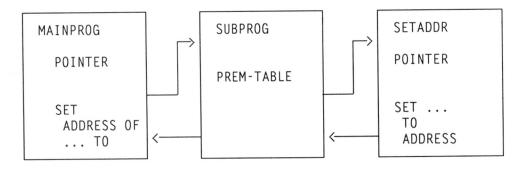

Here is the code:

```
TITLE 'Main Program'
IDENTIFICATION DIVISION.
PROGRAM-ID. MAINPROG.
DATA DIVISION.
WORKING-STORAGE SECTION.
01  WS1-WORK                  POINTER.
LINKAGE SECTION.
01  SUBPROG-AREA.
    05  SUBPROG-DATA-ITEM    PIC X(5) OCCURS 100.
```

```
PROCEDURE DIVISION.
1.
    CALL 'SUBPROG' USING WS1-WORK
    SET ADDRESS OF SUBPROG-AREA TO WS1-WORK
    ·    MAINPROG may now access the area, SUBPROG-AREA,
    ·    directly, without further CALLs to SUBPROG
    STOP RUN.
END PROGRAM MAINPROG.

TITLE 'Subprogram with sharable data area"
ID DIVISION.
PROGRAM-ID.  SUBPROG.
DATA DIVISION.
WORKING-STORAGE SECTION.
01  PREM-TABLE.
    05  PREM-TABLE-ITEM      PIC X(5) OCCURS 100.
01  MY-POINTER              PIC S9(9) COMP.
LINKAGE SECTION.
01  MAIN-POINTER            PIC S9(9) COMP.

PROCEDURE DIVISION USING MAIN-POINTER.
1.
    CALL 'SETADDR' USING PREM-TABLE MY-POINTER
    MOVE MY-POINTER TO MAIN-POINTER
    GOBACK.
    ·
    ·
END PROGRAM SUBPROG.

TITLE 'Subprogram that locates addresses'
ID DIVISION.
PROGRAM-ID. SETADDR.
DATA DIVISION.
WORKING-STORAGE SECTION.
LINKAGE SECTION.
01  LS-POINTER              POINTER.
01  LS-WORK.
    05                      PIC XXXXX.
PROCEDURE DIVISION USING LS-WORK LS-POINTER.
1. SET LS-POINTER TO ADDRESS OF LS-WORK
    GOBACK.
END PROGRAM SETADDR.
```

Note that SETADDR did not need to properly define the layout of PREM-TABLE, since it only needs to SET its address. SETADDR could be used to SET the address of any data area in any program, making this a reusable program.

While this technique has power, remember that MAINPROG's access to the premium table is dependent on SUBPROG. For example, if SUBPROG were dynamically CALLed and later CANCELed, MAINPROG would ABEND if it attempted to access the area.

Receiving data via a JCL PARM.

This technique is only valid for a main program, executed from the JCL EXEC statement. (Exception: An assembler main program could make this data available to subprograms.) Other than the previous example, this is the only occurrence where a main program has a LINKAGE SECTION.

First, we need an understanding of what a PARM is. Unlike other passed data, where we receive a pointer directly to the data, a PARM requires a different technique. The data from the PARM= parameter on the EXEC statement is preceded by a half-word binary field containing the number of bytes of data in the PARM. This data element is dynamically allocated and any attempt to access a larger PARM than that provided results in an ABEND (usually 0C4). For example, if we code

```
//     EXEC PGM=progid,PARM='07/24/91'
```

the data passed will be

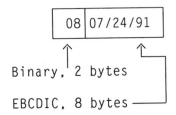

If we omitted the PARM, one is still allocated that looks like this:

```
┌──────┐
│  00  │
└──────┘
   ↑
Binary, 2 bytes
```

The main program would need something like this:

```
LINKAGE SECTION.
01  PARM-DATA.
    05  PARM-LENGTH   PIC S9(4) COMP.
    05  PARM-CONTENT  PIC X(8).
```

```
PROCEDURE DIVISION USING PARM-DATA.
1.   IF PARM-LENGTH = 8
         MOVE PARM-CONTENT TO...
     ELSE
```

... Reminder: If PARM-LENGTH had a value less than 8, the MOVE statement would cause an ABEND, since it moves 8 bytes.

3.2.10. Static versus Dynamic CALL Structures

When deciding whether to use static CALLs to modules or dynamic CALLs, there are several considerations. First, let's clarify the terms.

Static CALL: A static CALL is where the CALLing and the CALLed modules are bound together in the same load module during link-edit processing. (See Creating a Load Module for more information on the process.)

Dynamic CALL: A dynamic CALL is one that is not resolved until the run unit needs to transfer control to the CALLed module. In this case, the CALLing and the CALLed modules are each processed separately by the Linkage Editor. (See CICS/IMS/DB2 Issues for applicability in CICS.)

You can combine the two, using both static and dynamic CALLs within a run unit.

Considerations of a static CALL.

Static CALLs are the format at most shops. When you do static CALLs, you can improve the performance of your application. This is because all programs, being in the same load module, are loaded into memory together. (Note: The jury is still out on this. Some systems performance experts believe that, while static CALLs improve a single application, dynamic CALLs are better for overall computer throughput.)

An additional benefit is that all modules are located and their references resolved during the link-edit process. Assuming you check your listings from the Linkage Editor, you are assured that all modules are in place. Finding that a module is not available is preferable now, rather than during run-time when you might ABEND. This can also be useful documentation, having a complete listing of all modules of the application.

If the Linkage Editor is not able to locate a requested module, it can still finish creating the load module (depending on options used), but it prints a warning message about the missing module and sets an error condition code. The load module will execute properly *unless* the logic causes it to CALL the missing module. If that occurs, you will normally get an 0C1 ABEND, with a PSW (Program Status Word) showing the address of the ABEND somewhere around

00000004. This is because the CALL transferred control to location zero and MVS attempts to locate the next sequential instruction from zero. Some programmers attempt to correct this situation by changing the STEPLIB or JOBLIB because "the program didn't find the needed module." Don't fall into this trap. Remember, a static CALL must be resolved at link-edit time, not at run-time. (The JOBLIB/STEPLIB technique is valid, however, for dynamic CALLs.)

Static CALLs may be done by coding (full syntax not shown):

```
CALL 'literal'
```

where 'literal' is the PROGRAM-ID of the desired program, and you have specified NODYNAM as a compile option.

Considerations of a dynamic CALL.

Dynamic CALLs are the most flexible because you control them at run-time, not at link-edit time. Their use also introduces more complexity into the application logic. Because each module is a separate load module, every application that uses it will get the same version, a definite plus if a program is used by several applications. With static CALLs, all affected modules would need to relink-edit when changes were made. In a dynamic CALL, no relinks are needed.

An additional benefit, depending on your shop's system environment, is that you can control memory requirements depending on which modules are needed. For example, if you have a large module that is rarely needed, it doesn't take up memory during the times it isn't used.

Since dynamic CALLs are resolved at the time the CALL is executed in the run unit, the Linkage Editor is unaware of the need for the module. That means the link-edit listing that is so useful for static CALLs has little use here (other than to validate RMODE and AMODE status). More important for dynamic CALLs is to know in which load libraries the needed modules are. With this information, you can ensure the proper STEPLIB or JOBLIB statements are present. (Reminder: STEPLIB and JOBLIB DD's are mutually exclusive in a job step. MVS will search only one before searching through system libraries.)

If, at run-time, a needed module is not located, you will receive an 806 ABEND message, including a message with the name of the needed module (that is, you do not need to read the dump to solve this). If the module was too big to fit into memory, you will receive an 80A ABEND. The problem is corrected by locating the appropriate load library and making corrections to your STEPLIB or JOBLIB or by increasing the REGION. There is no need to recompile or to relink-edit. (Note: For dynamic CALLs, you can protect against these ABENDS by using the ON EXCEPTION and/or NOT ON EXCEPTION clauses of the CALL statement. For more information, see the previous chapter.)

Earlier, I mentioned that dynamic structures introduce complexity. That is because the application may now have both application logic in it and memory management logic. For example, while the CALL statement causes a dynamic module to be loaded into memory and given control, the CANCEL statement is used to release it from memory. A program CALLed again after being CANCELed will be in its initial state, with no saved values. Statements such as

```
CALL program-a USING data-namea
ON EXCEPTION
    CANCEL program-b
    CALL program-a USING data-namea
    END-CALL
END-CALL
```

can get you into trouble if CANCELing program-b did not free up sufficient memory or wasn't even in memory. These techniques can work well, but keep the added complexity of such techniques in mind.

An optional way to CANCEL a program is to define the program with the INITIAL clause on the PROGRAM-ID statement. For example:

```
PROGRAM-ID.  program-name  INITIAL.
```

This specifies that the program must be CALLed in its initial state. If the program is also CALLed dynamically, it is CANCELed when the GOBACK is executed. Note: This can have severe performance degradation. If a module requires reloading each time it is called, it requires electro-mechanical processes (to the DASD load library) that are much slower than electronic processes. When a program must always be in its initial state, I recommend writing the procedural logic to initialize all work areas each time the program is entered.

Dynamic CALLs are done by coding

```
CALL 'literal'
```

where 'literal' is the PROGRAM-ID of the desired program and you have specified DYNAM as a compile option.

or

```
CALL data-name
```

where data-name is a data element of PIC X(8), containing the name of the desired program. The settings of DYNAM and NODYNAM have no bearing on this syntax. This is the only acceptable format for dynamic CALLs in CICS.

As a final comment on managing dynamic CALLs, remember that the affected load modules must share appropriate RMODE and AMODE attributes. This is normally done by using the same RENT, RES, and DATA compile-time options. Otherwise, you can get some weird ABENDs because the modules won't be able to establish addressability to each other. (For more information, see Creating a Load Module and Specifying COBOL II Options.)

Converting a static CALL to a dynamic CALL.

Creating a dynamic structure once required that the decision be made prior to compiling the affected programs. Now, with COBOL II, you can convert a run unit with static CALL statements into one with dynamic CALLs. While you should recompile and relink programs to create a dynamic CALL structure when possible, the conversion approach is still an option (normally desired where source code is not accessible). The conversion is done by supplying an intermediate module between the CALLing program and the dynamically CALLed programs.

To convert a structure, IBM provides a module called IGZBRDGE. This is an assembler language macro program that, when supplied with the proper parameters, generates an object module with ENTRY points for the names of the modules you want to be dynamically CALLed. The syntax for the macro is

```
name   IGZBRDGE   ENTNAMES=(prog1,prog2,...progn)
```

where: name = the name you assign to the intermediate module (this can be any valid 8-character CSECT name)
proga though progn = names of the load modules that you want to dynamically CALL (these names must already appear within the CALLing program as CALL 'literal')

Using the macro will require you to get assistance from your systems programmers (they usually control access to IBM-supplied software and use of assembler macros). The steps required are

1. Run IGZBRDGE to create the interface module
2. With the Linkage Editor, create load modules of all CALLed programs that are to be dynamically CALLed
3. With the Linkage Editor, create a load module consisting of the CALLing module and the IGZBRDGE-created module.

3.3.   DEFINING, INITIALIZING, AND USING DATA AREAS

One of the main ways in which the professional programmer is distinguished from the novice programmer is the way in which data areas are defined and accessed. The approach used can affect memory allocation, the number of instructions generated, run-time efficiency, and program readability. Each of those topics is addressed in the following material.

3.3.1. Efficiencies in Data Definitions

This topic applies to two categories: memory efficiency and processing efficiency. Some of the guidelines have changed since OS/VS COBOL, especially for binary (COMP) data items. This section concentrates on the popular data formats: alphanumeric, packed-decimal, zoned decimal, and binary, plus implications for virtual storage allocation. While floating point data (COMP-2) does receive limited use, that format is not addressed in this book.

Memory efficiency.

With the amount of memory available in mainframes today, attaining memory efficiency may not seem to be an issue. While this is true for small, independent applications, it remains an issue for larger, corporate systems. The following topics might assist you.

Virtual storage constraint relief. The term "Virtual Storage Constraint Relief" (VSCR) refers to the process of reallocating memory from below the 16-megabyte address to above it. As mainframes increase memory, the increase will be in this address space and applications that don't take advantage of it will not benefit from the potential improvement. Realizing VSCR for an application includes allocation of both program memory and data memory. As this material is covered in more depth in specific topics, this is a summary list of that information.

Allocation of memory for programs. Whether a program is loaded above or below the 16-megabyte address is dependent on the RENT compile option. All program modules in a load module must have RENT for this to work. NORENT is primarily for compatibility with older programs. See Module Structures for more information.

Allocation of memory for data. Data areas are allocated above the 16-megabyte address if DATA(31) is specified and below if DATA(24) is specified. DATA(31) requires RENT. The compile option, NORES, also impacts on memory allocation as it restricts all memory allocations for addressability to be in 24-bit mode. With RENT, the DATA DIVISION is separate from the load module, but it is within the load module for NORENT.

EXTERNAL data and file definitions are allocated in 24-bit mode. See previous topics on sharing files and data for more information on when this technique is desired.

Alignment. First, remember that eight (8) bytes are the minimum allocated to 01-level entries (double-word alignment). thus,

```
01  REC-A   PIC X.
01  REC-B   PIC X.
```

requires 16 bytes, not 2. That is why I recommend that switches and accumulators be combined into common 01-level items not only to improve readability, but also to reduce unnecessary memory use.

Packed-decimal field sizes. Another concern is the number of bytes allocated for COMP-3 items. If you recall that packed-decimal items contain 1 decimal digit in the rightmost byte and 2 decimal digits in all other bytes, you will know that the right technique is always to specify an odd number for COMP-3 items. Consider,

```
05  FLDA   PIC S9(4)   COMP-3   VALUE +5.
```

appears in memory as

00	00	5C

,

which is what would be assigned if the PIC had been S9(5). The difference is that additional instructions will be generated to truncate the high-order digit due to the even-numbered PIC clause.

Processing efficiency.

Although you may have been adept at determining processing efficiency for OS/VS COBOL programs, you will find some differences here. How you define data elements, plus what compile options you select, will make a noticeable impact on your processing efficiency.

Processing efficiency by sign definitions. With OS/VS COBOL, my recommendation was to put S in the PIC clause for every numeric item. Now, I have a different recommendation, but let me first share some background information. COBOL II has the facility to be forgiving with signs (the new NUMPROC compile option), which means that it can generate some inefficient code on demand. Many shops, fearing that some of their programs potentially misuse signed data, opted for the least efficient NUMPROC option, NUMPROC(NOPFD), which is explained later. If you want to use the most efficient option, NUMPROC(PFD), you must establish data in the following format:

- If the data will *never* be signed, omit the S in the PIC, for example, PIC 99. If such a field has a plus (C) or minus (D) sign, you will get incorrect results on IF NUMERIC.

- If the data is *always* signed with C or D (never *F*), place the *S* in the PIC clause. (Note: A MOVE from a PIC 9 to a PIC S9 field will set the sign to C.)

If all your data qualifies, you may specify NUMPROC(PFD) for your compiles. If you are unsure about C, D, and F, specify NUMPROC(MIG) and test the results. Here are some examples of the number of instructions generated, depending on selected options:

```
05  DISP-1      PIC 999.
05  DISP-2      PIC S999.
05  DISP-3      PIC 999.
05  PACKED-1    PIC S9(15)    COMP-3.
05  PACKED-2    PIC S9(15)    COMP-3.
```

This table lists the number of instructions generated for each compile option for these example statements.

MIG	NO PFD	PFD	
3	3	2	MOVE DISP-1 TO DISP-2
2	3	2	MOVE DISP-2 TO DISP-1
2	2	2	MOVE DISP-1 TO DISP-3
4	6*	4	ADD 1 TO DISP-1
5	7*	5	ADD DISP-1 TO DISP-2
3	4*	3	COMPUTE PACKED-1 = PACKED-1 * PACKED-2

*Included a CALL to a COBOL II run-time subroutine for additional validation and adjustment.

The above table may indicate that MIG and PFD are alike because they generate the same number of instructions for these few examples. Don't assume that, as these examples demonstrate only a few situations, and the choice of these options also affects how conditional statements are processed (e.g., IF NUMERIC, IF POSITIVE). For information on that subject, see Handling Conditional Statements in this chapter.

Processing efficiency considerations with binary data. This was an easy decision with OS/VS COBOL because you had a compile option choice of TRUNC or NOTRUNC. With COBOL II, you can choose TRUNC(BIN), TRUNC(STD), or TRUNC(OPT). One IBM manual states that TRUNC(BIN) is the equivalent of

NOTRUNC. Another IBM manual states that TRUNC(OPT) is the equivalent of NOTRUNC. Unfortunately, both are correct. In OS/VS COBOL, NOTRUNC caused the data to be stored as a full or half-word (not truncated) and *also* generated the least amount of code.

In COBOL II, the process of generating the most efficient code and the process of not truncating data have been separated into two different compile options. If you use binary arithmetic for efficiency and do not have a concern for truncation, use TRUNC(OPT). If you use binary arithmetic to store the maximum number of bits in the half or full-word, use TRUNC(BIN). Here are some examples of the instructions generated for different options:

```
05  BIN-F1      PIC S9(9)    COMP.
05  BIN-F2      PIC S9(9)    COMP.
05  BIN-H1      PIC S9(4)    COMP.
05  BIN-H2      PIC S9(4)    COMP.
05  BIN-F3      PIC S9(6)    COMP.
05  BIN-F4      PIC S9(6)    COMP.
```

This table lists the number of instructions generated for each compile option for these example statements.

BIN	STD	OPT	
17	1	1	MOVE BIN-F1 TO BIN-F2
4	1	1	MOVE BIN-H1 TO BIN-H2
19	4	3	COMPUTE BIN-F1 = BIN-F1 * BIN-F2
19	6	3	COMPUTE BIN-H1 = BIN-H1 * BIN-H2
20	11	10	ADD BIN-F1 TO BIN-F2
7	6	3	ADD BIN-H1 TO BIN-H2
11*	4	3	COMPUTE BIN-F3 = BIN-F3 * BIN-F4

* The BIN option generated 11 instructions, plus a CALL to a COBOL II runtime subprogram for further data validity.

From the data in the table, there are clearly performance differences. If you rarely use COMP data, the choice of compile options for your applications may not be critical, but if your applications require COMP data, you should be sensitive to the performance implications.

Processing efficiency considerations for field sizes. When considering data efficiencies, we often think only of the arithmetic statements. Too often overlooked is the importance of field sizes where the MOVE instruction is used. For example, where the data types, sizes, and signs match, you will get more efficient data moves than when they are different. A small point, but significant if your application does a lot of MOVE instructions.

3.3.2. Coding Literals

Literals may be numeric, nonnumeric, or hexadecimal. I encourage removing as many literals from the procedural code as possible, except for simple situations such as where a zero or one is obvious (e.g.,. . . VARYING FROM 1 BY 1 UNTIL . . .). Here is a brief summary of common literal usage:

Numeric literals.

Length from 1 to 18 decimal digits, sign is optional, as is a decimal point. Number is assumed positive if sign is omitted.

Nonnumeric literals.

Length from 1 to 160 bytes, any EBCDIC character combination, enclosed in quotes or apostrophes, depending on choice of APOST compile option. If a quote or apostrophe must appear within the literal, it must occur twice, as in

```
'DON''T GET CONFUSED'
```

Hexadecimal literals

Length from 2 to 320 hexadecimal digits (1 to 160 bytes), enclosed in quotes/ apostrophes (depending on choice of compile options) and preceded by X, as in:

```
X'C8C5E7'
```

which occupies 3 bytes and, in EBCDIC, is 'HEX'

3.3.3. Defining a Table

If tables are new to you, you might consider reading the first four subtopics here, as they provide additional information on tables. This topic will explain how to define a table in WORKING-STORAGE. You may have heard terms such as *two-dimensional*, *three-dimensional*, or even *four-dimensional*. Let's get those terms simplified. The dimensions for a table are the number of search arguments that must be used to get a result. We'll take several examples to demonstrate this.

One-dimensional tables.

A one-dimensional table consisting of a single element type is merely a list. If unordered, I call it a laundry list because the only way to find anything is to read each item. This approach is useful if you have data that must be validated, where the validation itself affects the logic. For example, if you know one of your company's products is legal in ten states and not legal in the other 40, then a purchase order from the other 40 states should not be processed. To validate purchase orders, a table such as this might be defined using these sample two-character state codes:

```
01  LEGAL-TABLE-ENTRIES.
    05      PIC X(22)
        VALUE 'ALAZCOFLIDKSMAMONYOHZZ'.
01  LEGAL-TABLE REDEFINES LEGAL-TABLE-ENTRIES.
    05  VALID-STATE  PIC XX, OCCURS 11.
```

or this:

```
01  LEGAL-TABLE-ENTRIES.
    05      PIC XX      VALUE 'AL'.
    05      PIC XX      VALUE 'AZ'.
    05      PIC XX      VALUE 'CO'.
    05      PIC XX      VALUE 'FL'.
    .
    .
    05      PIC XX      VALUE 'ZZ'.
01  LEGAL-TABLE REDEFINES LEGAL-TABLE-ENTRIES.
    05  VALID-STATE   PIC XX, OCCURS 11.
```

Notice the redefinition does not need to follow the PIC clause format as long as it is faithful to the number of bytes represented. There is an eleventh entry here, ZZ (although any unique code would do). The purpose of including an extra entry for tables is to allow better procedural control. For example, a control field, such as ZZ, is for tables where the last entry can't be otherwise predicted or where the size of the table is subject to change frequently (in this example, for instance, the number of states in which the product is legal will probably change).

Another type of one-dimensional table contains multiple data element types, usually a search element and a data component. For example, an insurance company might have a table containing premium amounts by age. That could be shown

```
01  PREM-TABLE.
    05  PREM-ENTRY   OCCURS 99   TIMES
                                 ASCENDING KEY IS PREM-AGE
                                 INDEXED BY AGE-INDX.
        10 PREM-AGE          PIC 99.
        10 PREM-MALE         PIC S9(5)V99 COMP-3.
        10 PREM-FEMALE       PIC S9(5)V99 COMP-3.
```

This table has more depth and structure than the previous one. Also, where the previous table needed only to be searched for a match to make processing decisions, this table isn't so simple. Searching the table presents different amounts to charge for the insurance policy. The ASCENDING KEY clause specifies that this table must be in ascending order by age *if* a SEARCH statement is used to process against it (covered in Improving Table Searches). The INDEXED BY clause specifies an index-name (covered in the topic on subscripting). Searching the above table requires knowledge of one variable, age.

Two-dimensional tables.

A two-dimensional table is a one-dimensional table with an added dimension. Let's take the table in the previous topic and add a new dimension, a smoking/nonsmoking premium. Searching this table will require two variables: age and smoker/nonsmoker status. Here is one way of constructing the table:

```
01   PREM-TABLE.
     05   PREM-ENTRY     OCCURS 99   TIMES
                                     ASCENDING KEY IS PREM-AGE
                                     INDEXED BY AGE-INDX.
          10   PREM-AGE           PIC 99.
          10   PREM-SMOKE-OPTION  OCCURS 2.
               15   PREM-MALE       PIC S9(5)V99   COMP-3.
               15   PREM-FEMALE     PIC S9(5)V99   COMP-3.
```

This structure gives us four premium amounts for each age: two for smokers (male and female) and two for nonsmokers. Whether adding an INDEXED BY clause for the smoking option will improve performance will be a topic addressed in Subscripting versus Indexing. Tables of any complexity are usually initialized by reading a file of data and inserting data elements in the appropriate table entry. The PERFORM VARYING statement is effective here.

3.3.4. Initializing a Table

Initializing a table can be done in a variety of ways, usually dependent on how frequently the data changes and how complex it is. Here are some examples:

Redefine the table and store variable data

```
01   LEGAL-TABLE-ENTRIES.
     05     PIC X(22)
          VALUE  'ALAZCOFLIDKSMAMONYOHZZ'.
01   LEGAL-TABLE REDEFINES LEGAL-TABLE-ENTRIES.
     05   VALID-STATE PIC XX, OCCURS 11.
```

Initialize the table to spaces or zeroes with **VALUE** clause

```
01  LEGAL-TABLE.
    05  VALID-STATE   PIC XX   OCCURS 11   VALUE SPACES.
```

This feature did NOT exist in OS/VS COBOL.

Initialize the table to spaces or zeros at run-time

```
INITIALIZE LEGAL-TABLE
```

*Note: INITIALIZE was reviewed in Chapter 2. With one
statement, you can reset a table.*

Some programmers accomplish this by using something like this, which
should be avoided:

```
PERFORM 3400-RESET-TABLE VARYING STATE-CODE FROM 1 BY
   1 UNTIL STATE-CODE > 11
   .
   .


3400-RESET-TABLE.
    MOVE SPACES TO VALID-STATE (STATE-CODE).
```

This works, but it is unnecessary with COBOL II, it is inefficient, and it is
clumsy to code.

Initialize the table with variable data from a file

```
PERFORM VARYING AGE-INDX FROM 1 BY 1 UNTIL EOF OR
   PREM-AGE (AGE-INDX - 1) = 99
      READ FD3-PREM-FILE
        AT END
            SET EOF TO TRUE
        NOT AT END
            MOVE FD3-PREM-AGE TO PREM-AGE (AGE-INDX)
            MOVE FD3-ML-PREM-SM TO PREM-MALE (AGE-INDX, 1)
            MOVE FD3-FM-PREM-SM TO PREM-FEMALE (AGE-INDX, 1)
            MOVE FD3-ML-PREM-NOSM TO PREM-MALE (AGE-INDX, 2)
            MOVE FD3-FM-PREM-NOSM TO PREM-FEMALE (AGE-INDX, 2)
      END-READ
END-PERFORM
```

This example assumes that each record on the file contains the four
premiums for an age group. This is an example where an inline PERFORM can
be effective because the logic is contained within a few eye scans and does one
function.

3.3.5. Improving Table Searches

One of the problems with tables is that, as we become familiar with them, we forget that a lot of computer time is spent calculating addresses and making comparisons that prove false. For example, if a table is unordered, the only way to locate a valid entry is to start at the beginning and test each variable until the end of the table is reached or a match is found. If this is done rarely, it may not be worth the effort to improve the process. However, many tables are used frequently. Any steps that improve the process will reduce costs and resource use. Here are some options that can improve table searches:

Use SEARCH statement. The SEARCH statement has several benefits over the PERFORM VARYING. One, the SEARCH statement is complete, able to increment the subscript value, make the comparison, test for the end of the table, and execute valid conditions, all with a few lines of code. Each dimension in a table requires a separate SEARCH statement. The SEARCH statement isn't new with COBOL II, although many programmers have never used it. Also, the SEARCH statement requires that the table be defined with an INDEXED BY clause. This is advantageous since it relieves you from needing to specify it as you would with a PERFORM VARYING statement. Here are examples using basic syntax

A sequential search

```
SET AGE-INDX TO 1
SEARCH PREM-ENTRY
  AT END    SET AGE-ERROR TO TRUE
  WHEN PREM-AGE (AGE-INDX) = APP-AGE
     PERFORM 3300-EXTRACT-PREMIUMS
END-SEARCH
```

Equivalent code with the PERFORM would require

```
SET AGE-ERROR TO TRUE
PERFORM VARYING AGE-INDX FROM 1 BY 1 UNTIL
 AGE-INDX > 99
   IF PREM-AGE (AGE-INDX) = APP-AGE
       PERFORM 3300-EXTRACT-PREMIUMS
       SET AGE-INDX TO 99
       SET AGE-OKAY TO TRUE
   END-IF
END-PERFORM
```

The above SEARCH statement searches the table from beginning to end until the AT END condition is met or the WHEN condition is met (there can be multiple WHEN conditions). The PERFORM accomplishes this also, but requires several extra statements that may not appear obvious, and if omitted cause errors in processing.

A binary search

```
SEARCH ALL PREM-ENTRY
   AT END    SET AGE-ERROR TO TRUE
   WHEN PREM-AGE (AGE-INDX) = APP-AGE
       PERFORM 3300-EXTRACT-PREMIUMS
END-SEARCH
```

This format of SEARCH appears similar to the sequential SEARCH statement, but it is quite different. For one, it requires that the table entry have the ASCENDING/DESCENDING KEY clause specified and that the variable following WHEN be that data-name.

The benefit is increased processing speed for large tables. This is accomplished by a technique called a "binary search." To gain an appreciation of this technique, assume you have a table with 10,000 entries. Sequentially searching the table for a match would, on average, require about 5,000 comparisons per attempt. For example, if your match value were the 5,061st entry, the SEARCH (or PERFORM VARYING) would execute the comparison 5,061 times before finding the match. This is both expensive and time consuming. A binary search divides the remaining elements in half and checks for high or low. For the example mentioned, it would start at the 5,000th entry and test for high or low. Since ours is the 5,061st, it would test higher than the 5,000th entry. (Remember, the ASCENDING KEY or DESCENDING KEY is required for this option.) The logic would then split the remaining items and test the 7,500th entry. The process would continue, splitting and testing high or low until the 5,061st entry were matched.

While computers may use slightly different numbers, the example is still valid. The concept is to narrow the remaining entries, based on discoveries already made. In my theoretical example, the 5,061st entry is located on the 12th compare, not the 5,061st.

Since the SEARCH statement is dependent on indexes, you will want to check a later topic, Subscripting versus Indexes.

Arrange tables by probability of occurrence. Sometimes you know that of all the possible entries in a table, the majority of matches will match to a subset of the table entries. In that case, you may want to use a sequential search and initialize the table with the most frequently used data elements at the beginning. For example, if you have 100 job titles in a human resources table, but 95% of the employees have the title "Programmer," it wouldn't make sense to do a binary search to locate job title. Put the Programmer job title as the first entry in the table and do a sequential search.

There is a drawback to this easy approach. Over time the most probable job title may change. If, in our example, the department were restructured and programmers were reclassified as "Programmer/analysts," the performance of the application would suffer until changes were made to the table.

Arrange tables for direct access. This technique can rarely be used, but for that reason it is often overlooked when it is the best approach. Consider the case in which you want to print the name of the month but only have the number of the month. I've actually seen people do this inefficient technique:

```
01   MONTH-CONTENTS.
     05           PIC X(10)   VALUE '01JANUARY'.
     05           PIC X(10)   VALUE '02FEBRUARY'.
     05           PIC X(10)   VALUE '03MARCH'.
         .
         .

01   MONTH-TABLE REDEFINES MONTH-CONTENTS.
     05  MONTH-ENTRIES    OCCURS 12
             ASCENDING KEY IS MONTH-CODE
             INDEXED BY MONTH-INX.
         10  MONTH-CODE PIC 99.
         10  MONTH-NAME PIC X(8).
         .
         .

     SET MONTH-INX TO 1
     SEARCH MONTH-ENTRIES
       AT END
          DISPLAY ' INVALID MONTH'
       WHEN MONTH-CODE (MONTH-INX) = REP-MONTH
          MOVE MONTH-NAME (MONTH-INX) TO REP-TITLE
     END-SEARCH
```

The above example works, but with much unnecessary processing. A better and much simpler approach is to acknowledge that the appearance of entries within the table corresponds to the search argument (e.g., the seventh entry in the table happens to represent the seventh month), which gives us this simple approach:

```
01   MONTH-CONTENTS.
     05           PIC X(8)   VALUE 'JANUARY'.
     05           PIC X(8)   VALUE 'FEBRUARY'.
     05           PIC X(8)   VALUE 'MARCH'.
         .
         .
```

```
01   MONTH-TABLE REDEFINES MONTH-CONTENTS.
     05  MONTH-NAME      PIC X(8) OCCURS 12.
         .
         .

     IF REP-MONTH > 0 AND < 13
         MOVE MONTH-NAME (REP-MONTH) TO REP-TITLE
     ELSE
         DISPLAY ' INVALID MONTH'
     END-IF
```

This is a case where indexes are not beneficial, since the entry within the table is extracted in one statement. More on this concept in the next topic.

3.3.6. Subscripting versus Indexes with Tables

If you work with tables, you've probably encountered discussions on using indexes to subscript through tables versus not using them (not using indexes is generally called subscripting). First let's identify the issue. Each time you request access to a table element, the run-time code must calculate the location of the data. Consider the following data description:

```
01   MONTH-TABLE.
     05  MONTH-NAME  PIC X(8)   OCCURS 12.
```

If this statement is encountered,

```
MOVE MONTH-NAME (REP-MONTH) TO REP-TITLE
```

the compiler will generate appropriate code to take the value of REP-MONTH and compute how many bytes the proper data element is beyond the starting point of the table. For example, if REP-MONTH contained the value 07, the generated code would need to do the following (approximately):

- Convert REP-MONTH to COMP format, if necessary.
- Subtract 1 from the value (7 - 1 = 6).
- Multiply the value by the length of MONTH-NAME (8 * 6) to get the offset in the table.
- Add the result to the memory location of MONTH-TABLE.
- Store the value temporarily as a base address and execute the MOVE statement.

Now, the resulting object code from compiling that statement may not generate the code quite that way, but my intent is to demonstrate that some work is needed every time a table element's address must be calculated. All of the above must be done each time the contents of the search argument REP-MONTH is changed, whether subscripting or indexing is used. The difference is that with indexes the result is saved for future use. With subscripting, the calculations are repeated for every access where there is the possibility that the value has changed. (Note: this is dependent, but only to a degree, on the OPTIMIZE compile option.)

So, what are your choices? If the table is accessed only once for each change of the search argument, it makes no difference which method you use. This rarely occurs, however. Usually you will access the table several times before changing the search argument, meaning that indexes will serve you better than subscripts. An example in which the table search does not change for several statements follows:

```
IF MONTH-CODE (REP-MONTH) > 3 AND MONTH-CODE (REP-MONTH) < 7
    MOVE MONTH-TITLE (REP-MONTH) TO REP-TITLE
    MOVE '2ND QUARTER' TO PAGE-TITLE
END-IF
```

The above calculations would be done three times (once for the first comparison, again for the second comparison, and once again for the move) if REP-MONTH is not defined as an index. If REP-MONTH were an index, no computations would be needed since the offset would have been previously calculated. That can mean a lot to an application. (The OPTIMIZE compile option minimizes this, but the need to do a computation of some degree still remains when indexes are not used.)

The main issue, then, is how many statements are executed after changing the value of an index. Indexes can be changed by three statements: the SET statement, the SEARCH statement, and the PERFORM VARYING statement.

Together with the ASCENDING KEY and INDEXED BY clauses of the DATA DIVISION, this gives good documentation and efficiency to an application. If you haven't used these statements before, I believe you will find that they complement each other.

3.3.7. Using Large Table Space as a Database

This is a simple technique that was introduced in the previous chapter. There are no special coding requirements other than some form of table management technique. The big change is that you may define an 01-level item up to 16 million bytes. For example, if you are processing a keyed VSAM file, it may be much quicker to load the database into a table and use the SEARCH ALL statement instead of reading randomly from DASD. The limits of 01-levels changed considerably from OS/VS COBOL, giving this capability. Such a technique should not be used for EXTERNAL items, since they are allocated below the 16-megabyte address.

3.4. HANDLING CONDITIONAL STATEMENTS

With COBOL II, you need to be sensitive to a few changes in conditional statements. While these differences appear elsewhere, they are summarized here for ease of access.

3.4.1. ALPHANUMERIC Tests

In OS/VS COBOL you could code IF ALPHABETIC and know you were testing for upper-case alphabetic characters. In COBOL II you must use IF ALPHABETIC-UPPER for the same results. IF ALPHABETIC still works, but it accepts both upper- and lower-case text as valid.

3.4.2. NUMERIC Tests

IF NUMERIC works the same for most situations. The difference depends on your choice of the compiler NUMPROC option. Here is an example of where the difference lies:

```
05 DATA-FLD PIC S999.
   IF DATA-FLD NUMERIC
```

will be true with all options if DATA-FLD contains a signed, positive or negative, number. That means the sign would be either "C" or "D". If DATA-FLD contains an unsigned value (sign of "F"), the test will be true for NUMPROC(MIG) and NUMPROC(NOPFD), but it will fail for NUMPROC(PFD). These same considerations should also be used when using the IF POSITIVE, ZERO, or NEGATIVE tests. (See, Efficiencies in Data Definitions for more information.)

If you define data elements with the "S" (e.g., PIC S999), regardless of whether you anticipate a sign, you may want to use the NUMPROC(MIG) option to maintain compatibility with that coding technique.

3.5. MAKING A PROGRAM MORE EFFICIENT

Making a program more efficient can be tough work, especially if major flaws exist in the design or if the program is already written. This section summarizes various techniques that can improve a program's performance, but none of these techniques go beyond COBOL (that is, if the file is poorly structured or if the logic flow is inefficient, you'll need more than some performance tuning to resolve the problem). Several of these topics will refer you to other topics for more information.

3.5.1. File Blocking in QSAM

I'm still amazed at how this old-fashioned technique is ignored in many applications. Increasing the block size of a sequential file reduces the number of physical I/O requests that must occur, thereby reducing the elapsed time and cost of a program. Years ago many shops had standard guidelines such as "always block by 10." That may have been good advice in the early 1970s but no longer. A programmer doing small tests will not see the difference, but a full-scale productional run can be significantly affected. Since the maximum allowed in QSAM is 32,760 bytes, I recommend you use a block size as near to that as possible. If your DASD is larger than that (e.g., 3380s), use a block size that is slightly smaller than 1/2 the track size. Let's see an example:

Assuming you are using IBM 3380 DASD drives, the particulars are

```
Bytes per track:  47,476
Tracks per cylinder: 15
```

For this example, let's assume you have a record size of 376. Optimum blocking would be 32,712 (87 * 376), since this would give you 87 logical records processed for each READ or WRITE. Unfortunately, that leaves 14,764 bytes unused per track (47,476 - 32,712), or a wastage of 31 percent. That gives optimum I/O, but it compromises DASD usage. Let's try figuring nearer to half a track, 23,238 bytes [(47476 − 1000) ÷ 2]. By using slightly less than half the track, we can still get a good block size of 22,936 (61 * 376) and 61 logical records per block. Since 22,936 is less than half the size of the track, we get two blocks per track for a total track usage of 45,872 bytes (22,936 * 2). This is still an excellent block size and the DASD wastage is less than 4 percent, a significant improvement. (Note: Save your valuable time. IBM sells reference cards for their equipment so you don't need to do arithmetic. The card for the model 3380 is order number GX26-1678 and costs less than a dollar.)

The FD needs the clause

```
BLOCK CONTAINS 0 RECORDS
```

The JCL DD statement (output ONLY) needs the clause

```
DCB=BLKSIZE=22936
```

You will further improve I/O for QSAM files on DASD by allocating in CYLINDERS instead of TRACKS. While too deep for this book, this allocation causes fewer rotations of the DASD to transfer the file.

3.5.2. Data Formats

This subject is covered earlier in Efficiencies in Data Definitions. Here are my general guidelines:

- Always use packed-decimal for computational fields.
- Always specify an odd number of digits for the PIC clause.
- Always specify the sign in the PIC clause for computational fields.
- Always use indexes for tables. (If you refuse to accept my earlier arguments about indexes, then at least use COMP items for subscripts to minimize the inefficiencies.)
- Use COMP every time it is specified in an application or IBM documentation, since that normally means that either MVS or an application program expects it (but be careful of misuse of the SYNC clause, as that forces boundary alignment that may change desired record alignment).

If you're skeptical about guidelines beginning with the word Always, so am I. Even so, by following simple guidelines, I can concentrate on the programming assignment at hand instead of worrying about minor differences in performance. If you're convinced that binary arithmetic (COMP) is superior, review the earlier topic, Efficiencies in Data Definitions.

3.5.3. COMPUTE Statement

Years ago, I was advised to avoid the COMPUTE statement because it was inefficient. In hindsight, I was given poor advice. In test after test, the COMPUTE statement has been at least as efficient as other instructions, whether replacing a simple ADD with COMPUTE X = X + 1 or something more complex. The additional advantage of COBOL II is that, with OPTIMIZE specified, the compiler looks for sequences of arithmetic and saves those intermediate values for use later. The sequences can either begin the computation or be bound in parentheses to ensure they are identified. This can often create what appears to be amazing efficiency on a statement-by-statement basis. Consider this example:

```
COMPUTE A = A * (B / C)
    .
    .
COMPUTE Z = F * G + (B / C)
    .
    .
COMPUTE E = B / C
```

In all three statements, there is the sequence B / C. If the compiler determines the logic flow of the program cannot change the values of B and C between any two of the three statements, it saves the result of the division so it can be reused. In the last statement, for example, no division takes place. The generated machine code simply moves the result into field E.

While I encourage use of the COMPUTE statement, you need to be sensitive to the possibility of incurring large intermediate values that exceed machine capacity (see Chapter 7 for more information on machine capacities). As a general guideline, you can add the 9s in the PIC clauses to determine the largest intermediate value for multiplication or division. For example,

```
05  A   PIC  S9(15)   COMP-3.
05  B   PIC  S9(15)   COMP-3.
05  C   PIC  S9(15)    COMP-3.
05  D   PIC  S9(15)    COMP-3.
 .
 .

    COMPUTE A = A * B
```

will have an intermediate result of 30 digits (15 + 15), which is within the machine capacity for packed-decimal arithmetic. The generated machine code (using LIST compile option) would look something like this:

```
Assembler instructions          Compiler comments

ZAP    376(16,13),19(8,9)       TS2=0       B
MP     376(16,13),11(8,9)       TS2=0       A
ZAP    11(8,9),384(8,13)        A           TS2=8
```

You don't need to know assembler language to understand that this represents three instructions. The first one moves B to a temporary work area, the second multiplies the temporary work area by A, and the third moves the result to A. Very efficient. Now let's look at a different example:

```
COMPUTE A = A * B * C * D
```

This will have an intermediate result of 60 digits (15 + 15 + 15 + 15). Since this number is too large for the machine, extra code must be generated to programmatically extend and validate the intermediate values. Explaining the generated assembler code is too complex for this book, but I show it here to highlight what pattern of assembly language indicates less efficient code (again, using the LIST compile option):

```
Assembler instructions          Compiler comments

    ZAP    360(16,13),11(8,9)   TS1=0       A
    MP     360(16,13),19(8,9)   TS1=0       B
    ZAP    376(16,13),19(8,9)   TS2=0       C
    L      2,92(0,13)           TGTFIXD+92
    L      15,188(0,2)          V(IGZCXMU)
    LA     1,782(0,10)          PGMLIT AT +766
    BALR 14,15
```

```
          CLC   401(8,13),0(12)        TS2=25              SYSLIT AT +0
          BC    2,484(0,11)            GN=13(0005E4)
          BC    15,494(0,11)           GN=14(0005EE)
GN=13     EQU   *
          L     15,460(0,2)            V(IGZEMSG)
          LA    1,754(0,10)            PGMLIT AT +738
          BALR  14,15
GN=14     EQU   *
          MVC   360(16,13),408(13)     TS1=0               TS2=32
          NI    360(13),X'0F'          TS1=0
          ZAP   376(16,13),27(8,9)     TS2=0               D
          L     15,188(0,2)            V(IGZCXMU)
          LA    1,782(0,10)            PGMLIT AT +766
          BALR  14,15
          ZAP   11(8,9),416(8,13)      A                   TS2=40
```

First, instead of three instructions, you generate 20. However, that is just the visible portion. The highlighted instructions are the key to alert you to possible inefficiencies you may want to avoid. They represent the assembler language equivalent of CALL statements. The first is a CALL to module IGZCXMU, the second is a CALL to IGZEMSG, and the final CALL is to IGZCXMU again. While I have no idea how large those IBM-supplied programs are, I assure you they are each much larger than these 20 instructions. The guideline is not to look for these specific modules in arithmetic statements, but to watch for the pattern. (Note: You will see similar patterns in other, nonarithmetic instructions. In those instances, they are necessary for proper operation and may be ignored.) Whenever you have this pattern of instructions in COMPUTE statements and performance is important to you, consider using several COMPUTE statements, such as:

```
COMPUTE A = A * B
COMPUTE A = A * C
COMPUTE A = A * D
```

The preceding information is presented to sensitize you to possible inefficiencies. Yes, you can often avoid the appearance of these inefficiencies by coding many MULTIPLY and DIVIDE statements. They generate more code on average, however, since each MULTIPLY or DIVIDE statement edits and stores intermediate results, and they make the equation more difficult to read.

3.5.4. Compiler Options for Run-Time Efficiency

Some compile options have been discussed earlier in this section. This topic summarizes the impact on performance of various options and does not explain their functions in detail. A full discussion appears later in Specifying COBOL II Options.

Options that give maximum productional performance (some of them have implications on your data definitions):

Compile-time options

```
OPTIMIZE
NUMPROC(PFD) or NUMPROC(MIG)
TRUNC(OPT)            (has potential implications for CICS.
                      IMS, & DB2)
NOSSRANGE
AWO
NODYNAM
FASTSRT
NOTEST
```

Run-time options

```
NOAIXBLD
NOWSCLEAR
NOSSRANGE
LIBKEEP
RTEREUS   (IF main program is non-COBOL and frequently
           CALLs COBOL programs, this may impact on IMS/DC).
```

Options that generate maximum flexibility in the run-time environment, both for the application and for the computer:

```
RESIDENT   -(required for CICS)
RENT       -(required for CICS)
```

3.5.5. CALLs

A CALL statement generates a significant amount of executable code, often invisible. By invisible, I mean that the executed code is buried in the initialization code of the CALLed module, not in the CALLing module. Where a program is small (e.g., 50 statements or less), consider imbedding it in the parent program or using a nested structure, since either will minimize or eliminate some overhead code. If this isn't feasible, the most efficient CALL structure is the CALL BY REFERENCE format with the NODYNAM compile option. Don't worry about the GLOBAL and EXTERNAL options for data reference. Their use does not affect performance.

By including this information, I am not suggesting that you not use the CALL statement. I use it regularly. It has many benefits if a shop has reusable code or large applications. Just be aware that, of all statements, the CALL statement will normally execute the most overhead (nonproductive to the application logic) instructions.

3.5.6. SORTs

This chapter has a separate topic on SORT techniques and there is information on JCL for sorts further in this chapter. For a more thorough discussion, read those topics. What appears here is summary information.

First, assess your application data flow to see if the new sorted structure is needed in several places. If so, you will usually incur less cost by sorting the data once and saving to a permanent file, eliminating the need to resort the data later.

Second, consider using DFSORT to do the sort instead of COBOL. DFSORT is more efficient, and the control statements can be done in a matter of minutes, not hours or days. DFSORT is explained later in this chapter.

Third, never use the COBOL SORT statement format, SORT USING . . . GIVING . . . . Doing so accomplishes nothing that DFSORT could not do in less time with less coding and testing.

Fourth, consider using DFSORT control statements to replace an INPUT or OUTPUT PROCEDURE on those occasions where DFSORT cannot do all the necessary processing. This includes those situations in which an INPUT PROCEDURE is to do simple data selection and/or will reformat the data prior to sorting. This type of situation is much simpler to code with DFSORT control statements than by writing an INPUT PROCEDURE. (This technique has been available for years, yet many programmers are unaware of this possibility.) A program using this approach is in Chapter 8 (Sample Programs). See the section JCL Requirements for more information on the JCL for DFSORT and also see Chapters 5 and 6 for additional tips on sort applications.

Fifth, always use the FASTSRT compile option. If your SORT is anything other than SORT INPUT PROCEDURE . . . OUTPUT PROCEDURE . . ., you will receive improved performance.

3.5.7. SEARCH ALL

This is described previously in Improving Table Searches. If your application searches tables, see that topic. It explains and demonstrates the binary search process.

3.5.8. Indexes and Subscripts

This is described under Subscripting versus Indexes. If your application searches tables, see that topic. It explains and demonstrates the differences between use and nonuse of indexes to provide addressability to tables.

3.5.9. Data Structures and System Environments

There is no COBOL solution to this. I included the topic because you might be looking for a solution here. A poor data architecture can defeat the most well-written programs. Your data architecture should be designed prior to writing the programs that access them. If you believe your performance is being affected by poor data architecture or environmental considerations, see either your shop's data specialists about conducting a design review or your shop's technical staff to conduct performance monitoring of your application.

Some issues that may affect performance are mentioned below.

For VSAM files, check the control interval sizes, the free space allocations, alternate indexes, buffers, and keys. If you are using the defaults from Access Method Services, this should be investigated by a person familiar with VSAM. For more VSAM assistance, which is beyond the scope of this book, you might want another QED book, *VSAM: The Complete Guide to Optimization and Design* (See Chapter 9). That book addresses all issues that might affect VSAM performance.

For CICS applications, check your module structure, the number of EXEC LINK or EXEC XCTL commands that may occur within a transaction, and the number of I/O operations generated within a transaction. For more thorough information on CICS performance and design considerations, see the QED book *How to Use CICS to Create On-Line Applications: Methods and Solutions* (Chapter 9). The book covers all issues and tasks for building and executing CICS applications with COBOL.

For IMS applications, review how often your logic makes a CALL to IMS (this is NOT the same as how many CALLs are in your program). By restructuring your SSAs (and your logic), you might be able to reduce the number of CALLs. Usually, simpler programs require more CALLs, while sophisticated programs require fewer CALLs. Thorough coverage is provided in a more appropriate QED book, *IMS Design and Implementation Techniques* (see Chapter 9). That text is appropriate not only for addressing performance issues, but also for its complete coverage of the IMS/VS environment.

For DB2 applications, I can only refer you to your shop's data specialists or to a couple of special interest QED publications in Chapter 9, *DB2 Design Review Guidelines*, and *DB2: Maximizing Performance of Online Production Systems*. As with the other books listed here, these focus on design and performance in mainframe applications, covering the full spectrum of the named system environments.

For information on developing a DB2 application with COBOL, see the QED book, *Embedded SQL for DB2: Application Design and Programming* (Chapter 9, Related Publications). While examples in that book use OS/VS COBOL, it complements this book by its coverage of building DB2/COBOL applications for MVS/XA or MVS/ESA environments.

Earlier in this book I mentioned that COBOL II is not just a language, but it is also an environment. By environment, I mean that it is involved not only with compilation, but also with execution. The other subjects mentioned in this topic are also full environments. While your COBOL II program is the heart of the application logic, how the program interacts within these other environments affects the quality, value, and performance of your applications.

3.6.   MAKING A PROGRAM RESISTANT TO ERRORS

Is it really possible to make a program bullet proof? I don't think so, but I do know you can take steps to develop a program that will minimize ABENDs and other errors. In this topic, I have summarized various techniques that can help prevent an error.

3.6.1.   FILE STATUS

If you use VSAM files, this technique is old hat to you, but what about those QSAM files? COBOL II provides special services to QSAM files that use the FILE STATUS clause in the SELECT statement. For one, the program does not ABEND (honest!) even if the DD statement is absent. Of course, your program is expected to check the file status after each I/O to determine status and take appropriate action (e.g., after detecting that a file did not OPEN properly, your logic should ensure that no READ or WRITE went to that file). For file status codes, see Chapter 7. Here is a simple example showing the fundamentals (highlighted) to improve QSAM file integrity (some parts of the program are omitted). This example assumes that the absence of the file is acceptable (e.g., a file that is not always present). For that reason, the word OPTIONAL appears in the SELECT statement, although it is primarily to indicate that absence of the DD is anticipated. OPTIONAL also causes the status code to be different and supports CLOSE processing.

```
INPUT-OUTPUT SECTION.
FILE-CONTROL.
    SELECT FD1-WEEKLY OPTIONAL
       ASSIGN TO INPDD  FILE STATUS IS WS1-FD1-STAT.
DATA DIVISION.
FILE SECTION.
FD   FD1-WEEKLY
       BLOCK CONTAINS 0 RECORDS
       RECORDING MODE IS F
       RECORD CONTAINS 100 CHARACTERS.
        .
        .
WORKING-STORAGE SECTION.
```

```
01  WS1-FD1-STATUS.
    05  WS1-FD1-REC-CT   PIC S9(4)  COMP  VALUE 0.
    05  WS1-FD1-STAT     PIC XX.
    05  WS1-FD1-EOF-SW   PIC X                 VALUE 'N'.
        88 FD1-EOF                             VALUE 'Y'.
    .
    .

PROCEDURE DIVISION.
1.  PERFORM 1000-INITIALIZE
    PERFORM 2000-PROCESS UNTIL FD1-EOF
    PERFORM 3000-WRAPUP
    IF RETURN-CODE > 15
        DISPLAY 'SERIOUS I/O ERROR ON FD1'
    END-IF
    STOP RUN.

1000-INITIALIZE.
    OPEN INPUT FD1-WEEKLY
    IF WS1-FD1-STAT NE '00'
        SET FD1-EOF TO TRUE
    END-IF
    .
    .

2000-PROCESS.
    PERFORM 2100-READ
    IF WS1-FD1-EOF-SW  = 'N'
    .
    .                     process the data record here
    .
2100-READ.
    READ FD1-WEEKLY
      AT END
          SET FD1-EOF TO TRUE
      NOT AT END
          IF WS1-FD1-STAT NE '00'
              SET FD1-EOF TO TRUE
              MOVE 16 TO RETURN-CODE
              DISPLAY 'FD1-WEEKLY I/O STAT ' WS1-FD1-STAT
          END-IF
END-READ.
```

In this example, notice that if an OPEN error occurs, the READ statement
is not executed. This allows for different settings of the RETURN-CODE: 4
meaning that the weekly file was not present, and 16 meaning that it was
present but an I/O error occurred.

3.6.2. ON SIZE ERROR

There is nothing new here with COBOL II, just an old standby that is rarely used. If your applications could conceivably cause an overflow or divide by zero, this should be considered.

3.6.3. PARM Processing

Validating PARM lengths was discussed earlier under the section on module structures. For more information, see that section.

3.6.4. CALL Statement (LENGTH OF, ON EXCEPTION, and BY CONTENT)

These are all new features of COBOL II. The LENGTH OF clause lets a CALLed program validate the anticipated length of the passed data. The ON EXCEPTION clause is good for DYNAMically CALLed module structures, allowing you to prevent 806 or 80A ABENDs.

The BY CONTENT clause has some performance implications, but could be advantageous if your program CALLs other programs that need data from your program but are not to modify it. This not only protects your data, but it also prevents a CALLed program from inadvertently overwriting parts of your program through addressability to your DATA DIVISION.

All of these options of the CALL statement are explained in Chapter 2 and in this chapter under the section, Module Structures.

3.6.5. Data Validation

The 0C4, 0C7, 0C9, and 0CB ABENDs are probably the most familiar ABENDs in all shops, yet they can usually be prevented. Let's take them separately.

0C4 This ABEND is usually caused by a runaway subscript or index attempting to access unallocated memory. While it can occur for other reasons, the majority of programs ABENDing with 0C4 have an OCCURS clause. ABENDing can be prevented by testing the range of the subscript prior to use. Program testing can be supplemented by the SSRANGE compile option.

0C7 This ABEND is caused by using nonnumeric data in an arithmetic statement, which can be prevented by using the IF NUMERIC test. (See earlier topic, Data definitions, for implications of NUMPROC compile option.) Don't attempt to do your own range test for these two reasons:

1. If the field is PIC 99, you could get an 0C7 in your attempt to prevent one. This occurs because the generated code converts the data to numeric format and then compares it to other numeric values.

2. If the field is PIC XX, you could be accidentally "approving" nonnumeric data, getting an 0C7 anyway. Consider the following:

```
05  DATA-ITM PIC 999.
05  NEW-DATA-ITM REDEFINES DATA-ITM PIC XXX.

    IF NEW-DATA-ITM > '000' AND < '100'
       ADD DATA-ITM TO ...
```

In this innocent example, you need to be familiar with the EBCDIC collating sequence (Chapter 7). If you check it, you will find that "01 " (a zero, a one and a space) are between "000" and "100." In fact, quite a number of nonnumeric values are in that range (e.g., "03<") and several could cause the ADD statement to cause an 0C7 ABEND.

0C9 and 0CB These are, in fact, the same ABEND, a divide by zero. One is packed-decimal and the other is binary. It can be detected by an ON SIZE ERROR clause or by validating the divisor before the DIVIDE statement.

3.6.6. COPYbooks

The more data definitions, file definitions, common procedural statements, and program-to-program interfaces you put in COPYbooks, the less exposed you will be to programming errors. If you give the same programming specifications to 20 programmers, expect at least one of them to make a simple error that affects processing or ABENDs the program.

COPYbooks will not only reduce your exposure to misinterpretations, but they will also improve overall program documentation and communications among a project team.

3.6.7. RETURN-CODE Tests

While reviewed earlier in the section, Module Structures, RETURN-CODE is another technique to improve resistance to error. Anytime you CALL a program or PERFORM a paragraph that could have conditional outcome, ensure the program specifications include a status code to be returned. Doing so improves readability of the program, improves communication between the two modules, and provides incentive for the person writing the CALLed or PERFORMed code not to use a GO TO or issue an intentional ABEND. (The mechanics of issuing an intentional ABEND were covered in the topic Terminating a Program/Module, also in this chapter).

3.7. VSAM TECHNIQUES

This is *not* a treatment on VSAM programming techniques but a summary of new facilities available to you in COBOL II. COBOL II does not change the way VSAM files are handled, and all of these changes appear in various places in Chapter 2. They are here for a quick reference.

First, COBOL II provides a VSAM status code field to allow you to interrogate status codes from Access Method Services. Those codes are defined in the appropriate *VSAM Macro Instruction Reference* manual. (See Chapter 9 for the specific manual for your shop.) This is in addition to the standard file status field. (See chapter 7 for file status codes.) An example of a VSAM SELECT statement follows:

```
SELECT FD2-MASTER
    ASSIGN TO MASTDD
    ORGANIZATION IS INDEXED
    RECORD KEY IS FD2-KEY
    FILE STATUS IS WS1-FD2-STATUS
      WS1-FD2-VSAM-STAT.
    .
    .

    05   WS1-FD2-VSAM-STAT         COMP.
         10   STAT-RETURN-CODE     PIC 99.
         10   STAT-FUNCTION-CODE   PIC 99.
         10   STAT-FEEDBACK-CODE   PIC 99.
```

These data elements may be checked in addition to the normal FILE STATUS field. Notice that the VSAM status field is the second named field in the FILE STATUS clause. The FD for a VSAM file need be only

```
FD   file-name
     RECORD CONTAINS nn CHARACTERS.
```

In the above FD, the RECORD CONTAINS clause is optional. I suggest using it, primarily for its documentation function.

Another new feature from COBOL II that could affect VSAM processing is the addition of NOT AT END and NOT INVALID KEY to the I/O statements. These are explained under the topic Scope Terminators in Chapter 2.

The final new technique available to the COBOL II programmer is that the START statement now has an additional option for the KEY clause that improves readability. That option is GREATER THAN OR EQUAL TO. For example, instead of coding this:

```
START file-name KEY NOT LESS THAN data-name...
```

you can code this:

```
START file-name KEY GREATER THAN OR EQUAL TO data-name...
```

It is a small item, but this option lets you think positively instead of negatively to state the same condition. Anytime you can avoid using NOT, you reduce the odds that a rookie programmer will make an error in the future when maintaining your program. For more specific VSAM considerations beyond those addressed within the scope of COBOL II, QED publishes *VSAM: The Complete Guide to Optimization and Design*. See Chapter 9, Related Publications, for information on this and related IBM VSAM publications.

3.8. SORT TECHNIQUES

A COBOL SORT requires several considerations, not only to have it work correctly, but also, to have it work efficiently. Additional sort information may be found in these sections: Making a Program More Efficient (in this chapter), JCL Requirements (in this chapter), plus sections in Chapter 5 and Chapter 6. First, let's review how the sort takes place. Let's use a simple SORT statement, such as

```
SORT SD-SORT-FILE ASCENDING KEY FIELD-A
    INPUT PROCEDURE 2100-PROCESS-INPUT
    OUTPUT PROCEDURE 3100-PROCESS-OUTPUT
```

3.8.1. SORT Logic Flow

A common perception of the logic flow from the above is an implied PERFORM UNTIL statement of 2100-PROCESS-INPUT, followed by the sort, followed by an implied PERFORM UNTIL of 3100-PROCESS-OUTPUT. If that were true, you could view the process as similar to any other PERFORM structures. Instead, here is what happens:

1. When the SORT statement is executed, it does NOT transfer control to an INPUT PROCEDURE. Instead, it *dynamically loads* the SORT utility program (DFSORT, the same one used for stand-alone sorts) into memory and transfers control to that application, passing the addresses of any INPUT or OUTPUT PROCEDURES, plus the address of some sort control statements. (For efficiency, you should allocate more memory to the run unit than the application itself requires.)

2. DFSORT is now in control. First, DFSORT checks for the existence of a control data set that might have stand-alone control statements (ddname would be either IGZSRTCD or SORTCNTL). If present, DFSORT includes these with those received from your SORT statement. Next, it does an

implied PERFORM of your INPUT or OUTPUT procedure. This means your code is running subordinate to DFSORT, not subordinate to your parent paragraph with the SORT statement, and certain programming practices should not be done. These include using such statements as STOP RUN, GOBACK, or (horrors!) a GO TO to a different logic path in the application. For the application to terminate cleanly, you *must* return control back by the same path following normal structured practices. (If you're wondering how to stop a sort in progress, I'll get to that shortly.)

3. As each RELEASE statement is executed, DFSORT feeds the next record into the sorting process, which is occurring *concurrently* with your INPUT or OUTPUT processing. Likewise with the RETURN statement, each execution of it causes DFSORT to pass back the next record available from the sort. An important point, explained shortly, is that DFSORT also checks contents of a special register called SORT-RETURN *each time* it receives control from a RELEASE or RETURN.

4. As your code exits the INPUT or OUTPUT paragraph, DFSORT uses this as a signal to finish that sort phase or to return control back to the statement following the SORT statement. When control is returned to the statement following the SORT statement, DFSORT exits memory. If an error occurred at any time, DFSORT sets a nonzero value in the SORT-RETURN special register.

The following diagram is a symbolic representation of what is happening. The dotted lines represent the conceptual flow. The solid lines represent the actual flow.

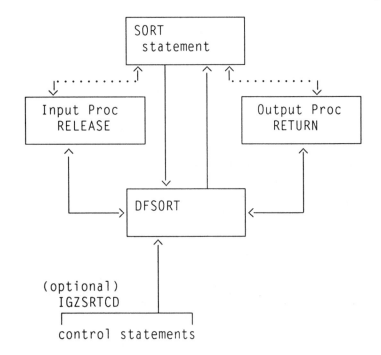

3.8.2. SORT Components

A COBOL SORT requires several components: A SELECT statement, an SD definition, an INPUT PROCEDURE of procedural code if the data is to be modified or selected prior to the sort, and an OUTPUT PROCEDURE of procedural code if the data is to be modified or otherwise processed after the sort. The optional INPUT PROCEDURE requires a RELEASE statement to transfer a record to the sort process and the optional OUTPUT PROCEDURE requires a RETURN statement to read records back from the sort process. An example sort program is included in Chapter 8 (Sample Programs). Let's look at each of the SORT components:

The SELECT statement

Since DFSORT allocates its own work files, this is a comment. Use:

```
SELECT sort-file-id ASSIGN TO SORTWORK.
```

The SD statement

Because the actual sort files are allocated by DFSORT, your goal here is to use the minimum acceptable syntax to COBOL II. All data fields that will be keys for the sort process must be defined within the 01-level.

```
Specify:   SD   sort-file-name
                RECORD CONTAINS nn CHARACTERS.
           01   sort-record-name.
                05 sort-key-a    PIC ...
                05 sort-key-b    PIC ...
                 .
                 .
```

The PROCEDURE DIVISION

First, a SORT statement must be used. Usually, there will be one or both of the possible PROCEDURES. The INPUT PROCEDURE, if used, needs to have a RELEASE statement somewhere within the logic flow (i.e, the RELEASE statement does not have to be in the named paragraph). This also applies to the OUTPUT PROCEDURE, in that the RETURN statement need not be physically within the named paragraph.

3.8.3. SORT Performance Tips

Terminating a SORT.

Earlier I reviewed the logic flow of a sort. You may recall that I stated that DFSORT checked the status of SORT-RETURN after receiving control via a RELEASE or RETURN statement. This is the key. If you are in an INPUT or

OUTPUT procedure and decide to terminate the sort or the application itself, follow these steps:

1. Set a flag so DFSORT knows to terminate. Do this by a statement such as:

```
MOVE 16 TO SORT-RETURN
```

2. Next, RETURN or RELEASE one more record. Since DFSORT checks SORT-RETURN first, the next record will not be processed. Instead, DFSORT will shut down and return control to your statement following the SORT statement.

3. Those two steps cause the sort process to terminate. Now you can terminate the application or whatever is appropriate. Use something such as this following your SORT statement:

```
IF SORT-RETURN > 0
    your error termination process goes here
ELSE
    your normal next process goes here
END-IF
```

Improving performance of a SORT.

Much of this was covered in an earlier section, Making a Program More Efficient. Here are some specifics.

1. Use an INPUT PROCEDURE (or the IGZSRTCD interface) to restructure your input records so that only the needed fields are sorted. Since much of the sort process occurs in memory, this increases the number of records that can be sorted this way. (How to use IGZSRTCD is explained in the next topic.)

2. Use selection logic to ensure no records are sorted that are not needed. For example, why sort 100,000 records when the OUTPUT PROCEDURE (or the following program) has logic that bypasses many of the records. This logic can be in either an INPUT PROCEDURE or the IGZSRTCD interface.

3. Specify the FASTSRT option. This improves I/O for any USING or GIVING clauses (i.e., ignored for programs with both an INPUT and an OUTPUT PROCEDURE).

4. Never use a SORT USING... GIVING... statement. A stand-alone sort is quicker and easier to code.

5. Specify more memory than you think you need. Because DFSORT is a "smart" program, it does the best it can with what it gets. This doesn't mean it is working efficiently, only that it is working functionally. Your technical staff may have guidelines for your shop.

6. Don't specify many SORT work files in your JCL. Modern sort techniques generally work best with fewer, not more, work files.

Using DFSORT control statements (IGZSRTCD).

Although seldom used, the SORT control statements may be used from within COBOL SORT programs. Their advantage is that they are easy to code and can eliminate the need for an INPUT or OUTPUT PROCEDURE, depending on the complexity of your requirements. They can also supplement processing if the program already has INPUT or OUTPUT PROCEDURES or both. For example, an INCLUDE or OMIT statement could determine what records are sorted or an OPTION statement could provide special performance information to SORT. When used within COBOL, the statements must have DDNAME of IGZSRTCD or SORTCNTL. This can be changed by the SORT-CONTROL register in a COBOL program if desired. The syntax is identical to that used in a stand-alone sort (remember, it is the same program).

Your choice of statements must coincide with processing steps of the application. For example, if you use an INREC statement to realign data fields, the data fields must appear in the SD record description as they will appear after the realignment. (Note: Don't show a smaller record size in the SD record description, however, as DFSORT opens the file before processing the INREC statement. That generates a run-time error.) Likewise, use of OUTREC would change, again, the record's description. For that reason, you cannot use both INREC and OUTREC in an application (nor can I think of a reason why you would need to). The format of each statement is in the section, JCL Requirements. Here are some suggested uses.

1. To select records for the sort: Use INCLUDE statement.
2. To omit records from the sort: Use OMIT statement.
3. To realign and shorten (lengthen) records prior to the sort process: Use INREC.
4. To realign and shorten (lengthen) records after the sort process: Use OUTREC.

A coding example is in the section JCL Requirements. For additional information on using DFSORT, see your appropriate reference manual (Chapter 9, Related Publications).

CONTROL STATEMENTS (in order of processing)

OPTION	provides temporary overrides to defaults
INCLUDE or OMIT	specifies what records to sort
INREC	reformats input records

SORT or MERGE   *<— provided by COBOL II SORT statement*
SUM   creates summary records and totals
OUTREC   reformats output records

Complete syntax on the DFSORT control statements is in the section JCL Requirements in this chapter.

3.9. CICS/IMS/DB2 ISSUES

Some of the material presented here appears in various other topics. This material is presented under the assumption that you know how to program applications for CICS, DB2, or IMS. In all cases, refer to your technical staff for specifics for your shop. CICS and IMS are complex system environments and there may well be differences from what is written here. There is also a topic in the next chapter (Debugging) about debug considerations for CICS, IMS, and DB2.

3.9.1. CICS Considerations

CICS receives major performance improvements from COBOL II, and most OS/VS COBOL programs do not require specific program changes to benefit from them. COBOL II simplifies several CICS processes and provides some features that weren't previously allowed.

Issues regarding module structure and compile options

1. Specify the option, COBOL2, when running the CICS translator.
2. If your shop is using CICS/MVS Release 2.1, specify the option, ANSI85, to use these features:
   - Lower-case characters in COBOL statements
   - Batched compilations
   - Nested programs
   - GLOBAL variables
   - Reference modification
3. A run unit must not have a mix of OS/VS COBOL and COBOL II.
4. Programs must use NOCMPR2, RES, RENT, NODBCS, and NODYNAM compile options.
5. IBM recommends you use TRUNC(BIN), although you may want to test other TRUNC options if your application makes extensive use of binary arithmetic.
6. Programs may not be CALLed from assembler programs, although they may CALL assembler subprograms.
7. While the DYNAM option is not allowed, the use of CALL identifier is valid with NODYNAM for CALLs to COBOL II subprograms.

8. Dynamically CALLed subprograms may contain EXEC CICS commands if running under CICS/MVS.
9. If the FDUMP, TEST, or SSRANGE compile options are used, the formatted information will be written to the temporary storage queue, CEBRxxxx.
10. The ON EXCEPTION and NOT ON EXCEPTION clauses are not allowed with CICS.
11. Programs that use macro-level CICS code will not compile with COBOL II, nor will those using BLL cells.
12. If you CALL another COBOL II program that will execute EXEC CICS statements, pass the DFHEIBLK and DFHCOMMAREA as the first two parameters. The CICS translator will insert the appropriate data definitions and adjustments to the PROCEDURE DIVISION USING statement for the CALLed program. Exception: When the CALLed module is a nested program, the PROCEDURE DIVISION USING statement must be manually coded. (Note: CALLing another program that also executes EXEC CICS statements was not allowed prior to COBOL II.) The LINK and XCTL commands may still be used for other forms of program transfer.
13. If the program(s) will use the reentrant feature, specify RENT during link-edit processing. (See JCL Requirements.)

Programming techniques that apply to CICS:

1. If you use EXEC CICS HANDLE statements, the HANDLE is suspended when CALLing a separately compiled COBOL II program (reinstated upon return), but remains active when CALLing a nested program. If the CALLed program will issue any EXEC statements, it must first issue an appropriate HANDLE statement to protect against possible ABENDs.
2. Do not use BLL cells. Instead, where SET or ADDRESS parameters reference BLL cells, specify the ADDRESS OF special register for the actual data area.
3. Do not write code that provides addressability for areas greater than 4K (usually done in OS/VS COBOL by adding 4096 to the value of a BLL cell). This function is provided for you by COBOL II.
4. The SERVICE RELOAD statement is treated as a comment, so *there is no need to code it*.
5. The LENGTH parameter is not needed, although it may be coded if desired. (CICS uses the LENGTH OF special register from COBOL II to access the length of the data area.)

6. STOP RUN is now a supported statement, but I encourage you to continue using EXEC CICS RETURN or GOBACK for compatibility.
7. You will improve transaction response time and use less virtual memory by converting EXEC CICS LINK commands to COBOL CALL statements.
8. If any EXEC CICS commands include reference modification (CICS/MVS only), be sure to include the length parameter. Otherwise, the CICS translator generates incorrect code. (Reference modification was explained in Chapter 2.)

If your shop has a CICS-to-COBOL II conversion software package, the conversion of BLL cells can be done automatically for OS/VS COBOL programs. Check with your technical staff. Here are some elementary (and incomplete) comparisons of how COBOL II replaces BLL processing. All differences are highlighted.

Accessing an area in LINKAGE SECTION.

OS/VS COBOL:

```
    LINKAGE SECTION.
        .
    01  BLL-CELLS.
        05  FILLER              PIC S9(8) COMP.
        05  DATA-REC-POINTER    PIC S9(8) COMP.
    01 DATA-REC.
        .
        .

        EXEC CICS ADDRESS CWA(DATA-REC-POINTER)
        .
```

COBOL II:

```
    LINKAGE SECTION.
        .
    01 DATA-REC.
        .
        .
        EXEC CICS ADDRESS CWA(ADDRESS OF DATA-REC)
        .
```

Reading a file

OS/VS COBOL:

```
WORKING-STORAGE SECTION.
    .
01  WS1-FILE-WORK.
    05  WS1-REC-LEN     PIC S9(4) COMP VALUE 100.
    .
    .
01  WS2-DATA-RECORD    PIC X(100).
    .
    .

    EXEC CICS READ DATASET('fileid')
        INTO(WS2-DATA-RECORD)
        RIDFLD(keyfield)
        LENGTH(WS1-REC-LEN)
        .
```

COBOL II:

```
WORKING-STORAGE SECTION.
    .
01  WS2-DATA-RECORD    PIC X(100).
    .
    .
    EXEC CICS READ DATASET('fileid')
        INTO(WS2-DATA-RECORD)
        RIDFLD(keyfield)
        .
```

Processing a large storage area.

OS/VS COBOL:

```
WORKING-STORAGE SECTION.
    .
01 WS1-FILE-WORK.
   05  WS1-REC-LEN      PIC S9(4) COMP VALUE 5000.
    .
    .
LINKAGE SECTION.
    .
```

```
01 BLL-CELLS.
     .
   05  ADDR-1          PIC S9(8)    COMP.
   05  ADDR-2          PIC S9(8)    COMP.
     .
     .

01  DATA-REC-A          PIC X(5000).
     .
     .
   EXEC CICS READ DATASET('fileid')
       RIDFLD(keyfield)
       SET(ADDR-1)
       LENGTH(WS1-REC-LEN)
END-EXEC
SERVICE RELOAD ADDR-1
COMPUTE ADDR-2 = ADDR-1 + 4096
SERVICE RELOAD ADDR-2
```

COBOL II:

```
LINKAGE SECTION.
     .
01  DATA-REC-A          PIC X(5000).
     .
     .
   EXEC CICS READ DATASET('fileid')
       RIDFLD(keyfield)
       SET(ADDRESS OF DATA-REC-A)
   END-EXEC
```

If you have a CICS application that accesses an IMS database (sometimes referred to as DL/1), see the next topic for additional information.

Earlier versions of CICS (e.g., version 1.6) shipped the DFHECI (CICS COBOL stub) module with AMODE and RMODE of 24, preventing your application from running above the 16-megabyte address. If your program link-edit listing shows an AMODE and RMODE of 24 despite specifying RENT and RES at compile-time, see your systems programmer to reinstall DFHECI with AMODE and RMODE of 31.

3.9.2. IMS Considerations

There are no special changes for IMS applications that affect the applications programmer. Some of the compile options have been streamlined to improve compatibility (e.g., COBOL II has no equivalent for the OS/VS COBOL compile option ENDJOB). Also, COBOL II offers your technical staff the ability to preload COBOL II applications more efficiently.

With COBOL II, restrictions on use of UNSTRING and INSPECT have been removed. Restrictions on ACCEPT, DISPLAY, and STOP RUN have been removed for IMS/DB applications, but since the restrictions still apply to IMS/DC applications, I suggest you do not use those statements.

Although not specific to COBOL II, the main programming concerns for IMS are

1. You do not need to code ENTRY DLITCBL. Use PROCEDURE DIVISION USING instead. It is easier to code and provides better readability.
2. For program termination, code GOBACK. Do not use STOP RUN.
3. Where all modules in a run unit are COBOL II and compiled with RENT, specify the RENT option at link-edit time. (See JCL Requirements.)

I won't specify compile or run-time options for IMS/DC applications, as your technical staff has already made some decisions here. The selected options are dependent on the mix of COBOL II and OS/VS COBOL programs and on whether the modules are preloaded. Typical IBM recommendations include RES, RENT, TRUNC(BIN), and DATA(24), as these allow applications to run in nonpreload mode or preloaded.

Some versions of IMS still run below the 16-megabyte address line, requiring that data areas from your program be located there. That is done by the compile option DATA(24). Check with your technical staff for more particulars for your installation. If your shop is running IMS/VS Version 3, Release 1, you may specify DATA(31). [Exception: CICS applications accessing IMS databases should still use DATA(24)].

For CICS applications, you may use EXEC DLI instead of the CALL statement if your shop is running IMS Version 1, Release 3, or later. As noted above, however, BLLs are not allowed. Once the scheduling CALL is completed, there are no other differences for CICS applications. Here is an example of the differences when using the scheduling CALL statement (differences are highlighted). See the previous topic on CICS for explanations of the differences.

Differences for a scheduling CALL for CICS/DLI programs.
OS/VS COBOL:

```
LINKAGE SECTION.
        .
01   BLL-CELLS.
     05   FILLER          PIC S9(8)     COMP.
     05   DLIUIB-BLL      PIC S9(8)     COMP.
     05   PCB-ADDR-BLL    PIC S9(8)     COMP.
     05   PCB-1-BLL       PIC S9(8)     COMP.
```

```
        05  PCB-2-BLL          PIC S9(8)      COMP.

    01  DLIUIB.
        05  UIBPCBAL           PIC S9(8)      COMP.
          .
    01  PCB-ADDRESSES.
        05  PCB-ADDR-1         PIC S9(8)      COMP.
        05  PCB-ADDR-2         PIC S9(8)      COMP.
          .
    01 PCB-1.
          .
    01 PCB-2.
          .
        CALL 'CBLTDLI' USING PCB-SCHEDULE
                             psb-name
                             DLIUIB-BLL
        MOVE UIBPCBAL         TO PCB-ADDR-BLL
        MOVE PCB-ADDR-1       TO PCB-1-BLL
        MOVE PCB-ADDR-2       TO PCB-2-BLL
```

COBOL II:

This example uses the POINTER technique described earlier in this chapter and in Chapter 2. It is created by modifying the DLIUIB COPYbook or by using a REDEFINES statement to place the POINTER.

```
    LINKAGE SECTION.
          .
    01  DLIUIB.
        05 UIBPCBAL           POINTER.
          .
    01  PCB-ADDRESSES.
        05  PCB-ADDR-1        POINTER.
        05  PCB-ADDR-2        POINTER.
          .
    01  PCB-1.
          .
    01  PCB-2.
          .

        CALL 'CBLTDLI' USING PCB-SCHEDULE
                             psb-name
                             ADDRESS OF DLIUIB
        SET ADDRESS OF PCB-ADDRESSES TO UIBPCBAL
        SET ADDRESS OF PCB-1 TO PCB-ADDR-1
        SET ADDRESS OF PCB-2 TO PCB-ADDR-2
```

An alternative way to code the last three statements in the above example follows. Because this technique uses EXEC CICS commands, the DLIUIB COPYbook does not need to be changed.

```
EXEC CICS ADDRESS SET(ADDRESS OF PCB-ADDRESSES)
          USING(UIBPCBAL)    END-EXEC
EXEC CICS ADDRESS SET(ADDRESS OF PCB-1)
          USING(PCB-ADDR-1) END-EXEC
EXEC CICS ADDRESS SET(ADDRESS OF PCB-2)
          USING(PCB-ADDR-2) END-EXEC
```

A sample IMS program is included in Chapter 8. The sample was written to be compatible with OS/VS COBOL and with COBOL II.

3.9.3.   DB2 Considerations

While there are several issues to address with CICS and IMS, DB2 is hardly a concern. I include this topic to reassure DB2 programmers that I didn't overlook DB2. If your DB2 application operates within the CICS or IMS environment, those considerations will apply. Other than that, here are the few considerations:

1. If you are using a DB2 precompiler prior to Version 1, Release 3, the generated IF statements from the SQL WHENEVER statement that contains a GO TO clause omits the END-IF. The END-IF must be added manually. (Later versions include it in the generated COBOL source.)
2. Whereas all types of dynamic SQL statements were not allowed with OS/VS COBOL, you may use them with COBOL II.
3. If you used an SQLDA (Structured Query Language Data Area) with OS/VS COBOL, you needed to write an assembler program to manage the address pointers. That still works, but is not needed with COBOL II. Instead, you may use POINTER variables with the SET statement. You will also need to define your SQLDA because the SQL INCLUDE for COBOL does not provide the code for it. Examples of an SQLDA, along with all other information about dynamic SQL statements, are included in the *IBM Database 2 Advanced Application Programming Guide* (see Chapter 9).
4. The COBOL II options that affect the DB2 environment are TRUNC and NOCMPR2. IBM recommends TRUNC(BIN) for DB2, as it does for CICS and IMS. If your application does not use binary arithmetic extensively, follow IBM's recommendation. If you do use binary arithmetic (COMP), you may want to test other options of TRUNC if performance is an issue. NOCMPR2 is required because of changes in COBOL II. (See Specifying COBOL II Options for more information.)

5. DB2 statements used by COBOL II are OPEN, CLOSE, PREPARE, DESCRIBE, and FETCH.

6. Non-SELECT statements, as well as fixed-list and varying-list SELECT statements, may also be used with COBOL II.

3.10. CREATING A LOAD MODULE

Creating executable code (called a load module in MVS) requires that the output from the compile(s) be processed by the Linkage Editor. This is because IBM language compilers generate a standard format dataset of machine code that includes nonexecutable tables of reference (e.g., list of CALLed modules that must be resolved). Certain compile options affect this process and there are other items you can specify for your program at the time of the link.

The Linkage Editor is an intelligent software product and can do many things with the object code it processes. However, because the Linkage Editor does not know the logic structure of the application, or which program should get control at run-time, there are specific concerns you must address for a successful link-edit. This section addresses all Linkage Editor considerations except JCL. JCL for the Linkage Editor is in a later section, JCL Requirements: Compile, Link, and Execute.

3.10.1. Static Versus Dynamic CALLS

The concept of static CALLs and dynamic CALLs was explained in the section Module Structures. If you have static CALLs to resolve, you must have the needed modules in object or load format accessible to the Linkage Editor via JCL DD statements. If you use dynamic CALLs, there are no concerns to the Linkage Editor in resolving these CALLs.

3.10.2. RESIDENT and REENTRANT Options

Reentrant At run-time, MVS checks to see what attributes a load module has so it can manage the load module correctly. Those attributes might be placed in the object module by the language compiler or in the load module by the Linkage Editor. This may seem redundant, but the processing done by each is different. For example, by specifying RENT at compile-time, the COBOL II compiler generates different object code so the program will be reentrant, as well as have 31-bit addressability. The module attributes are marked for 31-bit addressability, but are not marked as reentrant. That is done by the Linkage Editor.

When the option RENT is specified to the Linkage Editor, it sets an attribute bit so MVS will assume the module is reentrant. (Linkage Editor options are in the section, JCL Requirements.) When MVS loads a run unit that is marked reentrant, it schedules the run unit to take advantage of this feature, whether the run unit is or isn't reentrant. Don't make the mistake, then, of assuming that you can specify RENT at link-edit time and not at compile-time. Each serves a different purpose. Here is a definition of reentrant code to help you determine when RENT needs to be specified to the Linkage Editor.

Reentrant code First, reentrant code has no relationship to 31-bit addressability. The COBOL II compiler packages reentrancy and 31-bit addressability with RENT, but the two features could have been done separately. Although all applications can benefit from 31-bit addressability, only specialized applications benefit from being reentrant. By being reentrant, a load module is capable of being loaded once into memory and then multiple transactions can execute concurrently, using the one copy. This feature can be useful for high-performance on-line transactions, but it is of no benefit for batch transactions. Usually, your technical staff that supports on-line transactions can assist you with this, as the decision has some dependency on how the on-line environment is initialized.

Resident The RES option affects the size of your load module, the size of your Linkage Editor listing, and how your load module accesses the COBOL II run-time modules. Since RES means that COBOL run-time modules will be resident in the system and not in your load module, there are no CALLs in your object module to COBOL routines for the Linkage Editor to resolve. (Exception: There is always a CALL to IGZEBST that must be resolved by the Linkage Editor.)

3.10.3. Using the Linkage Editor

Despite its simple design, the Linkage Editor is one of the least understood of IBM's software. This is not an extensive treatment on the subject, but it should suffice for most applications. The JCL, options, and tips for use are in JCL Requirements. The control statements, however, are here.

Linkage Editor concepts.

First, let's review terms to be sure we're in sync. See figure 3.2 for a simple compile and link-edit for a two-module application.

In figure 3.2 (the datasets are double-lined), program MODA, with a CALL to MODB is compiled. The output object module is written to the SYSLIN DD statement. The object module has a table in it (referred to as a dictionary), listing all external references that the Linkage Editor must resolve.

When the Linkage Editor reads this as input (SYSLIN), it strips nonexecutable tables from the code and searches for any external references, in this case, MODB. If the Linkage Editor cannot locate MODB elsewhere (this is explained later), it searches a DD statement named SYSLIB and locates it. The module is read from SYSLIB and combined with MODA into an executable load module.

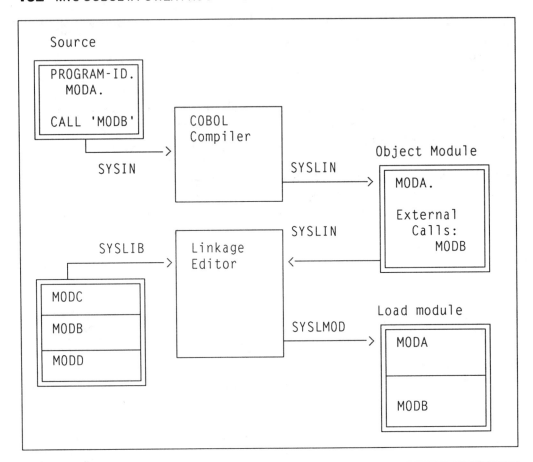

Figure 3.2. Sample flow of compile and link.

The Linkage Editor has no idea which module should receive control at run-time. Unless specified elsewhere, it assumes the first module read from SYSLIN should get control (in this case, MODA).

Now, let's back up and review the process in detail. Here are the basic logic steps as executed by the Linkage Editor, presented to help you determine what, if any, special considerations need to be made.

1. First, it OPENs and READs the SYSLIN dataset. That dataset may contain object module(s), control statements, or both. If it contained only object modules, any decisions to be made would use Linkage Editor defaults (e.g., which module gets control at run-time). If it contained only control statements (covered later), they would need to specify which modules to process and where to find them. Since object modules contain tables that identify the name of all modules CALLed by them, this becomes additional input to the Linkage Editor.

The Linkage Editor continues to read (and process in the order of appearance) control statements and object modules until either end-of-file is reached on SYSLIN or a NAME control statement (covered later) is read.

2. If *all* the object code needed to create a load module is in SYSLIN, the Linkage Editor searches no other libraries, follows any control statement instructions, writes out the load module to the SYSLMOD DD and is finished with that load module. (See step 4.)

3. If, after reading all input from SYSLIN, there were missing modules (as in our example of MODB), the Linkage Editor has a priority of search to locate the missing module(s). That priority is

   a. Was it concatenated in SYSLIN? If so, it uses it. This could occur when there are several COBOL compiles preceding the link-edit step or when JCL has concatenated several object datasets. The Linkage Editor will use all such modules up to end-of-file on SYSLIN or the appearance of a NAME control statement (explained later). Note: Concatenated modules found in SYSLIN are placed in the load module even if there are *no* calls to them.

   b. Was there an INCLUDE control statement specifying additional modules? An INCLUDE statement can identify object modules or load modules (not both) that are to be included in the new load module. Note: Modules specified on INCLUDE statements are included in the load module, whether needed or not. The Linkage Editor is just following your instructions.

   c. Was there a LIBRARY statement specifying where to search for the module(s) if still not located? This is useful if there might be a CALL to a unique module and you want the Linkage Editor to know where to search.

   d. Is there a SYSLIB DD statement? If this data set is present, the Linkage Editor will search there last. This is a PDS of load modules. This final search is often referred to as the automatic call library because it will be automatically searched unless one of the prior events occurs. The member name must match the name from the CALL statement AND the module name from the PROGRAM-ID. (Note: The Linkage Editor term for a module is CSECT (for Control Section). The Linkage Editor does not refer to a PROGRAM-ID name, but to a CSECT name.

4. After processing all the modules, the Linkage Editor writes the load module to the SYSLMOD DD dataset and names the load module. The name is done on a priority basis. The priority is

   a. Was there a NAME control statement? If so, the module gets its name from it.

   b. Was there a member name coded on the SYSLMOD DD dataset? If so, it gets its name from there. If a module already exists in the library with that name, it is overwritten.

c. In the absence of the first two options, the module is named TEMPNAME. If a module already exists in the library with that name, it is overwritten.

If end-of-file on SYSLIN has been reached, the Linkage Editor terminates. If the processing in step 4 was caused by the appearance of a NAME statement, the Linkage Editor starts over again at step 1. In this way, the Linkage Editor can create multiple load modules in one execution. COBOL II allows you to take advantage of this with the NAME compile option.

This wraps up Linkage Editor processing. The Linkage Editor's only function is to locate and bind all modules that you (or the object module) identify as being needed in a load module. Whether the modules are needed or not, whether control is given to the right module, whether the modules are reentrant or not, are decisions the Linkage Editor cannot make. It only follows instructions and makes assumptions in the absence of those instructions.

Linkage Editor control statements.

These are the basic control statements, presented with the options most commonly used. If you are responsible for a link-edit procedure that has additional control statements, see the appropriate Linkage Editor reference manual (Chapter 9). Overlay structures are excluded from this discussion. For the options that are specified via PARM to the Linkage Editor, see JCL Requirements.

Control statements follow traditional IBM syntax, i.e., they must begin at or after column 2, must not exceed column 71, must have a nonblank character in column 72 if continued to a following statement, and must begin in column 16 on any continued statements. In most cases, the examples shown can be combined into one statement if desired. Where a single member name is shown, there can be several, separated by commas. The examples shown are the most common format.

```
INCLUDE ddname                        <- For sequential object
                                         datasets
```

or

```
INCLUDE ddname(membername)            <- For partitioned datasets
                                         with either object or load
                                         modules
```

This statement is a demand that modules identified on the DD statement be included in the new load module. The ddname may be one of your own or you may reference SYSLIB or SYSLMOD if desired. The Linkage Editor includes them even if there are no CALLs to them and even if they are duplicates of modules already located. For example,

```
//SYSLIN  DD  *
     INCLUDE MYDD(MODB)
//MYDD  DD  DSN=MYLIB,DISP=SHR
//SYSLMOD  DD  DSN=LOAD.LIB,DISP=OLD
```

In this case, the Linkage Editor would search the dataset specified in the MYDD ddname and look for a member named MODB. Note that the name of the new load module will be TEMPNAME because no name is specified. (See above if you don't know how names are defined.)

```
LIBRARY   ddname(membername)       <- Specifies a PDS where a
                                      CALLed module is located.
```

or

```
LIBRARY   (CSECTname)              <- Identifies a CALL that is
                                      not to be resolved in this
                                      link-edit.
```

or

```
LIBRARY *(CSECTname)               <- Identifies a CALL that is
                                      never to be resolved.
```

The LIBRARY statement has two personalities. One format is used to identify where CALLed modules can be located when you want the CALL resolved via "automatic call library," but the member is not in SYSLIB. The ddname may be one of your own or you may reference SYSLMOD if desired. As with SYSLIB searches, the member name and CSECT name must match. The second format is used when a particular module should not be included, even if the Linkage Editor could locate it. The third option is used when a module reference should be ignored from now on. Here is an example, combining all three:

```
//SYSLIN   DD  DSN=&&OBJECT,DISP=(OLD,DELETE)
     LIBRARY  LIB(MODA),(MODB),*(MODC)
//LIB   DD  DSN=DAVES.LOADLIB,DISP=SHR
//SYSLMOD  DD DSN=LOAD.LIB(NEWPROG),DISP=OLD
```

In this example, the Linkage Editor would look for MODA in DAVES.LOADLIB, would ignore the CALL to MODB, and would remove permanently the reference to MODC. Note: This, of course, does not change the program logic. If the program logic still executes CALLs to MODB or MODC at run-time, an ABEND will occur. The load module name will be NEWPROG. The entry point for the load module will be the object module in &&OBJECT.

```
MODE AMODE(a),RMODE(r)        <- Specifies memory residency and
                                 addressing capability
```

```
     where  a = 24, 31, or ANY
            r = 24, or ANY
```

This is usually not needed, as it overrides the mode specified by the compiler. Don't use it unless you are well-versed in 31-bit and 24-bit concepts. AMODE refers to the addressability of the program, while RMODE refers to where the program may reside. The COBOL II compiler sets these automatically, depending on your choice of compile options RENT and RES.

This statement might be useful if you want a COBOL II module to be RES, NORENT and you want an OS/VS COBOL module to be able to CALL it or be CALLed by it. Specifying MODE AMODE(24),RMODE(24) would tell the Linkage Editor to set the load module attribute so your module would not be loaded above the 16-megabyte address, allowing programs with 24-bit addressability to interact.

As with other statements, you can fool the Linkage Editor because it only obeys your commands, but if programs aren't what you specify, anticipate some weird ABENDs. For example, you could specify AMODE(31) for an OS/VS COBOL program, but since it can't handle a 31-bit address, an ABEND is inevitable.

```
NAME        membername [(R)]   <- Names a load module
```

If used, this must be the LAST control statement for a load module. At this point, the Linkage Editor stops reading from SYSLIN and processes everything pending, creating a load module. After finishing a load module, it then picks up again reading from SYSLIN. If there are more modules or control statements, it continues to create load modules until end-of-file on SYSLIN. The (R) means REPLACE the module if one already exists with the same name. If (R), including the parentheses, is omitted, the Linkage Editor will not create the new load module if a member already exists by that name. (Note: COBOL II has the ability, based on the compile option NAME, to create this Linkage Editor control statement for you. In the section on JCL, we'll explore where this might be useful.) Here is an example, using several of the statements discussed so far, in which an object module has been created in a prior step:

```
//SYSLIN    DD DSN=&&OBJECT,DISP=(OLD,DELETE)
//          DD *
  INCLUDE  XTRAFILE(PROGC)
  LIBRARY  ALTFILE(PROGD)
  NAME   PROGA(R)
//XTRAFILE DD  DSN=LIBA,DISP=SHR      <- PDS containing PROGC
//ALTFILE  DD  DSN=LIBB,DISP=SHR      <- PDS containing PROGD
//SYSLMOD  DD  DSN=LIBC(MYPROG),DISP=OLD
```

In this example, the load module will be named PROGA, as that is a priority over MYPROG in the JCL. The load module will contain whatever object module(s) was in &&OBJECT, plus PROGC (even if not referenced). PROGD will be in the load module only if CALLed by one of the other object modules. The module that gets control at run-time will be the first module, as that is a default and no control statement said otherwise.

```
ENTRY        externalname        <- Specifies logical beginning of
                                    load module
```

where externalname can be PROGRAM-ID name or ENTRY name from the source program.

When the logical beginning of the program might be other than the first module's PROGRAM-ID name (CSECT name), use the ENTRY statement. This is useful when you are combining modules in different sequences and can't predict their order of appearance to the Linkage Editor. This statement is never needed on single-module load modules that have no ENTRY statement in the PROCEDURE DIVISION.

Consider an example where PROGA CALLs PROGB. Both have been previously compiled and linked. Now PROGB has been recompiled due to a change needed. Since the Linkage Editor assumes the first object module read in through SYSLIN is the entry point, an ENTRY statement is needed, such as the following:

```
//SYSLIN  DD  DSN=&&OBJECT      <- Contains PROGB object code
//        DD  *
  INCLUDE  SYSLMOD(PROGA)
  ENTRY PROGA
  NAME PROGA(R)
//SYSLMOD  DD  DSN=LIBC,DISP=OLD
```

PROGB will precede PROGA in the load module, although because of the ENTRY statement, PROGA will be the logical beginning point. Note: This could cause debugging complications if you assume that the entry point identified in a dump is the beginning of the load module.

```
REPLACE  module-name [(new-mod-name)]      <- Changes existing
                                              references
```

```
    where  module-name = a module or reference in a
                         FOLLOWING module
           new-mod-name = a replacement reference name
```

This is a seldom-understood control statement. It must *immediately precede* the module to which it refers. It is useful on three occasions.

1. When a new version of the CSECT has been created and relinked and you want to relink a load module to use the new version.
2. You created a new version of a module but with a different name. Without changing and recompiling all CALLs to the old name, this will change all references within the load module.
3. You accidentally INCLUDEd some modules into a load module that aren't referenced by the module. This statement can remove them.

Let's look at some examples:

```
//SYSLIN  DD  *
   REPLACE  PROGB
   INCLUDE  SYSLMOD(PROGA)
   ENTRY    PROGA
   NAME     PROGA(R)
//SYSLMOD  DD  DSN=LIBC,DISP=OLD
```

The above example tells the Linkage Editor to remove PROGB from the member in the following INCLUDE statement. Since there is no other input, the Linkage Editor searches SYSLIB for the new version of PROGB. This process is often referred to as a replace link. If PROGB were not referenced by any module in PROGA, it would be removed and all traces deleted.

```
//SYSLIN    DD  DSN=&&OBJECT    <- Points to SUBC module
//          DD  *
   REPLACE  SUBA(SUBC)
   INCLUDE  OLDLOAD(MODA)
   ENTRY    PROGA
   NAME     NEWPROGA
//OLDLOAD  DD  DSN=LIBC,DISP=SHR
//SYSLMOD  DD  DSN=LIBD,DISP=OLD
```

The above does several things. First, we have the object module for SUBC in the input stream (DSN=&&OBJECT). It is a replacement for a module called SUBA. The Linkage Editor will replace all references to SUBA with SUBC. The new load module is also being written to a different library. By omitting the (R) from the NAME statement, we ensure that if a module already exists by that name we don't replace it.

```
ALIAS   external-name        <- Provides alternate name for load
                                module
```

I include this statement although I am opposed to using it. The ALIAS statement, by providing another name to a program, can create confusion in program documentation. Another little trick it does is with ENTRY statements. If the external-name shown matches an ENTRY statement within the program, that ENTRY statement becomes the logical entry point. This violates the "one entry, one exit" concept of structured programming.

```
ORDER   CSECTname [(P)] [,CSECTname,...]   <- Arranges order of
                                              CSECTs in load module
```

The ORDER statement is rarely needed, except for CICS links in which a CICS module DFHECI must be the first CSECT in the load module.

```
//SYSLIN    DD  DSN=&&OBJECT
//          DD  *
   ORDER    DFHECI
   INCLUDE  CICSLIB(DFHECI)
   NAME     CICSTRAN(R)
//CICSLIB   DD  DSN=cics.library,DISP=SHR
//SYSLMOD   DD  DSN=LIBD,DISP=OLD
```

This section on the Linkage Editor was not intended to give you all possible information for using it. Instead, it was intended to help you understand the flow and to help you determine when you need various JCL and control statements. JCL for the Linkage Editor is defined in JCL Requirements.

3.11. SPECIFYING COBOL II OPTIONS

The COBOL II compile options are referenced throughout this book, often with partial explanations or examples of use. This section is somewhat more academic, explaining what each option does and its typical uses, rather than describing tips and techniques.

3.11.1. Options Available

The options available fall into three categories: (1) those you may specify at compile-time, (2) those you may specify at run-time, and (3) those you cannot specify at compile or run-time. I make you aware of that third category because, if your attempts to override an option aren't working, it may be because your company has prevented them from working. This ability to enforce compile options is new with COBOL II.

COBOL II compile-time options.

Since those options specified at compile-time are the most common, let's look at them first. Figure 3.3 lists them by general category. Several options appear in more than one column. The categories are

Performance: These are options that affect resource usage, either at compile-time or at run-time. "R" means the option affects run-time, "C" means the option affects compile-time, and "O" means the option affects input/output of the compiler, other than to SYSPRINT.

Documentation: These are options that affect the input or SYSPRINT output (normally, printed listings) from the compile.

Structure: These are options that affect the module-to-module structure, and the residency and addressing facilities of the run-time module.

Standards: These options provide opportunities your company may wish to use to monitor or enforce standards.

Test-debug: These options provide debugging capabilities but at the expense of extra resource usage. "C" is for compiler debugging, and is for use by systems programmers.

Run-time effect: These are options that have an effect on the run-time environment, either in required JCL, data formats, application logic, or options that may be changed from that specified at compile-time.

In reviewing the list, you may want to receive a list of the defaults at your company. You can get one by submitting any program for a compile in which you have included the SOURCE compile option. If you want a list of all COBOL II error messages, use this two-statement program:

```
ID DIVISION.
PROGRAM-ID. ERRMSG.
```

ADV   Options: ADV, NOADV
               Abbreviations: None

Option	Performance	Documentation	Structure	Standards	Test-debug	Runtime Effect?
ADV	R					X
APOST		X				
AWO	R					
BUFSIZE	C					
CMPR2*				X		
COMPILE	C			X		
DATA	R		X			X
DBCS						X
DECK	O					
DUMP					C	
DYNAM*	R		X			X
EXIT	C	X		X		
FASTSRT	R					
FDUMP	R				X	
FLAG		X				
FLAGMIG				X		
FLAGSAA				X		
FLAGSTD				X		
LANGUAGE		X				
LIB	O	X				
LINECOUNT		X				
LIST		X				
MAP		X				
NAME	O		X	X		
NUMBER		X				
NUMPROC	R					X
OBJECT	O					
OFFSET		X				
OPTIMIZE	R					
OUTDD						X
RENT*	R		X	X		X
RESIDENT*	R		X	X		X
SEQUENCE		X				
SIZE	C					

Figure 3.3. COBOL II Compile options. (* = CICS-sensitive)

Option	Performance	Documentation	Structure	Standards	Test-debug	Runtime Effect?
SOURCE		X				
SPACE		X				
SSRANGE	R				X	X
TERM	0					
TEST	R				X	
TRUNC	R					X
VBREF		X				
WORD		X		X		
XREF		X				
ZWB						X

Figure 3.3. *(Continued)*

This option is used with the WRITE AFTER ADVANCING statement. It adds 1 byte to length of 01-level entry. For example, to write a 133-byte physical record with the first byte for carriage control requires a 132-byte record definition with ADV and requires a 133-byte record definition (with the first byte not referenced) with NOADV. ADV gives better performance and retains device independence.

```
APOST       Options: APOST, QUOTE
                Abbreviations: APOST, Q
```

This option determines whether you will enclose literals with the apostrophe (') or with quotation marks (").

```
AWO         Options: AWO, NOAWO
                Abbreviations: None
```

This option specifies APPLY WRITE ONLY for any physical sequential datasets with blocked, V-mode records. AWO gives better performance.

```
BUFSIZE      Options: BUFSIZE (integer)
             Abbreviations: BUF (integer)
```

This option specifies how many bytes may be allocated by the compiler for the work datasets. Specifying BUF(32760) gives best performance.

```
CMPR2        Options: CMPR2, NOCMPR2
             Abbreviations: None
```

This option provides compatibility with COBOL II, Release 2. (Note: This version of COBOL II is not covered in this book.) The Release 2 implementation of COBOL II was a subset of ANSI 85 and there are some incompatibilities. NOCMPR2 should be the option you use to take full advantage of the features of COBOL II described in this book. If you have earlier COBOL II programs, use CMPR2 and the FLAGMIG compile option to identify potential incompatibilities. CICS and DB2 applications must specify NOCMPR2. Refer to the *VS COBOL II Application Programming Guide* (Chapter 9) for more guidance.

```
COMPILE      Options: COMPILE, NOCOMPILE, NOCOMPILE(n)
             Abbreviations: C, NOC, NOC(n)

             where n = W for level 4 errors (Warning)
                       E for level 8 errors (Error)
                       S for level 12 errors (Severe)
```

This option specifies whether a compile is to generate object code after detecting an error. COMPILE means to generate object code anyway. NOCOMPILE means to generate no object code, regardless. NOCOMPILE(n) means to stop generating object code if an error of that severity occurs. For example, NOCOMPILE(E) would mean to stop generating object code after appearance of the first level 8 error message. Syntax checking of the program is not affected.

```
DATA         Options: DATA(24), DATA(31)
             Abbreviations: None
```

This option specifies whether DATA DIVISION entries are to be allocated below or above the 16-megabyte address. Where possible, specify DATA(31). The primary use of DATA(24) is when you are maintaining compatibility with older, non-COBOL II programs. This option is for use when RENT is specified and is ignored if NORENT is specified. See Module Structure for more information.

```
DBCS        Options: DBCS, NODBCS
            Abbreviations: None
```

This option provides support for the Double Byte Character Set (DBCS), allowing use of non-English characters if the 256 EBCDIC character set is insufficient. There is no further reference to this option in this book. Most applications will specify NODBCS.

```
DECK        Options: DECK, NODECK
            Abbreviations: D, NOD
```

This option specifies that object code is to be written to the SYSPUNCH data set in 80-byte records. It is normally set to NODECK. See also the OBJECT option.

```
DUMP        Options: DUMP, NODUMP
            Abbreviations: DU, NODU
```

This option is not for application debugging. It is for use by your systems programmers when a compiler error is occurring and they are diagnosing it. This should normally be NODUMP.

```
DYNAM       Options: DYNAM, NODYNAM
            Abbreviations: DYN, NODYN
```

This option specifies whether CALL "literal" statements are to generate static CALLS (resolved by the Linkage Editor) or dynamic CALLs (resolved at run-time). For more information, see Static versus Dynamic Calls. For CICS, this must be NODYNAM. DYNAM may not be used with NORES.

```
EXIT        Options: NOEXIT, EXIT (options)
```

The various options are not shown here because your installation must specify what they are. EXIT is specified where an installation has one or more of the following:

1. A user-written routine that intercepts all requests for SYSIN statements (COBOL source), providing them via the user routine.
2. A user-written routine that intercepts all COPY statements, providing the source statements via the routine instead of from the SYSLIB DD statement.
3. A user-written routine that intercepts all output to SYSPRINT and reformats or otherwise processes it.

These are powerful features, allowing a company to (1) read all source statements or COPY statements prior to being processed by the compiler, (2) provide direct access to a source program management system internally instead of via JCL, or (3) provide reformatted or duplicate compiler output listings. For most installations, this is NOEXIT.

```
FASTSRT    Options: FASTSRT, NOFASTSRT
             Abbreviations: FSRT, NOFSRT
```

This option specifies whether you want DFSORT to optimize processing for a COBOL SORT application. FASTSRT can improve processing for any SORT statement that has either a USING or GIVING statement or both (i.e, a SORT... INPUT PROCEDURE...OUTPUT PROCEDURE would not be optimized). When FASTSRT is specified, COBOL II ignores it if the feature cannot improve your program performance. IF NOFASTSRT is specified, COBOL II will still produce information messages where optimization could have been realized.

```
FDUMP      Options: FDUMP, NOFDUMP
             Abbreviations: FDU, NOFDU
```

This option specifies that a formatted dump is to be produced at run-time in case of an ABEND. A SYSDBOUT data set is required (e.g., //SYSDBOUT DD SYSOUT=A). For CICS, the dump is written to the CEBRxxxx temporary storage queue (can be suppressed by EXEC CICS HANDLE ABEND command). The formatted dump is not produced if TEST was also specified as a compile option. For more information, see Chapter 4 (Debugging Techniques).

```
FLAG       Options: FLAG (x,y), NOFLAG
             Abbreviations: F(x,y), NOF

             where x and y =  I for Informational messages
                              W for level 4 errors (Warning)
                              E for level 8 errors (Error)
                              S for level 12 errors (Severe)
```

This option specifies whether error messages are to appear imbedded in the source listing (new with COBOL II). The x value specifies what error level messages appear at the end of the listing. The y value specifies what error level messages appear within the listing. The y value must not be lower than the x value. For example, FLAG(I,E) means all messages appear at the end, but only level 8 errors and above appear within the listing. NOFLAG specifies no error messages.

```
FLAGMIG      Options: FLAGMIG, NOFLAGMIG
             Abbreviations: None
```

This option flags migration errors for incompatibility between COBOL II Release 3.0 and prior levels. See CMPR2 for more information. Normally, this is NOFLAGMIG.

```
FLAGSAA      Options: FLAGSAA, NOFLAGSAA
             Abbreviations: None
```

This option flags statements that are incompatible with IBM's Systems Application Architecture (SAA). If your company has standardized on SAA, this should be FLAGSAA. Otherwise, it should be NOFLAGSAA. For more information on SAA, see Chapter 9 (Related Publications).

```
FLAGSTD      Options: FLAGSTD (options), NOFLAGSTD
```

This option flags statements that do not conform to the ANSI standard and specified subsets. The options are not listed here as they would be specific to your installation. If your shop enforces a level of ANSI 85 or a Federal Information Processing Standard, then your shop will be using FLAGSTD with some options specified. Otherwise, use NOFLAGSTD.

```
LANGUAGE Options: LANGUAGE (n)
             Abbreviations: LANG(n)

             where n = EN for mixed-case English
                       UE for upper-case English only
                       JA or JP for the Japanese language
```

This option specifies the language to use to print out the compile listing. This includes diagnostic messages, page headers, and compilation summary information. A special Japanese Language Feature must be installed to use options JA or JP. To print output in mixed-case English, specify LANG(EN).

```
LIB          Options: LIB, NOLIB
             Abbreviations: None
```

This option specifies whether COPY, BASIS, or REPLACE statements can be used. Since most shops use COPY statements, this should be set to LIB. There is no further reference to BASIS or REPLACE statements in this book. (The REPLACE statement that is used in this book is for the Linkage Editor, not the compiler.)

```
LINECOUNT    Options: LINECOUNT (n)
             Abbreviations: LC

             where n = number of lines to print per page
```

This option specifies number of lines to print per page on SYSPRINT data set during compilation. Specifying zero causes no page ejects. Since the compiler uses three lines for titles, there will be three fewer COBOL statements per page than the specified line count.

```
LIST         Options: LIST, NOLIST
             Abbreviations: None
```

This option specifies whether a listing of generated assembler code for the compiled program should be produced to SYSPRINT. This is mutually exclusive with the OFFSET option. If both are used, OFFSET receives preference. For information on using this listing, see Chapter 4 (Debugging Techniques).

```
MAP          Options: MAP, NOMAP
             Abbreviations: None
```

This option specifies whether a DATA DIVISION map for the compiled program is to be produced to SYSPRINT.

```
NAME         Options: NAME, NONAME, NAME(ALIAS)
             Abbreviations: None
```

This option specifies whether a Linkage Editor NAME control statement is to be inserted immediately following the last object statement for a program. The NAME statement will use the PROGRAM-ID. If NAME(ALIAS) is specified, NAME statements are also generated for all ENTRY statements. For examples of where this is useful, see JCL Requirements in this chapter. Usually the default for this is NONAME.

```
NUMBER       Options: NUMBER, NONUMBER
             Abbreviations: NUM, NONUM
```

This option specifies whether the compiler should use sequence numbers from your program in columns 1–6. If so, they are sequence-checked. To me, this was important when programs were on punched cards. Now, with most people using DASD to store source programs, I suggest using NONUMBER. With NONUMBER, the compiler generates numbers for the compilation and all diagnostics refer to those generated numbers.

```
NUMPROC      Options: NUMPROC (n)
                Abbreviations: None

             where n = MIG   for migration support
                       PFD   for preferred sign support
                       NOPFD for no preferred sign support
```

This option specifies how signs in data fields are to be handled by generated code. This topic is explored in Defining, Initializing, and Using Data Areas. Your shop probably has a companywide standard on this option. If, after reading the mentioned topic, you feel your application should use a different option, I suggest you test the application and discuss it with others at your shop. I say this because a book can rarely address the many possibilities that exist. If in doubt, NUMPROC(NOPFD) works, but at the cost of efficiency. The most efficient option is NUMPROC(PFD).

```
OBJECT       Options: OBJECT, NOOBJECT
                Abbreviations: OBJ, NOOBJ
```

This option specifies whether the object module is to be written to the SYSLIN data set in 80-byte records. OBJECT is required if the TEST option is also specified. See also DECK. Both options do the same thing. To generate object code, one of them should be on. I suggest setting this to OBJECT.

```
OFFSET       Options: OFFSET, NOOFFSET
                Abbreviations: OFF, NOOFF
```

This option specifies whether a condensed listing of generated code will be produced to the SYSPRINT dataset. This listing shows the beginning offset location of each procedural statement. See also LIST. If used in conjunction with LIST, LIST will be ignored. For information on using this listing, see Chapter 4 (Debugging Techniques).

```
OPTIMIZE     Options: OPTIMIZE, NOOPTIMIZE
                Abbreviations: OPT, NOOPT
```

This option specifies whether optimized code is to be generated for the compiled program. This is enhanced from the optimizing facility in OS/VS COBOL. When OPTIMIZE is specified, it not only seeks to optimize individual statements, but also to combine statements when possible. In addition, it will attempt to create inline PERFORMs when possible and to bypass any code that will not be executed. Because the generated code is often quite different on a statement-by-statement basis, you may want to specify NOOPTIMIZE during initial testing. NOOPTIMIZE also reduces costs if you do many compiles before putting a program in productional use.

```
OUTDD        Options: OUTDD (ddname)
                Abbreviations: OUT(ddname)
```

This option specifies what ddname will be used for DISPLAY messages at run-time. The option normally specified is OUTDD(SYSOUT).

```
RENT         Options: RENT, NORENT
                Abbreviations: None
```

This option specifies that the compiled program is to be generated with reentrant code. It also allows the program to be executed in memory above the 16-megabyte address. RENT programs may *not* be mixed with NORENT programs. RENT is required for CICS programs. RENT also allows use of DATA(24) or DATA(31). NORENT cannot be used with DATA(31). Unless you have special considerations, I suggest specifying RENT to take advantage of the extended memory accessibility. NORENT supports static CALLs to and from 24-bit programs. See RESIDENT for related information. Also, see the RENT Linkage Editor option in JCL Requirements and Options in the previous section Creating a Load Module.

```
RESIDENT     Options: RESIDENT, NORESIDENT
                Abbreviations: RES, NORES
```

This option specifies that CALLs to COBOL II run-time modules will be resolved at run-time, not during the link-edit phase. This produces smaller load modules that access the most current version of the COBOL II modules. RES is required for CICS programs. See RENT for more information. The setting of RENT and RES cause the following RMODE and AMODE settings to also be made for the module.

These options Allowable combinations		3 cause these settings	
		RMODE	**AMODE**
RENT	RES	ANY	ANY
NORENT	RES	24	ANY
NORENT	NORES	24	24
RENT	NORES	not allowed	

RMODE refers to where a module may be loaded. AMODE refers to the addressability it has within memory, either to data areas or to other programs.

```
SEQUENCE    Options: SEQUENCE, NOSEQUENCE
              Abbreviations: SEQ, NOSEQ
```

This option specifies whether the source statement sequence numbers are to be validated. Unless your program is on punched cards, which can be dropped, NOSEQ is more efficient and prevents irrelevant error messages.

```
SIZE        Options: SIZE (nnnn) or SIZE(MAX) or SIZE(nnnK)
              Abbreviations: SZ(...)

              where n = memory requirements
```

This option specifies how much memory is to be used by the compiler. To a degree, the compiler is more efficient if more memory is specified. My suggestion is to set it to a number that exceeds REGION size, such as 4000K, with the REGION at 2000K. Setting SIZE(MAX) could cause the compiler to use all memory in the system, compromising performance of other applications.

```
SOURCE      Options: SOURCE, NOSOURCE
              Abbreviations: S, NOS
```

This option specifies whether the source listing is to be produced. See the following section on JCL for tips on using this.

```
SPACE       Options: SPACE (1), SPACE(2) or SPACE(3)
              Abbreviations: None
```

This option specifies single, double, or triple spacing of the SOURCE listing from the compile.

```
SSRANGE Options: SSRANGE, NOSSRANGE
              Abbreviations: SSR, NOSSR
```

This option specifies whether debug code for subscript and index range checking is to be included in the object module. Debug code is also included to check reference modification. This can increase cpu use during running. Output from this option is written to the MVS message log (in batch, this appears as the JES log) or to the CICS CEBRxxxx queue. The program will be terminated upon occurrence of any detected error. This option can be affected by the matching run-time option following.

```
TERMINAL    Options: TERMINAL, NOTERMINAL
              Abbreviations: TERM, NOTERM
```

This option requests that messages and diagnostics be sent to the SYSTERM dataset. This was useful prior to full-screen programming environments (e.g., ISPF) when on-line programmers used typewriter terminals.

```
TEST            Options: TEST, NOTEST
                     Abbreviations: TES, NOTES
```

This option requests that object code be produced to run with the COBOL II Debug facility, COBTEST, either in batch or interactively. This option forces these additional options: RES, NOFDUMP, NOOPTIMIZE, OBJECT. Information on COBTEST is in Chapter 4.

```
TRUNC           Options: TRUNC (n)
                     Abbreviations: None

                where n = BIN    allow full binary value
                          OPT    optimize object code
                          STD    conforms to American National
                                 Standard
```

This option determines how binary (COMP) data will be truncated in your application. This is because binary data is stored as 2-byte or 4-byte values, regardless of the PIC clause. Your choice of TRUNC specifies whether the maximum binary value should be allowed, TRUNC(BIN) the American National Standard should be used, TRUNC(STD) or optimized code based on an assessment of the PIC clause and the field size, TRUNC(OPT). This option is discussed at length in a prior section on data efficiency. IBM recommends that you use BIN if your program uses CICS, IMS, or DB2. Because of the performance implications, you may want to test other settings for your application.

BIN allows the maximum value, regardless of the PIC clause. STD uses a generic approach, using only the PIC clause. OPT assesses the field size (2 or 4 bytes) and the PIC clause to generate the most efficient code.

There is no one-to-one correspondence with TRUNC options of prior COBOL compilers.

```
VBREF           Options: VBREF, NOVBREF
                     Abbreviations: None
```

This option generates a listing at compile-time of the different verbs used and how many times each verb is used. It can be useful to assess whether a program uses verbs that are unfamiliar to you or that do not follow your shop standards. NOVBREF causes a more efficient compilation.

```
WORD          Options: WORD (xxxx) or NOWORD
              Abbreviations: WD, NOWD

              where xxxx = 4-character name of a word table
              developed by your installation
```

This option allows a company to develop a table of verbs that are to be checked during compilation. For example, if ALTER or GO TO are not allowed, they could be placed in this table, and at compile-time generate a warning message developed by your shop.

```
XREF          Options: XREF, XREF(SHORT), XREF(FULL) or NOXREF
              Abbreviations: X, NOX
```

This option specifies whether a cross-reference listing is to be produced by the compiler. The cross-reference listing is at the end of the source listing and if SOURCE is specified is appended at the right of related source statements. XREF and XREF(FULL) generate a listing of all names. XREF(SHORT) generates a listing of referenced names. XREF(SHORT) and XREF(FULL) may not be used with versions of COBOL II prior to version 3.1.

```
ZWB           Options: ZWB, NOZWB
              Abbreviations: None
```

ZWB causes a compare of a signed numeric item with an alphanumeric item to have the sign stripped prior to the compare, e.g., a +5 (hex C5) would be equal to 5 (hex F5). Although I don't recommend it, NOZWB can be used if you compare numeric items to SPACES.

COBOL II run-time options.

These options may be different for different environments, e.g., CICS and non-CICS. These options are usually set for an entire shop. They are presented here so you may modify (some of) them at run-time. You may need to contact your technical staff for assistance in their selection and use. Figure 3.4 lists them by some general categories. Several run-time options appear in more than one column. The categories are

Performance: These are options that affect resource usage.

Documentation: These are options that affect the input or SYSPRINT output (normally printed listings) from the compile.

Structure: These are options that affect the module-to-module structure, and the residency and addressing facilities of the run-time module.

Standards: These options provide opportunities your company may use to monitor or enforce standards.

Test-debug: These options provide debugging capabilities, but at the expense of extra resource usage.

How to specify: These two columns specify whether your company defaults may be overridden and how. For information on how to do this, see Specifying Options at Run-Time and Specifying Options via Preassembled Modules.

						How to specify	
Option	Performance	Documentation	Structure	Standards	Test-debug	Use IGZEOPT	Use JCL
AIXBLD	X			X		X	X
DEBUG*	X				X	X	X
LANGUAGE		X					
LIBKEEP*	X		X	X			
MIXRES*	X		X			X	
RTEREUS*	X		X			X	
SIMVRD*	X					X	X
SPOUT		X			X	X	X
SSRANGE	X				X	X	X
STAE	X		X	X	X	X	X
UPSI			X			X	X
WSCLEAR	X			X			

Figure 3.4. COBOL II Run-time options. (* option ignored for CICS)

Before reviewing these, you may want to get a listing of your company defaults. This may be accomplished by submitting a COBOL II program for a compile, link, and execute. If you have no program, this one works fine:

```
ID DIVISION.
PROGRAM-ID. EXAMPLE.
PROCEDURE DIVISION.
1.   STOP RUN.
```

The run-time EXEC statement for the linked program needs this format:

```
// EXEC PGM=programname,PARM='/SPOUT '
```

The options will be listed on the JES log. These options will be those for the batch environment. For a CICS or IMS/DC environment, ask your systems programmer. Normally, you won't need to override, or even know about most of these options, other than some for debugging purposes. Here is an example of the output:

```
+IGZ025I Run-time options in effect: 'SYSTYPE(OS), LANGUAGE(UE),
+       NOAIXBLD, NODEBUG, LIBKEEP, NOMIXRES, RTEREUS, NOSIMVRD, SPOUT,
+       NOSSRANGE, STAE, NOWSCLEAR, UPSI(00000000)'
+        Default options overridden: 'NOSPOUT'
+        Maximum physical space allocated by the space manager was
+        '16384' bytes above 16 megabytes and '8192' bytes below 16
+        megabytes.
```

AIXBLD   Options: AIXBLD, NOAIXBLD

If this option is specified, the system checks for empty VSAM indexes at OPEN and invokes Access Method Services to build alternate indexes. This affects performance and also requires that a SYSPRINT DD statement be included for Access Method Services messages. NOAIXBLD means that VSAM indexes are already defined.

DEBUG   Options: DEBUG, NODEBUG

This option is effective when WITH DEBUGGING MODE is specified in the source program. This is the only reference to WITH DEBUGGING MODE in this book.

LANGUAGE   Options:

See this option above, under Compile-time options.

LIBKEEP   Options: LIBKEEP, NOLIBKEEP

This option causes all COBOL II run-time modules to be retained in memory during a run unit. This can increase performance, especially if COBOL modules are CALLed by non-COBOL main programs. In most cases, LIBKEEP should be specified.

MIXRES   Options: MIXRES, NOMIXRES.

This option is specified when RES and NORES programs are combined within a single run unit. It is primarily used for migration assistance to COBOL II, when NORES was the previous default. It should be used only if needed and not used as an ongoing standard. Considerations on using MIXRES are in the topic, COBOL II to OS/VS COBOL, in Module Structures.

RTEREUS   Options: RTEREUS, NORTEREUS

This option was discussed earlier in the section Module Structures. RTEREUS initializes the run-time environment for reusability. This option does not apply to CICS. It affects program structure and may or may not be set at your installation. Specifying RTEREUS for IMS/DC applications is dependent on several factors, including preload considerations and the use of GOBACK or STOP RUN. Check with your technical staff if you have concerns for IMS/DC applications.

SIMVRD   Options: SIMVRD, NOSIMVRD

When processing a variable length relative dataset, this option uses a VSAM KSDS to simulate that data organization. For more assistance, see the appropriate *COBOL II Application Guide* (Chapter 9, Related Publications).

SPOUT   Options: SPOUT, NOSPOUT

This option issues a message indicating the amount of storage allocated and the selected run-time options in effect. It uses the WTP (write-to-programmer) facility (in batch, this is the MVS JES log). In CICS, the message goes to the CEBRxxxx queue.

SSRANGE   Options: SSRANCE, NOSSRANGE

This option activates the SSRANGE object code generated during compile-time. This feature allows you to compile with SSRANGE, yet control its use at run-time. Using NOSSRANGE at run-time can reduce cpu usage somewhat, and it eliminates the need to recompile to activate SSRANGE. Many shops set the default to NOSSRANGE to prevent inadvertent use of SSRANGE in productional applications.

STAE   Options: STAE, NOSTAE

STAE causes COBOL II to intercept ABENDs, cleanup the run-time environment, and produce a formatted dump (if FDUMP was specified). STAE is the normal setting and is recommended for CICS and IMS applications.

UPSI   Options: UPSI (nnnnnnnn)
             where *n* = digit from 0 to 7

There are 8 UPSI switches. They are provided for backward compatibility if a shop is dependent on their use. These switches cannot be referenced if the option NOCMPR2 is set. Since NOCMPR2 is the preferred option to take advantage of the newest COBOL II features, the UPSI feature is meaningless at most shops.

`WSCLEAR      Options: WSCLEAR, NOWSCLEAR`

This option causes all external data records and working storage areas acquired by a RENT program to be set to binary zeros (other than fields with VALUE clauses). This can reduce performance. Another approach is to write initialization code in your program or use more VALUE statements.

Additional COBOL II options.

There are other options that you cannot use, but that affect COBOL II. They are listed here in case some of the information I've given you in other sections appears to conflict with what is happening to your code. These options are used at the time COBOL II is installed or modified by your systems programmers. If you believe the options are incorrect at your installation, you will need to see your systems programmers to determine the settings.

ALOWCBL(YES) This option specifies whether PROCESS or CONTROL statements may be imbedded in source program. The default is YES. It is required for CICS. (You will want to use these statements, since they allow programmers to control SOURCE output.)

DBCSXREF(NO) The default is NO. This option specifies some cross-reference options for DBCS (the double-byte facility for languages with extensive alphabets). If you specify YES, you must order more software. If your installation needs DBCS, this option must be set to YES.

INEXIT, LIBEXIT, PRTEXIT These are the three components that make up the EXIT facility. If your company uses one or more of these, they can be set to be the default by your systems programmer.

LVLINFO This is a Systems Engineering option to specify what level is used at your company. If specified, up to four characters may follow the IBM Release number. It is a means of keeping track of different releases in your shop's terms. Default is to just print the IBM level number.

NUMCLS(PRIM) This is the technical side of NUMPROC. This setting determines what signs NUMPROC will accept. NUMPROC(PRIM) is the assumption used in this book, since it supports signs that are either C, D, or F.

3.11.2. Specifying COBOL II Options via JCL at Compile-Time

The options you need to specify are those other than the installation defaults. They may be coded as follows:

```
//  EXEC coboliiprocname,PARM='option-1,option-2,...'

    Example: // EXEC COB2C,PARM='SOURCE,OFFSET,OPTIMIZE'
```

3.11.3. Specifying COBOL II Options Within the Source Program

There will be times when you aren't familiar with the JCL or when you want to keep a program's compile options with the source code. That can be done with PROCESS statements. A PROCESS statement may be anywhere between columns 1 and 66. There may be no spaces between options. You may use more than one PROCESS statement. The format is

```
PROCESS  option-a,option-b,...

Example: PROCESS  SOURCE,OFFSET,VBREF
         PROCESS  XREF,OPTIMIZE
                 ID DIVISION.
                  .
                  .
```

Other than for installation options that have been defined as not eligible for override, the PROCESS options take precedence over any in the JCL and over the installation defaults. You may use CBL in place of PROCESS if desired. (Don't confuse this with *CBL statements, covered in JCL Requirements.)

3.11.4. Specifying COBOL II Options at Run-Time via JCL

As noted, the run-time options may be specified via JCL at run-time or via a module called IGZEOPT. This topic addresses the JCL approach. The JCL option may be used if your program is capable of accepting a PARM at run-time (e.g., CICS and IMS programs cannot). The syntax is to code the PARM statement with the selected run-time option(s) preceded by a slash. Any PARM the application program is to receive must be to the left of the slash mark. For example

This example executes a program called MYPROG, and sets SSRANGE on (assuming program was compiled with SSRANGE). The second example has two logical PARMs, one for the application and one for the COBOL II run-time options. The first PARM is WEEKLY and is made available to the program via the PROCEDURE DIVISION USING statement. The second PARM is SSRANGE,MIXRES and is processed by the COBOL II run-time environment.

```
//    EXEC PGM=MYPROG,PARM='/SSRANGE'
```

or

```
//    EXEC PGM=MYPROG,PARM='WEEKLY/SSRANGE,MIXRES'
```

3.11.5. Specifying COBOL II Run-Time Options in Preassembled Modules

There will be times when you need to specify run-time options and can't use JCL (e.g., CICS and IMS) or you want to specify options that cannot be specified via JCL. (See Figure 3.4.) In those cases, your installation must establish a module called IGZEOPT for each combination of desired options. (IBM provides a facility that your technical staff can use to create this module.) You can include the module into your program during link-edit processing. You use normal IN-CLUDE processing (see the previous section, Creating a Load Module) to accomplish this. The reason this works is that COBOL II inserts a weak external reference (WXTRN) into your program for IGZEOPT. The module is never required, but if it is present at run-time, the COBOL II modules use it to establish options for the run unit.

Note: If COBOL II is new at your shop, the needed IGZEOPT modules may not have been created. Your systems programmers need to be told all possibilities that may be needed, so they can create them. At a minimum, this is usually at least one version with the setting for SSRANGE if opposite that of the shop default (e.g., if the default is NOSSRANGE, a version is needed with SSRANGE to support testing).

3.12. JCL REQUIREMENTS: COMPILE, LINK AND EXECUTE

Your installation will probably use JCL differently from what is shown here. This information may be useful, however, to assist you in improving performance or in understanding some of the processing steps. While you may have other facilities at your shop, such as on-line compile and test facilities, this section deals with the batch facility. It is a common format across most installations and is usually the least expensive.

3.12.1. JCL for Compilation

In most installations, JCL procedures (PROCs) will be used for the compile, since there is so much JCL to specify. See figure 3.5 for an example.

```
 1.  //COB2C PROC  OUT='*'
 2.  //COB       EXEC  PGM=IGYCRCTL,REGION=2048K,
 3.  //               PARM=NOSOURCE
 4.  //STEPLIB   DD  DSN=your.cobol2.compiler.library,DISP=SHR
 5.  //SYSLIB    DD  DSN=your.cobol2.COPY.library,DISP=SHR
 6.  //SYSPRINT  DD  SYSOUT=&OUT,DCB=BLKSIZE=133
 7.  //SYSLIN    DD  DSN=&&OBJECT,UNIT=SYSDA,
 8.  //               DISP=(MOD,PASS),SPACE=(TRK,(40,10)),
 9.  //               DCB=(BLKSIZE=3200,RECFM=FB)
10.  //SYSUT1    DD  UNIT=SYSDA,SPACE=(CYL,(1,1))
11.  //SYSUT2    DD  UNIT=SYSDA,SPACE=(CYL,(1,1))
12.  //SYSUT3    DD  UNIT=SYSDA,SPACE=(CYL,(1,1))
13.  //SYSUT4    DD  UNIT=SYSDA,SPACE=(CYL,(1,1))
14.  //SYSUT5    DD  UNIT=SYSDA,SPACE=(CYL,(1,1))
15.  //SYSUT6    DD  UNIT=SYSDA,SPACE=(CYL,(1,1))
16.  //SYSUT7    DD  UNIT=SYSDA,SPACE=(CYL,(1,1))
```

Figure 3.5. Sample COBOL II Compile JCL for MVS.

While the JCL at your shop may be different, let's review the sample MVS compile JCL in figure 3.5. You may find it is more efficient than what your shop is using. (Note: DD statements may be in any order.)

1. Statement 1 specifies any symbolic JCL parameters.
2. The REGION on line 2 ensures that a SIZE compile option exceeding 2048K won't access more memory than 2048K. (Having the SIZE option set to a higher value than 2048K allows the REGION to be increased if appropriate without also needing to change the SIZE parameter concurrently.)
3. The PARM on line 3 is an example of a compiler option that was not specified as a company default, but will be treated as such if no other PARMs are specified.
4. Statement number 4 should have the name of your installation's library where COBOL II is stored.
5. Statement number 6 points to a partitioned dataset for COPY statements. (COBOL II allows the block size of this data set to be double that allowed with OS/VS COBOL.)
6. The SOURCE, OFFSET, LIST, MAP, VBREF, and XREF information is written to the DD statement on line 6 (SYSPRINT). This defaults to RECFM=FBA, LRECL=133.
7. The DISP of MOD on line 8 allows multiple compiles to be in a job prior to a link-edit. This allows concatenated object modules for a multiple-module structure.

8. The DCB parameter on line 9 is the largest block size that can be processed by the Linkage Editor. If this is not specified on the JCL, COBOL II defaults to a block size of 80 bytes. Use this option to reduce I/O during compiles.

9. Lines 10 through 16 are work files. They are allocated to cylinders to minimize I/O. Their block sizes are determined by the setting of the BUF compile option.

10. The source statement input dataset, SYSIN, is not in this example, since it is provided by the programmer in the job stream. It must have a record size (LRECL) of 80 bytes and may or may not be blocked. Efficiency is increased if the dataset has a large block size, especially for big programs (by large block size, I mean 12,000 or more).

Tips to control the compile process.

Multiple standard options At most shops, there are usually several standard sets of compile options that people use. For example, it may be common at your installation to specify "SOURCE,OFFSET,NOOPTIMIZE" during testing and "SOURCE,LIST,OPTIMIZE,MAP" when compiling for productional use. Instead of requiring programmers to code all that and be subject to a coding error, you could set up standard combinations in a PDS using PROCESS statements (these were covered in a previous section, Specifying COBOL II Options). Using my example, you might code three PDS members (LRECL=80, RECFM=FB).

Member: USEDEF
This member would have one blank record.

Member: TEST:
This member would have this statement:

```
PROCESS SOURCE,OFFSET,NOOPTIMIZE
```

Member: PROD:
This member would have this statement:

```
PROCESS SOURCE,LIST,OPTIMIZE,MAP
```

Now, if we insert a SYSIN DD statement in the compile PROC and change the PROC statement itself (using the example in figure 3.5) to include these two statements:

```
//COB2C   PROC  OUT='*',OPTION=USEDEF
            .
            .
            .
//SYSIN   DD   DSN=your.library(&OPTION),DISP=SHR
//        DD   DDNAME=SOURCE
```

we could specify the desired combinations by coding

```
//  EXEC COB2C                 for defaults
//SOURCE DD....
```

or

```
//  EXEC COB2C,OPTION=TEST     for "testing" options
//SOURCE  DD  ....
```

or

```
//  EXEC COB2C,OPTION=PROD     for "production" compiles
//SOURCE  DD  ....
```

Multiple compiles There are two ways to do multiple compiles. One is to compile a main program and one or more CALLed subprograms in one step to link them into one run unit. The other is to compile multiple programs that are each to be linked as separate run units. Let's take them separately.

Compiling a main module and subprogram(s) Insert "END PROGRAM program-id." as the last statement in each program. This lets the compiler tell the various programs apart. The second step is to arrange the sequence of source programs in the order you want the object modules to be created. Then, one execution of the compiler creates all the object modules in the specified sequence, such as:

```
//  EXEC COB2C,PARM='SOURCE,OFFSET'
//SYSIN  DD   your.source.lib(MAINPROG),DISP=SHR
//       DD   your.source.lib(SUBPROGA),DISP=SHR
//       DD   your.source.lib(SUBPROGB),DISP=SHR
```

This generates the object code first for MAINPROG, then SUBPROGA, followed by SUBPROGB. From the information in the previous section, Creating a Load Module, you know that this minimizes or eliminates the need to code Linkage Editor control statements.

Compiling several independent modules Insert "END PROGRAM program-id.," as in the previous example, as the last statement in each program. This lets the compiler tell the various programs apart. The second step is to specify the NAME option (along with any other options) on the compile JCL. Then, one execution of the compiler creates all the object modules with Linkage Editor NAME control statements following each one.

This example generates the object code for PROGA, PROGC, and PROGB and places a NAME control statement after each one. From the section Creating a Load Module, you know that this causes the Linkage Editor, in one execution, to create three separate load modules with no need for Linkage Editor control statements.

```
//    EXEC COBC,PARM='SOURCE,OFFSET,NAME'
//SYSIN  DD    your.source.lib(PROGA),DISP=SHR
//       DD    your.source.lib(PROGC),DISP=SHR
//       DD    your.source.lib(PROGB),DISP=SHR
```

Limiting printed output with *CBL. You can control the printing of SOURCE statements, assembler statements (LIST option), and data maps (the MAP option). This could be useful (and save some trees) when you have a large program, have changed a few statements, and need to see the output from one or more of those three options (SOURCE, LIST, MAP). Here is how it is done.

1. Specify appropriate compile options via JCL or PROCESS statements. These must include those which you want to control. In our example of controlling source and assembler statements, we would specify SOURCE and LIST via a JCL PARM or PROCESS statements (if not already the installation default). This causes the compile to begin with the *options set on*. That is mandatory. If the options are set to NOSOURCE, NOLIST, or NOMAP, the next steps cannot take effect.
2. Next, immediately (or wherever desired) include a statement in your source program that is similar to the PROCESS statement. This is a *CBL statement also known as a CONTROL statement. The *CBL statement is similar to PROCESS, but it can only specify SOURCE or NOSOURCE, MAP or NOMAP, LIST or NOLIST, or some combination of the three. When encountered by the compiler, the compiler adjusts the compile options according to the *CBL options specified. The *CBL statement may begin in any column, starting with column 7. As with PROCESS, no spaces may appear between options. The reason to code the *CBL immediately is to negate any listings until we reach the part of our program we want to list. For our example, we would specify

```
*CBL  NOSOURCE,NOLIST
```

3. Then, immediately preceding the code you want a listing of, insert another *CBL statement, such as

```
*CBL   SOURCE,LIST
```

4. Finally, at the end of the code you want listed, insert another *CBL statement, identical to that in step 2.

Let's put all this together in an example using PROCESS and *CBL statements. Assume that SOURCE and LIST are set to NOSOURCE and NOLIST as installation defaults. Here is the example:

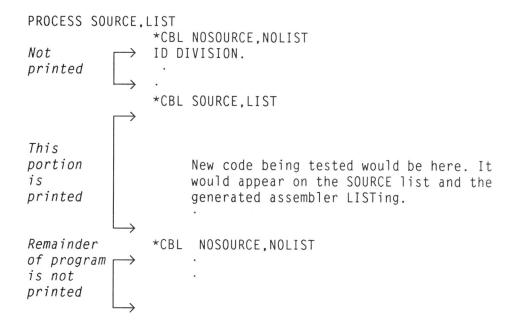

```
PROCESS SOURCE,LIST
                  *CBL NOSOURCE,NOLIST
Not         ┌──→  ID DIVISION.
printed     │        ·
            └──→     ·
                  *CBL SOURCE,LIST
            ┌──→
This        │
portion     │
is          │           New code being tested would be here. It
printed     │           would appear on the SOURCE list and the
            │           generated assembler LISTing.
            │              ·
            └──→
Remainder         *CBL  NOSOURCE,NOLIST
of program  ┌──→      ·
is not      │         ·
printed     │
            └──→
```

Using *CBL statements takes practice and adds work to the compile process, but this feature puts the ability to reduce paper usage in the programmer's hands. Prior to COBOL II, it was an all-or-nothing situation.

3.12.2. JCL for Link-edit Processing

The processing of the Linkage Editor was covered in the section Creating a Load Module. This topic deals with the JCL requirements. Here is an example of an MVS procedure to use with the previous MVS example for compiling:

```
1.  //LKED      PROC OUT='*'
2.  //LINK      EXEC PGM=IEWL,REGION=1700K,COND=(4,LT),
3.  //          PARM='SIZE=(1600K,800K),LIST,LET,MAP,XREF,RENT'
4.  //SYSPRINT  DD   SYSOUT=*
5.  //SYSLIB    DD   DSN=your.cobol2.runtime.library,DISP=SHR
6.  //SYSLIN    DD   DSN=&&OBJECT,DISP=(OLD,DELETE)
7.  //          DD   DDNAME=SYSIN
8.  //SYSUT1    DD   UNIT=SYSDA,SPACE=(CYL,(5,2))
9.  //SYSLMOD   DD   DSN=&&TEST(GO),DISP=(NEW,PASS),UNIT=SYSDA,
10. //               SPACE=(TRK,(10,20,5)),DCB=BLKSIZE=32000
```

Figure 3.6. Sample link-edit procedure for MVS.

To review the MVS link-edit JCL (Note: DD statements may be in any order):

1. Statement 1 specifies any symbolic JCL parameters.
2. Statement 2 specifies that, if a prior step had a severity 2 error (return code greater than 4), no link should be done. It also specifies the link-edit options you will normally require (RENT depends on the application). The SIZE option shown is intended to reduce your link-edit costs. Unlike the COBOL II compiler, which can take advantage of available memory automatically, the Linkage Editor must be told how much is available. In this example, I am specifying that it may use 1600K and should leave 800K of the 1600K for I/O buffers. This reduces I/O to SYSUT1 during link-edit processing and can reduce overhead to load the module at run-time.
3. Statement 5 must point to your COBOL II run-time library, since there is always an imbedded CALL to at least one of the modules.
4. Statement 6 assumes object code input is from the sample COBOL II compile procedure. This could be any sequential dataset with LRECL=80 and a block size not greater than 3200.
5. Statement 7 is a JCL technique that allows logical concatenation to SYSLIN via a DD name of SYSIN. That allows you to code

```
//      EXEC LKED
//SYSIN DD *
  control statements
```

instead of

```
//      EXEC LKED
//SYSLIN  DD
//          DD *
  control statements
```

6. Statements 9 and 10 specify the output dataset, in this case a temporary library with a module name of GO.

Selecting link-edit options.

The COBOL II compiler places several link-edit attributes into the object module, primarily the AMODE and RMODE attributes. The options that will normally affect you are as follows:

RENT This option marks the load module as reentrant. (Note: All modules must have been compiled with the RENT attribute.) Use this for modules where reentrant processing is desired (normally CICS and IMS/DC applications). See Creating a Load Module for more information on RENT.

REUS This option marks a load module as serially reusable. (This is not needed if RENT was specified—was used for OS/VS COBOL modules.)

LIST This option produces a listing of control statements used on the print dataset.

XREF Produces a cross-reference listing on the print dataset.

MAP This option produces a list of all modules in new load module on the print dataset.

LET This option lets the module be marked executable, even if errors occurred. (This is useful if some modules are known to be absent during a test.)

NCAL This option does not resolve any CALLs via the "automatic call library."

Be careful with options such as AMODE or RMODE (not shown). For additional information on the Linkage Editor (or AMODE and RMODE), see Creating a Load Module.

Naming the load module.

This is also explained in Creating a Load Module. The load module name is determined by this priority:

1. If there is a NAME statement, it is used.
2. If there is no NAME statement, but a member name is on the SYSLMOD JCL, it is used.
3. If neither of the above, TEMPNAME is used.

Linkage Editor Listing.

The Linkage Editor Listing may include weak external references (WXTRN), depicted as

```
IGZETUN $UNRESOLVED(W)
```

If the prefix of the module is IGZ, this is normal and does not require that you attempt to correct it.

3.12.3. JCL for Batch Execution

In executing a program, you need to consider these JCL requirements that are imposed on you by COBOL II. They are in addition to other DD statements your application may require.

Additional DD statements.

To execute your program, there are some JCL DD statements that are required in addition to whatever other JCL you use. They are

SYSABOUT To list any COBOL II ABEND intercept information. If this DD statement is missing, summary information is written to the MVS message log (WTP route code 11). For batch, this is the JES log. The data set format is LRECL=125, RECFM=VBA. For example,

```
//SYSABOUT DD SYSOUT=*
```

SYSDBOUT To list any output from FDUMP, if specified. This is also required for some options of COBTEST (Chapter 4). Dataset format is LRECL=121, RECFM=FBA. For example,

```
//SYSDBOUT DD SYSOUT=*
```

SYSOUT To list any DISPLAY information. Dataset format is LRECL=121, RECFM=FBA. (Note: This ddname is determined by the COBOL II compile option OUTDD. I assume you use SYSOUT). For example,

```
//SYSOUT   DD SYSOUT=*
```

SYSIN To process any input from an ACCEPT statement. Dataset format is LRECL=80, RECFM=FB.

Write after advancing and ADV option.

When writing reports, you probably use the WRITE AFTER ADVANCING statement. Remember the ADV option, which allows you to not include a byte in the 01-level record for the ASA control character. For example, if you are writing a report that is 115 characters wide (they don't have to be 120 or 132 as some people believe), you would code it differently, depending on the setting of ADV.

With ADV:

```
        FD  FD-REPORT-FILE
            RECORD CONTAINS 115 CHARACTERS
            RECORDING MODE IS F.
        01  FD-REPORT-RECORD PIC X(115).
                            ︿
                            └──────────────┐
                                           │
         .                                 │
         .                                 │
            MOVE field-name TO FD-REPORT-RECORD
            WRITE FD-REPORT-RECORD AFTER ADVANCING 1
         .
   //ddname DD SYSOUT=A,DCB=BLKSIZE=116
```

With NOADV:

```
        FD  FD-REPORT-FILE
            RECORD CONTAINS 116 CHARACTERS
            RECORDING MODE IS F.
        01  FD-REPORT-RECORD.
            05                 PIC X.         <- Not referenced
            05 FD-DATA-AREA  PIC X(115).
                        ︿
                        └──────────┐
                                   │
         .                         │
         .                         │
            MOVE field-name TO FD-DATA-AREA
            WRITE FD-REPORT-RECORD AFTER ADVANCING 1
         .
   //ddname DD SYSOUT=A,DCB=BLKSIZE=116
```

In the first example, notice that the FD and 01-level specify the actual size of the report, freeing the programmer from being concerned with machine dependencies. This still requires the JCL to acknowledge the real record and block size of 116 (record size plus ASA control character).

The second example, using NOADV, is the same size on FD, 01-level, and JCL. It requires different coding, however. The first byte of the 01-level must not be referenced and no MOVEs may be made to the 01-level name. I recommend

ADV, since I don't want to be concerned with accidentally modifying an ASA control character.

3.12.4. DFSORT Control Statements

This topic appears in several places. See also the appropriate sections in this chapter. This topic contains the control statements you would most likely use in a SORT application.

GENERAL Syntax All the following statements are coded as part of the IGZSRTCD (or SORTCNTL) dataset, which must be LRECL=80. All statements must leave column 1 blank and must not exceed column 71. Statements may be continued to a following line by ending a parameter with a comma and then coding the next parameter on the next line, again leaving column 1 blank.

INCLUDE and OMIT syntax (Use one or the other, not both.)

```
 INCLUDE COND=(st,len,ty,cond, st,len,ty  [,AND or OR]...)
 OMIT                          C'xxxx'
                               X'xxxx'
                               +number
                               -number
```

```
Where
    st       = first position of field
    len      = length of the field in bytes
    ty       = type of data, i.e., CH, FI, ZD, PD
    cond     = EQ,GT,LT,GE,LE,NE
```

For example, including records where positions 25–28 equal "LIFE":

```
INCLUDE  COND=(25,4,CH,EQ,C'LIFE')
```

Omitting records where positions 25–28 equal "LIFE" or positions 25–30 equal "HEALTH":

```
OMIT  COND=(25,4,CH,EQ,C'LIFE',OR,25,6,CH,EQ,C'HEALTH')
```

INREC Syntax (Only the specified fields will be in the sort record.)

```
INREC  FIELDS=(start,length,start,length,...)

              └ 1st field ┘ └2nd field ┘ etc.
```

For example, extract fields in positions 35–40 and 61–90, creating a sort input record of 36 bytes. (SORT is faster with shorter records.) Reminder: SD 01-level must show that these two fields are now in positions 1–6 and 7–36. While the new record length is now 36, the SD 01-level should continue to reflect the original length.

```
INREC FIELDS=(35,6,61,30)
```

SUM Syntax (has two different formats)

```
SUM  FIELDS=(start,length,type,...)
```

Fields must be FI, PD, or ZD. This summarizes data based on sort keys used. Fields being summarized must not be sort key fields.

```
SUM FIELDS=NONE
```

This option creates one output record where multiple records had the same sort key. For example, if you wanted to get a sorted listing by salesperson and the input file contained a record for each sale by salesperson, this option would eliminate the duplicates.

OUTREC Syntax (same as INREC, except it can insert binary zeros, blanks, or constants)

For example, reformat output from above to include 30 blanks, making the output record 66 bytes long:

```
OUTREC FIELDS=(1,36,30X)     <- inserts 30 blank bytes

OUTREC FIELDS=(1,36,30Z)     <- inserts 30 bytes of binary
                                zeros
```

For example, reformat output from above to begin with 10 blanks, followed by first 30 bytes of data, followed by a 13-byte literal, followed by the last 5 bytes from input record, creating a 58-byte record:

```
OUTREC FIELDS=(10X,1,30,C'literal value',31,5)
```

Example of SORT JCL.

Here is an example where a COBOL SORT program has a USING statement and an OUTPUT PROCEDURE statement. The OMIT and INREC provide all the logic needed to omit certain records from processing and to reformat the record to contain only the needed data fields for the OUTPUT processing. There are no

COBOL changes required to use the OMIT process, but the INREC requires the SD 01-level to reflect the new data positions.

```
//        EXEC PGM=cobol-sort-program
//SORTCNTL  DD *
    OMIT    COND=(26,2,CH,EQ,C'25')
    INREC   FIELDS=(1,5,6,20,26,2,28,2,47,2)
//    ·
//    ·                <- other DD's as needed
//    ·
```

SUMMARY

This chapter covers a lot of material, all of which is designed to help you be a better, more knowledgeable, more efficient programmer. Some techniques may appear not to work correctly in your shop. If that happens, first review the material to ensure you followed the guidelines carefully. Many of these techniques are not routinely used and you may encounter people who swear the techniques will never work. This is because for many years many of us have viewed COBOL as just a black box and had no understanding of it. You won't master all these techniques by reading. Keep the book nearby and try something new on your next program.

Debugging Techniques With COBOL II

This chapter will not teach you how to debug specific problems. Instead, the goal of this chapter is to ensure you know what information is available and how it may be used. As a professional programmer, your interest is in developing a foundation of knowledge on which to build, not to learn tricks for specific situations. Despite this statement, the first section of this chapter is a tutorial, presenting some concepts about dumps to readers with limited background. If you need special information about COBOL II dumps beyond what is covered in this section, see Chapter 9 (Related Publications).

Unfortunately, many programmers think debugging means reading dumps. Not true. Reading a dump is a last resort and should be postponed as long as possible. Additionally, with several proprietary dump interpretation software products on the market, the pain from reading system dumps is a memory. (Note: If your shop still reads raw dumps from the system, I suggest you encourage your management to investigate the dump interpretation software products available. They save a mountain of paper, reduce costly training time, and usually isolate most problems, often including a statement of the problem in plain language and how to solve it.)

COBOL II provides several aids to assist you in solving problems, including options for compile output, object code generation, and error interception. In fact, some problems that caused an ABEND in prior versions of COBOL cause only an error message and termination today. You will also notice that COBOL II provides facilities to let you be proactive in anticipating and resolving ABENDs.

Because the focus of this book is on helping you develop efficient applications with COBOL and not on teaching various work practices to solve problems, the debugging environment (called COBTEST) provided by COBOL II is not covered in depth. Another reason is that COBTEST is a separate product that may not be at your installation. For specifics on the compile options that support debugging, see Specifying COBOL II Options, in Chapter 3.

4.1. REMOVING THE MYSTERY FROM DUMPS

This section is a tutorial, taking some license with the actual specifics that occur. If you are comfortable with dumps and using compiler output to resolve them, you will find little here. You may even disagree with some of the details as I present them. The goal of this section is to ensure there is no mystery surrounding dumps for people with little experience. So long as a topic is mysterious, you cannot learn techniques to deal with it.

With many debug courses oriented around specific problems (e.g., "How to solve an 0C7," "How to solve multimodule problems"), junior programmers often view dumps as a mystery. Let's tackle that first. With a grasp of how the elements fit together, it is easier to develop a strategy for a variety of application problems.

4.1.1. 1. Why Is the Dump in Hex, Anyway?

Contrary to a popular belief, the computer does NOT do hexadecimal arithmetic (yes, you can buy one of many hand-held calculators that do hex arithmetic, but the mainframe cannot). Instead, the mainframe does binary arithmetic for memory management and uses hexadecimal as a shorthand format. (If a dump were nothing but 1s and 0s, life would be tough indeed.) Also, the operating system has no idea whether the data components of your program were EBC-DIC, binary, packed-decimal, or floating point. The common format for all formats is the bit configuration they use, so this is what you get. The operating system correctly assumes that the compiler with which you compiled your program will provide documentation to assist in locating your program and data elements. The operating system further assumes, also correctly, that the Linkage Editor listing will provide assistance in determining which program was involved in the ABEND. I'll cover that information shortly.

Do you need to be good at hex arithmetic? Although I may incur the wrath of many senior programmers, my answer is no. For most of us, we have a sufficient knowledge of hex if we can

- Write our name in hex
- Count from 1 to 20 in hex
- Write our age in binary, in hex, and in packed-decimal
- Using our fingers, subtract numbers such as 4A minus 3C

The above items aren't difficult and emphasize that what we need is the ability to recognize patterns. For example

- C4C1E5C5 is a pattern of EBCDIC characters ("DAVE")
- F2F5, 19, and 025C are patterns of the decimal value 25 in EBCDIC, hex, and packed-decimal. (No, I'm not 25, but it was a nice age when I was.)
- In the subtraction example, I know that 4A is greater than 3C. That also means I know that 3D through 49 are numbers that occur between these two. With my fingers, I can do whatever is needed there.

In most cases, the information you have from the compiler and Linkage Editor are hex numbers. Usually, all you need to do is search high/low and match values. You'll see that later. If, for your application, it is necessary to consistently do arithmetic such as

```
  3A2CD4        4C9A0F
 -2FC19A       +19CDF0
```

you should consider buying one of the many calculators on the market that do this for you. Why? They aren't expensive and their use removes a lot of drudgery. For a person to be a superior programmer, there are many skills to master that are more important than hex arithmetic, so why waste the time? I stopped teaching the details of hex arithmetic years ago and have no regrets.

Other questions you may have are, "Do I need to be able to convert decimal numbers to hex and hex numbers to decimal?" and "Do I need to be able to read negative hex numbers, i.e., master the technique of two's-complement notation?" Unfortunately, these two techniques can be frightening but are in many textbooks. Instead of answering those questions, let's turn them around. A better question is, "How do I eliminate the need to convert hex to decimal and cope with two's-complement notation?" Now the answer is simple. Just don't use the COMP format. That's all there is to it. Yes, you may still have to add or subtract hex numbers to locate programs or statements or data elements, but you never need to convert those answers to decimal and you won't be dealing with negative numbers.

From the above, you may wonder why some programmers use COMP. For one thing, they were probably taught it was more efficient (see Chapter 3 for more information). One of the reasons many programmers use packed-decimal (COMP-3) is that it requires no hex conversion in a dump. That in itself improves your productivity. If you would like to learn more about hexadecimal values, see Chapter 7.

4.1.2. Identifying Where Information Is Located

Earlier, I mentioned that the operating system assumed information was available to assist you in reading a dump. Using figure 4.1, let's look at how that information is constructed. For our example, assume a batch program, PROGA, has an ADD statement on line 23 of the program and that it will ABEND because of a bad data field. (In our example, it also CALLs PROGB, but that is incidental to the problem.) Here are the steps:

1. The first step, the compile, produces two important pieces of information. One, the SOURCE option shows that the ADD statement is on line 23. Two, the OFFSET option shows that it is in the range 2FC through 305. (Remember my comment about knowing ranges. ABENDS never occur where a failing instruction begins.) Those two items will be important in the event of an ABEND. The purpose of the compiler-produced information is to locate which statement or data element within a specific program caused the ABEND.

2. Next, the Linkage Editor prints a listing of how the load module is constructed. It shows that PROGA is at the beginning, with an offset into the load module of 0. You may also note that PROGA occupies addresses 0 through 4CEF and that PROGB occupies addresses 4CF0 through 52BF. The purpose of the Linkage Editor listing when debugging is to locate which program within a load module caused the ABEND (although this information is rarely needed when using compiler-produced debugging aids, such as FDUMP).

3. Third, when the program ABENDs, MVS has two outputs. One is a series of messages, normally available via the JCL sysout queue (JES) for batch applications. (The COBOL II run-time error intercept routines also put messages here.) The second output is the dump itself. The dump is produced only if there is an appropriate DD statement, such as SYSUDUMP or SYSABEND. (Check with your installation standards for which one you should use.) Information from MVS confirms in which load module the ABEND occurred.

Now, let's follow that flow in reverse, going from MVS to the Linkage Editor to the COBOL II listing. By following these steps as a standard routine, you will solve most of the ABENDs you will encounter. Sample listings of actual output will be in following topics. We're still on basics in this section.

From MVS. On ABEND, MVS prints that the load module was named GO, the ABEND was 0C7, and that the offset in the load module was 302. The dump shows the actual memory location, 32D2A2. Locating location 32D2A2 in the dump will be a waste of time because it will be all in hex. So don't do it. Notice also the MVS message saying offset 302. Where did 302 come from? MVS has *already* subtracted 32CFA0 from 32D2A2, giving a result of 302. This is the offset of the instruction beyond the logical beginning point of the load module. To confirm which program that is in, you look at the Linkage Editor listing. Reminder: MVS always shows the next sequential instruction's address, not the address of the offending instruction. When you locate the correct offset in the

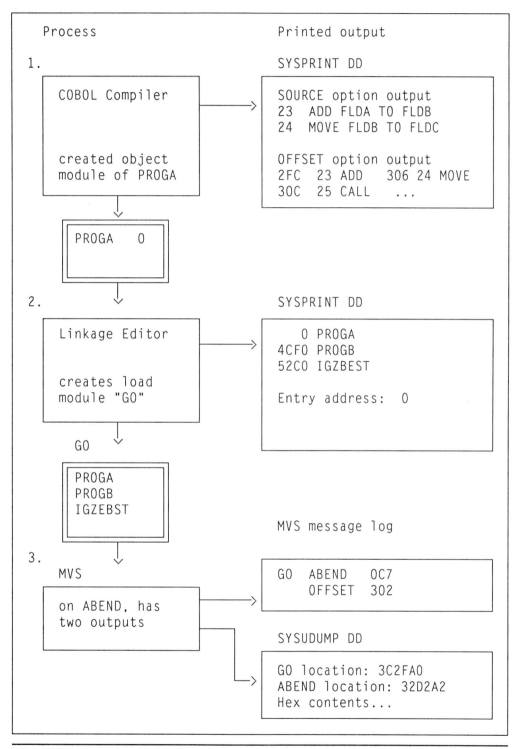

Figure 4.1. Sample of information to analyze a dump.

correct program, you will be looking at the instruction just beyond the one that caused the ABEND.

From the Linkage Editor. From this listing, you want to confirm the location of the ABEND from the physical beginning, not the logical beginning, of the load module. Since the physical beginning (always 0) matches the logical beginning (entry address) in the example, you know the offset of 302 needs no further adjustment. (Note: If the entry address (logical beginning) was other than 0, you would need to add it to the number from MVS to get an address relative to the Linkage Editor listing.)

Since the Linkage Editor listing shows us that instructions between relative location 0 and 4CEF are in the program PROGA, you now know in which program to search for the problem. Notice that you haven't done any hex arithmetic yet. When you are using debug facilities from COBOL II, you usually do not need to reference the Linkage Editor listing, as the error message will include the name of the offending program.

From the compiler listing. Here is where planning helps. If you compiled the program and specified none of the possible options to help in debugging, you should stop pursuing the problem until you recompile the program with some debugging options (see Chapter 3). Assuming you specified SOURCE (to list all source code and sequence numbers) and OFFSET (to show at what offset the instructions begin), you can continue with this problem. In our example, the OFFSET listing in figure 4.1 shows that location 302 occurs somewhere between the beginning of an ADD statement on line 23 and a MOVE statement on line 24. Again, notice that no hex arithmetic has been needed. This confirms that the ABEND was caused by the ADD statement on line 23.

A reminder about an OFFSET listing: Earlier, I mentioned that MVS always points, not to the instruction causing the error but to the next sequential instruction. For example, if the offset address had been 306 (the address of the MOVE instruction), it would still confirm the ADD instruction as the one causing the ABEND. Likewise, had the offset address been 2FC, it would confirm whatever instruction preceded this ADD statement. With the specific instruction confirmed, it is usually a small matter to determine whether it was FLDA or FLDB in the example that caused the 0C7.

Review. To review that flow again, all programs must go through three steps in their life. One, to be compiled into machine code. Two, to be transformed into executable code as a load module. Three, to be loaded into memory and executed. On an ABEND

- MVS indicates which load module.
- The Linkage Editor listing shows which program.
- The compiler listing shows which statement.

Bypassing any of those three steps can cause confusion in solving the problem. These steps are needed whenever MVS or the COBOL II run-time modules cannot identify the problem.

My suggested steps in solving a dump follow:

1. At the risk of offending programmers everywhere, I suggest not using the system dump information (e.g., SYSUDUMP DD) when testing a program, unless other approaches fail. A large number of ABENDs can be solved without wasting so many trees. If you get an unsolvable ABEND, you can always add the DD statement and reexecute the program. In most cases, it isn't needed. From my experience, programmers tend to read (or keep) everything the computer prints for a testing error. If that is true at your shop, you will get a productivity gain by not even seeing the unnecessary dump. For example, I once got an ABEND for misspelling a DDNAME. One of the system messages was "Missing DD statement" (or words to that effect). With that message, I corrected the situation in minutes. Despite this, MVS still produced a dump of 100+ pages for me to throw away. When I discussed this with several other programmers, many felt I should have read (or kept) the dump anyway. Why? Because it was there. Let's get out of that trap.

2. Read the system messages first. This may solve the problem. For example, if you meant to execute a program called GLOP, but coded EXEC PGM=FLOP on the JCL statement, MVS produces an 806 ABEND message, stating that the load module called FLOP could not be located. The problem is solved. No dump is needed.

3. Even if the system messages do not produce any clear solution, check them anyway for ABEND messages that have an OFFSET address or ABEND code. The OFFSET can be checked against your Linkage Editor listing to confirm which program was involved and the ABEND code may be sufficient in itself. For example, once I got an ABEND of 0C9 (divide by zero). Since I had just added a group of statements to the program, one of which was a COMPUTE statement with the divide operator, I knew where to look for the problem.

4. Unless your program has a complex link-edit structure, you can now go to the source listing and locate the offending statement with the OFFSET value.

Most of the time, these steps will do it for you. If they solve 90 percent of your problems, you will be viewed as a technical genius and you can then afford to seek additional assistance beyond that. Our goal in this topic is to remove the magic, not make you an expert. In the following topics, you will see additional information to assist you. If you desire to master every facet of dump reading, you may want to get the appropriate IBM manuals. (See Chapter 9, Related Publications.)

4.2. READING THE SYSTEM MESSAGES

Earlier, I suggested that you check the system messages first. Let's get a feel for that here. One of the most difficult challenges is being patient as you read the many messages logged during your job. Some are useful; some are not. Here is a simple example where a program received an 0CB (decimal divide exception) and, although there is a lot of information here, most of it is useless for this problem. I highlighted the useful data but, even with this aid, it can be difficult to bypass the other information. Since MVS never knows the true cause of a problem, it gives you every shred of information it has, leaving it to you to discard most of it.

In this example, the load module ABEND offset is 6C2. If I know the module to contain only one COBOL program, beginning at location 0, then I can proceed directly to the COBOL listing to locate the error. The dump, if present, can be tossed.

```
IEA995I SYMPTOM DUMP OUTPUT
SYSTEM COMPLETION CODE=0CB REASON CODE=0000000B
 TIME=12.41.54 SEQ=32563 CPU=0000 ASID=0052
 PSW AT TIME OF ERROR 478D2000 00006E22 ILC 6 INTC 0B
  ACTIVE LOAD MODULE=DKA10100 ADDRESS=00006760 OFFSET=000006C2
  DATA AT PSW 00006E1C - FD41D17B 9006F822 9008D17B
  GPR  0-3   00000000 00006FD0 0000A930 30006FDC
  GPR  4-7   000140B0 007EEE88 000067B4 0000A930
  GPR  8-11  0000EAB4 00007000 000067F4 00006B5C
  GPR 12-15  000067E0 00006E58 50006E06 00000000
END OF SYMPTOM DUMP
+IGZ057I An ABEND was intercepted by the COBOL execution time ABEND
+        handler. It is described by a corresponding IEA995I message.
```

This next message is indicative of the type of assistance COBOL II gives the programmer. What would once have been a difficult ABEND to solve is now a simple error message. The ABEND occurred when the program attempted to READ the file. Again, an example of an error where no SYSUDUMP DD is needed. This gives the program name, so the Linkage Editor listing also isn't needed. With the offset of 0516 from the message, the OPEN causing the error can be found from an OFFSET or LIST option.

```
+IGZ035I There was an unsuccessful OPEN or CLOSE of file 'PAY102' in
+         program 'DKA10200' at relative location X'0516'. Neither FILE
+         STATUS nor an ERROR declarative were specified. The I-O status
+         code was '39'.
```

These next messages don't give much information, except to tell you that the COBOL run-time intercept module is active and the SYSABOUT DD is missing. The SYSABOUT DD statement is used at ABEND to record information for you. For an example of SYSABOUT information, see Using FDUMP and SYSABOUT.

```
+IGZ043I A SYSABOUT error occurred. The ABEND information may be
+        incomplete.
+IGZ057I An ABEND was intercepted by the COBOL execution time ABEND
+        handler. It is described by a corresponding IEA995I message.
```

These examples are by no means complete or thorough. I hope you now have a better anticipation of the type of messages that COBOL II generates, so you may adjust your debugging technique accordingly. Our goal here is to work smarter, not harder. For information and detailed explanations of the run-time messages (all have the prefix of IGZ), see *VS COBOL II Application Program Debugging* (Chapter 9, Related Publications). Note: If the message has a prefix of IKF, it will be from the OS/VS COBOL run-time library, indicating a non-COBOL II component of your run unit.

4.3.   READING THE OFFSET AND LIST OUTPUT FROM A COMPILE

These two options, OFFSET and LIST, are mutually exclusive. If both are selected, OFFSET gets priority. I recommend that OFFSET, as a minimum, be specified for every compile where you anticipate executing the module. Without one of the two, you will be unable to identify a specific COBOL statement in case of an ABEND, and OFFSET uses less paper.

Here is an example, showing both the OFFSET list for part of a program, plus the LIST for that part of the program. In this example, the LIST option is needed due to the complexity of the ABENDing statement. The statement causing the error is the ADD statement on line 76. With so many data-names represented, the OFFSET listing is, by itself, insufficient to locate the problem. The LIST, because it shows every instruction, helps us identify the data field at the added expense of producing more paper at compile-time.

The messages from MVS. The messages from MVS show the ABEND occurred at offset 464 in the program. Using the number 464 as a search argument, you can locate the ADD statement in the OFFSET or the LIST output.

```
IEA995I SYMPTOM DUMP OUTPUT
 SYSTEM COMPLETION CODE=0C7 REASON CODE=00000007
  TIME=12.35.47 SEQ=09141 CPU=0000 ASID=0057
  PSW AT TIME OF ERROR 078D1000 843005CC ILC 6 INTC 07
    ACTIVE LOAD MODULE=GO        ADDRESS=04300168 OFFSET=00000464
    DATA AT PSW 043005C6 - FA32D1B4 D1BDF224 D1BD801E
```

```
GPR  0-3    00000001 0004C300 043005A2 00045090
GPR  4-7    00045090 84300674 007C5FF8 00007FD8
GPR  8-11   0004C300 00045210 0430020C 0430041C
GPR 12-15   043001E8 04303028 500323EC 800323FC
END OF SYMPTOM DUMP
+IGZ057I An ABEND was intercepted by the COBOL execution time ABEND
+        handler. It is described by a corresponding IEA995I message.
```

The SOURCE listing from COBOL II. The numbers to the right of the listing are produced by the XREF option and show the line numbers where the data elements are defined. The number 1, to the left of the COBOL statements in lines 75 through 78, shows the depth of nested statements.

```
000071
000072      2000-PROCESS.
000073          PERFORM 2100-READ-DATA                               80
000074          IF NOT END-OF-FILE                                   49
000075 1           MOVE FD2-EMP-NAME TO WS2-EMP-NAME                 34 53
000076 1           ADD FD2-DED1 FD2-DED2 FD2-DED3 FD2-DED4 TO WS1-ACCUM  35 36 37 38 45
000077 1           MOVE WS1-ACCUM TO WS2-TOTAL-DED                   45 55
000078 1           WRITE FD1-OUT-REC FROM WS2-OUT-REC.               27 51
```

The OFFSET listing from COBOL II. Notice how many statements can be identified in so little space. The OFFSET listing has the line number, the hex offset, and the verb. The OFFSET listing should be read from left to right, not from top to bottom. In our example, the offset of 464 occurs between lines 76 and 77, confirming the ADD statement. Because this ADD statement contains so many data-names, more information will be needed. See the LIST output for a comparison.

```
LINE # HEXLOC VERB      LINE # HEXLOC VERB         LINE # HEXLOC VERB
000062 00035A PERFORM   000063 000376 PERFORM      000064 00039A PERFORM
000065 0003B2 STOP      000068 0003C6 INITIALIZE   000069 0003E6 OPEN
000073 000428 PERFORM   000074 000440 IF           000075 00044C MOVE
000076 000452 ADD       000077 000488 MOVE         000078 0004AA WRITE
000081 0004E8 READ      000083 000532 MOVE         000085 00053A ADD
000089 00054C MOVE      000090 000558 WRITE        000091 000590 CLOSE
```

The LIST output from COBOL II. The LIST option is mutually exclusive with OFFSET. If you specify both, OFFSET takes effect. You do not need to know assembler language to use the LIST option. This lists every machine instruction generated for COBOL statements. To the right of each instruction are some abbreviated words and codes to assist you in deciphering what data elements are involved. It takes practice and an occasional leap of faith to interpret them, but it isn't difficult to survive here.

Since you know the address of the next sequential instruction is 464, you can determine that the offending instruction was at location 45E, the preceding instruction. That instruction, AP (for ADD Packed-decimal data) is adding the contents of temporary storage area # 2 (TS2-n) to the contents of temporary storage area # 1 (TS1-n). You know this from reading the comments at the right. (Note: Temporary storage areas are just intermediate work areas the compiler added to our program to accomplish various functions. The numbers of the storage areas used have no special meaning.)

```
00043A                  GN=12 EQU *
  00043A D203 D17C D18C      MVC 380(4,13),396(13)      VN=5           PSV=4
000074 IF
  000440 95E8 900A           CLI 10(9),X'E8'            WS1-EOF-SW
  000444 58B0 C020           L                          11,32(0,12)    PBL=1
  000448 4780 B22E           BC 8,558(0,11)             GN=3(0004E2)
000075 MOVE
  00044C D213 9012 8000      MVC 18(20,9),0(8)          WS2-EMP-NAME   FD2-EMP-NAME
000076 ADD
  000452 F274 D1B0 8019      PACK 432(8,13),25(5,8)     TS1=0          FD2-DED2
  000458 F224 D1BD 8014      PACK 445(3,13),20(5,8)     TS2=5          FD2-DED1
  00045E FA32 D1B4 D1BD      AP 436(4,13),445(3,13)     TS1=4          TS2=5
  000464 F224 D1BD 801E      PACK 445(3,13),30(5,8)     TS2=5          FD2-DED3
  00046A FA32 D1B4 D1BD      AP 436(4,13),445(3,13)     TS1=4          TS2=5
  000470 F224 D1BD 8023      PACK 445(3,13),35(5,8)     TS2=5          FD2-DED4
  000476 FA42 D1B3 D1BD      AP 435(5,13),445(3,13)     TS1=3          TS2=5
  00047C FA34 9002 D1B3      AP 2(4,9),435(5,13)        WS1-ACCUM      TS1=3
  000482 F833 9002 9002      ZAP 2(4,9),2(4,9)          WS1-ACCUM      WS1-ACCUM
000077 MOVE
  000488 D209 D1BE A063      MVC 446(10,13),99(10)      TS2=6          PGMLIT AT +79
  00048E D203 D1CC 9002      MVC 460(4,13),2(9)         TS2=20         WS1-ACCUM
```

If you look at the preceding instructions that are affiliated with the ADD statement, you find two statements, one at location 452 and one at location 458. Both are PACK instructions (a PACK instruction converts EBCDIC DISPLAY data to COMP-3 format data and moves the result to a receiving field). The first PACK instruction moves a data field called FD2-DED2 to TS1, and the second PACK instruction moves the data field FD2-DED1 to TS2.

Now things are beginning to take shape. The two PACK instructions moved FD2-DED1 and FD2-DED2 to the two temporary fields TS1 and TS2. The AP instruction that ABENDed was adding those two fields. Therefore, of all the data fields specified in the ADD instruction, the error was either FD2-DED1 or FD2-DED2. The other fields on the ADD statement on line 76 may also cause errors, but the program never got that far. At this point, you can look at those two areas in the dump. One of them probably has a blank in it.

That wasn't so hard, was it? Usually, the LIST option isn't needed, but it's nice to know it is available. If you sometimes find it difficult to locate the source statement with LIST, it may be because the program was compiled with OPTI-MIZE. While OPTIMIZE is recommended for productional use, its ability to restructure the program at the machine code level can make it difficult to match instructions to source statements. In such a situation, recompile with NOOPTIMIZE and rerun the test.

4.4. USING FDUMP, SYSABOUT, AND SSRANGE

4.4.1. SYSABOUT

The SYSABOUT DD statement, although not required, is used to record elementary information in case of an ABEND (for CICS, this information goes to the CEBRxxxx queue). The STAE option must be set for this to take effect. (STAE causes the COBOL II run-time error intercept code to take control in the event of an ABEND.) See JCL Requirements for specifics on the SYSABOUT DD. The purpose of using SYSABOUT is to determine the program name that caused the ABEND, including the date compiled. For me, that is all I get from it. Here is an example:

```
— VS COBOL II ABEND Information —
Program = 'PRTFILE' compiled on '04/17/91' at '12:35:37'    <— Useful
    TGT = '04303028'
Contents of base locators for files are:
    0-00007FD8                    1-0004C300
Contents of base locators for working storage are:
    0-00045210
Contents of base locators for the linkage section are:
    0-00000000
No variably located areas were used in this program.
No EXTERNAL data was used in this program.
No indexes were used in this program.                    <— Possibly useful
— End of VS COBOL II ABEND Information —
```

As you see, this shows you the PROGRAM-ID, the date compiled, plus some other bits and pieces. For most of us, the SYSABOUT information is only to confirm the name of the offending program. Since STAE is the default at most installations (see compile run-time options for more information), you may want to have this information. Getting the SYSABOUT information does not override other information sources, such as FDUMP.

4.4.2. FDUMP

FDUMP is a compile option that produces a formatted dump upon ABEND if the STAE run-time option is set. This option increases the size of your load module and the amount of virtual memory used, so it should be reset off (NOFDUMP) after testing applications that need high performance. If the application is volatile, new, or not performance-sensitive, you may decide to leave FDUMP set even when used in production. (See the next topic, A Proactive Approach to Problem Resolution for more information). Use of FDUMP is not dependent on the presence of the normal system dump (SYSUDUMP DD).

FDUMP requires the SYSDBOUT ddname for non-CICS applications and uses the CEBRxxxx queue for CICS applications. If you specify SYSDBOUT and SYSUDUMP, you will get both dumps. In most cases, you will find you don't need two dumps, as the FDUMP will usually be more than sufficient (and saves trees). See JCL Requirements for specifics of the SYSDBOUT DD.

FDUMP presents you with a format of the DATA DIVISION, using names from the source code, with the data converted for readability if needed. Additionally, it presents you with the line number and statement number of the verb that caused the ABEND if NOOPTIMIZE was specified, and the hex offset of the verb (remember the OFFSET and LIST features?) if OPTIMIZE was specified. This eliminates virtually all hex arithmetic when reading dumps, the need to review the Linkage Editor listing to determine what program caused the ABEND, and the need to review the dump to determine the value of various data fields.

Here is an FDUMP example, produced with the same ABEND that caused the SYSABOUT information:

```
VS COBOL II Formatted Dump at ABEND —
Program = 'PRTFILE'
Completion code = 'S0C7'
PSW at ABEND = '078D1000843005CC'
Line number or verb number being executed: '0000076'/'1'    <— line number in
The GP registers at entry to ABEND were                          source program
    Regs  0 - 3  - '00000001 0004C300 043005A2 00045090'
    Regs  4 - 7  - '00045090 84300674 007C5FF8 00007FD8'
    Regs  8 - 11 - '0004C300 00045210 0430020C 0430041C'
    Regs 12 - 15 - '043001E8 04303028 500323EC 800323FC'
Data Division dump of 'PRTFILE'
000023 FD PRTFILE.FD1-REPORT FD
FILE SPECIFIED AS:
   ORGANIZATION=SEQUENTIAL   ACCESS MODE=SEQUENTIAL
   RECFM=FIXED BLOCKED
CURRENT STATUS OF FILE IS:
   OPEN STATUS=EXTEND
   QSAM STATUS CODE=00                        <—File status information
```

```
000027 01 PRTFILE.FD1-OUT-REC X(37)
        DISP    ===> JOHN E. DOE              213.35
000029 FD PRTFILE.FD2-INPUT FD
FILE SPECIFIED AS:
  ORGANIZATION=SEQUENTIAL ACCESS MODE=SEQUENTIAL
  RECFM=FIXED BLOCKED
CURRENT STATUS OF FILE IS:
  OPEN STATUS=INPUT
  QSAM STATUS CODE=00
000033 01 PRTFILE.FD2-INP-REC AN-GR
000034 02 PRTFILE.FD2-EMP-NAME X(20)
        DISP    ===>JANE S. DOE
000035 02 PRTFILE.FD2-DED1 S999V99
                                                INVALID SIGN

    DISP    ===>+000.00
            HEX> FFF FF
                 000 00
000036 02 PRTFILE.FD2-DED2 S999V99
                                    INVALID DATA FOR THIS DATA TYPE

    DISP     HEX>  44444            <- This field has blanks (hex 40)

                  00000
000037 02 PRTFILE.FD2-DED3 S999V99
                                                INVALID SIGN

    DISP    ===>+020.00
            HEX> FFF FF
                 020 00
000038 02 PRTFILE.FD2-DED4 S999V99
                                                INVALID SIGN

    DISP    ===>+030.00
            HEX> FFF FF
                 030 00
000039 02 PRTFILE.FILLER X(40)
        DISP    ===>04000
    .
    .
- End of VS COBOL II Formatted Dump at ABEND -
```

In reviewing the sample FDUMP output, you noticed that it states the error was caused on line 76, the 1st (and only) verb on that line. If the program had been compiled with OPTIMIZE, the statement would have shown the hex offset, instead. Here is that verb and the 01-level entry it was referencing:

```
000033      01 FD2-INP-REC.
000034         05 FD2-EMP-NAME    PIC X(20).
000035         05 FD2-DED1        PIC S999V99.
```

```
000036          05 FD2-DED2          PIC S999V99.
000037          05 FD2-DED3          PIC S999V99.
000038          05 FD2-DED4          PIC S999V99.
000039          05                   PIC X(40).

000076          ADD FD2-DED1 FD2-DED2 . . .
```

Since the ABEND was an 0C7, you know that FD2-DED1 or FD2-DED2 probably contained blanks. By looking at the FDUMP, you can confirm this. Also notice how FDUMP points out incorrect signs—acceptable, but incorrect for this choice of the NUMPROC option. This could be useful information if the program logic had IF NUMERIC statements.

4.4.3. SSRANGE

SSRANGE is an excellent aid when testing a program that has subscripts, indexes, or uses reference modification and is not dependent on the SYSABOUT or SYSDBOUT DD statements. (Chapter 2 explains reference modification, and subscripting and indexing are described in Chapter 3). SSRANGE may be used with FDUMP or TEST and appears as a compile-time option and as a run-time option. This provides you with the opportunity to control its impact on performance. Here are your choices:

Compile option	Run-time option	
• SSRANGE	SSRANGE	Debugging is activated, with some impact on performance.
• SSRANGE	NOSSRANGE	No SSRANGE monitoring, but run unit may be activated by changing run-time option.
• NOSSRANGE	SSRANGE	No SSRANGE monitoring. Program must be recompiled with SSRANGE before monitoring takes effect.
• NOSSRANGE	NOSSRANGE	No SSRANGE monitoring.

Many companies have the run-time option default set to NOSSRANGE to prevent inadvertent productional running of programs with SSRANGE specified at compile-time. If you are unsure about your shop's default setting, see Specifying COBOL II Options in Chapter 3 for instruction on how to determine them.

That topic also specifies how to turn run-time options on or off. (There is an example of doing this in the next topic, but the example assumes you are familiar with the mechanics from Chapter 3.)

SSRANGE should normally be part of your proactive debug technique, covered in the next topic. Testing programs with untested subscripts, indexes, or reference modification without specifying SSRANGE is not professional.

4.5. A PROACTIVE APPROACH TO PROBLEM RESOLUTION

Usually, problem solving is done when a program is being tested, when you have time to use a variety of techniques to solve a problem. Sometimes, however, you are trying to debug productional applications and can't afford the luxury of extensive use of DISPLAY statements or other code modifications. Here are a couple of tips to use when the program won't cooperate. These tips work for all environments.

4.5.1. In Test Mode

First, compile the suspected (or untested) module with FDUMP and NOOPTIMIZE. Yes, this will affect performance, but if the program is having problems, you are not getting the desired performance anyway. I recommend NOOPTIMIZE because FDUMP, OFFSET, and LIST output from COBOL II are easier to use than when OPTIMIZE is specified. FDUMP, as explained previously, does increase load module size (due to the tables, not due to extra code) and also increases use of virtual memory. While you normally do not have debug code in productional applications, doing so will position you to get maximum usable information at the time of an ABEND.

Second, if subscripts, indexes, or reference modification code are suspect, include SSRANGE in the compile-time options specified. If you do not anticipate that one of these problems will occur, specify NOSSRANGE at run-time to minimize performance degradation. (See the previous chapter under Specifying COBOL II Options for information on setting options.) Now run the program. If it ABENDs, you will have the FDUMP output. If the problem appears to be one of the types that SSRANGE handles (and you specified NOSSRANGE at run-time), all you need to do is

1. If the module is executed by the JCL EXEC statement with PGM=modulename, change the PARM to '/SSRANGE' and reexecute.
2. If you were not running from the JCL EXEC (e.g., CICS or IMS),
   - Relink the module with a copy of IGZEOPT that includes the SSRANGE option.
   - Rerun the application and (I hope) solve the application.

- Since the load module now contains IGZEOPT with SSRANGE, you must remove it to restore processing efficiency, either by creating a new load module directly from compiles or by relinking with a RE-PLACE statement. (See Creating a Load Module in the previous chapter.)

Example 2 assumed the installation default for the run-time option was NOSSRANGE. If the installation default had been SSRANGE, you could have left it as is, running with degraded performance until the problem surfaced or linked a version of IGZEOPT with NOSSRANGE until the problem surfaced and then relinked to remove IGZEOPT to reactivate SSRANGE. The important item to remember is that IGZEOPT is an alternative to the installation defaults. Once placed into a load module, IGZEOPT must be removed if its options are no longer desired.

4.5.2. In Production Mode

This approach is more long-term than the previous one. If you have an application that isn't sensitive to performance concerns, you might want to use FDUMP all the time. This can be useful if an application is volatile or is being maintained by a less experienced programmer. With FDUMP, less experienced programmers build confidence more rapidly than if they continually face a hex dump, and problems are generally resolved more quickly. Unless the run unit is complex, I suggest omitting the SYSUDUMP DD also, relying solely on FDUMP. While some of you will dismiss the thought out of hand (because "we've always used hex dumps"), I encourage you to consider the option. (If your shop is using one of the available dump interception and formatting software products on the market, this may not be relevant.)

4.6. USING THE COBTEST FACILITY

COBTEST is a separate product from IBM and may not be installed at your shop. There was a similar (but not identical) product with OS/VS COBOL called TESTCOB. The COBTEST facility is embedded within your object module by using the compile option TEST. COBTEST runs with these options even if they are not specified: TRUNC(STD), NOZWB, NUMPROC(NOPFD). I want you to be aware of COBTEST, but it is not a focus of this book. I find it useful for the professional who uses test scripts and I have included some examples. The on-line environments are described but without details. For more information on work practices with COBTEST, or for a complete list of all commands and syntax, see *VS COBOL II Application Program Debugging* (Chapter 9).

4.6.1. COBTEST Debug Environments

One of the reasons some companies don't use COBTEST, or don't use it extensively, is because COBTEST does not support all MVS platforms nor does it provide equal services on those that are supported. This is unfortunate because COBTEST is a much-improved testing tool with COBOL II and has much to recommend it.

COBTEST supports three modes: batch, full-screen (TSO), and line mode (TSO). Full functionality is available only from full-screen mode. Full-screen mode and line mode are not available for CICS. Batch mode is available for CICS in a restricted fashion (using "CICS" and "batch" in the same sentence clearly speaks to restricted use). Line and batch modes are available for IMS, but require the IMS/VS BTS product. (See Chapter 9.)

Programs that run easily in TSO (e.g., DB2) and those that do not use CICS or IMS are the prime beneficiaries of COBTEST. Here are brief descriptions of the three modes.

Batch mode.

Batch mode is straightforward for batch programs using JCL. Instead of specifying the name of your program on the PGM= parameter, specify COBDBG, instead. For example, assume a program was compiled with the TEST option and linked into a load library called TESTRUN.LOAD, with a member name of DAVEMOD1. The PROGRAM-ID of the COBOL II program is DAVEPROG. To test in batch mode, my JCL might look something like figure 4.2.

```
 1. //jobname   JOB   ....
 2. //GO        EXEC PGM=COBDBG
 3. //STEPLIB   DD   DSN=TESTRUN.LOAD,DISP=SHR
 4. //SYSABOUT  DD   SYSOUT=*
 5. //SYSDBOUT  DD   SYSOUT=*
 6. //SYSOUT    DD   SYSOUT=*
 7. //SYSDBIN   DD   *
 8. COBTEST DAVEMOD1
 9. RECORD
10. QUALIFY DAVEPROG
11. SET WS3-TASK-CODE = '01'
12. TRACE PARA PRINT
13. FLOW ON
14. AT DAVEPROG.36 (IF (WS3-TASK-CODE NE '01'),
    (LIST WS3-TASK-CODE))
15. ONABEND (FLOW (25))
    //
```

Figure 4.2. Sample COBTEST in batch.

While the JCL in figure 4.2 is relatively simple, the function of each, plus a brief description of the control statements will help you get a feeling for the power of COBTEST in batch mode. The commands are read from the SYSDBIN dataset. The numbers were added for clarity.

Statement 2 executes COBTEST.

Statement 3 contains the name of the load library where the module to be tested was linked.

Statements 4 through 6 have been discussed elsewhere and are for any debugging output from this test.

Statement 7 is required for batch mode operation. COBTEST opens this input file to receive instructions. While I haven't explained these statements (and will not, extensively, in this book), let's review them here.

COBTEST DAVEMOD1 tells COBTEST the name of the load module to load for this execution.

RECORD tells COBTEST to create a log on SYSDBOUT of all commands.

QUALIFY DAVEPROG tells COBTEST the name of the PROGRAM-ID to which the following statements apply.

SET WS3-TASK-CODE = '01' forces an initial value into a WORKING-STORAGE field.

TRACE PARA PRINT specifies that a trace (similar to TRACE ON in OS/VS COBOL) of paragraph names is to be printed (default is to SYSDBOUT).

FLOW ON specifies that a log of paragraphs executed is to be kept by COBTEST (later referenced by line 13).

AT DAVEPROG.36 ... specifies that an IF statement is to be executed when the statement on line 36 is executed, in this case printing out the value of WS3-TASK-CODE whenever it is not equal to '01'. (The commands inside the parentheses, IF and LIST, are also COBTEST commands.)

ONABEND (FLOW(25)) specifies that, if an ABEND occurs, print out the most recent 25 paragraphs executed (similar to the FLOW option from OS/VS COBOL).

In the example, you would normally not want both a TRACE and a FLOW, since these two options overlap. A restriction of batch mode is that all commands are processed immediately, preventing any interaction. This restricts you to a limited set of commands, but batch mode has much to offer, as you'll see.

For me, I like to keep things simple, because there are so many skills that a professional programmer needs to have. I use standard batch facilities whenever I suspect a potential problem and that relieves me from mastering all the various commands. By setting up a test script of basic debug commands, I have a tool that can be reused with minor changes for many programs. I'll cover the use of test scripts in the next topic, after describing the other modes of COBTEST.

Line mode.

Line mode allows interaction from a TSO terminal and the syntax of commands matches those of batch mode. An added feature is that, by selecting commands, you can stop execution, modify values, and continue. Since it is the same product as the batch product, you would expect the TSO CLIST to appear similar to the batch JCL. It does. Since this is not a text on CLISTs, I won't explain their syntax here. If you need more information on writing your own CLISTs, you might explore the QED text, *MVS/TSO: Mastering CLISTs*. (See Chapter IX.) Here is a sample CLIST:

```
PROC 0
FREE DDNAME(SYSDBOUT)
FREE DDNAME(SYSABOUT)FREE DDNAME(LOADLIB)
ALLOCATE DDNAME(SYSDBOUT)    DSN(SYSDBOUT.JCL)   OLD
ALLOCATE DDNAME(SYSABOUT)    DSN(SYSABOUT.JCL)   OLD
ALLOCATE DDNAME(LOADLIB)     DSN(TESTRUN.LOAD)   OLD
COBTEST LOAD(DAVEMOD1:LOADLIB)
QUALIFY DAVEPROG
```

In the example, I created datasets of logonid.SYSDBOUT.JCL and logonid.SYSABOUT.JCL for the SYSDBOUT and SYSABOUT datasets. (For information on their data set attributes, see Chapter 3, in the section JCL Requirements.)

Notice that the COBTEST command is different from that used in batch mode. Not only does it execute the COBTEST program, it specifies in what DDNAME the named load module is in (in batch mode, it was in the STEPLIB DD). If I place the CLIST above in a dataset named DAVE.TSO.UTIL, with a member name of DEBUG, figure 4.3 shows what the screen might look like after typing in the TSO command.

As figure 4.3 shows, you will see a COBTEST message appear each time the software is ready for instructions from you. At this point, you could type in commands such as shown for batch mode and press the terminal Enter key.

A down side with line mode is that you can't see anything unless you request it. Much of this is (to me) a throwback to the early days of on-line terminals before CRTs. A programmer using TSO 20 years ago didn't have a CRT, only an on-line typewriter. In that era, line mode made sense. It still has use when used with prewritten scripts, as I mentioned earlier for batch mode. The Debug language is a rich language, allowing sophisticated test scripts to be developed and reused. This can eliminate the common problem in which a programmer, after typing in commands at a terminal for an hour or more, doesn't remember what was tested.

You can place prewritten scripts in a dataset (LRECL=80) and allocate to TSO with a DDNAME of SYSDBIN. For example,

```
ALLOC DDNAME(SYSDBIN) DSN(SYSDBIN.TXT) SHR
```

As with batch mode, use of SYSDBIN is limited. COBTEST will open and read commands from SYSDBIN if the DDNAME is allocated. All commands are executed immediately, so such use is usually limited to commands that are repeated, such as QUALIFY, RECORD.

```
--------------------- TSO COMMAND PROCESSOR --------------
ENTER TSO COMMAND OR CLIST BELOW:

===> EX 'DAVE.TSO.UTIL(DEBUG)'




IKJ56247I FILE SYSDBOUT NOT FREED, IS NOT ALLOCATED
IKJ56247I FILE SYSABOUT NOT FREED, IS NOT ALLOCATED
IKJ56247I FILE LOADLIB NOT FREED, IS NOT ALLOCATED
IGZ100I PP - 5668-958 VS COBOL II DEBUG FACILITY — REL 3.2
IGZ100I (C) COPYRIGHT IBM CORPORATION
IGZ101I COBTEST
```

Figure 4.3. Sample of COBTEST screen in line mode.

Full-screen mode.

Full-screen mode has all the commands available under batch and line modes, and several more. Whereas line mode can be invoked from a CLIST, the full-screen mode must be installed by a systems programmer to run as an ISPF menu. Check with your technical staff to see if this is available. Full-screen mode allows you to see source code during execution and to have several windows open on screen. Since this operates under ISPF, many of ISPF's features are available also. Since ISPF invokes full-screen mode for you, the COBTEST command is not appropriate in this environment, nor will it work.

This book's focus is on program development techniques, not work practices, so I avoided doing more than make you aware of the tool and present some techniques for packaging standard commands. For a thorough reference to COBTEST, see *VS COBOL II Application Program Debugging* (Chapter 9, Related Publications). You will need that manual since it includes all the error messages for COBTEST.

4.6.2. Sample Batch Mode Scripts

Here are my suggestions for some common COBTEST statements that you can use with most applications where you need simple, canned scripts. While the examples use batch JCL, the commands could also be used for DB2, CICS, and IMS applications. (See CICS/IMS/DB2 Debug Considerations.) With these examples, you must change the name of the load module on the COBTEST statement and the name of the PROGRAM-ID on the QUALIFY statement.

Sample trace.

Unlike OS/VS COBOL, where READY TRACE printed the name of every paragraph executed, this prints only the names where logic flow changed:

```
//GO        EXEC PGM=COBDBG
//STEPLIB   DD   DSN=TESTRUN.LOAD,DISP=SHR
//SYSABOUT  DD   SYSOUT=*
//SYSDBOUT  DD   SYSOUT=*
//SYSOUT    DD   SYSOUT=*
//SYSDBIN   DD   *
COBTEST module-name
RECORD
QUALIFY program-id
TRACE PARA PRINT
//
```

Sample flow trace.

This is useful where you are getting an ABEND, but do not know how the logic flow is creating it. This example produces a list of the 25 most recently executed paragraphs that caused a change in the logic flow prior to the ABEND:

```
//GO        EXEC PGM=COBDBG
//STEPLIB   DD   DSN=TESTRUN.LOAD,DISP=SHR
//SYSABOUT  DD   SYSOUT=*
//SYSDBOUT  DD   SYSOUT=*
//SYSOUT    DD   SYSOUT=*
//SYSDBIN   DD   *
COBTEST module-name
RECORD
```

```
QUALIFY program-id
FLOW ON
ONABEND (FLOW (25))
//
```

Sample subroutine test.

This is useful if you are testing a CALLed subprogram and have no module to
initiate the CALL or you want to test how it performs with certain variables.
With this script, a subprogram with PROCEDURE DIVISION USING can be
tested alone. In this example, the subprogram is a variation of one of the
examples in Chapter 8, DKA101BN. Part of that program is here:

```
LINKAGE SECTION.

01   LS1-RECORD.
      05   LS1-JOB-CODE          PIC XX.
      05   LS1-SICK-DAYS         PIC 99.
      05   LS1-VACATION-DAYS     PIC 99.
      05   LS1-ERROR-SW          PIC X.
              .
              .

PROCEDURE DIVISION USING LS1-RECORD.
```

Here are sample control statements to test it with a value of LS1-JOB-CODE
equal to '05'. (I continue to use the FLOW and ONABEND statement because,
being proactive, I don't want an ABEND to leave me wondering what happened.)

```
//GO          EXEC PGM=COBDBG
//STEPLIB     DD   DSN=TESTRUN.LOAD,DISP=SHR
//SYSABOUT    DD   SYSOUT=*
//SYSDBOUT    DD   SYSOUT=*
//SYSOUT      DD   SYSOUT=*
//SYSDBIN     DD   *
COBTEST DAVEPROG
RECORD
QUALIFY DKA101BN
LINK (LS1-RECORD)
SET LS1-JOB-CODE = '05'
TRACE PARA PRINT
WHEN TST1 (LS1-ERROR-SW = 'Y') (LIST ALL)
FLOW ON
ONABEND (FLOW (25))
//
```

This example introduced a new statement, LINK. You may have already figured out what it does. LINK establishes addressability for an 01-level entry in the LINKAGE SECTION. In practice, it simulates a CALL statement. LINK can be followed (not preceded) by a SET statement to initialize the field. In effect, the program is CALLed, passing a value of '05' to it. Once you have developed such canned statements, you will find this is easier than locating the parent CALLing program and setting it up to CALL the subprogram.

The WHEN statement is testing a switch in the program. Whenever the named data element has a value of 'Y', this statement will list the entire DATA DIVISION. Since this is a small program, it was easier to code than naming the fields with which I was concerned. Also, LIST ALL fits better in my philosophy of having several canned tools in my arsenal for program testing. (Note: While the command summary below may indicate that IF and WHEN are equivalent, they are not. IF takes place immediately, which is inappropriate for batch. WHEN tests constantly throughout the run.) Here is sample output from the script, as written to SYSDBOUT:

```
Printed by        ┌──── > RECORD
RECORD            │    QUALIFY DKA101BN
statement         │    LINK (LS1-RECORD)
                  │    SET LS1-JOB-CODE = '05'
                  │    TRACE PARA PRINT
                  │    WHEN TST1 (LS1-ERROR-SW = 'Y') (LIST ALL)
                  │    FLOW ON
                  └──── > ONABEND (FLOW (25))
                       IGZ100I PP - 5668-958 VS COBOL II DEBUG FACILITY — REL 3.2
                       IGZ100I (C) COPYRIGHT IBM CORPORATION
                       IGZ102I DKA101BN.000035.1
                  ┌──── > IGZ106I TRACING DKA101BN
Program TRACE     │    IGZ109I 000040.1
                  └──── > IGZ109I 000051.1
                  ┌──── > IGZ103I WHEN TST1 DKA101BN.000037.1
Output from       │    000025 01 DKA101BN.LS1-RECORD AN-GR
WHEN statement    │    000026 02 DKA101BN.LS1-JOB-CODE XX
condition         │           DISP    ===>05
being set         │    000027 02 DKA101BN.LS1-SICK-DAYS 99
                  │           DISP    ===>00
                  │    000028 02 DKA101BN.LS1-VACATION-DAYS 99
                  └──── >        DISP    ===>00
                       IGZ129I PROGRAM UNDER COBTEST ENDED NORMALLY
                       IGZ350I ******** END OF COBTEST ********
```

In the previous example, the program was to set LS1-ERROR-SW if it passed an invalid value. If you browsed through the program listing in Chapter 8, you noticed that only values of 01, 02, or 03 were valid in LS1-JOB-CODE. By asking for a listing only if the error switch was set, I confirmed that the program worked correctly for this set of test data. The commands were also listed because I included a RECORD statement.

All of this can also be used in line mode by establishing a SYSDBIN dataset as shown in the previous topic with the ALLOCATE command for TSO or by combining into the CLIST.

4.6.3. The Debug Language—summary

This includes rudimentary syntax of some of the commands I've shown you, so you can experiment with test scripts. I also include a brief description (no syntax) of the other COBTEST commands, so you will have access to them within one book. A complete description is in *IBM VS COBOL II Application Programming Debugging* (Chapter 9).

AT	This command establishes breakpoints in a program. This is helpful when you want to pause at a statement (not in batch) or execute other commands at a given statement. This is a major command for scripts.
AUTO	This command activates an automatic monitoring portion of the screen (full-screen mode only).
COBTEST	This command invokes COBTEST in line mode and specifies name of load module in both line and batch modes.

```
  ┌─ COBTEST ─┬─ LOAD(loadmodname:ddname) ─┬─────────────────────── ──><
              └─ loadmodname ──────────────┘└─ PARM('your_parm') ─┘
```

COLOR	Used only in full-screen mode, this command allows you to modify color attributes for your session.
COMMENT	Useful in all modes, this command inserts comments in your scripts and your debugging output.
DROP	This command deletes symbols established with EQUATE.
DUMP	This command terminates a debug session and prints a SNAP dump of storage areas. Goes to SYSABOUT if other than CICS, which goes to the CICS dump dataset.
EQUATE	This command allows you to use a shorthand technique to assign names for various parts of the

debug session. Where you will be developing complex scripts, this is a must.

FLOW

This command specifies to turn on (or off) an internal trace of program flow. The flow is printed by a second execution of the statement with different options. See example.

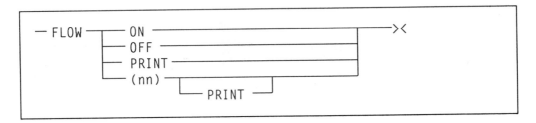

FREQ

This command tallies how many times verbs were executed.

GO

Starts or resumes execution of a program.

HELP

Not available in batch mode, this command provides information about any COBTEST command. In full-screen mode, ISPF will display information.

IF

A powerful debug command, it provides logic capability to your debug script. See example.

```
          IF (expression)   (command list)                    ><
```

LINK

Useful when debugging CALLed subprograms when you are testing them without the CALLing program, it sets up the LINKAGE SECTION addressability. This must be followed by the SET command to initialize the values of the variables. See example.

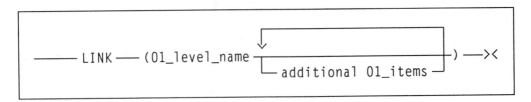

LIST

This command displays or prints data areas from program. See example.

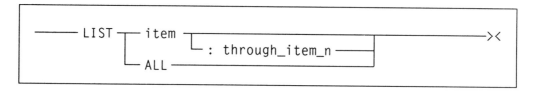

LISTBRKS

This command is a useful command when you've set many breakpoints with AT, NEXT, or WHEN commands and need a refresher on what is still set. This is helpful when you are in a debug session and wanting to determine the next step to take.

LISTEQ

Similar to LISTBRKS, this command lists all active EQUATEs in your program. Useful if you didn't write them down.

LISTFREQ

This command lists the number of times verbs were executed for all programs for which FREQ was specified. This may be useful if seeing the count of verbs gives you information on what was or was not properly executed.

LISTINGS

Available only in full-screen mode, this command gives access to the various source listings to be available during test.

MOVECURS

Available only in full-screen mode, this command moves the cursor between the command line and the source or auto monitoring area. This can be set to use an ISPF PF key. This command moves the cursor between the command line and the source or automonitoring area. This can be set to use an ISPF PF key.

NEXT

This command sets a temporary breakpoint at the next verb. It is useful when you want a breakpoint set from the current position in the program for one iteration.

OFF

This command resets breakpoints that were set with AT.

OFFWN

This command resets breakpoints that were set with WHEN.

ONABEND

This command specifies a list of commands to execute if the program ABENDs. It is very useful if you want information listed or other processes to occur only at ABEND. See example.

```
─────── ONABEND ───── (command list) ──────────────────>──<
```

PEEK	Useful only in full-screen mode, this command allows you to see the line number that is obscured by the AT breakpoint information on the screen.
POSITION	Available only in full-screen mode, this command causes the current line to move to the top of its area on the screen.
PREVDISP	In full-screen mode only, this command redisplays the previous screen (if done via ISPF).
PRINTDD	Not meaningful with CICS, this command specifies a DDNAME for RECORD output. Default is SYSDBOUT. Useful if you want to send RECORD information to different datasets during the debug session. Each occurrence of PRINTDD closes the previously open file.
PROC	A powerful command, it allows you to intercept CALLs to an existing (or nonexisting) subprogram. From this, you can specify SET commands that dictate what values to return to the CALLing program.
PROFILE	For full-screen mode only, this command brings up a screen in which you can change your default debug parameters.
QUALIFY	This command does double duty. It identifies the name of the PROGRAM-ID to which following commands apply. It also can qualify data names (e.g., where the same name exists in two or more programs being tested together). See example.

```
─────── QUALIFY────── programid ┬──────────────────>──<
                                └.─nested_program_id ─┘
```

QUIT	This command terminates the session.
RECORD	This command starts or stops recording of the debug session. It is useful for reviewing what hap-

	pened during a debug session. Records to the PRINTDD (default is SYSDBOUT).
RESTART	This command deletes and reloads a program, making it available in its initial state. It does not apply to CICS.
RESTORE	In full-screen mode only, this command restores the source listing area of the screen to the last point of execution.
RUN	This command causes the program to ignore all breakpoints and begin or continue execution. If the program does not ABEND, this command will cause it to proceed to STOP RUN or GOBACK.
SEARCH	In full-screen mode only, this command searches for a given character string. Similar to the ISPF FIND command.
SELECT	In full-screen mode only, this command is useful to see frequency counts for other than the first verb on a line. It is not usually needed, as most programmers no longer attempt to put more than one COBOL statement on a line.
SET	This command sets a variable to a value. It is useful when initializing areas or, at a breakpoint, changing them to monitor program logic. See example.

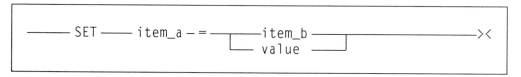

SOURCE	Available only for full-screen mode, this command opens, closes, or resizes the source area of the screen.
STEP	This command causes a specified number of statements to be executed before stopping execution and returning control to the terminal.
SUFFIX	Similar to SOURCE, this command opens or closes the suffix area for full-screen mode.
SYSCMD	This command is used with CMS. (This is the only reference to CMS in this book.)
TRACE	This command displays a flow of program or paragraph execution. See example.

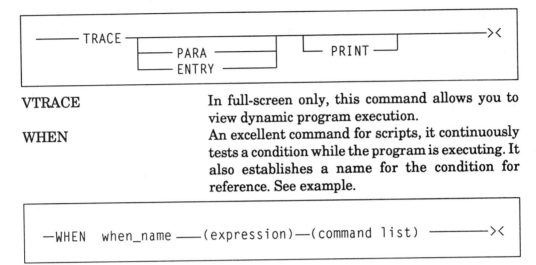

VTRACE   In full-screen only, this command allows you to view dynamic program execution.

WHEN   An excellent command for scripts, it continuously tests a condition while the program is executing. It also establishes a name for the condition for reference. See example.

```
—WHEN   when_name ——(expression)—(command list) ————————><
```

WHERE   Useful in line or full-screen mode, this command displays what statement the program is at during program suspension.

4.7. CICS/IMS/DB2 DEBUG CONSIDERATIONS

This section assumes you are familiar with prior topics in this chapter, so this section presents only those details that are unique for these environments. For instructions on the mechanics of using line or full-screen mode, see the IBM manual titled, VS COBOL II Application Programming Debugging (Chapter 9).

CICS debug considerations.

Most of these specifics for CICS were covered previously.

- Output from SYSABOUT or FDUMP or SSRANGE goes to the CEBRxxxx queue instead of to a DD dataset (where **xxxx** is the terminal-id of the transaction). If the CEBR queue has not yet been established at your shop, see your technical staff.
- COBTEST can be used only in batch mode, i.e., all commands must be prepared prior to running the CICS transaction. The commands must be stored in the CSCOxxxx queue. Commands follow the same syntax as shown previously and follow the same order. For example,

```
COBTEST loadmodulename
RECORD
QUALIFY program-id-name
        .
        .
```

- Changes to run-time options must be made via the IGZEOPT module.

A programming item to consider is that the EXEC CICS HANDLE ABEND command will bypass the COBOL II debug facilities.

IMS debug considerations.

IMS programs can use most test aids, but you must remember that it is not the only program in the run unit, even in batch mode. Here is a summary of IMS considerations:

- COBTEST may not be used in full-screen mode.
- COBTEST requires access via the IMS/VS BTS (Batch Terminal Simulator) software product from IBM. (It needs to be installed by your systems programmer.) See the IBM manual, *IMS/VS Batch Terminal Simulator Program Reference*, for more information (Chapter 9).
- SSRANGE and FDUMP should be used with the BTS product when testing on-line transactions due to DD restrictions in an on-line environment and the possible conflict between COBOL II's use of STAE and IMS/VS's use of STAE.
- Changes to run-time options must be made via the IGZEOPT module.
- The RENT option must be specified when using BTS.

DB2 debug considerations.

There are fewer restrictions for DB2, primarily because it works within the TSO environment, whereas CICS and IMS do not. Here are considerations for DB2:

- DB2 can use FDUMP, SYSABOUT, and SSRANGE, as described in earlier topics, with no restrictions.
- DB2 can use COBTEST in batch, line, and full-screen modes, but the mechanics for each are different. For batch, in the bind, the RUN statement should specify COBDBG (COBTEST's batch name) as in this example:

```
RUN PROGRAM(COBDBG) PLAN(xxxxxxx) LIB('cobolII.library')
```

  where 'cobolii.library' identifies the name of the load library at the shop in which the COBOL II run-time modules are stored. Your program library should be concatenated with this one, such as in figure 4.4.
- Running DB2 in line or full-screen mode follows the same concept as batch:
    STEPLIB must concatenate the COBOL II run-time library.
    The RUN statement should identify COBTEST, e.g.,

```
DSN SYSTEM(...)
RUN CP PLAN(planname)
```

For line mode, enter COBTEST as a TSO command.
For full-screen mode, use the appropriate ISPF menu.

```
//DB2RUN   EXEC PGM=IKJEFT01
//STEPLIB  DD   DSN=cobolii.library,DISP=SHR
//         DD   DSN=db2load.library,DISP=SHR
//         DD   DSN=yourload.library,DISP=SHR    <—Your
//SYSABOUT DD   SYSOUT=*                            load
//SYSDBOUT DD   SYSOUT=*                            library
//SYSTSPRT DD   SYSOUT=*
          .
          .
//SYSTSIN DD  *
DSN SYSTEM(...)
BIND PLAN(planname) ....
RUN PROGRAM(COBDBG) PLAN(planname) LIB('cobolii.library')
END
//SYSDBIN  DD  *
COBTEST planname
   .
   .                    <—COBTEST commands go here
   .
//
```

Figure 4.4. Sample DB2 batch COBTEST.

SUMMARY

In writing this book, I was torn about whether or not to include this chapter. Debugging is not a skill for building better productional systems. By following the guidelines in Chapter 5 (Program Design), problems will diminish. I finally decided to include this chapter because FDUMP and SSRANGE can help. I use COBTEST only for packaging scripts, not for interacting with a terminal.

While I attempted to be as thorough as possible in other chapters, I avoided it here. IBM's COBOL II debugging manual covers it thoroughly (it's over 300 pages) and you will need that manual anyway, since that is where error messages are located. Still, I hope you picked up a few tricks here that will help you be proactive in your approach to resolving problems.

The best programmers often do poorly at debugging or reading dumps. The better the code, the less opportunity to engage in debugging practices. Writing errorfree code is possible. Believe it and you will write it—but first you must believe.

COBOL Program Design Guidelines

Unlike the previous chapters that focused on exploiting COBOL II, this chapter focuses on program design. This chapter is presented because 1) some shops have no design guidelines at all, 2) others have design guidelines so outdated that no one uses them, and 3) still others have design standards that use terminology that prevents direct translation to the programming process. Effort has been placed on simplicity and clarity instead of more rigorous definitions of the design process. Emphasis has been placed on structure and style components, using COBOL II facilities where they enhance those issues. Some awareness of structured design and structured programming concepts is necessary to use these guidelines. This chapter relates to the next chapter, COBOL Coding Guidelines. Both are presented to assist you in evaluating and establishing your own program design and coding guidelines.

In reading this chapter, you may find areas in which this book is in conflict with your shop's standards. Since your shop has its own circumstances, this is anticipated. What I hope occurs is active dialogue on some of the differences and why your company's standards disagree with these. At too many companies, the standards manuals were developed with an unconscious awareness of the restrictions of earlier versions of COBOL. This is an effort to remove those restrictions. Too often, the programmer is criticized for poor program structure, when the real culprit was a design so convoluted that the programmer had to patch it together.

5.1. STRUCTURE VERSUS STYLE—DEFINITIONS

Quality finds its way into a program by two routes: structure and style. Good structure ensures the application does exactly what is required and also minimizes debug efforts. Style is a contribution by the programmer to ensure clarity in the structure. Here are my definitions.

5.1.1. Structure

Structure is an end product, not a process or a technique. Good structure is evidenced by balance and consistent decomposition of a program's components. Common examples of structure within the code are verbs such as CALL, PER-FORM, EVALUATE, INITIALIZE. Their appearance alone is not, however, proof of good structure. A program gets its structure during the Program Design phase of application development.

5.1.2. Style

Style is the approach taken by the programmer to achieve clarity, consistency, maintainability, and portability. Good style is simple, using as few syntax elements as possible to represent the solution. This is apparent in the coding by a uniform format with predictable and recurrent placement of both data and procedural items. A programmer will be able to absorb the structure and processes of a program designed with good style using a minimum number of eye movements. A program gets its style during the coding phase of application development. Most style aspects are addressed in the section, Program Layout Guidelines.

5.2. ACHIEVING GOOD STRUCTURE

These are practical tips to assist the programmer in developing good structure. Reasonable effort has been made to ensure these steps do not conflict with the majority of design processes being used.

5.2.1. Use Top-Down Development

This initial step is where you should do the JCL for batch processes and ensure all screen-to-screen interactions for on-line applications are complete. By doing this now, before getting into the details of each program, you ensure the structure is complete from the top down. For example, in doing the JCL you will complete all external names (e.g., DDNAMES, PROGRAM-IDs) required and may discover that some processes, such as the use of various utilities (e.g., IDCAMS, DFSORT) were overlooked. This step should also confirm what processes should be daily, weekly, on-line, batch, and so on.

A side benefit of this step is that it allows a programming team to start dividing the work effort, with senior programmers beginning program design while junior programmers begin coding JCL or statements for utility programs.

If documentation specialists are on the team, they can begin structuring the documentation for the system.

Note: If the application will use VSAM, IMS, CICS, or DB2, ensure the data design has been properly done. See the topic Data Structures and System Environments in Chapter 3 for more information.

5.2.2. Design Each Program from the Top Down

This is a major factor for success. Here are some techniques to assist you.

Decompose each box on the structure chart into subordinate boxes. Decomposition allows you to focus on the solution and not on the mechanics. Decomposition begins with a high-level statement of what is to be done. If you can state it in one sentence, you can depict it as a box on a chart. For example, decomposing a box called "Do final processes" might create these subordinate processes: "Print totals," "Update audit file," "Close files." Each description begins with a verb. Together, they represent the processing described by the parent box. Descriptions such as "Error routine" or "Handle I/O" are invalid; they can't be decomposed and reflect an incomplete decomposition. Where possible, the subordinate boxes should be shown from left to right in their anticipated processing sequence.

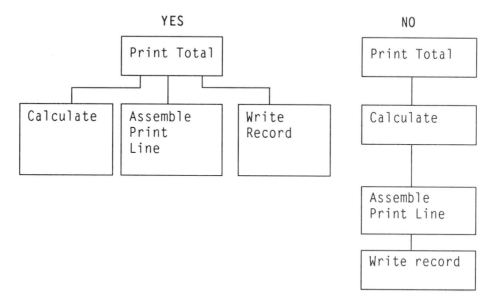

Represent one COBOL paragraph or CALLed subprogram per box. This ensures decomposition occurs and that too many functions aren't attempted within a single module. This can be easily tested. You should be able to fully code any module above the lowest level (e.g., after editing the third level of a structure chart, you should be able to code the first and second levels of the program). GO TO statements that are required during the coding phase are evidence that the decomposition was incomplete or incorrect.

Place control higher and action lower. By placing control (e.g., IF) in upper-level modules and action (e.g., COMPUTE) in lower-level modules, you contain the scope of each module. Moving action to a lower level is the management equivalent of delegation, whereas moving control to a lower-level is the management equivalent of abdication. Not following this guideline is a major reason that lower level modules must abort or GO TO another module to correct an error in the structure or resolve an issue caused by a higher module's abdication. Note: The authority to terminate the program (STOP RUN or GOBACK) should never be delegated to a lower-level module. This verb should appear only in the highest module.

Be sensitive to cohesion and coupling aspects. Here are basic definitions.

> **COUPLING:** The degree that two modules are dependent on each other. This should be low.
>
> **COHESION.** The degree that all the code within a paragraph or program relates to the purpose of the paragraph or program. This should be high.

For example, a module titled "Initialize work areas" might consist of many MOVE or INITIALIZE statements and even the loading of a data table. All of these processes are setting data areas to initial values before processing and therefore this module would have high cohesion (desirable). Here are some tips to increase cohesion and reduce coupling:

1. Isolate functions. For example, the READ of a file should be alone in one module (paragraph). Other examples might be "Compute withholding tax" or "Assemble print line."
2. Separate one-time processes from repetitive processes. This is often the first decomposition within a program, separating those processes that occur at program initiation, those that occur at program termination, and those that are repetitive.
3. Avoid setting switches to trigger action in peer-level or lower-level modules. This is known as pathological coupling, the tying of one module's actions to another's without higher-level modules being involved or aware. This defeats the isolation desired within modules and creates complexity in maintenance when higher-level modules are not in control of processes.

4. Avoid defining general-purpose modules. Modules such as "Do database I/O" are not functional and are difficult to debug. Instead, identify what must occur (e.g., "Read policy segment" or "Add beneficiary segment").

5.2.3. Use structured programming techniques

Structured programming is a process and a technique, not an end product. It is a process of building programs by a rigid discipline, following a technique of combining logically related components. Each of the five possible structures has one entry and one exit. (See figure 5.1.) With structured programming, all modules whether paragraphs or programs should also have one entry and one exit. Definitions for terms are given.

SEQUENCE: Verbs that manipulate data or cause an event to occur. This includes MOVE, ADD, and WRITE among others.

SELECTION: These are conditional statements that are often dependent on the particular implementation of COBOL to be easily used. These include IF, ON SIZE ERROR and AT END among others.

DO-WHILE: In COBOL, this is implemented as PERFORM and PERFORM UNTIL. By determining what condition should terminate processing, you prevent abdicating the decision to a lower-level module that must control the process with a GO TO. Repetitive processes should be controlled by the PERFORM UNTIL statement.

DO-UNTIL: Not available prior to COBOL II, this requires the WITH TEST AFTER clause in the PERFORM statement. Where the DO-WHILE tested a value prior to each repetition, the DO-UNTIL tests the control value after each repetition. The choice is often moot with COBOL, but does affect the resulting value of any data elements being incremented in the iterations.

CASE: Available only in COBOL II, this is executed with the EVALUATE statement. Because this verb has several different formats, you should be familiar with it; its capabilities may enhance your program design.

Structuring an application cannot be done by simple prose. Check your program design specifications to see if they 1) have an implied GO TO to return to the beginning to repeat the process for the next record, or 2) have imbedded alternate selection logic in the body of the processing specifications. These are two common errors that occur in developing specifications. They are usually avoided only by a conscious view of the entire application as a large DO WHILE or DO UNTIL.

SEQUENCE

SELECTION

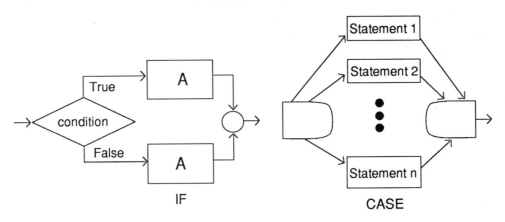

ITERATION

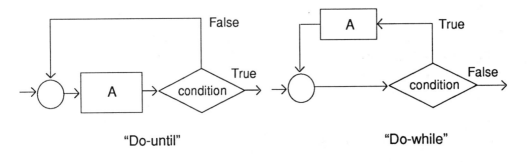

Figure 5.1. Structured programming components.

5.2.4. Use CALL and PERFORM to Transfer Control and Delegate Processes

This often begs the question "How big should a program be?" Do not subdivide a program into smaller programs based on some arbitrary limit, such as the number of modules (boxes) or the anticipated number of source statements. A program may stay a single program so long as its primary function is well defined. That consideration, itself, will ensure that the program stays relatively small.

5.2.5. Use Structure Charts with Consistent Style and Numbering

Consistency and the ability to readily convert a structure chart into code are key factors determining whether structure charts improve productivity. Also, since the programmer will develop paragraph names from this chart, the naming technique should be predictable. A sample structure should follow these guidelines:

1. Define one uppermost module.
2. Decompose each module in a left-to-right fashion.
3. Define names for each module consisting of one verb followed by at least one word, preferably two.
4. Assign module numbers to each box as follows:
   (1) Level 1 (top) Set to 0.
   (2) Level 2   Increment by 1000.
   (3) Level 3   Increment by 100.
   (4) Level 4   Increment by 10.
   (5) Level 5   Increment by 1.
   (6) Level 6   Increment by Alphabet (A, B, etc.)
5. Include a horizontal line across the box to depict CALLed subprograms.
6. Draw an angled mark across the upper-right corner to depict modules that are accessed from more than one module.

The benefit of the above numbering scheme is that each module's name contains its origin. For example, a box titled 1100 will be a subset of the box titled 1000. When this numbering scheme is carried into the program's paragraph names, there is a good one-to-one relationship that is easy to read and understand.

Simple Structure Chart

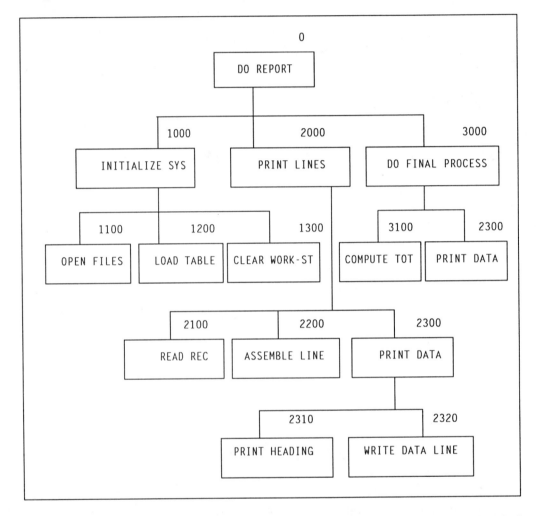

This example represents only one approach to the application. If coded directly from the structure chart, there would be 12 paragraphs (one is a prewritten subprogram and one is PERFORMed from two locations). It also demonstrates the style of the designer, since it depicts where files are OPENed, but leaves it to the programmer to determine where to CLOSE them. (Ideally, there would be a module numbered 3200 named "Close files.") Notice that all paragraphs other than the top one are to be PERFORMed (i.e., no fall throughs, no GO TOs).

The style of the programmer may also affect the final structure. For example, the programmer may determine that modules 1100, 1200, and 1300 consist only of one OPEN, one CALL, and a couple of INITIALIZE and MOVE statements. Being only four or five statements, the programmer might decide to put all of them in module 1000. As this is a style issue, there are no firm rules. If this occurs too frequently in the coding of an application, the structure can be defeated by ending up with a few very large paragraphs that are difficult to decipher and maintain. There should be periodic reviews during the coding process to ensure the structure is intact.

5.3. SORT DESIGN TECHNIQUES

Sorting has unique aspects because it is a separate program being activated under control of COBOL within the run unit. Here are some considerations to take whenever specifications indicate a sort is needed.

5.3.1. DFSORT versus a COBOL SORT

Consider using DFSORT instead of a COBOL SORT with INPUT/OUTPUT procedures.

DFSORT is advantageous when (1) the output will be used by more than one application, (2) the volume of records to be sorted is such that restart or recovery processing is not feasible, or (3) the speed of development is primary (DFSORT statements may be coded more quickly than COBOL SORT statements).

Consider a COBOL SORT when (1) the selection criteria is complex, (2) many of the data fields will not be needed after sorting, (3) the number of records to be sorted will be significantly reduced by using COBOL record selection, or (4) the sorted data is needed by a single application and run-time performance is primary.

5.3.2. DFSORT Control Statements Versus INPUT or OUTPUT PROCEDURE

Specify that the DFSORT control DD * dataset (IGZSRTCD or SORTCNTL) be used with SORTs whenever selection criteria are simple or the OUTPUT PROCEDURE does not need access to all data fields. This can reduce development and run-time costs. This technique combines the positive features of using DFSORT alone with the positive features of a COBOL SORT.

5.3.3. SORT Performance Issues

Consider performance issues of sort applications even though such information is not part of the user's requirements. The volume of records involved in a sort will be the major influence on run time and cost. This can be reduced by sorting only the records needed *and* by sorting only the fields necessary for subsequent processing. This can be accomplished by the IGZSRTCD control dataset or by an INPUT procedure.

5.4. SUMMARY OF PROGRAM DESIGN GUIDELINES

While not complete, the following represent highlights to remember in designing programs. Refer to the previous pages for specifics.

1. Do JCL and external processes first.
2. Decompose each program and module.
3. Do control processes first and action ones later.
4. Design each module to be a single paragraph or program.
5. Maintain one entry and one exit for each module.
6. Identify all modules with a verb.
7. Consider management terms such as *span of control*, *delegation*, and *abdication*.

SUMMARY

These design guidelines omit any COBOL examples and assume the reader is familiar with the terms and techniques defined in Chapters 2 and 3. I would appreciate hearing from you whether they help you organize the up-front part of your programming.

COBOL Coding
Guidelines

This chapter complements the previous chapter, providing a framework for program coding. As with Chapter 5, this section is provided because many shops either have no guidelines or their guidelines were developed in the 1970s. These guidelines may be used to help you develop your own coding guidelines, or you can use them as they stand. While Chapter 3 showed various ways of using COBOL for specific applications, this chapter focuses only on the mechanics of the coding process. I'm sure these guidelines differ from any your shop may have. How do I know this? Because most guidelines I have seen emphasize that the programmer should code every entry in a program. You will find the guidelines in this chapter are different:

- Code the fewest statements necessary for the application (optional entries keep getting dropped by ANSI, only creating future conversion headaches).
- Some verbs should never be coded. This includes some popular verbs.
- The period (.) is a curse and should be coded only to end paragraphs.

Surprisingly, most of these guidelines (other than new verbs) work fine with older versions of COBOL. In fact, the main reason people find it difficult to convert to COBOL II is because they are still coding syntax from ANSI 68, not because they were using the OS/VS COBOL compiler.

Examples of programs developed using these guidelines are in Chapter 8. You will notice that the examples do not follow these guidelines completely. I believe the programmer must have some latitude in interpreting any guidelines on the programming process.

Notice to OS/VS COBOL Readers: I do not encourage you to change existing programs so they incorporate new techniques. Programs that do not follow these guidelines should not be changed except when it will be beneficial. "If it ain't broke, don't fix it" is my motto for program maintenance.

6.1. GENERAL LAYOUT GUIDELINES

This section deals with general guidelines that apply to all divisions. Emphasis is on neatness and on preventing the program from becoming dense (i.e., having too many statements per page).

6.1.1. Format—White Space and Indentation Guidelines

Spacing

1. DIVISION statements should be preceded and followed by at least two blank lines.
2. SECTION statements should be preceded and followed by at least one blank line.
3. Paragraphs, FDs, SDs, and 01-levels should be preceded by at least one blank line.
4. Place each statement (this includes ELSE) on a separate line. This does not include clauses that are subordinate to a statement.
5. Place paragraph names on a separate line.

Indentation

1. Margin A entries (FD, SD, DIVISION, SECTION, Paragraph names, 01-level entries) must begin in column 8 and margin B entries (procedural statements, subordinate data definitions) must begin in column 12.
2. Entries that are subordinate (e.g., 05-level data definitions and related clauses) or are components of the same definition (e.g., FD) should be indented 4 columns and aligned in columnar fashion.

6.1.2. Use of Comments

Use comments liberally to make code more meaningful or to explain complicated logic.

1. Use the * in column 7 for comments.
2. At the end of the program, document every project that causes a change to the program. Here is an example:

```
*-------------------------------------------------------------*
*      MAINTENANCE LOG                                        *
* DATE    * WHO        *    DESCRIPTION                       *
*-------------------------------------------------------------*
* 05/26/90* ANNA LIST  *    CC12345 - NEW BILL OPTION         *
* 07/20/91* JOEL FIXIT *    NP23456 - NEW TERM RIDER          *
*-------------------------------------------------------------*
```

3. At the end of the program, place the COBOL II statement "END PRO-GRAM program-id." The END PROGRAM statement begins in column 8 and does not include a hyphen. The program-id must match that coded in PROGRAM-ID of the IDENTIFICATION DIVISION.
4. Place the TITLE statement at the beginning of the program and at the beginning of all parts of the program that would benefit, e.g. a SORT INPUT PROCEDURE.
5. Place comments as paragraphs, not as single lines interspersed between other statements. See examples in Chapter 8.

6.1.3. COPY Statement Use

Use the COPY statement for record formats and complex procedural processes that are used in several programs. COPY members should carry a comment line showing the last date changed and why, in addition to a comment line identifying the COPY member's function (e.g., STATE-NAME TABLE).

6.1.4. Resolving Compiler Error Messages

Resolve warning messages before maintaining the program. If the compiler generates a return code other than zero, you are receiving warning messages that could cause complications later. The compiler routinely is upgraded to change some warning messages to major error messages. Keep your program listings clean.

6.2   IDENTIFICATION DIVISION GUIDELINES

6.2.1. Specific Layout Guidelines

None, other than general guidelines specified previously.

6.2.2. Minimum Entries and PROGRAM-ID Guidelines

1. PROGRAM-ID must be eight characters long, matching the productional name of the program.

2. Enter one or more comment paragraphs to describe the purpose and functions of the program. These should be in comment format (* in column 7). Avoid generic descriptions such as "SORT FILE AND PRODUCE REPORT."

3. Use comments to provide information on AUTHOR and on DATE WRITTEN.

4. Do NOT use the COBOL elements, AUTHOR, DATE-WRITTEN, INSTALLATION, or DATE-COMPILED. They are obsolete elements.

6.3. ENVIRONMENT DIVISION GUIDELINES

6.3.1. Specific Layout Guidelines

None, other than general guidelines specified previously.

6.3.2. Minimum Requirements

1. The ENVIRONMENT DIVISION is not needed if there are no external MVS files to be processed (those processed with OPEN and CLOSE verbs).

2. The CONFIGURATION SECTION is not usually needed and should not be coded.

3. No I-O-CONTROL entries are usually needed.

4. INPUT-OUTPUT SECTION, followed by FILE-CONTROL, followed by SELECT statements are all that are usually necessary in this division (assuming external files are processed).

6.3.3. SELECT Statement Use and DDNAME Guidelines

1. The ASSIGN clause must specify "AS-ddname" for VSAM sequential files, but just "ddname" for QSAM sequential files and VSAM indexed or relative files. Example, where DDNAME will be MASTERIN:

```
SELECT FD-PAYROLL-FILE
    ASSIGN TO MASTERIN.      <- For QSAM & VSAM indexed or
                               relative files

SELECT FD-PAYROLL-FILE
    ASSIGN TO AS-MASTERIN.   <- For VSAM sequential files
```

2. For SORT files, use ASSIGN TO SORTWORK.

3. ORGANIZATION should be specified *only* for nonsequential files.

4. RESERVE clause should not be specified (use JCL if more data buffers are needed).

5. The selection of DDNAMEs for the application should not be left to the individual programmer. It needs to follow a predefined company standard. This becomes critical when multiple programs are combined into a run unit.

6.4. DATA DIVISION GUIDELINES

6.4.1. Specific Layout Guidelines

1. **Data-names.** Data-names must be sufficient for a knowledgeable reader to understand (e.g., FLDA is unacceptable). Data-names must be hyphenated and use a prefix convention that is consistent throughout the division.

   - FDs and SDs should have a prefix of FDn- or SDn- and end with the word FILE. (The phrases, LABEL RECORDS ARE and DATA RECORD IS are obsolete and should NOT be used.) The suffix "n" should reflect the file's relative number within the program. Examples:

   ```
   FD1-identifier-FILE
       RECORD CONTAINS nn CHARACTERS
       BLOCK CONTAINS O RECORDS
       RECORDING MODE IS F.

   (Note: nn refers to the number of characters in the
   record. For variable-length records, use RECORDING MODE
   IS V.)

   SD2-identifier-FILE
       RECORD CONTAINS nn CHARACTERS.
   ```

   - 01-level entries for FD and SD should retain the prefix of the file description and end with the term RECORD.
   - 01-level entries for WORKING STORAGE should have the prefix WSn- and end with the term RECORD.
   - 01-level entries for LINKAGE SECTION should use the prefix LSn- and end with the term RECORD. Examples:

   ```
   FILE SECTION              01 FD1-identifier-RECORD

   WORKING-STORAGE SECTION:  01 WS1-identifier-RECORD

   LINKAGE SECTION:          01 LS1-identifier-RECORD
   ```

2. **Format for subordinate levels.** Subordinate entries are indented four columns to the right of their parent entry. If the entry is an

elementary item, the PIC and VALUE clauses may appear on the same line. Subordinate entries should begin at level 05 and increment by 5. Their data-name should bear the same prefix as the 01Dlevel entry.

3. **Categories for 01-level entries in WORKING STORAGE.** Group like items together, such as in the following example:
   - 01-level entries that contain various switches and counters
   - 01-level entries that are used to store data records during processing
   - 01-level entries that are used to format print records
   - 01-level entries that are used in CALL statements.

4. **Definition of data types.** Specify data fields as either alphanumeric or numeric. Follow these techniques to minimize inefficiencies:
   - Use PIC X for all items that are not used in arithmetic or are not intrinsically numeric (e.g., a person's age is intrinsically numeric, whereas a part number is a coding mechanism that could become nonnumeric).
   - Define COMP-3 (packed) items as an odd number of digits, plus a sign, to ensure optimum code is generated.
   - Define COMP items that will contain a number of 9,999 or less as PIC S9(4) for optimum memory use.
   - Define COMP items that will contain a value between 10,000 and 999,999,999 as PIC S9(9) for the same reason.

5. **Definition of switches.** Define switches as PIC X and show a value of 'Y' if true and 'N' if not true. The name of the switch must specify a readily understood condition, with 88-level entries also provided, e.g.,

```
05 WS3-FD1-PAYROLL-FILE-EOF   PIC  X  VALUE 'N'.
   88  WS3-FD1-PAYROLL-AT-END         VALUE 'Y'.
   88  WS3-FD1-PAYROLL-NOT-AT-END     VALUE 'N'.
```

6. **Use of 88-level entries.** The 88-level removes literals from the PROCEDURE DIVISION, improving readability of the procedural code, and simplifying conditional statements. Use them wherever they accomplish this. Use a meaningful name that will be appropriate in the procedural code.

6.4.2. Minimum Requirements and Restrictions

1. Use SECTION names only when there are entries within them (e.g., the FILE SECTION is not required if there are no FDs or SDs to be processed).
2. Do not use the 77 level or 66 level entries. Instead, combine what would be 77 entries into a common 01-level. Common data types (e.g., counters, switches) are easier for maintenance than 77 level entries. Likewise, a

REDEFINES entry is clearer and more readily understood than 66 level entries.

3. Do not use the word USAGE and abbreviate PICTURE and COMPUTATIONAL. For example,

```
05 WS2-PAGE-COUNTER    PIC S9(5)    COMP-3.
```

6.4.3. Performance Considerations

To improve performance of programs, use the following guidelines:

1. **Define tables with indexes** and, where possible, in ascending order. This supports binary search techniques (SEARCH ALL) and is more efficient than using subscripts. Note: As a general rule, subscripts are no less efficient than indexes when the subscript data element is changed for each use. In all other cases, indexes are more efficient. For example,

```
IF WS-PREM-AMT (WS-APP-AGE) = WS-APP-PAID
    PERFORM 2300-PROCESS-FULL-PREM
ELSE
    IF WS-PREM-AMT (WS-APP-AGE) > WS-APP-PAID
        PERFORM 2400-PROCESS-OVERPMT
```

could cause the location within the table of WS-PREMDAMT to be calculated twice. With indexes, this additional calculation would not happen.

2. **Use S in PIC for numeric items** (e.g., PIC S999) if a sign is present. This reduces generation of object code that resets the sign after each operation.

3. **Use COMP-3 or COMP** for data elements that are involved in arithmetic operations.
   - Use COMP-3 for application data elements and accumulators used to assist the programmer. COMP-3 is more efficient than DISPLAY and more readable in a dump than COMP. For example,
   The number 123456789 would require this storage and would appear this way in a dump:

```
Data    Bytes
Type    required        As seen in a dump
DISPLAY   9             F1F2F3F4F5F6F7F8F9
COMP-3    5             123456789C
COMP      4             075BCD15
```

   - Use COMP only where specific subprograms or system functions require them. For example, PARM processing requires COMP. Also, use COMP for subscript control elements (i.e., where indexing is not being used).

4. If possible, define arithmetic items that are used in the same computation with the same number of decimal places.

6.5. PROCEDURE DIVISION GUIDELINES

6.5.1. Specific Layout Guidelines

1. Indent conditionally executed statements at least 4 columns beyond invoking statement. For example,

```
IF WS-FD-EOF-SWITCH = 'N'
    PERFORM 3200-PRINT-DETAIL
```

2. Place Scope terminators and ELSE statements in same column as previous statement to which it relates. For example,

```
IF WS-SALARY-CODE = 'H'
    PERFORM 2300-COMPUTE-HOURLY-PAY
ELSE
    PERFORM 2400-VALIDATE-SALARY-EMP
END-IF
```

3. Code statements that exceed one line to next line with a minimum 2-column indentation. For example,

```
MOVE ZEROS TO WS-HOURLY-RATE
               WS-GROSS-PAY
```

4. Develop paragraph names with a structure, such that the name of PERFORMed paragraphs is an extension of the parent paragraph. This should match the structure chart numbering scheme. For example,

```
2000-PRODUCE-FINAL-TOTAL.
    PERFORM 2100-CALCULATE-DATA
    PERFORM 2200-ASSEMBLE-TOTAL-LINE
    PERFORM 2300-WRITE-TOTALS.
```

5. Focus on function. Paragraphs with several functions tend to be large and can become difficult to debug.
6. Be conscious of the overuse of literals. They can lead to maintenance headaches. If a literal is used often, consider defining a WORKING-STORAGE data element for it instead.

7. Be conscious of the overuse of switches. With good design, fewer switches are needed. Switches are usually misused when a paragraph does not have the authority to take a specific action, but must set a switch to show a condition.

8. Code all paragraphs using structured programming elements such that only one period is used at the end of the paragraph.

6.5.2. Minimum Structural Requirements and Constraints

1. There must be only one STOP RUN (main program) or GOBACK (sub-program). Note: Do not use STOP RUN in IMS or CICS programs. For CICS, use EXEC CICS RETURN in the highest level module.
2. SECTION entries should not be used.
3. One paragraph, one period.

6.5.3. Program Structure Guidelines

Here is a summary of general considerations to assist you in coding the program.

1. Keep paragraphs small.
2. Code top-to-bottom, left-to-right.
3. Keep balance. Don't string out PERFORMs through a series of serially executed paragraphs.

4. Ensure all paragraphs return control to the PERFORMing paragraph.
5. Place control statements higher and action statements lower.
6. Place I/O processes in separate paragraphs and include a record counter for potential debug assistance.
7. Don't mix several functions in one paragraph. Decompose the paragraph so imbedded functions become new paragraphs that are PERFORMed from the original paragraph.

6.5.4. Use of Control and Action Paragraphs/Subprograms

Ensure PERFORMed action paragraphs return status when the outcome is conditional. For example,

PERFORMing a paragraph that can have multiple outcomes and then checking results:

```
PERFORM 2300-READ-RECORD
IF WS-EOF-SWITCH = 'N'
    ....
```

Making a decision first and then PERFORMing the action paragraph:

```
IF VALID-DETAIL-RECORD
    PERFORM 2400-PRINT-DETAIL
    ....
```

6.5.5. Preferred COBOL Statements

Appearance of any of the following statements within a program generally indicates that the program is using COBOL II facilities and good structure.

1. **COMPUTE.** Usually more efficient than other arithmetic statements, especially when more than one arithmetic operation takes place.
2. **EVALUATE.** See examples in Chapter 2.
3. **CONTINUE.** See examples in Chapter 2.
4. **INITIALIZE.** If you group common items together, such as accumulators, the INITIALIZE can reset all entries under a group name, numeric fields to zero, and alphanumeric fields to spaces.
5. **SET.** The SET statement has two formats, SET TO TRUE and SET to adjust indexes or POINTERs. (Reminder: When setting indexes, always test that the range of an index is within the table being accessed to prevent causing major program problems.) For example, if a table has 99 entries, you could program this:

```
IF WS-AGE > 0 AND < 100
    SET WS-PREM-INDEX TO WS-AGE
ELSE
    ...        <- process for invalid age goes here
```

6. **PERFORM and PERFORM UNTIL.** The presence of a PERFORM UNTIL denotes a DO WHILE or a DO UNTIL, both of which show the repetitive portions of a process. See examples in Chapter 2.
7. **SEARCH and SEARCH ALL.** Although not new, many programmers are unaware of their features. You are encouraged to consider their use. See Chapter 3 for more information. Here is an example of a binary search:

Assumed table definition

```
01  WS-STATE-CODE.
    05 WS-STATE OCCURS 50 TIMES ASCENDING KEY STATE-ID
            INDEXED BY ST-INDEX.
       10 STATE-ID       PIC XX.
```

Binary search, indexed

```
SEARCH ALL WS-STATE
  AT END
     PERFORM 2300-RECORD-STATE-ERROR
WHEN STATE-ID (ST-INDEX) = WS-APP-STATE
     PERFORM 2400-RECORD-STATE-VALID
END-SEARCH
```

8. **Nested programs.** Nested programs offer many benefits and their use is encouraged. For more information on nested programs, see the section Module Structures in Chapter 3.
9. **CALL extensions.** Extensions to the CALL statement, including clauses such as BY CONTENT, LENGTH OF, and ADDRESS OF provide opportunities to develop a cleaner module-to-module structure. Their use is not required, and there are many situations in which they serve no purpose.

6.5.6. COBOL Statements That Should Be Used with Caution

While the following statements are useful, consider them carefully before using them. They are listed here to acknowledge that situations may exist when they will contribute to structure and clarity.

1. **PERFORM WITH TEST AFTER.** This format works exactly like PERFORM UNTIL except that the test of the associated variable occurs after the PERFORM instead of before it. The difficulty is that programmers used to one format may have difficulty rethinking the logic flow.
2. **Inline PERFORM.** While it is no longer necessary to PERFORM outside a paragraph, this statement increases the size of a paragraph, increases the complexity of any paragraph, and increases the possibility of introducing an error into program logic. See the example in Chapter 2.
3. **Nested COPY.** The ability to include a COPY statement within another COPY member introduces administrative complexity to maintain the entries.
4. **Hexadecimal literals.** These are machine-dependent and require a knowledge of bit configurations. They are coded as X'literal', e.g.,

```
MOVE X'OF' TO WS-PROCESS-ERROR-SWITCH
```

5. **Reference modification.** This feature allows reference to specific bytes within a data element, e.g., MOVE WS-EMP-NAME (3:10) TO WS-EMP-NAME would move ten bytes, beginning with the third byte.

6.5.7. COBOL Statements That Should Not Be Used

Most of these elements violate structured programming techniques or could introduce external problems (e.g., COPY OF). Exceptions: The PERFORM THRU, EXIT, and GO TO are sometimes required to construct a meaningful structure with CICS applications. Other than for CICS, these statements should be avoided.

1. **ALTER.** Do not use.
2. **COPY OF.** This feature allows a programmer to specify from what library a COPY member will be extracted. This creates a dependency on the location of COPYbooks, which should be an administrative issue, not a programming one.
3. **PERFORM THRU.** PERFORM THRU requires a minimum of two paragraphs, encourages the use of GO TO, and violates the concept of decomposition. The format is never required and should be avoided. See exception for CICS.
4. **EXIT.** The EXIT verb only serves to place a paragraph name. Since it is linked with PERFORM THRU, avoiding use of PERFORM THRU should eliminate this verb also. See exception for CICS.
5. **GO TO.** Using GO TO indicates an incomplete or inadequate structure. In OS/VS COBOL, it was required to function within some restrictions of that compiler (e.g., SORTs), but no longer has validity. See exception for CICS.
6. **ENTRY.** The ENTRY statement gives a program more than one entry. Since this is a violation of structured programming, avoid its use. If a subprogram requires multiple entry points, write multiple subprograms instead. Also, it is not required for IMS programs.
7. **NEXT SENTENCE** clause. NEXT SENTENCE is an implied GO TO. Use other approaches, such as the CONTINUE statement, or rewrite the statement so NEXT SENTENCE is not required.

6.5.8. Compound Conditions

Conditions are used in IF, EVALUATE, SEARCH, and PERFORM statements. A compound condition is one that combines two or more conditions with AND, OR, or NOT. While these are useful, here are some guidelines to prevent problems.

1. Use arithmetic expressions with caution. They have two potential problems. The first is that if used more than once, you lose efficiency and should use a COMPUTE statement to store the result prior to the conditional statement. The second is that the computed value is not truncated into a PICTURE clause, preventing an exact value from being used (e.g., 10 divided by 3 is a never-ending quotient).

2. Use parenthesis around conditions to clarify and document what each condition is. For example,

```
IF A > B AND = C OR D is equivalent to

IF (A > B AND = C) OR
   (A = D)
```

3. Use NOT carefully. When possible use a positive test, not a negative one. Also, remember that NOT combined with OR is always true. Consider,

IF A NOT EQUAL 1 OR 2. The field, A, will always be unequal to one of those values, therefore the condition will always be true.

6.6.   COBOL SORT TECHNIQUES

Sorting has unique aspects, since it is actually a separate program being activated under control of COBOL. Here are some considerations to take whenever specifications indicate a sort is needed. For performance considerations or to determine whether to use DFSORT alone or a COBOL SORT, see Chapter 5 ("Program Design Guidelines"). For usage techniques, see Chapter 3.

1. Address SORT Performance Issues.
   * Sort only the records needed, not the entire file.
   * Sort only the fields necessary for subsequent processing, not the entire record.

2. Use paragraphs, not SECTIONs. The INPUT PROCEDURE and OUTPUT PROCEDURE must specify paragraphs, not SECTIONs. Use a single paragraph for the INPUT and OUTPUT PROCEDURES, i.e., do not specify "paragraph-a THRU paragraph-n."

3. Validate correct SORT execution. The SORT-RETURN special register will be nonzero if the SORT process terminated prematurely. This field should be tested immediately following the SORT statement.

4. Terminate a SORT correctly. If a processing discrepancy occurs during an INPUT or OUTPUT PROCEDURE, move 16 to SORT-RETURN, and then issue one more RETURN or RELEASE statement, (i.e, do not immediately issue a STOP RUN, GOBACK, or ABEND). This will

terminate the sort and will return control to the statement following the SORT statement, at which time you can test SORT-RETURN and then act accordingly.

5. Consider using the IGZSRTCD Interface. Using DFSORT's INCLUDE or OMIT statements with the IGZSRTCD DD statement (SORTCNTL is also allowed) may eliminate the need for an INPUT or OUTPUT PROCEDURE.

In developing a COBOL SORT, here are the basics for the COBOL statements that are used, assuming that both an INPUT and an OUTPUT PROCEDURE are needed. Some portions of the program are omitted. The action taken in this example for a sorting error is an example only.

```
SELECT SD1-sortfile-FILE ASSIGN TO SORTWORK.
    .
    .
    .
SD  SD1-sortfile-FILE
    RECORD CONTAINS nn CHARACTERS.
01  SD1-sortfile-RECORD.
    05  SD1-sortkey-a  PIC ...
        .
    05  SD1-sortkey-z  PIC ...
        .

    SORT SD1-sortfile-FILE
      ASCENDING KEY  SD1-sortkey-a  SD1-sortkey-z
      INPUT PROCEDURE 1000-SELECT-DATA
      OUTPUT PROCEDURE 2000-PRODUCE-REPORT
    IF SORT-RETURN > 0
        DISPLAY ' SORT ERROR OCCURRED' UPON CONSOLE
        CALL 'ILBOABNO' USING WS3-ABEND-CODE
    ELSE
        MOVE 0 TO RETURN-CODE
        STOP RUN
    END-IF.

  1000-SELECT-DATA.
    PERFORM 1010-READ-INPUT
    IF NOT WS-MASTER-EOF
        .
        .         <- Processing to validate or modify data
        .               prior to the sort goes here.
        .
        RELEASE SD-sortfile-RECORD
    END-IF.
```

```
2000-PRODUCE-REPORT.
    RETURN SD-sortfile-FILE
        NOT AT END
            .
            .        <- Processing of data after the sort
            .                    goes here.
    END-RETURN.
```

SUMMARY

Admittedly, the format of this chapter was different, rather terse, and procedural. The focus was on mechanics, not on logic or design. My goal was to give you a format for assessment. Many times, we don't know what we want to do until we hear someone else suggest what we clearly do not want to do. If this document helped you determine how you want to change your programming standards, I'll consider it a success. Your comments will be appreciated.

Summaries, Tables, and References

7.1. SUGGESTED COBOL COMPILE AND EXECUTION JCL OPTIONS

These options are presented here in summary fashion and, in many cases, options for different situations may be combined. For each situation, only the options that normally affect the category are listed (e.g., options such as SOURCE, SEQUENCE, and OBJECT do not appear). You should refer to Chapter 3 for specific options and to Chapter 4 for debugging specifics. You should also know your shop's defaults before using these suggestions.

7.1.1. Options for Syntax Compile

If you're compiling a program to determine whether it is coded correctly, but you do not intend to execute it, you incur minimum costs and resource use by coding:

```
NOCOMPILE,XREF,VBREF
```

7.1.2. Options for Routine Tests

Routine testing is for programs that have executed several times and are beyond the unstable phase. These options are proactive. (See Chapter 4.)

```
OFFSET,FDUMP
```

7.1.3. Options for Minimum Compile Resource Use

This option is for use when you want minimum resource use during the compile (see also, Options for Maximum Compiler Performance, following):

```
NOOPTIMIZE
```

7.1.4. Options for Debugging Assistance.

These options may be useful for instable programs or those that have not been tested. SSRANGE increases run-time resource use. Debugging options also require JCL at run-time.

Compile options

```
MAP,XREF(SHORT),OFFSET,SSRANGE,FDUMP
```

Run-time requirements

```
//SYSDBOUT   DD   SYSOUT=*    for FDUMP
//SYSABOUT   DD   SYSOUT=*    for COBOL ABEND messages (optional)
//SYSOUT     DD   SYSOUT=*    for DISPLAY statements (if any)
```

Note: If you specify SSRANGE, you must also specify appropriate information at run-time to activate the debugging code for this feature. That can be done in either of two ways:

1. On the EXEC JCL statement if your program can receive a PARM (IMS and CICS programs cannot). The format is

```
//stepname   EXEC PGM=pgmname,PARM='/SSRANGE'
```

(If your program also expects a PARM value, it must be coded to the left of the / mark.)

2. If your program cannot accept a PARM (CICS and IMS) or if you prefer not to use this technique, you can include the appropriate code at link-edit time. That is done by adding the following link-edit control statement and DD statement during the Link-edit step. The desired options must have been previously set in the module named IGZEOPT.

```
INCLUDE ddname(IGZEOPT)
```

See the section Specifying COBOL II Options in Chapter 3 for more information.

7.1.5. Options for Minimum Run-Time Costs

These options are for programs that are stable and you want minimum cpu use. You should check Chapter 3 for specifics of each option, since some might affect run-time logic.

```
OPTIMIZE,TRUNC(OPT),NUMPROC(PFD),NOSSRANGE,
NODYNAM,RENT,RES,ADV,AWO,NOTEST
```

7.1.6. Options for Maximum Compiler Performance.

These options are my personal suggestion for your shop to use as defaults for maximum performance by the compiler. These options should be used with the sample JCL PROC that is in Chapter 3. This supports a REGION size up to 4000K.

```
SIZE(4000K),BUF(32760)
```

Note: An additional step that should be considered is re-blocking your shop's COPY library if COPY statements are used a lot. COBOL II allows the block size to be up to 32,767, double the size that OS/VS COBOL allowed.

7.1.7. Options for CICS

CICS programs need the following options set. You should read the section CICS/IMS/DB2 Issues in Chapter 3 for specifics and additional considerations.

```
RES,RENT,NODYNAM,NOCMPR2,TRUNC(BIN),NODBCS
```

7.1.8. Options for IMS/DC

IMS programs normally use the following options. You should read the section CICS/IMS/DB2 Issues in Chapter 3 for specifics and additional considerations.

```
RES,RENT,DATA(24),TRUNC(BIN)
```

7.1.9. Options for DB2

DB2 programs are not as sensitive as those for CICS and IMS, although they benefit from the same options that improve performance (e.g., RENT, RES). You should read the section CICS/IMS/DB2 Issues in Chapter 3, for specifics.

```
TRUNC(BIN),NOCMPR2
```

7.2. SUMMARY OF MAJOR COBOL STATEMENTS

This section includes a subset definition of syntax for a subset of the available COBOL statements with emphasis on the major new facilities of COBOL II (e.g., you won't find the syntax for the ALTER or GO TO statements here, nor the more esoteric options of some of the other statements). Where any clause is omitted, it is noted. Statements that are not new and have no variables (e.g., GOBACK, STOP RUN) are omitted.

Where a loop is evident in the syntax, it represents an optional clause or repetition. Charts should be read from top to bottom, left to right. Each complete statement ends with "—><". Where, due to complexity, I redirected the flow of the syntax from right to left, I inserted arrows (e.g., <——<——) to assist you. Statements or clauses that are new with COBOL II are highlighted.

My goal was to provide a ready reference for the majority of statements that you will encounter, not provide a reference to every option. For explanations and examples of statements new in COBOL II, see Chapter 2. For complete syntax, see the *IBM VS COBOL II Application Programming Language Reference* (Chapter 9).

IDENTIFICATION DIVISION (obsolete clauses omitted).

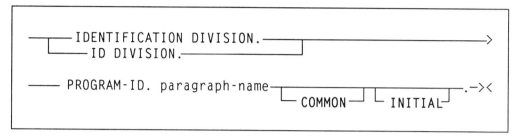

Partial ENVIRONMENT DIVISION (VSAM options and CONFIGURATION SECTION omitted).

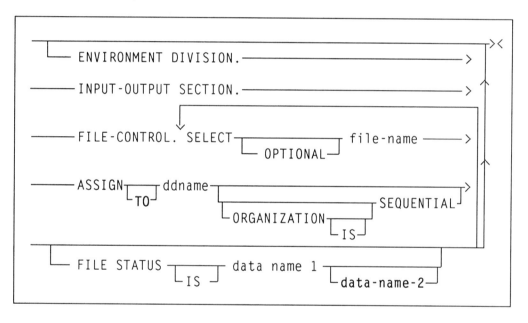

DATA DIVISION.

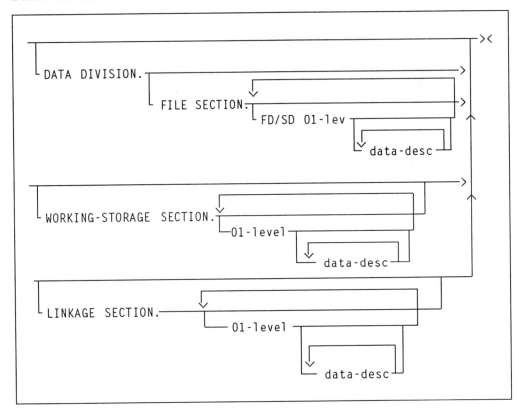

New USAGE and VALUE options.

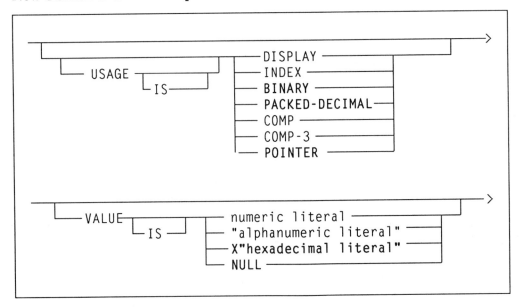

Partial PROCEDURE DIVISION (declaratives and SECTIONs omitted).

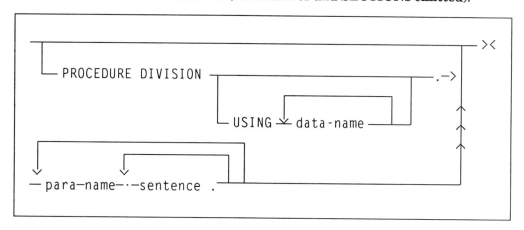

Relational operators.

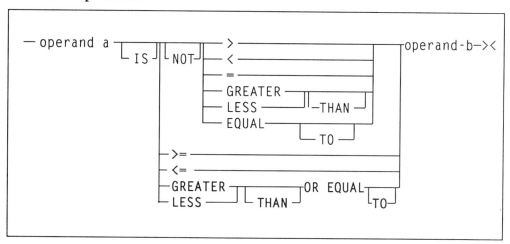

Precedence rules for conditions and arithmetic expressions. Elements are listed in the priority in which they are evaluated.

1. Parenthesized elements
2. arithmetic operations ←
   - 2.a. Unary operator
   - 2.b. exponentiation
   - 2.c. multiplication and division
   - 2.d. addition and subtraction
3. NOT
4. AND
5. OR

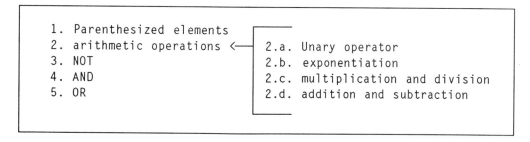

Class condition.

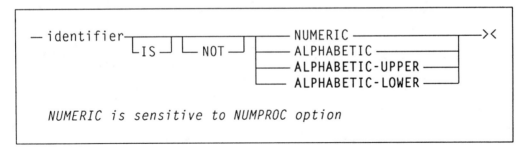

Sign condition.

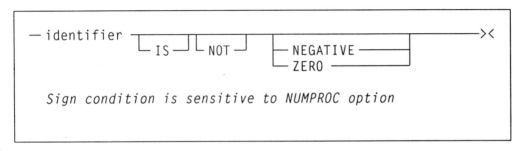

Reference modification.

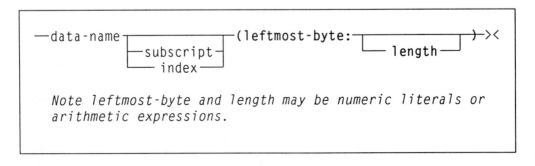

ACCEPT statement for system transfer.

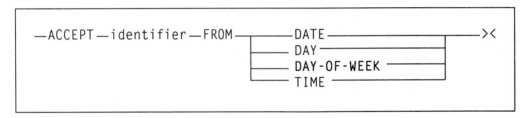

ADD statement.

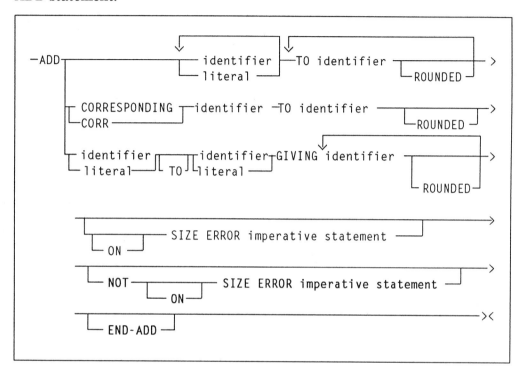

CALL statement.

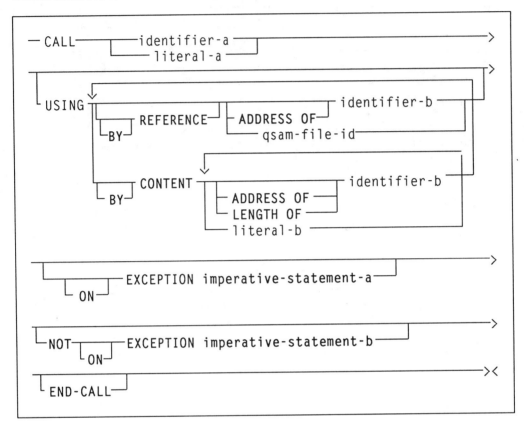

CANCEL statement.

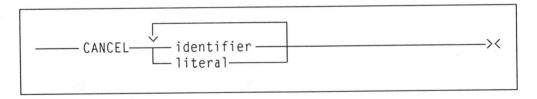

CLOSE statement (tape reel options omitted).

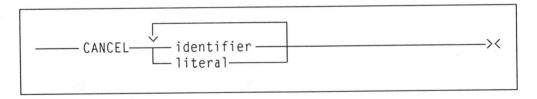

COMPUTE statement.

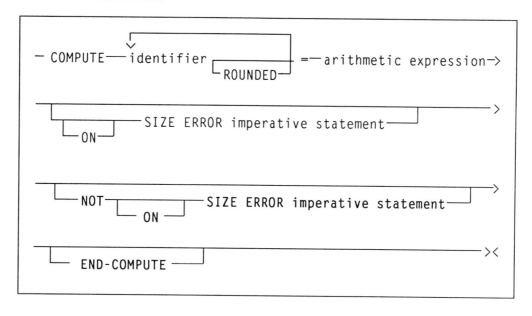

CONTINUE statement.

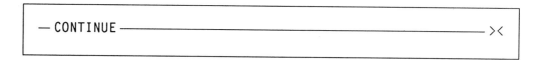

DELETE statement.

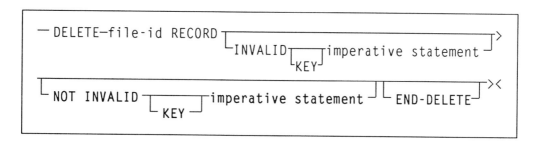

DISPLAY statement, abbreviated.

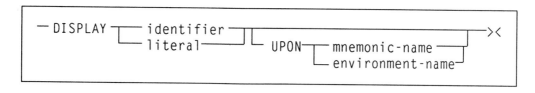

DIVIDE statement.

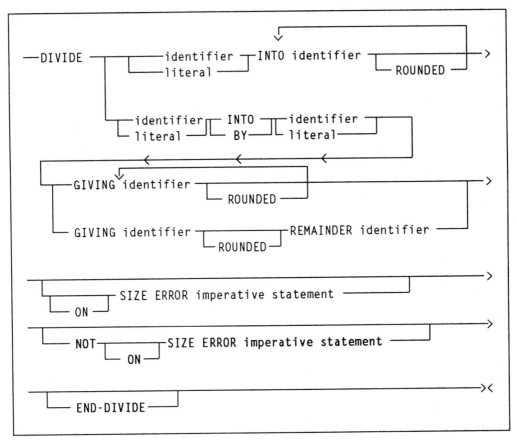

ENTRY statement.

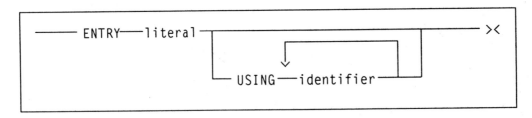

EVALUATE statement.

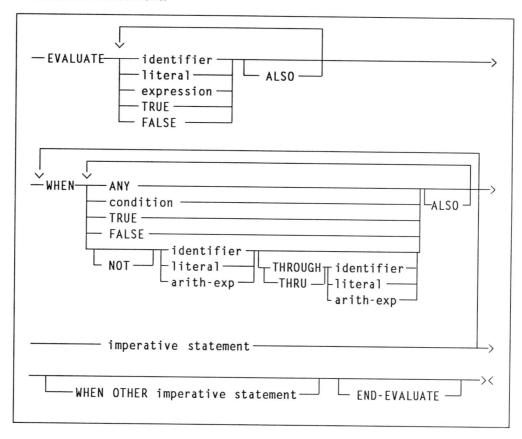

IF statement (NEXT SENTENCE clause omitted).

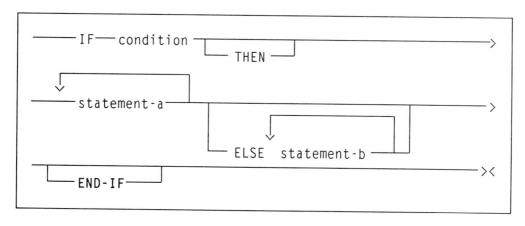

INITIALIZE statement.

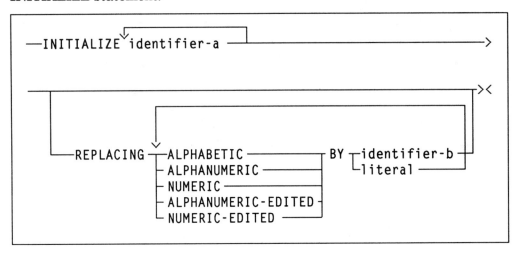

INSPECT statement.

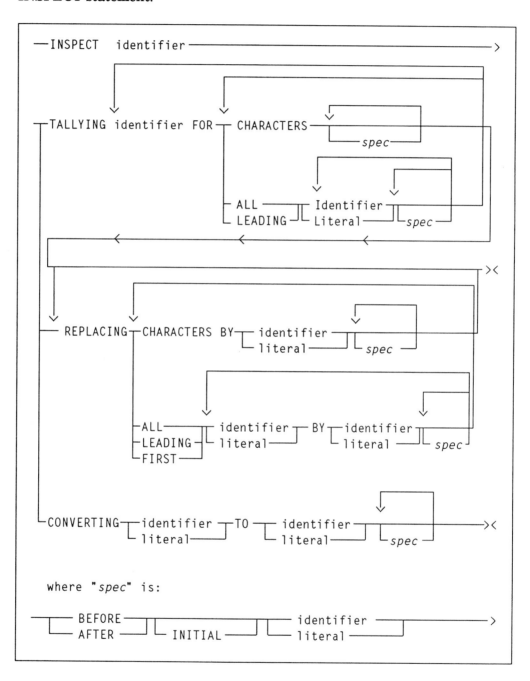

MERGE statement.

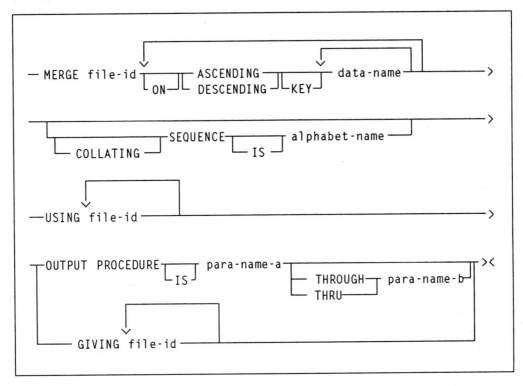

MOVE statement.

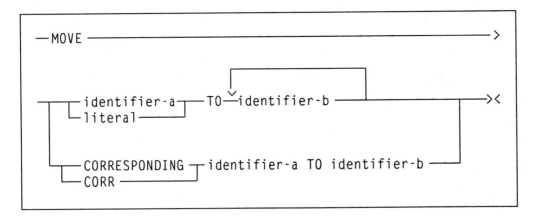

MULTIPLY statement.

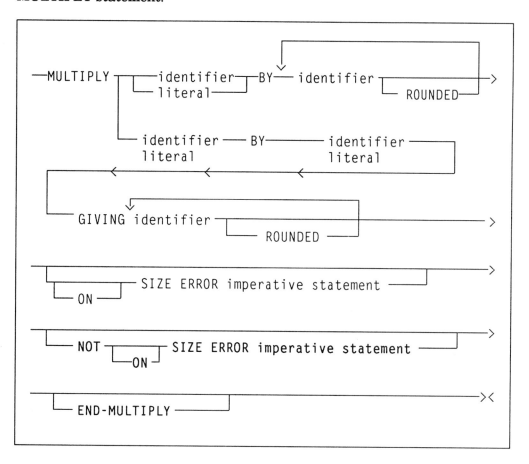

OPEN statement (tape reel options omitted).

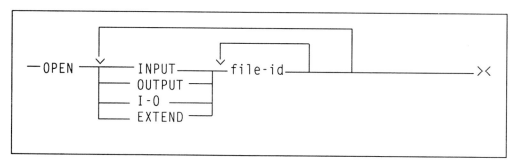

PERFORM statement, except Inline PERFORM.

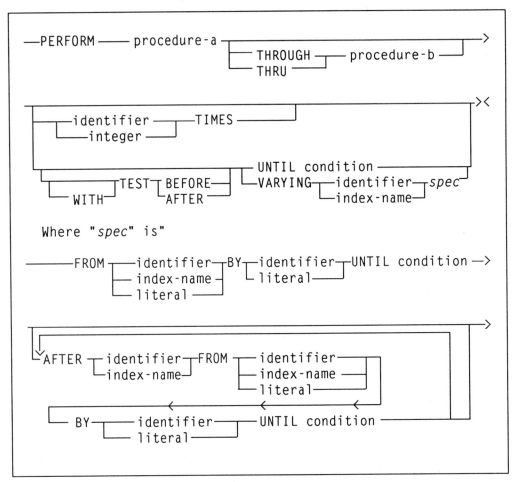

Inline PERFORM.

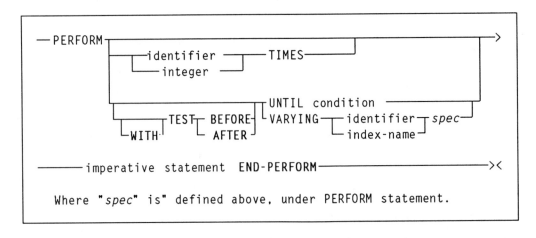

READ statement. AT END/NOT AT END cannot be intermixed with INVALID KEY/NOT INVALID KEY. NEXT has meaning only for VSAM.

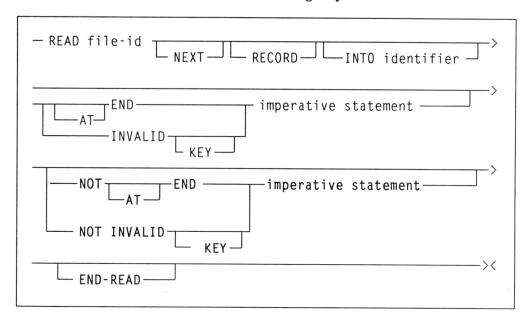

RELEASE statement.

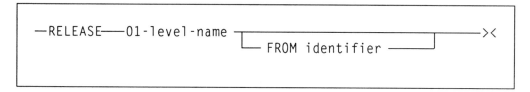

RETURN statement.

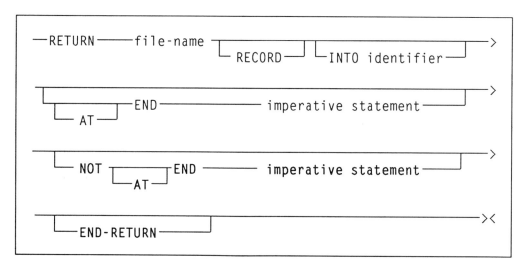

REWRITE statement.

```
— REWRITE 01-level-name ──┬─────────────────────────┬──────────>
                          └──── FROM identifier ────┘
──┬──────────────────────────────────────────────────┬─────────>
  └ INVALID ──┬───────┬── imperative statement ──────┘
              └─ KEY ─┘
──┬──────────────────────────────────────────────────────────┬─>
  └──── NOT INVALID ──┬───────┬── imperative statement ──────┘
                      └─ KEY ─┘
──┬────────────────────┬──────────────────────────────────────><
  └─── END-REWRITE ────┘
```

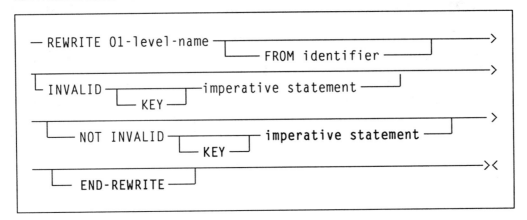

Serial SEARCH statement (NEXT SENTENCE clause omitted).

```
— SEARCH identifier ─┬────────────────────────────────────────┬─>
                     └ VARYING ──┬── identifier ──────────────┤
                                 └── index-name ──────────────┘

──┬──────────────────────────────────────────┬─────────────────>
  └──┬──────┬── END imperative statement ────┘
     └─ AT ─┘

  ┌────────────────────────────────────────┐
  v                                        │
──WHEN condition—imperative statement ─────┴─┬────────────────┬─><
                                             └ END-SEARCH ────┘
```

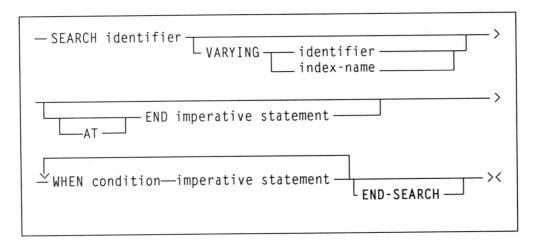

Binary SEARCH ALL statement (IS EQUAL TO omitted).

```
— SEARCH ALL  identifier ─┬──────────────────────────────────┬─>
                          └─┬────┬─END imperative statement──┘
                            └─AT─┘
            ┌─ AND ──────────────────────────────────────────┐
            v                                                 │
——WHEN ──┬──data-name — = ──┬──identifier ────────────────┬──┴─>
         │                  ├──literal ───────────────────┤
         │                  └──arithmetic-expression ─────┤
         └──────────── condition-name ────────────────────┘

——imperative statement ─┬──────────────────────┬──────────────><
                        └──── END-SEARCH ──────┘
```

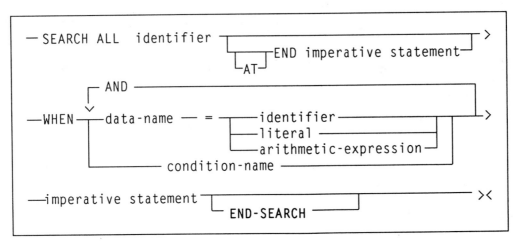

SET statement.

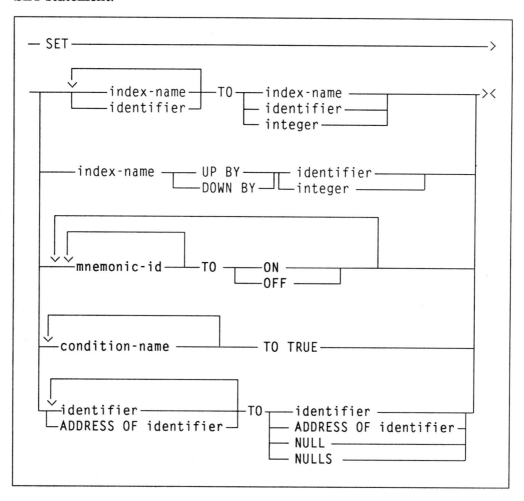

SORT statement.

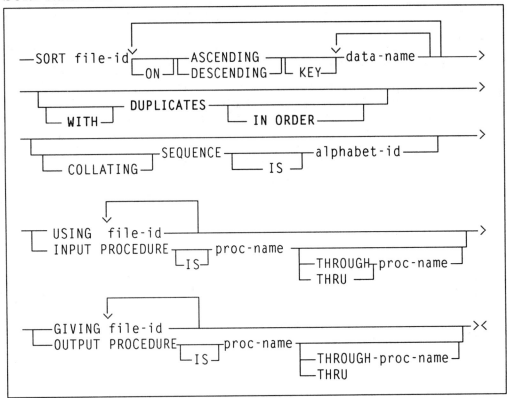

START statement (fully spelled operators, e.g., EQUAL TO, omitted).

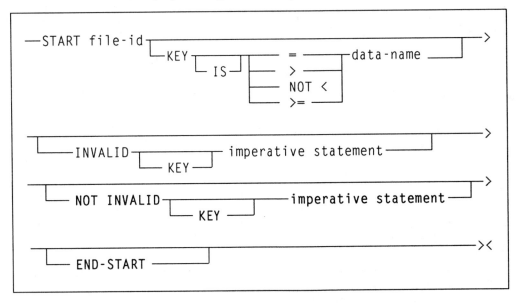

STRING statement.

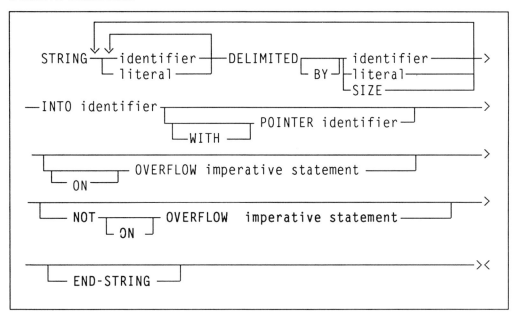

SUBTRACT statement.

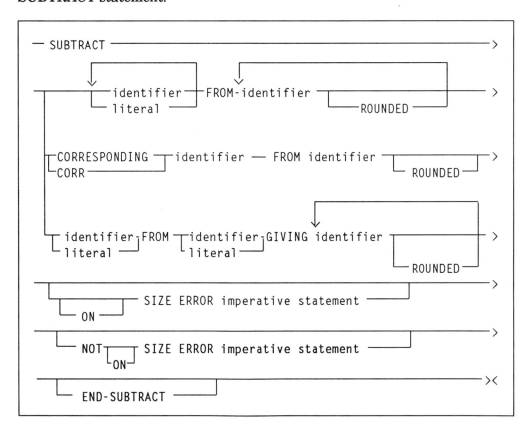

UNSTRING statement.

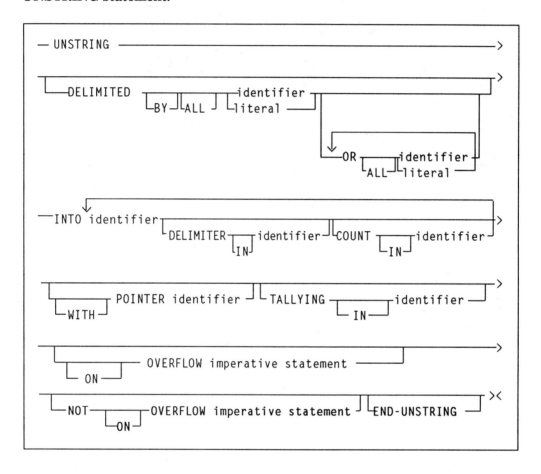

USE statement.

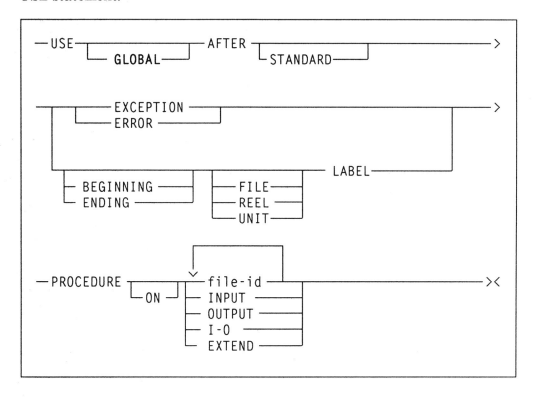

WRITE statement (sequential).

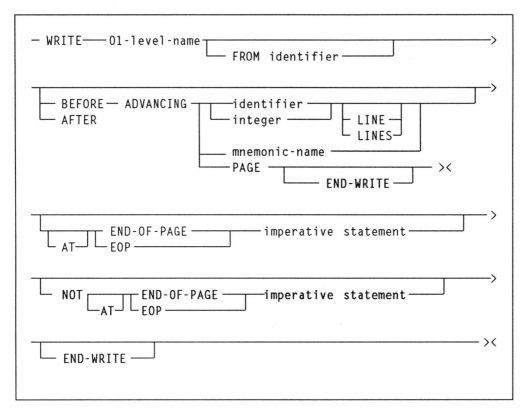

WRITE statement (non-sequential).

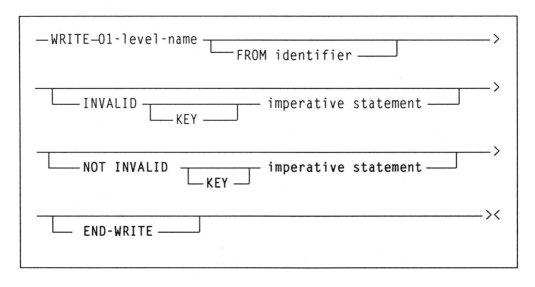

7.3. FILE STATUS CODES

This table of status codes is primarily for quick reference. The keys shown for COBOL II are for use with the NOCMPR2 compile option.

QSAM		VSAM		
COBOL II	OS/VS COBOL	COBOL II	OS/VS COBOL	
00	00	00	00	Successful completion
N/A	N/A	02	02	Duplicate key
04	N\A	04	00	Wrong length record
05	N/A	05	00	Optional file not present
07	N/A	N/A	N/A	Not a reel-type device, yet was specified
10	10	10	10	End-of-file detected
N/A	N/A	14	N/A	Relative rec # too large—sequential READ
N/A	N/A	20	20	Invalid key
N/A	N/A	21	21	Invalid key, sequence error
N/A	N/A	22	22	Invalid key, duplicate key or not allowed
N/A	N/A	23	23	Invalid key, no record found
N/A	N/A	24	24	Invalid key, attempt to write beyond file limit
30	30	30	30	Permanent error
34	34	N/A	N/A	Permanent error, violation of file boundary
35	93 96	35	93 96	File missing that was not OPTIONAL
37	93	37	90	Device conflict
38	92	N/A	N/A	OPEN error, closed WITH LOCK
39	95	39	95	OPEN fail, conflict of attributes
41	92	41	92	OPEN attempted for open file
42	92	42	92	CLOSE attempted, file not open
43	92	43	92	REWRITE attempted when prior I/O not proper
44	92	N/A	N/A	Attempted REWRITE with different record size

continued on next page

| QSAM | | VSAM | | |
COBOL II	OS/VS COBOL	COBOL II	OS/VS COBOL	
46	92	46	92	READ attempted (sequential), no next record
47	92	47	92	READ attempted when file not OPENed for input
48	92	48	92	WRITE attempted when file not OPENed for output
49	92	49	92	DELETE or REWRITE attempted - OPEN incorrect
90	90	90	90	Undocumented errors
91	91	91	91	VSAM password failed
92	92	N/A	N/A	Logic error
93	93	93	93	VSAM resource not available
94	94	N/A*	94	VSAM file position indicator missing (COBOL II with CMPR2 option)
95	95	95	95	VSAM file information wrong or incomplete
96	96	96	96	NO DD for VSAM file
N/A	N/A	97	97	OPEN successful - integrity verified

A more thorough review of file status codes is available in the *VS COBOL II Language Reference* manual. Sample scenarios are in *VS COBOL II Application Programming Guide* (Chapter 9).

Note: When using FILE STATUS for QSAM files, there may be situations in which recovery may be inhibited if the ERROPT=ACC parameter is not coded on the file's DCB parameter.

7.4. TABLES AND WORKSHEETS

7.4.1. Installation Options

COBOL II compile-time options
Use this section to fill in your shop's default options. For information on each option, see the section Specifying COBOL II options in Chapter 3.

Option	Sample Settings	Your Installation Defaults
ADV	ADV	_____
APOST	APOST	_____
AWO	NOAWO	_____
BUFSIZE	32760	_____
CMPR2	NOCMPR2	_____
COMPILE	NOCOMPILE(E)	_____
DATA	31	_____
DBCS	NODBCS	_____
DECK	NODECK	_____
DUMP	NODUMP	_____
DYNAM*	NODYNAM	_____
EXIT	NOEXIT	_____
FASTSRT	FASTSRT	_____
FDUMP	NOFDUMP	_____
FLAG	FLAG(I,W)	_____
FLAGMIG	NOFLAGMIG	_____
FLAGSAA	NOFLAGSAA	_____
FLAGSTD	NOFLAGSTD	_____
LANGUAGE	UE	_____
LIB	LIB	_____
LINECOUNT	60	_____
LIST	NOLIST	_____
MAP	NOMAP	_____
NAME	NONAME	_____

Option	Sample Settings	Your Installation Defaults
NUMBER	NONUMBER	_____
NUMPROC	PFD	_____
OBJECT	OBJECT	_____
OFFSET	NOOFFSET	_____
OPTIMIZE	NOOPTIMIZE	_____
OUTDD	SYSOUT	_____
RENT*	RENT	_____
RESIDENT*	RESIDENT	_____
SEQUENCE	NOSEQUENCE	_____
SIZE	4194304	_____
SOURCE	NOSOURCE	_____
SPACE	1	_____
SSRANGE	NOSSRANGE	_____
TERM	NOTERM	_____
TEST	NOTEST	_____
TRUNC	BIN	_____
VBREF	NOVBREF	_____
WORD	NOWORD	_____
XREF	NOXREF	_____
ZWB	ZWB	_____

* = CICS-sensitive

COBOL II run-time options

This may be separate for different environments. For information on how to determine these settings, see the section Specifying COBOL II Options in Chapter 3. Also, some of these settings cannot be overridden for individual applications.

Option	Sample Settings	Your Installation defaults	
		Other	**CICS**
NODEBUG	NODEBUG	_____	_____
SSRANGE	NOSSRANGE	_____	_____
STAE	STAE	_____	_____
AIXBLD	NOAIXBLD	_____	_____
SIMVRD*	NOSIMVRD	_____	_____
SPOUT	NOSPOUT	_____	_____
LIBKEEP*	NOLIBKEEP	_____	_____
LANGUAGE	UE	_____	_____
RTEREUS*	NORTEREUS	_____	_____
WSCLEAR	NOWSCLEAR	_____	_____
UPSI	00000000	_____	_____
MIXRES*	NOMIXRES	_____	_____

* Option ignored for CICS

Run-time options may be forced via IGZEOPT Assembler module. Global defaults are in IGZEOPD.

7.4.2. Compile Options: COBOL II Versus OS/VS COBOL

This list is to assist programmers familiar with OS/VS COBOL compile options who want to locate the similar option for COBOL II. For information on each option, see the section Specifying COBOL II Options in Chapter 3.

COBOL II Option	OS/VS COBOL Option Settings	Comments
ADV	ADV	
APOST/QUOTE	APOST/QUOTE	
AWO	n/a	
n/a	BATCH	Batch compiles are available by specifying END PROGRAM statement.
BUFSIZE	BUF	For OS/VS COBOL, this specified the total amount of memory for buffers. For COBOL II, it specifies the maximum per buffer.
CMPR2	n/a	
COMPILE	SYNTAX CSYNTAX SUPMAP	There is no 1-to-1 relation, although the function is similar.
n/a	COUNT	This function was moved to COBTEST.
DATA	n/a	
DBCS	n/a	
DECK	DECK	
DUMP	DUMP	
DYNAM	DYNAM	
n/a	ENDJOB	The ENDJOB function is always in effect in COBOL II.
EXIT	n/a	
FASTSRT	n/a	
FDUMP	SYMDMP STATE	
FLAG	FLAGW FLAGE	

COBOL II Option	OS/VS COBOL Option Settings	Comments
FLAGMIG	MIGR	Both compilers use it to monitor migration toward the current release of COBOL II. OS/VS COBOL only checks for ANSI 74 compatibility.
FLAGSAA	n/a	
FLAGSTD	FIPS	These two have similar goals, but are different.
n/a	FLOW	This function was moved to COBTEST.
n/a	LANGLVL	COBOL II does not support ANSI 68.
LANGUAGE	n/a	
LIB	LIB	
LINECOUNT	60	
LIST	PMAP	
n/a	LSTnnn	The LISTER feature is not available with COBOL II.
	LCOLn	
	L120/L132	
	FDECK	
	CDECK	
MAP	DMAP	
NAME	NAME	COBOL II provides extended features here.
NUMBER	n/a	
NUMPROC	n/a	
OBJECT	LOAD	
OFFSET	CLIST	
OPTIMIZE	OPTIMIZE	COBOL II does significantly more optimization.
OUTDD	SYS	
RENT	n/a	
RESIDENT	RESIDENT	

COBOL II Option	OS/VS COBOL Option Settings	Comments
SEQUENCE	SEQ	
SIZE	SIZE	
SOURCE	SOURCE	
SPACE	SPACE	
SSRANGE	n/a	
TERM	TERM	
TEST	TEST	
TRUNC	TRUNC	In OS/VS COBOL, this was a yes/no option. In COBOL II, it is a more complex issue. See Chapter 3.
VBREF	VBREF VBSUM	
WORD	n/a	
XREF	SXREF	
ZWB	ZWB	

7.5. HEXADECIMAL CONVERSION CHART

The following table represents some hexadecimal and decimal values. Notice that two hex values occupy a byte. The values shown are built from right to left, showing the hex and decimal values that each bit occupies within a binary value.

The techniques shown following the table are simple ways to convert from different numbering systems to others by using the table. I apologize to the mathematicians and others among you who prefer more elegant approaches. I use this approach because, unless hex arithmetic comes easy to you, it is a skill that is rarely needed. As I mentioned in Chapter 4 ("Debugging"), if you need to do hex arithmetic a lot, get a hand-held hex calculator.

Finding binary numbers.

The row titled "Binary value of bit within hex number" lets you see what bits will be on or off for any hex representation. The value will be true for any column, since this represents the bit configuration, not the numeric value. For example, the hex number A will have the binary value 1010 because A (decimal 10) is formed with the 8 and 2 bits on and the 4 and 1 bits off. This lets us determine the binary number directly from a hex number or construct a hex number from a

Hex	Dec	Hex	Dec	Hex	Dec	Hex	Dec	Hex	Dec	Hex	Dec
0	0	0	0	0	0	0	0	0	0	0	0
1	1,048,576	1	65,536	1	4,096	1	256	1	16	1	1
2	2,097,152	2	131,072	2	8,192	2	512	2	32	2	2
3	3,145,728	3	196,608	3	12,288	3	768	3	48	3	3
4	4,194,304	4	262,144	4	16,384	4	1,024	4	64	4	4
5	5,242,880	5	327,680	5	20,480	5	1,280	5	80	5	5
6	6,291,456	6	393,216	6	24,576	6	1,536	6	96	6	6
7	7,340,032	7	458,752	7	28,672	7	1,792	7	112	7	7
8	8,388,608	8	524,288	8	32,768	8	2,048	8	128	8	8
9	9,437,184	9	589,824	9	36,864	9	2,304	9	144	9	9
A	10,485,760	A	655,360	A	40,960	A	2,560	A	160	A	10
B	11,534,336	B	720,896	B	45,056	B	2,816	B	176	B	11
C	12,582,912	C	786,432	C	49,152	C	3,072	C	192	C	12
D	13,631,488	D	851,968	D	53,248	D	3,328	D	208	D	13
E	14,680,064	E	917,504	E	57,344	E	3,584	E	224	E	14
F	15,728,640	F	983,040	F	61,440	F	3,840	F	240	F	15

Binary value of bit within hex number / Bit position within byte

0 1 2 3	4 5 6 7	0 1 2 3	4 5 6 7	0 1 2 3	4 5 6 7
8 4 2 1	8 4 2 1	8 4 2 1	8 4 2 1	8 4 2 1	8 4 2 1
one byte		one byte		one byte	

binary one. If you can remember the hex numbers from 0 to 15, you don't even need the table. For example,

To convert E7C to binary, you examine each hex number and break it down into the appropriate bit value combination of 8, 4, 2, and 1, using "1" for on and "0" for off.

E becomes 1110 because it requires the 8, 4, and 2 bits.
7 becomes 0111 because it requires the 4, 2, and 1 bits.
C becomes 1100 because it requires the 8 and 4 bits.
Putting the result end to end you get 1110 0111 1100.

To convert 10110110 from binary to hex, you first mark the number off in units of 4 bits from right to left.

The rightmost 4 bits, 0110, represent 6 (4 and 2 bits).
The next 4 bits, 1011, represent B (8, 2 and 1 bits).
Our hex number, then, is B6.

Converting from hexadecimal to decimal.

To convert a number from hexadecimal to decimal, take the decimal value from each column that corresponds to your hex value and add the decimal values together. For example, to convert 05FA to a decimal value:

A in the rightmost column has the decimal value of	10
F in the next column has the decimal value of	240
5 in the next column has the decimal value of	1,280
TOTAL:	1,530

Converting from decimal to hexadecimal

Similarly, to convert a decimal number to hexadecimal, locate the largest decimal number on the chart that is not greater than your decimal number. Subtract it from your decimal number and mark its hex value. Repeat the above until done, finding the largest number on the chart that is less than the remainder, marking its hex value. For example, to convert the decimal number 1,100 to a hex value:

> 1,024 in the third column from right is nearest to 1,100. The hex value from that column is 4. The 4 will then be the hex number that occupies the third position from the right, since it came from that column. Our hex value so far is 4xx.
>
> With a remainder of 76 (1,100 – 1,024), our next decimal number found is 64 in the second column. Using its hex value (4 again) our hex value so far is 44x.
>
> Our final remainder is 12. Taking the hex value C from the rightmost column our final hex number is 44C.

7.6. EBCDIC COLLATING SEQUENCE

This is not a complete EBCDIC chart. The focus is on alpha and numeric.

dec	hex	char	dec	hex	char	dec	hex	char
0	00		125	7D	'	196	C4	D
			126	7E	=	197	C5	E
			127	7F	"	198	C6	F
63	3F		128	80	**	199	C7	G
64	40	SPACE	129	81	A	200	C8	H
65	41		130	82	b	201	C9	I
			131	83	c	202	CA	
			132	84	d			
			133	85	e			
73	49		134	86	f	208	D0	
74	4A	¢	135	87	g	209	D1	J
75	4B	.	136	88	h	210	D2	K
76	4C	<	137	89	i	211	D3	L
77	4D	(	138	8A		212	D4	M
78	4E	+				213	D5	N
79	4F	|				214	D6	O
80	50	&	144	90		215	D7	P
81	51		145	91	j	216	D8	Q
			146	92	k	217	D9	R
			147	93	l	218	DA	
89	59		148	94	m			
90	5A	!	149	95	n			
91	5B	$	150	96	o	225	E1	
92	5C	*	151	97	p	226	E2	S
93	5D	)	152	98	q	227	E3	T
94	5E	:	153	99	r	228	E4	U
95	5F	¬	154	9A		229	E5	V
96	60	-				230	E6	W
97	61	/				231	E7	X
98	62		161	A1		232	E8	Y
			162	A2	s	233	E9	Z
			163	A3	t	234	EA	
106	6A		164	A4	u			
107	6B	,	165	A5	v			
108	6C	%	166	A6	w	239	EF	
109	6D	_	167	A7	x	240	F0	0
110	6E	>	168	A8	y	241	F1	1
111	6F	?	169	A9	z	242	F2	2
112	70		170	AA		243	F3	3
						244	F4	4
						245	F5	5
121	79		192	C0		246	F6	6
122	7A	:	193	C1	A	247	F7	7
123	7B	#	194	C2	B	248	F8	8
124	7C	@	195	C3	C	249	F9	9
						250	FA	
						255	FF	

7.7. COMMON ABEND CODES AND MESSAGES

COBOL run-time module ABENDs.

When an ABEND occurs from the COBOL II run-time modules, there will be a message with the prefix IGZ associated with it. See *COBOL II Application Programing Debugging Manual* (Chapter 9) for an explanation of the error. If the run unit includes any OS/VS COBOL modules, the associated run-time error message will have the prefix IKF. ABEND codes from COBOL II will range from 1000 to 1999.

Common application ABENDs.

0C1 Often due to error in OPEN or attempted READ before OPEN. CALLs to nonexisting subprograms may also cause this.

0C4 Usually caused by subscript errors in COBOL. The SSRANGE option will identify this error. Other possibilities include incorrect specification of passed parameters in a CALLing/CALLed structure (e.g., one module passes one parameter and the CALLed module attempts to access two parameters. Other possibilities associated with the LINKAGE SECTION include mishandling of PARMs and failure to SET addresses with POINTER items, where appropriate.

0C7 Bad data in arithmetic operation. The OFFSET or LIST compile option can assist in identifying the offending COBOL statement. Usually caused when spaces are allowed to be in a numeric field.

0C9 or 0CB Usually caused by a divide by zero.

x37 Normally caused by data storage specifications. It may be too little DASD for an output file or incorrect JCL for a tape file.

1037 CICS transaction "fell through" the last statement in the program, causing an implicit EXIT PROGRAM statement to be executed.

Messages from other system components.

When an error occurs within MVS, an MVS component will usually issue a message. The prefix can be helpful in locating where the issued message is documented. Common prefixes are

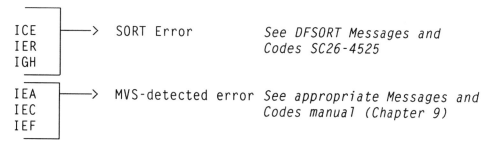

```
ICE  ┌──> SORT Error      See DFSORT Messages and
IER  │                    Codes SC26-4525
IGH  │

IEA  ┌──> MVS-detected error  See appropriate Messages and
IEC  │                        Codes manual (Chapter 9)
IEF  │
```

7.8. JCL SUMMARY

The information in this section is summary information. The intent was to combine various pieces of JCL information that are sometimes forgotten. For specific JCL statements and their options, see the appropriate JCL manual (Chapter 9).

7.8.1. Summary of Syntax and Major Statements

This depicts the basic statements of JCL and their description.

```
1 3        12       16    <── thru ──>      71
//NAME     OPCODE   OPERANDS
```

JOB statement Identifies the set of run units as one complete unit of work and identifies appropriate accounting information.

```
//jobname JOB      operands.....     comments...
```

EXEC statement Identifies the run unit that is to have control of the cpu. EXEC statements run in the order of appearance.

```
//stepname EXEC     operands....     comments...
```

DD statement Identifies a dataset that may be accessed by the run unit identified in the preceding EXEC statement.

```
//ddname DD        operands...     comments...
```

Comment statement Provides comments within the JCL.

```
//*        comments.........
```

Null statement Identifies the end of the JOB.

```
//
```

Delimiter statement Identifies the end of an in-stream dataset (optional).

```
/*
```

7.8.2. Summary of JCL Coding Syntax:

All JCL statements must have slash marks in columns 1 and 2. All entries must be between columns 1 and 71. Each separate component of a JCL statement must be separated by at least one blank. Components are name, opcode, and operands, as shown above. No space must appear between operands, except where a continuation is done to a following line. Comments may appear after the rightmost operand by placing at least one space before coding the comment. Operands may be continued to the next line by coding a comma at any legitimate point within the operand and continuing on the next line between columns 4 and 16. For example,

```
//PAY103   JOB       123456,'MONTHLY PAYROLL' monthly payroll
//PAYPRINT EXEC     PGM=PAYROLL,REGION=256K,
//   PARM='HOURLY'
//PAYMAST  DD  DSN=PAYROLL.MASTER.WEEKLY,DISP=(,KEEP),
//             UNIT=TAPE,DCB=BLKSIZE=13000
//
```

7.8.3. Coding Guidelines for JCL Positional and Keyword Parameters

In this summary, *operand* and *parameter* have the same meaning, since both are frequently used. Multiple rules are normally in effect concurrently.

COMMON RULES

- Positional operands precede keyword operands.
- Single quotes are needed if nonstandard characters are used.

- An operand is not required if the default is acceptable.
- Operands are separated by commas.
- Subparameters are also separated by commas.
- Parentheses are needed if any commas are used to separate subparameters.

POSITIONAL

- It is denoted by position, not by content.
- The absence of a subparameter requires a comma if more subparameters to the right are to be coded.

KEYWORD

- It begins with "keyword=".
- It may contain positional and keyword subparameters.
- Keyword parameters and keyword subparameters may be coded in any sequence.

Examples:

```
//JOBA    JOB    123456
```
one positional parameter

```
//JOBA    JOB    (123456,4321),SMITH
```
two positional parameters, the first having further subparameters

```
//JOBA    JOB    (123456,'RM-A',,,9999),'SALLY SMITH'
```
two positional parameters, the 1st having several internal subparameters and the 2nd using quotes because of an imbedded space

```
LABEL=1
```
one positional subparameter

```
LABEL=(,SL)
```
second positional subparameter

```
LABEL=EXPDT=91365
```
no positional parameters

```
LABEL=(EXPDT=91365)
```
as above (parentheses cause no harm when they contain a complete parameter list)

`LABEL=(2,SUL,RETPD=35)`	two positional subparameters and a single keyword subparameter
`SPACE=(TRK,10)`	two subparameters
`SPACE=(TRK,(8,2))`	two subparameters, one of which has further subparameters
`SPACE=(TRK,(8,,20))`	two subparameters, one of which uses first and third positional subparameters
`SPACE=(TRK,(8,2),,CONTIG)`	three positional parameters within a keyword parameter; the second has further subparameters, the third is not coded, and the fourth is CONTIG.

7.8.4. JCL DD Parameters for Sequential Datasets:

Many programmers try to remember the many parameters that need to be on DD statements and, as a result, often code them when they aren't necessary. The table below is an attempt to put some order to this.

			Non-JCL means to provide		
JCL	NEED	SL	CATALOG	JES	COBOL FD
UNIT	REQUIRED		X	X	
DISP	REQUIRED*			X	
VOL	REQUIRED***		X	X	
SPACE	DASD ONLY	X		X	
DSN	OPTIONAL**			X	
DCB	REQUIRED	X			optional

*Default is NEW,DELETE.

**Required for preexisting datasets.

***Your shop probably has some unit types defined (e.g., SYSDA) that do not require the VOL parameter.

In the table, the left column depicts the JCL parameter to provide a DD variable. The four columns on the right depict other means by which this information is provided. Where an "X" appears, the associated parameter may be omitted. If your shop uses system managed storage, the table may be incorrect. A definition or clarification for each of the terms in the table follows.

> SL means Standard Label (the dataset exists prior to the run unit).
> CATALOG means Catalogued dataset (The dataset exists prior to the run unit and is catalogued in either the system catalog or the temporary job catalog, i.e., DISP was PASS.)
> JES means Job Entry Subsystem (for SYSOUT and DD * datasets).
> COBOL FD means COBOL program, limited to RECFM, LRECL and BLKSIZE subparameters.

UNIT. Required, but is not needed if the dataset is catalogued or the dataset is processed via JES (either SYSOUT or DD *).

DISP. Unless a JES dataset, you must code it anytime you do not want the default.

VOL. Not needed for catalogued or JES datasets or those where your installation has predefined special UNIT types.

SPACE. For DASD datasets only, this need not be coded if the dataset existed prior to the current step or is a JES dataset.

DSN. This is required for access to any dataset created before this step.

DCB. Unless the dataset existed before this step or the COBOL program has information in the FD, this must be coded.

Catalogued Dataset:

```
DSN=SYS1.PROCLIB,DISP=SHR
```

Sysout (JES) Dataset:

```
SYSOUT=A,DCB=BLKSIZE=137
```

Uncatalogued Dataset:

```
DSN=XXX,DISP=OLD,UNIT=TAPE,
VOL=SER=123456
```

Temporary New Dataset: (with DCB in program)

```
UNIT=SYSDA,SPACE=(TRK,10)
```

7.8.5. JCL JOB and STEP Conflicts

Several JCL parameters appear on both the JOB and the EXEC statements. While the function of the variables is the same, the range varies. For example, the table shows that a REGION on a JOB statement sets the limit for all steps in the job, whereas REGION on an EXEC statement affects only that step, up to the limit of the JOB statement (i.e, if a JOB statement has REGION=150K and an EXEC statement has REGION=2000K, the step will be allocated only 150K of memory).

Parameter	JOB	STEP
REGION	Limit	Step
TIME	Entire job	Step
COND	flushes rest of job	controls one step
(JOB/STEP)LIB	If no STEPLIB	If STEPLIB

Note that JOBLIB and STEPLIB are mutually exclusive. MVS will check one but not both.

7.8.6. JCL for Tape Files

Many of us code JCL for tape files so seldom that we forget that additional parameters are sometimes needed. For the full syntax, see the appropriate JCL manual in Chapter 9.

LABEL= Is sometimes required because you might not have standard labels or you are processing other than the first file on the tape. Retention dates or expiration dates are coded here as well.

UNIT=AFF= This parameter allows tape files to share the physical drive of another file and can be beneficial when one file is processed prior to another file or several tape files are concatenated together.

VOL= Since tape files may have many volume serial numbers, this is sometimes needed to identify them. Also, if the file will have more than five reels, this must be coded.

DCB=DEN= Different tape drives create tapes with different densities. While this information is recorded on SL files, it would be needed to override defaults for a drive when file is opened for OUTPUT.

17 RIGHTMOST CHARS IN DSN I include this as a reminder that tape labels only record the rightmost 17 characters of a dataset label. Be sure not to focus unique naming standards on the leftmost characters, leaving some datasets with the same rightmost characters.

7.8.7. JCL: Using PROCs

Some programmers have trouble with PROCs, even though they do fine when coding JCL from scratch. There are a few differences in how the JCL is constructed.

PROC Keywords.

To assign a value to a keyword on a PROC statement, code

```
KEYWORD=value
```

To nullify a default value on a keyword on a PROC statement, code

```
KEYWORD=
```

For example, for a compile PROC set up this way with a default of LIST:

```
//COB2UC  PROC  OPTION=LIST
//COB2    EXEC  PGM=IGYCRCTL,PARM=&OPTION
           .
           .
```

you could code

```
//  EXEC COB2UC,OPTION=OFFSET
```

to replace the default value with a new value or you could code

```
//  EXEC COB2UC,OPTION=
```

to remove the PROC default (in this example, you would then get the installation default for that option).

Coding EXEC parameters.

When coding standard EXEC statement parameters (e.g., PARM, RE-GION), the overrides must be done in the sequence of the steps within the PROC. For a PROC with two steps, named COB2 and LKED, the following example would be appropriate, coding all parameters for COB2 before coding them for LKED:

```
//      EXEC COB2UC,PARM.COB2=SOURCE,REGION.COB2=2000K,
//          PARM.LKED=RENT
```

If stepname is not coded with the parameter, here is how each of the following EXEC parameters affects the steps in the PROC:

PARM	First step only, PARMs (if any) on remaining steps in PROC are nullified
TIME	All steps in PROC (not each step)
REGION	Each step
COND	Each Step

DD overrides.

Overrides to DD statements within a PROC are done in their order of physical appearance within each step. You need only code the parameter to be replaced, not the entire DD statement. Exception: For the DCB parameter, you need only code the desired subparameter, preceded by DCB=.

If overrides are not in the proper sequence, you do not get a JCL error at the time the job is submitted. In fact, you will receive no error messages if the job is capable of executing with the original values of the DD statement as they appear within the PROC. (No, this is not magic. Since DD statements are merged in the order of physical appearance, you end up with two allocations in the step. The OPEN process allocates the first one—the one from the PROC.)

7.9. ACRONYMS

This list represents many of the acronyms that a mainframe MVS programmer sees. Some are used in this book, some are not.

ABEND	ABnormal END
ALC	Assembler Language Code
AMS	Access Method Services
ANSI	American National Standards Institute
BAL	see ALC.
BLL	Base Locator for Linkage Section
CICS	Customer Information Control System

CMS	Conversational Monitor System
COBOL	COmmon Business Oriented Language
DASD	Direct Access Storage Device
DBCS	Double Byte Character Set
DB2	Database 2
DL/1	Data Language/One (See IMS/VS.)
DFSORT	Data Facility Sort
EBCDIC	Extended Binary Coded Decimal Interchange Code
HDAM	Hierarchical Direct Access Method for IMS
HIDAM	Hierarchical Indexed Direct Access Method for IMS.
IMS	See IMS/VS.
IMS/VS	Information Management System/Virtual Storage
ISPF	Interactive Structured Programming Facility
JCL	Job Control Language
JES	Job Entry Subsystem
MVS/SP	Multiple Virtual Storage/System Product
MVS/XA	Multiple Virtual Storage/Extended Architecture
MVS/ESA	Multiple Virtual Storage/Enterprise Systems Architecture
PDS	Partitioned Dataset
PL/1	Programming Language/One
QSAM	Queued Sequential Access Method
RACF	Resource Access Control Facility
SAA	Systems Application Architecture
SQL	Structured Query Language
TSO	Time Sharing Option
TGT	Task Global Table
VSAM	Virtual Storage Access Method
VTAM	Virtual Telecommunications Access Method

7.10. REPORT WRITER STRUCTURE

Report Writer is not covered in this book. This is a summary of the basic structure used. See Chapter 9 for the IBM reference manual.

Structure of DD to FD to RD.

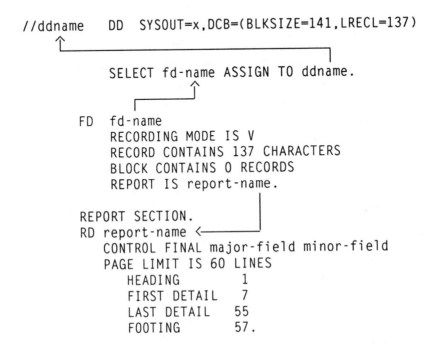

```
//ddname    DD  SYSOUT=x,DCB=(BLKSIZE=141,LRECL=137)


              SELECT fd-name ASSIGN TO ddname.


        FD   fd-name
             RECORDING MODE IS V
             RECORD CONTAINS 137 CHARACTERS
             BLOCK CONTAINS 0 RECORDS
             REPORT IS report-name.

        REPORT SECTION.
        RD report-name
             CONTROL FINAL major-field minor-field
             PAGE LIMIT IS 60 LINES
                 HEADING       1
                 FIRST DETAIL  7
                 LAST DETAIL   55
                 FOOTING       57.
```

Structure of data record clauses.

```
   01  RH       report heading
          PH         page heading
            CH          control heading
              DE           detail line(s)
            CF          control footing
          PF         page footing
        RF       report footing
```

Structure of procedural statements.

```
   OPEN                done once
       INITIATE        done once
            GENERATE   each detail
       TERMINATE       done once
   CLOSE               done once
```

7.11. COMPILER LIMITS AND MACHINE CAPACITIES

Compiler limits.

There are many limits on the compiler, most of which do not interest us. (Do you really care that you can have 999,999 source statements in a program? I hope not and I sure wouldn't want to have maintenance responsibility for it.) Here are some of the limits that are probably of more use to you in designing applications

Block size of copy library:

COBOL II	OS/VS COBOL
32,767	16,000

If your shop uses COPY statements extensively, you should consider reblocking your COPY library to reduce I/O.

WORKING-STORAGE total bytes:

COBOL II	OS/VS COBOL
127M	1M

With 127 megabytes available, this can change the way you design applications. In some cases, you may find an entire database might fit within WORKING-STORAGE for a batch application, allowing high performance direct retrieval.

	COBOL II	OS/VS COBOL
Number of data-names	16M	1M
Number of OCCURS levels	N/A	3
OCCURS value	16M	32K

The above three expansions open opportunities to build large multi-dimension tables for complex applications that would have been impossible with OS/VS COBOL.

LINKAGE SECTION total bytes

COBOL II	OS/VS COBOL
127M	1M

Combined with other options above, this allows sharing of large data areas with other programs.

Machine capacities.

When doing arithmetic, the compiler is aware of the maximum value that can be manipulated in the machine. When the compiler determines that there is the possibility for an intermediate or final value to exceed machine capacity, it invokes a CALL to a COBOL II run-time module to do the arithmetic operation procedurally. This keeps the logic intact and ensures correct numbers, but it could have a major impact on applications with many computations. Naturally, there are situations in which you can't prevent it, but an awareness of machine limitations may help you determine when it may be more appropriate to do several smaller calculations instead of one large one.

For packed-decimal, the largest number is 16 bytes, which translates into 31 decimal digits. In multiplication and division, the SUM of the two data fields (multiplicand and multiplier, dividend and divisor) cannot exceed 16 bytes, including the sign.

For binary numbers, the largest value for a half-word field is 32,767 and the largest number for a full-word field is 2,147,483,647. (Whether your program can contain those values is dependent on what TRUNC option you specified.)

From the above information you can see that packed-decimal is preferable anytime you are manipulating large numbers. (Yes, the computer can also do floating-point arithmetic, but you rarely encounter the need in business applications.) In fairness to binary arithmetic, its instruction set is faster than the packed-decimal instruction set, but to benefit from it you need to use TRUNC(OPT).

EXAMPLES of COBOL programs

This chapter is unique in this book. It is not a reference chapter and includes no new information. Instead, it contains complete source programs to demonstrate the guidelines presented in chapters 5 and 6 ("Program Design" and "Program Coding"). Some are COBOL II and some work with both COBOL II and OS/VS COBOL. The intent of this chapter is not to dazzle you with code, but to demonstrate some of the benefits of structure and decomposition, as well as a few of the new components of COBOL II. The focus is on structure and ways to preserve compatibility, not on using some COBOL II features. For examples of specific COBOL II statements, please refer to previous chapters.

Importance of style and simplicity.

If you've been writing "GO TO less" code for years, you won't find anything new here. However, if you are accustomed to coding all 4 divisions and think GO TO is a fact of life, I encourage you to walk through each example. All the programs demonstrate a bit of programmer style. I believe it is important to allow some degree of freedom for the programmer to code less-than-perfect programs.

The style of some of these programs conflicts with several major structured techniques, primarily in the initialization process. Some books suggest that the first record(s) to be processed should be read immediately after OPEN. I don't follow that belief. After years of teaching new programmers (and reteaching old programmers), I have found that many logic problems occur because of that practice. I have found programs to be simpler to code and to debug if you

1. Code one-time housekeeping processes in an initialization routine.
2. Code all repeated processes under the umbrella of a DO-WHILE (PER-FORM UNTIL) statement
3. Code one-time termination processes in a termination routine.

I included the IMS example because over the years I have heard complaints from programmers that it is impossible to use structured code with such a complex data structure. On the contrary, my approach is to blend the data structure with the program structure. Since IMS and structured programming both follow a hierarchical format, the two components can blend well.

Comments and small paragraphs.

I asked several programmers for comments prior to including these programs in the book. Two frequent comments were "Why are there so many comments in the code?" and "Why are some paragraphs so small?" Since you may have the same questions, let me give my response.

I include comments in code whenever I believe a rookie programmer may not understand the structure or the logic. I wanted to emphasize to you, the reader, where I was and was not, so you could follow my approach to structure. Also, while I often see comments in programs that explain a process, I have never seen comments that explain the structure—and this is exactly what most programmers need. Knowing what to do is usually straightforward. Knowing where in the logic flow to do it is sometimes impossible.

I compare programming to architecture. As an industry, we fail in teaching new programmers if we encourage them to use shortcuts for small classroom programs, hoping they will do differently on large, real systems. Consider architects: they follow certain disciplines whether they are building a one-story house or a 30-story building. A small building is a big building in miniature. We should do the same for programming: use specific disciplines, regardless of program size. Decomposition is decomposition is decomposition. Novice programmers who are taught to combine many small functions in one paragraph become senior programmers who write indecipherable paragraphs that run several pages long.

Knowing that somewhere, for some reason, someone will want to eliminate small paragraphs, I redid example 8.1 using COBOL II features, allowing the entire logic of the SORT OUTPUT PROCEDURE to be accomplished in a single paragraph. I don't recommend this type of programming, but the example does display how far COBOL has come.

Aren't the examples too simple?

These programs are indeed, simple. I've been asked on occasion to use more complex programs to demonstrate ideas in my programming classes. Unfortunately, 5,000-line programs only confuse students and drown them in the application's logic. These simple structures demonstrate techniques. Where the structure is simple, a program can be easily expanded and retain the simple structure. Also, when a program gets too big to grasp quickly, I break it into several programs. Life's too short to spend it wading through monster programs just to prove you can do it.

8.1. SORT EXAMPLE WITH COBOL II

If you're used to seeing SORT programs with lots of noise, such as SECTION headers, PERFORM THRUs, GO TOs, and EXIT statements, you'll find this to be quite different. The techniques in this program are covered in the section on SORT techniques in both Chapter 5 and Chapter 6. If the use of SORT-RETURN or the comments about IGZSRTCD leave you confused, I suggest you review those sections. This program also appears in other examples.

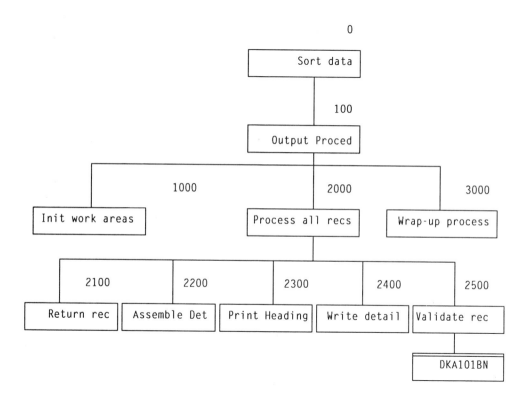

```
       TITLE 'SORT Program with external CALL'
       IDENTIFICATION DIVISION.

       PROGRAM-ID.
          DKA10200.

      *AUTHOR.
      *    David S. Kirk.
      *DATE-WRITTEN.
      *    April, 1991.
```

```
************************************************************
*      SORT Example                                       *
*                                                         *
*  The imbedded comments are tutorial and are not         *
*  meant to indicate you should explain the basics        *
*  of programs you write in this fashion, although        *
*  use of comments liberally is encouraged.               *
*                                                         *
*  There are several compromises in this example,         *
*  as the programmer's style is always a component.       *
*                                                         *
************************************************************


    ENVIRONMENT DIVISION.

    INPUT-OUTPUT SECTION.

    FILE-CONTROL.

        SELECT FD1-PAYROLL-FILE
            ASSIGN TO PAY102.

        SELECT FD2-PRINT-FILE
            ASSIGN TO REPT102.

        SELECT SD3-SORT-FILE
            ASSIGN TO SORTWORK.

    DATA DIVISION.

    FILE SECTION.

    FD  FD1-PAYROLL-FILE
        RECORD CONTAINS 74 CHARACTERS
        BLOCK CONTAINS 0 RECORDS
        RECORDING MODE IS F.

    01  FD1-PAYROLL-REC                     PIC X(74).

    FD  FD2-PRINT-FILE
        RECORD CONTAINS 132 CHARACTERS
        BLOCK CONTAINS 0 RECORDS
        RECORDING MODE IS F.
```

```
*  --------------------------------------------
* Notice that the record specifies 132 positions.
* Actually, the LRECL on JCL will be 133 if the compile
* option ADV is used. This keeps the program "machine
* independent," allowing COBOL to insert the ASA control
* character external to the program logic. If compile option
* NOADV were specified, the programmer would need to leave
* the first byte in the record untouched by the program logic.
*  --------------------------------------------
 01   FD2-PRINT-REC                        PIC X(132).
 SD   SD3-SORT-FILE
        RECORD CONTAINS 74 CHARACTERS.

 01   SD1-SORT-REC.
       05   SD3-EMP-NO-IN                   PIC X(5).
       05   SD3-EMP-NAME-IN                 PIC X(20).
       05   SD3-TERRITORY-NO-IN             PIC X(2).
       05   SD3-OFFICE-NO-IN                PIC X(2).
       05   SD3-JOB-CODE-IN                 PIC X(2).
       05                                   PIC X(43).

 WORKING-STORAGE SECTION.

    *  ----------------------------------
    * All counters and switches are combined in the following
    * 01 level.  This simplifies maintenance and saves memory use.
    *  ----------------------------------
 01   WS1-WORK-FIELDS.
       05   WS1-EOF-SW                  PIC X.
              88 ALL-DONE                  VALUE 'Y'.
              88 NOT-EOF                   VALUE 'N'.
       05   WS1-DATE.
              10   WS1-YY                PIC XX.
              10   WS1-MM                PIC 99.
              10   WS1-DD                PIC XX.
       05   WS1-ERROR-MSG               PIC X(16).
              88   WS4-JOBCODE-ERROR        VALUE 'INVALID JOB CODE'.
              88   WS4-GOOD-JOBCODE         VALUE SPACES.
       05   WS1-INCOUNT                 PIC S9(3)   COMP-3.
       05   WS1-LINE-SPACE              PIC S9(3)   COMP-3.
       05   WS1-LINECOUNT               PIC S9(3)   COMP-3.
       05   WS1-PAGENUM                 PIC S9(3)   COMP-3.
       05   WS1-PAGESIZE                PIC S9(3)   COMP-3
                                           VALUE +50.
```

```
01   WS2-HEADING-LINE1.
     05                              PIC X(40) VALUE SPACES.
     05                              PIC X(17)
                                     VALUE 'EMPLOYEE BENEFITS'.
     05                              PIC X(3)  VALUE SPACES.
     05   WS2-DATE-OUT.
          10   WS2-MM-OUT            PIC Z9.
          10                         PIC X VALUE '/'.
          10   WS2-DD-OUT            PIC XX.
          10                         PIC X VALUE '/'.
          10   WS2-YY-OUT            PIC XX.
     05                              PIC X(5) VALUE SPACES.
     05                              PIC X(5) VALUE 'PAGE '.
     05   WS2-PAGENUM                PIC ZZ9.

01   WS2-HEADING-LINE2.
     05                              PIC X(10) VALUE SPACES.
     05                              PIC X(3)  VALUE 'JOB'.
     05                              PIC X(10) VALUE SPACES.
     05                              PIC X(8)  VALUE 'EMPLOYEE'.
     05                              PIC X(5)  VALUE SPACES.
     05                              PIC X(8)  VALUE 'EMPLOYEE'.
     05                              PIC X(19) VALUE SPACES.
     05                              PIC X(4)  VALUE 'SICK'.
     05                              PIC X(5)  VALUE SPACES.
     05                              PIC X(8)  VALUE 'VACATION'.

01   WS3-HEADING-LINE3.
     05                              PIC X(5)  VALUE SPACES.
     05                              PIC X(14)
                                       VALUE 'CLASSIFICATION'.
     05                              PIC X(7)  VALUE SPACES.
     05                              PIC X(9)  VALUE 'NO. '.
     05                              PIC X(3)  VALUE SPACES.
     05                              PIC X(4)  VALUE 'NAME'.
     05                              PIC X(21) VALUE SPACES.
     05                              PIC X(4)  VALUE 'DAYS'.
     05                              PIC X(7)  VALUE SPACES.
     05                              PIC X(4)  VALUE 'DAYS'.

01   WS4-DETAIL.
     05                              PIC X(10) VALUE SPACES.
     05   WS4-JOB-CODE-OUT           PIC X(2).
     05                              PIC X(12) VALUE SPACES.
     05   WS4-EMP-NO-OUT             PIC X(5).
     05                              PIC X(9)  VALUE SPACES.
```

```
     05   WS4-EMP-NAME-OUT                PIC X(20).
     05                                   PIC X(6)  VALUE SPACES.
     05   WS4-SICK-DAYS-OUT               PIC Z9.
     05                                   PIC X(9) VALUE SPACES.
     05   WS4-VACA-DAYS-OUT               PIC Z9.
     05                                   PIC X(5) VALUE SPACES.
     05   WS4-ERROR-MSG-OUT               PIC X(16).

 01  WS5-DATA-PASSED.
     05   WS5-JOB-CODE                    PIC XX.
     05   WS5-SICK-DAYS                   PIC 9(2).
     05   WS5-VACA-DAYS                   PIC 9(2).
     05   WS5-ERROR-SWITCH                PIC X     VALUE 'N'.


 PROCEDURE DIVISION.
*  -------------
* This paragraph is the highest level.
* While there is no INPUT PROCEDURE, this program
* can still select which records to sort and can even have
* the data records reformatted prior to the sort. This can
* be accomplished by inserting an IGZSRTCD DD (or SORTCNTL
* DD) at run time that contains valid DFSORT statements.
* Example:
*   //IGZSRTCD DD  *
*       OMIT   COND=(26,2,CH,EQ,C'25')
*       INREC  FIELDS=(1,5,6,20,26,2,28,2,47,2)
*  -------------
 000-SORT.
     SORT SD3-SORT-FILE
                 ASCENDING   SD3-TERRITORY-NO-IN
                             SD3-OFFICE-NO-IN
                             SD3-EMP-NAME-IN
              USING FD1-PAYROLL-FILE
              OUTPUT PROCEDURE 100-MAIN-MODULE
     IF SORT-RETURN EQUAL ZERO
        MOVE ZERO TO RETURN-CODE
        STOP RUN
     ELSE
        DISPLAY 'SORT ERROR IN DKA10200' UPON CONSOLE
        MOVE 16 TO RETURN-CODE
        STOP RUN.
```

```
* ---------------------------------------
* The following paragraph is the SORT OUTPUT PROCEDURE.
* ---------------------------------------
  100-MAIN-MODULE.
      PERFORM 1000-INITIALIZE
      PERFORM 2000-PROCESS-ROUTINE UNTIL ALL-DONE
      PERFORM 3000-WRAPUP.


* --------------
* This paragraph does initialization. It is a compromise
* since it does everything in one paragraph. In a larger
* program, it should PERFORM a separate paragraph to OPEN
* files and one to initialize variables.
* The initialization part of a program should do nothing that
* routinely repeats, such as READing files or WRITEing
* headings.
* --------------
  1000-INITIALIZE.
      OPEN OUTPUT FD2-PRINT-FILE
      MOVE ZEROS TO WS1-DATE
                    WS1-INCOUNT
                    WS1-PAGENUM
      MOVE 999 TO WS1-LINECOUNT
      ACCEPT WS1-DATE FROM DATE
      MOVE WS1-YY TO WS2-YY-OUT
      MOVE WS1-MM TO WS2-MM-OUT
      MOVE WS1-DD TO WS2-DD-OUT.


* --------------
* This paragraph controls processing of each detail record.
* Because it follows the same path each time, it is simpler
* to locate problems in page headings or other conditional
* processes. The END-IF is used instead of a period because
*    it is more visible and less prone to problems and
*    it eliminates need to recode IF NOT ALL-DONE.
* --------------
  2000-PROCESS-ROUTINE.
      PERFORM 2100-RETURN-PAYROLL
      IF NOT ALL-DONE
          IF WS1-LINECOUNT GREATER THAN WS1-PAGESIZE
              PERFORM 2300-PRINT-HEADING
          END-IF
          PERFORM 2500-VALIDATE-JOB-CODE
          PERFORM 2200-ASSEMBLE-DETAIL
          PERFORM 2400-WRITE-DETAIL.
```

```
*  --------------
* This paragraph does the only RETURN of the input file.
* The END-RETURN statement isn't needed here, but minimizes
* problems if additional code is added later.
*  --------------
  2100-RETURN-PAYROLL.
      RETURN SD3-SORT-FILE
          AT END
              MOVE 'Y' TO WS1-EOF-SW
          NOT AT END
              ADD 1 TO WS1-INCOUNT
      END-RETURN.


*  --------------
* Because this paragraph does all of the assembly of the
* detail line, adding or changing fields is an easier
* process.
*  --------------
  2200-ASSEMBLE-DETAIL.
      MOVE WS5-JOB-CODE TO WS4-JOB-CODE-OUT
      MOVE SD3-EMP-NO-IN TO WS4-EMP-NO-OUT
      MOVE SD3-EMP-NAME-IN TO WS4-EMP-NAME-OUT
      MOVE WS5-SICK-DAYS TO WS4-SICK-DAYS-OUT
      MOVE WS5-VACA-DAYS TO WS4-VACA-DAYS-OUT
      MOVE WS1-ERROR-MSG TO WS4-ERROR-MSG-OUT
      MOVE WS4-DETAIL TO FD2-PRINT-REC.


*  --------------
* This paragraph prints all page headings, making it
* easy to keep track of page numbers or heading alignment.
* This is a compromise for readibility, as it does not
* PERFORM a single WRITE paragraph but repeats the WRITE
* statement for each heading line. In this case,
* the repeated statements make the ADVANCING options
* easier to see.
*  --------------
  2300-PRINT-HEADING.
      ADD 1 TO WS1-PAGENUM
      MOVE WS1-PAGENUM TO WS2-PAGENUM
      WRITE FD2-PRINT-REC FROM WS2-HEADING-LINE1
        AFTER ADVANCING PAGE
      WRITE FD2-PRINT-REC FROM WS2-HEADING-LINE2
        AFTER ADVANCING 3 LINES
      WRITE FD2-PRINT-REC FROM WS3-HEADING-LINE3
      MOVE 2 TO WS1-LINE-SPACE
      MOVE ZEROS TO WS1-LINECOUNT.
```

```
*  --------------
*  This paragraph prints all output except page headings.
*  --------------
   2400-WRITE-DETAIL.
       WRITE FD2-PRINT-REC AFTER ADVANCING WS1-LINE-SPACE
       MOVE 1 TO WS1-LINE-SPACE
       ADD 1 TO WS1-LINECOUNT.


*  --------------
*  This paragraph calls subroutine to validate job code
*  and set benefit data. Notice that the paragraph
*  handles not only the CALL, but does the actions
*  that it dictates. If error handling were extensive
*  it would be appropriate to PERFORM that portion in
*  a separate paragraph.
*  --------------
   2500-VALIDATE-JOB-CODE.
       MOVE SD3-JOB-CODE-IN TO WS5-JOB-CODE
       CALL 'DKA101BN' USING WS5-DATA-PASSED
       IF WS5-ERROR-SWITCH EQUAL 'Y'
           SET WS4-JOBCODE-ERROR TO TRUE
       ELSE
           SET WS4-GOOD-JOBCODE TO TRUE
       END-IF.


*  --------------
*  This paragraph wraps up processing. If there were final
*  totals or similar end-of-job processing, those would be
*  PERFORMed from here as separate paragraphs.
*  --------------
   3000-WRAPUP.
       CLOSE FD2-PRINT-FILE.
   END PROGRAM DKA10200.
```

8.2. THE SORT EXAMPLE WITH OUTPUT PROCEDURE AS ONE PARAGRAPH

This is the previous program, redone by decomposing within a single structure instead of decomposing to subordinate paragraphs. As I mentioned elsewhere, I don't recommend this approach to programming because it is difficult to maintain. It is included to emphasize the power of COBOL II in support of structured programming. Any senior level programmer can read this, but the goal of program design is to develop code that a less skilled programmer can maintain. Managers judge code by the ease of maintenance, not by the purity of style it may exhibit.

I omitted all except the PROCEDURE DIVISION from this listing. The tight structure was accomplished by Scope Terminators (END-IF, END-RETURN, and END-PERFORM), an inline PERFORM, and extensions to the RETURN statement. Periods are used only at the end of the two paragraphs.

```
PROCEDURE DIVISION.

000-SORT.
    SORT SD3-SORT-FILE
            ASCENDING   SD3-TERRITORY-NO-IN
                        SD3-OFFICE-NO-IN
                        SD3-EMP-NAME-IN
            USING FD1-PAYROLL-FILE
            OUTPUT PROCEDURE 100-MAIN-MODULE
    IF SORT-RETURN EQUAL ZERO
        MOVE ZERO TO RETURN-CODE
        STOP RUN
    ELSE
        DISPLAY 'SORT ERROR IN DKA10200' UPON CONSOLE
        MOVE 16 TO RETURN-CODE
        STOP RUN
    END-IF.


100-MAIN-MODULE.
* Initialization process
    OPEN OUTPUT FD2-PRINT-FILE
    MOVE ZEROS TO WS1-DATE
                  WS1-INCOUNT
                  WS1-PAGENUM
    MOVE 999 TO WS1-LINECOUNT
    ACCEPT WS1-DATE FROM DATEMOVE WS1-YY TO WS2-YY-OUT
    MOVE WS1-MM TO WS2-MM-OUT
    MOVE WS1-DD TO WS2-DD-OUT
* DO-WHILE loop
    PERFORM UNTIL ALL-DONE
        RETURN SD3-SORT-FILE
            AT END
                MOVE 'Y' TO WS1-EOF-SW
            NOT AT END
                ADD 1 TO WS1-INCOUNT
                IF WS1-LINECOUNT GREATER THAN WS1-PAGESIZE
* Page heading routine
                    ADD 1 TO WS1-PAGENUM
                    MOVE WS1-PAGENUM TO WS2-PAGENUM
                    WRITE FD2-PRINT-REC FROM WS2-HEADING-LINE1
                      AFTER ADVANCING PAGE
```

```
                    WRITE FD2-PRINT-REC FROM WS2-HEADING-LINE2
                      AFTER ADVANCING 3 LINES
                    WRITE FD2-PRINT-REC FROM WS3-HEADING-LINE3
                    MOVE 2 TO WS1-LINE-SPACE
                    MOVE ZEROS TO WS1-LINECOUNT
              END-IF
* Validate job code routine
              MOVE SD3-JOB-CODE-IN TO WS5-JOB-CODE
              CALL 'DKA101BN' USING WS5-DATA-PASSED
              IF WS5-ERROR-SWITCH EQUAL 'Y'
                  SET WS4-JOBCODE-ERROR TO TRUE
              ELSE
                  SET WS4-GOOD-JOBCODE TO TRUE
              END-IF
* Assemble detail line routine
              MOVE WS5-JOB-CODE TO WS4-JOB-CODE-OUT
              MOVE SD3-EMP-NO-IN TO WS4-EMP-NO-OUT
              MOVE SD3-EMP-NAME-IN TO WS4-EMP-NAME-OUT
              MOVE WS5-SICK-DAYS TO WS4-SICK-DAYS-OUT
              MOVE WS5-VACA-DAYS TO WS4-VACA-DAYS-OUT
              MOVE WS1-ERROR-MSG TO WS4-ERROR-MSG-OUT
              MOVE WS4-DETAIL TO FD2-PRINT-REC
* Write detail line routine
              WRITE FD2-PRINT-REC AFTER
                 ADVANCING WS1-LINE-SPACE
              MOVE 1 TO WS1-LINE-SPACE
              ADD 1 TO WS1-LINECOUNT
       END-RETURN
     END-PERFORM
* Termination routine
     CLOSE FD2-PRINT-FILE.
  END PROGRAM DKA10200.
```

8.3. CALLED SUBPROGRAM EXAMPLE WITH COBOL II

This program is CALLed by DKA10200, the previous program. Notice the missing ENVIRONMENT division and the use of EVALUATE and SET statements. In this example, the SET statement provides clearer documentation than using MOVE statements.

```
 IDENTIFICATION DIVISION.

 PROGRAM-ID.
     DKA101BN.
*AUTHOR.
*    David S. Kirk.

*DATE-WRITTEN.
*    April, 1991.


*  -------------------------------------------
* Validates job code and returns appropriate sick and
* vacation days allowed.
*  -------------------------------------------

 DATA DIVISION.

 LINKAGE SECTION.

 01   LS1-RECORD.
      05  LS1-JOB-CODE             PIC XX.
      05  LS1-SICK-VAC-DAYS        PIC XXXX.
          88 BEN01                     VALUE '1421'.
          88 BEN02                     VALUE '1014'.
          88 BEN03                     VALUE '2128'.
      05  LS1-ERROR-SW             PIC X.

 PROCEDURE DIVISION USING LS1-RECORD.

  100-MAIN-MODULE.
      MOVE 'N' TO LS1-ERROR-SW
      PERFORM 200-VALIDATE
      GOBACK.

  200-VALIDATE.
      EVALUATE LS1-JOB-CODE
          WHEN '01'    SET BEN01 TO TRUE
          WHEN '02'    SET BEN02 TO TRUE
          WHEN '03'    SET BEN03 TO TRUE
          WHEN OTHER   MOVE '0000' TO LS1-SICK-VAC-DAYS
                       MOVE 'Y' TO LS1-ERROR-SW
      END-EVALUATE.
 END PROGRAM DKA101BN.
```

8.4. SAMPLE SUBPROGRAM COMPATIBLE WITH BOTH COMPILERS

This program is the OS/VS COBOL compatible version of the prior program (DKA101BN). The EVALUATE and SET were replaced by IF and MOVE statements and the END PROGRAM statement was removed. Other than that, even with no ENVIRONMENT DIVISION, it compiles with no fatal errors under both COBOL II and OS/VS COBOL.

```
IDENTIFICATION DIVISION.

PROGRAM-ID.
    DKA101B2.

*AUTHOR.
*    David S. Kirk.

*DATE-WRITTEN.
*    April, 1991.


*  ------------------------------------------
* Validates job code and returns appropriate sick and
* vacation days allowed.
*  ------------------------------------------

DATA DIVISION.
LINKAGE SECTION.

01   LS1-RECORD.
     05   LS1-JOB-CODE              PIC XX.
     05   LS1-SICK-VAC-DAYS         PIC XXXX.
     05   LS1-ERROR-SW              PIC X.

PROCEDURE DIVISION USING LS1-RECORD.

  100-MAIN-MODULE.
      MOVE 'N' TO LS1-ERROR-SW
      PERFORM 200-VALIDATE
      GOBACK.

  200-VALIDATE.
      IF LS1-JOB-CODE = '01'
          MOVE '1421' TO LS1-SICK-VAC-DAYS
      ELSE
          IF LS1-JOB-CODE = '02'
              MOVE '1014' TO LS1-SICK-VAC-DAYS
          ELSE
              IF LS1-JOB-CODE = '03'
                  MOVE '2128' TO LS1-SICK-VAC-DAYS
              ELSE
                  MOVE '0000' TO LS1-SICK-VAC-DAYS
                  MOVE 'Y' TO LS1-ERROR-SW.
* This is the end of source.
```

8.5. SAMPLE SORT WITH A NESTED STRUCTURE

This program is the SORT program and its CALLed subprogram combined into a
nested program structure. Many parts of the SORT program have been removed to
focus on the nested structure. Notice that the CALL statement passes no data, the
CALLed subprogram has no PROCEDURE DIVISION USING statement, nor
does it have a DATA DIVISION. Because both programs now reference the same
data-names, debugging and documentation are improved.

```
TITLE 'SORT Program with nested CALL'
IDENTIFICATION DIVISION.
PROGRAM-ID. DKA10200.
ENVIRONMENT DIVISION.
INPUT-OUTPUT SECTION.
FILE-CONTROL.
      .
      .

DATA DIVISION.
FILE SECTION.
      .
      .

WORKING-STORAGE SECTION.
      .
      .

01   WS5-DATA-PASSED            GLOBAL.
     05  WS5-JOB-CODE                PIC XX.
     05  WS5-SICK-VAC-DAYS.
         10   WS5-SICK-DAYS          PIC 9(2).
         10   WS5-VACA-DAYS          PIC 9(2).
     05  WS5-SUB-DATA REDEFINES WS5-SICK-VAC-DAYS  PIC X(4).
         88  BEN01                   VALUE '1421'.
         88  BEN02                   VALUE '1014'.
         88  BEN03                   VALUE '2128'.
     05  WS5-ERROR-SWITCH            PIC X     VALUE 'N'.

PROCEDURE DIVISION.
000-SORT.
     SORT SD3-SORT-FILE
      .
      .


100-MAIN-MODULE.
     PERFORM 1000-INITIALIZE
     PERFORM 2000-PROCESS-ROUTINE UNTIL ALL-DONE
     PERFORM 3000-WRAPUP.
```

```
1000-INITIALIZE.
    OPEN OUTPUT FD2-PRINT-FILE
    MOVE ZEROS TO WS1-DATE
    .
    .


2000-PROCESS-ROUTINE.
    PERFORM 2100-RETURN-PAYROLL
    IF NOT ALL-DONE
    .
    .


2100-RETURN-PAYROLL.
    RETURN SD3-SORT-FILE
        AT END
            MOVE 'Y' TO WS1-EOF-SW
        NOT AT END
            ADD 1 TO WS1-INCOUNT
    END-RETURN.
2200-ASSEMBLE-DETAIL.
    MOVE WS5-JOB-CODE TO WS4-JOB-CODE-OUT
    .
    .


2300-PRINT-HEADING.
    ADD 1 TO WS1-PAGENUM
    .
    .


2400-WRITE-DETAIL.
    WRITE FD2-PRINT-REC AFTER ADVANCING WS1-LINE-SPACE
    MOVE 1 TO WS1-LINE-SPACE
    ADD 1 TO WS1-LINECOUNT.

2500-VALIDATE-JOB-CODE.
    MOVE SD3-JOB-CODE-IN TO WS5-JOB-CODE
    CALL 'DKA101BN'
    IF WS5-ERROR-SWITCH EQUAL 'Y'
        SET WS4-JOBCODE-ERROR TO TRUE
    ELSE
        SET WS4-GOOD-JOBCODE TO TRUE
    END-IF.
3000-WRAPUP.
    CLOSE FD2-PRINT-FILE.
```

```
TITLE 'This is the shortened subprogram'
IDENTIFICATION DIVISION.
PROGRAM-ID. DKA101BN.
PROCEDURE DIVISION.
1.  MOVE 'N' TO WS5-ERROR-SWITCH
    PERFORM 200-VALIDATE
    GOBACK.

200-VALIDATE.
    EVALUATE WS5-JOB-CODE
        WHEN '01'    SET BEN01 TO TRUE
        WHEN '02'    SET BEN02 TO TRUE
        WHEN '03'    SET BEN03 TO TRUE
        WHEN OTHER   MOVE '0000' TO WS5-SUB-DATA
                     MOVE 'Y' TO WS5-ERROR-SWITCH
    END-EVALUATE.
END PROGRAM DKA101BN.
END PROGRAM DKA10200.
```

8.6.   IMS SAMPLE PROGRAM THAT WORKS WITH BOTH COMPILERS

This program contains minor violating rules as did the previous programs. This is to be expected, rather than blindly accepting programming rules. Notice the balance of control and action, and that the status from PERFORMs is checked immediately. Keeping control at the higher level produces cleaner code. Note also that each paragraph contains only one period.

If you are familiar with IMS programs, you will notice it does not contain the usual ENTRY 'DLITCBL' statement. That requirement still appears in many IMS reference manuals, but it hasn't been needed since the PROCEDURE DIVISION USING statement became available.

The structure contains a DO WHILE within another DO WHILE. This lets the program use its own structure to access structured data.

This program compiles under:

- OS/VS COBOL with LANGLVL(1) for ANSI 68
- OS/VS COBOL with LANGLVL(2) for ANSI 74
- COBOL II for ANSI 85

yet follows all the guidelines in the book. Compatibility was preserved by including FILLER entries and by not using the END PROGRAM statement.

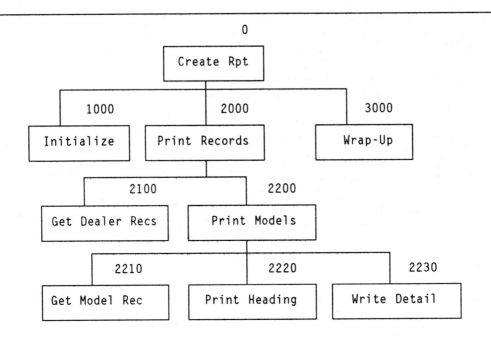

```
IDENTIFICATION DIVISION.

 PROGRAM-ID.
     DKA10300.
*AUTHOR.
*     David S. Kirk.

*DATE-WRITTEN.
*     April 1991.
************************************************************
*                                                        *
* PROGRAM: Reads a training database and prepares        *
* a simple report. The database structure is             *
*                                                        *
*                                                        *
*                                                        *
*                                                        *
*                                                        *
*                                                        *
*                                                        *
*                                                        *
*                                                        *
*                                                        *
*                                                        *
************************************************************
```

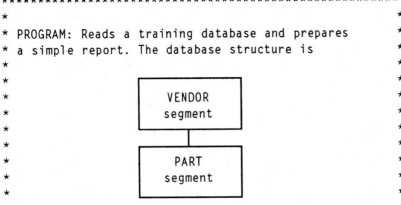

```
ENVIRONMENT DIVISION.

 INPUT-OUTPUT SECTION.

 FILE-CONTROL.
      SELECT FD1-PRINT-FILE
          ASSIGN TO REPT103.

 DATA DIVISION.

 FILE SECTION.

 FD   FD1-PRINT-FILE
      RECORD CONTAINS 132 CHARACTERS
      BLOCK CONTAINS 0 RECORDS
      RECORDING MODE IS F.


 01   FD1-PRINT-REC                     PIC X(132).


 WORKING-STORAGE SECTION.

 01   WS1-WORK-FIELDS-REC.
      05   WS1-EOF-SW                   PIC X.
           88 ALL-DONE                       VALUE 'Y'.
           88 NOT-EOF                         VALUE 'N'.
      05   WS1-PAGENUM                  PIC S999  COMP-3.
      05   WS1-SPACE                    PIC S999  COMP-3 VALUE 1.
      05   WS1-LINES                    PIC S999  COMP-3 VALUE 55.


 01   WS2-HEADING-LINE1-REC.
      05   FILLER                       PIC X(40)  VALUE SPACES.
      05   FILLER                       PIC X(17)
                                   VALUE 'IMS DL/1 WORKSHOP'.
      05   FILLER                       PIC X(3)   VALUE SPACES.
      05   FILLER                       PIC X(5)   VALUE SPACES.
      05   FILLER                       PIC X(5)   VALUE 'PAGE '.
      05   WS2-PAGENUM                  PIC ZZ9.
      05   FILLER                       PIC X(51)  VALUE SPACES.


 01   WS3-DETAIL-REC.
      05   FILLER                       PIC X(2)   VALUE SPACES.
      05   WS3-VENDOR                   PIC X(30)  VALUE SPACES.
      05   FILLER                       PIC X(1)   VALUE SPACES.
      05   WS3-PART-DESC                PIC X(20)  VALUE SPACES.
      05   FILLER                       PIC X(5)   VALUE SPACES.
      05   WS3-PART-PRICE               PIC $$$$,$99.
      05 FILLER                         PIC X(20)  VALUE SPACES.
```

```
* --------IMS WORK AREAS BEGIN HERE ----------------------------

  01   WS4-UNQUAL-VENDOR-SSA.
       05   FILLER               PIC X(9)        VALUE 'VENDOR  '.

  01   WS5-QUAL-PART-SSA.
       05   FILLER               PIC X(9)        VALUE 'PART    ('.
       05   FILLER               PIC X(8)        VALUE 'PARTYPE '.
       05   FILLER               PIC X(2)        VALUE ' ='.
       05   FILLER               PIC X           VALUE 'B'.
       05   FILLER               PIC X           VALUE '&'.
       05   FILLER               PIC X(10)       VALUE 'PARTPRIC >'.
       05   FILLER               PIC S9(6)       VALUE 000100.
       05   FILLER               PIC X           VALUE ')'.

* ##### VENDOR SEGMENT FOLLOWS
         COPY VENDSEG.

* ##### PART SEGMENT FOLLOWS
         COPY PARTSEG.

         COPY IMSFUNC.

  LINKAGE SECTION.

         COPY VENDPCB.

  PROCEDURE DIVISION USING IMS-DB-PCB.

  000-CREATE-REPORT.
      PERFORM 1000-INITIALIZE
      PERFORM 2000-PRINT-RECORDS
                UNTIL IMS-DB-STAT-CODE = 'GB'
      PERFORM 3000-WRAP-UP
      MOVE 0 TO RETURN-CODE
      GOBACK.

  1000-INITIALIZE.
      OPEN OUTPUT FD1-PRINT-FILE
      MOVE SPACES TO IMS-DB-STAT-CODE
      MOVE ZEROS TO WS1-PAGENUM.

  2000-PRINT-RECORDS.
      PERFORM 2100-GET-VENDOR
      IF IMS-DB-STAT-CODE NOT EQUAL 'GB'
         MOVE 3 TO WS1-SPACE
```

```
                MOVE VEND-NAME TO WS3-VENDOR
                PERFORM 2200-PRINT-PARTS
                        UNTIL IMS-DB-STAT-CODE = 'GE'.

        2100-GET-VENDOR.
            CALL 'CBLTDLI' USING
                GN
                IMS-DB-PCB
                VEND-SEG
                WS4-UNQUAL-VENDOR-SSA.

         2200-PRINT-PARTS.
            PERFORM 2210-GET-PARTS
            IF IMS-DB-STAT-CODE = ' '
                MOVE PART-DESC TO WS3-PART-DESC
                MOVE PART-PRICE TO WS3-PART-PRICE
                PERFORM 2220-PRINT-HEADING
                PERFORM 2230-WRITE-DETAIL.

        2210-GET-PARTS.
            CALL 'CBLTDLI' USING
                GNP
                IMS-DB-PCB
                PART-SEG
                WS5-QUAL-PART-SSA.

        2220-PRINT-HEADING.
            IF WS1-LINES > 50
                ADD 1 TO WS1-PAGENUM
                MOVE WS1-PAGENUM TO WS2-PAGENUM
                MOVE 1 TO WS1-LINES
                MOVE 2 TO WS1-SPACE
                WRITE FD1-PRINT-REC FROM WS2-HEADING-LINE1-REC
                        AFTER ADVANCING PAGE.

        2230-WRITE-DETAIL.
            WRITE FD1-PRINT-REC FROM WS3-DETAIL-REC
                        AFTER ADVANCING WS1-SPACE LINES
            ADD WS1-SPACE TO WS1-LINES
            MOVE 1 TO WS1-SPACE.

        3000-WRAP-UP.
            CLOSE FD1-PRINT-FILE.

    * THIS IS THE END OF SOURCE
```

8.7. SAMPLE STUB PROGRAM

One of the strengths of structured, top-down development is the use of stub programs. A stub program is one that does nothing, but must be CALLed from a program higher in the structure during early development stages. This allows subordinate programs to be executed, even though nothing is being done. Here is a simple stub program that works well. This example takes maximum advantage of the optional entries in COBOL II and the presence of the implicit EXIT PRO-GRAM code that is generated. CALLs to this subprogram will execute successfully and set a RETURN-CODE of zero. The END PROGRAM statement is optional.

```
ID DIVISION.
PROGRAM-ID.  programname.
END PROGRAM programname.
```

SUMMARY.

Other than the second example, none of these programs made extensive use of COBOL II. In fact, many of the examples demonstrated coexistence techniques, instead. If possible, I encourage a migration from OS/VS COBOL to COBOL II with deliberate speed. Continuing to code at the ANSI 74 level when you have access to ANSI 85 features is frustrating. These sample programs are not recommendations. Instead, they are examples of what you can code in a COBOL subset.

Large shops with a variety of CICS, IMS, and other environments may need to adopt a subset of COBOL, especially if many of the programs are reusable. Once you have your programs migrated to COBOL II, start using the new features. The use will refuel your momentum. Otherwise, you will find yourself continuing to code using older techniques. Until you feel comfortable with COBOL II's features, the pressure of the moment will constrain your growth. Don't let that happen.

Related Publications

One of the goals of all professional programmers is to have an adequate reference library, not full of concepts books or other books for novices, but those that contribute to building applications. It was with this in mind that I developed this list.

9.1.   FROM QED

These books from QED were referenced within this book because they share in the goal of helping the professional programmer develop better mainframe systems. Each book complements the material in this book by providing in-depth information about the various IBM platforms in which COBOL applications run. These books should not be referenced for COBOL-specific information or for examples of COBOL techniques. Their value is in their specialization in the topics specified.

These books may be ordered directly from QED. See the order card in this book or call QED at 1-800-343-4848. In MA, call 617-237-5656. Or fax QED at 617-235-0826

Embedded SQL for DB2: Application Design & Programming, CB308X, $34.95, $43.95

DB2: Maximizing Performance of Online Production Systems, CB2563, $44.50, $53.40

VSAM: The Complete Guide to Optimization & Design, CD3144, $39.95, $47.95

How to Use CICS to Create On-Line Applications: Methods and Solutions, CD1826, $39.95, $47.95

IMS Design and Implementation Techniques, 2nd Edition, CD2822, $39.95, $47.95

MVS/TSO: Mastering CLISTs, CD3195, $34.95, $41.40

DB2 Design Review Guidelines, CB2555, $90, $110

9.2.   FROM IBM

Your shop may already have a library of IBM manuals, but all too often they are out of date. This listing may help you confirm whether appropriate IBM reference material is available to you. Most of these books contain information you may need only occasionally if at all. These books were selected by me because they either provide more in-depth information about COBOL II or they provide information on the MVS operating environment. You should check with your technical staff to confirm what IBM publications are appropriate for your environment, as this list may be incomplete or list the incorrect IBM manual for your shop. Where books are shown in brackets, the books are mutually exclusive. For example, the following indicates that you need one of three possible JCL reference manuals:

    GC28-1300, MVS/SP JCL Reference
    GC28-1352, MVS/XA JCL Reference
    GC28-1829, MVS/ESA JCL Reference

Whenever using IBM manuals, you should check that the release level of the book corresponds with the level of software you are using. For example, if your shop is using COBOL II, Release 3.0, and your COBOL II manuals reflect support for Release 3.1 or 3.2, there will be features in the manual that won't function. Likewise, if your library's JCL manual specifies MVS/SP and you are using MVS/XA, there will be features available that you will be unaware of. When in doubt, check with your technical staff.

9.2.1.   For Programming with COBOL II

GC26-4047, *VS COBOL II Language Reference*. This is a complete definition of the COBOL II language, including all syntax.

SC26-4354, *SAA COBOL II Reference*. This defines SAA considerations for COBOL II. If your shop is committed to SAA across several platforms, this will help you.

SC26-4045, *VS COBOL II Application Programming Guide*. This provides a variety of tips and instructions for coding, compiling, and executing applications.

SC26-4049, *VS COBOL II Debugging*. This is a complete guide to debugging, including instructions on the debug language and mechanics of using COBTEST in batch and on-line. A complete presentation on dump reading mechanics is also included.

SX26-3721, *VS COBOL II Reference Summary*. This is a small book (not a reference card) that contains all COBOL II statements. It contains no material not found in other texts here.

SC26-4301, *Report Writer Programmer Guide*. This book provides syntax and other instructions for using the Report Writer Preprocessor with COBOL II. (This is a separate software product and may not be installed at your company.)

SC28-6483, *OS/VS COBOL Compiler and Library Programmer's Guide*. This book is needed if your run unit includes OS/VS COBOL modules. You will need this book to diagnose any run-time error messages that have the prefix IKF.

9.2.2. For CICS

SC33-0241, *CICS/OS/VS Application Programmer's Reference*
SC33-0512, *CICS/MVS Application Programmer's Reference*
SC33-0226, *CICS/OS/VS Rel 1.7 Messages and Codes*
SC33-0514, *CICS/MVS Messages and Codes*
SC26-4177, *IMS/VS Version 2 Application Programming for CICS Users*
SC26-4080, *IBM Database 2 Application Programming Guide for CICS Users*

9.2.3. For IMS

SH20-9026, *IMS/VS Version 1 Application Programming*
SH26-4178, *IMS/VS Version 2 Application Programming*
SH20-9030, *IMS/VS Version 1 Messages and Codes*
SC26-4174, *IMS/VS Version 2 Messages and Codes*
SH20-5523, *IMS/VS Batch Terminal Simulator Program Reference* (This book is needed if you will be using COBTEST for IMS applications.)

9.2.4. For DB2:

SC26-4380, *IBM Database 2 SQL Reference*
SC26-4293, *IBM Database 2 Application Programming Guide*
SC26-4292, *IBM Database 2 Advanced Application Programming Guide*

9.2.5. For MVS System Services

GC28-1300, *MVS/SP JCL Reference*
GC28-1352, *MVS/XA JCL Reference*
GC28-1829, *MVS/ESA JCL Reference*
GC38-1008, *MVS/SP System Codes*
GC28-1157, *MVS/XA System Codes*
GC28-1815, *MVS/ESA System Codes*
GC28-1374 and GC28-1375, *MVS/SP System Messages*
GC28-1376 and GC28-1377, *MVS/XA System Messages*
GC28-1812 and GC28-1813, *MVS/ESA System Messages*

GC26-4061, *MVS/SP Linkage Editor and Loader User's Guide*
GC26-4011, *MVS/XA Linkage Editor and Loader User's Guide Version 1)*
GC26-4143, *MVS/XA Linkage Editor and Loader User's Guide Version 2)*
C33-4035, *DFSORT Application Programming: Guide*
GC26-4051, *MVS/370 Access Method Services Reference*
GC26-4019, *MVS/XA Access Method Services Reference (Version 1)*
GC26-4135, *MVS/XA Access Method Services Reference (Version 2)*
GC26-4074, *MVS/SP VSAM Administration: Macro Instruction Reference*
GC26-4016, *MVS/XA VSAM Administration: Macro Instruction Reference (Version 1)*
GC26-4152, *MVS/XA VSAM Administration: Macro Instruction Reference (Version 2)* (These are the manuals that explain VSAM status codes)
GC26-4065, *MVS/370 Data Administration: Utilities*
GC26-4018, *MVS/XA Data Administration: Utilities (Version 1)*
GC26-4150, *MVS/XA Data Administration: Utilities (Version 2)*

Index